Royal Dragons

Marcus Sloss

Jace Cannon

ROYAL GUARD

Chapter 1

Yeah, That's Really His Name

THE TRAINING PIT came alive as the mail officer arrived. The murmurs reached me in the stands surrounding the pit, drawing my attention away from the little wooden dragon I'd been whittling. I set it down in my lap to listen to mail call with the rest of the king's finest.

I never got any mail, on account of not having a family, a lover, nor any people I'd call good friends, but a man could dream.

The once-a-week delivery always stirred excitement in any outpost, but it was especially distracting here in Olinios, where nothing significant ever happened. Half the soldiers stopped practicing entirely, pausing their hand-to-hand combat training as soon as they noticed the mail officer at the entrance. None of their superiors told them to get back to it, because the officers were watching the mailman now, too.

"*Mail CALL!*" the mailman boomed, unnecessarily. He already had our undivided attention. I could see him easily from the row of seats that surrounded the training pit, where I waited my turn with the other mid-class guardsmen. They were grouped around me, with the archers to our left and the ballistae operators to our right. Several bean-counter types leaned forward in the row ahead of us, taking up all the cushioned seats.

Across the pit from us, the mail officer raised his satchel and grinned. "Listen up! Got a big pile this week!"

An immediate hush fell over the crowd, the murmurs dying. He *never* had "a pile." The satchel was undoubtedly filled with a juicy array of love notes, family drama, and official news, but if he had more letters than normal, that could mean mass reassignments.

My stomach sank.

I knew a reassignment letter was inevitable. As a soldier who'd protected the city of Olinios for the better part of two years, I was due for a move. But after living my whole life wanting to be somewhere else, while making the best of what I could... Olinios was the first city that I didn't hate.

My gut kept on twisting as the mailman started calling names across the pit. *Please not me,* I thought. I wasn't ready.

My hope died when the officer called out, "Third-Rank Guardsman Warren!"

My shoulders slumped as I stood. I was the only "Warren" in the entire camp.

The mail officer kept waving my letter at the rows of seating, sweeping it at the crowd. Clearly, he hadn't seen me.

As I moved for the stairs, he paused to read the outside of the letter. "It's from a... Duke Biscuit?" The gruff man scratched his gray beard. "That's a new one."

I nearly fell down a step when I reached the stairs to the pit. *Biscuit? This isn't a reassignment.*

Down below, the mailman glanced away from me, scanning the row of fifty-odd faces. He found all of them staring at me, and he redirected his gaze to his target.

"Ah, it's for you then, boy?" he said, catching sight of me. I had a habit of going unseen even when I was right in front of someone, which—for a man my size—was really quite the feat.

"Yes, sir," I replied, still descending.

2

"You must tell us. Who's this Duke Biscuit?"

Laughter washed through the gathered soldiers, who rarely got any kind of entertainment. For them, this might as well be a comedy show.

I raised a hand as I stepped off the stairs. "Duke Biscuit runs Dasvilla City, far to the East," I said, loud enough for the whole pit to hear. "You lot probably haven't heard of the place. Most people call it Das. It's smaller than Olinios, but it's still got a duke, because it was always supposed to have a grand expansion."

"Why's he called Biscuit, then?" the mailman asked. "Does he like to eat? Is that it?"

I kept my eyes on the letter as I strode past the elite guards and mage teams, who had all paused to wipe their brows and watch.

"It's the name he chose when he got his dukedom," I called out. "See, the wilds around Das are full of deadly creatures. Biscuit felt he was being thrown at them, you know, like a kind of snack."

This earned a few snorts and chuckles.

"He was right, in a way," I added, weaving past a page that was leaning on a spear. The poor lad had fallen asleep standing up. They always worked those boys to the bone.

"The place never saw any expansion," I went on. "It's too dangerous. No one wants to live there."

The mail officer stopped trying to make a show of it. "You said Dasvilla?" he asked, quieter now that I'd gotten closer, looking around in case any of the elites also knew about the place. When none of the nearby soldiers responded, the mailman's face scrunched up. "Dasvilla... wait... Das, as in the Dasco region? In the shadow of the volcano, far to the north?"

I didn't answer at first. Dasvilla wasn't a well-known place, even though it was one of only nine cities with a duchy.

Aside from the abundant crops grown within its walls, it produced almost nothing to export, except for the firefruit.

Only truly brave souls could ever collect it, since they had to venture outside of walls to find the trees. This made Dasvilla's economy pitiful at best, and its ranking in the kingdom nearly irrelevant.

When I reached the mailman, I said, "That'd be the one."

The man frowned, but he handed over my letter. I accepted it with a sigh of relief. Most of my fellow soldiers didn't know much about me, and I liked to keep it that way.

However, given this clearly wasn't the dreaded reassignment letter, I found myself in good spirits. I decided to indulge everyone's curiosity.

"I grew up there," I shouted, pivoting to make sure everyone heard me. "My mum heard of a healer in Das who could fix her stomach pains. She used every last coin she had to book a dragonflight and pay for the treatment, but she died before it finished. I was left in the Dasvilla Orphanage... until I came of age, and enlisted with you lot."

"And then you found yourself in the other butthole of the kingdom... Olinios!" someone called out.

This earned a lighthearted round of laughter. It wasn't at my expense; it was just facts. Olinios was *not* a clean place.

"Yeah." I snorted, shaking my head. "Yeah, I guess I did." To the mail officer, I said, "Could be worse, though. The weather is much cooler here. Easier to wear heavy armor."

The officer didn't seem to hear me, as he was already delving back into his sack of papers, shuffling them about, probably looking for ones sealed in lipstick. Men receiving love letters were easier to make fun of than I was. *Little old orphan Warren.*

I stuffed my letter into my hip pouch before retreating back to my seat.

After I returned, a few of the other guards watched me, still curious. People usually opened their letters immediately on mail day. Most liked to hear the latest news or gossip right as it unfolded, not later.

Not me. Not today. And especially not with this mystery letter. It might not be a reassignment, but my relief was fading fast.

Whatever it says, I don't want anyone else seeing it over my shoulder, I thought, waiting impatiently for the mail officer to finish. Each time he pulled out a love letter, a familiar pang would race through me.

None of the love letters he bestowed would be for me, not now, and possibly not ever. My biggest love had been robbed from me over five years ago. I'd kept my heart closed ever since.

It wasn't my fault or hers, I told myself, just as I had countless times before. *There's no reason I can't love again, no reason I can't move on.*

Yet here I was, still alone and still brooding. Politics had been to blame. Our relationship had always been doomed to fail, and any hope of a letter from her had long since faded.

As for anyone else in my life, they all tended to vanish over time. My only true friend in the world was a bar stool at Karby's Tavern, and both of my parents were dead. All my former infantry buddies were assigned to faraway cities, and my current love life consisted primarily of ladies who lusted for my income more than my heart.

All of which made this mystery letter both troublesome and mysterious.

I knew *of* Duke Biscuit, sure, but I didn't know him well. I'd met his steward before, the Lady Etonia, because of her charity work at the orphanage, but I don't recall ever speaking to her directly. Her daughter had been kind to me as well, but neither one was related to Biscuit.

So what reason did the duke have to contact me?

I snapped out of my musings as the mail officer finally left the pit and everyone returned to their training assignments. The walls of Olinios didn't protect themselves, and the job of keeping the people safe was never over.

Or at least, it shouldn't be. Depending on the contents of this letter, the job might be over for me.

Chapter 2

Just another Field Day

I PREFERRED to fight with daggers. There was something about the feel of them sprouting from my hand, close to my skin, like a claw. They felt more like an extension of my body than a sword or spear, and I was better at using them.

Unfortunately, guardsmen weren't trained in small blades. Swords and spears were more intimidating, so that's what I was using now, as I sparred with Goderich, a fellow Third Rank nobody.

Our spears clashed and my feet danced while an officer watched, taking notes. He was a transplant officer, from the capital, and I'd forgotten his name. They often sent newbie officers out here when it came time to start promoting people. There was no one better to judge you than someone who had recently been judged; they were a lot harder on you.

It was a fuck-you-I-got-mine sort of thing.

"Hyaaagh!" Goderich cried, lunging for me, his spear going point-first. I knew it was a feint, because Goderich was smarter than that.

Over the past few months, as I'd finally let myself be comfortable in this ass-end of the empire, I'd started to let my real skills show. I'd been progressing through better and better opponents, moving up the combat rankings for my soldier class. Goderich was the top dog of the Third Class, and he wasn't dumb enough to jab a spear at an enemy and leave himself open if I dodged.

So I didn't dodge. I swung my spear down into both hands, making it horizontal, and slammed my spear down on his spear, just as he was feinting to one side. He'd intended to ram me with his armored shoulder, then trip me up, maybe bring a knife to his neck.

Instead, he lost his balance as his spear suddenly changed direction where he didn't expect. After I pushed down hard and the point buried itself in the mud, I surged forward and headbutted him, helmet-to-helmet. I'd be hearing the echo of that *clang* for the rest of the day.

"Agh!" he cried out, staggering back as I got a foot under me— and brought a knife under his chin. I hugged him close to me for good measure, abandoning my spear as I did so.

"Mortal strike!" the officer shouted, before Goderich could even notice the blade was there. I watched him blink through his dented training visor.

"That was damn fast, Warren," the officer said, noting something on his stone slate with a piece of chalk. "But I'd like to see you defeat someone *with* the spear, for once."

"I'm better with knives, sir," I said, stepping respectfully back from Goderich. "I play to my strengths, sir."

"That you do. Well. Seems you qualify for the Second Rank test next week—" the officer began, but a loud "Oi!" cut him off. He turned to see a man and woman coming up behind him.

Next to me, Goderich groaned—and it wasn't because I'd just beaten him.

"First-Rank Vanguard Fieran," the officer said coolly. Even as a newbie, he already knew who this bastard was.

Fieran, who absolutely *did not* outrank the officer, flicked a couple of fingers at the man. "Yeah, yeah, I don't got time for the pleasantries," he said in a raspy, growl-like voice that instantly grated on my ears. "Is this today's leading man in the combat rankings? I'm short an opponent, and I need some fresh fodder. Got a new mage on my hands."

At these words, my gaze flicked to the hooded woman standing behind Fieran. I couldn't see her eyes or hair, but she had a sharp chin and cheeks, and her skin was dark. She must hail from the wilds beyond the volcano, where Parshil's raw magic ran thickest.

I was surprised, though. People from the wilds rarely became citizens, and when they did, few were trusted enough to be allowed into the army, much less into a position as important as Warmage.

She also had a tattoo. I could see the pointed black end of it, at the bottom of one cheek. I had no idea what it could mean.

It seemed the officer had noticed the woman's complexion, too. "A new mage, you say?" he asked Fieran, probably bewildered. "I wasn't aware of any new transfers—"

"As I *said*, I haven't got the time nor inclination for pleasantries," Fieran interrupted. He beckoned to me with a disrespectful waving motion. "Come on, Birdie, spar with me. Not here, though, this ring is too small."

Birdie was a slur referring to Third-Rankers. I didn't scowl, though. People like Fieran didn't bother me. You see a lot worse, growing up in an orphanage.

I glanced at my officer, raising an eyebrow in question. He sighed and nodded his permission for me to leave. All the officers knew Fieran as the favorite of the city general, the man who commanded all of Olinios's forces.

For reasons no one could figure out, the highly competent city general treated Fieran like a son, giving him special privileges that were never revoked no matter how badly Fieran behaved. However, the two weren't related.

By this point, Fieran had already turned around and was tromping off, expecting me to follow. His mage partner had turned as well, completely silent. I followed them down a worn path, between two armor-repair tents, and into a much-larger mage training ring.

There, I passed by a groaning man as his own mage dragged him out of the ring. He must have just lost to Fieran.

"Top of his class in his home city, they tell me. A transplant and everything," Fieran said, stopping at the other end of the rink to turn and face me. He had the bronzed, mid-brown skin of a man from the north, completely free of stubble, meaning he probably shaved multiple times per day. His armor and padding were high-grade and vivid red, adding to the sense of vanity that I was getting from him.

At the same time, up close, his gray eyes struck me with their intensity. That color typically denoted nobility, although as far as I knew, he was a nobody.

Broad-shouldered and muscular, he had plenty of brute force to him while still being relatively lean. This made him agile when he fought.

And he *did* fight. Very well, in fact. It was the only reason anyone could think of to explain why the city general liked him: the young man *oozed* natural talent.

I threw a thumb back over my shoulder, indicating the Vanguard that Fieran had just defeated. "And you think I'll be harder to take down than *that* guy... why? I haven't got a mage."

Only the best of the best became Vanguards and got mage partners. A regular Guardsman would be helpless against a Vanguard and his Warmage, but all of them were deployed to the front.

That was, in normal circumstances. Today, though, I was feeling on edge. The letter still burned in my side-pouch, unopened.

It occurred to me that, if I beat Fieran right now, I would surprise my officer enough that I could probably ask to be relieved from training. Then I could open the damn letter.

Fieran shrugged at me. "My mage hasn't even had to use any

powers yet. I doubt I'll need her to beat you, so don't worry about that."

I cocked an eyebrow. "You aren't practicing with her?"

"Why bother? My old mage will be healed up this time next week. If I train too much with this one—" he inclined his head at the hooded woman "—then I might lose the stride I had with the old one."

His mage got hurt? I wonder how. I glanced around. "Aren't there some First-Rankers you can fight?" I asked him.

I wasn't afraid of fighting him. In fact, I wanted to. But I didn't like this situation. Why did he want to fight me *specifically*, when I was so far under his level?

"I've already beaten all the Firsties ten times over during basic training. You're what's left, even if you're only the best of the shit heap."

Fieran followed this comment with a pointed look at his fingernails. "Still, I've heard of you. You sounded like you'd last a minute or two, and I'm bored, and I've still got an hour left on the docket."

He fell into a stance with his sword out. "So, you coming at me or not?"

Ah. He's heard of me. That's not good, I thought, drawing a practice sword from a rack edging the ring. *I'm getting too noticeable. I'll have to work on falling back into obscurity again.*

I didn't like having the light shone on me. I preferred my life nice and quiet.

At the same time, I really wanted to get to my letter. It could get me booted out of town anyway, so I might as well go out with a bang—and put an asshole in his place at the same time.

I bent my knees, gripping my sword with both hands. "Ready," I said.

"Ready," he replied.

We waited, and the page assigned to the ring—the boy had been standing outside the barriers this whole time, silent, like a piece of scenery—followed our cue and shouted, "Start!"

Fieran came at me, faster than any opponent I'd fought in ages. He swung, blunt, testing me.

I caught his blade against mine, and pivoted to repel him, leaping clear of his backswing.

Upon missing me, he cut close again, forcing me off-balance. I leaned into my new center of gravity, falling backward and hitting the ground, rolling away as he brought the sword down.

Mud glooped against the back of my neck, through my mail, and I welcomed its coolness as I whirled. My blade met his greaves with a resonant *cliiiiinnnggg,* but he kept his feet, bringing the pommel down on my helmet.

I let him slam me into the mud.

"Pity," he said, stepping back to aim his final drive at my neck. With a blunted training sword, he'd only bruise me, but the battle would be considered won, since a pointed blade would have meant my death.

That is, if he'd landed the hit. As I faked struggling to get up, I paid close attention to his feet and his shadow, and when his blade came down on me, I jerked to one side. The sudden vitality in my movements caught him off guard, and he drove his blade into the dirt—

All while I planted a knife-tip right at the back of his knee.

He stiffened, feeling the cold, blunted edge of my training blade slide through his armor plates, getting up close and personal with his flesh. I pressed just the *slightest* bit too far, right where the blade had a little ding in it. The jagged edge would draw blood.

He was done.

"Disabling strike!" the page called out, unnecessarily. He sounded like he'd just woken up.

Fieran whirled on me, the blade sliding out of his plates. "The fuck?" he said, glaring. "That's not blunted!"

I peered at my knife, at the spot of red. "Wasn't it? Huh, must have gotten damaged somehow—"

What came next was raw instinct. If it hadn't been, I would have just let it all happen, because I didn't want people to know I was good enough to notice the abrupt stiffness in Fieran's stance in my peripheral vision. I didn't want people knowing how attuned I was to the quiet swish of fabric behind me, even in a raucous environment of clashing blades and knocking wood.

Sometimes, even I wasn't sure how I'd ever gotten this good. But the fact was, I knew how to keep myself alive.

I heard the mage coming for me.

I spun, catching her wrist, expecting to see a blade in her hand, or the glow of a burgeoning spell. But she held nothing. Our eyes met.

She had blood-red eyes.

This startled me so much that I didn't notice she'd stolen my knife until she punched me in the stomach with the weapon held fisted in her hand.

I grunted, collapsing backward. The woman brought her knee up, but I protected my face.

The strike still landed hard, and I got a better glimpse of her tattoo as my head jerked back. It was a tattoo of a blade, a knife, the handle above one eyebrow and the blade inked over her eye and down her cheek.

"I said I didn't need you!" Fieran growled.

He was talking to the red-eyed Warmage, and in response, she suddenly ceased her attack and stepped back.

Tensing, I looked up at her, only to find her gaze still stuck on me, as emotionless as steel. I caught movement from her hand— she was wiping *my* blade, not her own, on a kerchief she had pulled from her pocket.

She did it so fast I almost didn't catch it. The next moment, the kerchief was secreted away in her cloak, and she tossed me the knife.

"Halt!" a voice called behind me, and I recognized the newbie officer, who sounded breathless. I didn't look away from the mage, though—and she didn't look away from me.

She knew I'd seen the kerchief. *What the fuck was that about?*

The woman had just collected Fieran's blood.

"Did I hear right?" the officer said. "Did you just land a disabling blow—on a First-Rank Vanguard?"

He stopped short of saying *on that asshole.* I finally rose to my feet, daring to turn away from the woman.

"Got lucky," I told my new officer.

But with a pair of red eyes boring into my back, I wasn't feeling all that lucky today.

Chapter 3

What Does It Say?

As EXPECTED, I was allowed to return to my quarters early, as a reward for my accomplishment. Of course, Fieran stormed off before I did, without any officers giving him leave to.

I didn't care. Let the man throw his fit.

I was more concerned with the mage.

She'd vanished after the bout, but that was customary for Warmages. All of them were slippery buggers.

With her, though, her disappearance gave me a bad feeling. There was that instinct again.

I'll worry about it later, I told myself, as I wove my way out of the training pit. *Right now, I've got a letter to read.*

Before I could even make my exit, my feat was spreading in whispers through the pit. The news seemed to outpace even me.

Did you hear? I heard someone whisper near the gate. *A little Birdie beat City Prince Buttwad in a fight. Can you believe that? Serves the troll-fucker right.*

From there, the route to my bed was a short one. It started as a dirt path, which then led into a stone hallway that had been built into the huge, barren walls of Olinios. The enormously thick wall was meant to withstand sieges, but it wasn't the soundest of structures, given it was peppered with hollowed-out rooms.

When I reached my own door, I scowled. Someone had scrawled the words *Biscuit Boy* on the door with a knife.

My scowl slipped into an eye-roll. I was surprised Fieran could even spell the word *biscuit*. He might be talented in a hand-to-hand fight, but he didn't seem like the writing type.

I shot a glare down the hall, where the doors were painted red to mark their upper-rank inhabitants. Fieran—unfortunately—lived rather close to me, although he probably hadn't noticed that until today.

A dragon skull hung from his door like a door knocker, complete with a hidden bell.

As I watched, the bell rang rhythmically, a small noise caused by something thumping against the other side of the door. Fieran liked to make the bell ring when he had... company. Company that came from the city brothel. Company that didn't mind being shoved up against things as it moaned from the opposite side.

How did he even hire a prostitute that fast? I mused. *He must have some poor maid on standby.*

It was the guy's way of showing off, and it frankly disgusted me. So what if he could afford a prostitute? All the elites could manage as much. I'd be more impressed if the moans of pleasure ever sounded legitimate.

Why do they even let him keep that weird knocker? I thought. The skull was completely against protocol, and yet no one had ever removed it. As far as I knew, Fieran never got in trouble for having it—nor for anything else.

Yet he never bragged about being the city general's favorite. He never talked about himself at all. I shook my head, and left him to his entertainment. It was no business of mine.

My own room was small but private, and I entered it with

relief. I was grateful to have finally reached a rank where I no longer had to share a space.

A modest, dark lantern hung from the ceiling on a basic rope. The light required dragonfire to recharge it, but neither Olinios, nor I, were important enough to warrant a refresh. Dragonfire cost good money, after all.

My bed creaked in protest as I sat in the dark, my body heavy with battle armor. I wanted to take it off, but I was technically on stand-down duty for the next half hour. If the bell rang, I had to be ready to fight.

When the next shift was armored up and ready to go, I could finally shed the weight and find sleep.

With nothing better to do while I waited, I withdrew the letter carefully and inspected the seal. The sigil of Dasvilla—a cloud of fog ringing a tree—glared back at me.

Memories flooded my senses, most of them painful.

The Dasvilla of my childhood had been a beautiful, untamed, yet peaceful city; it was also isolated, and sharply divided between those with wealth and those without.

But outside Dasvilla's walls, the landscape of the Dasco region reigned supreme. The wildlands threatened to kill anyone who dared explore them, just like they did around every other city in the Parshil kingdom-only in Dasco, the land itself was dangerous.

Stonewood forests, as sharp and heavy as real rock; lava flows, creeping under the earth's crust; boiling rivers that filled the air with dense steam; and hot rain that sometimes turned acidic.

In short, if a man left the walls of a Dasco city, the surrounding environment would kill him, and it had a thousand ways to do it.

However, the danger didn't stop there. Like every other Parshil city, Dasvilla's wilds were not only filled with wild dragons, but also several brutal and savage peoples. These populated the lands in such numbers that no army could sally forth and cleanse them.

The Warmage's people had been one of them, once, although relations with them had improved.

Regardless, the great kings of old had once tried to claim Parshil's wildlands, but they'd failed to put a dent in the problem. In the end, only city walls could protect the populations of Parshil. There was safety *within* the cities, not without, which meant trade had to occur aerially.

To that end, all across Parshil, cities relied on dragonflights to get people and supplies in or out—but in Dasco, there was no alternative way of traveling that *didn't* get you killed.

I tapped the letter against my leg, knowing it had traversed a great and dangerous distance to reach me. Finally I slid my thumb under the letter's edge, breaking the seal.

I unfolded the parchment slowly, and read the first line.

Dear Guardsman Fourth Rank Warren,

I frowned. I was third rank, not fourth. Then again, I had only been promoted a month ago, and Olinios was far from the capital. Most people hated this outpost, avoiding it like the plague. Maybe word hadn't gotten around.

Then again, the rank on the *outside* of the letter was correct. Meaning someone more informed had addressed it. *One person wrote the letter, and another person addressed it. The person who addressed it was not allowed to read the letter itself, however. Sounds like a nobleman and his servant,* I thought.

I paused, unwilling to read further. Maybe this *was* a reassignment—to Dasvilla. The *other* ass-end of the kingdom.

It was unlikely, since reassignments normally came from the capital, but the worry was there. The fact was, I *liked* guarding the walls of this so-called *orifice* of a city. Sure, I hated this outpost just like I hated all of them, but I had found surprising prosperity here, with the above-poverty wages of a Third-Rank guard.

My comfort with this place was part of why I'd been promoted.

It would be a true disappointment to get reassigned, and I had every intention of disputing it when the day came.

However, I couldn't fight any orders in this letter. The seal implied as much. A duke's orders would be unavoidable. Might as well get it over with.

Below my name—which had been carefully printed in steady text—the handwriting switched to a flowing hand. Not Biscuit, then. Maybe a lady of his personal court?

The noblewoman from my childhood, Lady Etonia, managed his household. He also had several wives and a couple of daughters, last I knew. Perhaps one of them had written this?

The first line answered part of that question:

Lady Etonia Minax of Dasvilla has passed away.

I bit my lip. Biscuit himself wasn't the nicest guy, despite the joke of his name—but the steward of his estate had been an absolute angel. Biscuit had taken her in when her husband had died of mysterious circumstances. She'd been lonely without her lord, and couldn't bear to live alone. That's how the story went, anyway.

I was sad to hear she'd gone, but what did it have to do with me? I kept reading:

In her notes, she named a few heirs, in order. Your name was at the top of the list.

I blinked. *Um... what?*

It has been confirmed that you still live, and therefore you are summoned, in the name of King Kurto, to return to Dasvilla at once.

I reread the words, twice, then grunted in amazement, heaving out a long breath.

I'm Lady Etonia's heir? But I barely knew the woman. Lady

Etonia had been a motherly presence at the orphanage, but she hadn't taken any special interest in me.

She used to visit us all the time, to donate food and supplies. Unlike most noblewomen, she'd seemed to actually care. I remember having to learn how to sew, all because she'd delivered a large roll of cloth, needles, and twine. She had wanted us to be able to produce our own clothing, if the donations of old coats and pants ever slowed.

It had been a valuable lesson, one I never forgot. I had mended my own outfits from then on, even sewing new ones when I outgrew the old. Lady Etonia had been appreciative of my work when she'd come by to inspect us, but she'd never been overly inquisitive to me.

In short, we had never formed a bond, and we weren't great friends. I'd been just another orphan to her, albeit an orphan who was motivated to care for the whole group. My clothes hadn't been the only ones I'd mended.

At least, I *thought* I'd gone unnoticed. Clearly, I had missed something.

I thought back, scouring my memory for a reason Etonia might have left me her estate. She'd never sold it after her husband, Lord Lucian Minax, had passed; she simply hadn't lived there.

The only other thing I could remember about her was that she'd had a daughter. A daughter who'd taught me to write....

My gaze dropped to the letter. I knew that flowery handwriting. Lady Etonia's daughter had written this—and there was still a lot more to read. The first part had distracted me, but maybe the rest had answers:

Some years ago, the unusual passing of Lord Lucian Minax caused the Lady Etonia Minax great distress. To offer distraction, the wise Duke Kar Brennan—better known as Duke Biscuit—requested that Lady Etonia manage his estate in his stead, while a cause for her husband's death was determined. Now that she has passed, the death of Lord Minax has been determined to be natural, as has hers.

Without a son or son-in-law to inherit her late husband's estate, the law demands that another male must assume responsibility for the properties. Female heirs cannot inherit. The Lady Etonia only maintained control over the Minax estate due to an archaic law in the region, but that law no longer applies.

Furthermore, the business of the Minax family—Pinnacle Dragons Training and Breeding Company—and the family villa are in dire financial straits. While the Lady Etonia was occupied with the estate of Duke Biscuit, her own affairs fell to ruin. It will require hard labor, significant time, and substantial financial investment to fix both the business and villa. Otherwise, the entire estate will be liquidated once ownership is transferred.

We understand that you have no experience running a business or working with dragons; however, Lady Etonia selected you as her heir. By order of Duke Biscuit, you are to travel to Dasvilla quickly, where you will assume responsibility for Pinnacle Dragons Training and Breeding Company.

You have the right to refuse, in which case the estate will go to the next male on the list.

However, please note that the business and villa are former gems of the dragon industry. There are those who would kill to own an estate with such a strong reputation, albeit an estate that has fallen in popularity.

With the right leadership, this estate could be brought back to glory. It would then be worth a dukedom in itself.

Interesting, I thought, pausing. The daughter—I'd forgotten her name—seemed to be pushing me to take the estate. At the same time, she was warning me that doing so could be dangerous.

She wants me to accept... but she doesn't want to do so under false pretenses. She's hoping I'll do the right thing.

The next guy on the list must not be a favorite of hers, then. Otherwise she'd be punching up the whole "danger" and "hard work" bits.

On the next line of the letter, the writing switched back to a utilitarian hand.

21

The journey has already been paid for. It includes standard flights with commoner seating. You are to return within the month, and are hereby relieved of your soldierly duties until further notice.

In King Kurto's name, I command this.

Yours in trust,

Duke Biscuit.

Chapter 4

I Guess I Can't Date my Barstool Anymore

I STARED for a few moments more, until finally the entire letter caught up with me. A lord's estate—mine. My soldier career —over.

Any other man would be thrilled.

"Demons!" I cursed, shoving the letter away from me. It fluttered to the floor.

"Why would she even pick me? I know nothing about dragons!"

I dropped my head into my hands. My whole world had just changed. The question was, had it changed for the better, or the worse?

So much for staying out of the light.

The first thought that came to my head was that I should accept the villa, but not the dragon business. Most men could only dream of owning estates and villas, and I'd just been handed one for no reason.

That in itself was an easy decision; I could remain a soldier as long as I wanted, and then return to the estate to retire.

But running a dragon farm? A dragon farm in *distress?* That sounded dreadful. I was content where I was, and worse, I was completely oblivious to the inner workings of the dragon business.

All I knew about dragons were the basics—that they were integral to the kingdom, the backbone of the economy. Depending on their size and magical ability, they performed any number of tasks for the citizenry—

This thought was interrupted by a loud thump, and the sound of a bell.

I blinked and stood. That sounded like the bell from Fieran's door, the one inside his disgusting skull decoration. But it didn't ring again, and the loudness and suddenness of the noise raised the hairs on the back of my neck.

Can't hurt to check, I thought, crossing the small room to my door and pulling it open.

In the stone hallway, I found Fieran's door ajar, his skull-and-bell fallen just inside the threshold. Which meant it had fallen *after* the door had opened. I recalled the thump.

I moved.

He opened the door on someone, and they slammed the door into his head, and forced entry. The deduction raced through me as I leapt for his door and kicked it open.

In that instant, I realized this would be very embarrassing if I'd misjudged the situation, and Fieran and his prostitute had just been getting extra frisky.

But there was no prostitute. There was Fieran, and his Warmage. The cloaked woman straddled him, right there on his bed.

She had his hands around his neck. *They are* really *getting frisky,* I almost thought.

Then I realized his face was purple.

I drew my knife and swung at her, but she saw me and dodged. The air filled with the sound of gasping as Fieran finally got some air.

The woman pulled her own blade on me within instants, and suddenly she was on her feet, slashing, driving me back. If she could end me quickly, she could go back and finish Fieran while he was still weak and disoriented.

Good thing I wasn't going to let her end me.

Demons, I haven't had a fight this challenging in ages, a distant part of my mind mused. I had grown accustomed to using knives as a corollary weapon, something to be drawn as a surprise or as a backup, or when I got up close and personal.

Now, though, we traded blows as if we had swords. She mirrored my strikes, which meant she'd been trained by the best. Our blades sang against each other, and we grunted as crossbar met crossbar. With her free hand, she kept her palm open, maneuvering for balance and distraction.

Mine was the same. Like me, I knew she'd use that hand when I was supposed to least expect it.

We circled each other, swiping, tearing the fabric of her cloak and my under-armor leathers. I suddenly remembered the blood drop she'd taken from Fieran.

She took his blood, then came to kill him. She's a blood mage. They were rare, and known to be deadly in a make-it-look-like-an-accident kind of way.

It said something about Fieran that she'd been forced to outright strangle him, which would leave obvious marks. He must have survived several other "accidental" attacks first.

Forget Fieran. If I'm not careful, she might take my blood too, and who knows what she can do with it.

My back bumped into the wall.

I caught the flash of her grin as she went for my throat. I blocked—

With my bare hand.

My other hand, the one with the knife, I used to block the crotch shot I knew she was about to use. She was trying to surprise me, to use neither hand, but her knee.

She impaled her knee on my knife, and screamed.

Unfortunately for me, her first attack hadn't missed either. Her knife had gone clear through my palm, but she'd completely let go of it when I stabbed her.

Ignoring the ripping pain in my dominant hand, I brought my own knee up into her face. Kneecap met forehead, and her head snapped back.

She toppled right into Fieran's grip.

The man had gotten up, and he caught her by both wrists and yanked them behind her back. In a raspy voice, he said, "Gotcha, bitch."

Gritting her teeth, she glowered up at me as I pulled her knife out of my hand and sheathed it, blood and all. I reached for my own blade, and jerked it free of her knee.

Another scream tore my ears apart.

Fieran and I both flinched, and I was about to tell Fieran to get her to a healer when I felt something squirm at my belt. It was so foreign to me that I slapped my bloody hand to it.

Her blade. Her blade was *quivering*.

Something red shot out of the sheath.

I lashed out, trying to grab it out of the air, and I managed to slap the tiny missile down just enough that when it went for Fieran's throat, it missed, slicing into the space between his neck and shoulder.

I grabbed her at the same moment Fieran dropped her from surprise and pain, but she gave a monumental twist, somehow managing to wrench herself free of her cloak.

She hit the floor, rolled, and raced out the door so smoothly that I couldn't even touch her when I dove to stop her. I slammed into the floor as she rounded the door, fleeing, leaving a spattering of blood in her wake.

"Shit!" Fieran cried, sprinting over me to chase her. I surged to my own feet and raced after him.

She was easy to follow, with the blood trail, and with the dark blue leathers of a Warmage darkening the granite halls whenever we caught a glimpse of her. Shift change still hadn't happened, and the halls remained deserted, uncluttered.

She bounded through a door, into a stairwell.

She was going *up*.

How is she still running? Can she not feel pain? I thought. *Or did she cast a portable spell?*

These were rare, and expensive, but not unheard of. Portable spells were often used for invisibility, silent steps, healing, and the like. They were a favorite of high-class assassins.

I'd nearly caught up to Fieran by this point, fast as he was, and when he flung the stairwell door open, I tore through it first. He let me, knowing my momentum would carry me farther, faster.

I hurtled up the stairs, following the smears of blood. The woman ran like she hadn't been stabbed in the knee. If it wasn't a portable spell, maybe it was her blood magic. Could she cast a spell on her own blood? I didn't know.

"Get her!" Fieran called after me.

"What does it look like I'm doing?" I shouted back, slamming clear through the heavy wrought-iron door at the top of the steps. It lurched open, banging against the outside wall, and I had just barely caught sight of the woman again when she jumped clear off the side of the battlements.

I shouted something after her, and for that moment her slim figure seemed to hang frozen in midair. For the first time, I noticed her hair, braided close to her head in neat rows.

From this height, a jump would be fatal.

She fell out of sight—and a Mount-sized dragon rose before me, with the twice-damned woman riding on top of him.

They were already out of range of even my best leap, and I slowed to a stop, slamming into the low stone merlons running the full length of the wall.

27

Fieran cursed as he stopped too, and we were left to watch the would-be assassin sail into the evening air, her blood-red dragon darkening with each flap of its wings, until it finally blended into the pine forests of the southern wilds below her.

By this point an alarm had been sounded by the guards along the wall, and Fieran had vomited up more curse words than currently existed in my own vocabulary.

With a sigh, I turned toward him. "You should get that wound looked at."

He nodded at my hand without actually looking at it, his eyes glued to the horizon. "Look who's talking."

"Fieran, that's deep. You're going to faint."

"Fuck you," he said, in his permanently raspy voice. "You should have caught the bitch."

I remembered the handkerchief. He didn't realize it, but he had a point.

I turned toward him, lowering my voice before the other guards or a healer could arrive to us. I laid a hand on his shoulder and pulled, making him look at me.

"Fieran, that was a blood mage. She got your blood first, in the training pit. Only later did she try to kill you with it.

"But why get your blood first? To identify you? Fieran, is there something in your blood?"

His gray eyes seared into me. "Fuck off," he said.

But I could see the fear there. This man knew why that assassin wanted him dead.

His eyes fluttered suddenly. "Oh shit, I don't feel...."

And I caught the City Prince Buttwad a half-second before he hit the ground.

Chapter 5

I'm Outta Here, and I Don't like It

THE SUN WAS NEARLY RISING by the time I'd made my complete report—complete, minus the little bit about the woman testing Fieran's blood *before* she killed him.

The blood had told her something. She'd already gotten close to him by pretending to be a warmage. She could have killed him anytime, and called her dragon to swoop down and carry her away—but she'd needed his blood to know for *sure* if she should kill him.

Fieran had apparently passed that test.

The last lines of my report slunk through my head as I trudged back to my room, fully—and *finally*—relieved of duty.

Assassin rode a small-size dragon, breed unclear.
Personal riding dragons are well out of affordability range for all
but the richest nobles; this woman was therefore a professional,
likely hired by someone in the aristocracy.
Additionally, her mount was blood-red. This would suggest she
acquired a custom riding dragon to match her eyes and her
magic, which only adds to the expense.
Because of these facts, I would expect her to have either an
extremely wealthy benefactor, or a benefactor with connections
in the dragon industry.

In short, the woman might have been hired by someone like me. After all, I now owned a dragon farm.

The whole idea made me laugh out loud, and when I got back to my room, I slumped into my bed, exhausted. If I slept now, I might get a couple good hours of rest before my next shift.

Wait. I don't have a next shift anymore, I reminded myself. I shook my head, my thoughts foggy. Duke Biscuit had relieved me of duty, hadn't he?

Had my superiors been notified, though? Biscuit had provided for me to travel to Dasvilla aboard a dragonflight, but when was the flight? I hadn't been given any information about it.

Should I head to the platform now?

If only he'd sprung for a personal riding dragon, I thought bitterly. *If some nameless assassin has a dragon mount, then surely Biscuit has one, too.*

But no. He's sending me via economy dragonflight, being cheap. It didn't sit right with me.

I tried to be miffed about it, too, but my mind kept circling back to the assassin. Personal dragon mounts *were* rare, and thus limited to the upper class—so who had bought her one?

Dragons were too valuable to be used as mounts normally, so they cost a lot to own, at any size. The Mount-size ones were more useful to Parshil's economy if they were utilized for more important tasks than personal rides—but even Shoulder-sized dragons were more useful if they were used by the public.

As the smallest type of dragon, Shoulder-class dragons were hardly as tall as a man's waist, and often smaller. They were best known for delivering messages and parcels, hunting rats, or for their breath abilities, which had all sorts of uses.

The bigger the dragon got, though, the bigger the job it could perform. The Mount-class dragons were between the size of a horse and wagon, and used for much the same things.

Hauler dragons came next, about the size of a one-story building, like an inn. They typically pulled long trains of wagons or defended homesteads. They could be ridden into battle by squads instead of single soldiers.

Finally, Airship-size dragons provided the safest means of transportation above the deadly terrain between the cities, large enough to hold dozens of people and several structures, and sturdy enough to carry them long distances.

Then, there were the Behemoth-class dragons. Very few people had ever tamed one of those, and the only ones who had ever been friendly to humans were the four ancient Demons themselves.

All that summarized everything I knew about dragons, which was about as much as a children's book might contain.

And I'm about to inherit a dragon farm, I thought, shaking my head. What did I even know about dragon training or husbandry? I'd been told that they bred slowly and were hard to domesticate, which made for a tough business model.

They were also prone to escaping back to the wild, even if they'd been born in captivity. Lastly, they only lived for a decade or two. They might always be in demand, but they were tougher to raise than prize stallions, and only a little rarer.

Purchasing any fine animal required substantial wealth, and although dragons tended to cost triple, their training often came with a body count.

That's probably part of the reason why the rich love them so much, I thought.

And yet the assassin had a dragon.

Was she a noble in disguise, or just sponsored by one? Or had she gotten wildly rich by assassinating people?

I groaned and lay back on my bed, throwing an arm over my eyes. I hadn't even bothered to take off my armor.

But I couldn't sleep, even though every muscle screamed for rest. Tomorrow was gonna be a big day.

Me, own a dragon farm? I kept thinking. I'd been born poor, and becoming a soldier hadn't changed that. My recent promotion might have brought in more coins and a bit of status, but it was nothing compared to an estate.

Even in the army, I'd rarely had the chance to be near dragons and interact with them. The Dragoners—the men who rode dragons into battle—tended to be nobles, and they were an insular lot, protective of their mounts. Those dragons rarely saw action, and when they did, it was usually a rout—just a big show to make their riders look good.

After all, if you pit even a Hauler-class dragon against men on the ground, the dragon would win easily, every time.

So the Dragoner mounts were a status symbol. The crown didn't even buy them; they were usually purchased by their rider's wealthy families, or by those aspiring to climb the social ladder.

Four Demons, how I *despised* that ladder.

Children were starving in the streets, but the nobles would rather add a new pet to their collection or throw a new beast into battle than feed the citizens dying at their feet.

I knew it was their right to spend their wealth however they wanted, and dragons *did* create a whole economy on their own... but I grew up in an orphanage, sleeping on a stone floor, relying on the grace of a noblewoman to keep me clothed and fed.

Because of Lady Etonia, I'd tried hard to believe that wealth didn't define a person. Maybe she'd believed the same. Maybe that's why she'd chosen someone poor to inherit her dragons. Maybe she knew I'd put them to use and be practical, just like I'd done with that sewing kit all those years ago.

No, I wouldn't let my dragons sit in a cage looking pretty, and I certainly wouldn't use them to kill defenseless men, just to put on a show for my buyers.

Instead, I would use them for practical purposes... like sending assassins after my enemies.

Enemies. The word replayed itself in my mind. I picked up the letter again, scanning it. Something about the letter didn't feel right. It was the female author's way of wording it... of suggesting people might kill to have the estate.

Yet she seemed to want me to have it. There was no discouragement, only honesty. But why hadn't she signed it? Biscuit had signed for her.

Was she under his control, somehow? Had her mother been under his thumb, too? Is that why she included the suspicious story of her mother taking over Biscuit's estate, and of her parents' deaths being ruled "of natural causes"?

Four Demons, I was tired. I let the letter drop to my chest again, racking my exhausted, empty brain. What was the daughter's name again? J-something. Jocelyn... no, Joann....

Jolene.

At the name, a memory drifted back to me. I slipped into it easily, and my conscious mind gave way to dreaming, leading me into the past, and to sleep.

Chapter 6

The Turquoise Woman

"Dur... daruh... drag... on. Dragon?"

When I looked up from the slate, I found Jolene smiling at me, and my chest warmed. I'd been around girls all my life, but never ones so clean and so rich and so nice.

Jolene wasn't like the orphanage girls, and I craved her approval. On the rare times that she visited, I followed her around like a puppy, even though I was already taller than her —and when she had started giving reading lessons, I was the only one who never missed a session.

Today, we were blessedly alone, as her mother had taken the others on a field trip. It was probably the best day of my life.

"That's exactly right!" she said, pointing at the word *DRAGON*, which she'd scrawled on the slate for me to decipher. She sounded the word out for me again, pointing at each letter as she spoke the corresponding sound.

She was only a year older than me, but she knew so much more. At thirteen years old, I was in awe of every single syllable that she spoke.

When she was finished, she sat back in the rickety chair and tapped her nose with her chalk.

"That was a big word, too, Warren," she said. "Want to try a bigger one next? Or, better yet, is there a specific word you want to learn?"

I frowned at the question. I wasn't used to people asking me questions like that. What I wanted had never much mattered to anyone. Even my mother hadn't cared much about my opinions, but that had partially been due to her illness.

At the thought of her, my hand drifted to my chest, where the shape of a pendant was visible beneath my threadbare shirt. I rubbed the pendant, thinking. Jolene's smile faltered.

"What have you got under there, Warren?"

My gaze flashed back to her, to those swimming blue eyes of hers, framed by professionally curled ringlets of strawberry-blond hair.

Everything about her looked as if it had been sculpted to match a princess from a storybook... except for the crooked nose. And the blemishes, barely hidden by makeup. But everyone had those. I didn't care.

Just as my gaze landed on her, a crack of light broke through the clouds and arced down through the cleanest panel of the dusty old window. Suddenly the orphanage dining room lit up, and for the first time, I saw the brown speckles in her eyes.

The whole sight rendered me speechless, and I said, "What?"

"Under your shirt. Is that a necklace?" she asked.

I blinked. Normally, when someone asked what I was hiding, they intended to accuse me of stealing it or to take it away from me. But Jolene had everything, and again, she was *nice*.

I pulled the necklace out of my shirt. It was a raw turquoise, vivid blue and spattered with black, brown, and copper bits. The whole thing had been set into a gold base with a wide bezel to set off the stone.

Jolene cocked her head. "Oh—that's very pretty, Warren."

She sounded worried, and I knew why. "I didn't steal it. It was my mother's. I've had it since she died."

36

Jolene flushed for a moment, caught in her assumption, but then her bright face went sad. "I'm sorry. But I'm glad you still have something of hers."

I nodded. Jolene probably didn't even realize how impossible it was that I still had this necklace at all. The chain itself was long gone, stolen and sold by the first kid who tried to rip the necklace off my neck. I'd beaten up a dozen others since, for trying to get the pendant too.

In a way, the necklace was the reason no one at the orphanage bothered me anymore, excepting the adults. I was strong because of it.

Jolene took my silence to be mourning, and she reached for the pendant, her delicate fingers brushing mine.

"It's just lovely, Warren," she said softly. "Oh, what a treasure you have."

I almost snorted, but I managed a small laugh instead. I didn't want to laugh in her face, but I knew that she didn't mean it.

"I bet you have a hundred necklaces prettier than this," I said, letting it drop back against my chest. "You don't have to pate... pat... um."

She chuckled. "You mean patronize you? I swear I'm not." She ran a finger down the stone again, making my chest flutter at the pressure of her touch against my skin.

"It's raw stone, Warren," she told me. "All my jewelry is cut to be transparent and sparkly and perfect. But you can't do that with turquoise. It's meant to be polished and shone off in its natural form."

Her face fell again. "It's good enough, just as it is."

I watched her carefully, feeling as if there was something large here that I couldn't quite grasp. The sadness in her struck me— her, *Jolene*, the girl who had everything. Her eyes glistened, and I marked how similar they were to the turquoise... the color, the inclusions, the imperfections.

It's good enough, just as it is.

I gripped the stone again and raised it up, pulling the necklace over my head. "Here," I said, handing it to her. "If you really like it, take it."

She leaned away sharply, palms up in front of her. "Oh, no! I couldn't!"

I pressed it into her hand. "I mean it. It's safer with you than with me anyway." I closed her fingers over it, feeling the stirrings of something new, low in my gut.

I met her gaze. "It matches your eyes."

The young noblewoman blushed again, fiercely. "But it... to you... it must be so valuable to you! This is expensive, Warren, and you need...." She swallowed, struggling not to offend me.

"You need it so much more than I do," she tried again. "Besides, it was your mother's."

I shrugged and tried to put on a bigger show of disinterest than normal. It wasn't feigned disinterest; I really didn't care. I'd protected the object from theft all my life because I couldn't stand to see someone take what was mine.

But the memory in it, the value? It barely ever crossed my mind.

"I remember my mother up here," I said, tapping my head. "Not in some rock. Objects just weigh me down, really—I've got to protect them all the time around here.

"And I don't need the money, either," I tried to explain. "I'm joining the army when I'm old enough, and they'll pay me all I need."

I shrugged again and pushed the slate toward her. "Tell you what. I'll trade you my turquoise for the *word* turquoise. I bet that's hard to spell."

She smiled at the stone in her hand. It was a faint smile, wisplike. My stomach stirred again. I'd give her a thousand pendants if I could get even one of those smiles in return.

"I... don't even think *I* can spell 'turquoise,'" she admitted, rubbing her thumb over the rock.

I smiled back. I had her. I put chalk to slate.

"How about I write it badly, and you correct me just as badly?"

She giggled. "Sounds like a plan."

Chapter 7

A Dragonsteel Blade

THE NEXT MORNING, I woke up still thinking about Lady Etonia's daughter.

She'd taught me to write, and had helped her mother teach me to sew. Last I remember seeing her, she'd been growing like a weed. Her childlike radiance had faded, and she'd been suddenly built like a wooden washboard, all edges and no curves, and the pimples had exploded across her whole face, and no amount of makeup could hide them.

That storybook princess had vanished, and I'd been happy to let her go, to forget all about her. Jolene was way out of my league, pretty or not.

But now that I was remembering her, and now that I might potentially become a noble myself... other things about her were coming back to me. For example, she always had this sense of purpose whenever she set her mind to something.

Teaching me to write had been one of those things. And that smile... Demons, how did I still recall it so clearly? I think I even told her that I liked it once, when we were older. She'd pretended not to hear me.

Her mother had stopped visiting the orphanage shortly after I learned to spell *turquoise,* so Jolene had stopped coming, too.

But when I'd seen Jolene at a dance or in passing, we had always shared pleasantries.

I frowned. *We always shared pleasantries.* Now that I thought about that, it was strange. Why did it *always* happen? Almost like... had she been seeking me out?

We'd never had a romance. Nothing memorable had happened between us at all, aside from the time I gave her my necklace.

I wondered if she still had it. If so, it was probably buried at the bottom of some drawer somewhere, forgotten beneath all her prettier things.

I could ask her, I thought. *I never could before, but now I can.*

And with that small, almost insignificant thought, my decision was made. I don't know if it was the memories or just common sense, but I knew this was the last day that I would ever wake up in this room.

I was going to take what Lady Etonia had offered me.

I was going to see my old friend again.

Even so, it was hard to stand up from my bed and take off my armor. I changed out of it slowly, savoring the weight of each piece, the dents and dings that I'd put there with struggle and effort.

Not just me. Some of the marks came from the guy before me, I thought ruefully. *Now that I'm noble, I can afford my own armor, brand new and straight from the smithy.*

The thought was an oddly sour one, and I quashed it by donning the simple robes of a commoner—albeit one with a penchant for hooded cloaks, quiet boots, and dark colors. Even now, after years of soldiering, I preferred to keep to the shadows when out of uniform.

It was better to go unseen, in my experience. It had always been my natural instinct, ever since I was a boy. Another reason Lady Etonia never should have noticed me.

Something I have in common with that assassin, I guess.

42

Steering my mind clear of the dragon-riding blood-mage, I packed up everything I had left. The rest of my possessions mostly belonged to Olinios, so I couldn't keep them.

I tried not to miss my knives, my sword, and my weapons belt as I neatly wrapped them up in my pack, which I'd have to hand over to a superior officer. The shield I could keep, as I'd bought it myself after my standard-issue shield had proven too flimsy.

I shoved the rest of my meager belongings into my personal knapsack: some clothes, my mother's old scarf, and a decorative glass orb left behind on my bedside by a mysterious lover. Somehow, I'd never broken the thing, although I'd also never learned the name of the woman who had given it to me.

Wow, that had been a wild night—so wild that I didn't remember it. I think that's why I kept it around. My mother's pendant hadn't held my memory of her, so it hadn't mattered to me, but I'd forgotten the night when I'd obtained the orb. So, in a way, it *was* my only tie to a good memory.

Also, it shot out bands of blue-purple light when the sun hit it. As long as I could keep it whole, I'd use it to decorate my space, wherever I happened to go.

Lastly, there was the assassin's knife. I cleaned the blade and looked it over. To my surprise, the weapon was dragon-forged steel, the faint imprint of dragon scales carved decoratively into the handle. A ruby shone from the pommel and each crossbar.

More interesting to me, though, was the black-edged, seemingly hollow depression along the blade. If I had to guess, the thing could suck blood straight out of a victim, storing it somewhere within.

Another expensive artifact from an already-expensive assassin. Why did she even bother killing people, when she had such finery all around her?

But the well-wrought handle felt good in my hand, and I knew the metal could match just about anything. It would serve me well, if I took good care of it.

And that was it: I was done packing. I stepped out of my room without looking back. I'd enjoyed being a guardsman, and I knew I'd made a difference doing it.

For one, I had certainly helped Fieran. The bell-skull was off his door now, and I wondered where he'd scurried off to after the healers had gotten to him. I'd been forced to give a full report, while he'd mostly gotten out of it.

He really *must* have friends in high places.

Either way, my service had done something for the common people here, and that lifted my spirits. I'd guarded their walls, patrolled their streets, and even stopped by the orphanage with treats a few times.

I had been happy with my career and Olinios, but after a night's rest, I'd landed on two things.

One: I could do even more good with a dragon farm. I was being handed a villa and a business, and if I made enough money, I could give back the way Etonia had.

By the Four Demons, this would be a great boon even if I *didn't* use it to help my fellow man. Why wouldn't I want to live my life in luxury? Even just a few months of it, before the business failed.

Two: at the same time, I could decline becoming a Lord by selling the estate, after which I could return to soldiering. But why do that now? I could do it later, provided I kept the business afloat. It might even be worth more, once I put the work in. That kind of money could clothe all the orphans in the kingdom for a year.

In the end, I might as well give it a decent try and see if I liked being a noble. All the outcomes were good ones, provided I stayed smart about it. This was an impossible opportunity to come by, and I was grateful, just shocked.

I'd probably *stay* shocked for years.

On my way out of the wall-barracks, I stopped by the office of the watchmaster of the Olinios Guard. He was the top officer at any given time, second only to the city general, who wasn't to be bothered with matters like this.

I'd caught the watchmaster at a good time; his guard announced me, and he called me right in.

"Hey there, Karlen," I said, reaching my hand across his desk. The grizzled man raised an eyebrow, but he still shook my hand.

"That's Master Karlen to—" he began, but I cut him off.

"Not to me, it's not. I'm not a soldier anymore."

I handed over the letter as proof, and after a brief scan, he nodded.

"Right, right," he said. "I got notice of this yesterday, but it... ah...." He trailed off, then shot me a calculating look. He cleared his throat. "It must have slipped my mind."

I chuckled. "You mean with the excitement of the assassin?"

A shadow slunk across his face. "Something like that."

I cocked my head. Strange. "Did something else happen?" I asked.

He slapped the letter down on his desk and shoved it toward me. "No, I just forgot. Happens to all of us, you know. Even smart kids like you."

I knew a deflection when I saw one, but I didn't push. It wasn't my business anymore, if it ever was. I didn't miss the compliment, though.

Karlen raised a finger. "Stay here for a minute. I gotta send a message real quick, but I'll be back to inspect your gear. Don't worry, flights don't leave for an hour yet."

With that, he rounded his desk, and I saw his Shoulder-class war dragon for the first time. The hip-high creature plodded after him, its red tail swishing and its red tongue lolling. The rest of the creature was jet-black, a hybrid breed.

Hybrids were typically more docile, but they didn't win competitions for their beauty or their bloodlines.

Most officers had crown-issued war dragons at their beck and call. They were working dragons, used most often for messages, but they could also watch the wilds from the walls of the cities. From that vantage, they could raise an alarm well before a human could see any threat.

Officers also brought them into the wilds to help protect scouts and travel parties, when these were required for one deadly reason or another. War dragons were the kind I saw the most of, and I didn't hate having the well-trained ones on our side.

Karlen left with his dragon, but he returned only a minute later. He grunted, thanked me for my service, and was surprisingly warm in wishing me luck after he inspected my gear.

Next, he pulled out a set of official exit papers, filled them out, and stamped them. Upon handing them over, he said, "I've taken the liberty of arranging an escort for you, ah, Lord Warren. There will be a First-Ranker waiting for you at the platform to serve as a bodyguard."

I opened my mouth, but he held up a silencing hand. "No," he said, "I insist. If you're to be a lord, then it's my job to ensure both your safety and your good graces."

He lifted my exit papers and handed them over to me, bowing his head slightly. "I hope you remember Olinios fondly, milord. Safe travels to you."

With a frown, I took the papers. He waved me off, and I took my leave before either of us could say anything more.

It's already starting. People are treating me differently, I thought. Indeed, it seemed to be the case as I traveled to the bank. My fellow guards scurried past when they saw me, almost as if they already knew.

But they couldn't know, could they? I looked closer. No, the soldiers weren't scurrying because of me. They were just... scurrying. Guards all over the city proper were running-without-running toward the wall.

Something was afoot.

Chapter 8

Anyone but You

NOT MY BUSINESS, I thought. It was probably just last night's attempt on a guard's life. The news had reached people. Maybe someone had spotted the assassin somewhere else?

Not. My. Business. I repeated the words in my head as I forged a path to the city bank. I was used to people parting for me, but as the crowd thickened near the town square, I had to start shoving to get by. I wasn't in my uniform anymore.

When I finally entered the bank, I withdrew the majority of my fortune in the form of a certified dragonscale chit, plus some smaller, unenchanted chits for pocket change.

The fortune was modest, but it would serve me just fine on the journey, and it might even help with the failing business besides. I'd accrued it all over a decade of soldiering.

Keeping my hand clamped over my money chit to avoid pick-pockets, I headed over to the Olinios Roost, where I could finally start the long journey across the kingdom.

How long of a journey, I still wasn't sure. Routes to Dasvilla would probably be circuitous, since it wasn't a popular destination.

When the shadow of the Roost fell across me, I squinted up at the structure, which looked like a giant cage when backlit by sunlight. I hated these large Roosts, because they doubled as dragon traps.

It worked like this: every now and then, one of the huge Airship-size dragons would attract their wild fellows while flying between Parshil's walled cities. These wild dragons would then follow the domesticated dragons back to the Roosts, which were designed to trap untrained beasts.

The flight dragons knew how to work the mechanisms, to relax and twist in order to lift the bars. Meanwhile, the complex design of the three-story Roosts acted as a cage for any wild dragons that landed there.

The cruelty didn't stop with entrapment. After being captured, the dragons were restrained and put on display for passengers who paid extra to walk past the cages. I couldn't imagine going from a wild, free beast to a zoo animal.

Almost like becoming a soldier, I thought with a chuckle. Maybe I understood dragons better than I thought.

Anyway, once a month, most Roost operators put their captured dragons up for auction. I hated the whole process, where dragons were imprisoned for profit. It was too similar to what was done to humans through debt, indenture, or any number of other misfortunes.

At the same time, it was hard not to think it served the beasts right. Dragons had *attitude,* and lots of it. To remind myself of that, I opted to take the zoo route to the platform this time.

As I ascended the stairs, I had to walk past several of the wild beasts in their enclosures. Even tied up and restrained, the beasts watched all the passersby as if we were peasants. All dragons tended to think rather highly of themselves—until they were broken through hard training. Sometimes, not even then.

I might be the one breaking them, now. I didn't much like that idea.

While my knowledge of dragons was lacking, my direct experience with them was even more sparse. I had taken a few flights between duty outposts, over jungles or deserts so treacherous that the journey by land was near impossible. The kingdom had always covered the exorbitant costs for me, since I'd always flown on their orders.

The citizenry wasn't so lucky. Most couldn't afford to fly, and if they had to travel, peasants were often forced to face all manner of danger on the ground. Orcs, minotaurs, arachne, and wild dragons were just the beginning.

Far too many caravans went missing far too often for anyone's comfort.

Which makes me especially grateful that Duke Biscuit is paying for this trip, I thought. *Even if I don't want to return to Dasvilla, I still need to get there, and I can barely afford it myself.*

By my memory, however, Biscuit wasn't the giving type. I wondered if Jolene had made him pay for the tickets. What sort of relationship did the two have? Was she still living in Biscuit's estate, as her mother had? Was *she* now the one managing his affairs?

Another thought suddenly chilled me. Had he taken her on as a third or fourth wife?

She wouldn't accept that, though, would she? I tried to recall more memories of her, but most of them were unremarkable, foggy.

"Four Demons!" I cursed under my breath. "This woman is about to become my ward, and I hardly remember anything about her."

Since I was inheriting *her* family's fortune, that would make her my responsibility. Hopefully, the Lady Jolene Minax was a dragon expert and could be useful. Surely she had to know plenty about dragons, if she'd been born into a family of dragon breeders.

I crested the stairs and made for the ticket line, where the economy-class travelers waited to get their tickets stamped.

What am I even doing, taking on this business? I asked myself as the line ticked forward. *I don't even like dragons. And I don't know the first thing about breeding or raising them. I should just sell the whole thing.*

Then again, I *did* like a good test of skill. This might just be the challenge of a lifetime, and that thought alone made the whole adventure worth it.

When I finally reached the travel clerk, she caused me yet another headache by refusing to grant me passage. She said my ticket had been signed by a sigil she'd never seen before, and asked three times if I could prove it was real.

I stood there, dealing with her inability to process the ticket until her boss arrived.

"Yeah, that's Dasvilla's sigil," he said, stamping an approval. "Nothin' much comes in or out of there, 'specially not travelers."

Thankfully, the man asked no questions, and he even scribbled his signature on a one-week pass to prevent further issues. Turns out, mine wouldn't be a direct flight to Dasvilla, so I'd have to show the ticket again at the next Roost.

"Long layover you got coming," the ticket boss said, handing the travel certificate back to me. "Hope you got cash to spend, sir. Ignace is expensive."

I frowned and looked over my itinerary again as the ticket woman pushed me through. I hadn't read all the information on my original exit papers, but now that I was looking, I saw that the next stop was close—a mere two cities over—and after that, I had a layover of three whole days.

Three days. Three! And in Ignace, no less. Room and board was going to cost me a fortune in that hive of merchants and mistresses—but faster, earlier tickets would cost even more.

I chewed my lip. *Maybe Biscuit isn't so kind after all.* He'd found a way to *look* kind, while also stranding me somewhere that could bankrupt me in three days if I wasn't careful. Also, he was waylaying me for quite a lot of time.

I shook my head and boarded the dragon, taking the three steps up the side of the resting beast.

This was a green-and-white large-size dragon, another naturally mellow hybrid. I couldn't see its head from here, as it was tucked under another part of the platform. The beast was getting in a few more minutes of shuteye.

I could see its wings, though, folded just to the right of the steps. Even folded, they were nearly twice my height, rubbery and white, with delicate reddish veins.

The creature rose and fell with breath beneath me, making the platform seem to bob on an invisible river.

The flight would only take hours, so the economy seats were exposed to the elements. Raised buildings rose at each end, aerodynamically shaped, and large enough to house about a dozen high-class passengers in separate compartments. Rich people didn't have to contend with anything so plebeian as *wind*.

Shaking my head, I stood aside, pausing to look back at the city I'd grown to love. It was dirty, yes, and its peaked roofs might look like a bunch of broken arrowheads sticking up from a mire, but it had become home to me.

I scanned the walls wistfully, thinking of all the times I'd patrolled them, making the full loop of the near-perfect circle, then going back all over again. Easy. Repetitive. Safe.

But as I looked, that sense failed me. The city before me was anything but its normal self. There was a change in the air, in the movements of the people. They gathered at street corners, murmuring quietly. The shouts of merchants and hawkers had fallen silent.

Atop the walls, the guards had been doubled.

Seems a lot of fuss for a failed assassin, I thought.

How had the common people even gotten wind of the attack on Fieran so quickly? Soldiers loved to talk, but very few knew what had happened. They couldn't talk about something they hadn't seen.

Once again, I told myself it wasn't my business, and I forced myself to turn away. *Just pretend it's the city missing you,* I thought, allowing myself a small smile. False as it was, I found the thought comforting.

After counting the marked rows to find my seat, a flash of red caught my eye. Someone was exiting one of the wealthy cabins —a First-Rank soldier. I met eyes with them, and almost saluted.

My fist stopped halfway to my shoulder. I wasn't a soldier anymore. I didn't need to salute.

Besides, I didn't want to. The First-Rank soldier was Fieran.

Fieran stopped dead when he saw me, and he glowered. Of the two of us, he moved first, storming toward me.

"No," he said, his raspy voice even raspier. "No, not you. Anyone but fucking *you*."

I sighed. "You're my escort, then?"

He scoffed. "And you fancy yourself some sort of lord? Give me a windbreak."

With a shrug, I nodded past him. "What were you doing in there?"

"I was getting a shave, not that it's any of your business," he snapped. His face was smooth, so I believed him.

He sniffed. "All right. Just tell me where you're sitting, and I'll boot the guy next to you. Then we can sit and pretend this isn't happening for the next two hours."

I wanted to say, *You're hardly guarding me if you're not watching in all directions. In a seat, you can only really face forward.*

Instead, I replied, "That's fine by me."

It was going to be a long trip.

Chapter 9

A Shout in the Storm

TAKEOFF WAS UNEVENTFUL—WHICH, for me, was still an event. I'd only traveled by dragon a few times.

I found my seat by the numbers and letters gouged neatly into the wooden floor of the flight deck, which looked to be made of good northern oak. I made sure to get to my seat before Fieran did, reaching into my pocket as I went.

My next-seat neighbor was a young, dark-skinned woman with a suitcase in her lap and one large braid hanging down over one shoulder. Another woman from the volcanic wilds... just like the assassin had been.

However, there was nothing strange about that, In fact, it was far more common to see Velkans as servants than Warmages. She was clearly a servant of some type, but traveling alone, possibly between employers. Plus, she had one braid, not many. There was no trace of a tattoo on her face.

"Excuse me, miss," I said, "but would you mind trading seats with my... ah... my guard for ten coppers? He was a late addition to the manifest, you see, but he'll get in trouble with his superiors if he doesn't sit near me."

The young woman glanced between me, the scowling Fieran behind me, and the ten-copper chit in my hand. There was no telling which one of those three things made her decision—my kindness, Fieran's disposition, or the money.

She took the chit and rose, clutching the money as tightly as she clutched the suitcase. "Of course, sir. Sirs. Thank you."

"No, thank *you*," I tried to say, but she was already scurrying off. Fieran huffed behind me, and I moved forward, taking my seat so that he could take hers.

"She didn't even ask what seat number she was trading for," I mused, watching her reach the end of the row and look both ways. I turned to Fieran. "Would it kill you to be nicer?"

"She's a commoner," he sniffed. "You shouldn't have paid her. She would have left for nothing at all."

I sniffed back at him, annoyed. "All those lady friends you hired to come back to your rooms were commoners, too, and you paid *them*."

That silenced him, which was the best thing that had happened to me all morning.

About fifteen minutes later, the economy deck was full, with the exception of a couple of unclaimed seats. The young woman took one of them, and I was thankful there had been room for her. Sometimes these flights got overbooked.

It was another way the rich took advantage of the poor. Overbook a flight and hope a few people don't arrive, and if everyone *does* come, just boot some destitute sod off the dragon and make them sit around, waiting for the next one.

You do realize you're mad at yourself now, right? I thought. I rubbed my eyes, feeling more tired than I should have.

You're a noble now. Probably. Okay, maybe you're just noble-adjacent, but you might be keeping higher-class company soon, and you can't be thinking about the wealth disparity when you're going to need to be friendly. You can't make money off nobles that don't like you.

A bell tolled then, ringing near the front of the flight deck, but lower. It had to be hanging around the dragon's neck. As I watched, a man straightened at the helm of the ship, atop the front upper-class rooms. He must have been leaning forward to tug on the bell.

The sound signaled the dragon to start the flight, and it raised its head into the sky gracefully. The head was about as large as a hay cart, perhaps bigger. As the creature yawned, it cast a shadow with round edges across the deck.

"Must be a female," I commented. "Females have rounder snouts and fewer spikes, right?"

"You think they'd ever domesticate a *male* this big?" Fieran replied. "My, you really are stupid."

"And you're needlessly rude," I replied, looking up and down the dragon's neck, picking out the white scales among the green. "Anyway, I thought females were more vicious?"

He folded his arms. I sensed a harrumph coming. "Only when they have young to protect. Four Demons, Warren, were you born in a barn?"

I turned back to my unwilling guard. "It's possible. What about you? Were you born with a silver spoon up your ass? Because, for a man with no family crest, you are certainly acting like you're some kind of prince."

Fieran turned red, and he opened his mouth, but the dragon took that moment to spread her wings and flap them. For a moment, the great *fwoop* was the only sound in all of our ears.

Shouts of awe followed after, rising from the crowd that surrounded the takeoff platform. Those people were all well-wishers, there to say goodbye to loved ones; they had all been herded down to the next landing of the stairwells so that they wouldn't be flattened by the launch.

"Idiots," Fieran said. "It's like they've never seen a dragon before."

I scanned the crowd, picking out several dirt-cheeked children and a few ragged coats, hanging off the frames of adults.

"Many of them haven't," I said. "This is a rich man's mode of transport. Some of the people here are spending their life's fortune to send a family member on this trip, hoping they'll find employment elsewhere, and send money home."

I expected more snide comments, but Fieran fell silent, brooding. No matter. A moment later, several of the passengers cried out in surprise as the dragon leaned back on its haunches, tilting the deck backward at a harsh angle.

Inside the upper-class rooms, I knew the floor would be swinging to one side, making this part of the trip less jarring for the passengers who could afford the comfort. The whole thing —Roost, trap, zoo, deck, rooms, and dragon—was a true marvel of engineering. I wondered how I'd never appreciated it before.

Dragons have always been background noise to you. You only cared about the next duty station. But now....

Now, I was to make my fortune off these creatures. I had to pay attention. I had to learn.

The dragon flapped again, and my hand dropped to the arm rests to either side of me on instinct. I'd already tied myself in with the seat ropes, which were woven with dragon tendons for added strength, but takeoff was hardly for those with weak stomachs.

"I always fucking hate this part," Fieran groused. It struck me as an almost friendly admission, but I didn't have time to think it over before the dragon roared, tensed, and *leapt* off the Roost with its biggest flap yet.

Screams rent the air, and then we were rising. *Flap, flap, flap.* With every beat of the massive wings—each one nearly as wide as a city block—we rose higher, clearing first the buildings, then the guard towers, then the walls.

Somewhere close by, I caught the sound of someone vomiting. I closed my eyes, waiting for the beast to level out into a glide.

Someone screamed again, just one person this time, but wind buffeted against me so loudly that I barely heard it. A moment later—too soon—the same scream came again, cut off by a wing beat. I opened my eyes, squinting against the harsh wind. Why was someone still screaming? The worst was past.

"Help me!"

I went stiff in my seat and raised a hand, holding it in front of my face to cut the wind.

Then the cry came again, unmistakable: *"Help! Someone help me! Please!"*

Chapter 10

Some First Date This Is

"Do you hear that?!" I shouted at Fieran. Where was that voice coming from?

"I think I'm gonna be sick," he replied. He wouldn't be any help.

It has to be ahead of me. Otherwise I'd never hear it. Where—

There.

Toward the front of the flight deck, the servant girl who'd been sitting next to me was scrabbling at the wall of the nobles' cabins, her legs whipping side-to-side with each wing beat. She was clinging to the door handle of one of the cabins, screaming and sobbing in terror. With each surge of the deck, she nearly lost her grip on the handle.

The door had clearly been locked on her. Why wasn't she belted in? What was she doing there?

I gritted my teeth. I had a pretty good idea. Sometimes nobles saw a pretty face and... *encouraged* commoners to share cabins with them, suggesting it would make for a "more comfortable" ride.

I whipped an arm out, slamming my fist against Fieran's chest. "Your knife! Give it to me!"

"Blurp," he said, his face green. I rolled my eyes and reached into the small scabbard at his hip. I'd made the mistake of packing my only knife, the one I'd gotten from the assassin. The rest, I'd been forced to hand in.

Fieran caught my hand, his grip suddenly fierce, as if he thought I was about to kill him with his own blade. I didn't have time to mess about with him. I used my other hand to grab the leather flap housing his knife.

He went extremely tense, but as soon as I flipped back the flap, he loosened again. Strange. He didn't seem to care that I was going for his knife. What had he *thought* I'd been going for?

No time for that now. I retrieved his blade, gripping it tight and secure in my free hand; I'd packed the assassin's blade away with my things in the space under my seat. It was well within my reach, but all my possessions would be lost if I tried to open my pack during the flight.

Fieran let me go, and I sank back into my own seat on the stomach-dropping swoop between wing beats.

As a First-Ranker, Fieran had been given a draconium blade, sharp enough to pierce dragon flesh but not quite as strong as dragon-forged steel. Still, it made short work of the rope at my waist, which contained dragon ligaments that I couldn't have cut with a normal knife.

I could have just untied myself, but I wanted the rope longer, with the knot in the middle preserved. This way, it was long enough to loop through my belt and around my seat's arm rest as the deck rocked again. With the help of my hands gripping my arm rests, the loop of rope held me in place.

It was tough to stay upright, but I wasn't about to be torn away by the wind. If I lost my grip, the safety rope would keep me from falling... and I was no experienced dragoner. I *would* lose my grip, sooner or later.

My palms were already sweating.

In that first moment where I didn't dare move, I checked on the servant girl. She was still there. Why was no one helping her? Surely there were deck hands?

I saw them, tied into their own seats and facing the passengers. I could tell some of the hardened, sunburned men could see her. None of them moved. It was too dangerous, and who would risk their life over one meaningless serving girl?

Growling against the wind—it's not like anyone could hear me —I loosened the loop of rope in the space between wing beats.

As soon as I felt reasonably safe to do it, I started to stumble down the row of seats, stepping over and around other passengers. I could barely hear their shouts of confusion or anger as I looped myself in and out of armrests, ensuring that I wouldn't be taken away by the wind whenever the dragon beat its wings once again.

When I reached the end of the row, the young woman was miraculously still on board, her thick braid coming loose in a halo of wild frizz about her head. Her legs kicked weakly, her arms shaking. She was running out of strength, and still, no one helped her.

They weren't sworn to serve, I thought. *But I was.*

I staggered to the end of the row as quickly as I could, running past the outer seats to the front. I was just about to make a dive for the girl when the dragon suddenly banked, throwing me sideways. The momentum threw me to the deck, and I slid helplessly across the floor toward the railing.

Shit, shit, I thought. I was headed right for the spot where people entered the deck, and there were no balusters to grab there. I flung out my rope, but there was no way I could loop it around anything. I'd have to make a grab for the dragon itself, once I was over the edge—

A hand clamped around my ankle, stalling me. Someone shouted in effort and pain, an unfamiliar voice.

Before I could look back, the dragon twisted in midair, reveling in the joys of its flight. My savior swung me to one side, hurling me across the floor toward the young woman.

61

I didn't waste the chance. As I slammed into the base of the wall next to the girl, I looped my rope through the door handle, forced myself to my feet, and pulled her tight against my chest.

She screamed again, but feebly, and soon she clung to me with what little muscle she still had. We were standing up, but I pressed her into the wall, angling my legs and feet to make it easier to keep a hold on her.

When the flight started to level out, I looked over my shoulder. Back the way we'd come, I saw Fieran at the end of our seating row, curled into a fetal position on the floor, holding on for dear life.

He was the one that had saved me.

I'd taken his knife, which meant he'd gone to help me without the safety of a rope. It made no sense. The man despised me. Escort or not, if he failed in his task, the city general of Olinios would just cover for him. The man always did.

Yet he'd come to save me, and he'd risked his life to do it. Maybe he wasn't as bad as I thought.

For now, though, I kept these thoughts to myself, because there was nothing else I could do. I held the quivering girl close, ensuring a tight grip on her. I closed my eyes and waited for the flight to smooth out.

If it smoothed out. And if my own fading strength didn't give before then.

The girl squirmed in my embrace, but I held fast, pinning her. Did she think I had ulterior motives? Why else would she be squirming? I *had* to hold her fast, or I'd lose her.

Eventually, her panic must have subsided. She went limp, and let me do what was needed.

Hold on, I told myself. *Just hold on, for her.*

Minutes passed. Tens of minutes. The dragon continued to fly erratically.

I knew this would be a long flight, I thought as time passed. *But not* this *long.*

I thought of the captain at the helm, directing the movements of the dragon with his many reins, whips, and bells. Surely he'd seen me sliding across the deck, unmoored. The captain might not be able to see the girl from his position, but he must have seen *me*.

If not him, then his deck hands, who knew how to call warnings to him between blasts of wind. Some ships even had magical communication systems they could use, and this ship was nice enough to have that.

So why not level the dragon out? Why risk a passenger's life?

Unless... he's doing this on purpose.

It was a paranoid thought, but the suspicion grew as time passed. The captain and the dragon weren't making my continued survival easy on me, and when I stole a look at the deck hands to either side, I caught them looking my way and scowling.

I'm at the front of the crowd. If anyone hurt me right here, they'd be seen doing it.

Had the servant girl been bait? But who knew me well enough to guess I'd try to save her? Sure, all guards were called to serve, but I knew most of them wouldn't have risked their lives for a servant girl.

This was a trap, set for me, I thought.

I argued back at myself. *You're being paranoid. Stop it.*

But I couldn't stop. I was a brand-new noble, a former commoner. I was inheriting something that wasn't mine to inherit. I was exactly the type of person the upper class would want dead.

I was the first on that list of heirs. There were others underneath me. And Biscuit bought these tickets. Was it him?

I tossed these suspicions around in my head over the next forty minutes, until finally, we began to descend.

Chapter 11

Not This Again!

THE MOMENT the flight deck fell still upon landing, I unclipped my rope and stepped back from the woman. She exhaled, a half-cry, as I took my weight off her.

"I'm so sorry, miss," I said, catching her as she slumped. "I had to press against you, to keep you from falling."

Out of the corners of my eyes, I watched the deck hands. The crowd was getting up, and soon people would be milling about the deck. It would be much easier to gut me then, and find someone else to blame for it. Possibly this poor, shaking girl.

"It's... ah... quite all right," she said breathlessly, one hand reaching up to grip my bicep to steady herself. With the other, she seemed to be smoothing down her skirts.

Close as I was, I couldn't get a good look at her face. I remembered a pair of flat, dark eyes. Her orderly braids had become a pouf of dark frizz.

"Warren!" a gruff voice shouted, and I looked up. Fieran was stumbling toward me, still deeply green around the gills, gripping his stomach.

The young woman's whole body tensed.

I'm not sure what it was. My years of training, perhaps—a half-decade of practice in close combat, with the knife, the shield, the fist.

Or maybe it was just my raw instinct again, the intuition earned on the streets of Dasvilla as a child, during those late hours where the nuns didn't watch us.

It could have been the paranoia, too. Maybe I was just primed for it. Either way, when the woman tensed in my arms, my body knew what she was doing.

She moved fast, but furtive. I was faster.

I leapt back, catching her hand by the wrist.

She sneered at me, the knife in her hand flashing, and Fieran and I both recognized her at once.

"That's... that's her!" Fieran cried, stumbling backward. He fell on his rear and raised a hand to point at her. "The blood-mage!"

She'd sweated a lot during her screaming fit, and the makeup had drained away to reveal the sharp tattoo cutting down the side of her face. Her eyes weren't red—evidence that she was using a spell—and her hair was different.

But with the tattoo, the resemblance was obvious.

She rapidly brought a knee up. *That must be her favorite fucking move,* I thought, twisting to deflect her. She used the momentum to wrest herself free of my grip.

By the time I moved to grab her again, she was running. Fieran jerked after her, but I caught him by the belt. The assassin leapt over the railing—*another of her favorite moves,* I thought bitterly —and she stabbed into the dragon's still-folding wing with her knife.

When the dragon felt the pain, the whole flight deck whipped upward, but I'd seen it coming. I held onto Fieran's belt with one hand, and the door handle with another. We both toppled, but we stayed in the same spot.

Meanwhile, all the other passengers went sprawling. I was pretty sure I heard a bone break. Someone cried out, this time in sudden agony.

Fieran scrabbled to his feet as the deck rocked again, less violent this time. The captain was busy calming the great beast.

"Why did you stop me!?" Fieran shouted in his weird raspy voice, flinging my hand off his belt. "She's long gone now!"

I slumped back against the cabin door, breathing hard, exhausted from forty minutes of holding an assassin for dear life. Four Demons, why hadn't she stabbed me then?

I had her pinned. The whole time. That squirming? She was trying to get to her knife. But every time she moved too much, I only held her harder. It made me think she was slipping.

I shook my head, amazed at my luck. "She's an acrobat, Fieran. You saw how she jumped off the wall. She could have jumped onto the upper deck to get away from us, if she wanted to. Instead, she ran for the edge."

"So?" Fieran snapped. The half-growl, half-rasp of his voice made the word seem especially demanding.

"*So,*" I enunciated, "it would have been harder for us to follow her to the upper deck, but she didn't go that way. This means she *wanted* us to follow her.

"She was leading us, Fieran. You saw it. She would have flipped us off the ship if we'd run after her. She'd jump, and the deck would have rocked when we were still standing on it—and it would have been a *very* long fall off the Roost."

Fieran gaped like a fish for a couple of seconds as he processed this. To my surprise, he caught on rather quickly.

"She came here to kill me," he said. "To finish her job." He paused. "No, to kill *us.* She wants you dead now, too. When she tried to stab you—"

"She was going to say you did it," I finished.

"Then she'd wait to kill me in my jail cell, no doubt. And blame some other inmate for it, too."

I nodded. He was piecing it together about as fast as I was. This assassin was something else. We'd thought she had fled, but she had dogged us instead. She'd come up with a new plan on the fly, a public one that nonetheless kept suspicion off her.

My main question, though, was why she was after *me* now, in addition to Fieran. She hadn't cared before.

Revenge, maybe? Over me foiling her first attempt at Fieran? Or had she gotten my blood? Probably. My hand—healed now —had been bleeding all over us both.

What had she seen in *my* blood?

I'd think it over later. For now, I straightened, looking both ways. The damned deck hands were still scowling at us.

"I don't think she was working alone," I said. "We should go."

"Don't have to tell me twice. Get your bag, soldier, and let's get out of here."

I nodded and retrieved the knapsack from under my seat. It was only when I shouldered my bag that I realized Fieran hadn't brought one.

"Packing light, are you?" I said.

His eyes kept darting, scanning the crowd for the assassin. He was sweating, still afraid. Still *very* afraid. Did he know why she wanted him dead?

"Yeah, well, the assassin made an attempt this morning, too," he said. "So this is her third go at me."

I blinked. "Ah. So that's why everyone was in a tizzy in Olinios? Was it a more public attempt?"

"She tried to grab me out of the courtyard with her dragon. So yeah, you could say that."

I suppressed a shudder. We had to find a way to hide, quickly— but we had to do a much better job of it.

"Anyway, they'll give me what I need at the next duty station," Fieran added. After a beat, he said, "Only fools carry sentimental crap."

I remembered his silly skull with its bell. "Yeah," I said. "Only fools."

He said nothing, and together we hurried off the ship and down the Roost, keeping our eyes out for the assassin the whole way.

———

"If she comes back," I told Fieran later that evening, in our room, "we can't let her lead us. Acting on impulse nearly got me killed as it is. She played bait, and it was pure luck that I didn't pin her into a position where she could stab me."

Fieran sat at the rented room's single window, smoking a pipe he'd purchased on the way to the inn, puffing the smoke out through a crack in the glass. I'd tried to actually open the damned window, but he'd stopped me. *She could climb up here,* he'd said. *She could get us.*

I'd let him have his cracked window. There was no sense telling him I'd oiled up the window sill with what remained of my conditioning oil, which I normally used on my leather under-armor. He'd been stopping at the tavern for a quick ale at the time, and I didn't think he'd even hear me if I told him.

I sighed and lay back in my bed, which was one of four. We'd paid for the entire room, which had doubled the cost of our stay, but extra people meant more risk than I was willing to deal with right now.

Besides, it seemed this was the last available room in all of Ignace. We'd tried six other inns before this, but there was some sort of festival going on. I wonder if Duke Biscuit planned for that, too.

"You take first watch," I said. "I need sleep."

He didn't reply, just puffed away on his pipe. I leaned my head back to regard him.

"Fieran, why does this woman want you dead?"

"What? Hmm?" he said dully.

I reached into my bag, closing my hand on the glass orb, my only real possession aside from the assassin's knife.

"Don't play dumb," I said, setting the orb down on the night-stand beside my bed. "You heard me."

His dodgy eyes shot to me, then away again. Their gray coloring was stark in the dimness of late evening, almost as if they were glowing.

"My father is a... a dangerous man," he said finally. "People will go to any means to take away what he loves."

I raised an eyebrow. *That sounded like the truth.* I'd expected some half-assed excuse.

That's when it finally dawned on me. *"That's* why you were assigned to guard me. The city general knows your parentage, doesn't he? Probably the watchmaster, too. They sent you along to hide you from the assassin. To get you out of town."

I huffed a laugh. "Not that it worked."

Fieran took a long drag on his pipe, but said nothing, which was confirmation enough.

I wanted to ask who his father was, but the energy suddenly drained out of me. I'd have to *fight* for that information, and I was too tired to bother.

So I gave in, and fell fast asleep.

Chapter 12

The Demon of the Spark

I WOKE to the sounds of revelry in the street below our window, despite the fact the room was still dark. I rolled over and squinted into the glow of a portable lantern, glittering with the telltale shimmer of dragonfire.

Fieran was awake, still keeping vigil by the window. He held his pipe still, but it was dead, not even trailing smoke. Dark circles ringed his eyes.

"What time is it?" I murmured.

I expected to startle him, but he replied in his usual rasp, "Around four, I think." He must have heard me roll over.

I sat up, stifling a groan. "It was my watch two hours ago."

"I'm your guard. You don't have a watch."

As if any bodyguard can go a whole day without sleep, I thought.

Out loud, I said, "We both know your assignment is a farce, Fieran. Go to sleep. I'll watch until morning."

He shrugged one shoulder, still not looking at me. "Suit yourself. But I'm not going to sleep."

I squinted at him. He looked *ragged*. The assassin really had him rattled—and well she should. It was far stranger that I *wasn't* rattled.

It's because I expect her now, I thought. *She's lost the element of surprise, so long as I stay vigilant.*

I pivoted my feet off the bed and stretched my arms. "I think I'm going to pop into the bath house. They're less crowded this time of night."

"Suit yourself," he said again. He didn't offer to come with me. *Some bodyguard,* I thought.

After gathering up my spare clothes, I left the brooding Vanguard behind and headed for the baths in the basement beneath the tavern. The baths here were simple clay-tiled pools filled with lukewarm water—no flame dragons to heat them, and no frills. The long room contained four baths, all of them empty.

I slipped into one, and nearly fell back asleep.

Shaking myself awake, I washed the long day of travel off me, then drained my pool and set the pipes to fill it again with clean water. Somewhere down the line, a dragon with water lineage might be spewing water into a cistern-but more likely, the bath-water here was collected during seasonal rains.

Feeling refreshed and slightly more awake, I took the stairs up to the inn's entrance lobby, adjacent to the tavern. A burly man worked the desk at this time of night, wearing a single flower garland around his neck at odds with his gruff look.

I gave him the once-over. The day-shift innkeep had been a woman, but this man's muscles made sense, given the unscrupulous types that asked for rooms at four in the morning. He watched me with sharp, unhappy eyes, his nose curled in general distaste. I couldn't imagine why; I was clean, and a patron.

Maybe he just hated the night shift.

Despite his disposition, he accepted my dirty clothes and a five-copper chit, promising to have the clothes clean by morning.

And through all this, I *still* heard revelry—in the attached tavern, in the streets, in the distance. Festive bells jangled, bouncy string music played, all the sounds riding on a constant melody of laughter.

Curious, I stepped outside, keeping one eye peeled for the blood-mage while I observed the Ignace Dragon Festival.

As one of the Four Demons, Ignace was a creature out of history. The revered Behemoth-class dragon had been the Dragon of the Spark, so the festival celebrated her in shades of orange and red, the same colors she was said to possess.

For some reason, though, those colors were hard for me. If I hadn't been so bored, I would never have immersed myself in all this orange.

It was a hard aversion to explain. Too much of that color made my mind itch, like I was forgetting something, or like I had a hangover. It was somehow worse here, with all the scale patterns on the stall tablecloths and the spiky, orange drinking horns being filled with ale at every corner.

At the same time, the whole place was novel. The paper lanterns, which I'd seen strung across the streets in the daytime, were now lit with the flicker of candles, burning in a way that made my eyesight fuzz when I looked too closely.

Maybe there was magic in the air, or maybe it was just my old dislike of orange, come back to haunt me.

At first, I wished the place could have belonged to one of the other Demons. Emirosz had been a black-and-violet Behemoth, Pantalain a dull blue, and Grayle had been as golden as the sun on the horizon. Any of those colors would have suited me better.

Still, the street brimmed with people, and to my delight, almost all of them wore costumes. Soon, the colors faded from my awareness, and all I could think was that I was surrounded by dragons.

I felt like I'd wandered into a dreamscape. Tall, spiky dragon headdresses bobbed in the river of party goers, and I saw more than one cloth-woven red tail dragging behind someone in the dirt. Everyone wore red face paint on their cheeks, in the shape of a four-toed dragon talon, a sign of the Four Demons.

Even wilder, the ground was wet with spilled alcohol. The air smelled of cinnamon whiskey. At four in the morning, no less!

With Fieran sitting awake by the window, I saw no point in returning to my room without at least having a look around this bustling city.

Ten to one, the assassin was also asleep. Even if she knew where we had gotten rooms, she had no reason to think we'd leave so early in the morning. Besides, I'd keep an eye out for her.

Falling into a casual stride, I joined the flow of revelers along the edge of the road, keeping my distance from the nearest person. Without my realizing it, my body started to move to the music. I found myself clapping in time to the march, spinning and laughing, my feet skipping to every other beat.

Given my size and lack of costume, I drew attention, but this only led to people dancing up to me and handing me chains of orange and yellow chrysanthemums to help dress me up.

Some of the gift-givers—mostly young women, but also one man—fluttered their lashes at me, and winked. I felt my cheeks flush for the women, and for the man I just laughed and shook my head. I waved them all off, but I didn't miss the flirtation, nor the way it kept happening.

Subtle touches on my wrist, cheek kisses when they dropped the flowers over my neck. One woman's hand even brushed my belt.

What's going on here? I thought. I was somewhat handsome, sure, but not *this* handsome. I normally had to work hard to get this much attention from a single woman, much less a dozen in the span of a half hour.

Furthermore, the farther I marched, the more I started to see the figures moving rhythmically in the shadows of alleys, up against walls or behind stacks of crates. The occasional moan drifted out of the city's quieter places, accentuating the music. The few brothels I passed were doing brisk business.

So it's, ah... a sex thing? I thought, growing more nervous with each new flower garland I received. I quickened my steps and looked around, trying to place myself within my mental map of the city.

To my surprise, I realized the whole march was going in a giant circle that lined up somewhat with the city walls. When my own tavern finally came back into view, I stopped at a costume stall to get answers.

"Excuse me," I told the salesman—or perhaps saleswoman— who manned the little cart. They stood behind it in full costume, covered face-to-feet in orange-and-red regalia.

"I'm new around here," I explained, "and I'm wondering if you could tell me more about the festival?"

"Sure," a muffled voice said from inside the dragon mask. It sounded feminine, so I kept my ears sharp, checking to make sure she wasn't the assassin in disguise. "What would you like to know?"

I'd like to know why half the women in this march seem to want into my pants, I thought.

"Uh... is this like... a fertility thing? At all?" I asked.

She laughed good-naturedly, picking up a golden bracelet from her selection of wares and spinning it on her finger. "Something like that. It's the Nesting March, an old tradition celebrating Ignace's mate. He was a Behemoth class, wild and untamed. Legend has it that Ignace brought him a necklace of flowers every day for seven days, after which she agreed to lay with him."

Her mask dipped. "Oh, boy. You've got six garlands already."

Heat blossomed on my neck again, and I fingered the flowers against my chest. "What happens when I get to seven?"

The woman lifted her mask, revealing an older but elegant face. She winked one brown eye at me.

"Let's just say, if you don't start handing your flowers to other people, you are about to have a very nice night."

I laughed and stepped cautiously out of her reach. She replaced her mask.

"Easy, big boy. I've got no garlands to give." She indicated her own neck, where a single flower hung on a string. "I haven't participated since I was married."

I bowed my head to her. "Thank you. I'd better pass some of these on, then."

"I'm sure you will," she teased.

Chuckling and still a tad embarrassed, I left the stall, pulling a garland from my neck as I went.

It sounded like people spent the entire night exchanging garlands with people they found attractive, and that once a person gave or received a seventh garland, they... well. They took it as a fated encounter, and enjoyed each other.

There was a certain whimsy to the idea, and I almost replaced the garland around my neck, but thought better of it.

Having sex in the streets? Yeah, sounds like a great idea. There was no better distraction for the assassin to take advantage of. If she was tailing me, I would *definitely* get stabbed.

Hey, not the worst way to die.

With a promise to myself to return some other year, I ascended the wraparound steps to my inn and entered. I found the front desk empty, the burly night-shifter gone.

I frowned. That was odd.

Maybe he just went to the bathroom? I thought, leaning over the desk to check for blood. If the assassin had been here, she would have left some. There was nothing. The floor was clean.

Shrugging, I ascended the stairs to the guest rooms, but I wasn't the only one up there. I stopped at the top of the stairs when I found the innkeep pressing himself up against a young woman, kissing her neck. By my guess, she wore seven garlands.

But she wasn't enjoying his attentions. "I said *off!*" she murmured, pushing against him with one hand. He'd pinned her other hand to the wall by the wrist, and she twisted, trying to get away from him.

"Stop it!" she exclaimed. *"Stop!"*

"Shhh, baby," the innkeep growled between harsh kisses. He tugged at the edge of her glittering orange dress. "You've got seven garlands now. Just enjoy it—"

"Hey!" I shouted, stalking toward them. "She said no, sir. Let her go."

The innkeep shot me a glower. I knew that look, that hunger, the set of his eyes.

He wasn't going to stop.

Chapter 13

A Festive Encounter

I DIDN'T GIVE him a chance to protest, to say he owned this woman, to say it was *tradition* or that she *deserved* it, because she shouldn't wear such a pretty dress if she didn't *want* it. As he opened his mouth, I drew my arm back.

I punched him.

He went down with a *thud*.

I stood over him, rolling my sleeves up as he groaned. "Get back to your fuckin' post," I said. "If you don't, you aren't leaving this hallway with your nose still attached to your face."

I cracked my knuckles for emphasis, and added, "Some *other* parts might get detached from you, too."

"—Fucker!" he raged, trying to grunt his way to his feet. I kicked him in the chest, sending him down again.

Leaning over him, I said, "Go ahead. Test me. You're in no position to fight me, and that's *literal*."

He went still, grasping his chest and wheezing as he looked up —and up—and *up* at me. My height and build finally seemed to reach his tiny little animal brain. He gritted his teeth.

"Big talk for a *guest*," he said. "I could get you kicked out—"

"If you had any real power around here, you wouldn't be working the graveyard shift."

I flung a finger back the way I'd come. "Now *go,* before I do something that'll get me kicked out by the *city guard* instead."

With a low growl in his throat, the man nodded, and I allowed him to gather himself up. I stood aside to let him pass, keeping the young woman behind me.

"You're dead, asshole," he threatened uncreatively as he passed.

Normally, I would have said something to further provoke him, but I didn't want to force the girl to stick around watching us fight. She was probably traumatized as it was, so I let him go.

Turning, I finally got a good look at the girl. She was younger than me, by my guess, but her fearful face made her look younger than she probably was. She'd gone white as a sheet and sweaty. She knew what had almost just happened.

"Are you all right?" I asked.

She nodded weakly, opened her mouth, then closed it and swallowed. Despite the fear wafting off her, I could easily tell why the man had sprung himself on her. Her long, dark hair had been curled into luscious waves, and the sparkling dress hugged her curves so hard that half her chest had already escaped the fabric.

More than just half, I thought, my mouth going dry. After the man's grabbing, I could see the soft pink of one nipple just barely exposed. She was small, her waist and arms thin; an easy target, not strong enough to fight anyone off.

I stepped back to give her space, looking up and down the hall. "Which one is your room? I can guard it for you the rest of the night, if you want."

The girl shook her head. She had soft brown eyes, like the ones the assassin had pretended to have.

"I... I..." she stammered.

I held my palms out. "I can leave too, if you'd rather."

80

Finally she looked at me, really looked at me. There was a strangeness in her gaze, an odd mystery I couldn't name. I saw the fear, the adrenaline, but also something else. She was searching me. Thinking.

Oh, no.

"I... I don't have a room." Her head fell, so that she was staring at the floor now. "But I... could come to yours, if you like."

I groaned, running a hand down my face. "I didn't help you for *that*," I said. It wasn't the first time a woman had propositioned me after I'd protected her. As a guardsman, I often had the chance to save people from other people, and sometimes they were *too* grateful afterward.

"I know that!" she said quickly, reaching out to touch my bicep. I stiffened, and she let me go as if burned.

"I know," she repeated, her voice softer now, cowed. "But you don't understand. I want to. I *need* to. It's complicated... just, please?"

I crossed my arms, looking down at her, which was a mistake. That little pink spot of nipple, and all the flesh that surrounded it, was bringing back the stirrings of the revelry again.

"No one *needs* sex," I said. "People only say that when they're trying to guilt someone else."

She rubbed her arm, considering this. Her dress scintillated in the candlelight of the hall sconces.

"You... you're right. I *am* trying to guilt you." She looked up, and despite my best efforts, she took my breath away with the need in her eyes. Not sexual need, but something else, something economical but intense.

I had a guess. "You're pregnant," I said. "And you need some other guy to take the fall—"

She recoiled as if slapped. "No! I would *never!*"

I dropped my gaze to her feet and back up again, but I couldn't tell much about her. The costume looked expensive, but it was simple; she wore no jewelry, no mask, and no face paint, and her boots were plain brown leather.

She's not from here, or she'd have jewelry from other years, I thought. *She's poor, or she'd have matching shoes....*

But she still bought the dress, which probably cost her more than she could afford. She bought it to treat herself... and also to attract someone.

"If you need sex, why not have it with that guy?" I asked, nodding back toward the front of the inn.

She flushed, this time with anger. *"That* guy? He's a dick!"

I chuckled at her use of the word. *Vulgarity, eh? But only when I get it out of her. Demure otherwise. Possibly a servant?*

"Then tell me the truth," I said. I needed to know her story if I was going to ensure she stayed safe. If she went out into those streets alone again, seeking a different partner, it might work out even worse.

She glanced up and down the halls, then seized my hand by the wrist. Before I could react, she was already hauling me toward a door marked *Laundry.*

She pushed us through, into a room of tables stacked with clean linens. Washing bins lined the back wall, with clothes and towels hanging on a line above them. The air smelled of lavender water, heavy with damp.

I stopped on the threshold, stalling her. She let me go and turned.

"Please. I just want the privacy if I'm going to explain," she said.

"Fine." I twisted to shut the door behind me. "Then explain."

She hesitated, then slapped a hand to her mouth, squeezing her eyes shut. She murmured something against it and shook her head.

I crossed my arms again. "Didn't quite hear that—"

"He's going to make me his whore!" she blurted.

The statement nearly stunned me to silence. "What? Who is?"

"My lord is!" she cried, tears burning her eyes as she tugged up the hem of her dress. "I'm... I'm a servant in a great house. I used to work in the women's wing, but now... now I work in *his* wing. My master's. And...."

She hiccupped pitifully. "And he's finally noticed me. And no one is there to protect me anymore."

"Well, shit," I said.

Her eyes rose to mine again. "You know what I mean, then?" she asked.

Unfortunately, I did. "Why don't you leave his house, if it's so bad?" I said.

"I cannot," she replied formally, as if to hammer home that she had indeed thought about it, and exhausted the option.

"Both of my brothers work in the stables," She explained. "My lord would sack them both if I fled. All three of us would be separated, and likely destitute. They would have to join the army, and I might have to do worse."

She shook her head. "No. I cannot abide that."

My shoulders slumped. "So you snuck away during the Nesting March to have a last taste of freedom? Is that it?"

She paused for a moment, and then nodded.

Well, *this* was a predicament—except, it wasn't. Not for me. Not anymore.

"I could hire you," I said. "Your brothers, too. I just inherited an estate—"

But she was already shaking her head. "It's more than that. Please, sir, do not make me explain it all. The fact is, I can't leave. I must submit to my master—but I don't have to let it be the only thing I ever experience."

She took my hand again, drawing closer. I let her press up against me, and met her eyes. Her paleness had faded, and her gaze had grown hooded with real want.

"I want to be with someone good and kind," she said. "I want to be with someone like you."

With that, she reached for her neck, removed a garland, and looped it over my head. I was officially up to seven.

I swallowed thickly, but I couldn't deny that my body was reacting to her closeness, to the deep shadow between her breasts and the bedroom look in her gaze. My cock did its own calculations, and hardened.

I wanted to protest again, to tell her there were other ways—but I knew what it was like to have to make hard decisions. Having other people tell you they knew better, and having them offer pity and charity... it never helped.

It only made things worse.

My hand found her wrist, my thumb tracing the veins where her pulse thudded.

"How old are you?" I asked. "Don't lie."

"Twenty-one," she said, without hesitation. I believed her, but holy *Demons*, this woman was small.

"Are you sure about this?" I asked.

She nodded. "Yes. I'm ready."

I got caught in her gaze for another moment, then laughed. "Four Demons, I don't even know your name yet."

Her hand slipped around my neck. "It's better that way. Otherwise, you might try to come and save me." She cocked her head. "How about I call you Tall-and-Handsome? Hmm, maybe Tallan for short."

I ran a hand down her side, watching the fabric glitter in the candle of the laundry room's only lantern.

"I'll call you Shimmer, then," I said, and kissed her neck. She quivered against me, making my dick strain against my trousers.

"Demons, you're tiny. I might break you."

Her fingers found my belt. "Please do."

Chapter 14

Slow Burn

I SLID my hand under Shimmer's rear, and scooped her up against me. After locking the laundry door behind us—just in case, you know, *assassin*—I carried her to the nearest table, currently laden with folded towels.

She gave a delicious little cry as I sat her down on the linens. Turning her head, she said, "But haven't you got a room—?"

"Roommate," I said. "He wouldn't appreciate this."

Before she could face me again, I took advantage of her exposed throat, kissing a path down the underside of her jaw to her throat. When I bit her, she arched back, her breasts heaving against me.

I felt the fabric pull, and I slung an arm across her back, keeping her small form pressed hard against my mouth as I trailed hungry kisses down her collarbone to her tits.

When my mouth moved from the hard bone of her chest to the soft mounds below, I sucked hard at the giving flesh, taking the side of one breast as far into my mouth as I could.

"Ohh... that hurts," she moaned, and then more sharply, "Oh!" as I turned my head and found her nipple. It had popped free of her glimmering neckline, and for a moment I went hard on it, my tongue roving, teeth playing.

85

She pushed against my shoulders, but not hard, not like she really wanted to get away. Her breath hissed out.

"You—you're not very gentle, are you?"

I let her nipple escape my teeth, and looked at it, hard and pink. Using my thumb, I toyed with it, rubbing it back and forth.

"I can be gentle. You want me to be? You said you wanted to be broken."

Her brown eyes met mine, her lids hooded, eyelashes fluttering dazedly.

"I... I thought that was a figure of speech. I...."

She trailed off as I took her nipple into my mouth again and suckled, gently, bobbing my head with each tug and pull. Her chest rose and fell in a new, rougher rhythm as she watched me, her mouth open, a tiny choked noise at the back of her throat.

Then I bit her again. She threw her head back and cried out, her hands tightening on my shoulders.

"Which do you prefer?" I asked.

It took her a moment to gather the words to reply. Breathlessly, she said, "All of it. Give me all of it."

I leaned back, still standing off the table while I had her lying prostrate before me, her legs still clinging to my hips. I trailed a hand down her neck to her chest, where I tugged her sparkling dress down to set another nipple free.

With my other hand, I deftly flicked my belt open. "You asked for it," I said, diving back in.

She clung to me, her hands gripping the back of my head and shoulders as I bit into her. First I slid my tongue into her ear, making her moan and shudder; then I bit into it and tugged and forced her head to one side as I sank my teeth into the taut muscle of her throat.

Her hips bucked, her heat bumping against my stomach, inviting me. My trousers had loosened, my cock hard and unrestrained but not touching her yet, not at this angle.

I bit her again, hard, too hard to give her any plausible deniability come tomorrow. There would be a bruise.

"Fuck, Tallan, take me," she begged, suddenly and intensely. Her grasping hands turned to claws at my back, and she wrenched at my shirt, trying to get it off.

"You'll have to beg harder than that," I growled into the crevice between her tits, breathing in her warmth and heat and sweat. I mashed her breasts against my face, licking wildly with my tongue while my fingers depressed the raised knots of flesh to either side of me.

The dress slid further down, and I shoved her tits up to run my tongue along the sensitive line where her boobs met her abdomen. She bucked again, shoving towels off the table, making the wooden legs squeak.

I flicked my tongue along that sensitive space, making her squirm with sensation.

"Oh, Tallan—I can't—it's too much—"

And I'm barely getting started, I thought but didn't say. I gave her chest another violent squeeze before letting those perfect tits fall free to either side.

Demons, they were big on her, much too large for her frame. She probably cursed her bloodline, but I'd enjoy it.

Hovering over her now, I ran my hands down her ribs, along the scrunched orange fabric of the costume dress. The touch drew her gaze into mine, because we both knew where my hands were headed.

"Are you... are you going to do it now?" she asked in a timid voice.

My hands roved over the skirt, then under it, creeping in along the inside of her thighs. "Would you like me to?"

She bit her lip and looked down between her legs. "I thought I was supposed to—"

My fingertips met her panties, and slid underneath.

She released a stifled noise, and her arms seemed to cave under her weight as my finger hooked into the first fold of her sex, and drew down.

"Tallan... yes. I want you to take me," she said.

My finger drove deeper, into the hot wet of her, and rode up again. She tightened her legs against me and shuddered out, "Ooohhhh...."

With one hand she gripped the table's edge above her head, and with the other she gripped her own breast and squeezed tight. The sight of her nipple between her own fingers made my cock jump, and I almost set it free right then and fucked her.

I kept rubbing her, building up her juices, turning an already deep pond into an ocean of need. Four Demons, when I fucked her, there'd be no friction at all. I could go all night.

I found her nub.

"Oh!"

I'd known where it was, of course, but you had to build from the foundation if you wanted the palace to stand. I circled the fleshy bead with my thumb, taking my other hand away to stroke myself.

She pushed forward against me, forcing some of her dress back. "Yes... oh, Tallan... that feels...."

I dropped my gaze as her dress shifted back with her twisting, and I could see her sex for the first time. I had to stop stroking myself then, for fear I'd come too soon. Her pussy was almost as red as a volcanic dragon, and swollen. Her underwear was soaked totally through.

She was also hairless, top-to-bottom, a delicacy that caught me by surprise. Her naked folds were *extra* naked to me, pristine, maybe *waxed*.

I remembered what she'd said about needing to fuck someone tonight—needing it, but clearly also *wanting* it. I imagined her doing this, shaving herself clean; it was no easy task for someone with so many delicate bits. There was only one reason she would do this: because she wanted it to be perfect.

"You're a virgin, aren't you?" I said.

She tensed and looked up. "What? No!"

"You are. This is your first time."

She'd made it sound like this was a last gasp, a final hurrah—but it was so much more than that. A wealthy man wanted her, and he would have her, and she knew that.

But she didn't want him to be her first. She wanted something to dream about.

Well, if Shimmer wanted the time of her life, then she had come to the right place.

Chapter 15

The Right Man for the Job

I SLOWED my rubbing on her, trying to stifle my rush. I tended to get my partners off before me, if I could, but I knew how to make it last as long as I wanted. Subconsciously, I was tired and wanted to fuck and go to sleep.

But consciously, I wanted to give this strange girl a night she could never forget.

"I'm not a virgin, I'm really no—" she started to say, but that's when I pulled her closer and dropped to my knees. "Tallan?" she asked, her voice almost a screech. "What are you doing? Tallan? I can't see—"

I pulled her panties to one side, and kissed her.

Her legs boxed my ears, abrupt to the point of painful. She pushed on me, but I kept going, sliding my tongue up through the folds while my upper lip kept pressure on her clit. She writhed and pushed and moaned my fake name.

"Tallan, I can't... it's too much... stop...."

I pulled away, kissing the inside of her thigh. She shivered, and I licked the skin between her pussy and her leg. When I spoke, my lips touched her folds again.

"You sure you want me to stop?"

She stayed stiff a moment more, then fell limp. "No," she breathed. "I want more. But you should—"

"I'll get mine, don't worry," I told her.

Then I dove tongue-first into her body again.

Towels flopped off the table, the wood creaking as I went at her, as the tension inside her built and built. "Demons, Tallan. What are you—it feels—keep going. Like that, oh fuck, what *is* that—!?"

The words ended in a scream that could only mean one thing. The speed of it startled me, but there was no mistaking the pulse of her sex or the clamp of her thighs. I stood up, watching her mouth open as she moaned, as the pleasure I'd given raged through her.

I could have fucked her then, and she would have let me, insensate as she was. I couldn't even tell if she'd ever orgasmed before, by the way she gripped her breast and scratched the table like a beast.

Scooting her forward, I clambered up onto the table and pushed her dress higher, so it wouldn't get in my way. With her legs still around me and my knees folded beneath her, I finally reached for my cock, shoving my undergarments back so my stiff flesh could come free.

I gripped my shaft and fed it in between her folds, closing my eyes to savor the last pulses of her pleasure. My head was just sensitive enough to catch the echoes.

Then Shimmer was loose again, pleasure-exhausted, her big tits rising and falling with ragged breaths. She tried to sit up on one elbow, fumbling as if she'd forgotten how to use her limbs. Her dark eyes dropped to my cock. With her dress retreated past her navel, she could see my shaft, not my head.

She met my eyes. "Don't you want... I could use *my* mouth...."

My eyes dipped, and I stroked myself, plodding against her but not pushing through.

"I don't want your mouth," I said. "I want this—" I stroked myself twice, extra fast "—inside *this.*" And I nudged those perfect, glistening folds aside. Her entrance waited for me, so wet it would be easy.

A beat passed as I waited for her answer. "I... we can do it," she said. "But you were right, I really am a vir—"

I slid inside her.

Her words stalled, collapsing into a harsh, surprised moan. She was perfect, tight and slick and deep.

I went all the way, savoring it, treasuring the drawn-out hiss of her pain. It was often rough for a woman after coming, since orgasm made a woman's inner muscles go tense—in my experience, anyway, but that was limited. Still, I imagined it would hurt more if she'd never done this before.

I stopped when I was as deep as the angle would let me get, with about an inch and half of my cock exposed, and the rest buried between the protective folds of her hole.

I breathed hard to keep myself sane as I asked, "You all right? Does it feel okay?"

"It... hurts," she breathed, her tits rolling to either side of her chest, no longer propped up by her hands. She was gripping the table's edges now, as if for dear life.

I wanted to see those tits *jump.*

"But it hurts...." She closed her eyes. "Really good. It feels good."

"Just relax," I said. "I'll start slow."

And so I pulled out, achingly, every muscle in my body raring to go at her with full force. Her moan was long, croaky, and delicious. She'd gone native, the beast in her emerging. I would soon meet that beast with my own.

When my hips had swayed back just enough for me to see the ridges of my head, I swung back into her. I could feel the wetness grow.

"Tallan," she exhaled the next time I exited. I checked for blood, but there wasn't any. She was one of the lucky ones, but it would still hurt.

Unless I built her up properly, which I did, reentering her, just slightly faster this time. She breathed my fake name again, then said it, then moaned it, then *cried* it, and each time I went faster and faster.

"You ready?" I said, sweating, my rhythm reaching its breaking point.

"Yes, Tallan. I want you. I want you to come in me."

I laughed. "Oh, Shimmer. We aren't there yet."

Then I let her have it—all of it. Every single thing that I had.

I raised her thighs to either side of me and I fucked her raw, watching my cock surge into her little body, watching her tits flip and flop as she released a silent scream. I didn't stop, didn't slow—I only sped up, until we were only action, only *doing*. I lost all sense of self as my body broke hers.

I didn't even change position. I didn't need to. She was tight and wet and she was screaming for me.

"Yes, yes, oh Demons, yes!"

I closed my eyes as I felt my balls tighten, my body going beyond the point of no return. I lived within that crest, in that still moment of ecstasy.

"Come inside me!" she called out.

But I didn't.

Instead, I pulled free and spurted all over her stomach and tits, my mouth open and gasping as my arms turned to gelatin. I leaned over her on my hands and knees, still coming. I watched one string spatter over her nipple.

"Fuck, Shimmer," I said, shaking my head. "Fuck."

She was watching my cock raptly, possibly figuring out how cocks worked for the first time. Sure, she had asked me to come inside her, but did she know what "coming" looked like? She seemed fascinated, but not disgusted.

I licked my lips at the sight of her glistening with my cum, and not only with the beads on her dress.

Her arm extended down, and she closed a hand on my shaft. I sighed at the tenderness of it.

"Are they all... like this?" she asked.

I shook my head, chuckling. "Give or take." I'd been inside enough communal baths to know where I stood: nothing incredible, but not too shabby either.

"It felt so... big."

"That's because you wanted it. It always feels best when you want—"

I stopped myself, my eyes opening, the haze of lovemaking fading away. *Her lord. She won't want her lord, will she? I shouldn't say things like... no! I shouldn't let him have her! There has to be something I can—*

A knock sounded on the door, and I nearly had a heart attack.

"Oi, Rental! You in there? We got laundry. It's locked."

It was a woman's voice. "Shit, shit," Shimmer said, pushing on me. I backed off the table, and she slid off too, gathering her dress up.

"Sorry! Coming!" she said, waving at me to hide behind the door. I did so as she opened it.

"Buck up front says you'd better get it all done by sunrise, or you're fired," the woman's voice said, and from my vantage, I saw a pair of bronzed arms shoving a heap of clothes at Shimmer.

"He—I'm only working here for a few days, he can't fire me!" Shimmer cried, struggling to keep the clothes from falling.

"I'm just tellin' you what he said, girl. Now if you'll 'scuse me, some of us gotta work."

With that, Shimmer was able to close the door. She stood there looking baffled and exhausted.

I cocked a smile at her. "'Rental?'" I asked.

She released a half-mad-sounding giggle. "Yeah, they call me that because I'm just working here a little while. You know, exchanging work for a place to sleep until...."

Her words faded, and she blinked, looking up at me. Her eyes suddenly watered. "Thank you for this. I mean it. It was... thank you."

I smiled. "The pleasure was very much mine."

She shifted uncomfortably. "Yeah, I can feel that. All over me. Very sticky." She shook herself again.

"Anyway, I've gotta work now... I'd slipped out to see the Nesting March, and Buck caught me sneaking back in, so... I'm on a thin wing right now. But maybe, if you're not busy tomorrow...?"

I leaned close, past the pile of dirty clothes—some of which were mine—and I kissed her on the mouth for the first time. She gasped.

"I'm here for three days," I told her.

She blinked. "Oh, right. Three days?"

That was an odd response, but I'd clearly frazzled her.

"Three whole days," I confirmed. "So I'll see you later?"

She squeezed the pile of clothes close. "I... yes. Yes, I think you will."

It was nearly seven in the morning by the time I returned. I found Fieran fast asleep against the wall by the window.

I thought about tucking him in, but one man did not just lift another man while he was sleeping. It was bad form, so I left him be.

After checking the room for signs of any attempt at forced entry, I settled back into my bed.

Shimmer, I thought, a smile wisping across my face. I'd find her tomorrow, and I'd get her real name, and then I'd find a way to help her somehow.

I was about to be a lord, after all. There had to be something I could do.

I could marry her, I thought, and I laughed at the concept. If I was truly a lord, I couldn't just marry some maid... or maybe I could. Maybe it would piss all the other lords off. Maybe it would be hilarious. Who knew?

I didn't know her, but I still fell asleep warmed by the thought that I *could* marry. I could find a good woman, have children, support them, watch them grow. As a soldier, that future had been beyond me.

But anything was possible now.

Chapter 16

Food Always Tastes Better Afterward

OUR FIRST FULL day in Ignace was a long one, but uneventful. Turns out, the Nesting March had been just one night of a seven-night festival celebrating the founding dragon of the city.

The original Ignace, an orange volcano Behemoth, had been the first to bring settlers to the plot of land that would become her namesake city.

Many other cities of Parshil celebrated their founding dragons, and Ignace was no exception. At night, the tavern below us filled with rousing song and the clinking and occasional shattering of ale glasses.

During the day, music and singing moved past on the streets below our window. Sometimes I glimpsed red paper lanterns rising into the sky.

We stayed where we were the entire first day, holed up in our room. Fieran left once, ostensibly to report to his superiors, but he returned quickly. He'd cleaned up, possibly at the tavern's communal bath, but the sweat still seemed glued to his brow.

He must have shaved too, because his face remained baby-smooth, and he'd bought an entire wineskin of shaving cream somewhere.

I asked after Shimmer, calling her "Rental," and the maids assured me they'd pass on my message. I believed them, but the

99

laundry girl didn't visit me. She was working, so maybe she couldn't.

Or maybe she felt as trapped as I did, because aside from using the bathroom, neither I nor Fieran dared to leave our room. We both knew it would be easy for the assassin to kill us in the festival crush, and she would certainly be watching us now that daylight had landed.

Of course, we didn't know if the blood-mage had found us yet, but the woman seemed canny. She probably had. Even if she hadn't, we were safer inside.

We considered other options, but we weren't familiar enough with this city to lay any sort of trap for her. If I had to guess, she'd know the place far better than we did.

"Yeah," Fieran rasped, when I pointed that out. "Something tells me she's been around."

I nodded at that. I'd expected a protest from my bodyguard, or a request to hit the brothels, but I saw none of that. It seemed that the threat of death brought out the competent soldier in Fieran. He wasn't as moronic when his life was in danger.

Still, the hiding grated on me. If only I could catch the assassin and get answers. She was too good, though, and she had too many friends. I was now certain she'd paid off the deck hands and the captain of our flight. One of them had even tried to follow us in the crowd on the afternoon that we'd landed, and the whole lot had been gone again on the next dragon, switching with another crew before we could ask questions.

By the early afternoon of our first full day, I was restless. I woke Fieran up after my final watch was done.

"I'm going downstairs for some lunch. You want anything?"

He rolled over, mumbling in a soft, almost feminine voice, "I'm up, I'm up, damn you."

An instant later, he started to snore.

With a shrug, I locked the window, oiled the floor near the door, and turned the key behind me. The assassin would make a lot of noise falling over if she managed to get in, and Fieran had actually proven himself to have a bit of prowess, even if he was an ass.

Be nice, I told myself as I headed down the stairs to the tavern. *He did save your life.*

I missed a step. *Then again, he threw me right to the assassin. Delivered me right into her hands....*

Shaking my head, I continued on. I hadn't even reached my new estate, and already I thought the world was out to get me. I couldn't live my life jumping at shadows, or I'd be no better than a paranoid miser.

Two more days, I thought as I plopped myself down at a table facing the door. The caws and yips of trapped dragons filtered in through the open window nearest me. Our inn was actually built into the base of the Roost. This made it more secure, albeit smelly and loud; after all, we were surrounded by trapped, feral dragons.

The inn had a small tavern frequented by flight crews, which is how we'd known our own crew had left early. The Roost master drank an ale here every night, or so we'd been told. If two spots opened on a flight, we could trade in our tickets to the guy, and leave early.

"What'll you have?" the serving girl asked me, coming round to my table. She was wearing orange, to honor Ignace, and it made my mind burn just to look at it.

Color in darkness, smooth under my hand. The heat, the burning thrill of her gaze....

I shook the half-image from my mind, and looked at the server again. I'd taken to looking closely at every female I met.

The girl's eyes were dark-ringed and tired, despite her colorful clothes. She probably hadn't slept. I looked close, but she was too pale to be the blood-mage in disguise.

I ordered the biggest lunch she could bring me, and I found myself sitting pleasantly alone for a few hours nursing an ale and watching people mill past through the window. The inn was hunched next to the city's main thoroughfare, a road that ran past the base of the Roost.

From this angle, I had a good view of the Roost Road. It seemed more likely the assassin would try to get to us from this direction, although I wouldn't put it past her to brave the dragons.

Hours later, when the place filled for supper, an old man wandered in and seated himself beside me. I hadn't invited him to.

He tapped his cane on the nearest table leg as if testing its strength. "Where ya off to?" he asked me casually.

"Me? Nowhere. I'm just sitting here."

"Oh, I see that. I mean where you off to, when your dragon launches?"

I kept a wary eye on him as I sipped my ale. "How do you know I'm a traveler?"

"Clothes are too nice for this place," he said. "You've got a layover, longer than expected. Trying to save a buck by living low for a time."

He wasn't wrong. We hadn't bothered to ask around at the expensive inns.

"Dasvilla," I said. I could lie, but the truth would flush out my enemies faster.

He leaned toward me and offered a friendly smile. "Dasvilla? Nice place, that."

I looked him over, trying to determine whether he was a danger or not. He wore a light robe made from a fine material I didn't recognize, and he had a clean haircut that conveyed a respectable profession of some kind.

I considered my answer, keeping one eye on the Roost Road out the window. Afternoon sunlight made the sandy stone of the pavers glow golden, almost like a sun dragon's scales. The smell of fresh pastries and hot tea wafted from the tavern's back rooms and made my stomach rumble. That last big meal seemed so far away.

"Not as nice a place as this," I commented. "At least not the last time I was there. It has fewer dragons, though."

As fascinating and beautiful as the creatures were, their cries had never stopped even once throughout the night, even when the festivities died down.

Still, I was surprised there weren't more Airship-class dragons around; I'd only seen two since we'd been staying here, but the big beauties had only stopped by to offload passengers, not take on new ones. The Roost at Ignace featured three landing pads for loading and unloading, instead of the one that Olinios had, but none of them seemed to get a lot of use.

"To the contrary," the stranger said. "Dasvilla has plenty of dragons. There's a dragon husbandry business based there."

I eyed the man again. Above me, the floors groaned and shook as wild dragons ate, cleaned themselves, and rested in their cages. My eyes drifted up toward a blue-scaled Airship dragon who was about to take off from the landing pad. I could only see the underside of its throat from here.

Its scales shifted hue from stormy sea to clear night sky as it lifted off the platform, sending a heavy gust of wind down to the road and through my window. A color-changing dragon, then. Those were rare.

With the creature gone, its newly arrived passengers filed down out of the Roost. I was grateful none were staying for connecting flights, as this tavern was overcrowded already. Kin and strangers alike filed past the window, chatting excitedly as they marveled at the red-orange festival decorations.

"So, are you going straight to Dasvilla from here? Didn't know it had a direct flight," the man pressed. It seemed I had a talker on my hands.

He was nice enough, but the gem-encrusted dagger on his hip implied wealth. I knew better than to trust anyone wealthy, especially when he'd outright mentioned the business I was about to inherit.

I shook my head. "I'm on a long layover. Got to Ignace as quickly as I could, but I've got another flight to Bestune, then one to Ashkar, and finally one to Dasvilla."

"Why Dasvilla? Family troubles?" he asked.

I thought about it for a moment—about Jolene, and Etonia, and my long-dead mother, and all the street kids of the city I grew up in. I thought about everything that town meant to me.

"I... I guess it is."

Chapter 17

Honey and Hope and All that Good Shit

"Ah, so it's complicated, then?" the man asked me.

I shrugged. "Normally I'm left to my solitude, but not anymore. I might never have solitude again, after this."

"You're a soldier, then?"

I shot him a look. "How could you tell?"

He laughed, waving at me. "My apologies, son, but the matted hair gives it away; you lot *sleep* in your helmets, I swear. I should know. I used to serve on these very walls."

With that, he indicated the walls surrounding Ignace with a generalized up-high motion, even though we couldn't see the walls from here. His stare grew distant then, until a smile crept across his face.

"But that was ages ago. Now I trade honey!"

"Oh, that's... different," I said, unsure how to respond. "Why honey?"

He chuckled and gave me a conspiratorial wink. "It all happened because of a woman."

"Ah!" I chuckled with him. "Normally how it goes."

"Yes, yes. She worked at The Vineyard. That's a tavern—"

"In Ignace, yeah. I've heard of it." I'd heard whispers of it in the last hour alone, from half-drunk men at the tables around me. Only the most beautiful women were supposed to work there. It wasn't a brothel, though, so those women were unavailable, which only seemed to make them more legendary.

"Were you an officer or something? I hear it's expensive there." The mention of the finer tavern seemed out of place for someone who had once been a guardsman.

"Oh, no, I could never eat there. Never dated her, either. I was too lowborn, but...."

He trailed off conspiratorially. I decided to play along. "But?"

He paused as if deep in thought, reliving a memory. I let him, enjoying a shift in the breeze that suddenly promised summer heat and smelled like wet earth... anything to take my mind off the discomfort of sitting on a cheap wooden chair for so long. Or the greater discomfort of using a cheap bed for two more nights if a dragonflight seat didn't open up.

The old man broke his reverie and said, "You ever heard of Yemi bees?"

"The tiny little shits that leave blue marks when they sting you?" I asked, having encountered them more than a few times on scouting missions.

"Oh, yes. They're ubiquitous around here."

That was unfortunate, but I thought I knew where he was going with this. "They make honey, then?"

"Oh, yes. But I never cared much, at first. Hated the little fuck-ers. You see, during my time on the wall, Count Jiston ordered a lot of hunts, and I would usually be tasked with honey foraging because the man didn't like me.

"So, to save myself from the stings, I'd build a human decoy, smash the nests, and let the bees swarm the decoy while I tossed the broken honeycombs into my sack.

"I was good at it," the man went on, his eyes glazing again. "So good that I bragged about it to Belmy the one time I treated myself to The Vineyard.

"But my Belmy, well, she asked me nicely to *not* smash the nests. The next time I came in, she gave me a custom-made netting suit so I could take the whole hive out of the wilds and into the city.

"And, well, I did. She kept the bees on her roof with the dragons in her father's aviary, and she made decent profit and shared it with me."

Ah, I thought. If his love had owned an aviary, it made sense that he'd heard of Pinnacle Dragons in Dasvilla. Maybe he wasn't so suspicious after all.

Or maybe Pinnacle Dragons is bigger than I've given it credit for. Jolene's letter did say it had a reputation.

"Thing was," the old man continued, "Belmy's father married her off before I could woo her well enough to stop a proposed marriage. Once she got with child and her father passed, she pleaded with me to take over the bees, her passion, because I knew them somewhat. Her husband let her give it away; he loved her too, I think.

"I thought she was crazy, though." He sipped his tea with a shake of his head. "But honey is profitable, and since I enjoyed it, I put in for my freedom from soldiering and never looked back. Bees. Who'd have thought?"

The joy in his voice was something special. I could only hope to find that for myself one day. "I'm happy for you. I hope you found love eventually."

"Well, I thought I did. I married, but she always wanted more." The man drummed his fingers on the tabletop, and I got the sense the story wasn't over.

"Like a foolish young man, I wanted to give her that," he went on. "I wanted to make her happy. I expanded, starting farms in different cities to avoid transportation costs. Of course, this increased my income... which meant she spent more and I saw less of it.

"I eventually divorced her, because as we earned more, she grew more miserable, unable to hit the inner ring of the wealthy socialites all around us…. After months of suspicious activity, even the king agreed she was unreasonable."

The joy in his voice from moments ago seemed to have abandoned him. He sighed heavily. "I just hate being alone."

"Should have gotten two wives, or three," I said, trying to lighten the mood. The ultra-rich often had more than one spouse, men and women alike. It sounded like a lot of work to me.

He huffed a short laugh. "I'm too jaded. What if I got two bad ones, instead of one bad and one good?"

"You've got a point," I said, as a dragon the color of freshly cut citrines interrupted our conversation by squawking from a cage nearby. She launched at the ceiling of her enclosure, making the outer wall of the Roost shake with her impact. When she landed, she fell limp, moaned, and then emptied her stomach onto the floor. *Poor thing,* I thought.

"I really wish they'd give them bigger cages," I said.

"Try caging *that,*" the old man said. He pointed to a new, vivid ruby Hauler-class, just now landing on the middle platform of the Roost. "That's my ride to Bestune, and I get priority seating, so I bid you farewell."

"Safe flight," I said, rising to help him up, but he scoffed and waved me away.

"Safe travels to you, son," he said, by means of farewell. "I hope you find what you're looking for in Dasvilla. I'll ask around if I'm ever in town."

I watched him go, scanning the other patrons who also stood up. It was mostly people of wealth or those spending their fortune to relocate, judging by their scruffy clothing and the way they guarded their coin. I'd never seen such fearful eyes or clutching hands.

I spared a last glance at the man as he ascended the stairs at the base of the Roost. *I wonder why fate put you beside me?* I thought. *You started a business you never intended to start, and you did well with it anyway. Maybe I can, too.*

"Ugh, there you are," Fieran said, slumping into the seat next to me. "You ate supper yet? I'm starved."

Feeling much the same, I hailed a server. I ordered the stew from her, knowing that it would come out right away. They only had to scoop it into a bowl for us.

Fieran didn't protest, and when the food arrived, I covered his tab and stood. To the server, I said, "I'm going to watch the dragon launch. Is it okay if I borrow the bowl?"

The girl blinked, then inexplicably blushed. "I'm not sure if... ah... no, that's fine." She fluttered her lashes at me. "I trust you."

My own cheeks heated as she scurried away.

"How'd you get so lucky with the ladies?" Fieran groused.

"Dunno." I shot him a look. "Maybe I'm just *nice* to them."

He sniffed. "Whatever. You really going to watch the dragon?"

I nodded, stood, and lifted my bowl. "Dinner and a show, so to speak. I *am* inheriting a dragon farm, after all. I think I ought to get a good look at more dragons."

Fieran shrugged, but he rose too. After all, it was his job to guard me, farcical as that job might be.

We both carried our bowls and spoons over to the stairs, and no one stopped us as we ascended to the platform and sat on one of the benches lining the launch area.

Tucking into my food, I studied the red dragon as her passengers finished boarding. Her ruby scales glinted in the sunlight when she shifted closer to scratch her wing on an overhead support beam, making one of the passengers cry out as the floor moved beneath him.

This was a smaller, less-commercial dragon than the one we'd ridden in on, intended to fly shorter trips with fewer passengers. The dragon's captain sat in a special harnessed seat directly on top of her head, able to steer and see just as she did.

Meanwhile, the saddle on her back contained four benches with space for three people each. Bags went in the very front between her wings to balance the load. As a Hauler-class dragon, she was smaller than the hybrid Airship-class we'd ridden on the way here, but she could still carry twelve passengers easy.

This dragon had no cabins built onto her back, though. Instead, a slanted roof angled back from her shoulders, low to high; it would help wing lift while also offering shade.

The front row was for the wealthiest people, with the most wind-breaking and the most comfortable, padded chairs. All four front seats were already taken by people in ornate leathers —good solid traveling clothes that still had some style.

I counted the passengers behind the front, and my eyes lit up; two were missing. That meant two people who paid for a ticket hadn't shown up yet.

I scanned the area for the man I'd been told about, the launchmaster who liked to drink at the tavern where we were staying. When I glimpsed him near the entrance ramp, I set down my empty bowl.

"Hold on a second," I said. "I'm going to try to get us a ride."

The launchmaster grunted when I arrived to him. "Ticket?" he said.

I handed him the stamped papers that claimed I had a ride three days later. "I was just hoping to fill your two empty seats. There's, ah...." I mentally counted the cost of another two nights at the inn. "About eighty coppers in it for you, provided you delay the launch just ten minutes." After all, I had to return the bowls and grab our packs.

The launchmaster scowled at me. "These tickets are worth four hundred coppers, boy. That's forty silvers, and you've offered me eight."

My stomach dropped. I'd had no idea the amount was so high. "Well, they're worth nothing to *you* if those seats go empty."

"Let him on, Marty," a voice shouted, and we both turned to see the old honey-seller in one of the wealthy seats. He waved to me with a casual flick of his hand.

The launchmaster, Marty, didn't love the order, but he shrugged. "I'll delay ten minutes. If the original riders aren't here by then, you can pay me *two hundred* coppers, and I'll let you on."

I swallowed. That was steep—but still not much more than feeding ourselves for two more days during a festival would be.

Not to mention avoiding the assassin would have its own costs. She probably knew what dragon we had originally planned to fly on, so if we could sneak away early, we could elude her. She certainly wasn't among the dragon's current occupants; I'd made sure to check.

"Deal," I said. "Ten minutes."

With Fieran in tow, we made short work of running down the stairs, settling our bill, packing up, and running back up again. I hoped the assassin wasn't watching.

After a final call—which Marty himself shouted out to the dragon's captain—he let me and Fieran onto the flight.

We walked across the platform and over the narrow ledge to the back of the saddle. The musky scent of hay from the cages below mixed with the heated-leather aroma of the seats, but it wasn't unpleasant, and the view was lovely: the dragon herself was freshly washed, her shiny red scales free of dirt. They really did resemble rubies as they caught the light.

Fieran and I sat in a row that desperately needed a woman or child in it, given we'd been squished between two other burly types. We adjusted the best we could, eager to get underway. Marty gave the captain a thumbs-up, and a second later, the Hauler's massive red wings unfurled, casting a red shadow with a brilliant sheen.

The first beats washed cool air over the back row, and I felt myself grinning. Flying on the back of a dragon was taking my breath away yet again, and to my surprise, I found the experience lifting my spirits.

I'd almost died the last time I rode one of these things, and yet I was enjoying every moment of this. We burst into the air, my stomach floating from the sudden shift.

The dragon's wings flapped in unison as she angled her head toward the wilds, scanning the sky and the untamed lands for threats. A few minutes later, we were soaring high above the celebrating city, nearing some fluffy clouds.

I glanced over my shoulder to watch Ignace shrink in size. The festival was in full swing yet again, and the city teemed with oranges and reds and golds, with costumes and floats and long garlands of flowers. It looked like a volcano of its own, vibrant and boiling, full of power.

I hoped the assassin was down there, watching us leave, stuck for two more days before she could chase us.

When the city passed from sight, I fixated on the distance, where Olinios still existed, far out of my sight. Olinios had been good to me, with its friendly faces, and there was a certain barstool seat I'd miss. Now that I was growing accustomed to dragonflight, I had the space to mourn the passing of my own life, and to welcome the new.

I had considered selling the estate when I arrived, and coming back again. That thought no longer crossed my mind. While riding these beasts, and watching them in cages, and contemplating the way they fit into my world... well, I found myself curious.

How did a dragon farm exist? What would it be like to run one?

And could I be happy, tending to dragons? The way that old man had found joy in his bees?

I smiled to myself. *I can do that. I can save the business, stop assassins, and find my own calling.*

I was always down for a challenge.

112

Chapter 18

Shall We Be Off?

It wasn't until Fieran and I were high in the sky that I remembered Shimmer.

Demons! I cursed to myself, slapping a hand to my already-windblown face. I'd been asking after the young laundress all morning, bothering the server at the tavern about it. You'd think I wouldn't have forgotten her so easily, but I'd gotten swept up in the race to ride the ruby dragon out of town.

I dropped my hand and went back to gripping my seat's arm rests for dear life. *I'll send a message back,* I thought, but what would I say? I wasn't sure yet what my supposed inheritance would look like. I might not be inheriting much in the way of a fortune. I might just be inheriting a few silvers, a title, and a dragon farm that was more trouble than it was worth.

None of that would do Shimmer much good, unless I could hire her on to work for me. That seemed ill-advised right now, since I knew so little about what I would see once I landed in Dasvilla. I didn't think dragons needed laundresses.

Besides, I didn't want to step on Jolene's toes here. She should have inherited her mother's estate, not me—and she would have, if not for the antiquated laws of Parshil.

Wait... Jolene! That's the answer, I realized. Her letter had shown her to be competent, and if she was Lady Etonia's daughter, she would know how to handle this. I'd ask her how best to help Shimmer when I landed. She'd give me options.

With that at least somewhat resolved—after all, I hadn't promised Shimmer anything, so she wasn't waiting on me—I settled in for the flight.

This one was blissfully uneventful, and I spent my time making observations about the Hauler-class dragon we were flying on. Its ruby scales took on orange tones in bright sunlight.

If I remembered correctly, dragons with fire abilities were classified as Heat type. This particular Hauler-size breed was called a magma dragon.

Under the same typing, there were also flame dragons at Mount size, and volcano dragons at Behemoth size. Ignace, Demon of the Spark, was one of those. There were probably similar Heat breeds at Shoulder and Hauler size, but I didn't know what they were called.

I did know a few things, though, since Heat-type dragons were so ostentatious and well-known. For example, I knew that the magma dragon we were riding had an innate invincibility to heat, and it breathed lava spray instead of fire.

All heat-type dragons originally hailed from the wilds around the volcano Dasco, so in a way, this one was headed home.

After landing in Bestune, we bid farewell to the old man beekeeper and found a Mount-dragon charter that would take us to Dasco for the low, low price of half my remaining funds.

With a sigh, I handed over the money. We had outrun the blood-mage for now, but if we sat around Bestune too long, she'd catch up to us. Better to spend the coin and be safe.

The charter dragon turned out to be a hybrid, a half-sun and half-lake dragon. Its coloring was flat sea green with the occasional yellow scale, and its horns were clear like prisms. I didn't know what its abilities were, since hybrids could have unpredictable traits.

In the few minutes before launch, I hung near the captain to ask questions. She was a tall sun-tanned woman, clad all in natural leather, as bulky and muscular as a blacksmith. Her hair was a deep, luscious red, kept in a short tail. She wore flight goggles over forest-green eyes.

"So, what can this one do?" I asked. "I'm told hybrids can have all kinds of different abilities, while purebloods always have the same."

"That's true," the captain said, leaning over the front edge of the saddle platform to grip a rope she had dropped. "They tend to take on a little of each parents' powers, but those powers can mix any number of ways. Mostly, this one can swim as well as it flies, and it spits boiling water—which is more useful than it sounds."

I could imagine. Already-boiled water would be sanitized. This dragon would be a source of safe drinking water, if ever its passengers were stuck in a bad situation.

I leaned back against the banister of her captain's dais while she went about checking dials and muttering to herself, making tiny adjustments to her instruments as she went.

"And its parents?" I asked. "What can those types do?"

"Sun dragons are normally yellow or gold," she explained, moving to her steering reins now, reeling some in and hooking others to different supports in a complex array of equipment. "They've also got transparent horns and spikes. They spit concentrated light beams, which might as well be concentrated fire. They're impervious to attacks by nonliving objects—basically, weapons can't hurt them.

"Sadly, Seabreeze here didn't get that ability. We get shot at now and then, in Dasco."

So the hotlands still have their share of monster tribes, I mused to myself. Minotaurs could use arrows and ballistae. *I guess nothing ever changes in Dasco.*

As the captain finished up, she absently explained Seabreeze's other parental line, the lake dragons—not to be confused with their larger cousins, the ocean dragons. Apparently, their scales tilted between sea green, bright blue, and teal, dependent on the light. Their spikes were rough and beige-colored, as if the dragon's bones were made of sand. Lake dragons were impervious to poison, and they spat superheated steam.

Meanwhile, their navy-colored ocean cousins were impervious to drowning—they could hold their breaths indefinitely—and they spat lava, just like the volcano dragons, although the lava hardened rapidly into obsidian. If they spat from far enough away, it was similar to spitting arrowheads at an enemy.

"And that's all I got for you," the captain said, straightening to face me. "We're ready to take off. You good?"

I glanced at Fieran, who had seized the chance to snooze across several unused seats. "We're all set," I told the captain. "But thank you for telling me all this. I have a lot to learn about dragons."

She narrowed her deep green eyes at me, which served to darken the shadows inside her goggles. It was as if she suddenly recognized me.

"You're not—you're not the guy that's inheriting Pinnacle Dragons, are you?" she asked.

I offered a lopsided smile. "Am I so transparent?"

Her narrowed eyes suddenly jumped wide, and she dropped to a knee before I could stop her. "Milord! Forgive me for talking to you so familiarly—and for charging you passage. Please, accept a full refund. The owner of Pinnacle Dragons does not pay here."

For a moment I could only blink at her. "Why—why not?" was all I managed to ask.

She looked up at me, and for a second my animal brain took over. From this angle, I could see the tops of her breasts, bunched up under her leather riding jacket. They looked, ah... very *contained*.

"Seabreeze hailed from Pinnacle, milord," she said. "When I was a girl, I used to work for Pinnacle, and Seabreeze was my favorite. The old master was training him while I was there.

"When it came time for a sale, the master gave Seabreeze to me instead of selling him. Of course, I couldn't accept such a gift— but the old master said it was an investment. *Fly me where I need to go when I need to go there, and Seabreeze is all yours,* he said."

A confused chuckle tumbled out of me. "But that's not me. I'm the new master, not the old one. You don't have to keep holding this... tradition."

Shut up, shut up, I told myself. *She's offering you your money back. Take it!*

I needn't have worried. The captain was shaking her head vehemently, making the distracting flesh at her chest jiggle. I tore my eyes away, focusing on her face, but her tits remained in my periphery. I really needed her to stand up again.

"No, no, sir. I wouldn't hear of it. Seabreeze is everything to—"

"Please get up, Captain. You shouldn't be kneeling for me," I said, patting her on the outside of one shoulder. "Fine, I'll take the refund, but only if you tell me your name."

She rose, taller than me once more, the tantalizing skin now hidden behind her leather coat's lapels. From this angle, she looked much more modest, thank the skies.

"I'm Kenna, sir," she said.

I held out a hand. "And I'm Warren. Pleasure to meet you."

She shook my hand with both of hers, leaning into it. "Anything you ever need, just say so," she said. "Raising dragons is hard work, sir, but rewarding."

I nodded. "I'm no stranger to hard work, Captain."

Her gaze dipped to my biceps, and she grinned. "I can see that." She let me go, and pulled my payment from her pocket. The coins clinked in the pouch as she handed them over. "Well, milord. Shall we be off?"

Chapter 19

There's No Place like Home

WE LANDED at Dasvilla's large Roost an hour before dusk. A mountain rose over the city to the north, trailing a light stream of smoke that meant the volcano was active. I couldn't know for sure, but it appeared to be smoking more than it had when I'd left all those years ago.

Even with the smoke clouding the sunlight, the scenery was beautiful. A golden evening glow had settled onto my old home, making it look like a fairy tale setting. Aside from the increased smoke, Dasvilla seemed unchanged from when I left at sixteen.

I'd had hopes then, of becoming someone special. I didn't have those hopes anymore.

The Roost had been built to extend high above the city, with a clear view of the volcano in the distance. From this vantage, I could clearly see the city's delineation into two parts, separated by a steaming river: one side of the city was dirty and run-down, the other clean and, well, also run-down.

Clearly, Duke Biscuit's own fortunes hadn't much improved since I'd been here last, although what he did have was clean, if not perfect.

Both halves of the city were coughing up streams of evening smoke, marking the cook fires for the final meal of the day. Most of the populace was currently tucked into buildings, although light foot traffic trailed through the streets, and the Roost itself bustled with activity. The clang of hammer-strikes and the squeak of pulleys reached us from between the many supports of the Roost structure.

"Well I'll be burned," Kenna said, shading her eyes from the muffled sun. "They're fixing this old Roost. It's been falling into disrepair for years now. Must be makin' it pretty for you."

Close by, several artisans had stopped to stare at us. Someone had already sent a runner down the stairs. *Yeah, and they didn't expect me for several days yet. Maybe someone wanted to put on a show of prosperity for me, but I've arrived before it was complete.*

"Still looks rickety," Fieran said, kicking a fraying post. A few toothpicks of rotten wood chafed off.

"Yeah, but the Duke's keep looks better-maintained," I said, scowling. A tall stone building dominated the back end of the cleaner city-section, shining with a vibrancy that only came from constant upkeep. It had its own oval wall, with six towers spaced across it, which vaguely mirrored the oval-shaped wall of the city itself.

That hadn't changed at all, meaning it had been well-taken care of. The Dragon's Throat was the same too; the boiling-hot river ran past the castle and through an enormous iron grate at the base of the city's southern wall. I saw shapes in the grate that I didn't recognize, hard to discern at this distance.

"What's on the grate?" I asked Kenna, pointing.

Her face darkened. "Thieves. Biscuit has taken to drowning them, very painfully and very publicly. There have been... a lot more, lately."

A hot spike drove up through my center. They'd blister in that water, just as much as they'd drown. It wasn't a humane way to die.

"Is that an arena?" Fieran asked, the growl in his voice vanishing for a moment. "What for?"

An oval-shaped arena, even larger than the keep, stood not too far from the Roost. Despite being on the cleaner, eastern side of the city, it was still only a bridge away from the lower-class half of Dasvilla.

The building appeared shabby, mostly because large crowds tended to degrade new construction. It was missing most of its retractable oil-paper roof, with the streets around it clogged with food vendors and their milling customers. I thought I heard cheers on the wind.

"Used to be knight trials there," I said. "Sounds like that's still happening."

"It's not knights anymore, but yeah, there are still fights," Kenna said. "It's the only real entertainment around here, but they've switched to... well, you'll see."

She patted the side of Seabreeze's shoulder. "You gentlemen need anything else from me? I come through on Sundays, usually, but if you need me sooner, say the word."

Fieran turned and opened his mouth, but I didn't trust him to say something respectful, so I cut him off.

"We're good for now, thanks. I'll watch out for you Sunday. Come down to... wherever Pinnacle Dragons is, and I'll make sure to feed you a hot meal, as thanks for today." I couldn't recall, at the moment, where Lady Etonia's estate was, since I'd never actually been there.

Kenna nodded. "It would be my pleasure, milord. See you then."

With that, she mounted Seabreeze, her braid swinging out with her fluid movements. I admired the strength in her silhouette for a moment.

Fieran leaned toward me. "I wouldn't mind having that captain ride *me,* one of these days. With all that muscle, I bet she'd fuck me raw."

"Don't be crass," I growled, my mood souring again. Just when I was warming to him, Fieran goes and says shit like that. I turned and stalked for the stairs, and he hastened to follow.

121

"What? Can you blame a guy for admiring?"

"Yes, in fact, I can."

He scoffed as I led him onto the stairs, but he blessedly changed the subject.

"So you really used to live here?" he asked. "Where at?"

I pointed to one of the neighborhoods lining the Throat. "Lived with my mother over there for a minute."

Upon reaching a landing, I swept my arm to a hovel up against the western wall. "Then I lived in an orphanage there, until I came of age. After that, I had to work the fields for a while to afford passage out of the city."

With that, I pointed out the fields between the main city and the hovels against the wall. There was a solid half-ring of the fields, like a giant smile. The city designers would have shoved them right up against the walls, but they didn't get any light there in the shadow. Besides, if something attacked, the hovels served as a buffer—poor people dying just to spare a few crops.

"Did you not turn to soldiering right away?" Fieran asked, as if surprised by the idea.

"I didn't, no," I said. "I'd spent most of my childhood getting in and out of fights, and I was done with that."

"Really? What changed—oh."

I knew what he was thinking. King Kurto had established a military draft when I was eighteen, and thousands of commoners had been forcefully conscripted. The draft had since been revoked.

"I wasn't drafted," I said, scratching at the stubble growing along my neck. "But the draft was the reason I joined. I wanted to take the place of at least one poor sod who didn't want to be there."

After all, as much as I'd *thought* I hated fighting, I'd missed the rough-and-tumble street life during the year I'd been farming. The draft had given me an excuse to go back—even if I didn't approve of it.

Fieran was quiet for a long moment, and at the next landing, I turned back to glance at him. He was eying the fields, which currently sprouted large crops from the constant warm rain. Every cloud that climbed over the volcano ended up releasing a load of water on Dasvilla afterward.

"That draft really messed with a lot of people's lives," he said softly.

I measured my words. "I know. The king said the wildlands were more unruly than ever, but plenty of those original conscripts were sent East, when the worst of the fighting was off to the West."

"Yeah, and then we lost Parmisca just last year anyway," he said, sounding more sober than I'd ever heard him.

I nodded. Parmisca had been a real tragedy. An entire walled city, sacked by green elves and their monster henchmen less than a year ago.

"So, what did you farm, then?" Fieran asked, changing the subject.

I indicated the charred-black forest between the city and the volcano with an open hand. "Firefruit. It grows on those black trees. It's the best money here, and most guys are drawn to it, once they start wanting a wife and kids."

Although most of them never live to marry, I added mentally.

We had reached the based of the Roost now, and as we strode across the city road and onto a bridge over the Throat, none of the passerby seemed to recognize me. Oh, they *noticed* me fine; Dasvilla didn't have First-Rank Vanguards, so Fieran was drawing attention. However, no one called my name or showed any spark of knowing me.

I hadn't expected them to. When I'd left a decade ago, I had been strong but still scrawny, with only one summer's worth of built muscle. I might have been tall, but I'd also been dirty from living a hard life, and I don't think I'd had much facial hair, either.

Now, though, I was a high-ranking city guardsman with years of far less cushy infantry experience. This job had altered who I was at my very core. I'd left Dasvilla a hardened street kid, and I now returned a grizzled veteran. A decade of war tended to change a person.

My first and most important stop was the bank, because I loathed carrying around all my net worth. There was only one bank in the city, and of course it was on the nicer side of the river. No one on *this* side had money to spare for storing.

All the same, it was close to the Roost and to the arena—all the better to make your bets with. The three staple buildings were all part of the "Old Town" as some of the locals fondly put it.

The city had been founded the same way that most cities had: a set of crazy settlers had braved the wilds to reach fertile grounds and a water source, using a trained dragon to help them. Ours had been a magma Hauler named Das.

The settlers' first task had been to build a Roost, a wall, and a bank to encourage rich people to come and set up shop. It kept travel distance short for arriving nobles.

I found the bank with no trouble, depositing my money into my old account rather than go through the bother of dealing with Pinnacle Dragons' accounts yet.

The founders of these cities understood the importance of keeping crime down, so banks within the Parshil Kingdom were both extremely well-protected, and simple. A person or business deposited coins, then used ledgers for large transactions, requiring both parties to be present.

For now, I deposited the credit chip that contained most of my fortune, then kept the pouch of coins Kenna had returned to me. This left me with a decent chunk of copper coins and a couple of silvers, which I stashed in different spots under my traveling coat.

I was about to leave when an idea struck me. "Hey," I asked the teller. "Is my account still associated with a safe-deposit chest?"

These were used to store items rather than plain money. The teller flipped a page in his book, his eyes darting under his glasses.

"It appears so, sir."

Well I'll be cursed, I thought. When I'd left town, I'd hidden a special dagger in my safe-chest. I'd taken the blade off a minotaur when I was seventeen. The creature had breached the walls and gotten into the crops I'd been harvesting, and I'd somehow killed it with a gardening hoe.

"Who's been paying the safe-deposit fee?" I asked. As a kid, I'd been eager to keep the treasure safe, but I'd long since realized that the bank would happily toss the rusted old knife if I stopped paying for the place where it was kept.

The teller squinted at his ledger before his eyes widened. He regarded me with new respect.

"Says here the Minax accounts covered the cost," he said. "Signed by the Lady Etonia Minax."

Huh. That woman continues to be full of surprises, I thought.

"Do you wish to extract your item, sir?" the teller asked.

I waved a dismissive hand at him. "No, no, not yet. But I'll definitely come back for it." I already had the assassin's knife, and it was better quality. No sense dragging an old, blunt knife around with me. I might accidentally draw it, and get myself killed—and besides, I didn't care much for sentimental stuff.

Speaking of which....

I reached into my back, fished around, and pulled out the glass orb that my forgotten lover had given to me.

"Actually, can we add this to the safe-chest?" I asked.

The teller nodded. "Of course, sir. Just let me fetch it."

As he went to retrieve the chest, I let the orb reflect its violet-and-blue light across the wooden counter. It was a lovely thing, with a small diamond embedded on the underside, and no discernible source for the colored light.

However, it was a reminder of a woman I'd forgotten. As in, *legitimately* forgotten. I'd gotten drunk and woken up in an unfamiliar bed, with only the vague sense that something beautiful had happened.

For a long time, the orb had kept me curious, but now—now I had a new life, a new mystery, possibly even a new woman.

As I had done once before, and would do again, it was time to leave the past in the past.

After the bank, Fieran and I stepped back into the street to find the sun setting at a beautiful angle. For a moment, I simply stood back to regard the colors and sounds of my old home.

I'd never expected to return. Nothing held me here. My mother was long gone, and although I'd had many friends, they had been friends of necessity; fellow orphans and street kids, banding together for survival rather than brotherhood.

At least, that's what I'd always told myself. But standing here now, I found myself wondering after all the friends I'd had here. How were they doing? Were they married? Had they become parents, or maybe soldiers? How many of them were still alive?

My thoughts scattered as a thunderous sound broke my reverie. I startled, my hand going to my knife.

"What was—" I started to ask Fieran, when the sound repeated itself. I turned my head toward the enormous building rising up to my left—the arena.

I used to sneak into the so-called nosebleed section as a kid, climbing the outer walls of the arena to watch from the very highest seats if the stands weren't full. I'd nearly gotten myself killed trying to watch the hand-to-hand combat of the region's best knights. The arena used to be Dasvilla's one and only tourist attraction, but the place looked decrepit now.

But hadn't Kenna said it was still in use?

Shouts rose from the walls, followed by the clanking of chains. How could chains be so loud from so far? They had to be huge.

The original roar had also not been human. It was the cry of a monster, so loud that it dwarfed the raucous cheers that followed it.

No. Could it be...?

As soon as I suspected it was a dragon, I knew I was right. Dragons made all kinds of sounds across their many sizes and varieties, and this one sounded like twisting metal. But it wasn't the sound that told me I was right. I'd barely heard any dragons before.

All the same, I knew.

"Are they pitting knights against dragons now?" I asked no one in particular, my hackles rising. "I heard chains. Are they fighting *chained* dragons?"

Fieran stepped closer to me. "I've heard of this. Dukes and barons have been catching wild monsters to train men against them in arena combat. It used to be forbidden, on account of all the deaths, but the king has been turning a blind eye, because the attacks on caravans have been getting worse every year."

"But a chained dragon? It would be a sitting—"

BOOM!

The ground shook, and I staggered backward.

BOOM!

Now the ground wasn't the only thing shaking. I looked up, up, up the face of the arena, but the whole facade was moving. It took me a moment to understand the stone was crumbling away, a massive crack shooting down the yellowed sandstone.

Fieran cursed and grabbed my shirt, twisting to run.

At that moment, the entire wall blasted outward, and a great silver head plunged through.

Chapter 20

A Deadly Patient

THERE WAS no way we'd outrun the rain of stone, so I yanked on Fieran hard as I dropped to my knees. He came down with me while I whipped my shield up off my back, deflecting the first stone away from his face.

He reacted, retrieving his own shield in time to protect himself from the hail of rock. Bits of scree pummeled my shield as I took it back, using it to protect my kneeling body as best I could.

The rain slowed, but the decimation did not. The wall continued to bow outward, the crack spreading and splitting its greedy fingers across the stone face, the dragon's head leaning back to roar again.

The beast was enormous, an Airship-class, big enough to be used for commercial dragonflights. Very few Airship-class dragons were ever domesticated, as they had to be raised from an egg, which meant sneaking past the mother to raid a nest in the wild.

This dragon had *not* been domesticated. It was definitely wild, if it was being used in the arena. It was *acting* wild, too, raking its talons down through the audience stands until the crack gave even more. Thankfully, I didn't see people; they must have cleared the stands when the dragon started rampaging.

As we huddled, the front wall collapsed in a cloud of dust that swelled across the street like a sandstorm. I squinted against it, standing up when the rubble tumbled toward us—along with the dragon on top of it.

The beast was thrice the height of a man and the length of three houses, easily. Its silver scales shone dully, like freshly smithed metal that had not yet been polished. Chains linked all four of its feet so tightly that it could only take short steps. The links were each as big around as my head, and both of its wings had been forced closed with wing-muzzles.

It walked unsteadily, clearly hobbled by the bindings. Men in armor shouted amongst themselves in the arena behind it, but they didn't approach.

"What the hell were they thinking, bringing that in there?" Fieran exclaimed. "Airship-classes can't be contained like that! Are they *mad?*"

"It's going to trample half the city," I said, breaking into a run before I could even think. "We have to set it free!"

"Are you nuts? We need to kill it!"

I frowned at myself. He was right. I had no key for those massive locks. There was only one realistic way to protect the people of Dasvilla. I would have to kill this dragon.

Yet I couldn't bring myself to draw my knife as I closed the distance, reaching the edge of the scree and watching my footing as I darted and dodged amongst the rolling stones. Fieran shouted after me, but I didn't hear him.

The dragon roared again, but it had stopped moving. It merely perched atop the rubble of its former enemy, the arena, and looked about for a new thing to target.

The new thing it found was *me*.

Its silver eyes narrowed, its head dropping low. I noticed the low number of spines, and I guessed that it was female.

It roared at me, the flaps of skin to either side of its mouth rippling. I flinched, wondering what its breath ability was, and if that ability was about to disintegrate me.

Lucky for me, it was only a roar.

When the dragon made no move to snap at me, and just stared, I took a risk and threw my shield to one side. This improved my balance and saved some of my strength.

I was within twenty feet of the creature now, and I slowed on the uneven ground, both my palms up and facing out, placating.

"Hey now, hey," I said. "Let's not lose our heads here." *Especially not* my *head*, I thought.

Maybe it was being back in Dasvilla that did it, but I suddenly found myself trying to talk this dragon down, the same way I used to talk down bullies in these very streets. In my childhood, the kids under my protection used to run behind me all the time, a bigger kid always hot on their tails.

This, right here, is how I'd always dealt with them. *Hey now, let's not lose our heads.* The tactic tended to work, since I'd always been a large kid even when I was younger than the bullies.

Unfortunately, I wasn't bigger than this dragon.

Yet, it didn't attack. It bobbed its head sideways to look at me with just one eye, as if it could see better that way. With just one big step forward, it would have the clearance to bite me in half.

Movement behind it. My gaze flicked right, and the dragon noticed and whipped its head around to snap at the soldier coming up on its long, barbed tail. The man screamed and just barely escaped its jaws.

"Leave it alone!" I shouted. "The key. We need the keys! If it can fly away, it won't bother anyone!"

"No! Kill it!" someone replied, and I turned to find a crowd had gathered at a respectful distance.

"Kill it! Kill it!" someone started chanting, and more voices took up the call.

"NO!" I roared, louder than their moronic chant. I pointed at the arena. "It won't go down easy! If we keep trying to kill it, the thing will break more homes. It'll rampage! Now who's got the fucking *key!?"*

The chant mercifully died, but no one said anything. I cursed under my breath, shook my head, and then met the dragon's eye again. It had once again decided to plant its gaze on me, with one eye to the front, and one eye on its rear. The fighters would be stupid to try to approach it again.

Hands still up, I said, "It's okay, girl. It's okay. I'm just going to come closer, and get those chains off you." I took a step, paused, then took another. The dragon made no move toward me. "I don't mean you harm. I'm just going to get the bindings off you. Okay?"

To my surprise, the dragon grunted, a sort of deep-throated huff. It was almost like the thing understood me.

Either that, or it's barely containing its rage, I thought, with more than a little suppressed panic.

I crunched forward, my feet slipping on the loose sandstone. The dragon was deadly still, and it radiated something—anger, perhaps? I could feel it in the air, like a dense fog around the beast. It even seemed to have a color and feel to it, the tamed silver of the forge and the reverberating buzz of hammered metal. The creature was all potential, like the calm before a storm, only this storm was more deadly than anything that came from the sky.

Gradually, I reached its front talons. Its head loomed, still not moving, as if the thing had turned to solid metal. It creeped me out, and I knew that, without my shield, one wrong move would get me killed before I ever got to accept my new fortune.

I painstakingly lowered my hands to the manacle around the dragon's front left ankle. The manacle could have looped all the way around me and left several inches open, but it fit snug to the dragon's leg.

That's how big this thing was. The scale of the creature astounded me, even though I'd ridden on one just recently. For some mysterious reason, they seemed so much larger when their jaws were above you, rather than at the front of your flight platform, facing away.

Swallowing hard, I dared myself to look at the locking mechanism of the manacle. The dragon huffed, and I felt sure it was about to kill me because I'd broken eye contact—but it didn't.

Taking a steadying breath, I reached carefully into my pack, fished around, and found the sewing kit I used for uniform repairs. I retrieved the two largest needles and knelt in front of the manacle, setting to work.

I bet Lady Etonia never expected her sewing lessons to go to this, I thought, as I worked to pick the lock. After Lady Etonia had delivered sewing supplies to the orphanage, many of us had stolen needles and used them to try lockpicking. It was a tough skill to learn, requiring patience and practice, but it had served me well over the years.

The manacle snapped open.

The crowd gasped collectively, murmuring, and I moved to the next one, always walking as if the stones beneath me were eggshells. The dragon continued to twist its head this way and that, always keeping one eye toward me. Did it understand that I had weapons? That I was close enough to its flanks and belly to try to kill it? Were dragons that smart?

They have to be, I told myself, while working on the final manacle. *If dragons were dumb, this thing would have eaten me before I got this close. Instead, it's trusting me to help it.*

I didn't understand why, but I wasn't going to look a gift dragon in the mouth. When the last manacle clicked open, I set it aside and turned to the beast's head. I pointed at its wings.

"I can try to remove those too, if you can... ah...."

The dragon couldn't understand human speech, surely, so I mimed flapping wings, and then lowering one wing down. The dragon blinked.

"Lower. Your wing. Like this," I said, mimicking the movement again. I cupped my hands in a manacle shape, popping them open. "So I can remove the muzzles."

The dragon's eyelids twitched, as if it, too, were narrowing its eyes.

Then, it lowered one of its wings.

More whispers raced away from us, and someone shouted "Stab it!" while another demanded I lop off the wing, as if the flesh and bone would give like butter. I half-expected the dragon to snap at those people, since it almost seemed to understand me, but it ignored the insults and threats.

I picked my way over to the wing, and broke that lock, too. As soon as the wing-muzzle dropped away, the dragon made a new sound, a pleased rumble. It flapped the diaphanous silver wing, and something about the movement seemed cheerful.

"Last one," I said, nodding to the final wing. "Then you can leave here. All right?"

The dragon chirruped, like a high-pitched grunt—a far cry from the angry sounds it had been making before. Practically shaking with relief that this would soon be over, I took a final step toward the last wing.

I tripped.

I fell sprawling, but I didn't lose hold of my lock-picking needles. I knew I'd need them. They meant my survival.

Unfortunately, they were still sharp.

My hand landed against the wing, and the needles pierced the membrane, my weight dragging the impromptu blades down the wing in a bloody line. The dragon flapped, knocking me over as it roared. I rolled away on instinct, just as it snapped at the space where I'd been.

"Wait!" I shouted. "Accident, that was an accide... dent...."

My eyes held wide. As I'd spoken, the dragon had attacked, its jaws coming in for the kill... but it had stopped, and now the dragon's snout was not three inches in front of my face.

It huffed, blowing my hair back off my forehead. I completely forgot how to breathe.

"Didn't you hear him, idiot!?" a familiar raspy voice shouted. "He said it was an accident! Leave him be!"

Fieran, you moron, I wanted to say, but neither me nor the dragon moved. If the dragon did understand speech, it had ignored Fieran's words.

"It was an accident," I said again.

Those eyes narrowed to slits now, and it backed its head away, only a few more inches. It could still bite me in two pieces in a heartbeat.

I started working on the wing-muzzle anyway.

This one took longer, because my hands kept shaking and the blood from the wing had gotten onto my hands, making everything sticky. The more I sweated, though, the more blood I could get off my skin, until finally I had the proper grip to put the needles where I wanted.

The muzzle contraption opened with an audible *click*, loud enough to reset my heartbeat to match it.

"There," I said, stepping away. "You're free now—"

The dragon flapped its wing toward me, once.

I frowned. "I said you're—"

Another flap. There was something insistent about it. I surveyed the wing and its bleeding injury all over again.

I swallowed thickly. "Do you want me to sew it up for you?" I croaked. "It will hurt, but I've got ointment...."

I trailed off, praying to all the Four Demons that the dragon would just huff and take flight. The injury wasn't bad enough to keep it grounded.

Instead, it flapped its wing against me, almost like a little slap.

My hands trembling even worse now, I raised the needles up one last time.

After I sewed up the dragon's wound and poulticed it with my standard-issue cure-all ointment, the beast chirruped once, and took flight.

I watched its silver underbelly rise into the darkening sky, the gray lost against the oncoming night well before I stopped staring. I just stood there, in the middle of the collapsed wall of the arena, gazing at the empty sky like I was reading the stars.

When someone finally clambered up to me, I didn't even hear them. I nearly struck the heavens when Fieran clapped a hand on my shoulder.

"Hey," he said. "There's some guy here. Says you won something."

I turned to find the city watchmaster standing behind me. He looked chastened.

Good. He should be.

"What were you fucking thinking, bringing a wild Airship dragon into the arena?" I snapped, finally finding words again. I flung an arm out. "We were lucky this was all the damage it did!"

The watchmaster bowed his head at me. "I know, son. Trust me, I know. But the justicar ordered the dragon into the arena, and I'm unfortunately beholden to him."

This made me even angrier, because now I couldn't yell at the watchmaster for this idiocy, since the whole situation was out of his hands.

"To what purpose?" I growled. "Why on Parshil would a justicar want to endanger his city for—for what? Entertainment? Don't justicars swear to uphold the law? This is a soldier's pastime, not something for Enforcers to play around with."

He nodded. "I agree, sir. I agree wholeheartedly. But the justicar could not be dissuaded, and since he's probably on his way by now...."

The man trailed off, and I caught on.

"He's going to want to have a word with me, and it won't be pretty," I said, not bothering to hide my disgust. "This dragon was a prize, and I set it free."

"Yes," he admitted, "and while I would dearly love to know how you got that thing to understand you, there isn't time. Please, just take today's arena prize money, and go before this gets even messier."

With that, the man offered me a hefty-looking purse. I stared at it, a thousand arguments going through my head.

"Warren... maybe this is for the best," Fieran whispered behind me. "We don't want to draw too much attention when we only just arrived here...."

I nodded as he let the words hang. He was right, and I took the purse.

"I thank you, sir," I said. "We'll take our leave now."

The watchmaster looked like he wanted to say more, but the sound of horseshoes crossed over the river, and he nodded. Fieran and I hurried away.

When we were out of sight of the ruined arena, Fieran caught my arm and spun me.

"How did you do that?" he hissed. "How did you get it to obey you?"

I opened my mouth, then closed it. How could I explain?

"I don't know," I said. "But I think... it understood me."

He scoffed. "Yeah, right! But even if it did understand, why did it *obey* you? Dragons almost never listen to humans, especially not as perfectly as that one did. Not even after training with them for decades!"

I had no answer for that. No answers at all.

"I don't know," I repeated. "I'm just lucky, I guess."

He laughed and slapped my back. "Now *that,* I believe. You're one lucky fucker, Third-Rank Guardsman Warren. One lucky fucker indeed."

Chapter 21

The Girl with the Ice Dragon

THE CITY WELCOMED me with the sudden musky scent of after-dinner pipe smokers. I used to work a few of these alleys, mostly organizing other kids from the orphanage to help sweep businesses or haul shit buckets to the dump or the river. Work resulted in coins, which resulted in better food than what we normally got.

For us kids, the disgusting tasks were worth the sweets and real fruit, and work was better than stealing. Duke Biscuit's father used to chop off fingers for first-time thieves, and entire hands for repeat offenders.

I ground my teeth together. *And now his heir is boiling thieves alive,* I thought. *Apparently, like father, like son.*

Unsure where to go next, I decided to head for the keep, since Jolene likely still resided there. The closer we got to the tall six-towered building, the more dragons we saw. I'd forgotten how plentiful they were on the nicer side of the river.

"Is it just me, or does this city have more than the normal amount of dragons?" Fieran asked, dodging a stalking, wingless Mount-class dragon as it hauled a fancy carriage down the street. Once it was past us, it forced a horse and buggy off the road. Dragons didn't like to make way.

"It didn't when I was a kid, but then again, Pinnacle Dragons *is* based here," I said. "The business might be falling into ruin, but it's always cheaper to acquire or lease dragons close to where they were raised."

"Makes sense, but now that you mention it, most of the dragons do look old," Fieran mused, his gravelly voice turning pensive. "I'm guessing Pinnacle hasn't raised many new ones in a while. You've got your work cut out for you."

I didn't know how to take that, so I just said, "Thanks."

To better dodge further dragons, I stuck to the middle of the mostly-even cobblestone road. Dasvilla didn't have sidewalks like the larger cities did, connecting homes and storefronts directly to the road. Because of this and the unpredictable paths dragons took, a lot of the traffic stuck toward the middle, wanting to avoid blocking someone from using a door that opened inward while also keeping mobile in case a dragon-cart was threatening to run them over.

As for the people themselves, they weren't big on wearing fancy clothing unless they were nobles or merchant-class. Most of them wore common robes or working leathers, shifting to lighter outfits for the warmer summer season, and for good reason; the afternoon heat still permeated the city, even with the sun nearly down.

A few kids stared out of the alleys too, temporary transplants from the Hotside, which was the slang term for the poorer side of the city.

The kids watched the traffic pass with hesitant glares. No one tried to pickpocket me, even though I was ready for it. I was glad to see that Dasvilla still hadn't become a den for thievery; it just wasn't rewarding enough.

I knew better than to toss the kids coins, though, because not all of them would get to keep their own hauls. Many were forced to give their begging funds to adults back at home. Then again, maybe that had changed. I'd have to visit the orphanage with some donations here soon, to make up for being jaded right now.

As we passed one of the first two-story buildings, a beautiful woman—pale and dark-haired, like most people around here—waved at me from an upper-floor balcony. She smiled coyly from her lounge seat on the roof, her dress draped flirtatiously over a body that wore nothing else beneath.

It was always hot here, but only the wealthy dared to show themselves off like that; they'd have guards down below to protect them while they drank chilled firefruit wine and watched the sun go down.

As for the guards themselves, two types protected cities. The soldiers on the walls were mostly used to keep the dangers outside the city on the outside, although they could step into the city during brawls or riots as needed. In short, keeping the day-to-day peace was the realm of the guardsmen, led by the city general but mostly run by the general's watchmaster, whom we had just met.

Every city also had a justicar, who worked with his or her own team of Enforcers to serve as overseers, handling anything the guardsmen weren't equipped for. These elite soldiers made few appearances, but when they did show up, it meant bad news. They used their dragons to uphold the laws of the land, but sometimes that meant burning someone alive on the spot.

In a way, Enforcers *were* the law. All of them were highly educated in the capital, and they'd all trained in combat since puberty.

Each was assigned a Shoulder-class dragon which typically perched on their shoulders. The magical beasts were great at freezing or stunning disorderly drunks, but they trained with their Enforcers since they'd emerged from their eggs.

In that way, the Enforcers kept the tiny dragons to heel. Occasionally, a random citizen would sport a Shoulder dragon, too, but those were usually the mellower hybrids, and their owners had paid a pretty copper to get them. At one point, a well-dressed boy walked a juvenile dragon past us; the Mount-class creature was the size of a hound and still growing. It must have cost as much as a house.

In fact, when compared to other cities, Dasvilla was bursting with dragons. Mostly, the beasts blended into the background, only used as tools when it became necessary. Cats, dogs, and birds were also common, watching from balconies, stoops, or windows, waiting to see if humans dropped crumbs.

The closer we got to the keep, the more people seemed healthy and well-fed. If a person could afford food, it came relatively cheap here. The rich soils and reliable warm rains kept the fields producing in abundance, while the rocky forests were plentiful with firefruit for anyone brave enough to forage it.

At one point, I passed a vendor selling mystery meat on a stick. My mouth watered, but I didn't stop, walking instead to the nearest drink cart. An Enforcer stood over the cart, flirting with the young woman who was selling chilled ale there.

She was lovely, but unlike the noble I'd passed by earlier, she was dressed in thick clothing that didn't show off her body, including a kerchief which covered her hair. It was the sort of thing women wore when they *didn't* want attention. She had copper-colored eyes and alabaster skin, much too white for her to hail from Dasco.

As for her wares, I guessed that her ale had been magically cooled by the knee-high dragon curled at her feet. It was a calm pink-and-white hybrid, and it snoozed, ignoring the throng of traffic and the closeness of the Enforcer's own flame dragon.

Her dragon must be part snow or glacier-type, I thought, a faint memory coming to light and then fading from my mind again. *Maybe she brought it here from her homeland? She's been out in the sun all day, yet she doesn't have the slightest tan.*

Since she was distracted by the Enforcer—*oh come on, tell me where you live, sweetheart, and I'll carry you home later, it'll be fun*—I plunked two copper coins onto the counter. The vendor's eyes drifted to me, her fake-smile suddenly lighting into a genuine grin.

"Yes, sir? Fancy a drink for your parched... hey. Wait. I know you."

Her finger wagged, and it wasn't lost on me that she had dropped her conversation with the Enforcer the first chance she got.

I shrugged. "I'll have a mug. Two if you can answer my question."

She cocked her head at me, scanning me from head to foot even as she flipped the lid of her cart and filled an ale from some unseen, cold reservoir.

"What question?" she asked.

"I'm looking for Pinnacle's."

The vendor slid the ale across her counter, and something about the movement triggered a memory.

"The barn and fields, or the villa?" the Enforcer asked, cutting in. He folded his arms with a deep frown. His sunken eyes proclaimed that he wasn't sleeping much, but tiredness was no excuse for hounding a young woman.

"Not sure," I said. "Probably the closest one first. I was going to head to the castle, but they don't expect me there yet."

The Enforcer dropped a hand to the hilt of his sword. "Are you here to start trouble? You're not a debt collector, are you? You should know the Minax estate is under the Duke's protection."

A debt collector? That doesn't sound good.

"Uh, no. I'm not here for that."

"Good, because we don't like strangers who cause trouble," he explained, as if this were some grand secret.

I opened, then closed, my mouth, deciding to keep mum. This guy was just mad I'd interrupted his sad attempt at a courtship.

The serving girl poured a second drink, sliding another mug to me. "I can direct you to both places," she said, pointing down the hill at the nearest intersection. "For the dragon stables, go that way until you see the big barn on your left, with a sign out front that's seen better days. The Lady Jolene just passed by about half an hour ago, so she's there, not up the street at the old villa. I'm guessing you mean to meet with her?"

"Yes, in fact, I do," I said, passing the second ale to Fieran, who glared sourly at the Enforcer as he chugged it.

"Well, if you change your mind and want the villa, it's that way. Big blue building with a giant cage around it, can't miss it," she said, indicating yet another direction.

"However, if yer buyin' dragon eggs or Shoulder-class drags, my little Queen Collette should have an egg or two a few months from now." She nudged the pink-and-white dragon affection- ately with a toe. "She's a horizon-glacier mix, mated to another glacier, so her cooling ability is like to pass to her princesses and princes. Right useful in a hot place like this."

"I'll remember that," I said, smiling at her joyful nature while sipping my ale. Apparently, doing so gave me away.

"Oye! It's old Rennie! I knew I recognized you," the woman blurted. I blinked in reply, having no idea who she was. Her hand shot to her chest. "It's me, Becki! Don't tell me you forgot?"

My head tilted in confusion, but then I figured it out. The Becki I knew was three years younger than me, and she used to follow my lead during our alley days. She had this way of never being clean or pretty, and when I'd left, she'd been scrawny and sunken. Still white, though—whiter than snow, and always cold to the touch. And her hair....

I remembered now, why she kept it covered. She'd draw far more attention with that hair in the light.

"Well, I'll be burned," I said. "The scrawny little street cat grew up. Good for you." I leaned closer, and added behind my hand, "Glad to see you turned out just as ugly as I imagined."

Becki swatted at my shoulder. "Cad! You're not much better than a mutt yourself, you know."

Becki had always been blunt, loyal to a fault, and feisty. I had helped her a few times in rough spots, but she could mostly handle herself. As for the times she couldn't, well, it was because she'd had more than five opponents at one time. She could take out four with her fists alone, but anyone would struggle against five.

Sadly, with her pale skin and strange hair, she did sometimes attract five or more opponents at once... and they hadn't been there to beat her. Their intentions had been darker, so I'd always kept an eye on her, and we saw each other a lot.

I was glad to see she still enjoyed teasing and being teased. I don't think I could play the proper gentleman around Becki.

I opened my mouth, but I found I wasn't sure what to say. A knot of worry sank into my stomach. Eventually I had left her, growing up and moving on.

How had she fared without me, I wondered? She'd certainly turned out to be a looker, even without showing her hair. Those fiery gold-copper eyes and that winning smile would make any man's head spin, except maybe mine. I wasn't looking at her as anything more than an old, treasured friend.

The Enforcer suddenly stepped forward, his hand going to his sword.

"An old street kid?" the Enforcer said darkly. "You had better state your name and business here, *now,* because you sure look like trouble to me."

Chapter 22

That's a Really Big Barn

"Oh, don't be jealous, Garm," Becki said, slapping the Enforcer on the shoulder without sparing him a glance. "This here's Warren, one of the big kids I knew at the orphanage growing up. He kept a lot of us safe."

Behind her hand, she added, "Kicked the shit outta Arnie for cutting my hair when I didn't give him half my earnings. Went off to be a soldier."

Becki said all this like I was some sort of hero, but I didn't remember it that way. Arnie had been trying to do much more than cut her hair, but I didn't correct her.

"They hung Arnie last fall," she added, speaking to me now. She shook her head. "Some o' them fucks never learn."

She brightened then, pushing slightly back from the cart, as if she might run around it to hug me. I stepped back a smidge in case she did.

"Oh, Rennie," she said, almost a sigh now. "It really is so good to see you."

I almost corrected her to say *It's Third-Rank Guardsman Warren now,* but that wasn't true anymore, and I wasn't about to have an old friend call me "lord."

"Soldier, eh?" Garm snickered. "Got in trouble did ya?" He unfolded his arms, sticking his hands on his hips, upping his confidence. "Duke Biscuit is not the forgiving type."

"Uh, no. That's not it, but I'll be on my way. It was nice to see you, Becki. It's a damn shame you got the deep end of the ugly barrel, but I'll still kiss you if you want. Even if you probably taste like fish."

She laughed at this, and I topped off my joke by downing the last of my drink. Fieran had finished his own ale ages ago, and now he had his eyes turned toward the barely-disguised brothel across the street.

I'd nearly forgotten he was there, which struck me as odd. He had always been an attention-seeker before. Maybe the assassin was still on his mind? Or was it the Enforcer that he didn't like?

"Oh, like demons you get to run away like that," Becki said, following me away from Garm, who scoffed in frustration. "You'd better tell an old friend what brought you home."

I spared a glance for Garm, who clearly didn't like Becki giving me attention. I didn't want her in trouble with him.

"Really, Beck, I'll tell you soo—"

"Don't 'soon' me, Rennie. What happened? You come back to propose to Jolene?"

My ears burned. "That was when I was like, *fourteen,* Becki."

"So? I liked *you* at fourteen. We all can't be smart."

Huh. Did you? I thought, but I let the comment slide, opting for the truth. Anything to get her back to her cart before Garm started something.

"As of a few days ago, I'm, ah... I'm apparently the lord of the Pinnacle Estate," I said lowly.

Becki gasped in shock, hands flying to her mouth. "What? You're draggin' me. You mean after Lady Etonia...?"

"Yeah, she left it to me. I didn't see it coming either."

A wicked grin spread across her lips. She thumbed her pet ice dragon, who startled me because it was suddenly wide awake at her side.

"Well, now that you're rich, you owe me forty coppers for one of Collette's eggs!" Becki said. "I'll save one for you, of course. So you can have a dragon to remember me by."

"Why would I need to remember—I'm not gonna be *that* kind of noble, Beck. I'm not gonna suddenly stop talking to people. And split the demon's horns!" I cursed. "Forty coppers?"

It took me months to earn that kind of money, less so after my recent promotion... but I suppose none of that mattered now.

Becki prodded me in the chest. "You owe me, Rennie, for bein' a little shit all those years."

"A little shit? You were just saying how I saved your ass a dozen times!"

She plopped her hands on her hips. "What, you? A hero? You musta misheard me."

I released a baffled chuckle. "Forty coppers for the egg of a stray dragon, eh? That's airway robbery, Beck."

"There's none like her. It's a steal," Becki insisted, ducking forward to hug me from the side.

"She really is something, Rennie," she said quietly. "I found her fair and square. Life's been so much better with her there to help me. With you gone, I... I never thought I'd leave the alleys, but this little ice princess saved my future."

She leaned away again, her voice hardening. "So you're damn right it's forty coppers an egg. You'll only want to breed champions, after all."

I laughed again. "All right. If I have enough money, I'll buy one when the egg comes." It was the least I could do for an old friend, and the saleswoman wasn't about to take no for an answer.

"And for what it's worth, Becki, I'm proud of you," I said, nodding back at the cart. "Looks like you did well for yourself."

My old friend resumed grinning again, those metallic eyes glowing as if hot from a forge. "Welcome home, Warren. Rennie just doesn't suit you anymore, all grown up as a big and muscled man. Still poor though, if you're scoffing at one of my discounted eggs."

She paused, not letting go of my arm, which she still clung to. "Wait. You're strong, loyal, dependable, tall, smart, and... my, oh my. Jolene, you sly devil."

"Huh?" I asked, feeling dumb.

Becki released me with a mad cackle. "Like I said, the dragon farm isn't far down the road, on the left. Ten minutes at most. And Warren, please don't sell it." She wagged a finger over her shoulder. "These streets may define us, but its bullies don't...?"

She raised an eyebrow, inviting me to finish the sentence.

"Own us," I said. It was an old mantra we used at the orphanage. "It was nice to see you, Beck. Catch you later."

She pointed at me. "One egg. Forty coppers."

I nodded, and she spun around and headed back to her cart, the little Princess Collette trailing after her.

"You got a cute friend there," Fieran said a minute later, once we were out of earshot of Becki and Garm.

"Stay away from her, if you want to keep your dick on," I warned him.

He held up both hands. "Easy, boy. She's not my type."

I was about to ask if his type was the kind that could be paid to moan louder, but I opted to keep the peace instead.

We walked down the road quietly after that, with me wondering how many other dirty, scared orphans had found a way to fit into the city. Dasvilla was a decent place when compared to a junk heap like Olinios, but it was a prison just like all the other confined cities were. It was never easy for anyone but the wealthy.

I fought the urge to look back. *Maybe Becki was flirting with Garm. Maybe she just wasn't enjoying it, but... maybe she thought he was the best she could do.*

I hoped not. She didn't need a man; Becki had done just fine on her own. She'd just made me see that here, in this little spot so far from the king, there was more hope than I remembered. She hadn't needed a wealthy person's charity to get to where she was now.

But I did. Everything I'm getting came from Lady Etonia.

I sighed, my gaze wandering in the direction of the mass burial site outside the city, where Mom was buried deep under a flagstone to keep from being dug up by scavengers. Nostalgia washed over me. Etonia had been kind to me, and she'd left me an estate as if I were her own son.

But I wasn't her son. I didn't belong here.

"If only I knew hardly anything about dragons," I muttered. Maybe then, I'd feel more deserving.

Night was falling now, with the sky turning the same shade of pink that horizon dragons did so well to hide inside. A few general stores and farmer stands were still open along the road, offering their goods to those who passed. Prices were cheaper for food, but higher on tools; we didn't have much production here, at least not since the Pinnacle Foundry went dim.

I stopped at only one stall, spending more than I should have to purchase a new, basic sword, complete with sheath and belt. I might prefer knives, but I didn't dare go anywhere without a sword.

After that, the stalls gradually faded away as the buildings grew taller and the grassy grounds of the richest estates began. Several private Roosts peppered the ornate landscaping. I could see some of the dragons from the road, lounging around behind wrought iron fencing.

They looked lazy, bored, and straight-up *unused*, their potential economic usefulness going to waste, all for the sake of being put on display. Breeding dragons should have been highly profitable, and Lady Etonia had seemed so savvy. Had her husband been a terrible businessman, or had something else been going on?

Fieran maintained his sullen silence until the sun dropped below the horizon, when we finally arrived at a rickety barn three stories high. The main storage barn of Pinnacle Dragons had a pair of doors large enough to admit a covered wagon. The building stretched for a good two hundred paces deep and at least that wide. It ate up a lot of space and probably cost a fortune to maintain.

While the scope of the building was indeed grand, the sign that hung over the double barn doors needed work. It read *Pinncle ragons Train & ding,* with letters missing.

"Some inheritance," Fieran scoffed as we approached the door. It hung slightly ajar, so I pushed it open—

Only to be greeted by a dragon, running toward me at full speed. Its jaw opened wide.

And it lunged.

Chapter 23

Is It National Attack Warren Day?

THE SMALL SILVER creature shot right at me, and for a panicked moment, I thought it was going for my throat. Fieran gripped my shoulder, as if he were about to yank me out of the way.

Then the little beast angled to one side.

I tensed so that Fieran couldn't toss me as the dragon darted for the open door. It wasn't attacking, it was *escaping*.

Succumbing to my reflexes, I bent low and snagged the dragon by the nape of its neck. It instantly started to hiss and spit, enraged. I straightened, holding it up while it stopped snapping to inspect me.

"Let's get inside," I told Fieran. "We can't let the dragons get out."

"What? Right," Fieran said, sounding unusually breathless, his voice all rasp and no growl. He must have nearly panicked, too, but he'd kept his cool and stuck to his bodyguard role. I had to give him credit for that.

After Fieran slunk past me, I quietly closed the door with a foot. The small metallic dragon tilted its head in dismay, chirping and cawing. Other cries answered from the shadows, and I squinted into the barn.

Shafts of pale twilight cut down through the dusty air, hazy with smoke. It smelled of sulfur and, randomly, lavender. The barn was filled wall-to-wall and floor-to-ceiling with dragon pens, although most of them appeared to be empty.

It was like the wild dragon zoo in a Roost, only the cages were more comfortable for the dragons, and all the walls more solid. A wide corridor ran up the center of the barn, with stacked pens on both sides. A few of the closest pens were stacked six high, but they were empty; maybe they were for transient baby dragons? Most of the pens were double- or triple-deckers.

At one spot in the far distance, there was only a single pen between the floor and ceiling. It looked like the farther the barn went, the bigger the cages became. The pens must be sized according to their inhabitants, with many more Shoulder- and Mount-class dragons than Haulers. The place was too small to fit an adult Airship-class, but it could possibly hold juveniles.

A slight growl from one of the larger cages rose over the angry chitters of the other beasts, which then faded away. The growl also quieted the silver dragon I was holding; the little creature seemed very perplexed about being in midair without his or her wings having to flap.

Now that the dragon had calmed and my eyes had adjusted to the dimness, I peered deeper into the endless-looking barn. The place was built to house hundreds of dragons, trapping them behind bars, wood, and thorough organization.

It was dark now, with only one dragonfire lantern hanging over the main corridor to light the place. However, the ample skylights would allow for plenty of natural sunlight and fresh air during the day. Each of the ceiling windows could be shuttered, and each of them had escape-proof bars.

In the middle of the floor just ahead of me, a few feral-looking baby dragons lapped at a bowl of milk. They had vibrant, multi-hued scales that glowed ever so slightly in the dark; they looked like little living rainbows.

Eventually, the colors would settle and fully reveal their typing. There was some way to discern type before then, but it had to do with the patterns on their scales, and I wasn't schooled in the technique at all.

Hay lay clumped in piles here and there, and old dung crusted the wooden floors in too many places. Most of the cage doors were busted or hanging open on their hinges for no apparent reason. I hastily strode to the nearest one and peered inside, but it wasn't occupied, and didn't look like it had been in some time. The corners were near-white with spider webs.

Aside from the untethered babies, I only noticed four dragons total, all of them peeking out to see who was visiting. All in all, Jolene's letter had spoken the truth. The business was in distress, and the barn was nearly empty when it could hold hundreds.

"Demons," Fieran said. "This place is a dump."

I didn't disagree.

"Hello!" I shouted, and after a long few moments, I earned an echo. I didn't even know wood *could* echo. Or could it? Maybe there was a dragon back there mimicking me. I heard there were some types that did that.

Someone grunted above me. "We're closed!" a feminine voice shouted, from one of the cages on the second tier.

I set the baby dragon down, where it immediately came back to me, flying up to my shoulder to perch as if we were old friends. "I've got a letter for you," I called out.

A young woman with blond hair in a messy nest peeked out from one of the cages on the second floor. Her blue eyes focused on me, a bemused frown taking over her heart-shaped face. She was clearly trying to figure out who I was.

She unhappily huffed a strand of hair out of her eye. "If you're with the bank, they need to send Zelmor. I won't talk to anyone else," Jolene said with a sharp tone.

I recognized her, but she didn't recognize me. I wondered if that mattered. I reached into my robes, and extracted my summons. Before I could respond, Jolene grumbled, returning deep into the pen while hunched over. A second later she chucked a fire-red baby dragon out of the pen. It shrieked in the most pitiful way, as if its world was coming to an end.

"Fly!" Jolene demanded.

The baby closed its eyes, channeling its inner cannonball. I chuckled and caught it before it could land in the pile of hay Jolene had been aiming for.

"Oi!" Fieran shouted. He'd ducked at the same time I'd reached up to catch the dragon. "Those fuckers are eighty-percent spiky bits! Could you *not* throw them at us, please?"

In my hand, the little red opened her eyes. They were large, glassy, and vacant in the way only babies can manage. She cooed and nuzzled my hand.

With a shrug, I dropped her on my other shoulder. She nipped at the silvery dragon, who chittered back. They settled on opposite sides, tense with dislike.

Jolene's face appeared again. "Who else is with—oh." Her gaze dipped to Fieran's feet and back up again. She was noticing the guard uniform. "What do you want? I don't have money. Shaking me down won't get you the taxes any faster."

"We're not here to shake you down," I said as the red nuzzled my chin, having already forgotten the silver entirely. I leaned into the creature's tiny dragon kisses.

"Hey, stop that!" Jolene said, swinging her legs out over the edge of the cage. "Don't be sweet to that little hussy. She'll wrap you around her tail and never let go."

Jolene reached for a nearby sliding ladder and pulled it to her, turning to step down. Fieran leaned toward me, speaking lowly.

"She's got a point, you know. You do realize you're letting *two* untrained dragons within swallowing distance of your eyeballs, right?"

I blinked, turning to the red baby again. She kept nuzzling my jaw, rumbling contentedly. Had I really just thrown a dragon onto my shoulder like it was nothing?

I hadn't even thought about it. I'd just done it.

Jolene skipped the last dozen rungs with a smooth drop into a pile of dung, which burst into dust. It was old poop, then, left to solidify over time. Jolene winced when she landed, and I knew pain when I saw it; as she headed toward us, I could tell she was correcting a limp.

The young noblewoman was filthy, tired, obviously unhappy, and she stank of sulfur even from here. But beneath it all, I could tell she had turned into a fine woman. I was a bit surprised Lady Etonia *hadn't* had a son-in-law.

Jolene trudged up to us until she was a couple of paces away, then gestured at the milk cistern.

"Could you set the red one down?" she asked. "She needs to eat. They all do. Wait, why is Shiny on your shoulder? She's a little shit who hates everyone. Why isn't she chewing on you?"

I huffed in amusement, curling a hand under the red's belly and depositing her by the milk. "What's her name?" I asked.

Jolene folded her arms. "I named her Dull, because she's a dullard who likes to cling to idiots." She narrowed her eyes, and it was at this point that she fully inspected me, noting my straight back, clean haircut, shaven face, and probably my large musculature, because women always seemed to notice that.

She also cast Fieran a cursory glance, but seemed to accurately judge that I was the main event, and Fieran my hired hand. Her gaze returned to Shiny, who'd settled in to fake a nap, still clinging to my shoulder.

Dull and Shiny. I was either sensing a theme, or she'd gone through so many dragons that she didn't think too hard about naming them.

I tried to nudge the Shiny off my shoulder to join Dull by the milk, but she only dug her claws into the thick cotton of my cloak, pretending to sleep the whole time.

Giving up, I held out a hand. "Hello again, Lady Jolene. It's been a dragon's age. I'm Third-Rank... well, I *was* Third-Rank Guardsman Warren, and this is my, ah, temporary bodyguard, Fieran."

Jolene's plump lips drifted apart. She seemed to freeze in place.

Suddenly, her whole body became animated. "Oh shit!" she exclaimed, waving her hands at me. "No, no, no. You're supposed to visit the Duke first, then knock on the villa door for an inspection." Her hands ran down her face in frustration, until she seemingly caught a whiff of her armpits, her nose curling.

Her face flashed crimson red, and she abruptly looked like she might melt away. "Ugh, this day... but you're early. Far too early...."

Without warning, her gaze hardened. "Wait. I don't know you, either of you. You could be lying." Her hand ducked into a pocket, and she pulled out a whistle.

"Prove it," she snapped. "Prove who you are, right now, or I blow this whistle, and all my dragons go straight for your throat."

Chapter 24

A Very Dirty Woman

I WENT STILL, my hands up, placating.

"Jolene," I said slowly. "You know me. Remember? You taught me how to—"

"Oi, I've got your proof right here," Fieran interrupted, snatching the letter out of the breast pocket of my shirt. The move caught me by such surprise that I let it happen.

"What?" he said when he caught my raised eyebrow. "You've been fumbling with it the whole trip."

Jolene glanced between us, then grabbed the letter out of his hand, opened it, and then tossed it into the air in frustration when it confirmed her suspicions. She whirled to stomp away, shoving the whistle blissfully back in her pocket as she burned off her nervous rage.

I smoothly caught the letter and put it away again. Shiny growled on my shoulder, moving across the front of my shirt, her jaw aiming for my pocket.

"Hey, *no*," I told her, deftly catching her by her neck spikes again. "This is a piece of paper, idiot, not a snack." I tossed her to the ground, but only from waist height.

She landed stoutly, then tried to climb back up my boot. I

growled in the same way I'd heard that larger dragon growl earlier. Shiny backed off. That had settled it.

"Can you really sic all these dragons on us with that whistle?" Fieran asked, eyeing Jolene's back.

"I can't even get Dull to flap her wings when she's falling," Jolene said, grabbing a rake down from a hook on the wall. "You think I've got them trained to attack?"

I chuckled. "It was a ruse, then?"

"Not all the way," Jolene said, stabbing into a pile of hay. "The whistle scares them. There would have been noise and chaos, and it would have made you *think* they were attacking."

"Ah. So that trick has gotten rid of intruders before?" I asked.

She didn't reply, just moved dirty hay from the ground into a small wagon in the center of the aisle. I got the sense she was trying not to look at me, and keeping her hands busy so she had time to think.

I looked around. Which of the larger dragons had the growl come from, anyway? There were three that I could see, a silver and two hybrids, all Mount-sized, at or around my own height.

The door to the silver's cage looked a bit too rickety for my taste. If Jolene had blown that whistle, the silver probably could have broken down the door—and Demons forbid there be any fire-breathing dragons in here. Those wooden doors suddenly seemed ill-advised.

"What's that one's name?" I asked, pointing.

Jolene ran her hands through her messy hair and rounded on me again. "I thought you weren't due for three days yet," she repeated, not answering my question. "Ugh, you had to show up *today*, didn't you?"

"I got lucky with an opening on an earlier flight," I explained, holding both hands behind my back as I surveyed my new property. It was my attempt to at least *appear* lordly.

"So, this is part of the business, is it?" I asked. "It's in disrepair, but it's still functional. It's also in a good spot within the city, along a big road for easy trade, near the merchant's quarters."

As I spoke, I started to walk down the middle strip of the barn. Jolene fell in beside me, while Fieran took up the rear, looking into each cage as we passed.

"Well, yes, of course it's well-positioned," Jolene said. "My father built—"

"What happened to all your dragons?" I said.

She sputtered, and then her face went stiff. She ducked into a cage and took a flat shovel out of it, handing me the tool. I accepted it, frowning.

"They're either sold or dead," she said. "And you can take that and go dig up the dead ones if you want. Or you can do something a little more productive, and help me shovel some shit."

I stared her down. She stared back. That's when I finally saw it —the spark of anger, the little flash of *if my mother could have left all this to me, she would have. But she couldn't, so I'm stuck with you.*

I hadn't even been rude to her, and she already seemed to hate me.

"But you're a noble," Fieran interjected. "Don't you have, like, *servants* for that?"

Jolene threw her hands up, making an exasperated noise. A piece of hay randomly drifted out of her hair, dislodged by the movement.

"I don't even know where to start with that question," she snapped, still facing me, not Fieran. "All I know is that I have five hours of chores that have to get done, and no one is going to do them besides me. Morning inspections have to show a tidy shop, or they'll take the farm."

"Wait—they'll *take* it?" I asked.

"Yes. I've failed two inspections already, and a third failure will cost me the whole damned farm. And I had to go out today to get the taxes deferred another month, so I'm even *more* behind."

I had no idea how property inspection and taxes worked around here, but I didn't want to lose the place practically the same day I obtained it. It would suck to lose it just as soon as I got here.

Besides, I wanted to be in her good graces. We'd probably have to live together if she was going to be my ward, so to start off on a good foot, I should help out.

"Well, how about you explain a few things while we clean up the place?" I asked, turning to scan the corners of the nearest cage. "Just point me to the nearest pile of—"

"Oh, hells no," Fieran said. "I spent two days flying to get here with a Demons-damned assassin after me, and I don't even know what I'm doing here to begin with. I'm a guard, not a shit-scooper. I'll guard."

With that, he stomped back off to the entrance. I rolled my eyes.

"Ignore him," I said, hanging my bag on one of the many roof-pillars fronting the cages. "Tell me what to do."

Jolene eyed me for another moment, then obliged, pointing. "Dung in the corners. Drop it into a bucket, but be careful not to let it turn into dust. It sells as a fire-starter if it stays in cakes, and obviously, it's easier to clean chunks than dust."

"Got it," I said, heading for a corner. "We can take it a cage at a time."

She was already grabbing another shovel. "Thanks," she said, sounding relieved, as if she were unwinding a whole ball of stress. "So, what do you want to know? I had a whole spiel planned, but my brain is dead right now. Ask, and I'll answer."

I dropped my first pile of dragon deuces into a bucket. "Well, uh. How did you fail the other two inspections?"

She sighed. "Duke Biscuit and his wives very *conveniently*

keep me busy on inspection days. I'm not incompetent, Mr. Warren. Next question."

That got a smile out of me. "Fair enough," I replied, taking note of her hostility toward the Biscuits, which I'd probably share soon enough.

"How about this," I tried again. "Do you remember me at all?"

"Remember you? Have we met?"

Well, that answered *that* question.

"Never mind. Next question. Why is this place a... um, why is it not doing so well?" I had almost called it a *trash heap waiting to happen.*

I thought she might press me on whether or not we knew each other, but she didn't. Either she really was exhausted, or she was pretending not to remember me—but why would she do that? I was a nobody, and we never had a romance or anything. She might have taught me how to read, but if I'd forgotten her so easily, surely she had forgotten me as well.

"Well, the whole debacle started when my father passed away," she said. "That was what... fifteen years ago, now."

I nodded. "I remember. He died in his sleep, didn't he?"

Jolene shot me a glare. "That's what people say."

I swallowed. I'd drawn my own conclusions from her letter.

"You think—"

"He was *murdered,*" she said. "He died way too young, and from causes unknown. As in, there are a dozen accounts of doctors and apothecaries saying they couldn't determine a cause of death. They just found him dead."

She wiped her face, possibly to hide tears. "Our family mage-doctor even said a heart attack was unlikely, given his history. It was all very suspicious."

Jolene pivoted again, heading for one of the pens. "Anyway, that was where all the problems started. Mother thought he'd been poisoned, but our apothecary did an autopsy and said there was no evidence of that. *Hrrumph."*

With a hefty grunt, Jolene hauled open the pen, which had some sort of stuck hinge. She ducked inside and wheeled out a cart with fresh hay stacked on it. Then she returned to the shadows once more, and brought out another cart that smelled so sulfuric that I wrinkled my nose.

"The dung goes here," she said, pointing to the odorous cart. "It has to be taken to the local forge in the morning if we want him to buy any of it.

"As for this fresh hay, we need to spread it out after removing the old hay. I'd tell you to spread it thin, because it's pricy, but I'm already three—" her cheeks puffed and she unleashed a huff "—no, *four* days behind on spreading it. So lay down a thick mat, enough to hide the floorboards."

I nodded and kept working, never pausing to rest, even though my hands were a bit sore from sewing up that silver Airship dragon at the arena. I remembered hearing that Jolene's father died in his sleep. It had happened five years before I left the city.

"Damn," I said as it dawned on me. "That means your mother used the murder law for over ten years?"

Jolene cracked a rare smile. "Make that fifteen."

The kingdom had a rule: only males could inherit estates. Females could run them if the male was at war, sick, or indisposed. Basically, it was a petty law that encouraged women to marry rich little shits, but it did have loopholes.

One of those loopholes was that, if the estate owner died suspiciously, the widow could manage the estate until the killer was found. This prevented rivals from killing an estate owner without an heir and then swooping in to claim the whole thing.

Duke Biscuit had used this law to allow Lady Etonia to run her family business after her husband's demise, but he'd allowed it for far longer than was usual—especially if he *also* was the one who kept trying to make Jolene fail inspections.

"Duke Biscuit was kind to my mother," Jolene said, tossing straw. "Well, at least he *appeared* to be. I'm not so sure, anymore. However, things were very grim after Father's passing, and he did provide for us."

Juggling our shovels and buckets, we climbed to the next floor. I studiously didn't look up her skirt as she went ahead of me, although I wouldn't see much. She was wearing trousers underneath her dress.

"I'm sorry you had to go through that," I said, not sure how else to respond. "But—um, forgive me, but was your mother bad at running things? What happened to bring the farm to this state?"

She paused to haul up some hay using a pulley system. "Hmmm. Part of the issue was the help. Some of the staff refused to work for a woman, and those who did charged exorbitant labor prices."

She sighed. "We couldn't hire many new people, because firefruit-picking paid better and could actually be *less* dangerous. We could have had family help us, but that didn't work out."

"Family? There are other Minaxes?"

"Yes. I have two sisters, but one of them is in another kingdom and she didn't want to come back. My eldest sister had kids of her own to tend to—she's up to four of them now—so she's not able to help with the farm. Her husband never liked our parents, either, and he was openly hostile to Mother.

"And Mother, um, left all of them out of her last wishes," she added, as if she were embarrassed.

"Even your brother-in-law?"

"*Especially* him," she confirmed. "Anyway, when Father passed, this building was alive!" Her passion translated to an extra high throw of hay, off the side of the cage and down to an empty cart below.

"Every cage was filled," she went on, "and the floor was packed with overflow hatchlings ready to go to the market. Ah, those were different times. *Very* different times.

"But back to Mother," she said, focusing on the dung that had been hidden under a batch of stained hay. "She was certain Father had been murdered, so she spent half our fortune trying to find out how, and by whom.

"But, bless her heart, she never liked dragons. Her heart just wasn't in the business, and when money got low, she sold off our dragon stock... often at below-market rate, all to fund more investigations."

I remembered all the dragons we'd seen in Dasvilla. *Etonia must have sold them to anyone with a pulse,* I thought. *And Becki supposedly found one just wandering around somewhere, meaning they were either escaping, or too easy to steal.*

"She should have sold the whole business when it was still high-value," I said. "Then invested it in someone else's business. She could have provided for you, while still chasing her husband's murderer." I didn't add, *If he was even murdered to begin with.*

But what I'd said took things too far anyway. Jolene halted, making a jerking motion mid-swing. My stomach dropped unexpectedly. Had I just made her angry?

I shouldn't care—but I did.

"Are you calling my mother stupid?" she asked.

Here was the moment, then. The moment that would define us. Would she work with me, or would she hate me? Could we ever be friends again?

"Not stupid, so much as a bad businesswoman," I admitted.

She stared me down. I stared back.

Then the skies smiled on me, and she nodded.

"Unfortunately, it runs in the family."

Chapter 25

Cloud Breath

THIS TOOK ME ABACK. "What do you mean?"

"I'm no good at the business side of things, either," she said roughly. "Mother didn't handle Pinnacle well, and that's the sad truth of it. But I never stopped her. I never even noticed things were falling apart."

Jolene shook her head, her expression rueful. "At first, I was too young to understand the bad choices Mother was making. I wised up when I got older, but it was too late by then."

"Well, it wasn't supposed to be your responsibility, either," I said, relaxing. Jolene had always been intelligent, even if she now seemed a little more... *out-there* than I remembered.

But she's not antagonistic toward me. That's good, at least.

"Maybe, maybe not," Jolene said, stabbing her rake into a new batch of hay. "After I stepped in, we did keep things afloat until Mother died. That was when I learned just how much Duke Biscuit had been helping to prop up the business, and... he was done doing *that.*"

Another pause. "I can't blame him."

I raised an eyebrow. *There's something there,* I thought. *She keeps saying Biscuit is great, but she doesn't totally mean it.*

As I thought this over, I kept earning interested stares from the dragons. If I had to guess the genders by the sharpness of the spikes, the barn contained the silver purebred female I'd seen first, a gray-violet female hybrid, and a hybrid male in two shades of blue.

We weren't going into the occupied cages, though; it looked like Jolene had already done them before I got here. *Taking care of the dragons first,* I noted. That was a good sign of her character. She also petted the adults' snouts when they shoved up against the bars close to her. There was a lot of fondness there, clearly.

By contrast, the dragons seemed perplexed by my arrival, maybe unaccustomed to seeing a man in their midst. And while I had never really liked many animals—except maybe cats—I found myself feeling a new sense of intrigue and curiosity. I'd never been so close to so many dragons at once, and I hadn't expected to feel *comfortable* here.

"So, why are *you* still here?" I asked. "You could have married, and been able to inherit by proxy if Etonia left the farm to your husband."

Jolene sighed. "I should have, but to be honest, I love the dragons too much to leave them." As if to prove the statement, one of the baby dragons scurried up her back to rest on her shoulder, licking the milk from its lips.

"I'm also the youngest and most spoiled daughter," she added sheepishly. "Mother wanted to keep me close, especially after my older sister married into a trade partnership to please our father. Like I said, Mother hated that son-in-law. She didn't want me to go through that—but we also didn't expect her to die as young as she did."

"Sounds like it was a labor of love," I commented, stifling a curse as I broke up a dung patty. Heading down a ladder to grab a rag, I went on, "You loved the dragons too much to leave them, and your mother loved your father too much to care for the dragons."

"Something like that, yes."

We were silent for a while after that, while I scrubbed the dung-dust and she finished one of the larger cages next door. Thankfully, the flooring felt solid beneath my rag. It was rough and needed some new boards in a few spots, but it was all thick, quality wood. Meanwhile, most of the doors didn't fit properly in their frames when I closed them.

"Oh, don't close them," Jolene said, catching me doing it. "The babies like them open."

I grunted. "So that's why there's dung in the *unused* cages. We should keep them closed. Less work for us."

Jolene didn't reply as I flung my shovel contents onto the cart and wiped my brow.

"I suppose... we close them, then," Jolene said. "You are the boss now, after all."

I took a breath. "We can talk about that after I get some rest. Where should I sleep, anyway?" The piles of clean hay were starting to look way too good. "I should approach Duke Biscuit in the morning, not at night."

"You were supposed to do that first," Jolene grumbled, sullen again. "Then I'd have cleaned up the place ahead of time. But you can sleep in the villa. It's—*agh.*"

She'd been tossing hay off the edge of the second floor next to me, but she cried out halfway, her knee collapsing under her. I reacted, reaching for her. My fist curled into the back of her shirt, and I pulled her back to keep her from falling a full story.

This—paired with the shovel I was still trying to hold—cost me my balance. We toppled together into a pile of thankfully fresh hay.

"Oof!" she grunted, while I got a face-full of dry grass. I spat it out and looked over at her. Her face was twisted in pain, and she was rubbing her ankle with both hands.

I remembered her limp. "Hey, hey," I said, laying a hand on her shoulder. "What happened? What are you doing walking on that?"

169

She didn't answer, just shaking her head. She tried to stand, but I pulled her down again. She landed against my chest.

In any other scenario, my heart would have started pumping. But she smelled bad and I was downright exhausted.

"No," I said. "You are *not* working anymore." She tried to move again, but I stopped her. *"Jolene."*

"Stop it, please, just let me—the inspection—"

Her hands flew to her face, and I recognized the set of her lips, the quiver in her shoulders.

"It's not done," she sobbed. "It's not *done,* it's not—!"

I tried to take her hand, but she jerked away. "Please," she begged, her voice rife with tears. "Please just leave, Warren."

Warren. The way she said it, so familiarly.... *She* does *remember me.*

I tried to relax, opting not to touch her. She sat cradled by the thick pile of hay, her slim body shaking, her teeth grinding as she bit back her sobs. What had gotten into her?

Oh. Of course. It finally dawned on me that she had lost her mother only days ago, and now she was losing her dragons—to me—and she might be on the verge of watching the farm get taken by the bank or the king or who knew what else.

She was in pain, and lots of it.

"You want to know the truth?" she wept. "The truth is, my family is full of idiots. And I'm the worst of them all."

I touched her shoulder lightly. "Milady, that's not true—"

"Father dropped dead, like a moron," she cut me off. "Mother pissed off a lot of people trying to figure out someone to blame.

"And *I* left the doors unlocked one night!" she burst out. "I came back the next day to find every cage door open. Our guard, poor Landry, he had his throat slit...."

More sobs wracked her. "We found a few of the lost dragons,

170

but that was almost all the fortune we had left. Only four dragons refused to leave, bless them. Even Ravager left."

She vaguely indicated the barn, suggesting that the four loyal dragons were still here. "After that, we couldn't pay the staff. We could barely afford to pay our taxes. The Duke stepped in and started giving us trapped dragons from the Roost.

"But they were wild, too hard to train, and all our best trainers were gone by then. We managed, though... until Mother died. No cause of death, again. She was murdered, too; I know it. But no one killed her until the farm really started to fail, and it was only failing that fast *because of me.*"

She trailed off into open wailing then, and I pulled her against me. She allowed it. I don't think she was thinking clearly.

"Oi, what's with the waterworks?" Fieran asked, popping his head up over the ladder.

"Not *helpful,*" I hissed at him, but it was too late. Jolene curled her fists into my shirt, and totally let loose. My chest was sopping wet in seconds.

I sighed and moved to stand, dragging her along with me. "Come on, milady. Show me where the villa is."

"But—but—the inspection—"

"I have some of my own money. I'll bribe the inspector if we need to. Come on—"

"No, I couldn't ask—"

It went on like that for some time, with Jolene protesting and me insisting that she *come down the ladder, please, and let's find a nice quiet place to rest—*

"Chirrup!"

"Shit!" Fieran cried from the bottom of the ladder, and I whirled, only to see a silver shape skitter up over the edge. The hairs rose on the back of my neck; this was an adult dragon, a Mount-size, nearly as tall as I was. It must have broken out of its cage, hurtled past Fieran, and scuttled up here.

171

I reached for my knife, but the dragon was faster. It raced past me and leapt for the wall, then ran sideways along all three walls of the cage, forcing me to spin to keep my eyes on it.

"What the—" I said, just as I realized its mouth had been open the whole time. I staggered back, feeling strange. The air shimmered, as if with silver dust.

The dragon finally dropped to the floor, looking up to cock its head at me. My knees weakened.

"No... Tilly... no," Jolene said.

The world blurred. My head wobbled atop my neck. My grip on Jolene loosened. I glimpsed Fieran from the corner of my vision, his gray eyes wide as he looked at me swaying.

"Oh burning hells," he cursed. "Is that a cloud dragon?"

I didn't reply.

I just fell.

Chapter 26

The Spaces Between

Darkness.

It was the same dream again, and I was lost in it, in a darkness out of memory. My conscious mind railed against it. *Please. Let me out. Please, just let me wake up.*

It was like this most mornings, just before waking. The darkness would have me again. I'd sink into it, stuck between one place and the other. A dark so intense, it went beyond black. It was a nothing-dark, an ending-dark.

It was oblivion.

The whip. The last lash. "Shit, stop! You got his neck—"

I remembered the words, felt the heat on my skin. An injury, where my neck met my shoulder. My wrists hurt from the bindings. I still hung against the prison wall.

"Bandage it! Now!"

"But sire—"

"Help him! If he dies—"

"It's too late, sire. Look. It's too late."

The moments came back to me, out of order. Bright agony across my back. *I never lied,* I kept telling them. *I loved her. I loved her.*

173

"Who do you work for?"

I loved her.

I came awake hard and sudden, lurching into a crouch, my knife out and ready to go. The dark was still there, on the edge of my awareness, the blood still gouting from the side of my neck—

Fieran put his hands up in front of him and backed away. "Whoa, whoa. I'm not doing anything."

I squinted up at him through the hazy light of the... barn. *Right,* I thought, blinking. *We were in the Pinnacle barn. I was cleaning up, helping Jolene....*

I shook my head, rattling the memories around until they fell into place at the back of my mind. I rose to my feet, swaying and still dizzy. Touching my temple, I said, "That dragon...."

Fieran turned aside, so that I could see the silver-white dragon in question, curled up in a cage behind him. The cage door was wide open, but the dragon watched us curiously from inside, making no move to attack.

"It knocked us all out. You more than me," Fieran explained. "I just woke up. The smell of dung got me... one of the babies nearly pooped on my face."

He shuddered. "Took me a minute to get my bearings, I'll just say that. But then I went straight to you." He huffed a worried sigh, glancing around. "We were lucky the assassin didn't find us like that."

Fuck me, the assassin, I thought, stiffening. I peered up at the skylights again. A whole night and part of a morning had passed. The assassin might have discovered us missing and followed us to Dasvilla by now.

Fieran was right. We were lucky.

"What's her deal?" Fieran asked, nodding at the still-sleeping form of Jolene.

I considered my response as I looked at her, keeping the pale dragon in my peripherals. Asleep, Jolene looked so much more peaceful and less harried. Her blond hair nearly glowed.

She's like a sleeping angel, I thought. Despite her noble blood, she actually looked like she belonged here, in the hay, among dragons. A pang went through my chest as her breast rose and fell, the neckline of her soiled dress loosening, exposing just a little too much flesh.

A part of me wanted to lie back down and hold her just a little longer.

"She's a single woman struggling to run a business, with no money and no support," I said, shaking my head. "In fact, I think Biscuit has been actively working against her. It's amazing she got this far."

Fieran curled his nose at the nearest broken door hinge, looking like he might comment on precisely how "far" he thought she'd gotten, but he seemed too disoriented to complain.

The silver cloud dragon—maybe Shiny's mother?—continued to watch us without malice. Fieran caught me looking.

"We should kill that thing," he said, "before it conks us all out again."

I met eyes with the dragon, her silver gaze against my hazel.

"No..." I said slowly, tilting my head. "No, I think... I think she saw Jolene getting all upset, and it was her way of calming her."

Jolene had been nearly insensate, after all, blaming herself for the collapse of the business, worried about the inspector, and rambling about how she couldn't accept my help, she could do it all alone... I had to wonder the last time the poor woman had slept.

I turned my back on the dragon, suddenly certain it wouldn't harm us.

"They must really love her," I said, scanning over Jolene's sleeping form with admiration that went beyond her looks. In

175

that moment, I vowed to hire her as my steward, provided I inherited the farm as planned.

The dragons needed her. *I* needed her.

"Whatever you say," Fieran said tiredly. "So. You find out why her ma chose you to inherit?"

Sighing, I told him no. "But I doubt she has a clue, either," I added, "or she wouldn't have pretended not to know me. Anyway, we can ask later."

"Wait. She knows you?"

"I'm pretty sure, yeah. But she's hiding it."

Fieran sucked in a breath. "She was pretending?"

I remembered how she'd said my name—*Warren.* Not *Mister Warren again,* or *Milord,* or *Guardsman or Sir Warren.* Just my name, the same way she'd always said it.

"I think so."

Fieran chuckled. Something about the way he did it made me ask, "What?"

"Oh, nothing. I just have a suspicion as to why you were chosen."

I looked back at him, and opened my mouth to answer, but my eyes widened.

"Did you—did you *shave* before waking me up?"

Fieran blinked, then touched his cheeks. "Uh... yeah. Sorry. Nervous habit."

The man was fucking smooth again. I could have killed him. He was supposed to be so afraid of this damned assassin, yet he'd taken the time to *shave* before making sure his charge—*me*—was both conscious and safe?

And just when I'd started thinking he was competent. Demons, I was done with this.

"Come on, let's wake her," I said. "And let's go see this villa of mine, before—"

A loud *bang* on the barn door cut me off.

"By official decree of the king, you will open these doors, or we shall open them for you!" a stringy voice called out. I knew the sound of a bureaucrat when I heard one.

"Fuck, how early do these bastards get up?" I said, cursing as I rushed to the ladder. Fieran didn't reply as I sidled past him to go down. He leaned out over the edge to watch me go.

"What do you want me to do with her?"

"Nothing. She doesn't need this stress," I said, as the bureaucrat pounded again.

"If you do not open these doors in the next thirty seconds—"

I heaved open the barn door and jumped out of the barn, pausing when I found the business end of a battering ram in my face.

"What the hells?" I said, staring at it. Six beefy guardsmen were holding the thing up, with a reedy man standing off to the side, a scroll stretched between his hands. "I thought we had an inspection today, not a hostile takeover."

The bureaucrat sniffed. "And who are you?"

I squared up, displaying more confidence than I felt. "I'm the Lord Warren... Orpheus." I invented the surname on the spot, making a play on the word *Orphan*. In Parshil, only nobles received surnames, but he'd hardly respect me if I didn't already have one. "And you are?" I added haughtily.

He made an effort to square his shoulders, too, but it only made him look crooked. I wondered if he had scoliosis.

"I am Head Keeper Illowyn," he said, "and we *did* have an inspection scheduled today, Sir Warren—"

"Lord Orpheus."

Illowyn continued as if I hadn't spoken. "Is the current owner on site? If not, this is the last straw... milord." His gaze dipped to my traveling boots and back up again. "If you even *are* a lord. What is your business here?"

I finally closed the door behind me. "I'm the new owner," I said.

Illowyn laughed. He was skinny, tanned by the hot sun of Dasco, dark-haired and blue-eyed, with a goatee that was trying really hard to pretend it wasn't drawn-on.

He wore the robes of a crown Keeper, the scribe-type guys that upheld the kingdom's various "paper laws," meaning anything that didn't involve violence. The Enforcers often worked closely with them.

"Oh no, you're not," he said, glancing at his scroll. "Per article B of the Parshil real estate codex, chapter four section seven, any property which fails inspection three times concurrently is subject to repossession by His Majesty King Kurto. So, since you have failed this inspection, this property no longer belongs to you."

"Failed? But you just got here!"

He curled his lip and made a show of looking over at the cart full of dung that we'd rolled out front the night before.

"You were late to appear, which means an automatic failure," he said. "But something tells me you would have failed anyway."

Great. If I wasn't careful, this guy would talk circles around me.

"Well, fine, you have a point. But that three-inspection law only applies *per owner*," I declared, pulling this fact out of my ass without any idea if it was true. "If you would read a few articles down in your codex, sir, and you'll find that I now own this property, and therefore, this is only my *first* failed inspection."

The man sneered, but he dropped his gaze to his scroll and scanned the words there. "I see nothing here about this."

The page was titled *Real Estate Codex, Article B*. I folded my arms, putting on my best bluffing face.

"You'll want the next page. I see you only brought the one." *Overconfident bastard,* I thought but didn't say. "You may return to your offices and find it, and then if you would like to schedule the next inspection, sir, you can contact my retainers at my villa—"

"Rachel!" the bureaucrat suddenly shouted.

I heard a tiny peep at the back of the line of six guards, and a woman scurried up behind Illowyn.

She wore the same blue-and-copper robes, and wore thick-rimmed glasses. Her dark hair was knotted into a clumsy bun at the back of her head, with a few bangs fraying out of it like torn thread.

Like Jolene, this Rachel didn't look like she'd had any sleep for ages; the bags under her hazel eyes looked like little half-pools of watered-down ink. Her skin was fairly dark, enough so for me to tense and look her over to double-check that she wasn't the assassin.

Not enough muscle, I determined, after a moment. You couldn't fake a *lack* of muscle. This woman was only a scribe.

"Y-Y-Yes, sir?" she stammered, clearly nervous.

He tapped his page. "On the next page of this codex, is there a law stating that the inspection rule only applies per owner?"

I stared. He hadn't asked her to run back to their offices to check. He'd just asked her, as if she had some sort of photographic memory.

"Um. No, sir." Her wide eyes darted to me and then back again. "There's nothing like—"

"Hold on," I blurted. "I'll prove it. One second."

The words *shit, shit, shit* kept a steady beat in my head as I pivoted and hurled open the barn door. I snapped it closed behind me, hard enough to dislodge dust from somewhere over-head. My heart pounded.

That woman has a fucking eidetic memory!? This wouldn't be as simple as bluffing.

My mind raced, so fast that I didn't notice as Shiny ran up my

179

pant leg to my shoulder. I absently petted the small silver creature.

Then I looked at it, and an idea flared behind my eyes. I rushed to the larger cages and scaled the same ladder halfway.

"What the hells are you doing?" Fieran asked from the back of the barn, where he'd ostensibly been checking the security of the back door, if there was one. The barn went so deep it was hard to tell.

I didn't answer him, instead twisting on the ladder to look the other way.

"What's your name?" I asked the resting cloud dragon. Jolene had called it by a name.... "Tilly, is it?"

The Mount-class perked up and cocked her head at me.

I held a hand out. "Tilly, there's something I need you to do for me."

"They can't understand you, idiot," Fieran said, stalking up to the base of my ladder. "They can only catch basic commands, and only after plenty of training."

But I didn't believe it. I knew in my core that Tilly knew what I was saying. There was intelligence in those eyes—in the eyes of *all* dragons. The silver Airship dragon in the arena had listened just fine.

Tilly rose, and she wove her way to the door of her pen, her pale silver body scintillating in the soft light. I smiled at her. She understood.

"Here's what I need you to do."

Chapter 27

Lord Warren, the Dealmaker

Two minutes later, I caught one end of the battering ram with a hefty *oomph* as all six guards collapsed, fast asleep. I'd intended to catch Rachel, but I'd forgotten the ram, and I didn't want it breaking anyone's legs.

"Fieran!" I called, but he was already behind Rachel, catching her as she, too, faded into sleep. Both Fieran and I wore fabric over our mouths, torn from Jolene's sleeves. They didn't smell fantastic, but that only helped keep us awake.

"Good job, Tilly!" I grunted, lowering the wooden beam until I could drop it safely to the dirt-packed earth. The silver dragon towered over the two collapsed scribes as she stopped her very-effective circling, just now closing her mouth.

She watched me raptly, looking as curious as ever. She didn't run, but I'd known that she wouldn't.

"All right, grab some dung," I told Fieran. "Fresh stuff."

"You owe me for this," my bodyguard griped, but he gently lowered Rachel to the ground and scuttled back into the barn.

I checked each fallen guardsman for a pulse, just to be sure, and then knelt beside Rachel as Fieran returned with a pile of dung cradled inside a handkerchief. With a disgusted sneer, he passed it over. Holding the handkerchief by its clean ends, I swung the dung before Rachel's nose.

181

She made a face in her sleep, but her eyelids fluttered. I breathed a sigh of relief. Fieran had said that fresh dung had woken him up earlier, but I wasn't sure if it would work immediately after Tilly knocked people out, or if it would take more time.

Bad smells—or at least strong ones—break her spell, I told myself, taking another mental note about dragons.

"Hi there, Rachel," I said softly. "Don't be alarmed. You just, ah. Took a tumble."

She tried to rise, looking around, her expression hazy. "What?"

I didn't sugarcoat the situation. "Look. I used a cloud dragon to knock everyone out. They're fine, but you and I need to talk."

Her hazel gaze cleared, and her eyes cut back to mine. She recoiled slightly. "What do you want?"

"It's nothing untoward," I assured her, although under those robes, she appeared to be a rather buxom woman. In fact, now that I was this close to her, I could see just how lovely she truly was. The bulky robes, messy bun, and unnecessarily thick-rimmed glasses hid her beauty well, and I wondered if that was intentional.

"I just—well, I want to bribe you," I said matter-of-factly. "It's for a good cause, though."

I nodded back at the barn. "You see this place? I *just* inherited it, like days ago. I only arrived in Dasvilla last night. I know the place is a shambles, but its former keeper—the Lady Jolene, maybe you know her?—has been trying really hard to fix it up on her own. But she's just one woman, you see. Thus the failed inspections.

"But I want to help her," I insisted, leaning back so that Rachel could sit up. She rubbed her eyes under her glasses, but some of the tension had gone out of her.

"I want to keep this place in her hands," I went on, "to hire her as my steward, and return Pinnacle Dragons to its former glory. I... I really care for these dragons, Rachel. I know we can make something of this place. More than the kingdom can. They'll just foreclose, and you know it."

Her glasses plopped back onto her nose as she drew her hand away and looked at me, her gaze flat. I found myself impressed. She'd been ruffled at first, but now she seemed to see the situation clearly. I held my breath, waiting on her response.

She frowned past me, at the barn. "It does seem a shame," she said.

I nodded, probably too enthusiastically, but she ignored me. Instead, she looked around at the fallen men. To my surprise, the sight got a small, tinny laugh out of her.

"Wow... they all went down so easy." She faced me. "If I could bottle that stuff, would you sell it? The cloud dragon's breath, I mean."

My mouth hung open a moment. "I—"

"Yes, we can," Jolene said.

Everyone turned to see the now-sleeveless young noblewoman as she staggered out of the open barn door.

"If you can bottle it, we can sell it," she repeated, her face hard. "As much as you want."

Then it clicked for me. I turned back to Rachel. "You want a dragon's *breath*? As your bribe?"

Never mind that I'd never heard of bottling *breath*. Even if it could be done, that still begged the question: what did she need with knockout gas?

She bit her lip, her gaze sliding to Illowyn for a moment.

"Yes," she said finally. "But I want a lifetime supply. I can provide the bottles, but anytime I need more breath, I want to come back for it.

She leaned closer to me, suddenly intense. "And you'll sign paperwork saying so. I can't have you backing out."

A laugh tumbled out of me. *Amazing,* I thought. Here, I'd planned to calm down a hysterical woman, and instead Rachel had understood the situation and turned it to her advantage in instants.

She tilted her chin up. *"And* I want a share in the profits," she added.

Four Demons. Who is this woman? I blinked a few more times, then said, "Well, I'll be happy to give you all that, but how the hell are you supposed to *store* a dragon's breath in a bottle?"

"Very carefully," she said.

I raised an eyebrow and looked back at Jolene. "Have you heard of this?"

She nodded. "I've seen bottled breath once. It was bottled flame. The Biscuits had it, but they wouldn't say where they got it. Just one bottle, though. They sent it to the king as a birthday gift."

I rolled that through my mind. "That sounds... expensive."

"It is," Rachel said. "But I can provide the bottles. That cost won't fall on you. You just let me bottle the breath once a day. I promise I won't drain the dragon's power."

My mouth fell open. You could drain a dragon's magic? Furthermore, was this bottling business a new thing?

"Could I buy bottles from you?" I asked, my mind racing with possibilities, but she was already shaking her head.

"No. My supply is limited, and I'm still testing them. For now. But, if we're partners...."

She let the words hover, and I understood. When the bottles were commercially viable, it would benefit her to share that technology with me, if she had a percentage in the business.

"Deal," I said, opting not to discuss the precise percentage here. I stood, and Rachel seemed to want to say more—she probably noticed the lack of percentage, too—but she must realize she was already trying her luck. She took my hand as I offered it. I hefted her up.

She crashed into my chest.

"Oh," she said, her nose against my collarbone. I could now very much feel just how much endowment she was hiding. "I—I guess I'm still woozy."

She pushed away, a beat later than I would have expected. Her cheeks darkened with a blush.

Jolene strode past me, snapping her fingers. Tilly scampered to her side, the Mount tall enough to reach her shoulder.

"Tilly, Fieran, grab Red."

Red, I knew, was the only Hauler-class dragon in the barn. He was, inexplicably, yellow. He stood as tall as the three-story barn, and Fieran would have to lead him out the back wall, which doubled as a giant door.

"Red will take you to your offices by air," Jolene said, while Tilly and Fieran went to fetch the big beast. "He is a sun dragon, impervious to sight, meaning he can be invisible when he chooses to be. Father had him trained to do things like this. If you point him where to go, he will go there. The Keeper tower is easy enough to point out.

"Anyway, you'll want to add the addendum immediately to the real estate codex," Jolene continued, "so it's there when you return with Illowyn. He'll want proof right away."

Rachel nodded, although she looked unsure about Red as he poked his blindingly yellow, spiky head around the side of the barn. Fieran led him by a rope, with Tilly scampering happily between his legs as he moved.

"We'll need to be fast," Jolene said. "Or Illowyn will realize he got duped."

"I'll go quickly," Rachel said. "And I'll work up the contract—"

"Later," Jolene negotiated. "There's not time now. But we're good for it. You have our balls in a vice, and we all know it."

Rachel smiled, a little villainously. "Fair enough. Now—"

"Now, you get going," Jolene said, her voice resonant with authority. "Come on. I'll show you how to command him."

185

One quick flight lesson later, and Rachel was airborne. I watched her go, wondering why she'd been so excited by the idea of having knockout gas in her pocket.

I looked back at the guards and Illowyn. *Then again, I think I've got some idea.*

"She's pretty, for a foreigner. Nice rack," Fieran mused.

I scowled at him. "You do realize *you're* a foreigner, right?"

"My father wasn't," he snapped.

"That doesn't make you a full-blooded Parshin," I pointed out. His mother must have had darker skin, then, for him to turn out with that copper tone. She had probably been a servant, if I had to guess. After all, his father had been "someone important," and important Parshin men only married Parshin women.

He glowered and ground his teeth, but he didn't reply.

I said to Jolene, "All right. As soon as she gets back, we wake them all—" I indicated the collapsed men "—and make it look like Tilly got loose and attacked. I'll make it seem like I wrestled her into submission and saved them from her.

"Then Rachel says she does, in fact, remember the addendum I mentioned. We send them stumbling off while they're still disoriented; Rachel should help them along. We're lucky the barn is on such a large property, or else the neighbors would see all this."

I indicated the grounds around the barn, which were barren in more ways than one. Now that I was looking, the grounds appeared to have once been a fenced-in training area. The posts were gone, though, down to mere holes in the ground.

"They'll want Tilly put down, of course," I went on, "so she'll have to suddenly escape. You can do that, can't you, girl?"

Tilly bobbed her head at me, and I thought to myself, *Message received.*

Jolene didn't seem to notice, her lips parted. "You just thought of all that?" she said.

Fieran snorted. "There's no way Tilly will go along with something that complicated. She's just a stupid dragon."

"Oh, she will," I said, grinning. "I'll tell her we're playing tackle-the-dragon, and the loser just has to run away."

Tilly chirruped, perhaps in excitement.

"Now come on," I said. "Help me set the scene. Hurry, before these bastards get a good whiff of Fieran. If that happens, they'll wake up for sure."

Chapter 28

Lady Jolene, the Accountant

ALL IN ALL, the whole event went well. The inspectors woke up half-stunned to find me wrestling with Tilly. I managed to pin her and assert my dominance. Once she chirped in surrender, I loosened my grip. She flew away, like I'd told her to do.

After the show was complete, Illowyn left the property thoroughly suspicious of all of us, but he did leave. That was the main thing.

Breathing hard from my fake tussle with Tilly, I held an arm out to Jolene. "Care to lead me to my villa, milady?" I asked.

She giggled. "Oh, very well."

The noblewoman fell in beside me, her hand curled around my forearm. I suddenly wished I was sleeveless, too. I wanted to feel her skin against mine.

My neck and cheeks burned at the thought, and I studiously kept my gaze off her as we started walking along a well-worn path across the barren training fields, Fieran close behind.

"So," I began, but couldn't think of what to say.

She smiled. "So."

I swallowed.

189

We walked a little longer in silence, with me feeling awkward and her looking ridiculously radiant. I could not think of a single thing to say.

Jolene cleared her throat. *"Ahem.* So, it seems my mother chose well after all."

She sounded so satisfied, pleased even, that my shoulders released their tension. I suddenly felt very much at ease.

"About that," I said. "Do you know *why* she chose me?" I nodded behind us. "Fieran has a theory, but he won't say what it is."

Jolene peered over her shoulder, looking Fieran up and down. I glanced back to see him avoiding her gaze.

"Ah, *he* won't, will he?" Jolene said, turning back around. "Well, maybe it's to spare me the embarrassment. You see, Warren... I've had a crush on you since we were children."

I missed a step and sputtered, "What?"

She nodded sagely, as if this were some heavenly knowledge she were bestowing on me. "Yes. Quite silly, I know, but you always were so very sweet and so smart. And you grew up... well."

She glanced at my chest, then away again. "Anyway, I once wrote in my journal that I'd marry the stubborn-but-strong boy who ran the alleys with his little iron fist." She laughed. "I was fourteen at the time, but my mom was nosy. She read it, and never let it drop."

Jolene sighed as we crested a small rise. The path led back down into the city proper, turning to cobbles. Our villa would be somewhere among all the other houses, integrated into the human population. I had a feeling Jolene had spent most of her free time in the barn instead.

"However, she never did let the joke go," Jolene went on. "She got a little too serious about it, building you up in her mind as my fantasy savior."

Jolene turned her gaze up into the blue morning sky. "I think she saw you as this ill-fated soldier who never got a fair chance in life. She always was taken to flights of philanthropic fancy; she enjoyed the idea of 'bringing someone up from the rubble.' It was a little self-serving, but she meant well.

"Anyway, about a year after you left, she started to sicken. She wrote a will, and apparently, she threw you at the top. I'm not sure if her mind was going or not, but there it is. She hated my brother-in-law and didn't trust cousins. But she trusted *you*, and, well... this is going to sound silly, but—"

"—she thought you two would rekindle things," Fieran interjected, deepening his customary growl to emphasize his disdain for such fancies. "Like you were in a fucking storybook, or something."

Jolene sighed, but never missed a step. Meanwhile, I kept getting slammed with surprises, and it was all I could do not to trip.

"She thought we'd *get married?*" I blurted. "But I barely knew you, even then! And she didn't write me or anything, to figure out what kind of person I'd become. What if I'd grown up to be a gigantic ass?"

"Actually, I think she *did* do some research," Jolene said. "She said so in her final letter to me. It was included with her will and testament, but she didn't specify anything."

My mouth clamped shut, and I stifled a snort. I knew exactly what she must have caught wind of. It had happened five years ago, and although very few people knew about my little romantic dalliance and brief foray into politics, the people who *would* know would be nobles.

Either way, it had happened, and I didn't want to discuss it. I moved the conversation forward instead.

"And why did you pretend not to remember me?" I asked, letting her lead me across the street during a gap in carriage traffic.

"I... didn't want to admit to the crush." Jolene's face soured. "It was horribly embarrassing. Besides, I wanted to play the regal noble. I wanted you to take me seriously, because I'd planned to convince you not to sell Pinnacle."

"You thought I'd sell?"

"I knew you'd want to. Who wouldn't? After all, it's worth a lot of money—to a commoner, anyway. It'd be a pittance for a real noble, though."

I decided to let the dig slide. "Well, I'm not selling it."

She smiled again. "So I heard."

She must have overheard me speaking to Rachel, telling her I wanted Pinnacle, and that I intended to keep Jolene on as a steward, so she could stay close to her babies.

"The last time you tutored me, I was twelve," I said, shaking my head in disbelief. "Then your father passed. So it's been what, fifteen years?"

She shrugged. "Fifteen years since then, yes. Ten years since you left the city. You started farming in Dasvilla at sixteen, then joined the army at seventeen. That makes you twenty-seven now, right?"

I raised an eyebrow at her. *That was specific.*

"How much do you know about me?"

Jolene drew such a large breath that my traitorous eyes dipped to her cleavage, and my brain was momentarily overcome by the memory of her sleeping in the hay, her breasts still covered, but much more exposed, with golden dust motes sparkling all around her.

Then she abruptly started speaking, the words coming so fast that they nearly blended together. "You have thirty-two monster combat kills, which is a high number, seeing as how most units avoid monsters. After doing mandatory infantry service, however, you became a guard in increasingly distant outposts where you could only fight monsters from the walls."

I opened my mouth, but she kept right on talking. "Despite the obscurity you seem to be seeking, your peers respect you, your subordinates follow you, and your officers say you're reliably boring. Mother kept a report, but a page is missing, and I think it's because you had a wife who died in childbirth or something. I won't expect you to explain it."

She took a breath. "Anyway, whenever I turned down a suitor or had a bad breakup, Mother would bring up the old 'Warren joke' again. I got curious after a while and looked you up. And kept doing it. Call it a hobby."

I stopped walking, making her pause beside me. We now stood in a well-lit, cobbled alleyway scattered with small wrought-iron tables. They seemed to belong to a glass-fronted restaurant set into the alley wall. Music played from somewhere inside, a bard perhaps. It was a fancy spot, too fancy for me.

"That's messed up." I shook my head. "The 'Warren joke,' I mean. Your mother was pushing you toward some dude you didn't know."

"Well, she realized you were a loner, and that the king's army kept moving you. She'd taunt me that one of the barracks bunnies would snatch you up and that I should travel to see you."

Jolene collapsed into one of the diminutive tables, then seemed to realize she was in no condition to eat out, and stood again.

"I came out to one of your posts once, but you'd been reassigned before I could reach you. I took the opportunity to shop for dragons and got conned. The instant I tried to fly home, the dragon unlatched its own carrier and escaped, likely having done it a few times."

"Can't catch a break, can you?" I asked. A concerned-looking waiter was wandering toward us, but I waved him off. "You had a file on me. Gotta say, that's a little scary."

I scanned her eyes to see if she knew anything more, but there was no glint of wonder in her eyes. If she knew about... *her,* then there would be questions. So far, none had come.

"You can see why I didn't want you to know I remembered you," she said.

"Yeah. You'd look crazy," Fieran grunted.

Jolene swallowed. "Anyway." She tugged me forward, and we left the alley, much to the waiter's relief. "You're right that I can't catch a break. But forget that. You should know that my mother is buried with yours, so even if you aren't respectful to *me*, you should be so to her. After all, she upgraded your status from soldier to lord, purely from the goodness of her heart."

And out of a whole grave's worth of ulterior motives, I thought.

"Look," I said pointedly as we exited onto another busy road. "I'm forever grateful, and Pinnacle should have gone to you. It really should have. But it doesn't exactly add up, does it? I think she expected me to solve the murder mystery. That's the real reason she left it to a soldier."

One with a story, I didn't add. Etonia had probably known my secrets. She'd probably thought I had *connections*.

"Maybe," Jolene conceded.

I decided to bring the subject back to happy things. "Well, the barn at least had a lot of heart. I could feel the love for it oozing off you."

Jolene paused to curtsy. "Thank you."

It was so odd to have people curtsying at me. "I think we can make the place viable," I said. "I have some savings I can use to get us started, and it looks like we have hatchlings already. If we can keep things afloat until they grow—"

"Uh, about that! You see...." Jolene went pink again, pausing on the side of the cobbles where the carriages couldn't run us over. I swear, she was taking us in circles.

I sighed. "What is it this time?"

"Well... those babies aren't even mine. I'm being paid to make sure they reach adolescence, where they'll sell for more. We're not actually making many babies at the moment, and most of our future babies are spoken for to repay debt.

"And before you get angry, Useless, the big gray-violet storm dragon at the end, stopped laying eggs once Father died. I don't have the heart to sell her."

I very nearly threw my hands up in frustration. Useless was the biggest Mount-class in the barn, but apparently she was infertile, so not very valuable; Red was the yellow Hauler, well-trained, but he obviously couldn't lay eggs; and Tilly was the silver Mount-class whose cloud breath *might* have been worth something, but had now been pawned off to a damned assistant bureaucrat, who was *also* going to get a share of future profits.

And we couldn't sell her, either, or we'd break Rachel's contract and lose the whole farm anyway.

"Damn it, Jolene!" I burst out. "You should have sold this place. Three adults! *Three* dragons, none of them worth much. How the demons are you supposed to pay taxes with *that?*"

"It's not three. It's four. Scintillate laid Shiny's egg."

"Scintillate?"

"That's Tilly's full name."

"I already counted her. Useless, Red, and Tilly. The fourth one is the blue Mount-class, right? What's its name?"

"Dune. He's a beach dragon. Tilly's mate."

Well, at least that left us with *one* mating pair. It suddenly occurred to me that, as much as Jolene loved those animals, she would make for an absolutely hopeless accountant. I wondered if it ran in the family.

Jolene circled around to stand in front of me, crossing her arms. We were starting to draw the eyes of several passersby, and more than a few rooftop loungers. Everyone here wore more fabric than the heat warranted, and their hats made them taller than me.

"I've been paying the dues just fine!" Jolene protested. "I went outside the walls yesterday, and I brought back a whole peck of firefruit, earning just enough to pay off the interest. But the estate is in good shape. We can come back from this."

195

"Yeah, with *his* money," Fieran said.

I couldn't even tell him to shut up, because he was right. At the same time, Jolene's other words were catching up to me.

"You risked your life to go pick firefruit to pay *interest?*" I exclaimed.

"Yes, because I love them," she said.

She had me there. As much as I wanted to keep this woman far, far away from anything remotely *resembling* a ledger, I did want to keep her with the dragons.

"What was the plan, if your mother hadn't died?" I asked. "Did you think a magical fairy was going to fill your barn with dragons?"

She grumbled, her crossed arms tensing.

I pinched the bridge of my nose. "How bad is the debt? Be honest."

Jolene winced. "Trust me... you don't want to know."

I suppressed a groan. "Tell me anyway."

To my utter horror, she did.

Chapter 29

It's Only a Handful of Gold!

"THE ESTATE IS ONLY sixty gold in arrears," she said. My stomach dropped into my shoes.

While I struggled to speak, Jolene fidgeted awkwardly. "But it's only fifty-five if the babies reach maturity!"

As if that was better. "Sixty cursing gold!?" I blurted. "You gotta be shitting me." I'd barely brought ten gold with me, and that was my whole life's fortune. "What's the estate worth?"

"Please, can we go inside?" she said in a small voice, nodding at the gate beside us. I hadn't even noticed we'd stopped next to a gate. I looked up.

And up.

And up.

The gate had to be forty feet tall, as were the iron-barred walls around the perimeter, and the walls didn't even stop there. They continued horizontally from the top, forming an enormous cage around the absolutely *massive* three-story villa.

Jolene casually reached out and tugged open the door.

No key. No guards. Is she mad?

"I only recently moved back in," she explained, stepping aside to wave me through. "Duke Biscuit had been, ah, kind enough to house us for a long time, but his generosity... I don't want to take advantage of it anymore."

Fieran sniggered. "I'm sure you don't."

I practically staggered through the huge gate. "You—you kept dragons here, didn't you?"

"Father did, when I was a child."

"It... had to cost a fortune to build—"

"We used to have a fortune," she reminded me. "The problem now is that it's all gone."

I blinked at the building within the huge cage. It was three stories, ringed in balconies and littered in shutters and fanciful support columns. Dragons were carved into every conceivable space.

It was falling apart, too, making it look like something out of a nightmare. Weeds grew wild on the matted front lawn, where a dragon statue had long since collapsed. The stone was so thick with moss that it was barely recognizable as a statue at all.

And this is why they haven't sold the villa, I thought. *No one wants to live in a fever dream, much less one inside a cage.*

After closing the gate—*what is it with this estate and broken hinges?*—Jolene led me up the path, which was more rubble than stone.

"All told, the estate is worth a few thousand gold, but I've borrowed against all of that. So technically, we are worth negative sixty gold. Fifty-five if—"

"—the babies reach maturity," I breathed out. My knees felt weak, my whole body empty. This wasn't an inheritance.

It was a curse.

No. I shook my head and swallowed, dropping a hand to the knife in my belt, the one I'd taken from the assassin. *No. This place has potential. I can feel it.*

I turned to Jolene again. She looked like a lost puppy. She knew what sort of news she'd just delivered.

"I can fix this," I heard myself say. "But you're going to have to blindly trust me. And I mean *blindly.*" I threw out an arm. "Because, no offense, but it hasn't been going so well with you and your mother at the helm."

She sniffed, and I thought she might cry again. "Please. I'll do anything. This is all I have left of them."

"This is all sweet and syrupy," Fieran said, cutting between us to stomp up to the base of the villa's wide, ornate, yet decrepit front steps.

He threw an arm out at it and looked back at us. "But you both forget that someone *killed* for this. They killed Lord Minax, and then his wife two decades later."

"We don't know that," I said.

He scoffed. "Yeah, we do. Two deaths without causes? It's murder all around."

I swallowed. He'd come to the same conclusions as me—Etonia's mystery illness had settled it, in my mind—but he didn't need to bring it up right this moment. Jolene was not in the best state right now, and we had to be forward-focused. We had to take this one step at a time.

"And the killer wanted this place to fail, whoever it was," Fieran finished, dropping his hands to his hips to regard the villa. "Worse, they're still around and still doing murder. We've got to contend with that, not to mention our blade-faced friend."

"Blade-faced friend?" Jolene said at the same time I said, "We?"

"Yeah, we. My guard duty on you had no end date," Fieran seethed. He rounded on Jolene. "Who do you think did it? The murders."

Jolene didn't miss that we hadn't answered *her* question. "Who knows? Scorned lover from Mother? From Father? Maybe the competition? Although the competition's been doing great since my father died, so I'm not sure why they'd bother killing Mother now."

199

"Maybe a builder who wants to repurpose the space? Or a jaded client?" I suggested.

"We exhausted so many of those avenues already," Jolene said, shaking her head in defeat. "The list is long, but no one was ever arrested or even brought up on suspicion."

Sounds like it runs deeper than all of that, I thought, as a new suspicion gnawed at me. Maybe Lady Etonia saw her own death coming.

Maybe she chose me—and my history—for more reasons than her daughter's childhood crush.

Either way, it wasn't something we were going to solve just by standing here. I gestured for Jolene to go ahead of me to the villa, when I noticed the fallen statue again. Movement had drawn my eye to it, and I bent to look closer.

The statue opened its eyes.

"Oh shit," I said. It wasn't a statue at all. It was a real dragon, green, its scales half-covered with moss as if it had recently burrowed into the stuff.

Jolene and Fieran both spun to see what I was looking at, but I was already stepping closer. "Hey there," I said. It was a horse-sized Mount dragon, a swamp dragon by the color of it. It regarded me sharply with a pair of wild golden eyes.

"Four demons, that's Ravager!" Jolene hissed. "I thought she'd run away.... *Warren,* what are you doing? She's violent!"

"Relax, Jolene. She's not going to—"

The dragon lunged at me, claws out and teeth bared. I dodged right with a cry, but I still managed to slap it with an open palm. My blow landed against the dragon's head with a solid smack, and as she passed, I saw she was fat and out of shape.

She thundered to a stop, rounding on me, puffing air out her nostrils. I'd just wounded her pride.

I hissed at the green beast, stepping forward, ready to keep the fight going.

"Come on, Ravager. You wanna go?"

"I thought you said she wasn't going to attack!" Fieran shouted behind me. I ignored him, slapping my hands together threateningly and advancing on the dragon, broadening my shoulders to appear as large as I could.

The dragon's eyes darted, but finally, she shrank back. I stopped advancing, and she spat a gob of something at me, which I had to spin away to avoid.

It landed behind me, and a greenish haze rose from it. I forgot what swamp dragons spat, but most dragon spit was a bad idea to get on your skin, or anywhere close to your nose.

By the time I got my knife out to defend against further attack, Ravager had retreated. She shuffled away through the overgrown gardens, around to the front of the house and out of sight.

"Dammit, Warren," Jolene complained. "You scared her off."

"*Me?* Scare *her—?* Oh, forget it." I sheathed my knife. "I thought you said we only had four dragons."

"Well, I *thought* we did. Ravager ran off when my mother died. I thought she'd gone back to the wilds."

The little greedy place in my heart let the dragon's gender word echo: *she.* Maybe we had two mating females, after all.

"Looks like she got homesick," I said. "And she *should* be afraid of me. I'm her new master now, and I'm a soldier of war, not a coddled noblewoman."

At that moment, a red blur sliced across the edge of my vision. I drew a knife, only to have a tiny red shape flutter right past the blade to land unconcernedly on my shoulder, belching out a short stream of fire.

I scrunched up my face, smelling smoke. "What the—isn't this the red baby you threw at us yesterday? Dull?"

Jolene went dead still with amazement. "Un... unbelievable! Dull, you hussy!" Jolene straightened and threw her hands forward in an *are-you-kidding-me* motion. "I've been working with her for *weeks* to try to make her fly! Let alone to prove she can spit fire!"

And then, without any warning, Jolene rushed over and kissed my cheek. "Yes! Yes, yes!" she said, kissing me twice more before she shoved a fist at the sky and whooped. "She's mature enough to sell! That's five whole gold—"

"Don't get too excited," I said, scratching the little flame dragon on its snout. "I kinda like her. She might be worth keeping."

The dragon purred against my fingers like a cat, although the noise sounded more like fire crackling than a rumble.

"Okay, this is all fun and whatnot," Fieran said, "but can we please, please, *please,* find a bath?"

I eyed the villa dubiously. "Does that place even have tubs without something growing in them?"

Jolene scoffed. "Yes! Mother kept it very clean... on the inside." She shrugged and strode for the steps again. "She said it was best the outside looked like crap, so no one would try to steal anything."

"Great," I said, following her. "We're going to get baths, then. After that, we'll draw plans for how to save this estate."

I might not be knowledgeable about dragons or business—yet —but I knew a challenge when I saw one. I saw Pinnacle Dragons in the same way that Fieran had once seen *me* as a nice way to pass the time and hone his skills.

And, like Fieran, I didn't quite know what I was up against.

But unlike him, I would beat this opponent.

"I'm going to bring this place back to glory," I said. I was sure of it, the same way I'd been sure that Ravager wasn't going to attack—I'd been wrong, but also right; she'd just wanted to run away—and the same way I knew that Tilly could understand me.

This place was mine. I would *make* it mine.

"And *how* do you propose we pull off that miracle?" Fieran groused.

"We make plans," I said, patting Dull on the nose. "And this little one is a part of them. Aren't you, cutie?"

Jolene frowned. "So... you're planning to stay at the villa, then? Not with Duke Biscuit?"

"Yes, and you'll stay here, too. You need me, but I need your help as well. More importantly, if you want me *not* to sell this place and the villa, you better come up with some great ideas for how we take this mostly ruined business and turn it into something special. But, Jolene...."

My voice sank into a tone of warning. "You should know that no amount of seduction will change my mind. I know I'm your dream guy, but I belong to the dragons now."

Fieran snorted, and Jolene paused on the porch, as if she wasn't quite sure what to make of this. Luckily, she fell into deep laughter a moment later. The joke had landed the way I'd wanted it to.

"Are you *suuurrre* about that?" she teased, indicating her sweaty, soiled, and exhausted body. "I really smell my absolute best right now, you know. I'm in *prime* seduction condition. I will also snore like a soldier when my head hits the pillow. There's nothing quite like a good nasal serenade."

I laughed. "Oh, Jo. I think we're going to get along fine."

Chapter 30

A Close Shave (Literally)

JOLENE HADN'T LIED about the interior condition of the villa. There were no servants, but the whole thing was spotless and in perfect working order.

I took a bath in the first bathroom I came to, which I guessed was one of many. The claw-foot tub was twice my size and the water came out hot. Fieran guarded my door, waiting his turn.

Once clean, I emerged from water that had turned an embarrassing shade of brown. I pulled the plug and regarded my dirty clothes with disgust. I'd have to find some laundry materials around here somewhere; as a soldier, I'd been trained in handling my own things.

However, the bathroom was vast. Tiled floor-to-ceiling in marble, it contained ornate white furniture with gilded handles. Carvings and sculptures of dragons hid everywhere, some in plain sight, and some not. All of them seemed to be life-size, as if the late Lord Minax had instructed his artisans to make people jump all the time, thinking they'd seen a real hatchling out of the corners of their eyes.

One of the pieces of furniture here was an armoire, and I opened it to find a stack of plush towels. They would have sold for a decent amount. Lady Etonia did have her priorities.

After wrapping the towel around my waist, I exited the bathroom. Fieran turned casually when he heard the handle turn, then startled at the sight of me half-naked.

"All yours," I said, raising an eyebrow at his stubble-less cheeks, which had gone pinker than usual. "What? Never seen another naked soldier before?"

He looked away, his gray eyes lit with sudden anger. "You're not naked. And I just—didn't expect it. That's all."

I'd ask if he was into men, but all those moaning prostitutes said otherwise. I also knew I could be... *intimidating*, out of my uniform.

I'd built a lot of muscle in my spare time, both as an infantryman and a guardsman. Between having few friends and fewer hobbies, it was how I'd spent my spare time. Not to mention the scars all over my back. My cloak normally hid my mass and my marks.

"Four Demons, did you shave while I was in there?" I asked, trying to allay his discomfort. "Or do you just shave constantly, in the *hopes* that it'll grow back thicker?"

"Shut up," he said, shoving past me. "And stay by the door. I still have to guard you."

I shrugged and waited.

He emerged twenty minutes later with a spot of shaving foam on his face and his dirty clothes hanging off his clean body. He smelled of soap and dung both, and I shook my head at him. My bulk must have made him self-conscious, but he'd never been infantry. It made sense that he'd be a bit smaller.

I made no comment, and after that, I toured my new home—temporary though it might be. I walked the villa once, twice, and ultimately four times, unable to do anything other than grin. While the barn had been in bad shape, the marble-and-oak villa exuded a wealth I'd only ever dreamed about.

Jolene and Etonia had clearly wanted to pretend this villa was worth less than the barn, thus the shabby exterior. I could break the place down and sell it in pieces of material, and I'd make a fortune on that alone.

It *was* bare, though. The paintings, drapes, rugs, and other fine decorations were missing, but the soul of the building was something I instantly fell in love with. Her father had sunk his wealth into the flooring, the water catches, the multiple balconies, and the bathrooms, which all had working showers. I'd never even used a shower, and I wasn't sure yet how to go about it.

The place had five bedrooms—each one big enough to contain the entire children's quarters of my orphanage—and three living areas, two studies, a dining room, a whole half-floor of servants quarters, and multiple rooms that were probably closets, although they seemed far too large for that.

It was all way too much for me, but I couldn't help but enjoy pacing the building. In all of my wildest dreams, I'd never expect to be able to call a place like this home.

The home hadn't been built just for people, either, as evidenced by the giant cage. It soared well above the roof, which was decorated with perches and feeding troughs and large boxes that contained various oversized toys.

I figured the toys had once been given to dragons to play with. The roof must have been used as a communal place for dragons, and it was ingeniously designed for that purpose. A drain plumbed right off the eaves into the city runoff and sewage system, so all you had to do here was splash water and then shove any dragon droppings down the drain.

Cleaning this aviary—because really, it was an aviary as much as it was a villa—had to be infinitely easier than cleaning that damned barn. If I had to guess, this is what Jolene's father started with, raising dragons right outside his front door.

I found Jolene on one of my multiple passes through the house, and asked why she hadn't shifted the dragons to this open and airy exterior cage to finish out their days in comfort. The barn seemed a worse place by comparison.

"Oh, two reasons," she said, toweling off her wet hair while she spoke to me. She'd found another gown to wear, but it was looser and thus more revealing. She wore nothing beneath it, so the silk hugged her curves, making my heartbeat do treacherous things.

I was suddenly mad at myself for finding a luxurious robe to wear. I wouldn't mind showing off my bare skin to Jolene, especially without Fieran looming over my shoulder. The guy was on laundry duty right now; we'd both been willing to risk it.

Jolene lowered the hair towel. "Reason number one: Duke Biscuit has been paying for the upkeep here, in exchange for my mother's promise to stay at his residence. So if we had dragons here, we would also have to pay for the servants, and we couldn't afford that.

"Two: the Keepers made a law about it after my father died. Turns out, having dragons that close always made the neighbors nervous, but until my father died, no one had the balls to make a rule about it."

Either that, or he was greasing some wheels, I thought.

I shrugged one shoulder and peered out a window at the iron bars. You could see them from every angle within the building, so in a way, the place felt like a cage. It was still the nicest cage I'd ever been in. Far better than a stone prison cell.

"I guess it could lead to fighting, too," I said. "All those dragons loose and unsupervised around each other."

Jolene yawned into her hand, sleepily fluttering her eyelashes. "Nah. They were all quite well-behaved when my father was alive. He had such a gift with all of them. I love them, and they know that, but they are still animals. They won't respect you unless you're bigger and badder than they are, and I was always too much of a softie."

With that, she eyed Dull the Problem Child on my shoulder. "Something tells me you'll fare better," she said.

I left her to her afternoon nap, my mind whirring as I returned outside to look around the building. All the old anchor points of the business still remained, from perches to feeding troughs to little hidden nest boxes among the ferns. The whole space could be sectioned off to allow our Mount-class females their own territories, with the male Mount-class, Dune, cycling between them.

But I wonder what they eat, I thought, nudging a trough with my foot. It had been placed near a cistern that gathered clean water off the second story of the house, which looked like a cute little pond, but likely doubled as a dragon watering station.

So they drank water like the rest of us, or milk in the case of the babies, but were big dragons meat-eaters? I remembered reading somewhere that the environment couldn't support very many gigantic predators, so all the dragons' abilities developed from wild magic, rather than for hunting; and all their offensive spiky bits developed to protect them from other dragons and monsters, not for killing.

Then again, that applied to *most* of them—and dragons could be plenty vicious.

"Warren?" a voice called from the street, and I spun round to see my old friend Becki, peering at me between two iron bars of the cage.

She smiled. "Thought I'd find you here, instead of the barn. How's it look on the inside? I always wanted to see."

"Well, come on in, then," I said, beckoning to her. Her smile turned into a grin, and she leaned harder into the bars, draping herself over them. Her breasts pressed against the metal, tugging the neckline down, and she managed to show a fair amount of bare leg as she leaned on just one foot. Her pink-and-white ice dragon swirled around her legs, and the whole effect was almost flirtatious, but I didn't remember Becki being that way.

"I don't know," Becki teased. "I might not belong here. I might just dirty the place."

I was about to answer, but her frosty little dragon sniffed at the gate before entering through a hidden rat-hole under the base of the bars.

I chuckled. "Collette knows she belongs here. I think her mistress does, too."

Becki leaned back, her voice losing confidence. "Uh, yeah. She definitely knows this place. I found her, ah, near here. I figured she was one of the Minax dragons, but I, uh...."

"You didn't want to give her back," I said. "It's okay, I get it. She makes you a living. Jolene would have wanted you to have her anyway." *Because she always makes the worst financial decision, and that definitely would be the worst choice.*

Becki smiled sheepishly, which I found terribly cute. She glanced around. "Where is the Lady Jolene, anyway?"

"Napping, probably." After we all rested, we'd get to plotting, but I wasn't in any hurry just yet. "I'm not exactly doing well at sweeping her off her feet and rescuing her," I added, just to gauge how Becki would react.

Becki giggled, but her cheeks flushed. She still wore her head-scarf, and I suddenly wanted to see beneath it, to see if her hair had changed at all.

"Well, maybe you still think she's out of your league," Becki said, her voice going sultry. She finally creaked open the iron gate and entered the villa.

"But you're a lord now, aren't you? A big, delicious lord. You can take *whoever* you want."

All the air drained from my lungs as Becki raised a finger to my chest, parted the lapels of my robe, and touched me. She ran her finger down my chest all the way to my abdomen, biting her lips when she met the first rise of muscle.

It was all I could do to gently touch her wrist. "Becki... I'm not like that."

She pushed past my light grip, opening her palm on my pectoral muscle, her index finger dipping into my nipple.

"Maybe *I'm* like that," she said, leaning closer.

I swallowed. "Are you...? Like, as a second job?"

She tensed and shot me a glare. "What? No! I am *not* a prostitute."

I held up my hands. "I'm sorry. I'm just confused here."

She stomped backward and craned her neck to look up at me. "What's there to be confused about? You're a big sexy lord and I'm a horny peasant woman who used to adore you. Why *shouldn't* I want to act out one of the fantasies I've been playing in my head since my tits dropped? Especially now, while you're still not taken."

Not taken...? Did she think I was going to marry Jolene or something?

Marriage. Was this about that? Was Becki trying to get pregnant and trap me?

I cursed myself for even thinking such a thing. I'd seen the scum of the earth in taverns all across Parshil, but Becki wasn't a gold-digger. She had hated every single instance she had ever needed my help. She didn't *need no man,* as the saying went. I knew that about her, if I knew nothing else.

I also knew I was clean, and I was alone for the moment, and I'd had a wild day but still had energy to burn. I lowered my hands and reached for the hips of her dress. It was much more low-cut than the one she'd been wearing at her sales cart.

Tugging her closer, I leaned my head down. "Well, far be it from me to deny a woman such a lifelong desire. Besides, I've been wondering if your hair is still... weird."

She went loose against me. "Oh, you remembered."

I grinned. "Becki, your hair is *blue.* How on Parshil could I ever forget?"

Chapter 31

Nobility Does Have its Perks

I SNUCK Becki back to the same bathroom I'd used before, peeking into the entryway to check for Fieran and Jolene before I proceeded into the bathroom under the stairs.

Once she'd giggled past me, treating the whole thing like a game, I considered for a moment, and then pulled the tie of my robe out of its loops. I hung the tie on the door handle, a sign that I knew Fieran would understand. Jolene was hopefully fast asleep.

And what if she wasn't? I thought. *Why should you care what she hears? She has no claim on your love life.*

Yet I couldn't help seeing *all* of her, every time I looked at her. Dirty or sleepy, I remembered my old crush so easily.

I closed the door and turned.

Becki had her hands clasped behind her back, and she was giving herself a little tour of the bathroom, *ooh*ing and *aah*ing over the marble, the porcelain tub, the claw feet modeled after dragons. She opened a cabinet over a vanity sink and extracted a perfume bottle, sniffing it.

"Oh, I am so going to steal this," she said, although she did set it back in the cabinet. With that, she pivoted to smile at me, her shoulders forward as she rocked on her heels.

"So," she said, cocking her head at the shower. "You want to show me how that works?"

I chuckled, the sound somewhat faint even to my ears, and we both met up at the little square of open tile in the corner where the shower aimed down. There was a stone bench built from the wall, and a single panel of glass. A pipe led up to the gilded showerhead, which was full of little holes for the water to come out.

"I can try," I said, reaching for the handle. "But I've never used one either."

She reached out and grabbed my arm, cleaving to my side. "Oh? Then we can learn together."

My throat felt dry despite the residual moisture in the room. Who had I been thinking of? Jo-something? Who was that?

I'd gotten into this because I was a man like any other, but now I couldn't stop thinking of our childhood, of the various men I'd had to fend off for Becki. We'd been friends for so long, and I valued that... but she'd also been scrawny and underfed, and now that strange white skin glowed like alabaster under the candlelight of the bathroom sconces, and she had flesh in all the right places.

I was so aware of her presence beside me that I almost missed grabbing the handle of the shower. I felt clumsy, all thumbs, like a kid having his first time.

Stop it, I told myself, trying to read the etched instructions on the gold handle. *You're a lord now. And you've loved women beyond your wildest imaginings as it is. It won't be any harder to love this one.*

Finally I turned the handle to what I thought was the precise angle. "That should—" I began.

The water hissed out of the shower, drenching us both.

I sputtered, stepping out of the enclosure, towing her with me as she released a delighted shriek.

"Damn, that's cold!" I exclaimed, pulling my robe tighter against my skin.

Becki's giggles turned to a low hum in the back of her throat, and she slid her hands under my wet garment. "I can warm you up," she said, running her hands down over my hips. She spread her arms, pulling the robe aside.

She chuckled, this time deeply, her gaze raking over my cock. "Oh, it really is cold, isn't it...." Her voice sounded dry.

"Not for long," I said, my pulse thumping. My chilled cock twitched as I dropped my hands on her shoulders, shifting the fabric of her sodden dress aside, so it fell down her arms just a little.

Becki shuddered, I thought from cold, but then she said, "It's that big while it's *down?*"

I reached around her smooth shoulders, to her back, tugging on the tie that held the whole thing laced together. The bow came free, and her dress loosened.

She looked up, her copper eyes meeting mine.

I let the dress fall away.

She was perfect. Pristine. Like a snow-white statue in marble, shorter than me, but taller than Shimmer.

Shimmer. Shit. I forgot to send back for her....

You only just got here, I reminded myself. *You can ask Jolene about it tomorrow.*

I turned my whole focus back to Becki and her lily-white form. I'd never asked where she'd come from, to look like such an ice queen. I drew a finger down her fine jaw, along the tense muscle of her throat, between her perfect breasts. She was thin, her tits a nice handful—the sort you'd call perky, but I'd always hated that word. Her nipples were tinged slightly blue.

She sighed as I held her left breast in my hand, cupping it in the cage of my fingers. My palm rubbed the hard nipple as she swayed against me. My other hand sank down the delicate curve of her back, over her shapely ass. I gripped the round flesh and stifled a groan.

She made a sound, a half-peep, reminding me of her dragon. It occurred to me to wonder where it had gone, but the thought left me just as quickly.

I pulled her stomach tight to my cock.

Becki gasped and looked down to find me ready for her. It hadn't taken that much. Heat wafted over us, and for a moment I thought it was our own—but no, the shower had warmed up. Like a sweet summer rain, only hotter.

"How about you show me that hair of yours," I said, letting go of her chest to finger the edge of her kerchief. It had a pattern of little daisies, the sweetest of flowers.

But Becki wasn't sweet. She was deadly.

I watched her tits spread slightly as her arms rose, tugging on the edges of the kerchief. When the fabric flew free, waves of blue hair tumbled out.

Wave upon wave upon *wave.*

I stood dumbfounded, the head of my cock spotting cum on her navel. I remembered her deep blue hair—the color of ancient ice, of cold ocean—as a short skein, shaved close to her head. But she'd grown it out since I'd left, and apparently never stopped. It was tied with a ribbon every few inches, just to keep it in line, but it fell all the way to her feet.

It was also wavy, as if it had been braided recently. *There's no way that kerchief was holding it all in,* I thought. *She must have pulled a pin out, too... she was prepared for this. She took out her braids, and did her hair up special.*

She'd done this just for me.

"I've been growing it out," she breathed against my chin, never taking her gaze off me as she pressed her breasts to my chest. "I meant to sell it, you know. Haven't shown anyone. Not since I was a kid. Not until you."

Her voice was raw with barely-disguised craving. She abruptly nipped forward, her teeth grazing my chin, like a little dragon going in for a snack.

"You're just as... assertive... as I remember," I said, trying not to sound breathless.

"Mmm," she said, licking her lips. "And you're a little less forceful. I have to say, I'm a bit disa—"

I gripped her arms and spun her around into the rapidly warming spray. She laughed roughly as I stepped into the wet heat with her, and I pushed down at the spot between her shoulder blades. She crumpled onto the shower's stone bench with a moan, both hands flat against it, her ass slick with the falling water in front of me.

One of my hands clamped down hard on her hip, while the other parted her ass cheeks with two fingers. I nearly came early at the sight of her folds, hidden there. Like her nipples, her sex was tinged blue.

"What are you?" I breathed, running my fingers down her sex. When she jerked away, I held her in place.

"Just a m-mutt," she said. "Daughter of a whore and a foreigner. My mother—" Becki gasped as my fingers dipped inside her wet passage "—said he was too strange not to keep his child. She wanted to see—what I would *be*—"

The word cut off as my exploring fingers found her nub. I put pressure on it, exploring every fold I could see from this angle, and moistening everything that I couldn't. Her pussy was wet from the shower, but the wet was growing thicker, her body making ready for me.

"You're gorgeous, is what you are," I said, as intrigued as I was horny. I'd always known Becki's mother had been a prostitute who died young, but I'd figured her blue hair had come from some sort of magic spell. I hadn't realized it was in her blood, but I should have known—because there was another thing that was different about Becki.

She was always cold to the touch.

Marcus Sloss & Jace Cannon

Her sex was no different, and in that instant, I *had* to feel it. I stopped rubbing her and fed my tip between her cheeks. Then I pushed.

Her slick, delicious cold infused me.

I groaned as she groaned. It felt so strange, yet so incredible. She was giving and wet and easy to slide into, but *cold*. My balls quivered.

"Sorry... about that," she rasped.

I leaned over her, putting one hand on the wall. With the other, I took hold of her hip once again.

"Like you said," I murmured, "we've got to warm each other up."

I pulled out sharply, then I thrust back in.

She cried out, because this time I went to my full length, a length that had apparently impressed her. I made sure she got it all, her ass rippling as I rammed against her. I slid out, watching the bluish folds pull.

My cock shone between thrusts, glistening with her need. Her shoulder blades bumped back and forth with my rhythm, and she heaved back against me, meeting my force with her own.

"Warren. Fuck, oh Warren...."

"Yeah?" I replied, pounding into her.

"I—I want you so deep—"

I gave her what she wanted, harder each time, until I had her face pressed into the wall. She had to look back at me, her mouth open with want. I could see her right breast leaping with each thrust, the flesh swinging forward and back, just like my balls against her inner thighs.

"Milord," she said, wincing, not from pain but from pleasure. "Milord, my fucking lord, yes!"

Demons, I wasn't even touching her clit, and she looked like she might shatter just from this. The ache on her face was about to

218

do me in. Sweating in the spray, I decided to test her. I had just enough sanity left to do it, but not more.

"Where do you want it?" I asked.

She moaned, quivering. "Warren—"

"I'm going to come, Becki. Where do you want it?"

Her fingernails curled into the stone bench as I scrunched her up between my pummeling cock and the wall. She looked insensate, overwhelmed. That's where I wanted her.

"In... on me," she gasped. "Oh fuck, I wanna be stupid." Her copper eyes opened and stared back at me, flat with ecstasy. "Come all over me, Warren. I want to feel all that heat."

I gritted my teeth, hiding my grin, and gripped her hips with both hands now. Without warning, I yanked her backward, pulling out of her. She loosed a cry as I dropped her onto my sodden robe next to the shower, my movements careful but fast, because I didn't want to wait for this.

Back in the cold air, I flipped her, pulling her pussy close as I settled onto my knees. She was even more stunning from this side, the points of her nipples rolling. I grabbed her hand and shoved it against her pussy, positioning her index finger tight to her nub. I would do it myself, but everything was too slippery. I pushed my cock down and got it back inside her.

She nearly wept as I slid past the clamped fist of her walls. Her back arched, tits sinking back toward her chin. Her blue hair splayed all around us, the ribbons loose, the strands wet and snakelike. The whole thing looked like a drawing of a wingless dragon beneath her.

I spread my knees for leverage, and I fucked her.

Becki screamed out, "Warren!" and then she started cursing the Four Demons. Her finger did its job, working hard. I focused on it, holding back. I wanted her to come before me.

I crested, then stalled, my orgasm fisted in my balls. I thanked my lucky stars for the uncomfortable feeling, and kept going, pulling all the way out so my head could give her more sensation above her entrance. She writhed and moaned and begged.

"I need you to come, oh please come, come wherever you want, please—"

She'd lost all control now, and that's what unwound the knot in me. "Oh, shit," was all I said, before yanking myself out. My first spurt got as far as her cold, pebbled nipple.

By the second spurt, Becki was coming.

Her back arched again, which only served to get my cum across more surface area as she screamed out her pleasure. My heart still raced as white strings raced up her flesh, and her legs closed against me as her inner ache pulsed.

"F-f-f-fuuucck, Warren," she finally gasped, senselessly grabbing at her own sternum and smearing my cum across her stomach, which was sunken as she drew her breath deep. She finally met my gaze again, and I leaned over her, my loose dick trailing past her navel.

She said to come on her, not in her. She isn't trying to trap me. She wasn't doing this just because I'm a lord now.

I hadn't thought she was, but I'd needed to confirm it. Despite the cold of her body and the cool air outside the shower, that thought warmed me.

She wants me for me.

I kissed her on the mouth and said, *"Fuck,* Becki. That was good."

Her hooded gaze cleared, and she smiled. "I don't know," she said. "We should try again, just to be sure."

Chapter 32

Let's Get Busy (No, Not Like That)

We didn't get that chance. Not a moment later, a knock sounded at the door. I looked up.

"Just thought you should know," Fieran called, "the princess has risen."

I paled. *Oh shit. I better get Becki out of here.*

Becki giggled and slapped my chest. "Embarrassed of me already?"

I opened my mouth to say it wasn't that, but it *was* that, wasn't it?

"I just...." I ducked away, rising into a crouch. "I just don't want her to get the wrong idea about me."

Becki rose with me, cocking her head in interest. She didn't seem to be offended at all.

"What? That you, a single man, fuck women?"

I chuckled and stepped into the shower to hose off all the sex juices. She joined me, and I helped soap her off.

"I don't even know," I said. "I guess I had a crush on her. The same way you had one for me."

Becki laughed and slapped my chest. "On *Jolene?* You poor boy. That woman may be noble, but she's hopeless."

I couldn't disagree, so I didn't. "I know."

We were both clean now, but we didn't leave the warm spray, which was cooling. I circled Becki's hips with my arms, my hands spreading on her lower back.

I liked her. I trusted her. She was matter-of-fact, and not jealous. And holy Demons, that had felt good.

I wanted to keep her around. A part of me *needed* her. That piece of my old life, my old me.

"I want to hire you," I said. "You and Princess Collette, for the farm."

She laughed again, amused, her deep blue hair swishing as she tossed it.

"Hire me for what, Lord Warren?" she asked.

Grinning, I said, "I don't know yet." I kissed her and added, "But I'll think of something."

I had to resort to my sodden robe again, but a few minutes later we were dressed and back in the hallway. Fieran stepped aside as we exited, looking disapprovingly at us—or moreso, just at *me*. That I could handle, but I wasn't going to have him glaring daggers at Becki. She certainly had nothing to be ashamed of.

I, however, did. I understood that the moment I saw Jolene striding up the hall toward us. She stopped dead when she saw Becki standing there, and me next to her, in nothing but a wet robe. Jolene's mouth opened, but no words came out as she glanced between us, putting all the pieces together.

"Some house guest you are," Fieran muttered, which I thought was rich, given his behavior at the barn. He'd only called the place a dump half a dozen times.

Yes, but he's right. You should be better than him. You're a lord now, and it behooves you to be more discreet. Otherwise, you could soil Becki's reputation... and upset the woman whose home you're intruding on.

All right, maybe it was technically *my* home now, but she had every attachment to it. I needed to respect her connection to the place. This wasn't some back-alley tavern full of brawling soldiers. This was a *villa,* for demonssakes.

I rubbed the back of my neck, keeping the robe closed with my other hand. "Uh... Jolene. This is my old friend, Becki...."

Jolene blinked at me, then at Becki. "Hello," she said.

"Hi!" Becki said. To her credit, she didn't strike any poses or say anything racy. I struggled to find something to say.

"Sorry about this," I said, fluttering one of my soaked lapels at her. "I had to wear something while my real clothes dried."

It was an apology, but not for the thing right in front of her. Jolene's mouth snapped closed. I couldn't read her face.

She abruptly spun and walked away.

I let out a long breath. That couldn't be good. I tried to read her walk too, but she didn't seem to be *storming* off. Just walking, her skirts swishing casually behind her.

Maybe she's just fleeing an awkward situation?

Considering her personality, that seemed about right.

I sighed. "You'd better go," I told Becki.

She nodded and rose on her toes to kiss my cheek. "I'll stop by tomorrow, maybe?"

"Sure. Leave me a way to contact you, though, if I'm not in. Things are wild right now."

Her catty smile lit up the hallway, those bizarre copper eyes glinting. "Wild is *right,*" she said. "See you later, Milord. And Fieran."

She waved to my bodyguard, then left through the glass-paneled front door. She'd tied her kerchief again, now that she was going back into the public eye. I hoped she didn't sell all that hair before I saw her next. I had ideas on some fun things to do with it.

Fieran sniffed. "You're a busy man," he commented.

I let out a long breath of air, then moved to the stairwell.

"You aren't wrong," I replied.

Once my clothes had dried, I headed up to the roof and just stayed there for a while, enjoying the breeze while overlooking my grounds, and the city itself.

I could see plenty of Dasvilla through the bars, since this house was a story taller than most of the adjacent mansions. Rich people casually sprawled below me on rooftops, pretending that they weren't watching me. One of them even had some distance-lenses, although the woman only used them when I wasn't looking.

As I surveyed my new home, my hand wandered to my inner breast pocket, where two letters rested. One from my past, and one welcoming me to my future.

The roof's ornate trapdoor creaked, and it folded back, drawn by a pulley mechanism that could be triggered from either side. I turned to see Jolene stepping out, holding her skirts.

"Hey there. Where's your shadow?" she asked.

"Scouting the grounds," I said. "Again."

Fieran was paranoid, and not really about my safety. He seemed far more concerned for himself. Then again, maybe the Becki thing had embarrassed him by proxy, and he needed to get away from that, too.

Either way, I didn't mind being an afterthought. It wasn't that his presence was grating on me; it was that I was starting to like it. I'd gone a long time without friends, and although Fieran didn't count, he *reminded* me of friendship, and that was enough.

It was Dasvilla, this damned place. It made me remember friends, and home, and family both lost and found. It made my heart beat again.

Jolene wrested with her skirts some more, twisting the soft yellow fabric in her nervous fists. The color almost matched her blond hair, except for the notes of strawberry that graced the strands in the sunlight. Burn me, but she had lovely hair, all round waves and ringlets and yet somehow natural. Some women would *kill* for such hair.

I also noted that the dress was flattering, much more so than the one she'd worn to clean the barn in. Had she worn that for me? And the thin sleeping dress, too?

Of course she had. She'd admitted to the crush.

"Look," I said. "I'm sorry about Becki. That was rude. I should have been more discreet."

Jolene looked down. "It's your villa," she said.

The smallness of her voice was too much for me. I closed the gap between us with long strides, then took her hand. I lifted it to my mouth and kissed it, as formally as I knew how, lowering it again without making eyes at her.

"No, milady," I said. "It is *our* villa. I may be the owner, but it is *your* childhood home. You will stay here, just as you will continue to work with the dragons. I will keep you on as my ward if I must, but... I have a feeling your services will pay your way, just fine."

I leaned closer, dropping a grin. "And I mean your *dragon* services, just so we're clear. I *cannot* abide snoring, after all."

She bit her lip, still looking down, and then laughed out loud. Her blue eyes shifted to mine.

"Milord Warren, you are the most *shameless* flirt," she said.

I raised a brow. "Is it working?"

She blushed, making a move that was half waving me off, half fanning herself.

"Four Demons! I just saw you leaving a tryst with a commoner, and now you've got me turning red minutes later. How do you do that? Make me utterly forget another woman?"

225

"It'll be harder to forget her when she works here," I said.

Her joy faded several shades, and she sighed and looked away. "I do suppose you were too good to be true," she said.

I smiled. Some of the noble was leaking out of her.

"If I court you, Jolene, it will be the old-fashioned way. But I've got too much on my plate right now to deny myself a willing woman, so I won't. However, I won't hide it from you if I have a lover. Whatever relationship we have, it will not be built on secrets."

She nodded and set her shoulders. Our eyes met again.

"I understand," she said. "I will just have to get over you."

I grinned. "We'll see about that."

Chapter 33

First Meeting with a Snack Food

LATER THAT EVENING, Fieran and I headed to the duke's estate. Jolene went ahead of us, promising to alert the duke that we'd be coming.

"Ah, yes, the duke is waiting for you," the squire at the door told us when we arrived. "But unfortunately, you'll have to remove any weapons that are not visible. Forgive me while I search you."

Frowning, Fieran and I both endured a pat-down, giving up all the various knives we had hidden on our person. We were allowed to keep one sword and knife each, because we both had one in plain sight, on our belts.

As the squire worked, I looked him over. The man wore something close to guardsman officer attire, even though he was young; generally this meant he was a noble who'd gotten a leg up in the military. I didn't fault him for being high born, but it always bothered me that men like him got stationed in such safe places.

The dragon that perched on his shoulder was a bit much, as well. The Shoulder-size had two-toned scales with a gem-encrusted collar, of all things. The squire wore fine armor, even though his parents likely wanted him to avoid combat at all costs.

Fieran was my steady, silent companion, practically a shadow, as the squire bowed slightly and led us into the castle. The foyer was decorated with lush carpets, fancy paintings, marbled sculptures, and ornate weapons—nothing creative, as far as rich people's homes go.

I much preferred the eccentricities of my villa. I'd taken to calling it the Cage in my head.

Finally the squire turned us down an atrium, and the decor changed. Shoulder-class dragons lazed about the well-lit, glass-ceilinged room in golden cages, staring out windows into more atriums, all of them lined up beside each other, with different environments within. Heat rippled within the next one, and rough igneous rock dominated its landscape. Another looked like it was mimicking ice.

I glanced back at Fieran, who met my eyes. We were both thinking the same thing. *Is this where Etonia sold most of her dragons?*

I doubt she'd charged Duke Biscuit market rate.

I was starting to have my suspicions about this supposedly-friendly man, but I said nothing as the squire completed what was obviously an intentionally long tour. Biscuit wanted me to see this opulence, and to see where many of the wares of my company had gone to. This was some kind of flex, a show of power.

It was like he was saying, *Look at where all your dragons have gone to. Can't you see that I've already won?*

But what did he think he was winning? This display indicated gross negligence to me. None of these dragons were *doing* anything. They weren't being used for the betterment of Dasvilla.

It was no wonder the city hadn't grown.

We spent another half hour flowing through the estate's most expensive rooms, meandering behind the squire like a bored river, until we finally went up a set of stairs.

Once we reached the top, the young squire stood to the side of a set of open mahogany doors and announced me.

"Guardsman Warren has arrived, milord."

I didn't miss the exclusion of both my third rank and my lord title, not to mention Fieran.

"Lord Warren," I politely corrected, striding into the room. I stopped. Duke Biscuit sat at a long charwood table that I couldn't have purchased with all my life's savings put together, and he was facing an audience. I had just walked into that audience.

Ready for me, my ass, I thought. This was not how one treated a guest. The squire should have told me this was happening, and to come back later.

Instead they threw me at the back of a long line of supplicants that trailed up the center of the room, ending at Biscuit's table about thirty feet ahead of me. These people were commoners, and had apparently come to express grievances to their duke.

While the supplicants were forced to stand, representatives of the Dasvilla nobility reclined in the seating that lined the left and right walls of the room. They had three tiers of comfortable chairs with plenty of empty spaces where others could have rested while they waited their turn.

The nobles were probably here to put in a few words here and there, although most appeared to be engaged in idle chatter.

A woman sat beside the duke, her eyes on mine. I blinked at the clothing and sash of her station. I had nearly forgotten the duke had a wife, since he'd needed Etonia to serve as his steward, and she was the one I always saw as a kid. The duchess was a great deal younger than the duke. I didn't remember ever knowing her name.

"Ah, young Warren, there's the lucky boy now," Biscuit said from the table, cutting off the well-dressed young man who was standing in front of him. The guy must be a merchant, because he'd just been complaining about a trade deal he didn't like.

The front of the line seemed to be composed of those in the finest clothing, so even the line itself wasn't fair.

Either way, the duke was taking supplicants at the same time I arrived. This sort of thing didn't happen often, and the line was long. It looked like he'd started the whole thing right about the same time he'd heard I was coming. I didn't see Jolene anywhere.

Swallowing my annoyance and ignoring the stares of the nobles who attended this sad little court, I bowed at the waist, showing more respect than I already thought the man deserved. Fieran bowed too, ever my shadow.

"It is Lord Warren now, if you please," I told the duke, again keeping things polite. He was a rotund man, clearly not well-acquainted with diet and exercise. His pale skin looked washed-out beside the deep blue of his robes, and few wrinkles lined his noble gray eyes.

Here was a man supposedly on the very edge of civilization, touching upon the fierce wilds he was tasked with defeating, and he looked *soft*. The name "Biscuit" made even more sense now.

"Ah, already filling out those new britches of yours, are you?" the duke replied. He threw an arm at me and addressed the line of people.

"Can you believe it?" he boomed. "This man here inherited an entire lordship, estate and all, from a woman he isn't even related to. None of us in this room had ever heard of him. What incredible luck, don't you think?"

Talk about passive-aggressive, I thought as the peasants—who should have been able to relate to me—instead turned their jealous gazes my way. Already he was isolating me from my fellow man. I'd have to work hard to undo this.

I inclined my head. "My apologies, Your Grace. I did not know you were busy today, and I will not impose on these vital proceedings. The cares of the people must be addressed, for they are the ones we serve, and not the reverse."

With that said, I stepped to the back of the line. "I'll wait my turn. Please, continue—"

"What? Nonsense!" the duke cried, nearly hitting the merchant in the face when he waved me forward. "Come, boy, come. This frippery can wait until another day."

"Oh, I insist," I replied simply and loudly, albeit with a smile. "I was a commoner myself only days ago. I know how to wait."

His face darkened at that. Not even five minutes into meeting this duke, and we were already trading barely-disguised barbs. I could be setting myself up for failure—but I wouldn't allow myself to be walked on. It was up to the duke how he'd take it.

He glared at me. I glared right back.

Come on, old man, I wanted to dare him. *Show me what you got.*

Chapter 34

Playing Nice is Still Playing

THE DUKE LOOKED like he might keep pushing, but when all the scruffier people in the room looked his way, he just grinned instead. Appearances were important, after all.

"Humble, I see," he said. "Good, good, that's a fine trait in a noble. I'll see you shortly, Young Lord Warren."

With that, he turned back to the whining merchant. As I settled in for the long wait, I laid my hand casually on my knife, just to show those around me that I knew how to use the thing. When people stopped looking at us quite so much, Fieran leaned close to my ear.

"This guy is a piece of work," he said.

I nodded, still smiling. "Jolene might want us to stay here, but I can tell this guy doesn't. Why might that be, do you think?"

Fieran sniffed, and it occurred to me that he'd taken a very real interest in me and my new life. He was my bodyguard, yes, but we both knew that was a sham job meant to get him away from the assassin. His father was someone important, which is why he'd been targeted. This was also the reason he'd soon receive new orders, and then I'd be on my own against that same assassin.

So why did he care about my life?

I pondered this for a while, then turned my attention to the grievances of the supplicants, filing them all away at the back of my mind. As the line shortened and I got closer, I noticed the enormous Enforcer for the first time.

The beefy, sun-tanned officer didn't belong in this environment, and the spectacles on his nose were out of place. He sat several chairs to the left of Duke Biscuit, his face constantly buried in paperwork, marking notations as every supplicant passed through.

I blinked when I saw the insignia on his shoulder. *That's not an Enforcer. That's the justicar himself.*

I kept an eye on him, but he never once looked my way, not even when the supplicants were quiet and there was nothing to notate. If my instinct was correct, the man was avoiding looking at me.

Which meant I had his attention. A lot of it.

Finally, it was my turn to be front-and-center. I bowed with respect to Biscuit and his wife.

"Young Lord," Duke Biscuit said again, holding out a hand. "What a pleasure."

Young lord. Lucky boy. I didn't miss the disrespectful word choices that focused on my age. I shook his hand anyway. Better to get the full lay of the land *before* you start fighting your battles.

"The pleasure is all mine, Your Grace," I said. His grip was firm, but I met it with equal strength. "Former Guardsmen Third Rank Warren, and current Lord Orpheus-Minax, at your service."

I gave him my best winning smile, and then took his wife's hand to kiss it respectfully. She was a stunner, blond and blue-eyed just like Jolene—minus any red in her hair—but something about her felt empty, doll-like, cold.

"And this must be your lovely wife. Duchess, I regret that I don't know your name."

She withdrew her hand at the exact moment it wouldn't be rude. "I am Duchess Nola Laure-Brennan. Interesting, that you should attach the Minax name to your own. Are you betrothed to the Lady Jolene already? Or do you merely wish to sound important?"

The duke chuckled. "She does have you there, son. I've never heard of a commoner with a surname. Where does this 'Orpheus' bit come from? Are you sure you're not trying to boost your status?"

I met his eyes, still keeping a friendly face on. "It's derived from the word *orphan*, Your Grace. To remind me of where I came from."

This caused plenty of murmurs among the crowd, both noble and commoner alike. I might be the last in line, but several commoners had stayed behind to watch my first official meeting with the duke. I tried to take note of all of them, because these were likely the smartest of the group.

"And no," I added. "I am not engaged. I have simply inherited the Minax name, and I wish to honor its legacy, not erase it from the histories of Dasvilla. The late Lord and Lady Minax were good people."

This earned me some approving chatter from the commoner crowd. Etonia had done good work in the orphanage, and based on what Captain Kenna had said about Etonia's dead husband, Lucian Minax had been kind, too.

The duke's smile flickered, and he said, "Well, that is very... noble of you, isn't it. So, what brings you here this fine day?"

Your own squire brought me, I thought, keeping the snipe to myself, *although I'm pretty sure he got lost along the way.*

"Apparently Pinnacle Dragons is mine now," I replied, reaching into my robes. The squire had already disarmed me of my hidden weapons, so Biscuit didn't flinch at the gesture. I handed over the duke's letter, which I knew Jolene had actually written.

"I have followed the king's orders, as listed by yourself. It is my understanding that you are executor of the Minax estate, and so you must be the one to furnish me with the related titles and legal documents."

The duke looked over my letter, but I knew he wasn't reading it. It was an excuse to keep talking.

"Hmm, I must tell you, I found all this very curious. An orphan of unfortunate circumstances, inheriting a lordship? Quite peculiar." He looked up. "You should know that I requisitioned a full report on you, because this move shocked me so. Very interesting information in that report."

The justicar snorted suddenly, keeping his eyes on the paperwork. *Is that a threat?* I wanted to say.

Instead, I kept playing their game. I'd played it once before, after all.

"What can I say? I'm interesting," I said, hooking a thumb in my belt. "But so is the situation here. Imagine my shock upon hearing that a noble couple died mysteriously all those years apart, with an apothecary unable to determine the cause of death in either case! Such intrigue for such a boring city, I must say.

"Oh, and did I mention the murder of a guard and theft of dragons at the Pinnacle barn not long ago?" I turned to the justicar, my tone going colder. "Is there any sign the Minax estate will see justice from our justicar? Or has he already conveniently marked the case as unsolvable?"

The justicar was the lead Enforcer for any given city. Essentially, they laid down all the paper laws of a place, which included murder investigations. While soldiers tried to stop violence, Enforcers investigated the violence that still happened anyway.

If I understood the bars of rank on this guy's shoulder, this guy had seen some shit.

The justicar smirked, setting his pen down to lean back. "You should be careful of how you speak, regardless of your military standing. Foot soldiers should know their place," he said.

Duke Biscuit kept smiling; he didn't take my bait, but he certainly didn't want to defend me like I was one of his own, because I wasn't. Still, he was playing politics, while the justicar played a more basic game.

I opened my mouth to respond, but Duke Biscuit chuckled, cutting in.

"Lord Warren deserves more respect than that, Ormish," he said. To me, he added, "Please try to forgive him. He is only making a point for us all.

"So tell me, Lord Warren, why were you truly chosen? You must forgive our impoliteness, but I'm afraid you have blindsided us. Are you perhaps a conman, or former lover, who swindled the Lady Etonia? More importantly, are you here to cause trouble?"

"I am not," I said, reaching into my pocket to retrieve the second letter I kept there. I handed it over to the attentive duchess, who'd stayed quiet and frigid the whole time. Duchess Nola unfolded the parchment, read the missive, exhaled loudly from her nose, and then handed it back.

"Justicar Ormish, you're excused," the duchess ordered. When he stood, she eyed him darkly. "Cause no trouble with Lord Warren. Understood?"

He frowned, confused. They had probably had a completely different encounter all rehearsed. He couldn't have been here just to write reports; this man had seen combat, and lots of it.

He bowed deeply, despite his obvious confusion. "I... I only enforce the law, Your Grace. There are taxes owed, which should be paid upon transfer, or—"

"You will leave," Nola said.

Duke Biscuit half-frowned at his wife. "Surely he needn't—"

Nola leaned close to whisper in her husband's ear. His brow drew low, and he said quietly, "Are you certain?"

I alone was close enough to hear Nola's response: "The King's Hand is surely keeping tabs on him. We don't want to draw more attention."

Interesting. What were they trying to hide from the king, exactly? If I had to guess, Justicar Ormish had intended to ambush me here and try to ruin me by insisting I pay all the taxes up front. They wanted Pinnacle dead for good, but at the very idea of drawing the king's gaze, they'd sent Ormish on his way.

"I don't believe it. What did the letter say?"

"It says enough," I replied. "But if you need more, how about this?"

I leaned closer to whisper. "The King's favorite method of torture is whipping with a wind dragon's tail. I can show you the marks, if you are so inclined. They have quite the unique edge to them."

Duke Biscuit slumped into his chair, mouth agape. I could feel Fieran's confusion looming behind me. No one knew how the king and his Hand tortured people, because no one they tortured ever came back alive.

At least, nobody *common* knew. The nobles would be aware of the method, since the king would use the threat of that torture to keep them in line. Either way, it was a famous topic of conversation among tavern-goers.

People go into the dungeons, spill their secrets, and then never come out. Normally, people tell falsehoods under torture... but the King's Hand always gets the truth. Always.

Of course, I didn't know where the bodies went, since I had escaped the place alive.

The duke abruptly pounded the table. "This Supplication is over. Everybody out. Guards, escort the stragglers, then leave." He flicked his fingers at the nobles. "You lot, too. Begone."

You lot. He might be pitting commoner and noble against each other, but he was also making sure to keep the nobles a peg below himself.

The crowd—especially the high-borns—grumbled, but they left. I wondered if they had a nearer exit, or if they'd have to go through the maze of dragons like I had.

When it was down to just me, Fieran, and the duke and duchess, Biscuit said, "Well-played, Lady Etonia. Well-played." To his wife, he said lowly, "She chose the great hero himself to inherit. It appears she has won from the grave."

I was done listening to this, and I was done playing nice. "So tell me," I said. "Why did you ruin Lady Etonia? What did she ever do to you?"

Chapter 35

Do We Have a Deal?

I COULD HAVE HEARD a dragon's whisker drop in the silence that followed.

But really. *What did she ever do to you?*

It was clear to me that Biscuit had sabotaged the Minax estate after its lord had died. He'd taken Etonia from her home and business, making her into his steward—a job he already had a competent wife for—and giving Etonia work to do under the guise of being charitable.

That had distracted her from Pinnacle, and even then, he'd bought her dragons at what was likely pennies on the silver. Frankly, he'd allowed his ward to absolutely decimate her own holdings. If he'd had even one kind bone in his body, he would have helped Etonia hire a steward of her own.

I didn't know if he'd had her or Lord Minax killed, but he had never had their best interests in mind.

He stared me down for a moment, but eventually sighed and said, "I didn't *ruin* her, son. I simply allowed nature to take its course."

"You could have helped her. Stopped her."

"What would be the point of that? I prefer to watch people succeed or fail on their own. It is my deep belief that one must prove themselves worthy of a title. Of course, I give people openings to improve, but this sometimes leads them to prove they aren't worthy."

Like how you're worthy of leading Dasvilla? I thought. *Of expanding it into the wilds you haven't touched?*

I nodded behind me. "You're raising dragons. Dragons you practically stole from her. I saw several nests, Your Grace. You are a competitor of Pinnacle, not a compatriot. Is that why you killed Etonia? Because she finally realized what you'd been doing?"

The duchess shot to her feet. "You *dare*—"

"Calm, my love," the duke said, touching his wife on the wrist as she fumed. He shook his head at me.

"Such accusations, Young Lord. They are quite unbecoming. You've no proof of such a thing, because it is a lie. The Lady Etonia died peacefully in her sleep."

"Peacefully, my ass," I said.

The duke laughed. "My, you are a headstrong one, aren't you? But I suppose it makes sense, given your history." He tugged on his wife, and she reluctantly sat as he leaned toward me.

"Let me offer you a lesson, son. Businesses compete, and that is how it should be. But killing the competition? That is just bad form. If you'd known her late husband, you wouldn't think his sudden death so mysterious. He was a bigger man, living in excess, who drank heavily and fucked any woman who'd let him. Men like that often die of heart troubles.

"Besides, despite his gluttony, people loved Lord Minax. They *relished* in his presence, myself included. He had no enemies."

I straightened away from him. "We will see about that."

"Warren," Fieran hissed under his breath, a warning. I was pushing too far, but I wasn't going to stand here and fake my respect for this man a moment longer. He'd *ruined* Jolene's life, while smiling to her face. At *best,* he'd driven the kind-hearted Etonia into an early grave.

Yet he sat there and smiled, dancing his fingers across the table, a fake far-off look in his eye. I clamped my mouth shut. Whatever he had to say, I wanted to hear it. I wanted to know what story he told, so I could figure out how to disprove it later.

"Lord Minax had this way of warming any room he entered," the duke said wistfully.

He shook his head in feigned sadness. "The Lady Etonia adored him, and his death ate at her. She wasn't ready to lose him. After his passing, she started to find monsters in every shadow. None were real when she sent the guards to look."

He tut-tutted infuriatingly before looking back up at me. "I must say, if your goal was to upset the nobility of an entire city, you have succeeded in an incredibly short time," he said. "There's no better way to achieve that than by accusing your betters of crimes they didn't commit."

"You and I both know her death was not natural," I said. "And Pinnacle wasn't sabotaged on accident. A guard was killed, and nearly *every* dragon let free or stolen? In a city where *you* are angling to be her competitor? You're not keeping all those eggs I saw in your atriums. You sell them for profit, like any other dragon merchant."

Duke Biscuit never once lost his composure. "I do see your point there, boy. The incident with the unlocked barn was a shame. I lack proof, but I *believe* the sabotage was an orchestrated strike to remove Pinnacle from the business.

"As for myself, I am only a small name in dragon husbandry as of now, but there are much bigger players out there, let me tell you. I think those players reached a boiling point, and wanted Pinnacle done once and for all. It had been limping on for too long, you see."

"And Jolene?" I asked. He would only openly say so much, but I could learn from every word I got out of him. If I was lucky, he might even slip up.

Duke Biscuit furrowed his brow. His wife said, "The daughter."

"Oh, her. She is inconsequential. The only thing that matters is that villa."

I scoffed. Jolene wasn't inconsequential. He was pretending not to know who she was? Like I'd believe that.

"What's so great about that dump of a house?" I asked. A bizarre little corner of my heart hoped the house would forgive me.

"Why, it's one of the city's finer estates, despite its... peculiar architecture," the Duke replied, tilting back, clasping his hands comfortably over his protruding stomach.

"In fact," he continued, "I had hoped to purchase it from you, and to make you a very wealthy young commoner... but it seems you have no interest in that. Unless all this is an attempt to extort more money from me?"

"I'm not taking your money," I snapped.

The duchess leaned forward, setting her elbows on the table. She unleashed a wide and charming smile.

"Perhaps you will sell the barn, then? It did save our fledgling business significant money, due to our overflow issues."

I ground my teeth. *You conniving little bitch.*

"You paid Etonia bottom-of-the-barrel rates to rent space to raise dragons you'd stolen from her, as the business you illegally built got bigger than the business it had stolen from. I ought to be impressed with your nerve."

Biscuit patted his wife's arm. "Now, now, dear, don't incense him. He's already come in here with a chip on his shoulder."

"Yes, and a letter of protection from the King's Hand," she said coldly.

A sputter sounded behind me. "What?" Fieran said, speaking for the first time in ages.

The duke and duchess ignored him. "What is it you want, son?" Duke Biscuit asked. "Do you seriously want to rebuild Pinnacle Dragons? You should sell what you can, and run."

I shook my head. "Sell what? My debt? I'd get a handful of coins, and you know it. I bet you didn't expect me to see Jolene first, when I came to town, did you? Because if I'd come to you first, which was the plan—" Jolene had said as much "—then you would have conveniently left out all mention of Pinnacle's debts as you wrote up the sales contract. And I would have been stuck paying my debtors after you paid me, no doubt.

"Meanwhile, you'd get a new barn and new house, debt-free... and I'm *sure* you would have offered fair market rate."

The duchess didn't miss my sarcasm. "And you think you can run it? You think *you* can make it viable? You, a commoner, a soldier, a pretty-boy with a funny story to his name?

"Ha! You are welcome to try. We can always make our purchase once the banks take the estate away from you, and then you will walk away with no coins at all."

Duke Biscuit raised his eyebrows, and I sensed another dung-pile getting dropped.

"You should know that the crown gave Lady Etonia a break on her taxes, when her estate suffered damage during the break-in and release," Biscuit said. "That saved her five gold a month in taxes for a few years, but one word from us, and poof—" he waved his hand "—that goes away. In fact, you will owe *back* taxes.

"Essentially, if you keep any part of that estate, your taxes will double—and I will make sure the assessors come calling, well before the first of the year.

"Or...." He let the word drag out. "Or, you sell us the estate, *we* keep the tax break, and we take that saved gold and make a monthly charitable donation to the local orphanage. Or you could pocket it, if you preferred. Five gold a month for the rest of your life."

"Meanwhile, we will forgive your debts," the duchess added. "How does that sound?"

I tensed. He must have researched me before now, if he knew I'd come from the local orphanage. He also seemed aware that I cared about the place, and that I'd sent money back whenever I could.

I might have caught him off guard with my deductions, but he knew me well enough already, and he'd figured out what made me tick. *Some* of what made me tick.

The thing was, I didn't exactly have that much gold either, so this was probably a sweetheart deal. I only had a few gold to my name, even after years of serving in the army. And after that expensive trip he'd designed to drain me, I had even less.

So five gold a month, *forever*... that would allow me to live large, at least compared to my usual expenses. Despite the reek of bullshit coming off these people, any sane man would take this deal. This was a chance to rise from poverty *forever*.

But then Nola's words echoed inside me: *we would forgive your debts*.

Forgive. Not *pay off*.

Etonia was indebted to *them*?

Rage built inside me, but I stuffed it down into my icy, hard center. I'd started to like the dragons, sure. I'd seen their potential. But I needed to be realistic here. Reviving a business in a town where the reigning nobility would fight against me at every turn? That was a losing man's game.

I had to hedge my bets, and since these gold-blooded scammers seemed to like oddball agreements so much....

"I agree to your offer," I said, "on the condition I'm given a month to see if I can pay off the debts myself, and find a means of procuring consistent gold for the taxes as well."

Duke Biscuit snorted. "You can't be serious. It's impossible."

"And if you fail?" Nola asked.

"If I fail, I will come to you at fair market value, and expect you to fulfill your obligations to the orphanage on top of that."

I stuck out my hand. "That is my offer. So. Do we have a deal?"

Chapter 36

The Forgotten Suitor

THE DUCHESS SMILED. "He really *was* trying to extort us, darling. All that bluster, and for what?"

The duke nodded, shifting out of his seat in a smooth motion. "Bah. He came to negotiate fairly. When both sides win, it's a fair deal. We need to rejuvenate our dragon economy, and Lord Minax had big shoes you can hopefully fill, son."

He was faking friendliness now, because he thought he already had this wager in the saddlebag. To him, it was just delaying the inevitable by one extra month—which was nothing after fifteen years of waiting.

Biscuit offered his hand, and we shook on it. I pretended to believe he meant his words of goodwill, but inside, I knew a timer had started counting in their heads. They didn't think I could revive Pinnacle.

Demons, they were probably right.

"With a bit of hard work and determination, you can save Pinnacle," the duke rambled on, letting go of me. "Plus you already have a great dragon handler, do you not?"

I narrowed my eyes. "I do."

"Well, go on then, Lord Warren! You have paperwork to sign that needs to go to the king," the duke said, standing. "Thank you for being so understanding. I'm happy to see Jolene doesn't control you."

Whatever happened to not knowing who she is? I thought. *And since when is she the controlling type?*

She wasn't—but Biscuit was. Classic narcissist. He couldn't fathom why anyone would act for different reasons than him.

Nola stood as well. "I will take you to our scribe. We will get this signed now."

She started exiting before I could answer her, but I was done with this conversation anyway. I gave Biscuit a rather disrespectful bow of my head, and followed the duchess from the room. Fieran dutifully took up the rear. The two nobles had never once acknowledged his existence.

Now that Nola was standing up, the woman appeared to be taller than her husband, so I doubted they rarely stood beside each other. Biscuit didn't seem the type to want to be seen with a woman taller than himself. I wondered why he'd married her. Money, most likely. She must come from a powerful family.

We walked over a red carpet with paintings of dragons on the walls. I found them soulless compared to the homey etchings at my villa.

"And what of the dragons?" she said suddenly. "You were an orphan, then a common soldier. You have little experience with the beasts."

It annoyed me that it had taken them so long to ask this question. *Shows how much they care about their own dragons.*

"I'm not used to them, that's for sure. But I've got faith in them."

"Dragons require love and understanding," she said. "Or so my head breeder tells me. I never personally bother with the creatures. Jolene, of course, is quite passionate.

"But what about yourself? Do you have room in your heart for dragons?"

That was an odd way to phrase it. "I can't know for sure," I said, as she opened a small door into a private study with a scribe working at a desk in one corner. The sight temporarily made my mind drift from the conversation, and I said vaguely, "I've locked my heart away for a long time."

"Ah. How very romantic."

I blinked. *I shouldn't have said that. Demons, what made me say that? I don't think I ever really put words to that feeling.*

This woman wasn't friendly, yet she had still put me at a strange ease. She was as dangerous as Biscuit was. I wasn't used to dealing with these kinds of people.

While I stood aside, Nola shooed the female scribe away, then flicked through a stack of paper on the scribe's desk. After a dozen pages, she found what she sought, setting two versions onto the desk. She closed the door behind the scribe before sitting down with a quill and parchment.

"Guarding your heart is wise," she said, dipping the quill into an inkpot. She paused, nib hovering, and then shot me a heavy gaze.

"Then again, it is a very natural reaction to what you have been through. Having the king's only daughter ask you to run away with her... ah, but it was not to be."

I recoiled, and Duchess Nola snickered. "I see I guessed correctly, then?"

"Holy dung balls, man," Fieran whispered behind me.

I sighed. "It wasn't like that. I just rescued her."

"Wait. That was *you?*" Fieran asked.

Nola shrugged and began writing. "It's quite the story, don't you think? Princess runs away to the wilds, and a mystery soldier saves her—but she doesn't return for months. When she finally does come back, the kingdom rejoices... but that unknown hero is forever forgotten. Now I wonder why that could be?"

She clucked her tongue. "You want my guess? He stepped out of line, aimed above his station, and ended up in the king's dungeon for the effort. And yet here he is, still alive, with the king's protection."

I wouldn't call it protection, I thought, my teeth gritting. It was more a declaration stating that no one was allowed to kill me except the king himself, which the man dearly wanted to do.

Regardless, I didn't like her tone, and I didn't like what she was suggesting, either. Yes, I'd been in love once. But it hadn't worked out. I wasn't trying to save this dragon farm so I could get my old girlfriend back.

There was no going back. Not to that.

"You're lucky to be alive," Nola said, writing with sharp, scratching movements. "Our king is not one to suffer insolence. If anyone can do the impossible, perhaps it is you... but then again. Ah, then again...."

She let the words hang. The only sound was the spitting of the dragonflame lantern and the *shrit shrit shrit* of her quill.

I rolled my eyes, since she wasn't looking. Such drama. I know she was insinuating that she'd alert the king to my presence here, and tell him of my supposed attempt to gain status.

But had she even *met* the king's spymaster, his Hand? Because I had. The man knew where I was at all times; I was sure of it. I'd also never tried to make it hard for him to find me. My name was on the public rolls.

Besides, she and the duke didn't want attention. I had gathered as much. She was bluffing.

As if she could sense me thinking this, the duchess stopped rewriting her original contract to glance up at me.

"Justicar Ormish will be keeping an eye on you, also," she said, changing tack. "He's a former dragoner—"

"Who failed to promote to top officer, obviously, or else he wouldn't be stationed way out here," I finished for her. "I also ran into one of his Enforcers. Garm. The man seemed *ever* so competent."

Nola snorted. "Toothless. Nothing at all like his boss. He just had a baby, and all he wants is a third wife to share a bedroom with so he won't have to hear the baby scream."

"Interesting that you would know that about a common Enforcer."

This caught her off guard. The feather twitched in her hand.

I grinned. "Ah, so Becki *does* report to you. Is *that* why she came to my bedchamber today?" I shook my head. "How sad. I liked her, too. As I'm sure you know, we go way back."

Nola scowled, and I stifled a laugh. Becki might have come to my villa on Nola's errand, but she had come in other ways, too. By the time she'd left my villa, she had become no one's agent.

At the same time, her flirtation had been rushed, and quite obvious. I knew it hadn't just been her "acting out a fantasy." Becki wasn't the type to let fantasy drive her.

I'd keep an eye on her, to be sure, but now that Nola knew that *I* knew about her little agent, she wouldn't be able to trust anything that Becki said anyway.

"I should have known. You're terribly handsome," Nola said. "I must admit, I like you more with each passing second. Do you want my opinion, Young Lord? My real one?"

"Feel free," I said.

"Trade the villa to some rube, and get a lower noble estate. I should like to keep you around. We need more nobles who aren't so... discerning."

I recalled the empty seats during the Supplication. Three rows for nobility, but maybe a dozen people there.

"What? No one wants to answer to a man with a funny name?"

"Duke Biscuit is deftly ruling Dasvilla," she snapped. "Far better than his father."

I made no comment as her hand swirled through one signature, then another. Finally she waved me closer, lifting her blue eyes to meet mine. She kept crooking her finger, urging me nearer until she turned her head, and her lips brushed my ear.

"Princess Vanessa will be Regent Queen Vanessa if but one heart stops beating," she whispered. "I adore her, and I support her. I'm truly sorry your romance didn't work out, but I'll never help elevate you, out of fear of her husband and father.

"However, I will ensure you have a fair chance to succeed or fail without interference. Keep your estate in order, and you will keep it."

Of everything that had been said today, it was this that caught me most off-guard. We'd been playing games all night, me and the Biscuits, but it seemed that Nola's loyalties didn't strictly lie with her husband. She had motivations of her own.

"All right, Young Lord," she said, shoving the pages toward me. "These are your titles and such. Sign them. I will draft our other agreement and have it sent over tomorrow."

"Oh," I said. I hadn't realized that's what she'd been doing. I read the papers a few times, poring over each word, because I'd never gotten anywhere in life by trusting blindly.

Besides, trust was unbecoming of the next Lord Minax. After all, Lord Minaxes had a history of getting killed.

But everything was above-board. I signed, and officially became a noble, albeit the lowest-ranking one in the entire kingdom. Lord Warren still felt odd in my mind and on my tongue, but I knew the soldier in me still lived on, his blades ready.

Now if I could only figure out where to stick them.

Chapter 37

I Want to Steal Your Blood

We collected our many weapons from the squire at the front of the castle, and finally, we left.

I took a moment to look back at the six-towered building. When seen in relief against the stars, the castle looked like a sleeping Behemoth-class dragon, the towers like spikes ranging along its stone back. I could almost feel its presence, like a real beast close by. There was a scent of flame on the air.

The walk from the castle to the villa was a short one, but the night was calm and empty. It was late, but not too late; the sound of music drifted across the river from the seedy taverns on the far side, carried by the water.

When inside the walls of Dasvilla, you could *always* hear the Dragon's Throat, its waters rushing quietly. Steam rose from it, brightening the night air. Even if you couldn't hear the river, the steam marked its heat as it cut through the heart of the city.

Feeling nostalgic, I angled that way, for the steam and the music. I wasn't sure where Jolene had gone to after announcing to the Biscuits that we were coming, but I had no fear for her safety as of yet. She was not the heir, and didn't own the estate.

I was the one that people would want dead.

The thought made my skin prickle, and I remembered the assassin, who'd wanted me dead before I'd even known of my inheritance. Were the two related? It seemed unlikely. She'd been after Fieran originally, and had only come after me once she'd gotten a hold of my blood.

"Where are you going? Chasing a quickie with that new girl-friend of yours?" Fieran asked, his voice lower than normal given the insult it carried. He was probably thinking of the assassin too.

"I don't even know where Becki lives," I said.

"Well, this is where her cart was yesterday."

Was it? I looked around, and he was right. Everything looked different at night, especially on this side of the river. A few taverns were open along this stretch of road, but the music was muffled by thick walls and closed doors—things which poorer taverns didn't bother with.

Becki might well be out here selling cold ales on the street. It was always hot here, after all. The volcanic landscape saw to that.

"Oh shit, is that fog?" Fieran said, pointing ahead of us.

I chuckled. "No, just steam. It rolls off the river at night, when the air cools. Come on. It's thickest by the water."

He frowned, but I strode ahead, plunging into the wall of hot mist. It enshrouded me, swirling about my hands and arms like wild magic moving to my command.

Fieran clamped a hand on my arm. "I don't like this."

I sniffed the air and smiled. "Be ready," I whispered.

"What?" His gray eyes widened. "Oh, no. You're not saying—"

I hurled myself sideways, tackling him at the same moment I heard the beat of wings.

"Gah!" Fieran called out, his voice as high-pitched as a woman's.

Behind us, a pair of blood-red talons severed the fog, bobbed once in midair in time to another wing beat, and then dropped. A Mount-class blood-red dragon followed the talons to ground.

It had just dived for us, banked, and missed, before choosing to land instead. It could have risen back into the air, but the fog was too thick.

The assassin couldn't guarantee our deaths unless she was on the ground with us.

There was no mistaking the blood coloring of the human-height Mount, nor the black leathers on the leg of the assassin that rode him. My gaze trailed up over every lithe, deadly muscle of the woman, ending on her face as she stepped off the beast.

"So it *is* true," she said. "You sensed me."

It wasn't a question, and I *had* sensed her. What I had first taken to be the presence of the mythical castle-dragon had actually belonged to a real beast, and one that smelled like charcoal. A Heat-type, but what subtype, I didn't know yet.

"What do you mean, 'it is true'? What's true?" I asked, leaping to my feet again, dagger out.

Behind me, Fieran retreated into the fog, which was the right move. He could get lost in the hot steam, and try to attack her from behind—that is, if he wasn't abandoning me.

The assassin's own knives remained at her hips. They were the same strange make as the one she had given me, with the notch. They probably had hollow handles too.

Her orange eyes roved over me, the knife tattoo on her face swathed in shadow. She was darkness incarnate, from her skin to her purpose.

"Oh, I assure you." The woman flicked her hand back, procuring a razor blade between her middle and pointer finger. "You are never going to know."

I flung myself sideways again, feeling the blade whiff through my shirt and miss me by a hair. I rolled when I landed, trying to put distance and steam between us.

There was only silence and nothing where she had just stood.

My senses flared. *Behind me!*

I spun, narrowly avoiding the swipe of the blood-red dragon's claw. I planted a foot and rebounded, drawing my blade as I sliced for the neck. The strike landed, but not deep. The dragon roared in pain, a high trill, and retracted into the steam.

I surged after it, reaching for a horn, aiming to get leverage to stab it under the chin.

My hand stopped midair as something struck me across the middle, like a whip, but harder. I grunted, missing my mark. The dragon vanished, and I looked down to see a long line of blood hovering in midair, wrapping itself around me—

Oh shit. This couldn't be good.

My mind locked into fight mode, making calculations I couldn't consciously understand, and I sprinted in the *opposite* direction of where the blood had come from. The rope of blood began to constrict around just one side of me, and I yelped in pain. Closing like a thin fist, it could damage my organs in instants. If she sharpened it, it might cut me in half.

The constriction suddenly stopped, the blood dropping to the cobbles in a ring of red rain. A scream sounded ahead of me, female, and then the assassin was there, with Fieran on the ground at her feet, gripping his side.

I didn't question the scene, I just tackled her. She grunted.

Fieran found her and attacked, causing her to scream. This broke her concentration on the blood spell. She retaliated, injuring him.

The realities of the battlefield blinked through my head as she hit the ground underneath me. Her skull struck the stones, dazing her, and I grabbed her bloody knife and threw it away.

A splash sounded some moments later, but I barely heard it, because she'd revived. She formed a fist, a meaningful move.

I remembered the blood that she'd used to attack me.

I heaved off her, to the side. She cursed, and I pulled out of my roll to look back.

A sharp blade, red and liquid, hovered in front of the assassin's face, only a few inches from her own nose.

"You're using your own blood," I said. She must have the stuff stored on her, and she was manipulating it. She'd struck me with the rope of blood before, as a means of finding me in the dark with a long whip-tail of blood. The longer the rope, the more space it could cover, and the better it could locate me.

She only turned the stuff into blades when she knew her target's location, so that meant blades took more of her energy and focus than ropes did.

The hovering knife collapsed, dribbling down from midair to soak her chest leathers. I grinned, my suspicions confirmed. I knew how the stuff worked now. She was limited in how she could manipulate it.

She could only pull the blood *toward the person it had come from*. In this case, that was herself.

Smart. She must have circled me, then cast the rope out to find me. That's why it had only constricted and struck from one side; she couldn't pull it in more than one direction. Only toward its original source.

I aimed a knife for a throw, but she rolled away, vanishing. I crouch-ran back toward Fieran, but he'd left the spot where he'd fallen.

A cry, fabric whipping, the slide of a boot on stone. I dodged right, hand outstretched, catching fabric.

I shouted in pain as the weight of an entire man came down on my arm.

Fieran hit the wall of the canal below us, his feet sizzling in the boiling hot water. He kicked and swore, his hands scrabbling back at my straining arm.

He'd fallen off the stone edge of the river reservoir, not knowing where it was in the mist. Now he was being loud and the assassin could pinpoint us. And I could barely hold him.

257

"Grab my collar! Above you!" I said through gritted teeth, at the same moment I heard wing beats again.

Fieran obeyed, his hands clenching at the fabric around my throat. I twisted to one side, then screamed in blind pain as the dragon landed on me, talons-first.

But I'd turned, and the dragon had missed his deadly blow. One claw had instead glanced off my ribs, the other landing on stone.

I let go of Fieran and rolled flat to my back, with Fieran's weight still strangling me as he held my collar. Hands free, I drew both my knives. The dragon flapped to get away.

It was too late.

I brought my arms together, stabbing the dragon from both sides of its chest, skewering it. It screeched, the sound ripping through me.

I couldn't breathe. Fieran was cursing and slipping. I kept hold of the blades as the dragon panicked, flapping madly, trying to get away from the pain, so much pain.

It had power, enough for the flapping to haul Fieran up and over the edge. As soon as he was clear and I was gasping, I yanked my knives out. The dragon writhed into the steam and fled, wailing.

A horrible guilt cut through me. The dragon was only a beast, obeying its master, or possibly protecting its friend. I had likely just killed it with those stab wounds.

Feel bad later. Survive now.

Fieran suppressed a groan behind me, as if he had his own hand over his mouth. The assassin had stabbed him. She had his blood.

She could send a blade of his own blood shooting back at him.

He wore armor, but no helmet nor mail. I flipped around and cut through the side straps of one of his leg plates, tugging it off and throwing it over his face.

He caught it. "What the—"

"Hold it there," I hissed. "Stay dow—"

Clink!

A blade of blood smashed against the leg piece and splattered. If I hadn't covered his head with the armor, it would have gone through his eye.

I saw him paling, and I left him like that. "Keep covered! All sides!" I told him, before dodging to my left on silent feet to change my position.

I dropped low, waiting. The assassin fell silent. She might try to finish Fieran, but more likely, she'd want me dead first. If I was out of the way, Fieran would be easy prey. He was already injured, and he didn't understand her magic yet.

But I did. I was the threat.

Still crouched, I listened. *So much for making it look like a natural death,* I thought. This would look like murder.

Oh.

I had to stifle my own amused laugh. Murder *would* look natural, now. I was the new Minax, and the previous two had been murdered. If my guard and I both died in some alley, then the murder would be attributed to whoever had killed Lucian and Etonia. It would then distract from the real culprits just as much as a heart attack would.

Which makes me think this woman isn't related to the Minaxes. This is somebody else that wants us dead.

Something whooshed by over my head, ruffling my hair. Her searching rope. I noted the direction it was heading—straight toward her.

I sheathed both my blades and sprinted toward her. Crouching below the height of the hovering blood-rope would only work once. She'd figure me out.

That meant I had to strike now.

Shifting mist. Leather black. I pivoted on one foot, and lunged.

259

I got her by the back of her leather shirt. She grunted, silver flashed, but I was already spinning, using all my momentum to twist around and slam her into the ground. I dropped to a knee while she struck the cobbles. She tried to rise.

I put a knife to her neck.

She froze, knowing that she'd die before she could ever form a fist and use blood magic. I had her.

"Who wants us dead?" I said, my voice as gruff as I could make it. I pressed the blade harder into her skin.

Her body loosened under mine. She laughed. "I'm a blood mage," she said. "If you cut my throat, I'll just call the blood back into my body."

I twisted the knife, drawing blood. She tensed again. I let my smile show in my voice.

"Yeah, but you can't regrow skin, can you?"

She'd survive a cut throat, but only as long as she could keep feeding energy and focus into keeping her blood inside her—which wouldn't be nearly long enough for the skin, muscle, and ligaments of her neck to grow back.

"Who. Hired. You."

"You think you can just—"

"Listen, missy," I said, leaning close enough to lick the black braids that clung to her scalp. "I'm not playing this game. You tell me what I want to know, and I knock you out—or you just die, here and now."

A blink passed as she, too, made her calculations. She could die for sure, or die *maybe*. I was either merciful, or I wasn't. She was about to find out.

"I don't know who hired me," she snarled. "I never know. My guild passes orders down to hide their patrons."

I growled at this, but I believed her. "Why do they want us dead? And don't lie. You targeted us with blood. There's something in our blood that marks us."

"Hrrech," she spat, some sort of foreign curse, maybe. "Fine. Your blood is a general mark. There's a flavor in it that we're always told to hunt. I don't know why, but it's related to dragons. You can sense them, can't you?"

I'm not sure yet, I thought. *But something definitely seems strange with me. I knew where that blood dragon was in the mist. I knew it was watching us when we came here.*

And now that I'm around dragons more... I'm connecting to them, somehow. I think.

I didn't tell her this, though. I owed her nothing.

"And Fieran?"

She huffed out her nose, then said, "Oldest hit in the book. He's a bastard."

My knife drew more blood. "I said no games—"

"Agh, stop it! I mean a bastard *child,* you idiot."

I paused. "Of who?"

"Of the realest bastard of them all," she hissed back at me. "He's the bastard son of the dragons-damned king."

Chapter 38

Several Women Scorned

I WENT COMPLETELY STILL, stunned.

"That's all I know," she said. "Bastard princes gotta go. He'll be the third one I know of... this *week*."

Bastard prince...? Fieran?

Fieran was the king's *son?*

But there was no reason not to believe her. She was a blood mage; one vial of the king's blood, and she could target his offspring, just by sensing the similarities in the blood.

At least, I guessed it worked somewhat like that. There was a reason they'd sent a blood mage, as opposed to some other type of assassin.

The woman must have taken my silence as deliberation. "Please," she said, suddenly plaintive, her voice going feminine. "Please, I think you killed Vital... my dragon. She has a nest. Eggs. They'll be all alone. Let me go, so I can protect them."

My chest expanded. *Did she just say eggs?*

"Where?" I said. "Where are the eggs?"

She sniffled. "P-P-Please...."

"Cut the act. Where are they? I'll take care of them."

Silence. I waited. What kind of woman was she, really?

Her voice returned to normal. "Caliph," she sighed. Her body loosened again.

She knew what was coming: death. Inevitable as the night.

I raised my arm behind me—

She surged up.

The move threw me back, my knife going wide. I cursed myself. I'd meant to knock her out, but she must have sensed my weight shift, must have understood I meant mercy. She'd seized her last chance to finish the job she had started.

She whipped around, raised her hand. She'd pull her blood right through me.

The mist shifted behind her, and a bucket came down.

The metal container gave an impressive *ka-plunk* as it struck the assassin on the back of the head. She crumpled underneath it as a new form emerged from the steam. I got my footing under me, barely stopping myself from throwing my blade at the assassin's heart.

We would have killed each other. At the very least, she'd be dead. If that bucket hadn't shown up—

"You okay, Warren?"

My eyes went wide as saucers. *"Becki?"*

My ice queen stood before me, holding the bucket with both hands now. It was filled with frozen water, courtesy of Collette, no doubt. The dragon curled around her ankles, purring like a cat.

"Damn it, Becki," I said, hastening to pull off my belt. "What are you doing here?"

Sweat slicked her forehead. "I was sellin' my ales in a tavern. Then Collette started chirping. We went outside and found a dead clay dragon. So we followed the blood trail back here, and I heard your voice...."

She trailed off as I cinched my belt tight to the assassin's hands. Unfortunately, I had to keep her from forming fists, which was trickier. I settled for ripping my sleeves and tying one around each of her palms while she groaned.

"She's going to wake up. Collette, go get Tilly, from the Pinnacle barn."

"What? You want Col—"

But Collette chirruped and took off. She was already gone.

"How did you *do* that?" Becki breathed. "She never listens to me like that!"

I pointed into the steam wall, toward the river. "Fieran is injured. Can you go check on him? If he can stand, drag his ass out of here."

She blinked, but she understood fast, disappearing like the former street kid she was. I struggled to my feet, gripping the moaning assassin against me. She was small and thin, but all that thinness was muscle. A creature made for the dark, for sliding in and out of shadow, for drawing blood and using it as a blade.

It was a useful skill, that. A *very* useful skill.

And when she thought I was about to kill her... she told me where to find her dragon's eggs. With what she thought was her last breath, she saved them.

I willed Tilly to come faster. I didn't want to kill this woman. She knew something about me... something about my blood. And, she knew Fieran's secrets.

Fieran groaned behind me. Becki called him a baby.

And overhead, a silver beast roared.

I carried the assassin over my shoulder with Tilly keeping up my rear, puffing at the assassin's face whenever she stirred. Meanwhile, Becki let Fieran lean on her, and the two staggered home with me. Somehow, we managed to make our way back to the villa.

A light was on in the living area nearest the door. Jolene must still be awake.

"Shit. Let's keep it down," I whispered, stepping carefully onto the porch. Tilly took the first step behind me, and the wood creaked dangerously.

I turned. "Sorry, Tilly. I'll tie her up soon, so it'll be fine. Just hang out in the yard until tomorrow, okay?"

The cloud dragon blinked at me, silver eyes glinting, seemingly empty. But she stepped off the step. She could understand me. It was just eerie. Eyes were windows to the soul for people, but for dragons, they might as well be glass.

I cracked the door open, wincing at the whine the old hinges made—only to step into the foyer and hear crying.

"The fuck...?" Fieran groaned, trudging past me.

"Go upstairs and have Becki wrap that wound," I told him. "I'll see what's going on."

"I got it. Don't need her," Fieran grunted. "By the way, you're fucking wounded too, moron."

I chuckled roughly. "Your point being?" I nodded Becki toward him. "Help him out, if you can."

Becki huffed. "I'll try, but he's an ass."

Fieran groaned and stumbled for the stairs. Becki followed. I called out, "Jolene, we're back. I gotta go change, and then I'll be back down."

"Don't *bother*," she moaned back. Yep, she was definitely crying.

Caught between a rock and a dragon claw, I opted to take care of the more deadly woman first. I carried the assassin to my rooms and tied her to the bedpost of the giant four-poster. The bed was big enough for four people to get lost in, and I wasn't even sure yet if I could be comfortable there. I might just go back to the barn.

However, the wide posts made it easy to truss up the blood mage, keeping her arms spread to either side, her wrists each tied to a post.

I tied her feet together as well, and made doubly sure she had no weapons on her and nothing near her that she could use as a weapon. I knew my way around a good knot thanks to caravan duty in more than one past outpost, so I was fairly confident she couldn't escape.

Besides, she was still asleep. There were no strong smells to wake her in here.

Down in the main floor den, I found Jolene sniffling face-down on the green velvet couch. Shiny and Dull comforted her, nuzzling her arms as she cried into them.

"You all right, Jo?" I asked, looking around. The room was full of crates. "What's all this?"

"My things. My mother's things. Biscuit had it all dropped off." She paused to sniff, then looked up at me, only her eyes visible above the comforting ring of her arms. Those blue eyes were ringed red from weeping.

"Where *were* you?" she asked. "I... I've been worried."

"Oh, I, uh... we just stopped by the Keepers' offices. I wanted to see if maybe Rachel was there, with the contract ready. You know, for the bottled cloud breath."

It was the first lie I could think of that wasn't the good old "went to the tavern" excuse, and it made me wonder when we *would* hear from Rachel, or Illowyn, her Head Keeper boss. A new inspection would have to be scheduled, and we'd need to be ready for that, plus there were the tax people—

Calm down, I told myself. *One storm at a time.*

"But you were gone for *hours,*" she moaned.

"Hours?" I sat in the chair next to her. It was woven with thick thread, to look like green dragon scales. "Oh. You didn't know. The duke started a Supplication when we arrived."

She sat up. "What?"

"Yeah."

"But he... this...." She looked desperately around the room, her gaze flicking between every old crate.

"Is it your mom?" I asked. "Is it hard to see her things?"

Jolene didn't answer, but she dropped back into the couch and sobbed a bit louder.

"Do you, ah, want me to get Becki? We came across her on the way here."

Her shoulders stilled a moment, and then she cried into the cushion some more.

"I don't wanna see anyone," she finally said.

I gave a small, tired laugh. "I'm flying to Caliph in the morning. Fieran will need to heal, so it'll just be me. That's assuming you don't want to go."

Jolene glared at me with bloodshot, squinting eyes. "What? Fieran needs to heal?"

Becki eased into the big room then, sitting on another couch near the room's open, glass-paneled doors. There was no trace of blood on her, and she had deftly found someone else's old nightdress to put on. Fieran really hadn't wanted her help after all. Stubborn man.

Not just a man. A king's bastard.

Jolene was staring after Becki now. Clearly uncomfortable, Becki adjusted her skirts and folded her legs under her. Once she'd made room, her pink dragon hopped onto her couch, curling up at her feet.

I thought Jolene might say something like *Why is* she *here,* but she surprised me. "It's been a long time since we had... people here," she said. She looked at me. "It almost feels... better. What's this about Caliph?"

I sighed in relief, glad she'd given up the topic of Fieran, and even more glad to see the two women getting along.

"We have some dragon eggs to find," I said. "I got a tip, and I should be able to get them cheap."

"From the merchant there? Dagor? Ugh, the man's a snake," Jolene said. "Hold *all* his eggs up to the light to make sure they're fertilized, and that they're not fake and filled with dirt. It should look like flames are burning inside, when the sun hits them. It's the same for all kinds of dragons, just different color flame patterns. All the eggs should be cold to the touch, too."

She was rambling, and I missed most of the lecture. *Cold to the touch, eh?* I fought the urge to glance at Becki, whose skin had that same property. Could she be related to dragons somehow? That seemed unlikely. Once they reached adulthood, most dragons weren't cold.

"See, that's the sort of knowledge I'm missing," I pointed out. "I don't know a lot about dragons, Jo. I need you to join me in Caliph."

Jolene suddenly raised her voice. "As if I would help you! You *lied,* Warren. You sold Pinnacle! After years of struggling to keep it in the family, it's gone!"

I reeled. "What? No, it's not."

"You signed it away! My maid told me so. My maid... oh, fuck." And she stared sobbing again. "She's gone, too. Everything's gone!"

Well, you could hardly expect your maid to come with you, if she was on Biscuit's payroll, I thought. Jolene was going through something, though, and it would be cruel to point this out.

Becki scooted closer. "What's this about selling?"

"I didn't sell," I said. "I signed an agreement saying I'd get the business back on its feet in a month, or else sell it all to them at market rate."

"Oh... so, you basically *did* sell it," Becki said.

"Don't you start too," I replied.

"It's gone!" Jolene burst out, abruptly rising onto her hands and knees to glare right at me from only a few feet away. "The home I grew up in is *gone,* and he's going to put me on the street!"

"No, I'm not," I said calmly.

"Maybe we should hear him out, lovey," Becki said, fidgeting with the tie at the throat of her nightdress. "Duchess Nola sent me to spy on him, you know, but now I'm Team Warren for life. It could have been my big break, but I gave it up, just like *that.*" She snapped her fingers.

"He's got a way about him, see. If anyone can pull this off, he can. He's special. Special in general, and special to me. And maybe he's trying to be special to *you.*"

I looked at Becki, stunned, but she wouldn't return my gaze. I'd suspected she was a spy, but not that her assignment with me had been her "big break." What had I cost her?

Damn. I'd better not fuck this up, or she'll be out of a job. Jolene and I aren't the only ones whose futures ride on Pinnacle.

I cleared my throat and faced Jolene's enraged face again. On her hands and knees like that, I could see straight down her cleavage. It was... quite swingy at the moment.

Burn me. She's hot when she's mad.

"I'm going to rebuild Pinnacle, Jo," I said. "On my life, I swear it."

She stared up at me with those pitiful turquoise eyes, and said only a single word: "How?"

Chapter 39

Teacher and Student

"I've got ideas already," I told her. "I'll start here, at this villa, and then expand back into the barn once the business grows enough."

She dropped back on her knees. "Wait, what? You're not selling Useless, Red, Tilly, and Dune?"

I shook my head no.

"The villa?" Another no. She shifted a bit. "Okay, I'm sorry. I must have heard wrong."

"I'm sure you didn't. The Biscuits want you upset. They don't want you to stay and help me. They probably misled you, through your maid."

"Don't blame Aliese!"

"I wasn't blaming her. She's most likely a pawn." I sighed again, more tired than I wanted to admit to. The slice along my leg still throbbed, but I'd gotten a towel around it, and it had stopped bleeding.

"Duke Biscuit may be laughed at because of his name, but he's smart," I went on. "Or at least, his wife is. Either way, he's like you. He thinks this is a done deal. But just in case, he's hedging his bets, trying to turn my best dragon-keeper against me.

"It's already working. You don't believe in me.

"Well, I'll prove you both wrong. I might be poor, but I'm good at growing my savings. I put my money where it can do the most work."

Becki hid a smile behind her hand. "That's not the only thing he puts in that does work."

A flush bloomed on my neck, but Jolene didn't appear to have heard her. "You really think it can be done?" she said.

"I am going to rebuild Pinnacle *here,* but that process starts in Caliph. By going there, I think I can improve our odds. Our debts remain, but the taxes are at bay another month, and we have some capital. I'm just thinking about what to do next.

"So, do you have any ideas? Better yet, have you got any ledgers I can look through?"

Jolene frowned, cocking her head to think. It was so comical how silly this noblewoman could be. She was nothing at all like Duchess Nola, nor like any other noble I'd ever met. She practically acted like she'd been born in a dragon barn and then raised there.

"I'll get the ledgers for you," she said. "We kept them under Father's old bed. It'll just be a day trip to Caliph?"

"Yes."

"And you can purchase the ticket for me?"

"Of course."

Jolene released one final sniffle. "Okay. I need to pack. I do have some ideas, but we can talk on the flight."

I nodded, but she was already breezing past me to flee up the stairs. Once she was out of sight, Becki shifted to watch me.

"I'm sorry about the spying thing, Warren," she said. "I swear it wasn't like that when we first met, but Nola—"

"I know," I said, rising and crossing the plush golden carpet to her.

Her copper eyes swam with tears. "I'll never betray you again, Warren. I mean it."

I ran a thumb down her cheek. "You didn't betray me to begin with." I laughed. "Unless you become Garm's third wife, of course. Then we might have words."

She full-on guffawed at that, slapping my leg with the back of her hand. "Ha, no. Never."

Her smile faded. "But I *am* worried. Both the Minaxes died, and you could be next. Whoever killed them believed that Pinnacle was dead with them, but now you're here, and who knows what will happen?"

"I'll tell you who knows: no one," I said, cupping her jaw with a rough and calloused hand. She nuzzled into it, and I gently stroked her cheek.

"I'm way out of my element," I sighed out, "but not with a street rat like you, thank the flame. I'm glad to have you with me, Becki."

She took my hand and kissed my palm. "Well, you've given the best dragon farmer I know all the hope in the world, so you're already doin' something right. You also got me off cart duty, assuming you'll figure out where to hire me." Her copper eyes shone with sudden lust. "You should let me thank you for that."

I shifted my hand to the back of her neck, then slid my fingers into her hair.

"No thanks needed. Having you on my side is worth a hundred dragons."

"Are you going to kiss me, or what?" She bit her lip, eyebrows wagging. "We don't have much time before Little Miss Sob Story comes back, but maybe we can make it... quick."

That last word trailed off, heavy with disappointment. Jolene was thudding back down the stairs. I released Becki's hair, although I kept my eyes on her. She had no problem staring back.

"Here's this year's ledger," Jolene said, handing me a book as heavy as my old breastplate. She glanced between us, reading the situation. "Um, uh... you two never did say how you met."

273

I gestured out a window. "We had a history back in the orphanage. Anyway, I was serious about her working here. She's moving into the estate with us—if that's all right with her, anyway. She might still be in the duchess' pocket for a while, but we could play that to our advantage. I trust her."

"Oh, uh, were you like, lovers as kids?" Jolene guessed, standing awkwardly.

Becki shook her head. "No. He was never like that. He didn't take any lovers from the orphanage girls. He didn't notice us except to protect us."

Jolene was about to respond, but I cut her off with a massive yawn. "Ughhh. I gotta sleep." I fished into a pocket, pulled out a single gold coin, and flipped it to Becki.

"Watch the estate while we're gone, will you? Buy supplies, hire street kids for the house chores, maybe clean up the villa. I believe in you and in them. Jolene is going to be raising dragons, not doing common chores."

The young woman studied the coin in awe, blushing in shock.

"Wait, did you just make her a lady of the house, or me? Or both?" Jolene asked in a confused tone.

"She is. For now. Until I find a better use for her."

Becki finally closed her hand over the coin. "I've never handled a fancy house before. But I'll try."

Jolene brightened. "You can ask Alie—" She stopped. "Well, you could try to ask my maid, but... I'm not sure if she'll be up for it. She's not even *my* maid anymore.... I guess she never was."

Jolene's eyes grew red again. What was the story with her maid? There was something else going on there.

Becki blinked rapidly, as if she were only just now waking up. Without warning, she shot off the couch, rushed over to me, skidded to a stop, then rose on her tippy toes to kiss my cheek.

"Our estate will be in order by the time you return, Lord Warren, Lady Jolene. Enjoy your trip. I won't spend an extra bronze I don't have to. Now, to bed with you both. You need all the sleep you can get, if one of you's gonna learn to be a dragon farmer tomorrow."

Jolene's smile ghosted back onto her face. "Only if the other one can learn how to teach."

Chapter 40

Balls and All

I DIDN'T GO STRAIGHT to bed, despite Becki's order. First I showered and dressed my leg wound properly, and then I had a look at that fat ledger. I could make little sense of the thing... but lucky for me, I already had a Keeper for a business partner. Maybe Rachel could have a look later.

When I finally dragged myself back to my rooms around midnight, I found my bed already occupied.

A low fire burned in the hearth near the bed, and the flames shed enough light for me to see the single, small form that lay moaning under my sheets. I closed the door loudly, so that she could hear me.

"Warren?" Becki asked, her movements stilling. I strode over and flipped back the covers.

She lay there naked and flushed, her hand gripping something between her legs—a crystal candlestick that I'd placed by the bed.

"Couldn't wait for me, huh?" I asked her, unbuttoning my shirt.

She took her hand off the candlestick, leaving it wedged between her swollen, blue-tinged lips. "I know how busy you are. I just came to smell you, on your sheets."

As I took off my shirt, I once again admired her white form, like snow against my blue linens. Her slightly blue nipples and sex, with the crystalline rod shoved inside it, and the splay of blue hair in a halo around her.

"You're welcome to get off to me anytime," I said, unbuckling my belt. "But the shower didn't have to be a one-time thing. Not unless you want it to be."

She nodded, rising up on her elbows to watch me. I dropped my pants first, then my underthings, and crawled onto the bed on my knees.

I didn't assume the normal position, however. I went the other way, my head toward the foot of the mattress.

"Let me help you," I said, grabbing the candlestick.

She pressed sideways, and I lifted my knee up. "Only if I get to help you," she replied, sliding between both my knees. She took hold of my ass, and guided my cock down to her, arcing to fit it into her mouth.

I closed my eyes, letting the cold sensation consume me, and then I started thrusting the candlestick. I made sure my thumb caught her nub with each thrust inside her.

The glass was slick with her desire and chilled from her strange magic, and as much as I wanted to come inside her, I knew I had to be careful about *where* I came. I didn't need a bunch of little heirs running around.

I was slow and tired, just there to enjoy myself, there to build up, not break down. As she took me awkwardly down her throat and teased me with tongue and tooth, I leaned down on one arm and watched as the candlestick made her folds flicker, her desire going soupy around it, wetter with each passing moment.

She came first, her legs snapping together, the cry in her mouth rumbling the head of my cock. I pulled out the candlestick and tried to drop it on the bed, but it rolled off, hit the floor, and kept rolling toward the low fire in the hearth.

I felt a momentary relief that it hadn't shattered, before I rolled onto my back so that Becki could finish me.

It didn't take long. Her tongue played along the ridge of my head, and she sucked mercilessly on the first two inches of my cock before randomly taking me to the back of her icy throat.

The cold of it is what ultimately did me in. It was too strange, too different. A shiver of pleasure built into the frigid cracking of ecstasy, and I groaned as my cock gave up the ghost.

She kept me in her chilled mouth until my warmth seeped away, my spurts fading to nothing, my breath stolen. Then she dropped me and spat into the blanket.

Smiling, she curled up against me. "Am I officially your lover now, then?"

I pulled her close, my body still thrumming. "As long as you want to be."

"Oh, I think that might be forever," she said, before looking up with those odd copper eyes. "But can I ask... why do you trust me? You shouldn't. I'm an agent of the duchess."

I planted a soft kiss on her nose. "It was when we had sex the first time. I made it pretty clear I was losing control. Still, you didn't try to get me to come inside you. If you had ulterior motives, you would have wanted that. Getting pregnant could give you control over me, and that could improve your status in life."

She stared at me, seemingly amused despite the lack of smile on her face. "Warren, you're really some—"

Shattering glass made me shoot up in bed.

I rolled sideways, snatching a knife off my discarded belt almost faster than an attacker could blink. But when I looked up, wielding it, totally naked—

There was no one there.

"Oh! The candlestick," Becki said, swinging her legs off the bed. "Look!"

279

I followed her gaze, and there on the hearth was a pile of glittering glass roughly in the shape of the candlestick.

My knife dipped lower. "How did it break?"

Becki was slipping into her dress, likely to go get cleaning supplies. "It probably got too hot," she said. "I made it cold, you know, because I'm cold on the inside. Then it got hot. When glass gets too hot after being too cold, it can shatter."

I frowned. I hadn't known that.

"Maybe you shouldn't use glass for your pleasure anymore," I suggested.

She laughed, rounded the bed, and pulled me into a kiss.

"Why would I need glass, or any material at all, when I can just find you and have a big cock instead?"

The next morning, well before my flight, I slipped out of the Cage and onto the street.

I remembered where the Keepers worked with no trouble; like many kingdom employees, they worked in the local castle. I entered the front hall of their tower in all my best clothes, which wasn't saying much, at least not yet.

The interior was paneled opulently in marble and gilt, further proving the dukedom of Dasvilla was doing just fine financially. I waited at the front counter, a monstrosity in black marble, and I mused over what I'd seen last night. The nobles at the Supplication had been well-dressed, and the halls of the castle very well-appointed. The castle itself had great upkeep, every inch of it shining.

By slowly taking over Pinnacle's market share in dragons, the duke and duchess had likely gained control of travel in and out of Dasvilla—and anyone who controlled travel controlled the transport of goods.

They were making money hand over fist, selling to their little cadre of hopeful nobles at top dollar.

The only question was *why?* Why were the nobles even here, in this nowhere-nothing backwater? And why were they earnest enough to send representatives to a Supplication? It hadn't been many, but nobles usually avoided that sort of drudgery. And the three rows of seating? *Three?*

The duke expects to attract more and more nobles. He's making them some sort of promise... I'm just not sure what it is, yet.

Either way, they had a monopoly on wares within Dasvilla, and no one probably even realized it.

"Yes?" a woman's voice said. "Oh, it's you."

I turned to see Rachel, the brown-skinned scribe from yester-day, behind the counter. Her glasses flashed as she looked around, probably checking to see if anyone saw me with her. The movement made her long single braid swish. Scrolls crin-kled at her chest, where she held them close.

"I came to pick up our agreement, if it's been drafted," I said lowly.

"Shhh!" she hissed, leaning closer to me, the armful of scrolls flattening against the edge of the counter. "You do realize I could get in trouble for that, right?"

"Oh yeah. And you can get in trouble for this, too," I added, sliding a face-down sheet of paper over to her.

She blinked at it, then flipped it over, adjusting her glasses before reading. Her hazel eyes widened and she met my gaze again.

"I can't get you all this!" she whispered. "I'll lose my job!"

I tapped the sheet. "You're about to have a five percent stake in Pinnacle Dragons. You get me this information, and that five percent stake will be worth a helluva lot more money. You won't *need* this job when you make better money."

She chewed her lip, but I could see the wings beating behind her eyes.

"If I do this for you... I need you to do something for me," she said softly.

"Rachel, you already have me by my balls. Your wish is my command, balls and all."

Chapter 41

Survive and Thrive

"Are you sure you're all right with leaving your guard behind?" Jolene asked, her mouth right next to my ear, so I could hear her against the wind. She was squished up against my side on the first row of dragon seating, close enough to nix the bite of the wind.

When the seating manager had asked if he could sit two kids beside me, and I saw the desperate parents, I had nodded. They turned out to be teenage boys, so the flight on the turquoise Airship-class dragon was tight.

This dragon was male, extra spiky, and so long that there were more than four rows, but as soon as he flapped his majestic wings, all my worries faded.

The flight was long and was going to last hours, but at least I'd been given an excuse to get closer with Jolene. The unintended snuggling had helped her warm up to me. She still thought I had a good chance of losing Pinnacle, but she no longer believed I had no chance at all. She told me so, yelling it right in my ear as soon as we left land.

So much for talking on the flight, I thought. Jolene must be used to flying via cabin.

As for her trust in me, she had gone from my biggest critic to my biggest supporter. Even if she hadn't, I would have understood.

She might seem overly emotional, but she grew up in that house, that barn, that business. She hadn't wanted to lose any of it, and she hadn't wanted to lose her mother either, but the laws of the land had stolen her parents and heritage from her. The fact she could still chuck dung out of a barn mere weeks after her mother's passing amazed me.

I admired her determination. I found strength in her. Even when she had no reason to believe the estate would stay within her reach, she had still given the dragons the attentive care they deserved. She would prove to be the best possible steward, I was certain.

As for me, I was starting to really lean into the whole dragon farming idea. I'd lain awake brainstorming last night, and Becki had thrown in a few ideas too, and I was already anxious to implement some of it. It was in my personality to make the best of a situation, but I truly felt that this could become something great.

We just had to survive—and *thrive*—for one month.

I turned my mind back to Jolene's question: *Are you sure you're all right with leaving your guard behind?*

Should I tell her the truth, and say we'd caught an assassin last night? Fieran was the one best equipped to watch the woman. His life was forfeit if she escaped, after all—and I didn't want him here with me anyway. I needed to think about his parentage some more.

I hoped he was careful with his blades when he shaved around the assassin, though. I was starting to think he shaved out of nervousness, and that woman would love to exploit that.

Regardless, I didn't need a guard at all, if my assassin had been captured. Then again, the assassin might not be the only person after me. I'd have to keep an eye out all the time.

"I can handle myself," I told Jolene, nearly yelling in her face to get the message across. I pretended to get bumped by one of the boys, and shifted closer to her. "How are you feeling?"

"I just can't stomach the thought of losing Pinnacle," she said after a moment. I was glad she was being honest with me, but I'd have to earn her faith with time.

"You have, or had, your soldiering," she explained. "I have my dragons. They define me. That barn was my whole existence for almost twenty-seven summers, and now you're not even using it!"

"It's only being rented for a month," I countered. "And the hatchlings are still there."

Last night, one of Becki's ideas was to offer the stalls of the barn as storage space for the local nobles. *They've all got so much stuff, you wouldn't even believe it,* she'd said. *They're constantly buying new things to impress each other.*

I didn't doubt that, after seeing the Biscuits' multiple atriums. So I'd set Becki on the errand of offering rental space. She knew the kinds of rough-and-tumble men we needed to hire as guards, but as the duchess's spy, she also knew a lot of nobles. They even respected her, because her affiliation with Nola was a sort of open secret among them.

In short, Becki was going to milk that connection, making it seem like the storage venture was affiliated with the duchess. *I'll get them clamoring to hire the space, don't you worry. Everyone wants the Biscuits' favor around here.*

That open-secret thing made me laugh, though. Nola had thought she could fool me, when everyone else knew her game? *The new guy in town is always a rube, right? Well, not when he's actually* from *the town... and the wrong side of the river to boot.*

Anyway, I'd planned to move the business into the Cage and keep it all close to home until we grew. We had so few dragons that we didn't need the barn, and this way, the building would earn money until we grew large enough to fill up its pens.

Jolene unleashed a long breath. "I know. It's temporary... I hope." She spat some wild hair out of her face, before adding, "Besides, I have to admit that I'm emotionally tied to the estate, so much so that I can't make rational decisions about it. *You* can.

"Meaning you probably did what was best for Pinnacle. To survive, we had to downsize. I'm coming to terms with it, I think."

I pretended to be surprised, my eyebrows shooting up my forehead. "Oh? What's that you said? Hold on, I need to write this down." I tried to get into my coat, but the angle was bad. Jolene frowned and reached into my pocket, taking out my pad and charcoal pencil.

I shot her a deadpan look, took pencil to page, and said, "On the sixteenth day of Sivonth, Jolene admitted to being irrational."

"What? I did not!" She slapped my hand. "Har, har, very funny."

I started writing anyway, making her scowl. *Jolene is at her most lovely when the wind plays with her hair. She looks like a lightning dragoness made human, on a righteous quest to get vengeance for her clan's wild dragons, captured by city humans most foul.*

"Ugh, *that* much writing?" she asked, leaning close to try to see it. I made an I-bet-you'd-like-to-know face, and pocketed the sheet of paper. I left a corner out, so she could try to steal it.

She exhaled dramatically, reaching behind her head to grab her hair in one knot, if only to keep it at bay in this wind.

"Okay, on to today's lesson in dragon husbandry!" she called out. "On the subject of eggs! How do you tell if they're old or fresh?"

"Uh... I'm not sure," I admitted.

She nodded. "I could hardly expect anything else from you, could I? You've spent your adult life being a soldier. Well, starting today, you're a student of the dragon sciences."

A slow smile lit her face, and her bright eyes twinkled. I knew, in that moment, that I'd have a great teacher.

"Let's begin with the anatomy of an egg."

Chapter 42

She's a Bestiary!

"Not all dragon eggs have scales, but the vast majority do," Jolene lectured. "An egg with no scales is likely fake. Not all dragon eggs are shiny when fresh, either, but the majority are. A dull egg is likely fake."

Now I was taking *real* notes, even with the wind against me. I aimed to be a diligent student.

"All dragon eggs need to be kept warm," she continued, keeping her voice loud above the gale. The wind had lessened now that we'd slipped into a glide, but it was still there.

"If the egg is cold, or not being kept somewhere heated, it is either dead or fake."

Fake, fake, fake. Apparently selling fake eggs was common.

"Not all dragon eggs hatch, even when they are kept warm," she added. "And only fertilized eggs hatch. The best way to see if the egg contains a growing dragon is to lift the egg up to the light, then see if there is living flame within. This flame can darken with time, showing a hatchling and its activity, but the flame pattern should always be apparent, and flickering.

"In addition, mothers will abandon unhatched and unfertilized eggs, so you may stumble on a nest of eggs and get excited, only to find they're all stillborn."

Here's hoping the assassin's dragon left them somewhere perpetually warm, I thought. I hadn't yet told Jolene that I was headed into the wilds. On the way to the villa last night, I'd stopped by the poor dead clay dragon, as Becki had identified it. The assassin had said its name was Vital, but its life force was long gone by the time I reached it.

Still, I could sense the space where it had been—almost like I could sense a hole in the world, left by the dragon. I'd paused, Tilly behind me. With the unconscious assassin slung over my shoulder, I'd tried to memorize that sense. I'd use it to find Vital's eggs.

After that, I'd paid some local drunks to haul the beast behind my barn. I'd bury it when I got the chance.

Jolene hadn't stopped her lesson while I pondered all this. "To get the flame pattern to appear, simply hold the egg up to a light source behind it, and knock on the egg," she said, pretending to hold up an egg in front of her. "The interior will almost always react, if it is a viable baby."

"Okay, so do hunters go into the wilds and find eggs, then hold them up to a flame to see if they're fertilized? Have you ever gone nest hunting?" I asked.

She snorted. "No, I don't have a death wish. The wastelands we fly over have a food chain, and we humans are near the bottom. Four Demons, even *domesticated* dragons are deadly. I've lost two different fingers so far just training them! I had to have a healer reattach the same pinkie three times."

My mouth dipped open. I hadn't realized she was quite *that* resilient.

"But, uh... isn't Caliph one of the greatest dragon-hunting areas there is?" I asked, in the most casual way I could. That fact had come from Becki, too.

Jolene frowned again. She wasn't buying what I was selling.

"Just fly Red out and hunt dragons around Dasco Mountain," she said. "No one bothers *those* dragons. The dragons around

Caliph, though? They're on high alert all the time, because their nests are constantly raided."

She said this like it was the most obvious thing, but I knew it wasn't. If people wanted to catch dragons, they'd go where it was easiest. Yet Jolene knew an easy place that *nobody went to.* That's because only she knew about it.

It seemed she had more knowledge on this subject than anyone. I was damned lucky to have her.

"We could try to catch another male breeding dragon out there," I said. Right now, we only had Tilly and Ravager still able to lay eggs, but only Tilly wanted to mate with Dune. Seems dragons weren't nearly as polyamorous as humans. They took on one or two partners at a time, or none at all.

Jolene shook her head. "Uh, no. You just buy sperm from males. The math works out, unless you have a wild alpha you can stud. They're the top of their herd, though, and near impossible to catch. But females will *always* mate with an alpha—and males will always mate with a female alpha—even outside their current bonded pairings.

"This can cause interbreeding, though. You need to be careful not to let bloodlines cross."

"So every herd has an alpha male and alpha female?"

"No. Every herd has one or the other... just one dragon that's bested all the others. Gender barely matters to them, but males do typically win, as their spikes are sharper and can more easily pierce the flesh of opponents."

Hmm. I'd like one of each, I thought, staring out over the igneous promontories and charwood forests that peppered the hotlands below. Dasco Mountain was visible in the distance, offset slightly from the volcano. It looked run-down, like the volcano's unhealthy twin.

A series of small birds suddenly cawed past us, somehow not seeing the dragon until the last second. I soon saw why: small dragons chased the birds, panicking them as they tried to score an easy meal. They were either hatchlings or full-grown Shoulder-class dragons, hardly larger than the birds themselves.

Our ride banked, bringing big fluffy clouds into our sight line. They floated along a calm horizon, a part of the kingdom where heat wasn't constantly rippling the air. The capital was that way, and so was my past. The image seemed frozen before me as we soared over the reaching black charwood trees, which were slowly interspersing with greenery the closer we got to Caliph.

"So, about the sperm," I said, trying to cheer myself up with a silly subject. I grinned when it made her blush. "Do you just needle-inject the eggs in the nest with the sperm? Sounds messy."

Jolene looked at me like I was crazy, although the blush remained. "No! The female goes in heat, and then you put her on her back, stick a tube in her lady bits, and drip the semen into her."

My face scrunched up, forming a sour expression without my permission. I thought of Captain Kenna, who apparently used to work at Pinnacle. I couldn't imagine her doing something like that.

"You *drip* it? Into her *bits?*"

Jolene took one look at my face and belted out a laugh. "Wait, you thought you could fertilize eggs *outside* of the body? If only! That would be too simple."

I spread my hands. "Not a farmer," I reminded her dryly, earning a giggle. She shook her head at me, amused, and then turned so her back faced me, removing her waist restraint as she did so.

I instinctively slung an arm in front of her chest, but when she turned back, she guided my arm around to her back. She snuggled into me, getting comfortable. Startled for real this time, I pulled her close.

"You, uh... you could fall."

"Oh, no. Holiday is a smooth flier."

"Holiday?" I asked. "Wait... you *know* the dragon we're on?"

"Of course I do. I know all the dragons around here. I raised half of them."

Damn, you're growing more useful by the moment. "You're incredible," I said.

She didn't look like she'd heard me. "Well, Lord Warren, I appreciate you trying to learn and all," she shouted as the wind rose, "but I'm going to lose my voice if we keep doing it this way. I still have much to teach you, young hatchling, but for now, let's enjoy the ride."

I squeezed her again. "I was already enjoying it. How couldn't I, with such a gorgeous woman so close?"

"Oh no, not a charmer. No wonder my mother loved you," Jolene said, slipping an arm into my coat, her hand on my ribs. If she tried to snuggle any closer, we'd be naked.

She's just cold. She didn't pack a coat, and it's chilly in this wind.

Then again, she knows what a dragonflight feels like. So why didn't she pack a coat?

I stopped asking myself these questions and just decided to enjoy her closeness. The view really was something else. I stole a bit of the teenager's space next to me, so that Jolene could get her arm a little farther around me. I felt her smile against my shoulder, instead of tears.

If she knew I still intended to take her egg-hunting, she wouldn't be quite as happy as she was now. And when I took her *dragon*-hunting? Well, that would be worse.

So I savored it. Her breath, her windblown hair, the warm spot of her mouth against my shirt, and the sensation of her nice, round chest bunched up against my side.

Mmm, better stay calm there, stud, I told myself. She was close enough to notice if I got excited.

She was soft, though. Easy. Not coddled, but still a noble. She had no combat experience, no idea what it was like to hunt or fight.

Maybe I'll leave her behind and pay a guide, I thought. *I can give her the choice, at least. She might not be up for the wildlands.*

Not to mention I might not want to risk her.

Whether she came with me or not, hiring a guide seemed like a worthy investment. Either way, I hoped the Caliph wildlands would reward me for my bravery—if it could even be called *bravery,* and not madness.

Wildlands, here I come.

Chapter 43

Let's Go Make an Omelet

WE ARRIVED in the early afternoon, after a long and gentle flight which left some of Jolene's drool on my sleeve. She slept like a dragon with a full belly, even on the flight.

I didn't mind. No complaints.

Once we landed in Caliph, I opted to start my tour along the city walls, so that I could keep my senses alert, and see if I could tell which direction Vital's nest was. I could already feel the eggs in my mind, like a whisper.

I didn't like the feeling. It seemed odd that I'd never felt it before I'd received this inheritance. Had I gotten the ability between Olinios and Dasvilla somehow? Or had I always had it, and just never noticed? And what *was* it? Magic?

I doubted that. All citizens of Parshil were tested for magic as children, including orphans. The ability to develop magical talent was a rare trait, passed on through blood, and there were no mages in my family history. At least, my mother hadn't believed so, before she passed.

So it had to be *new* magic, which was much stranger. Magic came about through bloodlines, certain wild beasts (such as dragons), or it was affixed to items via spell-casting.

But I hadn't acquired any new items recently, except maybe the letter itself, and a few basic, ordinary weapons. I doubted that these things had spells attached to them, but I could check later, to be sure.

But picking up an innate, magical power somewhere, by happenstance... that shouldn't be possible. Yet it sure seemed innate to me.

The more I encountered dragons, the more obvious my bizarre sense became. Each dragon had an aura, a sort of mental scent that placed it in front of me, or inside a building, or even a street over... now that we were at the market, I could tell how many dragons worked within a hundred feet of us.

Furthermore, each dragon's aura changed based on their current temperament—it smelled charred when they were angry, and felt like sunlight when they were content. The colors of the auras tended to match the dragons' coloring, too, but it changed brightness depending on their age.

The assassin said it was in my blood, I thought. *But what did she mean? Did my parents pass it down, or is it like a poison?*

I'd ask when we returned, provided Fieran kept the assassin from escaping. For now, my new abilities were an asset to Pinnacle. If the last few days were any indicator, then if I kept training my new senses, they'd only get stronger with time.

"This seems... ill-advised," I said, after a large laborer shoved me aside on the battlements of Caliph, nearly pushing me over the parapet. "I mean, having your Merchant's Row on the *walls,* where wild dragons and monster tribes can see them? A dragon could swoop down and snatch that chicken right off its spit!"

I pointed to the other side of the battlement, where a vendor was roasting a chicken over a portable dragonflame. He sold pieces of it to passersby, and seemed to be doing good business.

"Oh, the dragons have learned not to do that," Jolene said, guiding me back to the center lane. "There are net-throwing ballistae set up every fifty feet or so. They get shot out of the sky if they try to steal anything, and sold into slavery by the city guard."

I'd never heard of a city guard making money like that. It stank of corruption to me.

"And the tribes of the wildlands would be seen well before they scaled the walls," Jolene added, pausing beside a jewelry cart. I noted the object that caught her attention: a gold necklace in the form of an extended dragon's wing.

I leaned over and procured a gold coin. "Let me buy it for you."

She blinked up at me. "What? No. We're broke, Warren."

I shrugged and moved to hand the vendor the coin, but Jolene caught my hand.

"Stop. I can't wear it anyway. I was just admiring the crafts-manship. I've, ah... seen this metalworker's art before. She calls herself Gem, and you can see her signature there. It's a little diamond."

She pointed, and indeed, a small diamond marked the inner corner of the gold wing, too small to be decorative.

"Why can't you wear it?" I asked. The poor vendor's face fell as I took back my coin.

"Will you stop getting off-topic? I'm supposed to be teaching you dragon facts, not to mention we're supposed to be looking for eggs." She turned away. "Come on, or I promise I'll lose you."

Given how packed the battlements were, I believed her. I tossed the vendor an apology copper and chased Jolene down again.

The street traffic only got worse from there, condensing at every intersection of the Caliph city wall. In hindsight, I prob-ably should have deviated to the less busy side, where appoint-ment-style businesses were run, but markets said a lot about a place.

They also said something about Jolene. She seemed at ease with busy streets, undeterred by the constant din of noise and smoky air from the cooking and smith fires.

Here, the rich smell of burnt wood fought against the scent of a city packed with dragons, not to mention the animals farmed to support them. Oxen mooed below us, corralled in big pens, and more than half of Caliph was protected pastureland. Apparently, it was known for beef and wool.

When I reached Jo again, I pushed our wooden hand-cart on ahead of us. My first purchase on the wall had been the cart, and some cages of various sizes to load it with.

Jolene had complained, saying the cages would cost too much to take back on the dragonflight, but I didn't plan to take them back empty. The items could also be resold at a loss, which I planned to do, but only after I filled each one with a beast.

As soon as I came up beside Jolene again, she began another spiel. "Every dragon has a special breath ability and a special invulnerability. For purebloods, these traits are set, but for hybrids they can vary. Generally, hybrids are less powerful but more specialized. Given they have a better temperament, this often makes them more useful."

"Hmmm," I said, as a table full of dragon-hunting supplies caught my eye. A toothless woman worked the stand while several children toiled behind her, taking instructions on how to properly oil leathers and string the metal wiring of egg carriers.

I stopped Jolene next to it, but she just kept talking. She had been in a good mood all day. Her smiles had been enormous as she'd pointed out all the gorgeous dragons sweeping over the bustling city. The place was ten times the size of Dasvilla.

But even so, it had fewer dragons.

"There are dozens of types of dragons," Jolene stated as I looked over the hunting supplies, "but they all fall under several main categories:

"Earth dragons, such as clay, stone, and sand dragons. Sky dragons, such as cloud, wind, and horizon. Water dragons, such as ocean, snow, and mist. And then Heat dragons, such as flame, lava, and lightning.

"Also, there are the lesser-known Forest dragons, sometimes misclassified as Earth dragons. Those include birch dragons, mangrove dragons, and other types that associate closely with specific flora."

"You don't say," I said, selecting my equipment with a finger and a raised eyebrow at the vendor. I flashed her a coin, and she got the hint. *Pack it up, but don't let my companion see.*

"Each variety is defined by its set breath and invulnerability traits," she said, still oblivious to the contents of the table as her eyes tracked a lovely sky-blue dragon far overhead. "They also come in different colors and sizes that allow them to hide in their given environment.

"Of course, hatchlings have a whole rainbow of colors until their scales settle. It is said that the patterns match their personality, or perhaps spell out their name amongst their kind."

I turned to face her, trading coins for a rucksack behind my back. "Are some varieties more dangerous than others?" I asked.

"Well, they tend to mirror their environments. In general, Water dragons are ponderous but powerful, while Earth dragons prefer to be still and stay hidden. Heat dragons are volatile, and Air dragons are fast. But hybrids can have all kinds of personality traits, especially since most are raised among humans. Dragons don't crossbreed very much in the wild."

I indicated for her to walk again, and she did. I slung the new rucksack over my shoulder when she wasn't looking, and rose up on my toes. About half a parapet away from us, a platform extended out over the wall. It was marked with a fabric sign reading "TOUR THE WILDS."

As we neared it, Jolene schooling me the whole way, I looked out over the jungle wildlands to check for Vital's essence again. Unlike Dasvilla, Caliph was surrounded by lush forest, not hot igneous rock and woods of living stone. It was humid here, but cooler, more pleasant overall.

Next, I turned my attention from the jungle wilds to Caliph itself. It was the capital of the dragon trade, according to Jolene.

For a lady who adored dragons, it was heaven. Eggs sold here for cheaper, since they were easy to transport from nearby nesting grounds of most types.

However, the captured dragons were wilder here. Most couldn't be trusted not to flee, and needed to be moved via caravan or special-ordered transportation flights.

Because of this, and the fact that the region brought in the most wild dragons, almost all of the biggest and best dragon farms were based in Caliph. The selection was huge, and smaller dragon species weren't too much extra to transport. Throw an egg in a bag with some other items, and its transport cost nothing extra.

"Speaking of human-raised dragons," I said, "is there any benefit to raising them from eggs?"

"Oh, yes. Not only are they easier to tame and train, but hatching a dragon creates a bond with the owner. You could never get that kind of bond from a wild dragon who'd been caged as an adult. Those kinds of dragons are resentful forever, no matter how many human friends they might make."

I missed a step when she said *bond.* "They bond to their owners? You mean like normal pets do?"

"Demons, no. It runs deeper than that. You get a sense of them."

"What sort of sense?"

She then proceeded to exactly define the sensations I'd been experiencing lately: "You can sense their aura. It's like a color, but it can help you determine their mood and location. I can do it for Ravager, and I've had other bonded dragons in the past— but it's a rare achievement.

"Regardless, the hope for a dragonbond is what keeps people buying eggs instead of keeping only to hatchlings, which are a sure thing. Eggs are *not* a sure thing, and can easily be faked."

So that was my power? I had a dragonbond?

But how could I have a bond with every single dragon I came across? No, that couldn't be right.

"Oh, look!" Jolene exclaimed, running up to the sales cart a few paces down from the TOUR THE WILDS place. The cart sold "commemorative eggs."

She picked one up to examine it. "These are sometimes viable, just considered too damaged to sell. Their flames are dim, and sometimes they die or the hatched dragons are weak, but they're really cheap. I'll find all the good ones here, and we'll throw them in the cart!"

Once again, I noticed how Jolene seemed to know something no one else did. If even a few eggs could become dragons, then someone would have cleaned the vendor out by now. But they hadn't. Even the vendor looked like he might argue, but thought better of it.

She started passing eggs to me, all of them cold to the touch. I dutifully held them up to the light. The flame patterns crackled, dim but still obvious.

"You might not be able to see the patterns on these," Jolene said. "The more dragonbonds you've had in your lifetime, the better you're able to see them."

I swallowed. I could see the patterns clear as day.

"So, uh... why are dragons so plentiful here? You said they can find all kinds in Caliph, except for a few types." We'd come too far from the volcano to see many Heat varieties, and because Parshil was landlocked, ocean dragons and their ilk were rare.

"The main reason is the rich and deep lakes around here. They're positively *stuffed* with fish," Jolene said, delving so far into the barrel of eggs that I couldn't see her elbows anymore.

"Those fish travel to shallow streams in abundance," she explained. "A different variety spawns each month, so the food source is constant.

"But fish aren't the only plentiful thing. A lot of the trees grow nuts around here, which attracts extra birds, squirrels, and all

301

sorts of abundant wildlife that falls on the bottom of the food chain."

She quieted for a moment, shoulder-deep in the barrel and fishing around for something at the bottom. The vendor, a pimpled ginger-haired teenager, looked at her like she was growing mushrooms on her head.

"Dragons eat squirrels?" I pressed. "Seems like a snack to them."

"Not even, except for Shoulder classes. No, it's goblins that eat small animals; they are too lazy to hunt bigger things. A lot of goblins leads to a lot of orcs, since the two usually group together. But the rich lands also attract both trolls and minotaurs.

"All of these groups are territorial. Every once in a while a supreme warlord unites all these races, but for the most part, they fight each other to gain territory or just because they feel like it. And do you know what endless fighting leads to?"

I swallowed, glancing at the wildlands again. Maybe I shouldn't go out there to find Vital's nest... even though I could feel it now, and quiet clearly. It seemed to be located near a gigantic pile of rocks in the distance.

Smoke rose out of the top of the formation, though. Maybe some wild races had already found the eggs?

"Fighting leads to nothing but death," I said quietly.

"Exactly!" Jolene peeped, emerging from the barrel with a black prize in her hand. She inspected it, grinning. "Battles lead to corpses! And after those fights, dragons feast."

Ew. I didn't realize they were like buzzards.

"Don't worry, they only like fresh bodies...." Her face fell, and she sighed at the egg before handing it to me. "Here, take this one too. It looks dead, but if I'm wrong and it hatches, we'll get a star dragon. Those are valuable."

I took a look, backlighting the egg against the sun. I didn't see flames at first, but when I squinted....

There. A dull flicker. I had life in my hand—I had a future.

Now if I could just find a hundred more eggs like this one, and Pinnacle Dragons would succeed after all.

Chapter 44

Jolene the Dragon Queen

WITH THE EGG still held up to the light, I twisted to get into my new rucksack. I extracted the egg bandolier and took off my coat and shirt right there on the battlement, so I could equip the bandolier.

Women whistled at me, making Jolene look up. I hastened to strap on the long band of metal egg cases, and I put the star egg in the center cage. The bandolier was made to protect eggs and keep them warm, while also preventing them from impeding movement too much. It wasn't *perfectly* practical, but I needed all my belt space for weapons.

Finally Jolene finished her survey of the barrel, whirling around to drop another six eggs in our cart. The vendor cleared his throat, and named a price. He'd inflated it, but I paid him anyway. I had a feeling I'd gotten more than my money's worth.

"Let's go next door," I said to Jo. "I want to see about this tour business."

"But I thought we were going to see the egg vendor?"

"You said he was a conman."

"He is, but he's cornered the market here. Anyway, what's the point of a wildlands tour? We're not here for that, and time's a-wasting."

I pushed the cart toward the tour proprietor anyway. The broad-shouldered woman sat at a podium next to her launch structure, reclining as she read a pamphlet, her face hidden behind it. She had her feet resting on the back of a gray stone dragon, a big Mount-class. Its saddle seated two, so I imagined she used it for her tours.

"Caliph is special, Jo," I said. "It's a place where fortunes can be made by the bold. And that's what I want to do today."

She frowned at my cart. "Wait. Is that salted meat?"

I'd stopped at a food vendor at one point, grabbing some rations that'd last for a few days. Jolene finally clued in when she saw it. She tugged on my arm.

"What are you planning, Warren?"

The heavy traffic in Caliph didn't exactly let us stop, so I pushed right up against the stone dragon, making it open one lazy eye at me.

"Well, I meant to spend some time in the wilds while we were here... but I need to talk to a guide first. I was curious if you wanted to go?"

"What!? Me?" Jolene blurted.

"Of course. It'll be dangerous, naturally, but I can do the fighting. You'll just be my naturalist."

She worked her mouth like a fish, at a loss for words for once. "But—but going into the wilds is dangerous! And you have all our...." She whispered behind a hand. "All *your* wealth is on you."

"About that. There's more at the bank now."

She looked flabbergasted. "How much is more?"

"I won an arena fight against an Airship dragon. I guess it's kind of a lot?"

"An arena fight? Against an Airship-class?!" she exclaimed.

She was hopeless. I handed her a pouch of coins. "If it makes you feel better, you can hold our money. We're business partners after all, and I trust you. Are you sure you don't want to come with me?"

"Out there?" She pointed toward the exact pile of stones I meant to visit. I nodded, and she shook her head. "Maybe next time. I'm anxious enough all the time as it is."

"Okay, then I need you to go into the market and take notes on everything. I mean *everything*. Do you know what arbitrage is?"

Her long locks swayed when she shook her head.

"When was the last time you came to Caliph to trade in dragons?" I asked. "Like actual dragons, not eggs."

"Oh, uh, six, no... seven years ago, with our old steward," Jolene answered. "Oh, arbitrage. I remember that word... it means buying low and selling high. You want me to study the market here, so we can sell things back home?"

"Yeah. I absolutely do. Dasvilla is the laughingstock of the kingdom, a backwater. Our lord is literally named Biscuit. No one goes there except Captain Kenna and the Duke's own dragons."

As I said this, the tour guide dropped her pamphlet to look at me, probably impatient for me to ask her prices. However, I kept my focus on Jolene.

"This means Biscuit has cornered the Dasvilla market on all kinds of things, or given licenses over to his nobles, to encourage them to curry favor with him. We can sell for much less, though, and Becki can do it through backdoor channels. It won't work for long, but it should boost our cash flow."

This, I had learned from my morning meeting with Rachel. After my balls comment, she'd asked me back to her desk. With her boss absent, we'd had an entire office to ourselves. That had proved a more productive meeting than I'd thought.

I might still have a job to do for Rachel, but she had already done good work for me.

Beside us, the dragon continued to watch, but the tour guide had raised her pamphlet again.

"If you're going to stay, Jolene, then I need your full focus on this," I said, gripping her arm—not too hard—to emphasize my point. "No getting distracted by dragons. *Focus,* Jolene. Focus on what makes the most profit. Find out what we should buy to maximize gains."

This job was a better one for Rachel, but if Jolene could get the numbers, then Rachel could parse them.

Jolene's blue eyes darted about while she mulled over how to answer. "I... I don't know."

"You're a noble, Jolene. Act like it. Flash your Minax signet ring around, and smile that gorgeous smile of yours. You'll get answers better than I will."

Jolene nodded slowly, still fidgeting. "Milord. I—" She glanced up at me, then hugged me out of nowhere, as if the act had taken all of her courage.

"I can't lose you. Warren. If you die out there, they'll kick me out, sell your assets, and give me nothing. I'm not even related to you."

I returned her embrace, cupping her head against my chest, if only for an excuse to touch her silky hair.

"This inheritance dragonshit isn't fair, so we can't be either." I tugged her head back to look at me, ignoring the people who had to go around us.

"I'm going to rebuild this business, Jolene, and then I'm going to give you a hefty stake of it. Fifty percent after Rachel's cut, if you want. That makes it a contract, then, not an estate. You don't need to be related to me for a contract to stay in place when I die.

"And at the end of all this, if we're successful but I decide this is not for me, all the value you brought to the table will be returned to you. I'll make it right. I promise."

Her blue eyes watered, like living tide pools. "Warren, that's...." She choked up. "But it's the *wilds*. What if you die?"

I chuckled. "Then fate takes me from this world. You lose everything, and I lose *more* than everything, but how is that any different from how it would have ended for you anyway? Would any of your mother's other male choices have saved a farm barely worth a few gold?"

"Well... no."

"I have to take risks to make money, Jo. But these are calculated risks, and I know what I'm doing when it comes to the wilds."

While she mulled this over, a full flight of dragons soared overhead, passing low enough that their personal gusts of wind carried the vendor's pamphlet away. I finally glanced over, and my chest constricted with surprise.

Captain Kenna shot me a wink, then crossed her arms and lowered her hat, pretending to settle into a nap.

Half-dazed, I patted the change purse I'd given Jolene. "Once you have your information," I said, "find a mage hub and place a distance-message to Rachel of the Dasvilla Keepers. She'll direct you in how to spend that wisely. Listen to her as if our lives depend on it, because they do."

She tentatively bounced the pouch of coins. "You...." Jolene pinched her eyes closed. "This is too much pressure."

I dipped my head in answer, guiding her hand to safely store the coins at her waist pouch. "You can do it, Jo. No one wants this to succeed more than you do. Just... keep your hands on your pockets."

"I *know* how to avoid a pickpocket, Warren. I might make poor *financial* choices, but I can navigate a city with the best of them.... Fine. I'll study everything I can while you gallivant around playing dragon-hunter."

I bent down and gently kissed her cheek. "You can always come find me. I could use your expertise out in the wilds."

"And share a tent with you? No. No thanks on that! How long will you be gone?"

I laughed. "I'll return within three days, or not at all. In which case, sorry I failed."

"You won't fail, Warren," she said seriously. "Mother chose well and—" she slipped her arm around mine "—and I ought to thank you for being the hero I needed. I.... Thank you."

She sniffled while straightening her back, trying on a smidge of pride for once. "You're something special, Warren. I'm shocked you're not married."

I recognized the beginning of a whole new conversation. "Come on, Jolene. It's time for me to leave—"

"Just a few more minutes," she interrupted, her eyes swimming with tears. She really was afraid for me. "Please."

I sighed again, and humored her. Kenna didn't seem to be in a rush, anyway.

"Truth be told, I've been engaged before," I said, earning an immediate stare. "You could say that a noble stole her from me. I'll tell you more if I make it back safely."

Jolene leaned against my cart. "Was she cute?"

"The prettiest girl in the entire kingdom, but it was young love. Young love that was destined to never work for an orphan commoner like me," I said, unable to hide the pain. "She never tried to reach out after we parted. As far as I'm concerned, she's long gone."

"Oh. I'm sorry." She brightened. "But you made it, Warren. You made it, and you're exactly what Pinnacle needs—a knight with a good soul, doing good things."

I shook my head, sucking in a guilty breath. "I've killed defenseless troll camps, punched a whore who tried to rob me, kicked a kid who somehow got a hold of my purse inside my robes, and I took advantage of a vulnerable woman in a laundry room just last week."

I winced, remembering Shimmer yet again. I'd asked Rachel to look into her situation, but I didn't know Shimmer's real name. Rachel didn't think I'd ever find her without it.

"Vulnerable how?" Jolene asked.

"She wanted to fuck the first guy she saw who wasn't a complete asshole," I said.

"Well, seems like she achieved that goal, given you're not an asshole," she said. "Besides, given the way Becki looks at you, I'm guessing you gave that laundry woman a very good time.

"Anyway, I'll keep all that in mind. Thanks for warning me, you horrible, no good, dirty rotten scoundrel, you," Jolene said. Her eyes drifted to take in an emerald green Shoulder dragon fluttering over traffic. "But you changed the subject. Your lost love, who was she?"

"A silly girl who met a silly boy. Life isn't about happy endings. It's about harsh realities, but I can promise one thing," I said. "I respect your passion for dragons, Jolene. It's true love. I... I don't know what my true love is."

"You know, if you keep being so demons-damned sweet, I might apply for that job," Jolene teased, pushing off the cart. Our time was up.

I chuckled. "Be well, Jolene the Dragon Queen. Be well. I shall return to you soon. Pinnacle Dragons won't stay small forever."

Jolene cocked her head, glanced at the vendor, then kissed me on the mouth.

"You'd better keep that promise," she told me. "I'll stay at the Lake Maiden. Find me when you're back."

Then she turned, and vanished into the crowd.

Chapter 45

Into the Wild Green Yonder

"MY FEE ONLY INCLUDES A SINGLE NIGHT," Kenna warned, leading me deeper into the jungle.

After Jolene had left, I approached Kenna. "So. You run tours in your off-time, do you?" I asked.

She tipped up her hat and grinned. "Makes more money than doin' nothin' at all."

"What about Seabreeze? The dragon you use for flights?"

"I rent her out to merchants during the slow times of the week. This here is Old Charlie." She patted the stone dragon.

I nodded. "All right, here's my offer: your full daily rate plus ten percent of my take, if you serve as a hunting guide instead of just a tour guide."

She frowned. "Don't know nothin' about catching dragons, just findin' em."

"All you need to do is help me find where they're hiding. You leave the catching to me."

We set out of Caliph on a warm afternoon wind, flying over a worn road packed with people. The road split within the first hundred paces, then again, and again, with the roads getting less congested and quieter each time.

"Why are we following roads when we're airborne?" I yelled at Kenna.

"To check for bodies," she said. "You can tell what killed them based on the bodies."

I swallowed. These lands apparently contained dragons, minotaurs, orcs, trolls, *and* goblins. Why anyone would walk out here without a full contingent of guards with them, I had no idea. I had my work cut out for me.

I pointed over her shoulder, since she was seated ahead of me. She wore flight goggles, and I now wished I had purchased some of my own.

"That formation. Can you take me down there?"

"That place? It's occupied!" she said. The stones were still smoking, as if something burned far within.

"I want to see it," I replied. "You can charge me for the detour."

I had a feeling I'd be paying extra for this as she nudged Old Charlie toward the pile of massive stones. As we drew closer, I could see the rocks were so large that only a Behemoth-class dragon could possibly lift them—that, or some type of magic.

And something *had* piled them here. There was nothing natural about this formation. It looked like a tower of massive oyster shells. Around it, the earth had been gouged with terrifyingly deep claw marks. The earth didn't degrade naturally in that way.

"It's called the House of Cards," Kenna offered, flying low over the formation before banking to do another pass. "Dragons usually nest there, but those rocks don't look balanced. One of these days, it's gonna collapse!"

I wasn't so sure. The stone appeared to be weathered. Maybe Behemoth dragons had more architectural sense than people gave them credit for.

I pointed a finger down. "Can you drop me off, then come back when I wave at you?"

Old Charlie gave a strange, lutelike roar. I took it to mean *you have got to be kidding*.

"Are you crazy?" Kenna said, still yelling over the wind.

"Yes," I replied. I could feel the pull of the eggs more strongly than ever. I'd suggested this direction for our hunt, because the call of Vital's essence was stronger here, like a pulse. It was louder than the dragon herself had been—because there was more than one life down there.

I thought of the commemorative eggs, the ones with the completely still flame pattern. Unfertilized eggs had no flames at all, but you could still see a flame, frozen in time, when the light of a young life had gone out.

Kenna banked again. "There are dragons in that formation, handsome. Wild ones."

"I know."

"You're from the city. You don't understand—"

"Take me down, Captain."

She fell silent, then clucked her tongue at Old Charlie. I didn't blame her for thinking I was a dead man. I really *didn't* understand how all of this worked. I should be out of my element.

But I felt it, that pulse, the steady thrum of life in those stones. It called to me like the memory of a loved one, now lost. There was no evil, no hunger, no rage.

"I won't land him to drop you," Kenna warned me. "We'll get close and give you a big flap to jump off. If you live, we'll pick you up via your arm. It'll hurt like a bitch. You might pull something."

I tapped her to let her know I'd heard.

"You've got an hour," she said, tilting into a slow dive.

Another tap, a low swoop, and one leap of faith, and I found

315

myself on the moss outside the House of Cards, my ride fading into the distance overhead.

I took a breath, tasting the air. It smelled like a good cigar, but cleaner; it felt like I was inhaling good clean air instead of smoke, but the clean air smelled of clove. I sensed friendliness here, and after taking a few steps, my conscious mind understood why.

There were no bones around the House of Cards.

Moss encircled the place, bereft of any corpses, old or new. Nothing feasted on prey here. That gave it more than a friendly air; it felt *sacred*. Dragons were beasts, and this was a dragon home. It *should* have bones around it, even just a few of them. But there were none.

They keep this place clean.

I didn't approach. I sensed tension in nearby trees, and the tension had a Hauler-size feel to it. Previously unseen dragons watched me raptly from the forest, like guards. But they weren't acting. Not unless I moved closer.

With a wave in the direction of both the hidden Haulers, I retreated into the jungle tree line and settled down behind a bush. If I wanted to infiltrate that place and secure Vital's eggs, I needed to know what I was up against.

Five minutes. Ten. A half hour passed, and I was starting to wonder if I'd run out my time. Nothing was happening out here. The guard dragons didn't move. I did get a glimpse of some small dragons, maybe a dozen of them, moving in and out of the holes and chittering.

Now that I was close, the force of the presence in the House of Cards felt even more enormous. It felt like as Airship-class was curled up beneath it.

Forty minutes. Damn. I might have to take my chances—

But before I could finish the thought, a wild dragon appeared overhead. I rubbed my hands together.

Here we go.

Chapter 46

House of Cards

THE GRAY DRAGON landed with an impact that made the ground shake beneath me. She had a rabbit in her mouth, the type of snack food that Jolene said dragons didn't bother with. I watched, rapt, as she lumbered toward the House of Cards. It was definitely a she, with that rounded head and smaller size.

As I watched, she put her nose into the stones—and then past them. Her entire head vanished into the stone edifice.

Holy shit, I thought, heart thumping. *Is that place an illusion?*

But no. I stood up and jogged left, trying to get a better view. The guard dragons tensed again, and I stopped before I forced them to make a move.

From this angle, I could see that the she-dragon had not stuck her head through an illusion. She'd just stuck her head into one of many holes and crevices between the stacked rocks. Half her neck was down inside it, too, as if the place had been designed for a dragon's head—not its body—to get into it.

Crunching and squishing noises came from the hole as well, and the dragon's neck moved slightly, proof that it was chewing. It was eating the rabbit inside the hole?

It dawned on me. *She's feeding babies. She's crunching the rabbit up, and feeding her hatchlings.*

This wasn't just Vital's nest. It was a whole *hotel* of nests.

Ingenious, I thought, as the pieces fell into place. *It was built for this purpose! The nests stay out of sight, so many in one place... and the heat underneath must be a natural hot spring or something. The heat rises through, keeping the eggs warm without mothers resting over them.*

And that's why full-grown dragons can't get in; it saves room. It can house so many more nests than a traditional nesting ground!

As for the small dragons, their purpose was clear now, too: they were tending the eggs and hatchlings, because only tiny dragons could fit their whole bodies in that place. I couldn't tell if these guys were big hatchlings or adult Shoulder-sizes from here, but I suspected the latter. They had to be nurse-dragons of some kind.

It really was a smart design, and I had to wonder at who—or more likely *what*—had built it. The dragons used it so naturally. I doubted that big dragon mother understood how the place worked; she just reacted to the design in an instinctual way, according to her nature.

And no one had ever noticed this? No one had ever dared to get close?

Because anyone who's ever had a dragon Bond can sense that there's a huge Airship-class under that pile, I realized. *Except it's not an Airship dragon at all. It's hundreds of eggs, close together!*

While these revelations struck me one after the other, the gray mother backed away and took flight again. Once she was gone, one of the guard dragons bugled at the House of Cards. A little blue dragon poked his head out.

The guard dragon bugled again, and the dragon looked at me.

It's giving him instructions. Amazing!

I didn't move as the blue Shoulder dragon wove through the moss toward me, stopping a good five feet back. I'd already shrunk into a crouch to make myself smaller and less threatening.

"Hey there, bud," I said, holding out a piece of salted meat. "Don't worry about me. I'm not here to hurt anyone or take anything. These eggs don't belong to me, do they?"

I couldn't desecrate a place like this with theft. Dozens of mother dragons relied on it, and it was ancient, sacred. If I cleaned it out, they'd either abandon it, or come after me in droves.

The spiky little dragon chittered—*pip pip pip*—and then darted forward, snatching the meat from my hand. Somehow, I didn't think he'd be so friendly with someone who didn't have the strange dragonbond that I did.

I retrieved another piece of meat. "I've got a job for you, boy. If you do it, I'll give you lots of meat."

"*Pip pufft?*" it replied, its little voice half-chickadee and half-wind-in-the-door.

I nodded toward the House of Cards. "There's a nest in there whose momma won't be coming back. I've come to take them somewhere safe and raise them. If you bring the eggs to me, you get a piece of meat for each one."

"*Puff whoosht?*" it replied, like a question. I had to make an educated guess based on the senses I was getting from it, but what else could it be asking except, *Which nest?*

"A clay dragon's nest. One whose mother hasn't checked on it in a long while. One that feels like... ah... like a claw scratching wet clay." I scratched the tree next to me. "Like this, but on clay."

I don't know what possessed me to describe the sense that came off Vital, a sense shared by her children, but the sky dragon cocked its head and watched my scratching with interest. It peeped like a baby chicken and looked at me.

"So, what do you say?" I asked.

"*Peep peep grrrowlll,*" it said, its voice first cheerful and then low in warning. Before I could reply, it slithered off back to the nest. I couldn't tell what it had meant.

A yes, maybe? With a warning? Maybe it thought I was tricking it. I waited. Five minutes until Kenna came back.

Blue burst into the air, wings flaring—the nurse dragon shot out of the rocks, then dove at me. I held up an armored arm, just in case, but I could see the blood-red thing in its talons.

It banked the same way Old Charlie had when he'd dropped me, and then it released its payload gently onto the moss.

"Good job, buddy!" I said, tossing it a piece of meat. "Can I have the rest?"

"Peep peep!"

No growl this time, I noted as it turned, flapping high enough to dive theatrically back into the formation. Maybe it had investigated my claims or something? And it had come to the conclusion that the mother really *hadn't* been back?

It dropped an egg before me twice more, and I caught it both times. It refused to return after that, growling, so I figured this was all I would get. Possibly, these were all the eggs that Vital had laid. I hadn't asked the typical size of a nest.

By now, I could see Kenna's dot in the distance, heading back. I patted the little blue dragon on its crown without thinking. It leaned into my touch, not aggressive at all.

"Well, then... thank you. Here. You earned it."

I dumped a half-day's rations of salted meat on the ground for the beast. The critter fell upon it with relish, burping between bites. One of the guard dragons rumbled jealously from the trees.

I laughed at the display and secured the third egg to my bandolier. All three appeared to be alive and vibrant and very close to hatching. The silhouetted babies took up the whole egg, so that very little light could pass through.

Seems I had arrived just in time, or those little guys would have nothing to eat.

Kenna was close now, so I waved. "You'd better go," I told the nurse-dragon. "She won't take me away if you don't."

It scarfed down its last piece of meat like a heron inhaling a fish, and then it waddled off before stopping to look back at me.

Our eyes met. I felt quiet. A strange peace overcame me. It felt like the moment before falling asleep, when the haze of consciousness is almost gone, but still lingers.

"Grr-rrak," the dragon said, a relaxed but guttural noise. Then it left me there, teetering, in a daze.

Wing beats sounded. "Your arm!" Kenna shouted.

I raised an arm, and what came next was pain.

My arm still ached by the time we landed and unpacked our supplies. As Old Charlie took to the sky to scout for us, Kenna placed her supply bag on the cart.

From there, she ran beside me along one of the roads out of Caliph, headed for some dragon nesting grounds she had scouted before.

"You can only find the path on the ground," she'd said. "It's too hard to spot from the sky."

Each of us took a turn pushing the cart. I had switched to simple leathers, and now carried a sword on my back. Most of the supplies rested on the cart's bed.

And that was our hunting party: two people loaded up with traps and carriers, nothing more.

Since we'd started the day later than I would have liked— after a full morning shopping trip with Jolene, plus a detour at the House of Cards formation—I made Kenna earn her pay, pushing her hard. We jogged for a solid hour until she slowed, guiding me off the beaten road and down a narrow game trail.

Up to that point, the sky had seemed at peace, with minimal clouds and no sign of a breeze. A few dragons soared overhead, but each carried riders. We'd yet to see what we wanted: wild dragons.

As soon as we left the road, the jungle quickly swallowed us. The vegetation grew thick with lush bushes, tall trees, and a lack of visibility I found disturbing. As the game trail narrowed, Kenna had to help carry the cart at the front to get it over roots and rocks.

We came across all sorts of birds, small rodents, and even monkeys as we traveled. Several of the animals were worth something as pets, but hardly enough to risk traveling too far from safety. If we lost sight of the path, we might never find it again.

Not even five minutes into the jungle, a spindly brown Mount-class dragon burst out of the brush in front of Kenna, breaking into a run, aiming away from us. She grabbed at her rope, but the beast was already gone.

"I may have paid too much," I teased.

She frowned. "That was a mangrove dragon, not very common. But yeah, let's leave the cart for now. No one is going to come by and steal it. This area is infested with threats."

I remembered what Jolene had said about dragons liking to eat fresh monster corpses. That meant they lived near monsters, so we might find orcs and goblins before we found dragons.

After parking the cart, I pulled out an axe, and proceeded to chop down a few branches and shrubs, using them to hide the vehicle. Once it was partially covered, we set out. I marked our path by quietly marking trees at eye level.

Large fronds crept over the game trail and I quietly cut them as I went. My goal was efficiency over silence. Kenna readied her bow with an arrow nocked, taking up a position behind me.

I tried to stay quiet with each step as we dove deeper into the jungle, casting an occasional glance back at the markers to make sure they were visible.

The sun had just started to set, giving the canopy an angled glow, when the quiet forest began to make sound again. For the past hour, we had failed to disturb anything except small forest critters, but now I heard the gurgle of running water up ahead.

I didn't slow, hoping the river would be a safe spot to camp for the evening. Kenna would insist we start heading back at the sun's zenith tomorrow, so I was acting a bit recklessly with my speed by this point—and because of that, I almost missed the trip wire.

Almost.

When I held up a closed fist, Kenna tensed behind me, her eyes finding the same string of animal guts stretching across the path.

I didn't know what tripping it would do, but I cautiously stepped over it while scanning the jungle. A few paces away, a very obvious pit had been covered with shrubs. Someone wanted the path guarded, but had done a poor job of it.

I stepped over the pit and toward the river, which glittered in the fading sun beyond a stand of mangroves. I slowed to observe what rested on the other side of the riverbank.

A half-dozen orc females lay sleeping there, out in the open, protected by brother males. It seemed like the group of them were just waking, stirring and rising to sit up, smacking their lips, their eyes still drowsy. The monsters bore pale gray skin with hints of green, all of them at least a head taller than me, with the males on par with the females.

The group seemed to be living out of a single shared tent. A small fire had burned down to embers in front of it. It wasn't a real camp, lacking any long-term assets like walls or trenches.

If I had to guess, these were outcasts sent to fend for themselves from the main tribe, or they were a hunting party.

I bit my lip, thinking. Orcs were ruthless, more than capable of killing an entire caravan. Afterward, they took the women and children to eat. Every time I'd ever found an ambushed caravan, it had been horrifying. The brutes didn't try to mate with captured humans, but they did find breasts and human babies a delicacy.

Because of this, I never showed an ounce of mercy to orcs—and I wasn't about to start now.

Chapter 47

Not a Bad Haul

BEFORE THEY COULD SMELL me coming, I burst out of the jungle and sprinted toward the group; I had to keep speed on my side. Kenna hissed a curse after me, then probably turned and fled. I didn't care.

I still held my sword, but I pulled a knife, too.

The sword rested in my right hand and the knife in my left. There was no time to switch weapons for the shield on my back, so I spent my energy covering the distance. I reached a stretching male orc who was smacking his lips, smiling hazily.

I swung my sword at its neck.

At the sound of blade and bone, another orc turned around. It shrieked as it saw me, but I was already sliding the blade out of the dead orc's spinal column and slicing through the next.

A female orc shot to her feet, but I reached her before she could do much more than face me. Even unarmed and caught off guard, a fully grown orc was dangerous. They could bite, or gouge with their tusks, or use the long claws at the tips of their fingers to rip skin apart, and they'd win just about every wrestling match against a human. Unlike trolls who were mostly fat, orcs were all muscle. This female could crush me with her biceps alone.

So I threw my knife instead of closing the distance. The blade lanced straight into the female's throat, lodging into her spine. I stabbed another orc with the sword instead of watching the female die. Most were easy pickings, still asleep at my feet.

I yanked my blades free with each kill, barely noticing as the mortal wounds gushed torrents of purple blood. I thrust and severed and cut. A primal roar erupted from another male, and I spun. It stood over the female I'd killed with the knife, eager to seek vengeance for its mate.

It charged me with a rock it must have snatched off the riverbank. I reached for my other knife to throw it, but I fumbled my grab. Orc blood had gotten onto the handle, a notoriously slippery substance, and the knife slipped right out of my grip.

The thing was almost upon me. I raised my sword, but this was going to hurt—

It roared and dropped, an arrow sprouting from its calf. Before it could recover, I sliced my sword across its neck from the side, yanking to pull it free of the muscle.

The body twitched. Thick purple blood rapidly oozed out of the wound, drenching the rocks underfoot.

Only the females were left.

For the most part, female orcs weren't allowed to fight; they generally only carried frying pans or skinning knives as weapons, since their status came from cooking the tribe's meals. With the males dead and the females scrambling to arm themselves, I carried out the grim task of erasing the rest of the blight.

Slaying female orcs wasn't exactly fun for me, but we made short work of the grim. One by one, the female orcs fell to our attacks, until the only sound that broke the bloody silence was the squalling of a baby orc.

I looked unhappily at the tent. I hated to kill children of any creature, but it had to be done. Every single male orc had to kill a human to become an adult within the tribes, so every single baby would cost a human life.

Kenna, however, had fewer qualms than I did. The baby's cry suddenly fell silent, and Kenna exited the tent with a purple-stained machete in one hand.

"Cut off their right ears," she said. "They're each worth a bounty. We can split it fifty-fifty."

I made no comment on the fact that I'd killed most of the creatures. I was just pleased to be making money.

"There's a bounty on orcs? Since when?"

"Since the king got it into his head to clear the entire eastern front of Parshil, I guess," Kenna said, already kneeling to remove the right ear of the nearest corpse. "There's a bounty on *anything* in the wilds between here and the sea."

She swiped a hand across her brow. "And that's not even mentioning the count of Caliph. He wants to wall off the whole damn road, so he can start sending ships of goods far abroad. He's using the king's bounties to advance that agenda."

Well, that was entrepreneurial, to say the least. The sea must be twenty miles from Caliph, which was a lot of road to wall off. But you wouldn't hear me complaining.

Once I had seven ears stuffed into one of the egg cages on my bandolier, I slit the dead throats of all the orcs, opening up their guts to attract dragons. According to Jolene, dragons would go crazy for the recently-murdered body of an orc.

In short, these bodies would make for impeccable bait. This had been my plan all along.

"Ya know, when you told me you wanted to use dead orcs as bait, I added ten coppers to your price right then," Kenna muttered, coming to stand beside me and survey our fresh carnage. "I thought you'd cream your pants and go running when ya saw 'em. Instead, seems we might have a busy night. Dragons should show up in no time."

As I set about building and setting traps using the bodies, Kenna disassembled the orcs' tent, collected a few weapons from inside it—some of them could be resold—and worked

327

silently in tandem with me. We finished at about the same time.

"We should get back to the cart," Kenna said. "The blood will be on the wind now."

I finished tying the last rope, and we were off, running back through the jungle and following the notched trees to the cart.

The two of us didn't say a word for a long time as we worked the cart closer to the site of the slaughter. Once we got within sensing range of the place, the sun had fully set.

"You stay behind," I said. "I'll go scout."

"What? No way. We should both stay here. What gets caught will still be there by morning."

I shook my head. "No. I need to watch." That would tell me what traps worked best, and how the dragons reacted to each.

"Fine, I'll go with. I can lasso an ox with the best of them, so if something looks like it'll run, I can snag it."

I stifled a grin. Kenna might pretend otherwise, but she wanted in on the action.

When we arrived back to the riverbank, the first dragon was already picking over the fresh corpses. It was shorter than I was, its skin shiny and red-brown, like copper. Stunted spikes clustered on its head, back, tail, and shoulders. I'd never seen this type before, nor ever seen a dragon with so many spikes.

"I don't recognize that variety," Kenna said. "It's probably a juvenile Hauler, maybe even an Airship. Juveniles can change a lot into adulthood."

"I don't care what it is; I'll take it. The more varieties, the better," I said, hoping we'd come across another rare mangrove dragon.

We gave the copper-colored dragon some time to hit a trap, but it didn't, so Kenna flung a looped rope.

She missed.

Kenna grunted in disappointment while the dragon shrieked and took off. It didn't go very far, landing on the other side of the river to glare at us. Its eyes were the same copper as its scales, tinged in gold. Its aura color matched, but the aura itself was dense. This thing would eventually grow larger.

"What was that about being worth the extra silver?" I asked Kenna, but I didn't mean it. She'd found us the orcs, after all.

"Hah. Never should have told you about the bounties," Kenna grumbled, settling back behind the bush we were using to spy from. She lowered her voice and added, "Didja know the duke doubled it after Parmisca fell? He wants to show the people he ain't weak, but all it shows is deep pockets. I'm not complaining, mind."

Parmisca was Parshil's westernmost city. It had fallen to monsters last year.

"Trust me, I appreciate the honesty," I whispered back. "And you're great with the arrow."

Kenna smiled, the compliment clearly tickling her. "Yeah, well, if you would have charged in against more of the bastards, I'd have fired one arrow, panicked, and ran."

"Somehow I doubt that," I said. "Come on, nothing's happening. Let's try to set up the big trap while we can."

She didn't argue, and I knew I'd sense any dragon coming from a decent distance, so we returned to get the supplies from the cart. The reinforced cage was the heaviest thing we'd brought along, so we soon worked up a sweat as we lugged it back to the site and popped it open.

The thing wasn't too different from what fishermen used for crabs or fish. Dragons would have to work their frames through a narrow opening, then struggle to get out again, because of their wings.

Together, we shoved a female orc with glazed eyes into the trap, then reset the orc's tent loosely over it to make it all look less human. I nearly slipped moving back to our hiding spot.

"Shit, there's blood and guts all over the place," I said. If we had to move fast to catch a dragon, we were screwed.

"Still, it beats hauling tourists," Kenna replied. "Okay, now we really *do* need to hide. Let's move back to that pit, see if anything fell inside it."

I agreed, and we made our way back to the game trail. We stopped before the pit and pulled off the leaves to find several human daggers at the bottom, implanted in the earth with the blades crudely facing up. I shook my head, chuckling, and Kenna helped me climb down to pull the valuable weapons out of the ground.

I put them into my bag, and to my amazement, she didn't ask for a cut of the profits.

"These weapons didn't come from some random tribe," I said. "These belonged to a team of soldiers, probably out on a raid mission."

"Poor bastards," Kenna said.

I dug out some kindling from my bag and set a tiny fire at the bottom of the hole to give us some light. From there, we disarmed the two string traps we found in the area. They both triggered a good spear to fall when the wires were tripped. Those would sell for decent money, too.

"Not a bad haul," I said.

"One soldier's bad luck is another man's treasure, I suppose," Kenna said, sitting at the edge of the hole so her feet could catch some of the heat. "Hey, Warren? Since you seem like someone who listens to advice, let me share some. Eggs are worth far more than wild dragons ever will be. You're on a fool's errand with this."

"What do you mean?" I said, settling in next to her. "Dragons are worth ten times an egg. I mean, they're economically viable. They can actually do things, do *work*. Eggs can't."

"Yeah, but a wild, untrained dragon is not going to sell. You can sell a healthy dragon egg for the same price as a wild adult dragon, maybe more. It depends on the market."

"Because the client can raise it and form a dragonbond?"

"Not just that. Any dragon that's been raised from birth by humans, even crummy humans, is going to be more tame than a wild dragon."

That did make sense. "But if I have a male and a female—"

"You can't just put two wild dragons together and get them to lay eggs, at least not without a long time spent acclimating them to each other. And you're even more screwed if you catch an already-mated dragon. An alpha can work, but it's not like every other dragon wants to jump its bones just because it's an alpha."

I rocked back and leaned on my hands, peering up through the jungle canopy at the starlit expanse of the heavens. *Jolene did tell me that buying dragon goop and inserting it into the females was financially the better and safer choice.*

But if that were true, I could harvest the males' sperm, set them free, and still keep the females. Right?

"It's like this," Kenna said, pulling up a patch of grass and tossing it into the pit. "You throw any house cat in a box with a feral cat, and the feral will kick the shit out of the house cat. The two aren't about to mate.

"It's no different with dragons. Even the late Lord Minax didn't bother with this tactic.

"He wanted to, though. He'd been working to engineer the Roost at Dasvilla to serve as a sort of dragon aviary, where they could move in and out at their leisure, without being trapped. He said the key to breeding wild dragons was to put them together in a place where they have room to flee their disputes."

"Is that how dragons die? From *disputes?*"

"Amongst each other? Yes. You'll even see that from farm-raised dragons. There is always some sort of hierarchy, at least within each size class. And outside that, smaller dragons always bow to larger ones. For example, Behemoth dragons can command any other size class, but Haulers can still command Mounts and Shoulders."

331

I nodded while she spoke, thinking of the repairs being made to the Roost. Were they enhancing what Lord Minax had started to do, or were they undoing his work? Maybe I should get involved there. I bet Rachel would know something about it.

Kenna brought a hand to her chest and flicked a button on her shirt, opening it a little further down her chest. It was getting hot here, and her tawny, sun-darkened skin had grown sweaty. It glistened in all the right places.

"Lucian Minax tried to mimic an aviary with his house," she said. "You know, with the cage around it? Only he filled it with sweet and lazy dragons who were happy to be there, instead of wild assholes who want to kill you."

She sighed, fanning herself with the loose corner of her shirt. "My point being, never underestimate a feral dragon."

I was working hard to keep my eyes off her tits, but she wasn't making it easy on me, and I was starting to think she was doing it on purpose.

"Do people normally avoid doing what I'm doing?" I asked. "I mean, what do experienced dragon hunters do?"

"They come out here with traps," she replied. "But the catch is only really worth it once they have eggs to sell. It's always, *always* about the eggs."

I asked her to elaborate, and so she did. She gesticulated as she spoke, then looked at me intensely to make sure I was getting it. The thing was, as she moved, she seemed to be getting progressively closer to me.

"So I'm not saying going against the norm is bad," she concluded, now mere inches from me. "Trapping is a tried-and-true method, but often it's to follow a mother to her nest or to knock a male unconscious and drain his baby-makers. Or it's to collect rare breeds, which can be worth it even when they're wild.

"But a single nest of eggs can pay for five trips into the wilds, and you don't have to fight orcs to get them. You just have to distract the mommas." She bumped my shoulder, then leaned close to my ear.

"And something tells me, my dear Lord Warren," she breathed, "that you're very good at distracting hot mommas."

Chapter 48

Curiosity Killed the Human

My neck heated. She was flirting with me.

I patted her knee, letting my hand linger slightly. "That's all good advice, Kenna. I respect it. I just figured every down-on-his-luck sucker would be out hunting dragon eggs, and I prefer to hunt things that can actually kill people—that *have* killed people."

I tapped the spear lying next to me with a fingertip. "So if killing orcs meant I'd have bait for dragon traps, I was all for it. Besides, I don't have time to wait for a dragon to mature. A mature, *tame* dragon is worth what? Ten times a viable egg?"

The expression on her face softened. Her hand moved for my knife, attached to my belt, caught between us. She ran her finger along the handle.

"You are very interesting, Lord Minax-Orpheus. A visionary who deals in blood."

"And coins," I said, lowering my voice to match hers. "But you've just given me the key to that part. I need an aviary—for ferals."

"Good luck with that," Kenna said, her gaze dropping to my mouth. She leaned closer.

Whoosh.

We both looked up as a shadow obscured the stars for half a moment.

Damn. That had to be a Hauler, at least.

I killed the fire with a handful of dirt to keep the new arrivals from seeing us. We'd both gone tense, and we stayed that way as we took our legs from the trap hole and crouched low behind the bushes nearby.

Kenna peered in the direction of the dead orcs, which were just barely visible through the foliage from here. I joined her, checking my senses. The copper dragon was still near, but it had been joined by several others that seemed to cluster around it.

From our vantage, we caught sight of a Shoulder dragon crawling into the top of the big trap.

"Well, that's a good start," Kenna whispered. The dragon was already stuck, it just didn't know it yet. But if anything much larger tried to free it, the trap would break.

I reached down to grasp one of the ropes we'd left here, tied to the tree with a lasso at one end. I had never been good at throwing lassos, but I'd learned the basics during my stint as a farmer, leading oxen.

Beside me, Kenna picked up her own prepared rope. She was ready to prove she was the expert she'd claimed to be, even after her earlier miss.

"If it's too big," I said, "we don't try to bind it. We just loop a spike so that we scare it and it runs."

"Why?"

"Because we can't take an Airship-class home with us," I said.

"So you *do* have some common sense," she whispered, grinning. "Which, for a former guardsman, is a rarity. By the way, you'll have to explain it to me sometime, how a guardsman can just wake up one day and learn he's a lord. Did you just fuck the right woman, or what?"

I readied my rope to throw, watching the shadows move among the corpses and carefully tracking everything that so much as *sniffed* at the cage trap.

"It's more that the right woman had a crush on me, I guess. Trust me, I don't believe it, either."

"I don't know, noblewomen really like tall, dashing commoners, especially when they're covered in blood and gore." We shared a chuckle and she added, "You probably think I'm kidding, but no, really. Noblewomen are all raving mad for bloody men."

Sounds like someone else I know, I thought.

Beyond us, the dragons were all busy eating. There were enough bodies that it would take time. Neither of us actually needed to act unless the cage was threatened or one of the dragons came after us, so I said, "I'll take the first shift."

"Ha, don't worry. We're not sleeping tonight," Kenna warned.

She turned out to be right, because not even ten minutes later, two dragons snarled at each other above the same corpse. There was no way anyone but a deaf man would sleep through that.

For the next half hour, we listened to the terrible, gut-twisting sounds of teeth scraping on bones, until it became clear the dragons were becoming too numerous. The big presence I'd sensed—the Airship-class—still hadn't appeared, instead choosing to lurk in the forest. Its aura had a silver coloring to it, and it felt somehow... familiar. Had I encountered it somewhere before?

After the copper dragon finished its own meal, it let loose a cry. After that, the Airship-class finally shifted—along with a dozen others that had been waiting their turn on the copper's chosen orc—and I wondered why the bigger dragon had waited to eat after so many of its small companions had gone first.

My answer came when something big landed beside the cage with a jarring thud, strong enough to make the dirt rise in a cloud around its feet. Dozens of small dragons scattered off the corpses to make room, some of them hissing away into the jungle and nearly touching us in their hurry to be gone.

Kenna didn't waste that chance. The moment she got a good line on a fleeing dragon, she tossed her lasso. This time, she hit her mark, pulling tight to lash the thing around its middle. It went down.

"Damn," I said. "I think that was a Mount."

She didn't even gloat. "We gotta scare the big one off, or your trap is doomed," Kenna hissed, deftly tying the new dragon to an exposed root.

I faced the river clearing again. By my count in the bad light, the cage trap had four dragons in it already, and several of the smaller rope traps had snared the ankles of another two dragons.

However, none of our prisoners had realized they were trapped yet. Their dinner still had meat left, after all.

Well, they noticed now. Sounds of distress peeped and squealed from behind the cage's collapsible bars as its inhabitants tried to flee the approach of the Airship dragon. A Shoulder dragon screeched and then started splashing loudly in the river, its ankle snare pulling tight as it tried to take flight. Worse were the sounds of bones splitting and crunching.

The Airship dragon prefers bone marrow... yikes.

It had let its buddies feast on the soft bits, but whatever kind of dragon this was, it didn't like sharing its favorite snack. My stomach turned with each passing second as I kept my eyes glued on the cage trap, knowing I might end up battling a dragon the size of a house just to keep my haul.

Fighting an orc or two was nothing, but dragons were far more intimidating. They were larger, smarter, and easier to spook. If one ran over you or fell on you in the heat of battle, you were dead—even if it was running away.

"All right, on me," I said. "Let's make this bad boy do a dine-and-dash."

I pulled a torch off my back, where I'd had it crossed with my sword. With a flick of my magic-enhanced tinderbox, I set the torch to burning, quickly lighting the tar substance on the fabric-wrapped tip.

Will all those glassy eyes turning to me, I rose to my feet. I held the torch tight in my left hand while I drew my sword with my right.

Kenna notched an arrow behind me, and together we stepped out of the tree line.

When we exited, a pair of massive silver orbs shifted from the trap to us. I didn't slow, edging closer to the monster. It was silver or perhaps gray, the difference hard to discern with the torch flame in my field of vision. The shadowy dragon sniffed intensely in my direction. Its head backed up and turned sideways, as if it had smelled something strange. Inquisitively, it started to watch me.

I paused. I'd expected anger or posturing. Instead, the dragon retreated, stepping across the river and sitting on its haunches on the other side. The copper dragon had done much the same, and the two now sat together like old friends.

"All the bodies are scraped clean, except the one in the cage," Kenna noted.

Inside the trap, the four Mount and Shoulder-size dragons kept munching on the dead orc's corpse, with several fixating oddly on his feet. The body still had plenty of meat left, but the bones themselves were visible now, and the Airship-class might want to eat their marrow. The cage might have filled up with dragons, but our catch meant nothing if the big gray Airship smashed it.

"Hello," I said, trying to portray confidence. The trapped dragons panicked at this point, crashing into the walls of the trap in their fight to get free. I winced, wondering how badly they were hurting themselves. None of them were able to break through.

I started advancing on the Airship again, approaching the tent-covered trap. When I reached it, I flipped a few hook locks to keep the smarter dragons from escaping once they were calmer.

"It's locked," I whispered.

"We need to run," Kenna said.

I shook my head, sensing the big dragon's anxiety. The Airship was a female, judging by her smoother head and smaller size—as big as a two-story house, instead of a three-story one. She was hungry and curious, but definitely skittish. She could have fought me, but I could read it in her eyes: she didn't want to risk her meal or her life.

And then it hit me. "It's the dragon from the arena."

Kenna nudged me. "What dragon? What arena?"

"I set it free the day I arrived in Dasvilla," I replied. "That's why her aura—why she *looks* familiar."

I squinted, scanning the aura closely. "She wants to be left alone," I said after a while, not entirely sure how I knew that. "She won't attack if we don't."

"You're mad if you think that—"

But I was already walking away from Kenna, stalking toward the river's edge to put out my light. As soon as I took my gaze off her, the big dragon snatched a skeleton off the stones and burst into flight.

"You're out of your demons-filled mind!" Kenna exclaimed.

I grunted. "So I've been told."

"I mean it! You're nuts!"

"Sometimes a man is told to rise to the occasion, only to surrender and die when he falters."

"What the curses does that even mean?" Kenna shot back, her face souring.

"It means let's get on with extraction." I tucked the darkened torch under an arm and grabbed a hold of a long side handle on the outside of the cage. We'd caught three apparent Shoulder sizes and one adolescent Mount, which was a great find, but too big for the cage.

Kenna didn't argue. She just grabbed the other side. We heaved the cage off the ground, infuriating the dragons within. They nipped at each other in pure frustration. I didn't even begin to study them because they weren't mine, not until we crossed the city's gates.

I did have to set them down once we reached the cart. From there, we went back to gas, muzzle, and bind the two Shoulder dragons that had fallen into snares. Once they, too, had been dragged back to the cart, I cleared a space on the vehicle for the cage.

All the while, the copper dragon watched us. I didn't try to catch it again.

⸻

When we were ready to lift the cage trap onto the cart, Kenna bent her knees to match mine while our relit torch pissed the dragons off. They kept spitting their various breath types at the flame, so we'd placed it at the front, away from both of us.

I counted off. "Three, two, one...."

An ice dragon killed the flame with its cold breath, but we ignored it, grunting with every ounce of our power until we got the cage onto the cart. With the fire out and the cage stabilized, we proceeded to clean up our mess.

Once finished, I tossed my supplies back on the top of the cart, extracted a new torch, and lit both torches again. Once I had them going, I set them in holders on the side of the cart, lighting up the path ahead of us.

Upon seeing the dark forest, a wave of worry washed over me. *That was reckless,* I told myself. I'd been mad to take my eyes off the big silver Airship dragon, and my mind replayed the moment over and over while we finagled the cart across the worst parts of the game trail.

The more I thought about it, the more I thought the big dragon had remembered me. More importantly, I had sensed its mood.

And the more I thought about it, the more it seemed like dragons *liked me*. I had no idea why.

One thing was certain: the guards at the gate were going to be in for one heck of a story when Kenna and I arrived.

That was, *if* we arrived.

Scanning the darkness, and with Old Charlie watching over us, the two of us plunged into the night.

Chapter 49

Hot Water

WE FOUND a place to camp inside the walls of a construction outpost about halfway between our trap site and Caliph.

For a fee, the soldiers manning the post allowed us to set up a tent inside their walls. It was noisy, as carpenters were busy building a watchtower within the enclosed area, but we wouldn't get waylaid by orcs or trolls in the night. Worth the cost just to have a good rest.

While Kenna set up the tent, I found the lead soldier for the site, an Officer Second-Rank. These guys were the types that got put in charge of small operations, like scouting, recon, and road-clearing. This was an offshoot of the latter.

As I handed over the spears we'd found in exchange for a few silver coins, I asked, "Is the count serious about building a road all the way to the ocean?"

The officer grunted, his muddy skin flushed from drink. I'd caught him on his off-hours, but he'd been bored enough to look over my unexpected wares—which he had, unfortunately, recognized. I think that was why he'd been drinking. Half his scout parties weren't returning.

"Aye, he's plenty serious. Problem is, he puts more value on a foot of road than he does a soldier's life." He turned, leaning the spear against the wall behind him with the other one I'd reclaimed from the orcs. We stood in a sort of common room, a hastily-constructed log cabin housing a keg of ale and a crackling fire. He'd bought the knives off us too, and they lay scattered on the low table between us.

I laced my fingers together, thinking. We'd caught a good variety of dragons, no two the same color, but I didn't know which were hybrids and what abilities the purebloods had.

I leaned closer, tapping the table. "Now *that*, my friend, is dragonshit. A soldier is worth more than a damned road." I shook my head, not bothering to hide my anger. "But hey, I've got a question. How much value, monetarily, do you think the count is putting on each foot of road?"

Soldiers cost money, after all, to feed them and pay them and house and equip them. If the count was sinking all that into a road—

"It's worth a handsome copper, that's what. I just bought my own weapons back from you, didn't I?" the officer said, waving a hand at them. "And look, we've got ale. Keg after keg of it. I got requisition money out the ass, so long as I show results. And we *are* gaining ground, little by little."

My thoughts whirred, as if a wind dragon were passing through my head. "Well, friend, I'm hoping to have a nice little surplus of Mount-class tame dragons by month's end. I can rent them to you at volume, at a reduced cost, to help keep your men safe."

Even a Mount would be a decent deterrent against orcs, but if I could get my hands on a Hauler....

The officer huffed in disbelief, eyeballing me as he raised his tankard. "No dragon obeys a stranger that easily," he said, taking a swig. "It's taken months of training each one, and you'd get rental income the whole way. I see your game."

"No game," I said. "Just an offer. It's not a sure thing, and you don't have to sign anything."

He put his lips to his ale, and just watched me like that, before putting down the drink again.

"You're green at dragon-raising, son, I can smell it on you. But sure. If you can get me some tame, *pliable* Mount-classes, or even Shoulders, anytime in the near future, I'd pay all I got to rent 'em. It ain't gonna approach the normal rental rate, though, so it depends what discount you're talking."

I suppressed a smile. Once a dragon knew that it was walking around with orc bait—read: a human—it would be happy to trail behind said bait and protect it by eating any orcs that came along. At least, the dragon would after I was done with it. Dragons tended to prefer scavenging the freshly dead, but if I could convince them to actually attack....

"I'll start with a low introductory rate," I replied. "Then, when we prove our efficacy, I'll take the count for all he's worth—but no more."

That ought to make him think twice before throwing troops in the meat grinder. He couldn't pay all the death fees to the families if he had no money in the budget for anything but dragons.

The officer cocked an eyebrow. "You sure are confident, son. I hope for my troops' sake that you can put your money where your mouth is."

I rose, and we shook hands. "I hope so, too," I said, because he had a damned good point. Why did I think I could do this? All of this? My ideas with Becki, the sneaky merchant trick with Rachel, training all these new wild ones with Jolene, and now this? Was I mad?

As I walked out of the building and headed for the tent, I thought about this new confidence, this new feeling inside of me, and I realized something: it was the dragons. Somehow, I'd never really been in proximity to them for more than the duration of a single flight.

But now that I was getting to know dragons left and right, they had awakened something in me. Whether it was some huge, unnatural dragonbond or something else entirely, I didn't know —but for the first time since I'd loved and lost, I had meaning again.

These dragons were the purpose I'd been looking for. And when anyone gave me a purpose, I went out and did it right.

———

After dropping off my things in our double-size tent and paying a few guards to watch the dragons, I told Kenna I was headed to the baths.

She stretched her arms up behind her head, following me out of the tent. "Sounds like a plan, boss," she said.

In these sorts of encampments, the bath house was always located opposite the latrines, so I headed in that direction. The communal house appeared rickety, and when we stepped through, I found a series of six wooden barrels and a Mount-size rainbow-scaled dragon. All the barrels were empty, which seemed odd for this time of night.

The bath attendant handed us each a sizable piece of jerky. "Throw the jerky in the barrel you want, and ol' Suds here will fill it up with hot water."

I scratched the dragon under his chin, which was just above my head. "A geyser dragon, I'm guessing?"

The attendant nodded. *Good. I'm getting better at identifying them.*

After I had the dragon rumbling in pleasure, I looked around the huge tent and found only one corner with a privacy curtain. "You should take that corner, Kenna—"

But she'd already thrown her jerky into a barrel. Suds lumbered forward to snap it up, and then the sound of torrential rains hissed up from the bottom as the dragon vomited up hot, clean water that smelled slightly of boiled eggs.

I stepped back on instinct to avoid the spray, then caught myself staring as Kenna threw off her blood-encrusted coat.

"What are you doing?" I asked.

"What's it look like I'm doing? Bathing. You never bathed in a camp before?"

She was unbuttoning her shirt now, and the attendant was blushing. The man spun around to face the wall as the tanned bulges of her tits appeared, one inch at a time.

My mouth dried out, my cock twitching. As soon as the other guy stopped looking, Kenna shot me a grin, then flung her coat wide.

I nearly choked on the mere sight of those breasts, and my face heated as I threw my own jerky in the nearest barrel. The dragon descended upon it, then followed its training and filled my barrel.

"There's a reason they have privacy areas, you know," I said. Women existed in the armies, just like anywhere, but most didn't want to be harassed while they bathed.

"Yeah, and there's a reason no one else is in this tent," Kenna said over the sound of roiling water. "Cost me a pretty penny, you know."

My eyes shot wide, and I spun to point out that the attendant was still here—but he wasn't. Only the dragon remained.

As for Kenna, she now sat in her bath, her tits resting on her crossed arms atop the lip of the barrel. Her pink nipples were hard and tight, and she'd let her red hair down. It was only just long enough to be pulled into a tail, yet it fell in a nice wave, framing her chest.

Her smile left no room for imagination. She grinned cattily up at me, swaying her hips side-to-side, making the water swish. Her tits glistened with moisture as she said, "Won't you join me? Or are you a rare breed of Loyal Noble, who won't fall to temptation when a woman tries to lure you away from your betrothed?"

"Jolene and I are just friends," I croaked, as the dragon stopped filling my barrel.

"Sure you are." She didn't believe me.

The multicolored dragon yawned, then curled up on the ground beside my barrel to nap. Shaking myself—*all* of myself, right down to my poor, bereaved cock—I stepped up the small stool beside my own barrel and slipped into the water. Soap hung on a cord from the side, and I started scrubbing in earnest.

"Oooh," Kenna moaned, flipping over, dropping her head over the lip to watch me upside down. This made her tits flatten against her chest, the nipples pointing to the ceiling. She kept swaying, making the flesh move and bob. "Tell me what you're doing."

"I'm cleaning myself," I said.

"Yes, but what *part* of yourself?" she asked, one hand very obviously dipping into the water, reaching for the crux of her legs.

I ducked under the water, all of me, then breathed out as I rose and shook my hair out. I scrubbed at it, turning the water purple with orc blood.

"My hair," I said. "The back of my neck."

"Mmmm. I'm washing my thighs."

Sure you are, I almost said, to throw her own words back at her. Instead, I commented, "You would sleep with me even if I was engaged?"

She laughed, making her tits jump. My cock moved to match, and I took it into my hand and started cleaning it.

"Commoners like me don't get noble dick very often, at least not by choice," she said lowly. "I kinda want to know what it's like, that's all."

"My dick's no more noble than the next guy's."

She raised an eyebrow, her eyes dipping to my navel.

"Hmmm. Care to prove that?" she said.

Chapter 50

One of a Kind

I WAS ROCK-HARD NOW, with both my shaft and balls squeaky clean. I hurried to clean the rest of myself off.

"You didn't really answer my question," I said. "You would help me cheat on a woman?"

She shrugged, straightening in the barrel, running her bar of soap up over her tits and then back down into the water.

"What can I say? I'm not a morality Enforcer. I get turned on when I see brave men kill monsters. And you killed *a lot* of monsters, *very* bravely. I can't help it if I'm horny. Now tell me what you're cleaning now—"

I rose from the water loudly, making her whip around. Her slight intake of breath at the sight of my ass made me smile, and when I faced her, her deep green eyes dropped straight to my dick. As I stepped toward her, that gaze went hazy with hunger.

Then I rose onto her stool and took the back of her head in my hand. "I'm cleaning your dirty mouth out," I said.

I didn't even have to exert pressure. She shoved her mouth onto my cock like she was starving for it, instantly taking me the full length to the back of her throat. Her moan was so deep, so satisfied that I felt the vibration of it against my tip. I sighed, sinking my fingers deeper into her hair.

Three times she took me all the way to my base, until her throat closed and she made a choking noise. Then she backed off to tease my head and recover. She readjusted, draping her tits over the edge so I could see them under my reddened shaft. The nipples gave tiny, arousing little jerks as she sucked me deep again.

"You've been a bad girl, flirting with a man you thought was engaged," I said, and she moaned, cocking her head to one side and taking me into her cheek. Her teeth expertly grazed the ridge of my head, the pocket of her cheek catching my tip in a gentle, wet hug.

She pulled off. "I've been naughty. Punish me."

Turning her head the other way, she went down on me until her throat pulled tight. She took her hands out of the water and gripped my ass, one finger on each hand just low enough to tickle by balls from behind.

They swung as I arced my hips against her, and with her grip on me, she started tilting her head first one way, then the other, sucking my cock the way a normal woman might kiss a mouth. With each turn of her head, my tip had something new to savor —the twang of a molar along its biggest vein, the flick of a tongue over the fleshy ridge, the swirl between cheek and throat as she sucked me in a circle, every side of my penis getting a different sensation.

She moaned when the vein quivered, and one hand came around to hold my balls. She massaged them, and I knew she'd find them ever so slightly hardened, ready to burst. I pulled out past her pinkened lips, teasing her mouth with my head.

"Confess your sins, and I might forgive you," I said.

She heaved a breath, tits rising. With my cock still against her mouth, she said, "I want you inside me. A betrothed man."

"I'm not betrothed."

She licked me. "Maybe not, but a noble woman loves you." Every word brushed my throbbing head in a slight puff of air, her lips never breaking contact with my hot, ready skin.

"What do you want me to do to you?" I asked.

"I want you to make me dirty—"

I thrust into her mouth, cutting off her words with a loud *mmm!*

Pulling out, I said, "We're in a bath. It's going to be very hard to make you dirty."

She brought her hands up under my balls, then stroked them both up my shaft. She guided the whole member into her mouth, and sucked a few times. I leaned forward to see her ass in the water, big and wide.

She retracted, tickling my tip with several licks. "I'm sure you'll think of something," she said.

I bent my knees a tad more, then rode my dick up through her tits to her mouth. She received me with a moan, and I dropped both hands on her shoulders and started thrusting in earnest.

"Warren—give it—so big—yes," she said, fitting in one or two words each time I rode her tits, until I could press past her mouth again. I didn't go deep there, but her tongue played with me, her want obvious. Her toes curled in the water, her legs tight together, but she didn't dare use her hands to please herself. She knew what she'd done.

"You bad girl," I said. "You're gonna make me come."

"I'm sorry—please—I want it—on me."

I shuddered and forgot her tits, ramming deep into her throat. Her surprised cry buzzed against my head, and she squeezed my balls, and it sent me well over the edge.

Ecstasy knotted up in my mind, then unwound sharp and fast, the overwhelming crack of a mental whip. I groaned at the intense pleasure and yanked back, my cock bobbing up into her face. I gripped the shaft and aimed my seed, watching it lick across her lips, her chin, her tits. The white fluid oozed down into the crevasse of her boobs, and I ran my head over her, smearing it.

"Oh yeah, make me dirty," she moaned.

I dropped my cock and took one breast in each hand, gripping them hard, rubbing them together against my loosening shaft.

"Touch yourself," I said, pushing on her shoulder. As she backed away, I stepped into her barrel. The water remained hot, so much sensation against me. As my cock dropped in, the water held it in suspension, keeping it hard.

Kenna backed away to the opposite side of the barrel, which wasn't far at all. As I took my cock gingerly in my hand, my gaze dropped to her spreading legs, and the pink flower ripe for the plucking.

She ran both her hands down over her tits, leaving one behind to tease her own nipple as the other hand roved over her navel, until her pointer finger found her clit. I watched her rub the nub, and I stroked myself in time to her movements, drawing closer.

"I want you," she moaned. "Oh Warren, I want you."

"You want me? Earn it. Make yourself come."

"I can't. Not without you. *Please.*"

I let go of my poor tired cock. I wasn't letting the erection go, but it needed help to keep hard. I stepped up to her, bent my knees, and took one of her thighs in my hand. I folded it up and out of my way.

Slowly, I urged my cock into her. I groaned at the tension inside her, at the thick moisture and heat, so different than the water in the barrel. Her whole body shuddered, nipples jumping. I took hold of her other leg, and with languorous, unhurried movements, I thrust.

I began with small thrusts, meant to harden me, but it was plenty for her. That finger started pressing harder, circling in jagged, practiced movements that I wanted to memorize. I watched her deep pink folds enclose me, again and again, her body wide for my taking. Her hand on her breast gripped ever harder, turning the tanned skin white, the nipple paling. I could still see my cum on her mouth, on her chest.

"Demons, you're so big, you go so deep, *oooh,*" she said.

"Shut up and come," I told her. "I want to make you dirty again."

She nodded. "Yes, milord. I'll come for you. Just watch me. I'll—"

By the time her breath hitched and her channel spasmed, I'd gotten hard enough. I shoved her shoulders and head back against the edge of the barrel, and she threw both of them backwards, tits bobbing up as she released a sweet, fevered cry.

"Warren! Oh, fuck me, yes, *Warren*—"

I slid out of her, heaved her up, and edged my cock against her other hole.

"Now for the real punishment," I told her, making a circle as I opened her wider. It gave her time to tell me no, but instead she kept moaning in release. I pushed into her, and she cried out louder.

"Milord! You're too big. Too big for that... *Demons....*"

I eased into her, past the tight hole into the looser heat beyond. The water smoothed my passage, and when I'd buried myself to full length, she reached for her sex and curled two fingers into herself.

"Punish me," she said. "Warren, *punish me.*"

I kept it slow at first, which was the best way to do this, watching her flinch and moan, flinch and moan, flinch and moan. With time, the flinches faded, until only moaning remained. Then I went faster, her body adjusting around me.

I started losing myself to the possession of it, to the way this tough woman opened to me, letting me into every hole in her body. "Naughty girl, naughty, naughty. You get what you deserve."

Her fingers worked faster beneath the water, our joining warped beneath the surface. My gaze sank into her folds, and I went faster, tunneling into her, my dick still sore and taking punishment all its own.

Finally my pleasure came, and I called her name as the second surge of cum spat into her ass. I stayed there, draining myself. It was so good to come inside, even if it was a different hole.

"Stay," she said. "Just a little longer... stay...."

So I kept holding her until she came, too.

Afterward, in our tent, we didn't bother with separate beds. "You're really not engaged?" she asked, curved close against me, a tough woman made soft in our sheets.

"I want to court her, someday. But right now's not that day."

She laughed, because even here, Kenna wasn't the type to giggle. "I'm just one of many, aren't I?" she asked.

For the first time, I kissed her on the mouth. "Maybe. But you're still one of a kind."

Chapter 51

Warren the Crazy

"WELL, which is it? Lord Minax-Orpheus or Guardsman Warren?" the watchmaster asked.

Since we'd arrived before sunup, he was the only one who could open the gate of Caliph to let us in. Our arrival hadn't caused a massive stir, since dragons were hauled out of the jungle all the time—but the sheer numbers in our haul did cause the bored second-rank guardsman to get his boss when we'd requested entry into Caliph before sun-up.

Now that I stood before the watchmaster, I smiled. I accepted both documents back from him. "Oh, in this case, definitely Lord Minax-Orpheus. I only showed the other document to verify my identity."

"Four Demons.... Pretty sure you caught a bog dragon, but it'll take a dragon expert to figure it out. Plus one digger, a soil dragon. Farmers would pay a small fortune for eggs from either one of those. Not the wild ones, though. They're notoriously hard to train."

As he spoke, he jotted notes on a piece of parchment, focused on his paperwork. "Anyway, not a bad haul, kid. Now for the bounties. Valmin, verify their freshness, then burn them."

His adjunct picked up the orc ears one at a time, sticking a finger into the severed flesh part to get a fresh squish. After each inspection, he tossed them into a communal fire on the outside of the wall.

"Verified. Oi, Watchmaster. What happens when you send two third-rankers into the bush?"

His superior sighed. "They kill orcs, capture dragons, and do it in less than a day, apparently."

The adjunct laughed. "The joke doesn't work anymore, does it?"

No, it didn't. I remembered that same joke from my time in the guard. *What happens when you send two third-rankers into the bush? The whore charges them double, of course.*

"You hear that, recruits?" the watchmaster of the Guard said loudly over his shoulder. "This former third-ranker just pulled in a small fortune in orc ears with nothin' but a dragon captain to help him. You all gotta step up your game!"

With that, he handed me the parchment, sucked in a deep breath, and shouted, "Open the gates!"

I clasped forearms with Kenna, handing her half of the bounty for the ears while the gate rose ponderously off the cobbled road in front of us.

"Oh, no. You keep it," Kenna said. "Use 'em to get that farm up and running proper-like."

I glared at her. "We had a deal."

She smiled. "I don't recall no deal. You'd think I would, on account of me gettin' money for it. Anyway, it's high time you get a bath, milord. You're covered in blood." She bowed her head. "Well met, Lord Warren the Crazy."

I dropped the pouch at her feet. "Don't you 'well-met' *me*, Captain. You earned that. And if you don't think so, then you can earn it later." I leaned closer. "I could use some eyes and ears in the Roosts around here. And maybe a few extra stops in Dasvilla. Let's just say I'm keeping you on retainer."

She scoffed and slipped a foot under the pouch. "Oh, milord," she said, and with a rapid heft of her foot, she kicked the pouch up into the air. It landed square in the middle of my cart. "I'll be your retainer for free, if it means I get to stop by your manor now and then for the... ahem... *royal* treatment."

I rolled my eyes and picked up the cart by the handles. "Fine. You're my retainer, and I'll pay you in orgasms, apparently. But that still doesn't account for the fact I promised you half the bounties, and I keep my promises. So now I owe you a dragon. A Hauler."

"A Hauler? I already got two to run my flights," she called after me as I rolled away. "What would I need another one for?"

"To start your fleet," I replied. "And I'll take 10%."

Her laugh chased me, and my spine tingled pleasantly as her eyes followed me a little while longer. I'd make sure to invite her to dinner next Sunday, when she flew through the Dasvilla Roost.

On my way to Jolene's inn, I had to pause at a particularly busy intersection, which was odd for this time of morning. It was still dark, with color only just tickling the horizons and yet a long line of carts rumbled past. It appeared they were full of cobblestones and road-building supplies, with Mount dragons pulling them, prodded along by sleepy-looking masons.

As I waited for the convoy of carts, a stray cat picked its way out of an alley, wandering over to curiously inspect my haul. I picked a chunk of gore off my leathers and tossed it down to the cat. The feline neared the chunk of orc, sniffed it with a wrinkled face, then outright gagged in a very dramatic manner.

"Fair. All too fair," I said. I remembered watching the dragons feast on feet and bone marrow. They certainly had a refined sense of taste.

The interaction kept a smile on my face until I reached Jolene's inn, which was situated across the street from the bank. The city was stirring by this point, with early risers quietly opening doors up and down the street before shuffling down the side-paths toward their jobs. I paused to watch the nothingness happen. It felt ghostly and mundane, like a life I could have lived.

To the left of the inn's front door, a guard leaned against the wall. He watched my arrival with scorn, looking wide awake. He must be used to the overnight shift.

That reminded me of the overnighter at the inn at Ignace, which reminded me of Shimmer. I hoped Rachel had answers for me when I got back.

"We're closed," the guard groused.

"Lady Jolene is needed. She'll want to be woken. Five bronze," I offered.

He sighed. "I'm a guardsman. Can't accept tips."

"Ah, babysitting duty. I remember that from my time as a third-ranker." I looked him up and down. "But why in common clothing?"

The man noticeably warmed toward me upon finding out I'd been a guardsman. "Less obtrusive to the common folk. City General's got us posted all up and down the streets lately. The count wants the city cleaned up before the guys from the capital come through to see how the road is going.

"Anyway, no tipping. I'm just here to do my job, but thanks. I'll go find your lady."

Once he departed, I set five bronze coins on the ground near the door regardless, and waited. He returned only a few seconds later, bending down to pick up the coins as if he just happened to find them there. I didn't meet his eyes, and he didn't meet mine.

Five minutes after that, a very disheveled Jolene appeared in a nearby window, the shutters opening to both sides so that she could peer out. I was glad to see her showing a little caution, as I'd instructed. She could have just come right out the door, blindly trusting the guard.

Behind her, a pair of kitchen maids were setting up for the morning meal. Pans clinked and bellows whooshed. As Jolene squinted toward me, I stepped forward into the dragonlight that pooled before her window, knowing her vision hadn't yet adjusted to the dark street.

"Warren?" Jolene blurted. "Are you covered in blood?"

"Yes. Didn't get much chance to do laundry in the wilds." I bowed chivalrously toward her. "Fret not, my lady, for I remain unharmed. I simply found some human-killers on my travels, and I removed them from existence, as was my duty."

The guard snorted in approval—or maybe at my stoic voice—but Jolene said, "Lords don't go around hunting trolls, Warren. They have men for that."

"It was orcs, milady. An entirely different thing."

"You know it's not."

I smiled.

While she tried to think of another way to say *For fuck's sake, Warren, stop trying to get yourself killed,* the clop of horse hooves made me look back the way I'd come. Now *this* soldier was wearing his uniform. The all-black Enforcer couldn't be mistaken for anything else.

For a moment I thought he was coming for me—I certainly did seem to be the main character in everything lately—but he rode on past. When he drew close, however, a low rumbling hiss sounded from under the inn's front steps. Frowning, I hopped off the porch to peer beneath it.

There was a dragon under there.

"Seems we have a curious visitor. Were you following some of your friends?"

The rest of my dragons were quiet inside the cage trap in the cart, not sleeping, but definitely afraid. I'd thrown the orc tent fabric over them to keep them calm. I patted my shoulder, inviting the dragon to come up.

"Come on up here, little buddy, and I'll make sure you're reunited with your friends."

By this point, the Enforcer had slowed and was turning around after all, so he played witness alongside Jolene and the guard as the not-so-little dragon edged out of the shadows and sniffed at my feet.

It was far too large to ride my shoulder, nearly adult Mount-class in size. I stared in awe, unable to comprehend how it had fit itself under the porch. In the shadows, its color was unclear.

Jolene was still blinking away sleep. "What kind of dragon is that? It's so spiky."

I didn't get a chance to answer before the Enforcer got close.

"Wait, is there a body in here?" the Enforcer asked, picking up a torch to wave over the covered trap cage. "Demons! Feet too. Damn, that used to be at least eight orcs. Who are you?"

"A man on a mission," I said with a grin, keeping an eye on the wild, unfettered dragon. It might look to the Enforcer like it was my pet, provided it didn't attack him.

Jolene blanched from her spot at the window. "Wait, you caught a dragon with a *corpse?*"

"No, I caught seven dragons with eight corpses." I shrugged. "Seemed logical at the time. Anyway, sir—"

I turned to reply to the Enforcer's question, but he was turning green. His head jerked left and right, trying to fight his stomach. He lost the battle and vomited right there in the street, splashing his meal across the cobblestones.

His own Shoulder dragon peeped out of the riding cubby on his back, crawled to his shoulder, and hopped onto the cage, probably hungry. The dragons inside nipped at it, not wanting to share. The big horse nickered as if it were laughing.

The Enforcer snatched his dragon off the frame, tucking it under his armpit as he abruptly rode away, pretending that he hadn't just embarrassed himself. He'd never even gotten my name.

As soon as he was gone, the shadowy dragon fondly nuzzled against my leg like he'd done it a thousand times. I patted him and sighed, adjusting the tarp to better hide the gory mess beneath it.

"Come, Lady Jolene. I need someone to help me get these dragons into their personal cages for our return flight home."

"Oh for demonssakes, Lord Warren," Jolene scolded, dragging herself inside while closing the shutters. A few seconds later she popped out the front door. "Have you no decency, bringing your kills into a civilized city?"

"Hmm?" I murmured, already busy removing supply items from the top of the cart. I realized it wasn't rhetorical when she folded her arms.

"What?" I asked. "The only good orc is a dead orc. I've lost too many friends to their raids. Demons to them."

"By the flame! Warren, there's seven dragons in here, not one. And that thing at your feet makes eight...."

She trailed off, stepping close to me to get a better look at my new buddy. She smelled of honey soap, and she looked more rested than I'd ever seen her. Her cheeks gleamed with vitality, where once they had seemed sunken. I mourned the fact her cloak was cinched all the way to her throat.

"Those back spikes... I've never seen a hatchling with anything like that."

I blinked at the dragon, which chirped. "How can you tell it's a hatchling? Could be an extra-large Shoulder."

She tapped its snout, which would have been insane for anyone else to do. She had mentioned losing fingers, though, so I figured she often touched without thinking.

"No teeth," she said. "Just a line of cartilage. A sort of beak. Babies have that until it hardens, then breaks off when they start cracking bones. Teeth grow in from beneath it.

"Also, it's got a real high-pitched chirp, its spikes are still stunted, and its scales haven't settled on a pattern yet. The iridescence is what gives it away for most people, but the light is bad right now."

Another good find then, I thought. On further inspection, I realized the dragon was copper-colored, his scales flashing in the dragonlight.

"Oh, I recognize you," I said, scratching him behind a neck spike. "You're the one we *didn't* catch."

"You mean it followed you? From where? I still don't recognize the breed."

"We saw this one in the forest before," I said. "I think he followed the rest of them here. They had clustered around him in the woods."

"Maybe he's an alpha? But no, he's too young," she said, her face lighting up as she lifted the tarp to peer inside. "Holy Demons, Warren! *You did it!* And are those eggs too? Three eggs! A whole nest!

She squealed, rushing around the cart to look at every dragon from all angles. She clapped her hands and grinned like a little kid, then ran to hug me, only to change her mind at the last moment when she remembered all the orc blood I was wearing.

Jolene patted my shoulder instead, then cinched the rope belt on her cloak tighter and redid her bedtime ponytail.

"All right, let's do this!" she said. "It's time to bring our new babies home!"

Chapter 52

She's Not My Wife!

WE RENTED space at the Roost to prepare our shipment. Every dragon found its way into a different cage, which Jolene said was important until we knew their temperaments.

I had filled eight of my ambitious ten cages. I stuffed the eggs into the last one, securing them with my tent and bedroll to make sure they wouldn't get broken.

When we were finished, I dropped the final bag of supplies on the ground and sat on a bench. I'd handle selling all my stuff back in a minute, but for now, I needed an update from Jolene's end.

"So, how'd your studies go?" I asked her.

She was busy looking over every dragon, taking notes, identifying them and letting them sniff her.

"Oh, decent," she said distractedly. "Ironically, the highest-cost market item right now is wild male dragons. A lot of people in Dasvilla have bought dragons for a song from Pinnacle, but most of ours were female, and now everyone wants to mate them with something big and strong."

"I thought you said that wouldn't work."

A little green dragon snapped at her, and she scolded it. "Bad! *Bad...!* But yeah, it won't work. It'll be a big mess. Those nobles just want the status of owning their own arboretum, like the Biscuits have. The duke's made them even more of a status symbol over there.

"Anyway, we can buy unruly dragons that no one wants in Caliph, and sell them for double in Dasvilla. They're pretty decent guard animals once they've got a month of training, so it's not some con."

And I'm wondering where they will hire that training from, I thought, grinning. If the Biscuits even offered that service, we would undercut it.

Jolene stuck her hand into another cage and pointed at a rather plain small dragon, mottled yellow and brown.

"That's a wild hybrid, and it's half gold dragon. They're common near commercial cities like Caliph, since they follow merchant caravans around.

"In Dasvilla, though, even a half-gold sells for a gold piece. Nothing crazy, but to fly him home is only a few silvers, so the profit margin is there. You just have to find a buyer, but we can't flood the market with them, or their value will go down. Might be better if we drained it first, since it's male."

I had some idea what she meant by "drained." After all, Kenna had done it to me the night before last, and once again on a rest stop today.

"Uh, shit. I was hoping he was worth more," I grumbled.

"Well, no. He's the most common dragon seen around people. Still, he sells for way more in Dasvilla than anywhere else."

I found this fact curious. The Biscuits had basically stolen Pinnacle away a dragon at a time over fifteen years, but they had the creatures all breeding in their greenhouses. It didn't seem like they were making use of their own market. What was their game, if not to sell dragons? I'd seen a lot of nests full of eggs.

"This girl, though," Jolene went on, pointing to a bicolored white-and-pink, similar to Becki's Princess Collette. "Twelve gold easy, maybe fifteen, and she's eating this orc leg with abandon because her stomach is definitely swollen with eggs. I could have altered Pinnacle's future with her alone."

"Oh, great," I said happily. "Then I did well."

"You sure did. I've got a feeling this copper one is worth even more, but I'll have to get out my bestiary to try to identify him."

I patted the little guy, who had graciously hopped into a cage for me. "Aw, him? I don't know. I might not want to sell him," I said, but Jolene put a hand on mine when I went to open the cage and scritch my new buddy under his chin.

"Uh, Warren. Don't. We need to get them all to the Roost for an early flight home, and if we open the cages, we risk them slipping out."

I pulled my hand back. "They won't have to be exposed to the wind, will they?"

"No. I already booked us a private cabin, essentially a confined space. This brown one over here, he *especially* can't be taken out without a secondary enclosure around him. He's liable to eat your face off."

I didn't say anything about how she'd been petting the beast a few minutes ago. "What kind is it?"

The guard in the aisle between Roost rooms suddenly spoke. "He's a juvenile clay dragon. They're right killers. A lot of the adventurers and officers use them because they're great at sniffing out orcs."

Jolene and I both startled when the man spoke; he'd been standing there so still for so long. But I couldn't blame him for being bored.

He smirked at me. "Wait, how do you not know that?"

"He big man. He hunt. He smash. He catch," Jolene joked in a monkey-like voice. I rolled my eyes while the guard bit his lip to hide a smile.

I tilted my head at her, raising one eyebrow.

"Oh, fine. He's actually very smart, but this is new to him," she told the guard.

Satisfied, I scanned the brown dragon again. I thought back to Vital, the blood-red dragon that the assassin had ridden. She must have been a hybrid clay dragon, not full-blooded, since she'd been brown-red and not full brown.

"Anyway, a clay dragon is worth a bunch to the right bounty hunter and...." Jolene ducked, peering up through the cage. "Aw, it *is* a boy. Darn. That means he's not worth as much and he's harder to train, but they're still semi-rare. We could sell him here, but only if we *don't* drain him. The right buyer will be able to tell."

"No. We're not selling." I said.

Jolene folded her arms. "No?"

"No. We're a dragon farm, so we need dragons. I can always catch a female, then we skip the stud fee. We already discussed this," I said, grunting. "I'm not in this for wild eggs. Our goal is to improve Pinnacle, and Dasvilla by extension. Meaning a warrior dragon who eats faces is something we could use."

She sighed again but didn't argue, instead pointing at the second-to-largest dragon before the copper hatchling. "This is a horizon-quartz hybrid. They're diggers, always going after geodes, but also really fast in flight. You can use them to send messages, or lead them up and down a freshly picked field. They'll churn it into fresh soil ready for planting in a day or two if you have enough of them.

"Outside of that, they're rather docile and boring, easy to domesticate and breed. They're not great at pulling or hauling, but they're vegetarian, so less threatening than most dragons overall."

"Damn, girly," the guard said. "You know your shit. Whatcha doing with that guy, exactly?"

She ignored him, but I shot him a look, and he paled. He did have a point, though. Once again, I found myself impressed with her knowledge.

"This one also looks like Collette, Becki's dragon," I said.

Jolene hovered our dragonflame lantern over the hybrid, high-lighting the pink-and-white scales. "Hers is part snow while this is part quartz. Far less pretty, too—more white than pink—and it's male. But he can breed with Collette, and they might knock out a pure horizon dragon."

Now *that* gave me pause. "What? Two hybrids can make a pureblood?"

"Yeah. There's a one-in-four chance, if the hybrids share a type."

Well, I'll be damned. That expanded my breeding options even more.

Jolene huffed, rubbing her hands together happily. "Five males, two females, and one is pregnant. Plus your lady copper. Great haul."

I didn't notice until now that my hand had wandered into the huge hatchling's cage, and I'd been absently petting its head spikes for some time. It purred in that thunder-like way dragons had.

Damn, I was just as bad as Jolene when it came to sticking my hands where they could be bitten off. I wondered if it had something to do with the dragonbond.

Wait. I did a double-take. Did she just say this was a female? I looked at the dragon again, but it remained just as spiky as ever. The males were supposed to be spiky.

I let it pass for now; Jolene could tell the gender later. "And if we sold them all here?" I asked her.

She tilted her head from side to side, mulling it over for a few seconds. "Fifteen, maybe twenty gold if we're lucky. Almost all of that goes to the pregnant one. But all her eggs could be sterile, and they'll value the dragon as such without proof of her breeding, so selling her now is just a bad idea."

"And in Dasvilla?" I asked.

"Selling seven dragons takes time at the market, but not too long. Like I said, they want males. They would see the value." Jolene puffed her cheeks then exhaled. "Fourteen gold probably for the males all together, minus your clay dragon. And they'd gamble on the eggs being good for this female, so we could get five more for her."

"Nearly thirty gold," I mused. That was almost a year's worth of orphanage funding, at least back in my day. "Good. I think I like being a dragon farmer."

"No, you like killing monsters," Jolene said. "The dragons are just a perk."

I snorted. "We can argue about which part is a perk later. For now, the sun's rising and our flight leaves in a few hours. We'll load the dragons first.

"After that, I've got to sell some of these supplies back to town, and use that money to find me a few more females at market. The rowdier they are, the cheaper they'll be, and I'll want the absolute cheapest."

"But—don't you plan on using the supplies again?"

"No. I can build more cage traps myself, now that I know how they function. Now come on. We've only got so much space in one of those staterooms, and I want it full to brimming with dragons."

Jolene curtsied. "I'll go find a porter to help us load them up." Her blue eyes rose to mine, and I found her gaze moist with emotion. "And Lord Warren... I'm very proud of you. Very. Thank you for saving Pinnacle."

With that, she scampered away, practically vibrating with excitement.

"Ain't seen a woman that excited since my ma saw me out the door," the guard said, proving he'd been eavesdropping the entire time. "Congrats on yer marital joys, chum. I can never get my wife that happy."

I heaved out a long breath. "She's not my wife. Just dedicated. She drove her business into the ground trying to make her pets happy. She's going to be pissed when she realizes I'm focusing on profit."

He laughed. "Whatever you say, chum. But seems to me that *she's* not the one wanting to keep them all."

For the first time, I took a good look at the guard. He was just like the guy at the inn—an appointee of the count, stationed to keep Caliph crime-free until the important nobles arrived. And after that, they'd be sent off to the road-clearing once again, leaving the commoners to fend for themselves.

"Yeah, well," I said, my gaze drifting to Jolene's retreating form. "Some things are worth more the longer you have them."

"Only if you treat 'em right nice," the guard replied.

I smiled. "I completely agree."

Chapter 53

Anatomy Lessons (and Not the Fun Kind)

THE EARLY MORNING crew at the Caliph Primary Roost—the town had four landing roosts, one for each direction of the city —welcomed us with huge smiles. I'd expected the overnight crew to be grumpy and sour, but I was pleasantly surprised by their hospitality when we brought up our dragons for loading.

"Ah, this one's a beaut," the porter said, grunting as he set down the cage with the large hatchling inside. He then knelt down and patted the top of the cage, as if he were petting the dragon itself. "Ah, that copper's pretty in the sunrise. Ain't you pretty, girl? Ain't you?"

And there it was again—someone calling my copper dragon a female. "How can you tell it's female?" I asked. "I thought the males were spiky, with sharp snouts. It has both of those features, even if the spikes aren't fully grown yet."

I could sense the creature through my mystery bond, but at such a young age, it didn't have much sense of its own gender. Typically I could only sense gender if the dragon was a mother, or in heat, or territorial. Other than that, gender didn't quite factor into their auras.

"It's the jaw shape," the man said. "It's wider. There's more room inside the mouth to hold food for long periods, so they can kill something and store it to feed to their hatchlings.

"And the scales under the chin are finer. That's so they can stretch the skin to store food. Sometimes, they can use it to store their eggs for short travel stints, as well."

I gave a low whistle. This guy knew his stuff, and so had the guard down below, in the cage area of the Roost. If I had to guess, people who loved dragons tended to go into dragonflight jobs, in order to be around the creatures more often.

As the rest of the crew happily fed the remaining orc viscera to their big fliers, the captain let us bring our cages into a private room at the front of the flight·platform. This was an Airship-class dragon, so the stateroom was small but doable.

Unfortunately, the pregnant pink dragon somehow escaped during transfer. The staff helped us corral the mischievous wildling into her cage, laughing the whole time, and feeding her treats. According to them, dragons grew far more docile after a heavy meal.

It seemed they were right, because she fell asleep once they had her back in position. I reinforced the cage lock and tied a burlap sack over it, just in case.

Overall, the packing process was enjoyable, and I could *feel* the passion rolling off Jolene and the workers. It was rubbing off on me.

I paid their manager for a day's worth of housing, then gave the crew a bonus out of my arena money. Jolene gave me the side-eye at my over-generosity, but I had a feeling I'd be back here again soon, and I could use all the goodwill from the Roost workers I could get.

"Sometimes, you invest in people, not just merchandise," I whispered to her afterward, as the ship's first mate graciously led me to a communal shower the crew used on the Roost.

"Case in point: they're letting me use their facilities to clean the post-battle grime and blood off me. One of them even let me buy a pair of clothes off him. They didn't have to do that, now did they?"

"I guess not," she grumbled.

"Otherwise, I would have had to rent a room just to wash. And that would have cost even more, right?"

She didn't answer, just took my dirty clothes and left to throw them out. But I figured I'd given her food for thought.

After we neatly stored all the dragons, the manager of the Roost cages offered to house my next haul of dragons at a cheap rate.

"The small variations are easy enough to handle," she explained. "The Roost has ample space to keep them confined. This *is* the dragon trade capital of the kingdom, after all."

"So I've heard. But if it's so popular, why are the cages empty? No one seems to be renting."

The older woman harrumphed. "Yeah. We gotta keep half the place empty at all times now, count's orders."

"You mean half of it is set up as a trap."

She nodded. Most Roosts served multiple purposes. They were flight platforms, storage areas, and large-scale traps for wild dragons, depending on which level you were on. Each level could be converted to a different use fairly easily, just by moving a few wall partitions around.

"Yeah. He wants the lands cleaned out so that—"

"So his road project can go faster?" I guessed.

She snapped a gnarled finger. "Right on the silver, son. Everything's about that road project anymore."

I had to agree. It seemed the count had involved absolutely everyone in his little pet project, and now, he wanted the king involved, too.

A road to the ocean. I turned to the horizon, where the nearmythical body of water supposedly existed miles off. I'd never seen it, but I bet a whole bevy of Water-type dragons lived there, rare in Parshil, and ripe for the picking.

In fact, why hadn't the kingdom built a settlement out there anyway? And why bother with an actual road?

I pondered this as Jolene and I headed back into the city, since our flight left in late afternoon. By this time, the sun had risen and the city roared with life. My first stop was to a tea-cart, where I gulped down an energy tea and ordered a nice breakfast wrap filled with eggs and chicken meat.

Jolene was thin, a bit malnourished honestly, probably from working herself so hard. So I bought her a wrap, too. She scarfed down the food, her table manners not unlike those of a dragon.

She clearly didn't worry about how I'd react to her, and most men might have been disturbed. I smiled the entire time, in wonderment. What sort of parents had she had, that she'd become so down-to-earth while still being noble? I wished I could have gotten to know either one of them. I'd known Lady Etonia to be a good woman, but now I had even more to thank her for.

When I ordered a second breakfast from another vendor, she didn't ask for any, but I handed her half of the pork skewer and she nibbled on it until we neared the entrance to the creature market. She popped her fingers into her mouth before we arrived, cleaning herself off.

A stern determination took over her face as we stepped through the archway into a gated pasture stuffed with tents.

I was certain she missed her dragons, but the excitement of Caliph was making her eyes glimmer again.

"Okay, dragons are plentiful everywhere," she said, "but it is important to remember just how much bigger this market is than anything else in the kingdom. The only market that rivals this one is the capital in Parshil.

"In both locations, it will seem like dragons are so plentiful they should be cheap, but look at how many people are here early in the morning. There are never too many dragons."

Images danced through my head, daydreams of tens of thousands of dragons teeming all over Pinnacle.

"Got it. Noted," I said. "Buy early, don't take the merchandise pool for granted."

"Which means *no haggling,*" Jolene said. "At least not until you have more training at it. Anyway, lets talk about utility types. There are hundreds of dragon varieties, but most are classified by their usefulness.

"For example, farming breeds are always in demand, typically by the crown, which pays good rates and then rents them to farmers at whatever cost keeps the crops growing steady. Farming dragons are typically herbivore-capable—meaning they can live without meat, although they're encouraged to eat rodents—since farm workers are afraid to work with carnivores. In fact, omnivores are often valued just for that one trait. I know, it's hard to wrap your head around, but—"

"I know this stuff, Jolene. Most cart-pulling dragons have molars rather than fangs. I've had to feed them as a soldier, when I was attached to caravans and such," I said, before holding up a finger.

"One rule remained the same even with leaf-eaters, though: don't stick your hand in *any* dragon's mouth, unless you have a grudge against your fingers."

Jolene proudly smiled. "Excellent. So, those are the Farm types. These typings are usually given along with their age, gender, and variety type during the sale process.

"For example, you might see a dragon listed as *Farm-1 Hauler, Cloud Horizon female.* That would be a Farm-utility, 1-year-old Hauler dragon, that's a cloud/horizon hybrid, and a female."

I was having trouble paying attention to her. She'd led us to the back of a long line that snaked into a huge closed tent; various roars sounded from within.

"Seems pretty self-explanatory," I said.

"It is, until you get the con-men trying to tell you a Combat-7 is actually a Farm-1, and you get yourself killed buying an experienced fighting dragon rather than the relaxed farming dragon you'd been told you were buying.

"Mislabeling is rampant around here, so beware. Some types sell better than others, and merchants are here to make money."

Our line inched forward. "And the other utility types besides Farm?" I asked. "You mentioned a Combat type?"

"Yes, the Combat type is used for violence of some sort. Those are the killer breeds that you normally see with adventurers or guardsman officers.

"Then there are Pet breeds, which are typically used as companions or for household chores.

"Transport types are those both large and docile enough to be trained for commercial dragonflights. Airship-size breeds are common for that, but some Haulers are used for it, too.

"Meanwhile, Mercantile breeds are better suited to ferrying goods or people around on the ground. Then there are Spell breeds, who are more varied, with more subclasses."

"You mean the ones suited to unique purposes because of their given magical abilities," I said.

"Yes. There are others, too," Jolene summarized, "but those are the main assignations." She took that moment to buy a clay mug of tea from a vendor who was walking up and down the queue selling drinks.

"But not all breeds always do what they're classed for," I guessed.

She nodded and took a sip of her tea before answering. "Exactly. Some businesses have guidelines, but the kingdom itself doesn't, so merchants can class things however they want —especially with hybrids, whose abilities can vary widely."

I smiled. Jolene was talking into her tea, trying to drink and speak at the same time.

Finally she gulped the last of it down and added, "The market itself is a bit chaotic, especially in areas where the Keepers aren't keeping close tabs on the market, but like I said, it can get extremely organized in some places, too.

"For example, in Caliph, there is a set of guidelines all the dragon farmers follow. Most of them have permanent shops, but they're in a sort of union that guarantees certain things to the consumer.

"Those standardized shops are the place to go. They'll also be anxious to sell off stock that's not producing for them. Sometimes they'll sell females that are out of cycle, or if they have more eggs than they have room to hatch, you can get them cheap in bulk.

"They're not concerned about the small fry, just about offloading them. They make their money on their trained animals, and the rest is window dressing to them. Some will also take favors or trade in advance, if they know that you're a farmer too."

My stomach dropped at that last part. *Oh no, Jolene. You didn't....*

Chapter 54

For the Love of Dragons

"LET ME GUESS," I sighed. "You did exactly that, and we owe lots of these guys money and favors."

She dropped her gaze to the side, looking like a chastised kid. "I... I thought I had to. I always thought our luck would turn. Mother didn't know."

By the Four Demons, this woman loved her dragons. If her mother had gotten her a tutor in economics, instead of planning for some soldier to save them, I think Pinnacle would be thriving already.

"It's all right, Jo. Just tell me—how bad is it?"

"It's... well. We owe something to everyone. But not enough for them to hate us... unless Pinnacle goes under. Then—"

She didn't get to finish. We'd reached the front of the line.

"Two bronze a head," said the guy at the front. He stood behind a tall wooden lectern, like a scholar at a guild hall or something.

I glanced at Jolene. "We have to pay to buy dragons?"

"Only the good dragons. Just do it. It'll be worth it, I swear."

Shaking my head, I held up two fingers for the man, paying four copper for us both to enter. The fee also bought me a white twine to wear around my wrist. Jolene got the same treatment.

She saw me looking and said, "It's so that we can go back in again if we leave."

Wow. This place had alarms going off inside my pockets. I scanned the crowd milling near the front of the tent, watched by a line of hulking mercs to either side.

They all wore the white twine, too. Maybe they changed the color of the twine daily so people couldn't sneak in multiple times on the same entrance fee? But couldn't the visitors buy their own colored twine?

I voiced this to Jolene, and she said, "The bands have a spell cast on them. At least, that's the rumor. I've never tested it. Not after I saw them throw a guy out, once. A dragon picked him up and tossed him. Broke his arm. The guardsmen said there was nothing they could do; he'd been trespassing on private property."

I raised my eyebrows. *Brutal.* Once we passed the line of leering security guards, I paused at a giant keg next to the fabric walls of the tent. I assumed it was water, since there were no guards or vendors manning the thing. It was unbearably hot here, and a drink sounded lovely.

"Do I gotta pay for this, too?" I said, pouring from the keg's tap into my traveling mug—only to find out it was ale.

"You'll pay with your good sense," Jolene said. "The booze is free here, but it makes people spend more. I'd dump it, if I were you."

I settled for sipping it. It was shitty, but it was liquid, and that's what mattered in this heat. The tent stretched for a good hundred feet ahead of us, and people were being funneled to either side. I could see stands of seating, like back at the training pit in Olinios.

I stopped. "Wait. Is this an auction house?"

"Sort of. There's always a main auction going on in the center, and they've got a sound-enhancing spell." She indicated a man at a table, who was currently exchanging a handful of coppers for what looked like a white dinner plate with the number 33 on it.

"You can buy into the auction, but don't bother," Jo explained. "You won't be able to afford anything they sell in the middle. The owners of the livestock have to pay just to show them. It's all so they can get top dollar for their best dragons."

After hesitating for a moment, I forced myself to move past the auction sign guy. My funds were dwindling. I wouldn't be able to buy any big fancy dragons just yet.

Jolene pointed along the edges of the arena—because that's what it was starting to look like, an arena. Vendors lined the oval fencing that enclosed a large dirt field. Dragons were everywhere; tethered to posts, in cages, magically kept asleep on carts for easy transport to their buyers.

The people attending the place never crossed the fencing, always staying in the stands or milling in front of the vendors. It was a circus in here.

"The center is magically reinforced in case a dragon tries to eat someone in the audience," Jolene said. "So you can only visually inspect the stock. If you like something, you and the vendor agree on a price, and he delivers it to you at the end of the sale day. Or you can hire a porter to get it delivered right away."

"And all of these vendors are farmers?"

"Yes—well, they're *representatives* of farmers. Pinnacle used to have a salesman here, too. The place itself is all owned by the dragon farmer's collective—you know, the thing that standardizes everything. They use the proceeds to uphold their rules."

Yeah, and I'm sure someone's greasing their pockets, too, I thought, as I distantly heard a voice cry "SOLD, FOR 500 GOLD! TO THE MAN WITH THE RED-FEATHER HAT!"

That was enough to buy a mansion, if my math was right. Yeah, I wasn't about to join in the auction.

381

"It's pretty overwhelming in here," I commented. "How do you propose we find two cheap dragons in this mess? Is there a spot for dragons that no one else wants?"

"Leave it to me. I know how to get things cheap," Jolene said, taking my hand and carving a path for us through the melee. She ascended the stairs when she got to them, taking me into the rows of stacked seating. It was quieter here, and she let go of my hand, still walking along the rows.

"Are you sure we can't keep using the barn?" she asked. "All these wild dragons are going to be a nightmare, but if I put Useless back at the villa, the wild ones should be able to coexist in the barn, so long as they each get their own cage. That's a problem for us in the future though."

"Useless is aggressive? How is she going to fare with Ravager in the Cage?"

I hadn't forgotten the half-wild swamp dragon that I'd thought was a fallen statue. I had her cowed for now, but she *had* attacked me. It could definitely happen again.

"It's a villa, Warren, not a cage," Jolene chided. She hadn't warmed up to my nickname for the place. "And you don't need to be afraid of Ravager just because she attacked you."

I stood dumbfounded for a moment, stopping right there in the stands. Jolene stopped and turned, cocking her head.

"I would think that's a *very* good reason to be afraid of a dragon," I sputtered.

"Oh, *pish,*" Jolene said, flapping her hand. "Ravager's a sweetie. She's just protective, is all. I think she sensed I was mad at you. She's ancient for a dragon, way older than she looks, and I was a toddler when she hatched. We've grown up and gotten old together, and she's like my best friend.

"You may have a way with dragons, but our bond is very intense. I was *gutted* when I thought she'd fled."

I sipped my ale with a nod. "Ah. I see then. Sorry for slapping her, I guess?"

Jolene started walking again, and I followed. "Oh, no, that was a good thing to do. Dragons aren't as fragile as us—a slap to them is more of a sharp tickle. But they do respect physical force, and she felt enough from you to back down.

"But thanks for apologizing anyway. She's a grouch, but I love her. I'm really very excited to go back and see her again. There hasn't been much time."

I made note of that, and turned my attention to the clientele here. As expected, most weren't commoners, because what commoner would drop two coppers just to enter a tent to buy things in?

"Okay, so this tent is where the serious buyers go," I said, returning to the task at hand. "The high-price auctions mean that the nobles and their families shop here, and when they're not interested in the auction dragon, they're shopping the vendors. So the collective gets good clientele all around."

"Yes, and because of the guidelines, they also get quality service, healthy animals, and sometimes they can even return a purchase."

"So the farms themselves are the money-makers in Caliph. There's no merchants or middlemen?"

"Oh, you can find resellers in the market area we just left. But yes, the farms are big names around here. The biggest ones...." Jolene sighed in admiration. "They can have three barns burn to the ground, and still be fine."

"But you don't get deals from them unless they have bad stock," I said.

Jolene hopped up on the bench of seating and started walking on it, her arms out to her side to keep her balance. She was enjoying this whole teaching thing.

"Okay, back to it," she said, spinning back toward me. She held up a finger. "The term 'deal' in the dragon world is a fallacy. All dragons are expensive, but they are still valueless as individuals unless they are correctly utilized."

Yeah. She was in the zone.

"Expand on what makes a dragon valuable," I asked, sitting down. I let my eyes wander the crowd below, thick as a Behemoth dragon's tail near the fencing that surrounded the sales arena.

Over the center of the tent, a hole had been cut in the fabric to let in cheap light, since lighting the whole place with dragon-flame would be costly. Through the hole, a light scattering of clouds threatened to worsen, its edges dark gray. I closed my eyes when a breeze found me, but it fled just as soon as it came.

"Collette is a great example. That dragon hated me. We just.... *Argh.* We didn't get along at all, and she never once cast magic for me. She couldn't pull anything, she couldn't do tasks; all she did was rot away in a cage, being bred every cycle."

As she spoke, I noticed a few more animals in the ring. A pair of stray cats wove in and out of the feet of a pair of collared Mount-classes, their owners riding them as a part of some sort of demonstration.

However, because shopping for dragons was expensive and the market had a cost to enter, no vagrant or orphans lingered in any shadows. I was a little surprised not to see any pickpockets. Two copper was a cheap price to pay for access to so many distracted rich folks—but maybe the collective "took care" of them, too.

"Then she met Becki after the whole breakout incident," Jolene went on, "and she and Collette became inseparable. Some dragons are absolutely worthless to certain owners, you see. If Collette had had a return option when I bought her, I would have returned her, absolutely—but she didn't, and I ate a loss on her when the sabotage happened."

I got the sense Jolene was keeping us here while she waited for something, so I stood and climbed to the back of the stands. I flipped open a panel of the tent to look at the market area that surrounded it. Those stalls didn't sell dragons at all.

I saw clothing, dragon apparel—*people buy hats for their dragons? Seriously?*—jewelry, trinkets, saddles, cages, and more.

Basically, anything you could buy *for* a dragon, it was sold outside this tent.

All of it looked pricy, because it was. Only wealthy people or agents of the crown bought dragons. Or farmers, like little old me.

"I think I get it. The value is perceived, not guaranteed," I summarized.

She snapped her fingers, drawing my gaze back toward her grin, toward those eyes just swimming with fervor. In that moment, something inside me swelled and then ebbed again. It was like desire, but deeper.

I wanted to feel that same love for something. And I wanted that love felt for *me*.

Chapter 55

Life, Color, Power

"Exactly!" she said. "You've got it! Now you're ready to really shop."

I peered dubiously down at the nearest dragon vendor, who'd just given a price way out of my range to a passing noble. The nobleman bought the damn dragon, another clay. I was certain he had just overpaid.

"I'm not sure if there's going to be *anything* here that we can afford," I muttered. I'd earned enough coins from the orc bounties to cover the trip so far, but it hadn't exactly ballooned my purse after all the things I'd had to buy to catch and house the dragons. Funds were still tight, even if I could sell the males in Dasvilla.

"Oh, nonsense. You just have to know where to look," Jolene said, as an older couple strolled along the stands a few rows beneath us, holding hands. Did people seriously pay the fee to enter, just to do nothing besides walk, talk, and gaze?

"So illuminate me. Where do I look?"

Jolene slapped a fist into her palm for emphasis. "Now, if you know what you're doing," she said in a new, gruff voice, "you'd think you should veer away from the big farms with their big prices, but their guaranteed results are why smart money uses them."

At first I started nodding, because it was a decent pitch, and she'd already said as much. Then I recognized it for what it was: a pitch.

"Your father liked to say that, didn't he? The smart money bit?"

She laughed and dropped the voice, still standing on the seats. She seemed so at home on her own two feet, in her own body, that I wasn't even afraid she'd lose her balance.

"Maybe, but it has truth to it. Just step outside this tent. That's where you'll see people selling dead eggs as live, injured dragons as healthy, and mislabeling dragons in the hopes of fooling someone."

I jumped up onto the seat with her and slung an arm over her shoulder. "Well, they won't fool me. Because I've got you, right?"

She held my forearm with her hand, and leaned into me, making us both sway. I knew she could be clumsy sometimes, but this was purposeful. She was definitely flirting with me.

"I'd roll my eyes, but you're completely right," she said. "You might be tall, dreamy, a lady-killer, *and* an orc-killer, but you have a lot to learn about dragons."

"Yeah. So everyone keeps saying." I'd never hidden my ignorance. I'd only worked to remedy it. Shouldn't I get a little credit?

I went to remove my arm, but she snatched my wrist, keeping me close. My hand rested against the flat of her chest, too close to... other things... for my comfort.

"But even if you had lived in Dasvilla all your life, you probably wouldn't know the right things about dragons," she told me. "Dasvilla is a bit of an outlier. It's big on farming, so it buys plenty of Farm-utility dragons, no shock there. And while Pet-utility dragons make for cute collector's items, they're not what makes Dasvilla tick."

She nodded me toward the back of the tent, to a section of vendors that teemed with little rich kids and, surprisingly, cages full of farm animals. An entire stretch of cages inside the arena fencing hosted chickens, chickens, and nothing but chickens, so-help-us.

At first I felt like scratching my head, but then it dawned on me. The next cage held ducks, then chickens again, then pigs, then a pair of bevows—semi-aquatic algae eaters—in a tank. I recalled that bevows were fast-growing and able to breed quickly, yet very easy for predators to catch.

"Where do we get the food to feed the dragons?" I asked, letting a smile grow on my face. I'd let her have the floor for her answer.

"Well, ever since a late payment from Father to Bewbers Farm caused a falling-out between them, we've had to switch to a worse food supplier. When we couldn't afford that anymore, I started paying the street ki—I mean, the local orphans for rats or loose chickens.... Four Demons, that makes me sound horrible, doesn't it?"

I frowned at the chicken cages. *I guess we're too poor to buy feed here after all.*

"Sounds like something those kids would love doing," I said honestly. "Go on. Tell me the rest."

"Okay, but yeah, the rats and things were never enough. Typically I just go to the market and try to haggle or, ah... take up credit with as many different vendors as I can.

"The plan was to avoid upsetting people, so I could spread out the debts," Jolene admitted. "But only until we could afford to pay them back!"

You sweet summer child. That was never going to happen, not at the rate she and her mother had been going. *Four Demons, if only they had hired Rachel....*

I was looking forward to seeing the scribe again, and to seeing how she could magically turn my new dragons into profit, to maximize her 5% take.

"In Dasvilla, is there open farm space unused inside the city?" I asked, returning to the topic of feed. Jolene shook her head. "Okay, yeah, so feeding dragons seems important.

389

Should we breed chickens somewhere? They grow fast, right?"

"Oh, for certain, but chickens are pricier here than in Dasvilla. Not by a lot, but we definitely want to buy them locally. Feeding chickens is cheaper in Dasvilla, too, making them more prolific and thereby affordable. Bevows are no good, because our water's too hot."

With that, she nodded me toward the far side of the farm-animal chaos, and I sighed and stepped off the seating to approach it. She took my hand again, and it felt natural this time. She was making excuses to touch me more and more.

I should tell her about Kenna, I thought. If she wanted me to woo her the proper way, she'd have to wait until the farm was profitable. Until then, I didn't want to pretend to be someone I wasn't.

"So," I said, "assuming we attempt to raise chickens, we obviously need to feed them. Chickens will eat just about anything, right?"

"Yeah, and that makes them great to have around, but my dragons always chased them away." Jolene pointed at the first dragon eggs. "Alright, let's test something."

Thankfully, she led me down to a stand *past* the farm animals, where a pretty woman sat reading a book with an array of eggs sitting before her. She wore a wedding band on her wrist, tangled with the entrance twine.

In front of the eggs, a sign read *HEALTHY EGGS! You touch, you break, you buy! Costs vary.*

Magical lanterns to both sides of the woman cast light through the eggs. However, when I reached out, my hand stopped in midair as if I'd thrust it into mud. The air rippled in front of me.

I took my hand away, and the air stilled again. My hand was fine, not even a tingle. I looked at both sides of it, curious.

It's that barrier thing, I thought. Seems we couldn't touch any of these eggs, as they were behind the magical barrier in the center arena. The fencing even rose up between us; it should have reminded me. I wonder if it was the source of the barrier, or if that came from somewhere else.

I also wondered at the sign: *You break, you buy.* Did some people have a way past the barrier? If so, they probably paid for it.

"These are eggs nearing hatch. That means high-value, since they are proven viable but haven't hatched yet. Once they hatch, there is a good chance they will form a dragonbond with the first animal or person they see, which of course makes them more manageable."

I admired the eggs. They were so vivid, each one's flame pattern so clear, so alive... a red egg that looked like a polished ruby, a pale green one that looked like crusted verdigris, and a bright green one that looked like leaves behind glass.

"Ah. So I don't need to hold these ones up to the sun?" I said.

"No. If you can touch them, you can test them by knocking on them, but I wouldn't advise it. I knock my own eggs, but never a merchant's egg," Jolene said, while the woman continued to read, disinterested.

These eggs, I noticed, each had a number and a price on a little card beside them. Meanwhile, lock-boxes hung from the front of the fence, within my reach. Each one had a number matching an egg.

So you put the money in, with your name, and they deliver the egg later... and she never even has to interact with you.

"Anyway, instead of knocking on an egg, you can just snap or clap next to the egg to get the baby's attention. These are all healthy eggs, from Shoulder varieties."

"How can you know that? There's no size class on those cards, just numbers."

"This is a minor noble's station, not too different from what Pinnacle's table used to look like. He's known for just one size class of dragon, and I've never once seen him deviate."

This woman must be that guy's wife, then. "Okay, so these are all at what stage, and what is needed to hatch them beyond this point?" I asked.

Jolene offered me a coy smile. "I was hoping you could tell me. Check under the table; she has more stock."

I crouched down and found three crates full of blankets and hay, encircling several dozen smaller eggs about the size of my fist. I studied them using my new senses, and now that I was looking for it, I could tell what set these apart from other varieties: magic wafted off them, in higher concentrations.

That's because smaller dragons are more likely to cast spells for their breath ability, I told myself.

I ran my hand back through my hair, and focused on the auras of each egg. They pulsed with life, with color, with power.

All right. Let's see what I can do.

Chapter 56

Who Wants to Be Normal, Anyway?

AFTER MY INSPECTION, I said, "These eggs are very developed, but they still need a heat source. They'll hatch in six days... this one seven." My finger pointed at them one at a time, going left to right.

"Healthy, healthy, a sweetheart, avoid this one, this one will have two colors and—"

The woman snapped her book closed and glared at me. Apparently, the barrier didn't silence us. Not sure why I'd thought it did. I guess I'd just gotten lost in my—what was it? My magic? My dragonbond?

"If you want to do my job, feel free," the woman snapped. "If not, leave me the hell alone. I'm reading here."

Jolene blushed and made apologies, yanking me away from the stand. She led me over to another vendor with a row of eggs. This one had far more warning signs about touching, but all in fun, colorful paint strokes. I guessed this vendor sold to children, while their noble parents paid the bill.

Jolene whisper-hissed at me, "Warren! What the curses was that?"

I blinked, and then realized what she meant. My stomach dipped uncomfortably. Why did I keep doing things like that without consciously meaning to?

"I don't know. I just, uh... *looked* into the eggs and saw they were healthy," I said.

I pointed back the way we'd come. "That breeder we just passed was good. And these." I returned to the table in front of us, where the male vendor watched us curiously. "These ones are mostly healthy," I said quietly, "but the purple one on the end is dying."

The vendor's eyes widened, and he snatched up the egg. Jolene was already tugging me away again.

"Keep doing that," she said. "Judge things. Here, these!"

I walked up to the next line of vendors, making commentary as I strode from one to the next.

"Good, good, that one's gonna be big, good, bad, that one's not a Shoulder-size, sick, that one's a hybrid, this one is different, we don't want it—"

"Different how?" the male vendor behind the station interrupted, a puzzled frown on his face.

Once again, Jolene yanked me away from the booth until we stood in the middle of the stands again. "What the hell has gotten into you?"

I feigned innocence, even though the game was up: I'd have to tell her about my abilities now.

"You wanted to test me, so I told you what I saw," I said, still dodging her question. "I've never been dragon-egg shopping in my life—not before that barrel on the battlements, anyway. So if I'm being weird, I'm not aware of exactly how."

I sucked in a deep breath and leveled my gaze at her. "So what the hell has gotten into you to treat me like I'm crazy? I really don't appreciate that."

Her face twisted, quickly converting from troubled to comforting. "Oh, I'm sorry, I didn't mean to... Warren, you.... Look, humans can't see more than a floating image inside the shell. Look at that egg."

She pointed to one in a traveling cage on the belt of a noble, who was sitting in the seats nearby, eating sandwiches out of paper wrappings with his little son.

"In that, all I see is an outline moving." She turned to the shop owner whose eggs I'd just been judging. The merchant lifted his egg and squinted at it through a small magnifying lens, trying to see what made the dragon "different." He shrugged, giving up, setting the egg back on its little stand.

"What did you see?" Jolene asked.

"A pulsing aura with a monochrome hue shining *around* the casing instead of inside it," I said lowly, so the noble nearby couldn't hear. I wasn't exactly sure how I'd seen it either, but I could see the coloration and vibrancy as a code in a way. Something inside me translated the colors and tones as if it were second nature.

While it was odd, I was done questioning it. Whatever it was, it was going to make me lots of money.

"And how was it different? What did the aura mean?" Jolene pressed.

"It meant the thing had two legs, not four," I answered. "A birth defect."

She stared for a moment. "A defect? Or a different beast? Wyverns only have two legs."

I scratched my chin. "No. I think that one was just defective. And wyverns' eggs look different, right?"

"Well, they do look similar to dragon eggs, but they're distinctive because...."

Jolene trailed off, blinked, then abruptly hugged me. "Warren, I'm sorry, but you could really tell that the baby was defective just by looking at it? Because that's incredible!"

"What? Seeing an aura around dragon eggs that conveys information isn't normal?" I asked, with only a faint hint of sarcasm.

"No, it's not. But if you can really do that... I can teach you so much! No one can do what you can. You could pick nothing but females? *From eggs?*"

"Well, I can't tell gender yet, but I'm guessing I could figure it out once I study them some more. But I can tell the health really easy. There's an aura inside every egg, and the healthier the baby, the bigger the aura. It's the goop around them in the shell." I pointed at the noble's egg. "That one will hatch by the end of the day."

"You gotta be cursing me." Jolene batted her eyes at me, mystified and impressed—before she suddenly pressed a finger to my lips. My eyes widened.

"Stop, Warren. Please stop talking. If we have an advantage, telling anyone else about it is a very bad idea.... They'll catch on eventually, but until that happens, we should be careful about this."

I grunted, dipping my head in agreement. She had a point. The longer I hid my abilities, the more money we could make.

Jolene gasped, out of nowhere. I was starting to see that she often did things out of nowhere.

She seized my arm. "I'm going to take you somewhere, and we're going to hone this skill right now!"

Once again, I let her drag me. I'd have to find a messenger to contact the captain at the Roost, because I was pretty sure we'd be missing our flight.

Chapter 57

Whoops, I Fell!

"Now, what's a bad egg look like?" Jolene asked. We sat huddled in the private room on board our dragonflight, having barely gotten here in time to board. The ground swooped and swayed beneath us as the dragon beat its great wings, but inside, we were sheltered from the wind noise.

I rubbed my sore knuckles and said, "The auras are just weaker. I assumed weak auras meant the baby wouldn't survive or thrive."

She scribbled something on her scroll. I was pretty sure she was going to write a whole grimoire on just me and my abilities. I hoped she'd be careful with it.

"Hmm. We'll have to test it," she said. "We'll match your feelings and sensations up to the flame patterns."

"Oh, about those. I think I see them better than you do. They're all a part of the aura."

She shot me a jealous look, then scribbled down some more. I felt like I suddenly had a biographer narrating my life wherever I went.

"What happens to cause an egg not to thrive, anyway?" I asked, mostly to take my mind off the lurching feeling in my stomach. I was getting used to these flights, but during any form of ascent, it was hardly smooth sailing. Good thing every state-room came with a complimentary bucket.

"It goes like this," Jolene said without looking up. "A mother dragon sits on a nest and waits for her babies to hatch. When four eggs hatch and one doesn't, she leaves the fifth one with the others, who continue to keep it warm.

"She then finds a sheltered place for the hatchlings and the egg, and starts feeding the babies pre-digested food. Sometimes the fifth egg hatches late and it's fine, sometimes it hatches with defects, and most often, it doesn't hatch at all. Those are the basics."

"Yeah, but *why* don't they thrive? Can you pop the egg open and see what happened to it?"

Jolene huffed. "Opening an egg early is always bad. Always. That's not just me guessing or farmer superstition, it's just naturally bad, because the baby is going to be underdeveloped no matter which way you look at it.

"If it isn't hatching on its own, something is wrong with it; by cracking it open, you force it to enter the world underdeveloped. This leads to numerous health issues that there are simply no fixes for."

She still wasn't answering my original question, and I told her so. Jolene laid down her parchment and met my eyes.

"It could be anything. The egg could have been on the cold side of the nest. An insect might have gotten into it and done damage. The mother might have caused a hairline crack during laying. There have even been documented cases where a female of *one* breed laid an egg in another breed's nest, and the mother's heat just didn't match the egg's needs the same way.

"Or, an egg just needed an extra week because the dragon inside was simply larger-sized. The magical concentration in the nearby area—or within the baby itself—might be imbalanced, as well."

That last part got my attention. "You mean late bloomers could be *stronger*, magically?"

"Potentially, but if they are, they are also more volatile. Imbalanced magic is harder to control for mages, and it's the same for dragons."

I nodded, wondering how many powerful eggs I'd left behind because I'd seen them as weak.

Except... I was looking at their auras. Not their flame patterns, or anything else that other people seem able to see.

Maybe I'd been a good judge of power after all. Only time would tell.

"So it can be worth hatching even late dragons," I summarized.

"Yes, but big farms like the ones back in Caliph sell all their risky eggs, hoping to get any value before they're turned into pig or fish food. Buyers on a tight budget are willing to take the risks those big farms don't have time for.

"However, some of those cheapskates are in a big hurry, and they'll hatch babies early, and have twenty die before they get one that survives. This one survivor is usually very large or very strong, or else it wouldn't survive early opening, so those people end up getting what they want... but it's just a horrible practice. Sadly, it's a big part of the secondhand dragon economy. You can make a couple gold if you're lucky, or—"

The room tilted suddenly as the flight dragon banked, and Jolene toppled toward me with a distressed *eep* noise. With my back against a dragon crate, I caught her, but her arms ended up in my lap.

She blushed so red, she looked sunburned. "Are you—" I started to say, but then the damned dragon performed another maneuver that made the room *spin*. The ceiling became the floor, and I shouted as we slammed into it, and then began to slide back toward the door as the dragon dove.

At least, I hoped it was diving. If it was *falling*, we were going to die.

Jolene clung to me as we thunked against the wall by the door, still sitting on the ceiling. My brain couldn't make sense of the change in perspective. I held Jolene close and checked the cages, but they miraculously remained in place, thanks to all the extra knots we'd used to secure them to the walls and floor.

Jolene was quivering, both arms around my neck, her face tucked against my jaw. She pulled her knees to her chest, and I held her in that position, my arms tight around her entire folded body.

My pulse raced. The pressure against the wall eased, but only just; the dragon was still diving. Why?

Focus on getting us strapped in, first, I told myself. *If we fall wrong, we could break our necks.*

The bench, desk, and bed of the stateroom were all covered with dragon crates, but the hammock still swung from a peg on the wall. We'd taken down one end, but the other was bolted in to prevent threats.

Grunting, I used all my strength to rise against the diving momentum of the dragon, lifting the fragile Jolene along with me. She was tense, frozen, unthinking—which could happen when fear overtook a person.

With a cry of effort, I reached out and grabbed the hammock. The fabric bunched thick in my hand, like good rope, and I pulled my entire body toward it.

"Jo! I'm gonna let go of you. Hold on!"

I had to take my arm from around her, and she screamed and sagged, nearly falling. Her response was to cling even tighter to me, nearly breaking my neck as she put all her weight around it.

With my hands free, I could now go hand-over-hand up the hammock. Grinding my teeth together, with a vein popping in my neck, I pulled—

The dragon leveled out again.

I didn't let go, cursing as the room righted itself and flipped us both. I lost all my senses for a moment, everything going black.

I came to with the rope still in both my hands, and Jolene's body pressed between me and the wall beneath the hammock peg. She groaned as my vision spun.

I tried to back away to keep from crushing her, but the centrifugal force remained intense, and I was distracted by the open cage door now pushing against my head. It must have flown open somehow during what *felt* like a giant barrel roll. I looked over at the cage, dazed, and the copper hatchling looked back at me, huddled in the far corner of its trap.

"Go... see what's happening," I rasped, still trying to push away from Jolene, who strained against me. My weight was killing her.

The hatchling crept forward. Somehow, against all rhyme or reason, the force of the flight-dragon's movements didn't seem to affect the hatchling.

"Go!" I shouted, making it flinch and recoil. "Shit, I'm sorry... just please. Please make sure the big dragon is okay."

The copper dragon peeped at me, the sound birdlike and tiny. Then the little female scurried out of her cage.

I watched, heaving mightily against my own weight, as the dragon skittered over the door, then did something I couldn't see. The locked door swung open a moment later. A ravenous wind hurtled in.

The dragon seemed unaffected by it, her outline flickering amid the onslaught. The other dragons screeched and keened, but they couldn't escape. The copper turned around the corner of the doorway, and vanished.

I don't know what I was expecting her to do—but I hoped she would get it done fast.

Chapter 58

Copper Genius

By THIS POINT, I had Jolene pinned but able to breathe again. She'd somehow gotten turned back toward me, and her legs were wrapped around my hips while my forearms were pressed to the wall by my head. Struggling to turn her neck, she finally looked at me.

"Warren," she breathed, the sound raw, her eyes hooded—most likely from a head injury. The momentum pinned her arms to either side of her, so that to anyone seeing this without context, it very much looked like I had her pinned against the wall.

My cock certainly felt that way. It twitched against all reason, and her eyes widened slightly, although she remained dazed.

Well, that was no good—neither the head injury, nor the erection.

"Jolene. Jolene! Listen to me!"

Her lips moved, but no sound came out. Her gaze drifted, eyelids closing.

I ducked close, shoving my nose against hers, turning her face to mine again. I got as close to her as I could while still being able to speak. Our lips brushed as I tried to keep her conscious.

"Jo! You're not done teaching me. Keep teaching!" Anything to keep her awake.

"I... but...."

"We were talking about eggs. Ones that don't hatch right."

"Oh... when you buy the weak ones...." She squinted, as if not sure she was answering the right question. "Make sure to pick a bad egg... every now and then. If we pick the best of the bad... every time...."

"No one will believe it's luck," I finished for her. "Tell me more!"

Jolene blinked rapidly, responding to my closeness—to *all* of my closeness. Her legs loosened and dropped lower, twining with mine.

"We... we're not exactly sitting on thousands of gold... to rebuild," she said. "So pick the absolute best, and one or two bad ones, and say nothing...." Her gaze slid again. "The dragons are watching you."

I shot a glance left and right, and it was true. A dragon stared at me from every cage not still covered by a tarp.

In that moment, I realized this wasn't new. The dragons were always watching me, always curious about me. It went back pretty far, too; I could remember this same intensity in their gazes during my time as a guardsman.

It was hard to tell when it began, but I remembered the first time a dragon had stared at me: on that fateful dragonflight away from the capital, after my torture, a porter dragon had stared me down the moment I stepped off the flight deck.

I'd felt like a mouse standing before a hungry cat, then. But I'd become stronger since then. I think the dragons could see that, too. There was no longer scorn in their eyes.

All this ran through my head in that frozen moment, and before I could speak, the room twisted again. I went flying like a dog in a rolling barrel, and Jolene screamed, but she'd gotten enough wits back to hold onto the hammock.

I crashed against several cages, breaking one before thudding to the ground. My vision blurred as I slid toward the open door.

The wind had quieted. The ground remained resolutely beneath me; the flight dragon had leveled out. I grabbed the door frame, my whole body aching.

The copper dragon landed next to me with a series of clicks as its claws touched the ground, and then it flapped its wings once more, and settled into place. A streak of blood dribbled from its mouth, down its chest, and in a stripe across its left flank.

"Oi!" a man shouted, running toward us using a guideline. I recognized the first mate.

Still disoriented, I struggled to rise. The man soon had his hands under my armpits, helping me up. The wind blew, but we were on the lee side of the captain's platform, so it was quieter here than anywhere else.

The man reached for my door handle, bracing himself so he wouldn't get tossed out if the flight dragon banked again—but then he stopped cold, his eyes locking on the copper dragon, as if he was only just now seeing it.

Once again, I got the feeling the wind was having no effect on the beast. It just calmly stood there, unruffled, as if this was the ground on a calm summer day.

"Can you do something about that dragon?" the first mate shouted. I couldn't remember his name.

"Copper, in!" I said, nodding to the stateroom. The dragon stretched out its neck and trotted past us. The first mate remained tense the whole time, but I groaned and got my feet under me. One of my ribs felt like it might be broken. I'd need to see a healer back in Dasvilla... another cost. Great.

Finally, the first mate seemed to shake himself awake, and he helped me into the room and closed the door. I sat on the floor against the wall, holding my side, breathing lightly. A tiny brownish-white dragon—the one whose cage I had broken— nuzzled my arm, and tucked itself into me, resting its chin on the wound.

The first mate, a skinny, close-shaven man with a wind-burned face and green eyes, just stared. "You keep your dragons loose?" he asked.

"Not on purpose. But they're well-behaved... enough," I rasped. Damn, this was hurting bad.

The man watched Copper—I might as well give the dragon a name—with especially wide eyes. "And that one... she's yours, too?"

"Yeah. Why?"

The man ran a hand back through his hair, his feet spread and planted to accommodate any more sudden shifts of the flight dragon. As for Jolene, she had sunk to the floor just like I had, her blond hair wild and wind-blown, her face sweaty and pale. She looked lucid, back to herself, but she wasn't meeting my eyes. I worried the crates would get loose and fall on top of her.

"Wait," I said, my thoughts sharpening. "Wait, we were falling. Or diving. What happened?"

The man swallowed so loudly I could hear it, even over the wind from outside. He nodded at Copper, who sat eerily still next to Jolene, making no sound at all.

"We was—we were in free fall, milord," the man stammered. "Our big girl Bessa got a bird in her eye, just flew right into the socket. She went mad from the pain—well, you felt it."

My eyes slowly returned to Copper, to the blood streak staining her chest.

"Your dragon, it... she flew next to Bessa's head. And Bessa calmed right down. I don't know how, milord, but she calmed her, and then... then...."

All my pain suddenly fled, and I straightened. "What happened? Say it, man."

"Your dragon got into her eye!" the man blurted. "I don't—I don't know how, we could barely see anything, but next thing I knew, your dragon had a bird in its mouth and Bessa... Bessa's eye is destroyed, and she'll need a healer mage, but she can land us."

I staggered upright, the brown-white dragon crawling up my leg, then my back as I stepped toward Copper. I reached to pat her gleaming head, and she looked up at me, and *shivered*.

Her form broke apart at the edges, like smoke, and my hand passed right through her.

"I'll be damned," the first mate said. Carter—his name was Carter. "It's got a spell. Dragons that big never have spells—"

I shook my head. "No. It's her invulnerability. She's invulnerable to... shit, I'm not sure." The dragon's aura suddenly seemed so big, bigger than all the others combined, and it was dark and misty and diaphanous, like a veil over a corpse on a dew-dappled morning.

I raised a questioning eyebrow at Jolene, but her cheeks went rosy and she looked down to study her skirts. "I don't recognize it either. It might be an ore dragon, but it would have to be a very big one, because those are Shoulder-size."

I let out a low whistle. If even *Jolene* didn't recognize Copper, then it had to be a rare type. The creepy way it reacted to the world made me think it was special somehow.

It stretched its head forward, and nuzzled my hand. It was solid again—and so was I. My pain had gone, and the brown-white Shoulder dragon had draped itself across my shoulders. It was snoozing, as if it were exhausted.

I tapped my ribs. They had been healed.

"Well whatever it is," Carter said, "I'll tell you one thing. That dragon just saved all our lives."

Chapter 59

Let's Call it Intuition

NEEDLESS TO SAY, we got a refund on that trip, and a promise of free flights in the future. My accidental heroics with Copper had saved us all kinds of money.

So of course, Jolene wanted to spend it.

"Just on the way, on the way!" she begged, dragging me through Dasvilla's market square now. Steam wafted over the edge of the Throat and between the stalls. I didn't want to be here right now. I'd had my fill of markets, and I hadn't slept last night, either.

"Just to walk through," I gritted out, because one road through Dasvilla was as good as any other.

Wherever we went, people stopped to look at us, mouths opening as they recognized Jolene and—by extension—me. Word had obviously traveled about the new lord at Pinnacle.

"Look, the shoulder Pets follow your motion!" Jolene whispered right next to my ear, surreptitiously pointing to every Shoulder-size we passed. To a dragon, they all did turn to look at me when I passed.

"Even the Mounts are getting out of your way! And Bessa the flight is resting her head on the side of the Roost, look—she's watching us!"

I didn't want to look, didn't want to see the poor dragon's ruined eye.

I dropped my arm across Jolene's shoulders. "Yeah, the looks are getting more intense... and they obey me. Mostly. Shiny, Red, and Dull liked me from the beginning, but Ravager attacked." I wondered if she'd attack me now, or if I'd changed enough to have her obeying me, too.

"Ravager already submitted to you. And Copper is following you around like a hound now," Jolene said. "We should get her a leash, even if she doesn't need one. People are uncomfortable."

That was true. Copper followed me like she hadn't been feral a mere day ago, but her lack of restraints had the market-goers giving us a wide berth.

I wouldn't call the dragon meek, though—more like the still, silent type. *Very* silent, and so bizarrely still. She even looked still when she *moved*.

We needed to get her away from prying eyes before someone recognized whatever type of dragon she was, and decided to try and steal her or something.

Jolene waved at a booth selling hundreds of eggs all in rows, lit by the sun, without candle or magic. I nearly fell asleep right there in the street. I was *so done* with eggs.

These ones were stood up on hot, carved stones that the seller kept periodically reheating in a little coal fire beside the booth. The wares were divided into price sections. For the vast majority of the eggs, they were dull in aura, if not completely blank. That meant this woman was a reseller, and probably not worth my time or money.

A sign on the first row of eggs read:

Farm-Utility Rejects!: Drop an Egg

4 Silver
Buy an Egg
3 Silver

Just buy the eggs, don't drop them, silly.

The sign perplexed me, but other passersby seemed unconcerned as they picked up eggs without even asking the seller. A noblewoman in a hat that looked like a birdcage lifted one up while I watched, holding it against the cloudy sky to inspect it. I reached into my bag and grabbed a small torch, lighting it with a flint. I still wanted to see the interior so I could learn more.

Jolene barged right up next to the birdcage woman and said, "Heya Missa! How's business?"

She was speaking to the seller, an older woman with curly gray hair. Jo had caught her halfway through chastising a little vagrant boy for trying to take off with a dead egg. Then again, maybe no one knew it was dead.

When Missa saw Jo, she slapped the boy's hand with finality, and allowed him to scamper off. Then she plopped into her chair, where she could watch who left with what. She armed herself with a fake smile and aimed it at Jolene.

"How's business, you ask? Like shit."

At the curse word, the birdcage woman harrumphed, replaced the egg, and shuffled indignantly off. Missa didn't even seem to care.

"Oh no!" Jolene said. I already knew her well enough to sense she was faking her concern. "What's got you down, Missa?" she asked.

"Demons got me over a barrel with debt, that's what. Farmers want more, buyers wanna spend less, and I'm caught in the middle, but what's new really?"

"Oh yes, I hear you, everyone's wanting more for less," Jolene scoffed, obviously playing a role.

Missa had two other tables, each with different utility types of so-called "Reject" eggs. Trying hard to keep myself awake, I started on the Combat-Utility Rejects and only went three down and stopped.

"Madam Missa," I said, "do you have a basket I could use?"

The old woman had mostly ignored me up to this point. Not anymore. She looked as if someone had exploded something in her face. "Whoa! Who's the hubby material?"

I wasn't in the mood, so I just picked up the egg I wanted and kept searching. Five eggs down, I found a baby dragon with a shell that felt as tough as iron when I tapped it. The baby inside was healthy, strong, and the best purchase I'd seen all week.

"I'm Lord Warren Orpheus-Minax, Former Guardsman Third Rank, Orphan, Champion of Dasvilla Arena apparently, Monster Slayer, and the current guardian of Lady Jolene. There's more, but that should cover it." I tossed Missa a purse, then turned to Jolene.

"What do weak baby dragons eat? Because we're about to have two of them." I showed her the eggs.

She immediately pegged them as Spell-class hybrids. "Most babies will eat any sort of meat. Why?"

Missa frowned. "What's this for?"

I reached into a pouch on my belt, popped some jerky in my mouth and chewed it aggressively.

"Warren?" Jolene asked, as I placed the iron egg on a bare stretch of table.

I slammed my fist down, shattering the iron egg.

Both women shouted something as the egg split down the center. I hit it again. This time, Jolene grabbed my arm.

"Stop, *stop!* Warren, we were just talking about this, babies need time—"

But it was too late. The egg broke open with a loud *snap,* and a little head poked through and immediately started squalling.

I freed the keening dragon with one hand, then pulled slivers of half-eaten jerky from my mouth and shoved them down her throat. The pale white creature munched greedily until I'd run out of jerky. Then, she burped.

I glanced up at Missa, who had watched all this with a strange, bemused grin.

"Seems I, uh, seems I've lost out," Missa said, because I'd purchased this healthy little dragon for only three silver when it had been an egg five minutes ago. "Well, she looks strong. Trust *my* wares to be strong. A capable baby, to be sure. How interesting. Yes, very interesting...."

She trailed off, clearly torn between trying to take credit for the beast and being completely mystified by the fact it was so healthy.

"Warren, she's going to be worth a hundred times what you paid!" Jolene said brightly. This made Missa scowl, but Jolene didn't notice.

I tapped the dragon on the nose, winking at it. The thing bit me.

"It would have died on the table if I'd left it," I said. "The shell was too hard. A few more days, and it would have suffocated."

Jolene sniffed, coming over to inspect the little white dragon, which was now twining around my hand, fawning over me, begging for more food. I added a bit more jerky to my mouth and started to chew.

Missa asked, "As, so it's more than a lucky guess. But that doesn't make sense. Lots of varieties have hard eggs. Unless you knew somehow. Did ya?"

"I won't lie to you," I said. "What is she?"

Missa's expression darkened. She hadn't missed my complete lack of an explanation. Damn, I was too tired to be keeping secrets right now.

Jolene scooped up the white dragon. "A snow dragon. They're sentry dragons. She's not frail at all. She shouldn't have been in the reject pile to begin with."

The poor little dragon curled up in Jolene's hand and fell asleep, her belly stuffed even before I could give her the next course. I plucked the egg off the ground, handing it to her. "If I didn't break her out, she never would have been free," I whispered. "There was a defect in the eggshell, not the dragon. Her pattern must have looked weak, because she's essentially been suffocating."

Jolene nodded, then said to Missa, "I'm shocked you don't just hatch all your eggs and hope for one like her."

"It's too risky," Missa said unhappily. "Even if they hatch, they're sick. Usually."

Jolene cuddled with the little snow dragon as if it were her daughter. Something about the sight of them brought a good feeling back to me. I didn't feel so tired, all of a sudden.

"That one's all yours," I said. "You look good together."

Jo went still for a moment, and then looked at the ground. Why did she keep doing that? Ever since I'd inadvertently had her against the wall during that free fall, she'd been unable to look right at me.

"Thank you, Warren," she said quietly. "She's perfect."

Missa frowned, walking around the counter to return my purse. "You can have the eggs free, if you tell me how you knew."

"I can't explain it. But, may I ask a question?" I said. Missa nodded.

"If your eggs ever accidentally hatch on their own, do you just sell them to recover the costs?" Another nod. "And you lose money doing this?" This time I earned a shrug.

"I ain't rich." Missa patted Jolene's back. "This girl has lost more money playing that game than I can count, ever since she's been this high." Her hand went to her knee.

Jolene's father had liked to let her gamble on eggs; he'd intended to teach her a valuable lesson. It hadn't stuck. He'd *meant* to teach her that life wasn't fair and that weak dragons weren't what you built a business on.

Instead, Jolene had just fallen in love with dragons. She wanted to save every one.

A random woman eyed the tiny baby in Jolene's hands as she strode past us. The dragon was unbearably cute, and iridescent like most babies, its white scales scintillating with a rainbow of colors.

I asked the passing woman, "You like her?"

Startled, the woman stopped walking and looked at me. She paled, recognizing who I was, which was honestly a feat. Had people been passing my portrait around town or something?

"She's precious," the woman stammered. "A real gem! Too tiny for me to manage, but very pretty," the woman said, handing Missa three silver coins and selecting the prettiest egg. "My little niece will like this... anyway, maybe I would buy a dragon like that when she's older. Will it be for sale later?"

Jolene didn't hesitate. "Pinnacle Dragons and More, in East Dasvilla, has several Shoulder-size adults and younglings for sale as we speak." She gazed up at me fondly. "Lord Warren just brought in *eight* wild dragons last night alone, and we have quite a pile of viable eggs."

"How sweet! The family business is revived! I shall have to stop by. You're such a cute couple."

Before we could respond to this, the woman sauntered off again.

Missa giggled. "That egg's not for her niece. She just likes gambling, and then pays her young relatives to try to raise them to the adolescent stage if they hatch." The old merchant watched the woman fade into the crowd. "That snow baby sure is healthy. I would have figured she'd be weak."

She was still fishing for information. I changed my mind on the spot, and decided to give it to her; as a reseller, she might make a good ally in the Dasvilla market.

"Her egg was the issue, not her," I said, walking down the line, touching a few more eggs with vibrant hues, including the first one I'd picked out. "You can hatch this one... and this one... and this...."

Missa followed behind me, turning each egg on its side, rotating them atop the heated stones. She marked the ones I touched with a faint X, in chalk. By the end of the line, I hadn't found another baby like the one I'd saved, but all of them had a chance, and I said so.

Missa raised an eyebrow, shooing another customer away when the man tried to buy something. "Those are viable? How can you tell?"

"Call it intuition," I said, before lowering my voice. "And I mean that. It's only *intuition*, if anyone asks. Are we clear?"

Chapter 60

No Secrets between Friends

"CRYSTAL, CRYSTAL," Missa said, without so much as a knowing smile. She really wasn't the friendliest woman.

I could see her calculating, though. None of the eggs were big, and hatching them would be a gamble, but with my help, she could sell them at a higher value for being "certified viable." Without any standardization, that "certification" could come from anyone.

Something wet struck my arm, and I squinted up to see the sky darkening.

"I owe you one, young lord," Missa said with a flutter of her fingers, dismissing us as she unfurled rain protection over her tables, closing her business to outsiders.

As we left, Jolene said, "She's a good woman. I think you handled it well."

"I hope so. Let's see what some of these adventurers are selling," I said, wrapping an arm around her lower back. The rain was reviving me somewhat. It felt good to be back in Dasvilla.

I walked deeper into the maze of egg sellers, going to a spot where the owner seemed like a grumpy, sour old man.

"Oi, keep away from the merchandise," he groused. "I don't want none of them wet."

I stayed back, surveying from afar. All of his eggs were massive, and he clearly had a thing for Airship-class dragons. I frowned, seeing movement in all the eggs, but not seeing anything that seemed *alive*. "See anything ya like?"

"No, Sir. I sadly don't."

He was playing a con. I wasn't sure what it was, and I wasn't a dragon egg Enforcer, so I let it go—but one thing was for Demon's sure. I wasn't doing business with him.

I moved toward the next big reseller of duds, who also had quality eggs. Among the duds, a sign read: *Do not touch. 1 Gold Per.*

Out of the ten, one had the same iron-egg affliction as Jolene's new snow baby. The difference was, this male was sickly and further along in his suffocation, likely beyond saving. He had stayed in the shell for too long. I sighed, extending a palm near the shell but not on it.

Somewhere behind me, a dragon roared, causing the reseller's other patrons to flinch. The shell cracked at the same moment, then split apart at the deep fissures. Without a doubt, the egg was going to hatch.

I stepped back and waited, thankful for the distraction of the roaring dragon; I didn't think anyone had seen me tap the shell. The baby dragon spilled out of the disintegrating egg, sliding across a glob of embryonic fluid. I caught him before he could fall off the table.

He curled into a ball, then breathed his last.

My heart sank, and I stroked his head, closing my eyes. A young man popped up from behind the reseller's table, and he blinked at the dead baby dragon.

The reseller finally noticed the scene. He shot to his feet. "What happened?"

The boy said, "He touched the egg and it erupted and he caught the baby and it died."

"It was sickly. I didn't kill it," I clarified. "I just saw it hatching and reached out."

"No ya didn't," the boy said. "Ya touched it, and then it broke, not the other way around. I'm Baron Iglin, who's you?"

"Lord Warren," I said, rising with the dead baby. This kid was pretty young to be a baron, but that happened from time to time. He must have slipped away from his minders.

Baron Iglin eyed me unhappily, gesturing for the seller to take the corpse. The old man reached out, surprisingly gentle about it. "I'm sorry for your loss," I said.

"It's just a dud egg, he gets them all the time. Ugh, you stink," Baron Iglin said, wrinkling his nose. "What's that shit crusted all over you?"

The old man looked exasperated, but he didn't tell the boy off. Jolene pulled on my sleeve with worry-filled eyes, having set her snow baby in a sling across her chest. "Let's go home, milord."

She didn't need to tell me twice. I turned around—

At the same moment, the voice of a small dragon roared close by, sounding pained. It was the smallest dragon-voice I'd heard outside of our own hatchlings. Something was going on.

I shook my head when Jolene kept tugging me. "No. I want to see where that's coming from."

Jolene's face fell, and I realized she'd been trying to get me away from whatever was happening. Resolute, I stalked up to the last vendor, which happened to be the biggest of them all.

Jolene fidgeted, clearly wanting to be anywhere other than near this booth. She especially seemed to be hiding her face from the young man who was currently dusting the eggs on display.

The sky darkened with each passing second, and when we reached this final booth, the clouds opened up and wept.

"Hello," I said to the young man. He had already put a tarp over his wares, and he instantly gloated upon seeing us soaking wet, while he himself wore fancy striped robes without a single damp thread.

He turned on his salesman's smile for us. "Hello, soldier," he said, correctly guessing my profession while offering his hand. "I'm Baron Maki."

"Warren. I take it you're from a big farm?" I asked, and he nodded. "What city is your farm in?"

"Here. I'm local," the man replied.

Huh. I still hadn't met any dragon breeders, aside from the Biscuits, who seemed to be amateurs. Jolene was now hiding behind me, so the two must know each other.

I was about to say something, when another customer called out. "Oi, Baron! I got three silvers for this one here."

Turning, I saw the man had pointed to a ruby-colored egg. This so-called Baron Maki inclined his head and instantly abandoned me.

"Feeling lucky, Iann?" Maki said, taking the silvers from the old man's hand. "Go on. Don't leave me in suspense."

The old man rubbed his hands, and Jolene straightened in a way that made me glance at her face. She looked stricken.

"Warren, we should go—"

No sooner was that last word out of her mouth, than the old man picked up the red egg, and slammed it onto the ground.

I took an involuntary step forward. "Hey!"

But the man didn't notice me. He was groaning. "Not another dud!" he lamented.

"Better luck next time, old friend," Maki said, turning to wave a boy out from the back corner of the shop area. "Clean this quickly, Ork, before the rain spreads it everywhere."

I barely heard him as I stared at the dead hatchling on the ground. It was fully-formed, and there was no bad smell. If the old man had kept the egg warm another couple of weeks, the creature would have been ready to hatch.

I made a move toward it, but Jolene caught my arm. "Warren, no."

"They just murdered a hatchling!" I hissed at her.

"I know. Shh." She kept her voice low. "This is what Maki does here. He buys unwanted eggs in bulk, and sells them to gamblers. If the egg hatches, they make money, but most don't. Some are dead already, but sometimes—"

"Sometimes they kill an innocent dragon!"

"I know. But it's just how it is. And if you make trouble for Baron Maki, he'll make trouble for you. Please, just try to stay calm."

I did try, with all my might, but watching that shop boy clean up a perfectly viable dragon nearly sent me into a rage. I suddenly saw the vast array of eggs in a new light.

Gambling. He's gambling with infants' lives.

But Jolene was right. I couldn't afford to pick fights with other local merchants, not until Pinnacle was fully established. A local merchant would have connections he could use to ruin me if he wanted to.

I might survive it, but I'd already pissed off the Biscuits. I had to slow my barrel roll, or else plummet headfirst into the ground.

So when Baron Maki came back to us, I tried a new tack, and plastered a friendly smile on my face. Gesturing over at the man's large offering of eggs, I said, "I was wondering... for the right price, could I buy eggs from you in bulk?"

Greed manifested in his dark gaze. "Oh, yes, sir. There are plenty of unwanted eggs to go around.

"However, you should consider my selection first and foremost. Some of my eggs are wild, which means we have no idea of their quality. The chances are better.

"Ah, and I see you brought the lovely Jolene. Hello, darling. Good to see you again."

Maki punctuated this slick comment with a smooth wink. Jolene said nothing. If the man recognized her, then he definitely knew who I was. I couldn't trust a thing he said, but of course, I'd already known that.

"Ah! Is that a snow dragon poking out of your pocket, Jolene?" Maki asked. "Quite the pricey beast for Pinnacle. How's business? Going well, then?"

He said this almost hopefully, so I gave him what he wanted. "We've emptied the barn," I said. "We're consolidating."

Maki frowned, twisting his face in pure shock. "Huh? We?" Lots of blinking. "And who are you, pray tell?"

Finally, Jolene stepped forward. In a small voice, she said, "Lord Warren, this is Baron Maki. He has a main farm in Caliph and a satellite farm in Das. He has visited Pinnacle often over the years, purchasing stock on behalf of his farm. Always at a fair price, I might add."

Somehow, I didn't believe that.

"Oh, Jolene. Do tell him the rest," Maki said, his voice sly. "There can be no secrets between friends, after all?"

Jolene looked like she wished the thickening mud would suck her straight into the ground. But she nodded, and I thought, *Here we go.*

Chapter 61

The Crack of the Egg

"WE ALSO... AH... COURTED," Jolene managed to say. "Or we tried to, but I never gave it the proper time," she rushed out. "It was my loss."

Jolene breathed deeply, looked up, and finally completed her introductions. "Baron Maki, this is Lord Warren Orpheus-Minax, Guardsman of the Third Rank, and the heir that my mother appointed."

"I'm sorry for your loss," Maki said.

I schooled myself, fighting not to scowl. That line had been ambiguous, and we all knew it.

Jolene curtsied anyway. "She's missed, but I have a guardian now. He is trying his best to realize Father's dream of a... *bustling* dragon market in Dasvilla. Not that having Mountain Heights Farm isn't sufficient, of course."

I could read between the lines. This guy must be a powerful player in the Dasvilla dragon market.

He wagged a finger at me. "Wait a second. I heard about a tall and mysterious new lord who somehow saved a flight dragon from free fall this morning," Maki said with a respectful nod. His finger drifted between us. "Are you two an item, then?"

"He's a free spirit, but he treats me well," Jolene said. That was a nice way to put it. "But he's not using the barn," she added under her breath. "And at this rate, we're going to need it."

Maki seemed to have caught up at this point. "The estate was always all you needed," he told Jolene. "Not any man." He turned to me again. "My newsboy said you chased off an all-black Behemoth on that flight. Is that true?"

It wasn't, but I'd happily ride the coattails of that story. "I wanted to keep my dragons safe, and I was willing to, shall we say, *take steps*," I said.

"And you wanted to save the other people on board, of course."

He was trying to catch me in a lie, but I hadn't admitted to anything. "Of course."

"Against a Behemoth that can eat you in one bite, no less! I haven't even *seen* a Behemoth in what, five years now? Brave, but crazy. Come, come, what can I help a friend of a friend with? It's great to hear Jolene is well-cared for," Maki said, flashing a charming smile at Jolene.

"Becki moved into the estate," Jolene blurted, clearly struggling to handle the situation. "Shit, sorry. Becki knows Maki."

The man's gaze narrowed. "Yes, Miss Becki worked at our Das farm for a bit. I thought she was keen on becoming a second wife, but she always was trying to get information out of me. She was the duchess's creature."

I was getting bored with all this, so I surveyed his unhatched wares. A lot of the eggs he was offering held no aura at all, and the majority of them were quite faint. I decided I didn't like this side of the business one bit.

"You should be wary of her," he said, meaning Becki.

A flash of lighting flared through the gray clouds. The rain was still light and somewhat enjoyable, but the distant storm felt more violent.

"I'm wary of everyone *aside* from Becki. We were kids together—"

424

I stopped talking, pointing a finger at Maki as we walked by several eggs that reached knee-high.

"Ah, see, I almost gave you free information. Suffice it to say my good friend Becki had a troubled life, and I was there for her when no one else was. I was there for many of the orphans of Dasvilla," I added. "Hey, can I ask a dragon question?"

"Dragons are my everything," Maki smoothly answered. The rain intensified. "What's on your mind?"

"Some of these baby dragons would survive if you simply opened their eggs, then force-fed them, with constant warmth and attentive care," I said matter-of-factly. "So why haven't you done so?"

"Ah, I will answer as my father would, but I don't always agree with him." He tucked his hands behind his back, not bothered by the rain. "Should they be saved for being weak? This world is harsh and brutal. What good is a dragon who'll probably never be of quality to breed?"

I narrowed my eyes. "Ah, I think I understand. So you choose to run gamble pits instead, killing potential dragons for a handful of coins?"

Maki's face darkened, and Jolene rushed to cover for my rudeness. "He's a warrior, not into dragons at all," she said uncomfortably.

Maki snickered. "Opposites attract, and no offense, Jolene, but your mother has always made poor choices. Warren is already bringing dragons home to you which you don't have the room or means to care for. Although I do find myself a sucker for a good story." His next grin had teeth. "I heard you loved a noblewoman, and lost. What was that lovely lady like? Do tell."

This comment lit a fire in me. It had been obvious from the beginning that he knew who I was, but now he'd let the dragon out of the bag.

"She was stubborn, fiery, a straight bitch," I said angrily. My voice softened, because how could it not? "But so cursing pure that I died for her. I mean, nearly died." Sometimes I wasn't sure which.

"You look hale for a nearly dead man," Maki teased.

"Huh, yeah. Life is a mystery sometimes." I turned my gaze on a large, knee-high egg at the back of the row. Its shell appeared to be crusted from fire damage—or perhaps erosion of some kind?

It looked terrible, but I could tell the issues were superficial. The egg must have rolled down a hill into a fire pit or something, but the baby dragon inside was in pristine health, a gorgeous purple-something with black accents.

"I like to gamble, and I had a good day," I said. I pointed to the egg, which was the ugliest one he had. "How much for that one?"

"That one? For Jolene, a gold. It's normally a bit more, since it could be an Airship or at the very least a Hauler. It was wild-caught, you see, so really it could be anything."

Jolene tugged my sleeve. "It's a week beyond hatch time, and it looks like it suffered magical damage," she cautioned.

Maki's smile flickered. He didn't like being caught out by a competitor.

None of that mattered. I could feel the raw power inside the egg. Lightning crackled across the sky with a nearby *boom.*

I handed Maki my purse, knowing he wouldn't dare steal it or take more than he should. "Here. Fish it out while I do this next part."

Jolene frowned. "Wait, Warren... you can just take the egg with you. You can't go opening a bunch of eggs without a carrier."

"We won't need one. Have you confirmed my purchase?" I asked, admiring the egg.

He handed me back the purse, and I tucked it away with a nod.

"It's always sad to see people gamble and lose," Maki said, "but I do hope that's not the case here."

Maki's words were sincere, in a snide sort of way. I hugged the egg while the storm turned darker with each passing moment.

The egg's inner aura pulsed with a repeated thrum until I felt it *connecting* to me. In that brief moment, I realized I had an aura as well. From what, or how, I couldn't fathom, but it surrounded me, like a cloud of orange flame.

The sky boomed, dragons roared, my vision faded. In that moment, I was somewhere else—back in that darkness between space and time, with the blood on my neck and the memories fading.

That's when I heard the crack of the egg.

Chapter 62

In the Distance

JOLENE SHOOK MY SHOULDER, and I came out of my momentary trance, taking my hand off the egg. A crack really had formed on its surface.

Huh. Well, I'll be damned.

"Come, my daughter," I whispered, shuffling backwards to give her space on the ground. The seam on the huge egg split deeper and deeper, until a perfectly healthy dragon smashed out of it, remarkably tiny given the size of the egg. I could have fit it into my coat pocket.

The casing crumbled around the little beast, falling in hundreds of pieces at my feet. I reached into a pouch and fed the black-and-purple dragon a chunk of jerky. I didn't bother chewing it first.

The baby dragon had a strong, wide snout. Where some dragons tried to swallow or strangle prey, this one's serrated beak would eventually turn into fangs, which it could then use for shredding anything it grabbed hold of. The purple and black colors wouldn't blend in during the day, but it reminded me of a panther in the night, stealthy and lethal. It had no trouble ripping up the jerky.

"You're going to be a glutton," I told the creature. "Aren't you?"

It took Baron Maki that long to get his words back. "A night dragon... How?" he asked in dismay. "I... I'm afraid I have to report this to my lord."

"Do so. The transaction was witnessed, and she'll only answer to me," I said, scratching the dragon's head.

Night dragons were rare, but they were the smallest known Airship-class, so they weren't much good for transporting large groups of soldiers. Because of this, the royals liked to use them as flashy personal mounts. This would be my first-ever Airship-class, even before I'd found any new Haulers.

Jolene practically shook with incredulity. "Only royalty rides night dragons into battle... but they're almost never used. I didn't know you had a breeder?"

"We don't," Maki said coldly. "Either one of our hunting parties found her, or the king's Roost traded her on accident. But he's right, she's bonded to him already. He literally called her out of her egg with... with magic. Honestly, I don't know what I just witnessed... but perhaps Count Jasper might have something to say about it."

I didn't recognize the name, but Maki had farms in both Dasvilla and Caliph.

"Is that the guy that runs Caliph?" I asked.

"Yes, Count Jasper, King Kurto's seventh or eighth cousin," Maki said with a grunt. "By the flame, Father is going to be unhappy to hear that I sold you the egg for a gold."

"Jolene," I corrected. "You sold *Jolene* the egg for a single gold, and you likely had a good reason for it."

He winced. "Do me a favor: she's got enough problems, so keep her out of yours." I raised an eyebrow, surprised to see real feeling behind the man's eyes. Maki went on, "Please. Her mother was killed, and it weighs on my soul. I fear every day that it might happen to her."

I couldn't tell if this was a threat or not. "Any idea who may have done it?" I asked.

"I won't speculate," he sniffed, a bit too quickly. "Accusations are so easy to fling—"

"Thanks for the help, Maki," Jolene cut him off. Her tone had grown defensive. I wondered if she finally, *finally* wanted to stop shopping.

"It was my absolute pleasure," he lied, staring at the night baby who now squatted by my right foot. I was pretty sure she'd just peed.

"Ya going to stable her at the main Roost?" he asked.

I didn't answer. "I appreciate the time and the dragon, Baron Maki. It was a very good deal," I said, dipping my head at him. Without further ado, I collected the night dragon and strode out of his shop area. The night dragon latched tight to my arm as I cradled her; it made me wonder if she might be infused with magical strength of some kind. Damn, there was so much to learn.

Once we got a good distance from Maki, I nudged Jolene. She visibly awoke from her thoughts.

I asked, "Did he actually like you?"

"Huh?"

"Maki?"

"Oh. Yes. He came by and helped with the barn while Mother was still around. I was a very eligible bachelorette back then, even if I'm not the prettiest." I scoffed and she blushed. "Maki tried to get me to go out, and he was very sweet, but he has a wife and three kids already. He never talked about them."

"Why would he? First and second wives don't normally get along."

That was just a fact of life, although nobles took great pains to *pretend* their multiple spouses got along like big happy families.

"It just didn't seem sincere, to never mention or bring them," she admitted. "He comes with a family already, which I could have accepted if he wanted me to actually *join* them. But he preferred to pretend they didn't exist, and even that much deception isn't attractive."

Jolene glanced up at the dark sky that poured down rain, which ran over her soft face in fervid rivulets. For a moment, she looked like a storm angel, as if she could just throw out her arms and take all the sky into her.

"Sorry about shutting down back there," she said. "Seeing Maki is always nerve-wracking. But you can sense dragons, Warren!"

She spun toward me. "The question is—why? You never had a dragonbond before. I know your parents weren't special, no offense. You're not a lost prince or something, unless you came from another kingdom... but someone would have found you if that was the case...."

I let her carry on like this for the next twenty minutes until we reached the Cage. I didn't even bother drying off, just tromped right up the steps and slopped through the door.

We both collapsed at the nearest table. Our new dragons had not arrived yet, probably because the porters at the Roost would hold them until the rain stopped. I pulled out my purse and tallied what was left. We were down to less than four gold, and that included all of my savings.

This didn't upset me, though. Far from it. I had found not only meaning, but *power* in this business. It finally felt like my decade of hard labor had served a purpose. Something important was going on, and I was being swept up in it. I wanted to know: to what end?

The king would hear about the night dragon I hatched, and his cousin Count Jasper might act aggressively to steal her from me. I'd have to deal with that. And then there was the assassin, still upstairs, with answers that needed unlocking. And of course, I had all these new dragons to feed and hatch, with barely enough money to feed them for long.

But I had Becki, and Rachel, and even Fieran... and Jolene. She leaned into my side, already asleep.

I mumbled to myself, "The future is bright, isn't it, Jo?"

A flash of lightning lit the room, and I found my gaze drawn up and out the tall foyer windows. In the afterimage of the flash, I saw a full-grown dragon in the distance, quivering with storm-light, and I had to wonder: *What comes next?*

Chapter 63

You Argue a Lot for Someone that's Tied Up

I WOKE up the next morning at the sitting room table, with Jolene stirring at my side. I blinked awake, the world shaking back and forth.

"Warren? Warren!"

Turning, I found Becki standing next to me, shaking my shoulder insistently.

"Warren, it's Fieran. Come quick!"

Alertness shot through me at the worry in her voice, and I rose to my feet, nudging Jolene aside so that she wouldn't fall over. She mumbled awake with a snort.

"Wha...? What?"

Becki closed a hand around my wrist. "Upstairs!" she said. "Please, I don't know what to do."

She led me for only two steps before I broke into a run, racing ahead of her and up the stairs to the mezzanine where I'd left the assassin.

The assassin! I kept thinking. *Did the assassin attack Fieran? Is he dead? Did she get away?*

Behind me, Becki was saying, "I'm sorry, I'm so sorry, he told me not to come in, and I didn't check on him all of yesterday, I just didn't have any time—"

I cut her off by throwing the door open, a knife already in my other hand. I stopped just over the threshold, taking in the scene.

The assassin was still there, lying at the foot of the bed, either dead or asleep. Her wrists were still bound, but not her feet, except that one ankle was tied to a bedpost. The Mount-class cloud dragon, Tilly, lay curled around that same bedpost, her head resting at the foot of the bed.

Seeing Tilly indoors made me startle, but then my eyes traveled up the mattress to Fieran. He laid still, the blanket thrown off him.

The bed beneath his body was stained red.

The injury, I thought. I rushed forward, checking his pulse. It throbbed weakly under my fingertips.

"I thought I told you to get a healer?" I said, turning to Becki, trying to keep the accusation from my voice.

"I tried! Fieran sent her away. He said he was fine, that the wound had closed up!" Becki replied, coming closer. My instincts kicked in and I held a hand out to stop her.

"Stop! No closer," I said, backing up to check on the assassin. If the woman was faking that stillness, she could jump up and stab me, or take Becki hostage.

Becki paused at the door, her face pale. "I knocked this morning. I fell behind in the cleaning and since I saw you were home, I wanted to make everything look nicer—but then he didn't answer when I knocked. No one did. I came in—"

I waved for her to stop talking and knelt beside the assassin, holding my knife at her dark throat. I checked her pulse, too—alive—and then checked her bindings. The skin of her wrists had gone raw, but the ropes remained tight. She wasn't faking. She was dead asleep.

As I moved to get up again, Tilly turned her head toward me, lowered it, and huffed at me. The dragon bobbed her head toward the assassin's face.

She's been knocking her out, I realized. I sighed from relief, but the feeling passed quickly.

"Not yet, girl," I told the dragon, petting her head, which was about the size of a damn dinner plate. Even as a Mount, she barely fit in this room. Fieran must have brought her in here to keep the assassin at bay, but if the woman's wrists were raw, that meant she'd tried to escape hard enough that Fieran had been forced to resort to Tilly.

With that head shake, Tilly was asking if she should keep breathing on the assassin. I didn't want her to, not yet. If Tilly breathed on the blood mage, it might be hours before I could wake her up again, and I might need answers soon.

I rose again, and pointed at the insensate woman. "Watch her," I told Becki. "One twitch, and you shout a warning."

"Okay. Okay, Warren," Becki said, sounding panicked.

I cast a last look at our prisoner. *He should have just killed her,* I thought. I know he'd wanted to. Yet Fieran had obeyed my commands, even though he wasn't truly beholden to me.

I'd wanted to interrogate the assassin, and instead of protecting himself and me by just slitting her throat, Fieran had done what I'd asked.

And it might have gotten him killed.

"You enormous idiot," I said, pulling up his shirt to check the wound in his side. I was the wrong color around the edges. It stank.

"An infection," I said, patting the man's cheek. His skin was smooth, even now. But how was that possible? The man couldn't have shaved in the past half day, at least.

That didn't matter. He stirred, mumbling.

"Fieran! Oi, idiot! What were you thinking?"

I heard steps in the hall, and I twisted to yell, "Jolene! Go find me that brown-and-white Shoulder dragon, the one we caught in Caliph. I need it now!"

The blond noblewoman popped her head in, saw the scene, nodded, and was gone again. She would get it done.

I slapped Fieran on his cheek again. "Fieran! Talk to me."

"No... no healers," he rasped.

I looked over the wound again, and had to swallow bile. It was bad. *Very* bad. Fieran must have known that.

Yet he'd refused the healer? Why?

"Warren!" Becki cried.

I was on the assassin again in instants, my knife back to her throat. Her eyelids fluttered, and no wonder. Bad smells woke a person from Tilly's cloud breath, and the room was rank with infection.

"Don't you dare move!" I growled, debating whether I should just end the woman right here and now. "Your knife, the one you cut him with. Was it poisoned?"

This infection had gotten too bad, too quickly. It wasn't normal.

"Blood... blood poison," the assassin rasped, before smiling.

Fuck. I hadn't considered that her blade might have been laced with anything.

"Get him water," I told Becki. "And get the damn healer back here." There was nothing else I could do for Fieran at the moment. I didn't know how to stitch a wound, much less heal an infection, or cure a poison I'd never even heard of.

Prodding the assassin's neck, I said, "How do we cure it?"

Becki's footsteps disappeared down the hall, then the stairs. She'd get the water and healer, but I didn't think either one would do much. Dasvilla wasn't prosperous enough to have a magical healer, and if this was an unknown poison, a regular healer wouldn't know what to do.

A cold smile spread faintly across the assassin's lips. She coughed once, then said, "I can cure him."

I fought to keep calm. "Then do it!" I demanded.

Her eyelids fluttered, those red eyes showing through. "What's... what's in it for me?"

"What's in it for you? You don't *die,* that's what."

"If I die, the cure goes with me."

Damn. She had me there. My mind raced. I had her dragon's entire clutch of eggs. Would that work? No. No, she would still be a prisoner even with the eggs. I could threaten to smash them if she didn't help....

But I couldn't do that. I couldn't smash even one dragon egg, much less three. I'd seen Maki's customers doing just that yesterday, and it had sickened me to my core. I couldn't do it. I just couldn't.

Fuck, when did I get so soft? I thought, knowing that there was only one other thing that would sate the assassin. But at that moment, Jolene burst into the room with the little brown-and-white dragon in her arms.

"Here! I've got him!"

I didn't ask how she'd gotten the creature so quickly. The porters must have dropped them off this morning, but if so, they'd come early. The reedy light dripping in through Fieran's window was still twilight, and the storm still rumbled overhead. No porters would travel in that, at least not without a tip that I couldn't afford to give them.

"Put him next to the wound," I said. "Stay out of reach of *her,* though."

Jolene nodded and rushed to the bed, keeping close to the wall by the door so the assassin couldn't grab at her. She lowered the strangely pliant dragon toward Fieran.

"What... what do you want me to do with him?" she asked, her voice trembling. At that moment, Becki appeared with a tin jug of water, but I waved her back.

"Just put him by the wound," I repeated. "He'll know what to do."

Chapter 64

So You Do Care

Biting her lip, Jolene released the dragon. The creature looked at me and chirped.

"Heal him," I told it. "I know you can."

Back on the dragonflight, when we'd fallen into a dive and I'd had my ribs cracked, this dragon had laid its little head on me—and the next thing I knew, I'd felt fine again, as if my rib had never broken at all.

Bones didn't just heal on their own. There was only one thing that could have happened.

With a small, throaty peep, the dragon lowered its head and chuffed against Fieran's wound. The man groaned sharply as pain rocked him, but he gritted his teeth to cut off his own cry.

Becki and Jolene watched, mesmerized, as the wound closed up. I kept my eyes on the assassin, whose own glare hadn't changed. She was still smiling at me, and she grew more lucid each moment.

"It healed!" Jolene breathed, and I chanced a look at Fieran. His wound had gone smooth, as if the cut had never been there.

But the dark splotch of the infection remained.

"A root-mineral hybrid," rasped the assassin. "How very lucky...

that you found one with that trait. I think the chances are... one in twelve...."

I edged the knife blade higher up her throat, under her jaw, where she could feel the full length of its finely honed edge. "Why isn't he waking up?" I demanded.

"Root dragons... close gaps. Mineral dragons affect skin." She laughed darkly. "The right hybrid can close wounds, a rare but useful trait.... Neither of them can cure blood poison, though. I'm the only one here that can do that."

"What's the antidote?" I said through gritted teeth.

The assassin remained dead still as she spoke. "There isn't one. It's not a real poison. It's *blood* poison. An infection... of the *blood.*"

Blood. The assassin was a blood mage.

"You can cure it?"

"Yes."

Our gazes locked. I knew what she wanted, and she knew I knew.

"Fine. Your freedom," I said. "You heal him, and *don't kill him* afterward, and I let you go."

"Warren... no," Fieran said, making me glance up. He had curled up into a half-ball, one hand gripping his closed wound, the other reaching toward me. His voice was so thin, so soft, nothing like the rough growl he always spoke with. "Please. Just kill her... you are too... important...."

"Shut up, Fier," I snapped at him.

To the assassin, I repeated my offer. "Heal him, and you go free. But you fucking try *anything,* and you're dead—and all three of your dragon's eggs get smashed, too."

It was an empty threat, but she wouldn't know that. Her eyes widened slightly.

I smiled. *So you do care about those eggs.*

She didn't look nearly as happy when she nodded. I gripped her by the front of her leathers and yanked her forward, slicing through her wrist bindings with one swift movement.

At the same time, I whispered into her ear, "I'm wearing those eggs on my person right now. I can smash them before you'd have a chance to get them off me, and Vital's babies will be dead, just like that."

With my threat delivered, I cut the rope tying her to the bed, and waved an arm.

"Everyone out. Out of the *house.* Jolene, I want you both outside with Ravager protecting you in case this bitch gets any ideas."

"But—but Warren—!"

"Just do it!"

Both women scurried out, way out of their depths with all this. Meanwhile, the assassin rose, rubbing her bloody wrists. I flashed her one of the eggs to prove I hadn't been kidding; I still wore them across my chest in the egg bandolier.

Scowling, she turned to Fieran, holding a hand out to me. "My knife. The one you stole from me," she said.

I bent a knee and tugged it from my boot, offering it to her hilt-first. She took it.

"I'll have to cut him," she warned. "Not deep, just enough." Her voice was breathy, and I realized she always sounded that way, like she was hiding her voice in shadows just as much as her body.

I held out a hand, and the root-mineral dragon sluggishly crawled over to me and clawed at my arm. I lifted the poor guy up to my shoulder, where it clung weakly about my neck, quivering in exhaustion.

That healing must have drained him. He's so small, I thought. He probably couldn't do this more than once a day.

"Do it," I told the assassin, watching her closely. I saw every flicker of her movement, and then judged it, using my vast knowledge of combat to rapidly determine what she was about to do—but true to her word, she didn't tense up to eviscerate my friend.

Fieran shook, raising a hand to stop her, but she just slapped his arm aside and pressed the blade to the dark bruise of the infection.

Blood pooled, a mere pinprick of it, but the welling liquid flattened out as her strange notched blade pulled the blood into its hollow core.

"I'm going to hold it here. It will take time," she said. I found myself grateful that she was narrating what she was doing. "In the meantime, tell your cloud dragon to back the fuck away."

I nodded at Tilly, who had raised her head to watch the proceedings with rapt concern. "Go on, girl. Go to Jolene, in the yard."

The dragon retracted from Fieran with a low, unhappy rumble, her eyes flicking to Fieran's face. Fieran lay now with his eyes closed, his breathing labored. He had no strength left to defy me or the assassin. He stood on the very threshold of death's door.

As for the knife, blood still seemed to be filling it—traveling up the notch and through the filigreed handle in a bright red vein. At the same time, the bedding beneath the hilt was turning red as some of the blood dripped out of the blade.

The blood is passing through the blade, I thought, trying to understand. *And it's circling around the hilt, and back down the other side and into his body again... but some of the blood is still draining out....*

"You're filtering it," I said. "Pulling all the blood out and putting only the good blood back in."

"Very astute, dragon man," she said. "Yes. That's how you cure blood poison. And you're lucky—only a few blood mages ever learn it."

I reminded myself to be certain that her knife was empty of blood again before she finished, or else she could use the blood to kill Fieran later. If she had a person's blood, she could send it back toward them at high speed in any shape she wanted. She could slit them open with a blade of their own blood.

As she worked, I said, "What do you need to give your superiors, to prove you killed a target?"

The assassin glanced at me, her red eyes clearer than ever. I didn't like seeing those red eyes awake; it seemed like the most dangerous color in the world.

"We must take the whole head," she said. "And the blood within the head must match the mark. It's the only way to be certain."

I swallowed. "So... there's no way to fake mine or Fieran's death."

The assassin faced away from me. "Yours? No. But your friend here...." She paused. "There is a pill that... *he* can take, which can mask his heritage. If you give him this pill, I can take a vial of his blood, and that will be enough."

*"Ohh*kay," I said, dragging out the first syllable. "You're saying *he* can take a pill, but I can't? And a *pill?* A pill that—what? Cures you of having a king's blood?"

Saying this out loud made me wince, and I shot a look at Fieran, but he didn't stir. He didn't know yet that I was aware he was the king's bastard.

"In a manner of speaking," the assassin replied. "I will say no more on the subject. But I can give him the name of the pill, and when he goes to take it, he will understand."

I tried and failed to make any sense of this. I pointed at Fieran.

"And you'll leave him alone? If he takes this pill? Why?"

The assassin closed her eyes, her expression darkening in concentration. "I must focus," she said.

"But you won't get paid if you don't kill him—"

"I will be paid if he takes the pill and gives me his blood, which will prove he has taken it. One of the ingredients leaves a lasting blood marker."

"But why didn't you offer him this chance before?"

"Let's just say I learned something new about him. Now *let me focus,* or he could still die."

I fell silent, watching as her eyes darted back and forth under her lids. It wasn't just her knife that was curing Fieran; the assassin *herself* was using magic to filter his blood. She could probably tell the spoiled blood from the healthy blood, and had to direct one type of blood to flow out of the knife, and the other type to flow back into Fieran's body.

She was saving him. Saving her target. Yes, she would be free afterwards—but she was doing what I'd already asked of her. There was no reason for her to tell me how to save Fieran later on. She had not traded that information for anything that would benefit her.

Which meant she could be making all this up, but why would she choose such an unbelievable story? I mean, a pill that cured a person of their parentage? What?

Yet this supposed pill would do nothing for me. She'd need my head. Once I let her go, she would still go after me.

A long sigh drained out of her, and she dropped the knife on the deep red sheet, swaying. I acted without thinking, moving to catch her—but I stopped myself in time. She was surely faking. She'd stab me just as soon as I touched her.

She collapsed to the ground with a series of loud thumps.

"Whoa!" I said, my knees bending involuntarily. I gradually sank next to her, careful of any trick, but the fainting was real. She'd drained her power nearly dry to save her former target.

She'd dropped the knife already, but I kicked it away just in case, then lifted her head into my lap.

"You... promised," she murmured.

"I know. You're free to go."

"Must sleep... not here."

"I'll put you up in the town inn."

446

She nodded, breathing low and ragged. What a strange situation, to have my own assassin at my mercy, trusting me like this.

"I could kill you now," I whispered.

That same cunning smile flickered over her face again.

"Ah... but then you'll never know what you are, dragon man...."

"My name is Warren." I paused. "What's yours?"

"Wouldn't you... like to know," she replied.

"I would. Very much," I told her.

But by that point, she was fast asleep.

Chapter 65

Mystery Bottles

I HAD the assassin's body halfway down the stairs when Becki caught up to me.

"Warren," she said, "you should have told me you had a healing dragon. If we bottle its breath, we can make really good money!"

I stopped mid-stair and turned to her, my muscles barely straining under the weight of the petite assassin. Leave it to Becki to think of making money when we all had bigger concerns.

Still, it sparked a question that had been skittering around in the shadows of my mind for some time.

"First Rachel with the cloud breath," I said, "and now you with this healing breath? Why haven't I heard of this bottling thing before?"

She blinked, then tapped her chin. "Actually... I'm not sure. Rachel's the one who gets the bottles, but you're right. I've never seen this sort of thing for sale elsewhere."

I glanced toward the keep. Another mystery behind that wily accountant, and not one I was going to tackle today.

"What are the limitations of bottling dragon breath, anyway?" I said. "Do you know?"

Becki nodded. Of course she knew. If something had the ability to make money, then she'd know everything about it. Which only made it stranger that she didn't know where these bottles were coming from.

"I only know that when a dragon uses its breath power, it drains energy. Whiles its imperviousness ability is innate, its breath ability has a cost. So you can only harvest so much breath at a time before a dragon collapses or even dies."

I frowned, remembering how the healing dragon had collapsed around my neck. "But Tilly had no trouble keeping the assassin down for a day and night with her cloud breath."

"Yeah, but she's older and bigger. The size and age of a dragon determine the size of its power reserve. Also, some breath abilities cost more energy than others. Like, I think transformative powers—like fixing a wound—cost more energy?

"Anyway, I don't know the details, this is all just stuff I've asked Jolene on the fly, but Rachel's contract gives her a bottle of cloud breath for every day that passes, and Tilly hasn't shown any bad side effects that I know of."

I bounced this information around in my head, weighing my options. "So the healing dragon's breath will probably drain it quickly, since it's small and young, and the power is transformative?" I asked.

She dipped her head. "Most likely."

"Be careful then. You can bottle its breath, but only as much as it can spare without its day-to-day life being impacted. But don't sell the bottles just yet. And give me the first bottle."

"But—but they could sell for a fortune!"

I huffed a laugh. "Somehow I think they will *cost* a fortune. I'm guessing those bottles won't come cheap."

"Maybe Rachel will rent them to us?" Becki said hopefully.

Over my shoulder, the assassin stirred. I waved Becki back up the stairs.

"Go back and keep an eye on Fieran. Do the bottle thing tomorrow. But remember—the first bottle of healing breath goes straight to me."

At the rate I was going, I'd need it before long, and the healing dragon wouldn't always be close. Better safe than sorry.

"Of course, milord," Becki said, bowing. "Until then... please keep yourself safe."

After slinging the assassin's limp body over Tilly's back, the dragon and I delivered the assassin to her own room in one of Dasvilla's three inns. The room was exceedingly cheap, since very few people ever visited this city, but my savings was going as fast as ever. I needed cash flow again soon, or I'd be charred.

I also needed a way to protect myself, and get Fieran the pill that supposedly cured a person of having a hit out on them.

When I laid the dark-skinned, scarred woman on the bed in her second-floor suite, she roused a little, eyes opening to look up at me.

"Mmmm," she said, her gaze hooded. It was the sort of sound a lover might make, and with her small, deadly frame beneath me, I found the murmur unnerving.

"The pill for Fieran," I said. "The name of the pill."

"Ask... any apothecary. Nightweed root," she said. "*You* can't ask. Has to be Fieran."

I cursed aloud, but under my breath. I'd never heard of nightweed. And why couldn't I fetch it myself, anyway? This got more mysterious by the minute.

"Fine," I said, standing up, looming over her. I didn't feel like pulling a blanket over her slim body, or giving her any other type of comfort. "I'll pass the message on, but there's one more thing you should know."

I leaned close to the woman, very close, so that our noses nearly touched. Her eyes widened at my nearness, the hooded look fading, as if she'd been in a dream and was just now waking up.

I prodded my own chest with a thumb. "I'm keeping Vital's eggs on me at all times," I said. "So if you try to kill me, you risk killing them."

Her face hardened, but she said nothing. I straightened. To her, those eggs could just be *eggs*. Maybe she hadn't cared about Vital as much as I'd thought.

Either way, it was my only leverage. I'd be burned if I didn't use it.

Once I had assured myself that the assassin was safe in her lodgings, I slumped back home, still exhausted from yesterday's trip. I never seemed to get a good night's sleep anymore, and judging by the person I found on my front stoop, I didn't think I'd be headed back to bed anytime soon.

I didn't bother ascending the few steps to the porch. I just sat on them. "What is it, Rachel?"

The woman looked up from a scroll she'd pinned to a slate in her hands. She must have rung the doorbell and then just stood there, reading through her notes, waiting to be let in.

I heard voices on the breeze, meaning Jolene and Becki were still in the yard, on the other side of the building. They wouldn't have heard her ringing the bell. How long had Rachel been standing here, scribbling?

"Ah, there you are, Lord Warren. I've come to take inventory and, I'm afraid, to deliver several sets of bad news."

I leaned by head against a porch post. The sun had crested the mountainous horizon by this point, but the day around me was still soft and moist, the air hazy with drifting steam and unspent rain.

"Our new inventory won't arrive for a while yet," I said. "The porters should bring the dragons over by tonight, though. What's the bad news? Give it to me, all of it."

"Well, regarding that servant woman, the one you called Shimmer... I'm afraid I made no headway in locating her. There have been no reports of missing maidservants anywhere in Parshil over the last week, so whoever she was, she hadn't been running away. She must have been on a trip sanctioned by her master. I'm afraid that was my only hope of finding her, without having her actual name."

I sighed. "Fair enough. You said there was more?"

"Yes." She lowered the scroll-and-slate, tapping it against her leg. "Our ruse with the inspections has stopped buying us time. While I was able to fabricate the addendum you requested, Head Keeper Illowyn has simply rescheduled his inspection of the barn."

We hadn't even *begun* to clean the place out. "Wonderful," I said. "When was it rescheduled for?"

"This afternoon."

I groaned. The inspection was *today?* And here I was, barely able to stand under my own power, with my only helpers busy already, and hardly enough funds to hire laborers... if the duke hadn't already paid off all the city's laborers in exchange for them *not* helping me. I wouldn't put it past that man's wife.

"Damn. Well, we will deal with it somehow. Jolene and I... I don't know. I guess we'll try to have the barn ready in time."

"You had better, or else you will be fined five gold. If you cannot pay the fine, the Keepers will repossess the barn."

My eyes flared wide open and I whipped my head toward her. "Five gold! I've barely got three-and-a-half gold left!"

"Then you shall lose the barn."

Ice cold, I thought. This woman was useful and voraciously intelligent, but a little bit soulless, if you asked me.

"Tilly," I said to the dragon, "go fetch Jo and Becki and bring them here."

As the dragon moved to do as she was asked, a man walked up to the front entrance of the Cage, paused near a metal box there, and then moved on again. It seemed we had received some mail.

With resignation, I rose to grab whatever he'd given us. I had a feeling *it* would be bad news, as well.

Rachel followed me, and I pulled a letter from the box. It was written in a fine and feminine hand, but it was addressed to Jolene.

"Here. This came for you just now," I told her when she arrived. As she ripped it open, I set Becki to the task of discussing the acquisition of those magic breath-bottles with Rachel, and the two women left to collect her daily allotment of cloud breath, leaving me alone with Jolene.

Unfortunately, I now had to ask Jo to return to mucking out stalls with me, once again in a furious hurry. Otherwise, her precious barn would be repossessed.

Before I could drop the news, Jolene scanned the letter and gasped, slapping a hand to her mouth. Tears instantly began to well in her eyes.

I wanted so desperately to sigh again, but I held it back. I laid a hand on her shoulder, but I couldn't hide my tiredness when I asked, "What is it this time?"

She shook her head, scrunching her eyes closed. "It's my friend. My old maid from the Biscuits' keep, Aliese."

I nodded. She'd mentioned the woman before.

"The duke, he's... oh, Warren, it's just horrible."

There was no patience left in me. "Out with it."

Sniffing back tears, she handed me the letter. I flipped the parchment over, and read:

My dearest Lady,
The worst has happened. I returned from an errand to find you
gone from your rooms, and Duke Biscuit waiting at your desk,
asleep. I will not say the state in which I found him, but suffice it
to say that the worst has come to pass. You are gone now, and my

master wants what he wants. He will take it from me when he wakes.

Just know that serving as your maidservant was my honor. I shall miss our friendship and the peaceful life we led, but all things must end. Do not mourn for me. I have taken nightweed root, and with that done, I can accept my lot. I must do this for my brothers in the stables, and for you. The duke must focus his attentions on someone, and if not me, he will harm others.

Thank you again for being the best friend a woman could have.

All my love,

Aliese

"She's going to him!" Jolene wailed. "After all our machinations, she's giving up and *going to him!*"

I reread the letter, stunned. What was that about nightweed root? After the assassin had *just* talked about it? The coincidence was hardly believable, and it took me another read for the situation itself to dawn on me.

"Your maid," I exhaled. "Without you there—"

"The duke is after her!" Jolene sobbed, crashing into me, her head against my chest. "He's been eyeing her this whole past year, ever since he saw her in the bath. We tried so hard to make her look ugly and dull, but he was peeping and he saw her and... and...."

I shoved the letter in my pocket and seized her by the shoulders. "Jolene. She *just* sent this. We can stop it, but we have to go *right now*. But I need you to get Rachel back for me... and I need something else."

"You can stop it? Then ask for anything. Anything!"

I swallowed. "You're not going to like it."

Chapter 66

Before the Fall

WITH YET ANOTHER valuable piece of paper in my trusty pocket, I let a squire take my weapons at the door of the keep. My mind whirred with new information.

Nightweed root, I kept thinking. *It's not possible....*

It was amazing, really, how a letter from a maid I'd never met had solved so many mysteries at once. My stomach felt feathery with nausea. So many secrets, around every corner.

"Focus," I muttered to myself. "This isn't about Fieran. It's about Aliese."

I didn't know the girl, but I knew perfectly well what intentions Biscuit had for her. I wasn't going to let it happen on my watch.

After handing over all but a single hidden knife, I finally made it into the expansive foyer of the keep. I peered up its immaculate, wide staircase carpeted in furs, and very nearly bulled my way up the stairs without stopping to speak with the steward.

"If milord would please wait," the squat steward told me, bowing barely half as low as he probably did to any other noble, "then I shall alert His Grace to your arrival—"

"Where are Jolene's old rooms?" I demanded. "I'm not here to see the duke. I'm here to pick up some of my lady's things."

The steward's eyes darted behind me, noting my distinct lack of company. I'd told Jolene not to come with me. I didn't need her emotions giving up the game.

If she broke down crying upon seeing Aliese, the duke would keep the maid just to hurt us. His wife was more on the pragmatic side, but I'd seen my share of lords. They always had to come out on top, consequences be damned.

Besides, three weeks from now, he'd have my farm. Why should he give me anything, if it could help me keep hold of Pinnacle? I had to control this narrative... and I had to do something that Jolene might not forgive me for.

It was time to drive another hard bargain.

I watched the steward closely as his mouth opened to answer me. He wouldn't tell me where Jolene's room was. He knew what I'd find there. He had also been given instructions never to let me anywhere without the duke or duchess's approval.

Still, if I was looking, he'd give me my answer. His eyes slid upward, to the left, for just a moment. Paling, he said, "Milord—"

I didn't wait to hear his excuses. I shoved past him, fast and hard, so that he couldn't protest and the squire couldn't come after me quickly enough to stop me. I took the stairs two at a time, hearing armor clank as the squire gave chase.

Up and to the left, I told myself. There were two doors on that side of the expansive mezzanine. I chose the door whose window would look into the courtyard, with all its dragon atriums. Jolene would shrivel up and die if she couldn't look upon her dragons.

Gripping the door handle, I pushed, but it didn't open. I nearly kicked it in, but I needed plausible deniability. I pulled my secret knife from its sheath on the underside of the egg bandolier, and ran it up the crack between door and door frame. In most old buildings, that was enough to slip the lock, provided the room wasn't housing anything important—and to the Biscuits, Jolene had never been important.

The lock thunked, and the door drifted inward. I pushed it open and stepped through, hiding the knife in a pocket.

Jolene's room was incredibly tidy, not a single mote of dust in the air or on any surface. A dainty bed, shrouded in lace, took up the center of the room, while a miniature library and sitting chair consumed the left corner.

And in that corner stood Duke Biscuit, his hands around a young woman's waist as he loomed behind her. She was dressed as a maid, in copper-and-blue livery, with a blouse that covered her from wrist to chin, an apron that padded her figure, and a floor-length skirt. She looked bulky and unattractive, which I knew was the point.

But that face. I knew that face.

Her eyes widened. "Tallan?" she whispered.

I almost said her name, the one I had given her. Instead I let the word echo through me.

Shimmer. Aliese is Shimmer.

I had found my lost damsel, after all.

As I stood there, recovering from the shock, Duke Biscuit took his mouth off Shimmer's neck and looked at me. His surprise darkened instantly to anger.

"What is the meaning of this?" he nearly shouted. "Martins! How has this man gotten into the keep!?"

The steward scurried up behind the guard, who had stopped at my back, paralyzed, unsure what to do next. The steward started bowing and making excuses, but I didn't hear them.

Shimmer. No. This was too big of a coincidence.

Except... except maybe it was the *opposite* of coincidence. I suddenly understood. I had met Shimmer in Ignace, where Duke Biscuit had *known* I would be staying. He must have sent her to spy on me, a job she was ideally suited for; as a maid, she could easily find seasonal work during the festival and hide among the staff of any inn.

And she'd found me, all right, because not many inns had still had rooms left to find. Four Demons, she might have even bribed the inn to keep a room open for me.

But instead of reporting on me, she'd been *rescued* by me, and then she'd asked me to take her to bed. I could tell from the way Duke Biscuit held her that he hadn't ordered her to do *that*.

So her story about finding love before her master made her his slave... that had been true. I somehow doubted she'd given Biscuit a good report, either.

I set my stance and took my eyes off her. Now wasn't the time to be surprised. Now was the time to *act*.

I pulled the sheet of paper from my pocket.

"Oh, good. Seems I've found you, Your Grace," I said, striding forward. The steward moved to grab me, then thought better of it. The staff here wasn't used to people barging past them, disregarding their rules and their precious propriety.

I had the element of surprise and confusion, and I wasn't going to waste it.

Duke Biscuit stepped angrily away from Shimmer. Damn, I'd been just in time.

"You haven't been announced," he said to me. "You can't just waltz into any room you please—"

"I've come into a spot of trouble," I said, slapping the paper down on the small table next to the reading chair. "I need more labor, and wouldn't you know it, I'm having trouble finding anyone to hire. It's almost as if someone told all the laborers in Dasvilla that it would be against their best interest to work for me."

Biscuit eyed the paper, his blue eyes flashing. I doubted he'd paid off any laborers himself, but it was certainly something his wife would do. It was a guess on my part, but he'd believe it anyway.

"What is that?" he asked.

"The title to the barn and its surrounding properties," I said. "And it's all yours, Biscuit. I will sign the barn away to you right here and now."

Greed flickered in his eyes. Without the barn and its training fields, I'd have even less chance of making Pinnacle prosperous again.

At least, that's what he would think. I had my own plans for the Cage, but I could leave that out of the conversation.

"How much?" he finally said.

I straightened. "I wish to purchase the indenture contracts of one maid and two strong young men. People already in your employ—no tricks, no pulling random drunks off the streets and throwing them at me. In fact—" I pointed at Shimmer "—I want her. You're Aliese, right? Jolene spoke very highly of you."

Shimmer looked like she hadn't breathed since I'd walked in the room. She weakly pointed at her own chest. "Me?"

I didn't answer her, instead tapping the title to the barn again. I didn't want to look like I cared about Shimmer specifically. I just wanted to look fucking desperate.

"There will need to be a stipulation," I said. "If I ever offer you twice the barn's current value, you have to sell it back to me, no questions asked."

Duke Biscuit had the gall to laugh out loud. "Well now, my young lord, that is very ambitious of you. And where do you think you will come up with that much gold in a mere three weeks, before your venture fails and Pinnacle is mine?"

"That's for me to worry about," I said, but not before I let a spot of panic leak into my expression and my voice. I had to *look* like I was at my wit's end here.

It would fool him, if I played my cards right. People believed what they wanted to believe.

The duke's face changed from amusement to cold calculation, and he picked up the title and scanned it. "You do realize that

461

the labor of three people over three weeks is a drop in the bucket compared to the barn's value?" he said.

"I don't want three weeks. I want their full indenture contracts." Jolene had told me that Aliese was indentured, and now that I'd identified Aliese as Shimmer, I knew her two brothers had to be indentured as well. The boys, supposedly twins, worked in the Biscuit's stables; she'd told me that back in Ignace.

It was for them that Shimmer had chosen to stay with her lord instead of trying to run away.

"Yes, but your business will succeed or fail in a mere three weeks," Biscuit said coolly. "I will purchase the barn, but only if the indentures revert back to me upon the dissolution of Pinnacle Dragons."

I pretended to consider this very seriously. "Fine," I said through gritted teeth.

Without hesitation, Duke Biscuit snapped his fingers. "Martins! Fetch me our Keeper—"

"No need," I said. "I brought one with me. She's out front. But your Keeper can check her work."

Duke blinked, and then his lips curved into a serpentine smile. "My, my, but you *are* anxious. Has something happened?"

"That's none of your concern," I snapped. "You." I pointed to Shimmer. "Go find the two strongest laborers on the property. Stable hands or something. People that are good to work with, no miscreants. Then return here with them."

Her mouth worked for a moment, but finally, she bowed. "Yes, milord! Right away, milord."

She didn't scurry out the door—she *bolted*. She didn't want Biscuit to have a chance to change his mind, and frankly, I didn't either.

Duke Biscuit looked up from the title to watch her go. For an instant, his lust was evident on his face.

Then he muttered to himself. It sounded like *Three weeks.*

I swallowed a grin. He thought he'd have his little toy woman back in three weeks, when I failed at this impossible endeavor. Little did he know that he'd never have Shimmer—not ever. I would die before I let it happen.

Then again, I could die much sooner, and for less.

How far can I get, before I fall? I kept thinking.

Only time—the next three weeks—would tell.

Chapter 67

There's Always a Maid

After the deal was signed, I didn't come home. I sauntered right up to the nearest gate and paid one of my last gold to pass through, borrowing a basket from a fruit picker on the way. They were all headed inside the city for midday, when the heat of the wilds became most oppressive.

I didn't care. I craved the heat. Anything to distract me from what waited for me back at home.

Fieran—and the secrets he'd kept.

I wished it weren't the case, but I'd grown to trust Fieran. I'd laid my life in his hands, and he'd laid his in mine.

Now, I knew the truth about him. It felt like a betrayal, but I just needed time. Time to process, to understand, before I came at him with anger. I knew there was a reason for the secrets.

So I'd think about it while I drove my body to its limits. I'd empty my mind of everything else.

Jolene found me at midday, arriving via Ravager. She dropped into the stand of firefruit trees where I was hacking away, cutting iron-hard stems twenty feet off the ground.

I doubt she could have seen me very well from the sky; Ravager must have served as her eyes. These damned dragons could find me wherever I went. Copper had already shown up an hour ago to watch me from the branches of the trees.

"Oh, Warren. Why don't you come home?" Jolene asked, stepping off Ravager's back with a wineskin of water. "Aliese and her brothers just arrived, and we all want to thank you. What are you doing out here?"

I didn't look down through the knife-sharp branches at her. "Go back, Jo. I need time alone."

She hesitated, then picked her way carefully across the black rock below my tree, avoiding the glowing segments and steaming cracks in the earth. The volcanic land here was deadly, the air unsafe to breathe for too long. I kept a ripped sleeve of my shirt tied over my mouth, a simple trick that cut the poison in the air but did nothing for the sulphuric smell.

"At least take some water," Jolene said, holding the wineskin up toward me. "Here, Shiny can fly it to you."

That drew my eye to the young silver-white dragon. I held out a hand, and she bit into the wineskin near the spout, flapped hard, and rose into the branches, deftly maneuvering between them before landing on my wrist.

"There's a good girl," I said, scratching her behind her head spikes before taking the wineskin. I was suddenly parched, and I drained the whole thing. Jolene could probably hear my chugging even twenty feet below.

"I'll leave another skin hanging on the tree for you," she said after I finished. I dropped the skin, and she caught it. There was a fresh silence after that, and I shook my head and sawed at the nearest firefruit stem with a grunt.

The fruit hung almost out of my reach, and I had to stretch my arms as far as my arm muscles would let me. Everything within easy reach of the ground had been stripped bare by gatherers, and the only firefruit left was dangerous to collect.

One needed resistance to heat and a lot of strength to cut through the bone-hard stems, and although the hot bark was painful against my bare skin, it wasn't bad enough to blister or burn.

If I had to guess, Jolene was down there stewing in both anger and gratefulness. I'd sold the barn, but saved her friend... and then I hadn't even come home to talk to her about it.

That was rude of me, but it had been an overwhelming week, and it wasn't about to let up anytime soon. A lot of conflict remained for me, and I just wanted to spend one long, hot day thinking about only one thing, or nothing at all.

Of course, it wasn't to be. "Update me," I said.

Jolene turned to Ravager and started rubbing her down with a dragon brush, making the green dragon lower her head and start rumbling.

"We have our new dragons back at the villa now. Once the storm cleared, the porters went to deliver our full shipment, only to find the cages empty... but the new dragons just flew straight to us. The porters arrived a little while ago with the eggs and cages, though. They tried to apologize for all the dragons escaping, and I think they about died from relief when they found out we had them all."

I shot Copper a sidelong glance, and the dragon just stared back at me, her copper eyes simmering.

"Now I wonder how that could have happened," I mused.

"Aliese's two brothers went to the barn to get the rest of our original dragons," she went on. "They already knew how to handle the duke's dragons, so the transfer is going well. Soon everyone will be at the Ca—at the villa."

"It's okay to call it the Cage, you know."

She didn't reply. I could feel so many unsaid words in the air between us. I wanted to tell her I'd get the barn back. I wanted to promise her the world—but I couldn't do that.

The truth was, I'd dug myself a very deep hole, and I'd pulled her to the bottom of it with me. There was a good chance we would never climb out.

467

"And the house? Does Aliese think she can manage it on her own?" I asked. I hadn't saved her purely out of the goodness of my own heart, after all. I *did* need a maid. I'd been asking far too much of Becki, and that had led her to drop the ball on Fieran. I'd asked her to take care of not one but *two* side businesses—one of which was still a secret—and the house, and the barn, all at once.

That was untenable. She and Jolene needed help.

"Yes. She's already cleaning in earnest," Jolene replied, so softly I had trouble hearing her. As I strained to catch the words, I managed to saw through the firefruit stem, and the vivid orange fruit dropped to the ground.

I cursed, snatching for it and missing. I wasn't worried it would bruise—only that it would end up in one of the many cracks in the earth, and either melt into the lava below, or simply be lost forever.

The round fruit hit the ground near Jo's feet, and not a moment later, Shiny swooped down and caught it by the stem on the first bounce. Flapping hard, the silver hatchling returned the fruit to me.

"Thanks, girl," I said, taking the boiling-hot fruit by the stem. When I did so, I noticed the stem was shorter than before. I eyed Shiny's sharp fangs. *Hmmm.*

Popping the fruit into my wire basket, I gave Shiny a soft command and watched her scurry ahead of me to the next firefruit branch.

"So Aliese has got the house well in hand," I said. "Are you having trouble emptying the rooms? Anything hard to give up?"

"No. Most of the furniture and heirlooms are long gone," Jolene replied. "Becki says we'll still have enough space to perform the storage service for the nobles she recruited already, just by using old bedrooms and studies. Aliese's brothers are going to go pick up the items when they're done transferring dragons over."

"And the inspection?"

This finally earned a laugh out of her. "The barn failed inspection. Illowyn recorded the failure before he knew you'd sold the place. Rachel says Duke Biscuit will have to pay the fee now.

"Technically, this was a final failure and the barn is supposed to be passed to the crown, but Biscuit will make a back-door deal with Illowyn, and everyone knows it. They both hate you now, by the way."

I chuckled, resting my chin on the heel of a palm as I watched Shiny bite through a firefruit stem in a single dainty chomp. The fruit fell, but using my other hand, I caught it with the basket.

Shiny looked at me, cocking her head. I held up a finger. "One piece of jerky per fruit," I said. "You're not going to stop at just one, are you?"

She gave an excited peep and moved on down the branch to the next fruit. Seeing no point in still being up here, I started to climb backwards down the branch.

"Honestly, you have them picking *fruit* for you now?" Jolene breathed, as I dropped to the ground to find three firefruits already waiting for me. Jolene had raced to save one from a crack, but the others were easy enough to scoop up.

"I don't think just any dragon could do it," I said, looking up to watch Shiny. I knew she was part cloud-dragon, but I didn't know her parentage. "Who was her father, by the way?"

"A pure-blooded lava dragon. We had to sell him."

I nodded. Lava dragons probably had magma breath, or something similar—I was still learning—while cloud dragons like Tilly had knockout-gas breath. A mixture of the two could definitely be something caustic.

"I think I know her breath ability," I said. "She can melt through iron by breathing on it. Not sure what she's invulnerable to, though. I guess time will tell."

"Fascinating," Jolene mused, her eyes still glued to Shiny. "There are so many uses for that...."

As she trailed off, it struck me just how beautiful she truly was. She'd chosen to wear a dress to come see me, a fancy riding dress with slits up to the thighs, but a dress all the same. It matched her hair, golden with hints of pink to it, a lovely ombre gradient starting at a low-cut neck and ending at her ankles.

A chain of some sort also hung in between her breasts, but the jewel was lost to the cavernous dark. I followed it with my eyes, then found her face again before she could catch me looking.

Don't go lusting after her just yet, I told myself.

But my body had other ideas.

Chapter 68

I Know How Trolls Work

I shook myself, both mentally and physically. *She deserves to be wooed properly,* I kept thinking, *and you don't have the time for that. You can't give her less than she deserves.*

With all the worries of Pinnacle breathing down my neck, I was no good for trying to earn myself a proper wife—because Jolene deserved that. She was a noble. She wouldn't want to be a woman scorned by a man with... I counted... *two* other lovers.

Three, if you counted Shimmer, but of course that relationship would have to stop now. I would not let Shimmer believe she owed me anything like that. I was *not* Duke Biscuit.

Yet despite all these arguments, I found myself closing the distance between us, curling an arm around Jolene's back, and pulling her close before I could even think. Half-panicked by my own movement, I tried to cover myself by hugging her, when everything in my body screamed for a kiss.

"Thanks, Jolene," I croaked out. "For the water. And for being an incredible steward."

I pulled away, but she leaned into me, and so I paused, my arm still on her back. She met my gaze as firefruit continued to thud to earth behind us. I heard a hiss as one dropped into lava, but even though it was worth nearly a silver on its own, I couldn't tear myself away from Jolene's eyes.

"Why are you out here, Warren?" she asked, her hand on my chest. It was like she didn't even notice my closeness, like she didn't even know I'd sold the barn. Her eyebrows merely dipped with concern for me.

Four Demons, I wanted her in that moment. I wanted to take her right there against Ravager's flank, hooking her legs over my hips like we'd done on accident on the dragonflight. I wanted to slip inside her and see that mouth open in pleasure as I rocked her over the edge of oblivion.

Shit, I was getting hard, and this was not the time nor place for any of that. Besides, none of that same want showed on her face. It was all me, while she was all business.

I backed off a bit more. "I learned something today that has me upset. I'm working it out in my head." I paused. "Also, I wanted to keep the eggs warm."

I indicated the bandolier strapped across my chest, although I'd adjusted it so the egg cages clung to my back, not my front, where I couldn't damage them while climbing on my stomach. I wore no shirt, just the bandolier and the sleeve over my mouth, plus a pair of sweaty pants and boots.

"The assassin is gone," Jolene whispered. "Fieran checked the inn."

Fieran. The anger rose again, but it was less now.

He was afraid. So afraid. And with good reason, too. I might have done the same, in his shoes.

"I figured the blood mage would leave the moment she woke up," I said. "She's a real tough demon-horn, that one."

I almost asked if Fieran had gone to take the nightweed root— but I didn't. That was his choice, not mine.

Jolene's hand on my bare chest turned into a claw, but her eyes dipped away from my face. She bit her lower lip before saying, "Are you hiding from the assassin? Out here?"

"Not hiding. Just keeping away from the people I care about. If she tries to kill me here, Copper will see her coming... besides, she has no dragon and no money. She'd have to risk walking out here to get to me, and the hot ground isn't the only threat."

It was a temporary runaround, but another benefit of hunting firefruit. No one was likely to bother me here. No one except trolls, that is.

Another firefruit hit the ground and then burst into flame with a *whoosh* behind me. Jolene sighed. "Well, I'll leave you to it. The firefruit will bring in quite a lot, and we're letting it go to waste by just standing here. I should get back and start making the dragons comfortable."

I hefted my basket, fighting my every urge to toss it aside and kiss her. *She deserves better. A real courtship. Not a quick fuck in the wilds.*

I managed to turn away to start collecting the fruit. "I'll stay out here just long enough to cover our next three weeks of food bills," I said. "How much do you think we'll need?"

She gave me a number, and I nodded, calculating. With all our collective dragons now headed into the aviary around the villa, I had to set about solving our new biggest issue: food. Feeding myself, Jolene, and our various new hires was really simple. To feed an aviary full of dragons was something different—not to mention we had to feed the hatchlings Jolene had agreed to raise to adolescence, which were no longer housed in the barn.

So I needed to earn some income to help float the business, but Jolene had been right: I shouldn't be risking my life finding excuses to kill off a few monsters.

If I died, Jolene and all my new employees were fucked, except maybe for Rachel. Firefruit was damned hard to harvest and dangerous to touch, but it paid even better than bounties did, at least by the pound. Picking the fruit killed a dozen young peasants every year, but I was more resilient than your everyday commoner.

Besides, I liked hard work.

"Kenna told me the crown is paying near a silver apiece for firefruit, and Copper seems to like eating it," I said, pointing to the mystery dragon still up in the tree.

"Whatever she really is, we want her growing fast so she can start breeding. Anyway, I should have enough by nightfall."

"Yes, I heard. The king seems to be hoarding the stuff. Just... please come back with the second-shift day laborers, will you?" Jolene said. "The trolls around here are more vicious than they were in your childhood, and they can appear right out of the ground when the sun goes down."

I swung my arm to catch a falling fruit with the basket. "I know how trolls work, Jolene," I said softly. "But I'll return soon, I promise."

Jolene hesitated there, still standing next to Ravager. Finally she walked up to me. I turned around and said, "Is there something—?"

Jolene flipped open my cloth mask and kissed me square on the mouth.

"Thank you," she said. "Thank you for Aliese."

Then she spun on her heel and nearly ran back to Ravager. I watched her mount and take off with my jaw on the ground, her golden dress like sunlight behind her.

I finally closed my mouth and thought, *Nothing could surprise me now... knock on wood.*

And I tapped my knuckles on the tree, just in case.

Chapter 69

Harvest Season

When the second-shift laborers emerged from Dasvilla to start harvesting fruit in the cooler hours of the day, a group of orphans streamed out alongside them. I recognized the kids by their ragged clothing and numbered marks on their hands.

The women who ran the orphanage would mark the kids daily in permanent ink, just to let other people know the kids belonged somewhere and weren't running wild. If one misbehaved, a person could report their number, and the kid would be disciplined. I used to be number twelve.

Upon seeing them, I sent Copper to fly above them and watch for threats. "Stay high, though. I don't want you to scare them."

I didn't like seeing those kids out here. Orphans were always eager to earn income—that was no different than it had been in my time—but we'd never been mad enough to go after firefruit. Sure, we could climb trees with the best of them, but other laborers would stake out their favorite stands of trees and beat anyone who crossed into their territory.

"Oi!" I said, waving once the kids got close. "Over here! I'll pay for your help."

Most of the locals were afraid to hire orphans, because "if you help 'em once, the little rats never stop coming." It was a rude assessment, but not wrong.

Well, I *wanted* to see them keep coming. It was funny how, if you only ever looked for opportunities, you started seeing them everywhere.

"I'll pay you for a sip from your wineskin," I told the first boy, offering him a silver. He took it greedily, palming it before I could have stopped him, even if I had wanted to.

After I downed a healthy swig of his mineral-tasting water, I asked, "How's the old building doing? The orphanage?"

The two oldest kids, a boy and a girl disguised as a boy, glanced at each other. "It's fallin' apart, lord sir," the girl said.

My face fell. I should have visited before now. "Is that because Lady Etonia is gone?"

"She hadn't been round much," the boy replied. His skin was brown, like Fieran's skin, which might be why he hadn't been adopted. Foreigners never got much respect in Parshil. "But we learned to sew and read 'cause of her and Lady Jo. The little ones miss 'em both."

I fell into a crouch beside the two leaders, holding their gazes.

"Do you know who I am?" I asked them.

They shifted nervously. "No, sir," the girl said. She was the braver one, then. I guessed she was thirteen, maybe fifteen at most. The boy was older, but he seemed to defer to her.

I looked past them. The gates would stay open for another few hours.

"How about you help me collect firefruit? Full pay, of course. Half the take to the orphanage." I lowered my gaze. "Plus a silver for each of you, to spend how you like."

A gasp of excitement ran back through the gathered children, but the dirt-faced girl narrowed her eyes and looked up at the tree I'd been climbing. Like the rest in the little area I'd staked out, the only fruit remained in the highest branches.

"I'm sorry sir, but no, we ent gonna climb to the tops for ya. We lost two kids last year tryna do that. They fall off and break their necks. It's too far."

My stomach curdled. "That's terrible." My voice had dipped to a growl, but I brought it back up again, taking a breath. "No. I just want you to catch the fruit. I've already got a picker. See?"

With that, I held out a hand just as Shiny dropped a firefruit into it. I caught the round, red-orange object with ease.

When I looked at it, my old aversion to the color orange took hold of my stomach for a moment.

Eyes like glass. Scales like opals. A dead arachne, torn to shreds, while I stood with a mere sword in my hand.

I shook off the feeling. The girl's eyes widened and she looked up at the tree.

"What? You already got a kid up there?"

"Not a kid." I leaned closer, whispering close to her ear. "A *dragon.*"

The orphans murmured again at my conspiratorial admission, and I whistled at Copper to come down. She alighted behind me like a loyal hound, and I could swear she'd grown from today's firefruit snacks alone. Her head came up to my chest, where before, she'd reached my waist.

I patted her. "This one will protect you all from anyone trying to take your spot or your fruit."

I pointed up. "There's also a hatchling up there doing the harvesting. You'll need to pay her in jerky, but I'll give you some silver to run back and buy some. I just don't have the time to do this myself right now."

I'd made enough to cover the rest of the month's food bill, after all, and it was time I moved on to other tasks. I patted the girl on the shoulder.

"It'll be a tough job, even if it sounds easy. I'll need you to collect the fruits, which are falling all over the place, so you'll have to watch your feet. You also have to keep the harvesting dragon happy, and keep the kids and dragons safe from anyone trying to steal them.

"Also, make sure the fruit gets to *Rachel* at the Keeper's head-quarters. She'll get the best price, and pay you your half up front. Then return the dragons to me at the end of the day.

"Plus, I'd better not hear you were taking all that money for yourselves. It goes to the orphanage. That's non-negotiable."

Her eyes had grown wider with each new responsibility. She was starting to realize this was the real deal.

"Uh, yes sir. I can do that, sir. Milord."

"You don't have to call me Lord. I'm just Warren to you lot." I shot one of the nearby eight-year-olds a wink, making the little girl blush.

To the leader, I went on, "Anyway, do all this for me, and you can do it again tomorrow, right up until the firefruit trees are bare. Copper can go out each morning to stake a claim for you, so you've always got something to harvest.

"But *only* if you stay honest. I'll know if you don't.

"So, kid. What do you say?"

Chapter 70

Let's Play Games

I STAYED with my new workers until dusk, giving them tips on how to work with the dragons while keeping other workers away.

When night started to fall, I sent the lead orphan, Tiff, to Rachel with the goods, making sure Copper stayed close and looked menacing. I might just send Ravager tomorrow, because she was bigger and a lot snappier.

"It's all thanks to you, Shiny," I said, patting the Mount-class hatchling with real affection.

Normally, the fruit at the tops of firefruit trees went to seed. The trees themselves could only be cut apart by magic, and doing so was highly illegal since it damaged the trees' ability to reproduce the next year. So, people weren't able to just cut trees or branches down to harvest them.

That meant directly picking each fruit by hand, but the only people who could get close enough to saw off the stems were kids. This was especially dangerous work, because the branches were either too smooth for good purchase, or too sharp to be safe to climb on.

Children got killed every year doing this for their families, and rage coiled in my gut to think people had hired orphans for it, too. Tiff was a smart kid to outlaw the job among her own clan

479

of orphans. It showed what she truly valued, and I was pretty sure I could trust her.

When I ushered the orphans inside the city gate at the end of the day, the Dasvilla watchmaster observed from the wall's edge. We nodded at each other, both with respect. We'd had plenty of adults try to steal our fruit, and although they had failed, rumors of what we were doing had spread. Apparently, the watchmaster approved.

Becki also stood inside the gate, handing out coins to each worker one at a time. I'd sent an orphan to her with a message—plus one to Rachel—and Becki, at least, had come through for me. Those coins were her own money, since I hadn't had enough silvers on me to pay the kids.

I waited until the gate closed behind us to approach Becki. She was being watched by the troops on the wall. When coins got passed out, trouble sometimes followed, so the guards were helping to keep the process smooth.

"Lord Warren, I must say, a single day outside the city and already people are starting to notice you," Becki said, shifting her gaze to the main street of Dasvilla, where Duchess Nola walked her house-sized Hauler dragon down the street, away from me.

The huge blue beast towered over the duchess, large enough for her entire entourage to ride it—and they were. About a dozen maidens of her court were seated atop a sort of palanquin, but all of them seemed to be turned in their chairs, looking at me.

"Her maidens tried to steal a peek when you were out there," Becki said, nodding toward the wilds, "and the guards had to kick them off the battlements because the dragon was ruining the masonry. Seems you are quite the lady-killer. Should I expect more additions to the Cage here, soon?"

"I'm completely content with the lovely lady I already have," I said with a grin, throwing an arm across her shoulder.

Becki snickered. "You say that, but there are rumors claiming you sleep alone. And as long as people think you're an eligible bachelor, you'll become prey for the ladies-in-waiting."

"Do I?" I asked.

"Do you what?"

I leaned my mouth next to her ear. "Do I sleep alone?"

Her moon-white skin flushed bluish, that strange magical cold emanating off her. She slapped my shoulder lightly.

"I've taken my own room in the Cage, thank you very much." She paused. "Although it just *happens* to be right next to yours."

I laughed and bent down to pet Collette. She rubbed against my hand, grinning in the doglike way some dragons did. I frowned and plucked a scale from her teeth.

"Wait, is she eating dragons?" I asked.

Becki looked lovingly down at her pet. "Oh, definitely, but only wild ones. She flies off to the north once a day or so. I think she found a mate out there, and he keeps feeding her treats, because she acts *very* satisfied whenever she comes back.

"But she knows better than to hunt around town. People kill dragons that go after their stock."

I eyed her stomach, wondering if Collette was already pregnant. "Can we feed her chickens in exchange for her wild dragon prey? As in, can she bring them back alive?"

My most entrepreneurial partner laughed as if I'd just made a great joke. "If I could just tell a dragon to do something specific like that, then I wouldn't be selling ale on street corners, or pitching empty mansion rooms to rich people as storage units."

She slipped her hand into mine, bumping her shoulder against my arm. "But if you want to ask her, knock yourself out. Maybe my little princess will listen to you."

I silently resolved to do just that, when I saw the duchess stop far ahead of us on the road, in the market area. Some of her ladies even came down off the dragon to look over the same stall as their mistress.

"Maki," I growled, my lip curling.

"Ah. I see you've met yet *another* person who spent effort trying to leech away the last of the Minax wealth," Becki said. "Speaking of which. The Biscuits lowered the dragon egg standard pricing today."

I groaned. "Tell me that doesn't mean what I think it means."

"Yep. We won't be seeing any more imports for a while. That's probably why the duchess is stopping to check Maki's stock... he's got the only eggs left in town."

Great. Now I'd have to pay to leave town—or I'd have to venture far into the wilds—if I wanted more eggs. Oh well. I had enough to hatch for now, and if the duchess bought all of Maki's stock, that was good news for me. The ones he had left were all duds.

"Is it just me, or does it feel like we're at war?" I asked. "Wait here a minute. I need to see the duchess. After that, I'd like a meal and a bath with a beautiful woman. You can let me know if there are any volunteers."

I walked away, but Becki didn't have a tactful bone in her body. She shouted to my back, "Your wish is my command, Big General Warren! I'll be taking applications for women to warm your bed this night!"

I suddenly had a good idea why people thought I was single: Becki was the one perpetuating that rumor. I shook my head while a grin spread across my face. It was ingenious, in a way.

If I wasn't "taken," then the nobles of this town would be more likely to be nice to me, in the hopes that their daughters and sisters might catch my eye.

Duchess Nola was deep in conversation with a handmaiden as I approached, but she cut the woman off with the flip of a hand. She wore a classy summer dress, in a light blue that softened her hazel eyes. She wore her hair in a bun, likely because of the sweltering humidity.

Her towering male dragon had a deep blue coloration, his eyes yellow. I had a feeling that Nola's true persona matched the dragon much more than the dress.

When I stopped and bowed to Nola, her dragon laid down, forcing some of the maidens out of the way. It didn't look like Nola had commanded him to do that, and she shot the beast a pissed-off look.

"Reginald!" she scolded. "Get back up this instant!"

The dragon had its eyes on me, though, and I dipped into an awkward bow. "He's showing respect, that's all. Aren't you, Reginald?"

The dragon rumbled, and Nola scoffed. "More theater from you, Young Lord? Do you ever tire of such tricks? And you are bowing in the wrong direction. You are *my* vassal, not his."

I didn't argue, merely granting her a second bow. No one could miss who I'd bowed to first.

An attendant ran up to Nola then, curtsying at me. With a coy smile, she said, "So *this* is the famous Lord Orpheus-Minax! I must say, he's more handsome up close."

"Shut up, Jasmine, you are *sixteen,*" the duchess snapped, scowling.

"Your pardon, milady, but I'm sixteen and two seasons," Jasmine replied demurely, grinning up at me. I didn't meet her eyes. *Way too young.*

I extended a hand to the dragon, and Reginald gently pushed the young maiden out of the way to accept my scratch on his snout. "It is nice to make your acquaintance, Lady Jasmine," I said politely, trying to make it clear I wasn't interested.

Young noblewomen like her were always chasing after big scary men like me, and it rarely ended well, because most big men that went after young girls were *actually* scary. As for me, I just looked the part.

"A messenger came yesterday, claiming a most absurd story," the duchess said. "I was stopping to see Baron Maki here to confirm it. Is it true you hatched a night dragon from this very stall?"

"Yes, I did," I said. The hatchling was currently resting with our other babies, living her best life.

Nola raised her chin imperiously. "Well then, I'll have you know that this news shall upset the king. While there is no law against a night dragon bonding with someone outside the royal family, it is highly frowned upon."

Duchess Nola narrowed her eyes. "It is *also* frowned upon to sell a building that has an impending inspection date *the same day* of the sale. You have cost my husband a great deal of money."

Here we go again, I thought. By the Four Demons, how I *hated* these political games.

All the same, I had to learn how to play.

Chapter 71

Big Happy Family

I SPREAD MY HANDS, feigning ignorance. "Is that so? Why, Your Grace, I am aggrieved by this news. I had no knowledge of any such inspection. Are we certain it was made public?"

There was a pause where something flickered behind her eyes. Nola knew as well as I did that no one had *officially* come to tell me about the inspection. Rachel hadn't been ordered to do it. She'd done is as my business partner, not as a Keeper.

Scheduling impromptu inspections without notice was not a good look... and if anyone looked into it too deeply, the duchess's own husband could be implicated.

She knew it as well as I did, so she changed the subject, her tone flat: "I would suggest you stay out of trouble, Lord Warren. For good this time. I will not give you any more warnings."

I bowed again. "My Duchess, I fully support you, Duke Biscuit, and the people of Dasvilla, but I will not be cowed before such vague threats. I have broken no laws, yet you tell me to watch myself? Might I remind you that I make enemies everywhere I go by simply *existing*?

"If you know that history, you should also know that at some point, a man has to stop being walked over. Better to die a martyr than a doormat," I said, letting my last sentence hang.

485

She pinched the bridge of her nose, before releasing it to roll both her wrists in the air in front of her. I'd seen other ladies make the same odd movement, as if they were unwinding all their stresses, like unspooling thread from an invisible bobbin.

After a breath, she said, "Since you are here, I will let you know that His Grace the duke has reviewed your application to rent exterior farmland. He approved, mostly because the land you requested is well-known troll territory. I can't imagine what you intend to do with it, but my husband surely wishes you dead."

I smiled at her candor. She was apparently done bandying words with me, and we both knew the true powers of this war were standing right here, right now. The land rental was another idea of Rachel's, and it had worked.

"But be prepared, Lord Warren," Nola added, "if we start to suffer deaths outside the walls because you are on some sort of... *troll* crusade, you'll be held responsible, no matter how many bounties you hand in."

"Your Grace, the dragon population in Dasvilla is growing each day, and the demand for dragon feed is growing with it," I replied. "Soon, I won't be able to feed my dragons because your husband will buy up all the feed before I get a crack at it.

"Therefore, I felt it was time Dasvilla expanded its supply of chicken, beef, and other meats, while also growing the grains to support them. To do this, I need to plant fields, and there are no more open fields within the walls of Dasvilla."

"Too many dragons! Oh, *please*," a different attendant cut in. The woman swished forward, her skirts clinking with bead-work, another blue-eyed, blond-haired lovely with an imperious air. "We own a fraction of the dragons the other dukedoms do."

Duchess Nola craned her head back with a long and flustered exhale. "Lord Warren, this is Second Duchess Oscilla, my sister-wife. She is more than *happy* to leave Dasvilla at any opportunity, to vacation abroad where she can let others know the many weaknesses of the home city she hates."

The duke's got one big happy family, I see, I thought, inclining my head at Oscilla, who was now holding her rotund stomach as if to advertise she was pregnant.

"Well met, Second Duchess," I said, not taking the bait. I'd already waded into enough politics for a lifetime, and there was no point arguing with nobles who were convinced they were right. I might be new to dragons and relatively new to farming, but I sure as the Four Demons could see the math didn't work out.

Dasvilla could not sustain the dragons I intended to bring into it, and if I was going to make Dasvilla the dragon hub it deserved to be, I had to start laying foundations now.

"By the way, Your Grace, thank you for expediting my land request," I said to Nola. "It shows just how serious the rulers of this great city—"

"Great! Ha!" Oscilla scoffed. At this point, most of the duchess' retinue wanted to be anywhere else. The entire group of them —even Jasmine—shifted uncomfortably, suddenly keeping their eyes on their feet.

"You may be handsome," Oscilla went on, "but you are a kiss-ass."

Is she drunk? While she's pregnant? I did see a maid in the group with a tray of wine glasses, so I wouldn't put it past her.

I bowed again. "Whether you share my opinion or not, it is my belief that Dasvilla is a grand city. It merely has potential that has not yet been utilized."

Oscilla rolled her eyes. "Ha! Men. You think you can change everything. Watch your back, orphan. The lords of this town hate grand-standers more than they hate crazy, bleeding-heart noblewomen who hurl false accusations for dozens of years at a time."

I didn't miss the jab at Lady Etonia. It felt very targeted, and I reminded myself to look into Oscilla's background when I had the chance.

"Funny, how the mere mention of my love for Dasvilla seems to upset its own people," I commented, unable to help myself.

Duchess Nola unleashed what could only be described as a full-on witch cackle. "Oh, but he *is* entertaining! First he bargains away the inheritance of a lifetime, then he claims he has killed a whole tribe of orcs, *then* he supposedly 'saves' a dragonflight from crashing, and not a day later he bonds to a night dragon... only to *complain* he is getting too much attention?"

Nola shook her head at me. "My dear young lord, living the way that you do isn't exactly a good way to stay quiet."

"He isn't doing any of that for attention!" the younger maid, Jasmine, interjected. Her sweet face had flushed with anger, apparently on my account. "I'm Viscountess Jasmine, by the way, since neither of my mothers wants to introduce me properly."

Jasmine's pointer finger leveled Copper, who'd fallen asleep with her head curled around my boots. "That is an Airship-class, at least, Mothers," she said. "An Airship! You can tell by the groupings of spikes.

"He hasn't been here a week, yet he's already acquired both a night dragon and another Airship, not to mention whatever he's got picking fruit for him. He has upset not only the king, but also the local government, from duke to Enforcer right down to the Head Keeper, yet he's not afraid.

"Why does a guardsman elevated to lord not fear a king's wrath? That is the question we should be asking. We should show him respect, not disdain."

"Why isn't he afraid? *Why?* Because he wants to hang!" Oscilla blurted.

I was starting to understand why Duke Biscuit kept Oscilla away from his courtroom.

Jasmine shook her head. "You are foolish, Second Mother. First Mother is supporting him, even though she doesn't wish to appear to be doing it. Her own agents guard him, for drag-onssakes!

"The ruling class have also paid heed to her message, to let him win or fail on his own, and to stay out of his way. Can you not see that he has the potential to help Dasvilla prosper, after so many years of Father's mishandling? You should learn from Duchess Nola, Second Mother, for she is far less foolish than you."

My eyes were wide by this point, and I actually whistled. This kid was as sharp as a fang.

Oscilla's face purpled, but she didn't storm off or cause a scene. When Duchess Nola said nothing, Oscilla turned her wrath on me.

"Who exactly *are you*, to speak like this to your betters?" she seethed. "And you had better give me a good answer, sir, or I will call up my cousin the justicar to get an even better one out of you."

Chapter 72

Caution, Wet Floor

"I'M JUST a simple orphan with a tragic backstory," I said, rapidly tiring of this conversation. I'd only come over here to see if there was any movement on the farmland application, and maybe to make a few friends among Nola's court.

"And young Jasmine here is right," I added. "It is my goal to make Dasvilla better, and I would be honored to have your assistance in that. But for now, my dear ladies, we must part."

I bowed and began to walk away without further ado. Copper woke as soon as I moved and stuck to my right knee again, scanning the street ahead of me.

I headed for a tavern, ignoring the ladies as they broke into chatter behind me. I was hungry, and I could rent a bath there instead of having to draw one myself at the Cage.

Copper kept up with ease, weaving through the evening traffic and never letting me out of her sight. I got the sense she really hated it when I went indoors, and it was no different when the short walk ended at the boisterous tavern I'd been looking for.

The young dragon—we still didn't know what she was—flew to perch on the roof to wait for me, every movement betraying her dislike of the situation. At the same time, she didn't seem the least bit worried that, at night in border cities like this one, rooftops could become hunting grounds for Behemoths.

Like her master, she seemed to have no problem living life dangerously, and that danger quickly found me again. Once inside the loud and crowded main floor, I hailed a young lad who managed the heated baths. I paid, shedding my sweaty pants into a cleaning bin, and I let the work of the day fade into the hot water around me.

Only five minutes had passed when an Enforcer entered the baths, all by his lonesome. I recognized him as Garm, the man who had wanted to take Becki as a second wife.

I'd expected someone to try to find me alone at some point, and that moment was now. I rose out of the water, and he didn't protest, merely unsheathed his sword with a wicked grin.

"I'm just here to talk," Garm said, his disarming voice at odds with his smile.

Even if he was telling the truth, I didn't care. I threw my egg bandolier on over my head—the thing never left my sight—and I confidently strode across the tiled floor between us, completely naked, saying nothing.

At the last second, he understood the only discussion I wanted was the violent kind.

"Hey, hey, wait—"

I swung a punch, and to his credit, he blocked with his arm and didn't attempt any sword strike. This gave *some* credence to him wanting to just talk, but so many things had me angry.

Shimmer's predicament, the raised egg prices, and Fieran and his secret... not to mention the orphans who had died picking firefruit, and the idea that Nola was even remotely on my side, playing games with me, *always* playing games....

So many small horrors, like knife cuts, notching ever deeper inside me. I needed to hurt something *right now*.

I head-butted Garm without any warning, then reeled back, shaking the stars out of my vision. His sword clattered to the porcelain floor as he cried out, and I pushed his weapon away with a foot. He swung at me, and I jerked my shoulder out of his reach, so that he punched a pillar behind me.

He shouted in agony, then shook out his hand. A knuckle stuck out of the skin, white and bleeding. He started swearing up a storm.

"Fuck, Warren, I just want to—"

My right fist slammed into his stomach with enough force to double him over. "Argggh! What the—milord, please!"

I punched his right thigh, numbing his leg until he plopped down into an awkward sitting position. At the same moment, an attendee opened the door to see what the commotion was. I glared at the young man, but he stood frozen. I was a bit surprised that he didn't flee.

"Fetch my robes," I commanded.

"But... but the Enforcer, sir—"

"This Enforcer slipped on the wet floor, and he's fine. You may leave him to me."

The boy hesitated, watching the groaning Garm, but the difference in rank between us was clear. "Yes, m'lord."

He vanished, and I sat on the bench on the other side of the small room with my foot resting on Garm's fallen sword. "What do you want?" I growled at him.

"Four Demons! I just came to tell you to give up the night dragon. Justicar Ormish promises protection for the dragon, a...." He hissed from pain. "A great trade. His words, not mine."

Protection? What exactly does that mean?

"No," I said simply. "The dragon is bonded to me. Ormish will have to try to capture her like everyone else plans to."

This gave Garm pause. *What? You thought I hadn't seen the gold coins in people's eyes at the very sight of my purple-black hatchling?*

People would be out to steal her in no time. I had Useless on permanent guard duty.

"Everyone knows you'll kill anyone who tries to snatch her,"

Garm conceded, loosing another pained grunt. "Unless you introduce the new buyer and try to transfer the bond."

"Hey, look at me. Garm." I snapped my fingers, getting his attention. His blue eyes drifted up to match mine.

"There ya go. Now listen closely. I'm not your enemy, but I'll go to war with you if you piss me off, and you'll lose. The duke and duchess don't like your boss, you know that? And what exactly is he offering *protection* for?"

Garm kept clutching his hand. "The Biscuits and the justicar are good friends—"

"No duke is *good friends* with his justicar. Nobles hate to share power, and they hate oversight even more."

At the Supplication meeting, the justicar and the Biscuits had obviously plotted to disinherit me. However, the moment I'd foiled their plan, the Biscuits had sent the justicar packing.

He was their tool. Nothing more.

But if he was trying to intimidate me in a bath house, of all places, then he had ulterior motives as well. He'd wanted me disinherited just as much as the Biscuits, but why? His motivations couldn't be the same.

"At least you know how to play the game," Garm said.

"Speaking of, buy me two months, Garm, and I'll replace him," I said. "Maybe if you do well, you could be the next justicar around here, at least until the king slots another failed officer into the position."

The bathroom attendant arrived then with a set of robes. Behind him, the tavern bouncer loomed. I used a foot to slide the sword back to the Enforcer. Everyone saw me do it, and we all knew what it meant.

"You should be more careful on wet floors, Garm," I said.

He didn't look at me. "Message received, milord."

It had better be. I was done being hunted and toyed with and used, and if anyone ever tried getting me alone in the bath again, they wouldn't walk out with their balls still attached.

The bouncer chuckled. "Hit yer head a bit hard, didja?" he said to Garm. "Well, I'll make sure the ladies have a look. Come on, lemme help ya up."

I left the two men to it, snatching my still-wet, half-scrubbed trousers from the attendant's hands and stuffing my legs into them, back in the hallway. Copper chirped approvingly as I exited back onto the street.

The truth was, my situation was only going to get worse. If the justicar of this city—the absolute *epitome* of law and order— was trying to shake me down for my dragon, he wouldn't be the last, and likely wasn't the first.

I also wouldn't be the only target. The Biscuits and the justicar and who-knew-who-else would go after Jolene next, since Becki was protected by her affiliation with Nola. And what about Aliese and her brothers? What about Rachel, even Kenna?

People were relying on me, many more than I'd planned on. With that in mind, I had to devise a plan to lay low for a bit— and that plan sure as shit wouldn't involve living in a luxury villa with multiple unprotected entry points.

An idea began to form. Jolene was going to hate it, but if she wanted to save Pinnacle Dragons, this was the best way forward... I hoped.

Chapter 73

Housekeeping!

THAT NIGHT, I avoided Jolene. I knew my deal was going to make her emotional, and already, I hated to see her upset—in part because I wasn't sure what to do, but also because I wanted badly to hold her. And holding her was a bad idea. I was worried I wouldn't be able to control myself if I had her against me like that.

I had been poring over some of the Pinnacle documents in my rooms for several hours, trying to make sense of the business and its debts, when a soft knock sounded at my door. Frowning, I called out, "Come in."

The door swung wide, pushed from the other side, and an ancient cleaning cart appeared over the threshold. Nothing that still remained in this villa was new anymore.

Shimmer stood behind it, wearing her apron of station. She trundled the cart into the room.

"Shimm—" I started to say, then stopped as she turned.

She wasn't wearing anything under her apron.

It had taken me a moment to notice, but now it was obvious. Her tawny skin shone slightly orange in the light from my hearth, her ass so round and smooth that my hands itched to grab it. As she faced me again, I caught a glimpse of side-boob that made my heart race. I'd forgotten just how big those tits were when they weren't smashed up inside a uniform.

She curtsied daintily at me. "Milord," she said. "I'm just making my rounds."

"In *that?*" I choked out. What sort of cleaning had she done for Lord Biscuit?

"It's a special uniform, to be used only for your rooms." She pushed the cart forward. "Do you like it?"

I wasn't sure what to say, so I went with, "Yes?"

She parked the cart by my desk and pulled a feather duster off the front, then stepped around the edge of the desk top toward me. She curtsied again.

"If Master would pardon me, I saw some cobwebs under this desk when I did my first survey of the manor, and I would hate for Master to be bitten by a spider. May I?"

I swallowed thickly, knowing there wasn't a single cobweb anywhere near my feet. "Shimmer—Aliese. You don't have to do this."

She cocked her head at me. "Do what, milord?"

I held out a hand, indicating her bare collarbone down to her bare legs and feet. "This. I didn't get you out of Biscuit's keep so I could have a... a sex slave, or something. You aren't beholden to me. You can live your own life. I never expected you to—"

She caught me off guard by placing a hand on my knee and leaning so far forward that I could see the darker flesh of one nipple under her sinking apron.

"Milord," she said lowly, "please let me get the cobwebs."

I searched her eyes, my blood spinning, my cock responding like the idiot that it was.

"Um... very well," I said, pushing the chair back to make room for her.

She smiled, her brown eyes flickering with firelight. With her weight still on my knee, she bent down and knelt in front of me. For a moment she hovered there, her hand drifting to my thigh, the crevasse between her tits making my stomach feel light.

Then she shifted in place, ducking under the desk and revealing her backside in all of its glory.

Oh, fuck, I thought. What had I been doing before she came in? And why hadn't I been dreaming of that perfect ass, those plush thighs and the dainty dip of her back, the waist where my hands would fit perfectly? And those two ties of the apron, so easily pulled, and the little shakes of her side boob as she fluffed her duster around?

I laid my hand on her lower back without thinking, and she stilled momentarily, then set back to her completely fake work, dusting slowly, sensuously.

"I'm sorry, Master, but there's something way back under here. Give me just another few moments," she said, and her head ducked low, her ass rising up, her back arching. Her sex came into view, the pink-and-red folds, the faint glisten between her bronze thighs.

"Take as long as you need," I said, running my hand upon her back over her ass, and then under it. She shuddered, moaning ever-so-softly as I traced a finger where her butt met her thigh and then ran it up into her pussy.

I dipped my finger between the folds, pressing it up and down again, watching the way the flesh curled around my fingertip. I dipped into her, finding her inner channel wet and tight. My other hand had found my cock already, and I absently stroked myself through my pants.

She pushed back against my hand, shoving my finger deeper. With my ring finger, I added pressure to her nub.

"Oh..." she breathed out. "If, um, if Master could help me...."

"I'd love to help," I said.

"I've found some dust. But it's really far back. Could Master push me in deeper?"

499

I rose from the chair, pulling my hands off and out of her. "With pleasure," I said, undoing my belt. I'd made it clear that she didn't owe me this, yet here she was, offering it to me.

I thought vaguely of Becki as I pulled my cock out and shook free of my trousers, wondering if maybe she'd be angry about this, but it's not like she and I were exclusive. In fact, she seemed to think of me as a "good time," not a boyfriend. I hadn't made any promises to her.

After this... will I need to? Will I have to choose one of them?

I was a soldier. We were famous for sleeping around. Surely neither of these women expected exclusivity from me... but I had better ask, to be sure.

Tomorrow, though. Not right now.

"How deep do I need to push you?" I asked.

Her knees parted slightly, spreading herself out for me. "All the way."

I couldn't see her head under the desk, just her back and her ass and her pussy, and it was hot—just a hole there for me to fuck into oblivion.

I levered myself down, putting one hand on the desk and gripping her hip with another. I pressed the tip of my head to her opening, and pushed.

"Tallan," she breathed, her old nickname for me, as my skin went taut against her folds. The outside of her sex was still somewhat dry, exposed to the air like it was, and I had to work myself in, to wedge past the tension of her entrance.

The friction made us both sigh, and then my path smoothed out, the ridges of my head popping past her folds and into the tight muscle inside her. I sank into the warm sheath, feeling every twitch of her muscle, every bump of her sex as it rode past the most sensitive part of me.

"Deep enough?" I asked her.

She swayed back against me. "I'm not sure... try again...."

All the authority had gone from her voice, leaving only raw need.

"You tell me when you've got it, all right?" I said, pulling out.

"I will—"

I plunged into her.

She moaned, and that was enough for me. Tugging her back against me with each thrust, I went to *town* on her, ramming my cock into her at full speed. She slicked up and started to cry out.

"Master yes... Master, take me. Yes. Master's cock is so big...."

Damn, that's hot, I thought, without slowing. Her ass shook and jiggled and her folds swelled up, wetter every moment. I had to throw my head back, to take my eyes off her to keep from coming.

It was almost like fucking a desk, but it was warm and wet and it moaned for more.

"I missed you—I wanted you—take me. Take me, Tallan—"

My leg was starting to cramp from the angle, so I gave her one more good thrust and pulled out, my cock bobbing. I stepped away from the desk and plopped into the old armchair by my fireplace as she scooted back and rose on her knees to look at me.

I beckoned to her with a finger. "You can't make Master do all the work, Shimmer. Come here and shine my cock with your pussy."

She bowed her head, then rose and strode to me, slipping into my lap one knee at a time. She looked down, frowning, and I used a hand to guide myself into her. Her eyes closed in ecstasy.

"Oh, milord. You feel good."

I laid one hand on her ass, and with the other, I lifted the loop of her apron over her head and let it fall open. Those big tits fell practically in my face—

I blinked.

"You got a tattoo."

Her eyes opened, and she looked down at the dragon she'd had inked around one breast, as if the little beast was nesting around the curve of her flesh. I gripped her and raised both tits to better see the orange-red dragon underneath.

It was Ignace, one of the Four Demons, from the festival where we'd first met.

Something fluttered inside me, and it wasn't lust. *Orange scales, red eyes, always watching, always knowing.*

"Do you like it?" Shimmer asked, breaking my strange reverie.

I swallowed. "Yeah. It's sexy." *And looking at it is like recalling a dream.*

"Ignace is the Demon of the Spark, did you know that?" she said, leaning both her tits against my face, cupping my chin and making me look up at her.

"I got the tattoo to remember you by. The nameless lover who took my virginity, like a spark in the night. Only that spark was supposed to die off. Instead, he found me again."

She kissed my forehead. "Now I get to feel his flame whenever he wants me. *Anytime* he wants me. I'm his."

"Shimmer...."

She made space between us, then tilted my face back to kiss my mouth, flicking her tongue over my own.

"Everything Biscuit wanted from me, I want to give to you," she purred. "I'm your servant. Your toy. I want to make him jealous and punish him. But also, I've dreamt of your cock every night since you took me. I don't want any other man. Only you."

My dick twitched inside her, begging her to start fucking me. "All right," I said. "But you can change your mind anytime. And you should know that me and Becki—"

She tapped my nose. "Oh, I know. I asked her. First rule of

being a servant is *don't step on your boss's toes.* Technically, she's my boss."

My mouth felt so dry, my heart thudding. "And she said...?"

"She said *have at it.* That she's not your wife. She just said I should have no expectations, and I don't... except the expectation that you take me when you please."

Damn it, Becki, I might love you, I thought, widening my knees, which opened Shimmer up to me even more. Her head lolled back, her lips parting as I sank just a tiny bit deeper.

I thought of Jolene, but that was a relationship to pursue later, when I *did* want a wife. Right now, I just wanted the farm up and running... and to fuck beautiful women who wanted to fuck me back.

"You know how to do this, Shimmer?" I said, bouncing her slightly on top of me. Her tits gave a sweet little jiggle. "After all, you were a virgin, what? A week ago?"

"I can figure it out," she said, pushing my face flush to her tits. She rolled her hips up, and sent me instantly into bliss. I groaned against her skin, listening to her sweet, quickening breaths as her channel rose up to my tip and dropped down again.

She gave me as much sensation as possible, rising, circling me, then swinging forward, sheathing me to the base. Her sex went thick with juice again, spilling between us, making a mess of my balls the more she gave it to me.

Not one to be left out of the festivities, I worked a hand into the pile of apron between us and dug through until I found her trigger. The clit had swollen, and with just a tiny touch, she moaned, so I kept my rubbing soft and sweet as she buried me inside her.

"Oh, Master. Master, come inside me."

I nodded, circling faster. "I will."

"You can. You can come in me."

"I know."

Jolene had mentioned that Shimmer had taken nightweed root. After that comment, I knew exactly what that root did. It was a shame Shimmer had gone to such extremes, but it had been too long since I'd come inside a woman. There was something special about that moment of hot, fierce connection.

There would be no babies made this day.

Shimmer came down hard, moaned wildly, and breathed out, "Master feels good. I want his cum. Oh... oh... *oh,* fuck, Warren... *yes....*"

Her sex tensed, then rippled, and she jerked to sudden stillness. In response, I took my hand away and used my own hips to keep us going. She recovered and rocked with me, still shuddering, still crying out wordlessly, her tits bouncing against me in time to my thrusts.

My cock throbbed, wet and anxious, until my balls spasmed and cum raced up my shaft and shot into her. I groaned through gritted teeth, riding it out, my neck muscles tense as I felt every spurt purged from my body into hers.

We fell still, gasping together. "Does Master feel clean?" she whispered.

I chuckled lowly. "No. I feel dirty as hell."

"Then tomorrow, I shall clean you again."

Chapter 74

Once Upon a Time

I woke to the faint glow of distant morning. My curtains had been sold for extra cash long before I'd arrived here, and I could see the sky clearly beyond my row of tall windows, the inky night dancing the edge between the witching hours and sunrise.

An urge rose in me, an instinctual need to take flight and taste the potential of the new day on the air.

I rose and stretched, suppressing a yawn so as not to wake Shimmer, whose small, naked body cleaved to my side. Carefully, I peeled away from her, setting my bare feet down onto the wooden floor whose rug had also been sold.

I sat for a moment in the barren room. No wall hangings, no furniture aside from the bed. Some might call it sad, but I felt it was enormous.

I was accustomed to emptiness—the cold economy of orphan beds, of a soldier's trunk and lamp, of walls scrubbed clean when an officer got bored. I had no possessions aside from that odd glass orb, but it remained in the bank with my old unclaimed knife.

No, to me this room was not empty, but simply vast, endless, a collection of cold hard shadows in sharp corners. If nothing else, the assassin could not hide here. I stepped quietly to the window and found Copper asleep in a window box that was far too small for her, even without any flowers inside of it. My watchdog against the assassin.

I should have asked her name, I thought. She couldn't always be "the assassin."

Turning this thought over in my mind, I tapped on the window. Copper raised her overly spiky head and peered at me with her deep copper eyes, and I pointed up at the sky. She made no move to show me she understood, but I simply felt that she did. I'd find out soon enough.

With my bodyguard notified, I slipped into the fresh pair of trousers that Shimmer had laundered for me. They felt papery clean against my skin, a thin but crisp material. I thought of the sky again, of the urgent energy running through my veins, the tension in my wings that made me yearn to take flight.

I don't have wings, I thought, rolling my shoulders. I must have been having dragon dreams.

With a soundless shrug, I headed for the door. Might as well sate the curiosity inside of me, this bizarre, wild need in my shoulders.

I ascended the servant stairs through the house, since they were closer to hand, passing through empty hallways and rooms already filling with rich people's things.

Becki had been hard at work today, and we needed the money, but one day I hoped to be rid of this junk. I preferred the calm simplicity of empty rooms with open windows and unlocked doors. There was freedom in the mental silence of an uncluttered nest.

Rubbing my eyes, I made my way to the pull-down door to the roof, but I found it open, a breeze whispering down the unfolded steps. I expanded my awareness, but sensed no danger. I hadn't even picked up a knife, which gave me pause. It was almost as if I'd fallen under a spell, and I stopped to think clearly, pinching my arm, even running a quick math problem through my head.

No. I was me. It was just something about this time of day, the *possibility* of it all. Today could be anything. I could fly anywhere.

Fly. I couldn't fly.

"Damn, what was in that bathwater last night?" I muttered, climbing the unfolded steps.

"Oh! It's you," said a voice.

I paused with only my head through the trap door, and my stomach tightened when I saw Fieran sitting on one of the long stone benches within the fenced pseudo-courtyard of the roof. Copper sat at his feet, her head on his knee. She'd listened to my command to meet me up here, after all.

"Huh. She's taken to you," I said, rising the rest of the way out of the trapdoor. I closed the gap between us, hesitated, and then sat beside Fieran.

He'd gone tense. I'd given away what I'd known the moment I hesitated. I shouldn't have done that. Nothing had changed between us because of... the secret.

Not *his* secret. That was the wrong word, but it would do for the moment, until all the air was clear between us.

Copper rumbled insistently, because Fieran had frozen mid-scritch. He loosened again, taking comfort in the dragon. I wondered if that was why she was here with him, because she knew what came next would be hard. Or maybe it was something more than that. Maybe the growing dragon felt a kinship with Fieran, because they both had secrets burned into their cores.

One was not who he said he was, and the other was an unknown, an enigma. I had no idea what either one would become.

I clasped my hands before me, resting my elbows on my knees. I tasted the air like I'd wanted to, feeling it drift along my scales —my *skin*.

"Something got you feeling weird?" Fieran asked, probably in reaction to my bathwater comment.

"Yeah. I feel fucking draconic this morning," I said, trading a secret for the one I knew was coming.

I sighed. "There is something weird about me, Fier. I'm too close to them. Every minute I spend near them, something inside me grows. I know it sounds crazy, but I feel it. I feel like something's *coming*, but inside me."

He nodded, then chuckled. "That's what she said."

I didn't laugh. "You would know."

Cold, like a death fire between us. We stood suddenly on a precipice, with our friendship on one side, and a future of enmity on the other.

"I'm sorry," I said softly. "You don't deserve that." There was a reason he'd kept these secrets, and the assassin was one of them. It's just that, somewhere along the way, I thought we'd crossed that line into friendship. Then again, I hadn't told him about the princess either.

It hit me. *I hadn't told him.*

"You know, then," he finally said, shifting in place, scratching Cooper's head faster. He wore his trousers, but only a simple white sleeping shirt that someone must have scrounged up for him. Something without all the blood.

I kept thinking, too fast, my mind aflame. *I never told him. I had secrets too.*

Here I'd been, selfishly thinking of the lie he'd been living, when hadn't I been doing the same thing?

"I want to tell you something, Fieran. Can you listen?" I asked.

He kept his eyes down. "I will always listen to you, Warren," he said softly. "Always."

There was no hesitation in the words, and no judgment. I spoke to the sunrise, or to my clasped hands, with his gray, royal eyes burning into me, and the naked breeze caressing my chest.

"I met a woman," I said.

Chapter 75

Shaving Cream

"I WAS A SOLDIER THEN," I went on, "a young veteran by that point, top of my rank and moving up fast. They put me on a solo mission in the wilds near the capital. I was supposed to be tracking a specific minotaur shaman and its entourage, and I'd been getting close, when I found her. A beautiful woman and— and no one. No one else."

My mind fuzzed, like it always did when I thought too closely about this memory. "She looked like you, now that I think of it. Tall for a woman, gray-eyed and red-haired. I imagine your hair is red under that dye?"

He swallowed. "Yeah," he said.

I nodded. "I bet it's a bitch to keep it from staining at the roots. Anyway, she was pale, obviously full Parshin." That was the biggest difference between her and Fieran, but I didn't say that. He knew.

"Just lovely, you know, a real sight to behold. Sitting there in the middle of a huge clearing in arachne territory, just...." I tried to remember. "Demons, I think she was brushing her hair. Right there in the middle of a forest."

I tried for a moment, then, to get lost in that memory, but the warmth of it had faded away. There was a burgeoning sense of *orange,* like heat, which I couldn't place. It came with the memory every time, but always escaped recognition. I liked to think of it as the haze that follows love at first sight, but I'm hardly the romantic type.

I clamped my hands onto my knees and set my shoulders. The sun burned at the horizon before me, lighting up the rocky expanse of the wilds.

"Anyway, I fell for her. How couldn't I? You know who she was by now. The princess. Running away from her father, alone in the wilds—and there I was, a capable soldier, appearing just in time to protect her."

Fieran blew air out his mouth. "No shit?"

"No shit."

"Crazy noble bitches," he said. "They really think they're fucking immortal, I swear."

Normally, I'd tell him off for calling my ex-lover such a name, but he wasn't exactly wrong. I'd met enough nobles since to think they were *all* a little crazy, male and female alike. They all felt untouchable in one way or another, and very few understood how the world really worked.

Even Jolene had her moments, although she was more down-to-earth than most.

"I tried to get her to go home, but she wouldn't hear of it, and I had no choice but to accompany her on her mission to run away. I kept her safe while she got the need for freedom out of her system. She got into my heart, because of course she did. We were lovers, and then we were caught."

"I heard of you," Fieran said. "The man who rescued the princess from the wilds. That was all a story to avoid scandal, I'm guessing?"

"Yep. The king wanted me dead, but she argued for my life. Honestly, the details are blurry even now... Four Demons, that's what love will do to you. But she wasn't pregnant, so we had that going for us. She had a kid later, but it was over a year after we split." I scoffed. "I guess some people move on faster than others.

"Anyway, I survived the torture. Because there *was* torture. Whipping, mostly.

"I don't remember much of it, thankfully—just that the king and his men kept trying to get me to admit that I'd led Vanessa on, that I'd seduced her because I wanted something. Status, maybe, or a way to get close to the king, to assassinate him.

"But I meant only to love her, and they didn't like that answer."

Which led to the darkness, I thought, but didn't say. *The blood gushing from my neck, and the darkness....*

"There was some sort of scare, where I almost died... I think. It's hazy. But the king seemed relieved I was alive, and he stopped the torture and let me go, with a protective order declaring me a hero, protected in full by the crown.

"In reality, he hates me. He just didn't want to tell his daughter he'd killed me, because he was sure that she'd never forgive him."

I shook my head, because I had my doubts about that. Vanessa had never once tried to contact me. And the kid she'd borne *right away* with her new husband... the *name* she'd given that child....

I gritted my teeth. She had a strange way of showing me she remembered me, and to this very day, it still hurt.

"But after letting me go, the king swore that if he ever saw me again, or that if I ever tried to see his daughter again, he would kill me," I went on. "So I left, laid low, tried to stay quiet, to get used to being alone.

"I know the King's Hand keeps tabs on me, but no one's ever tried to off me until the assassin, and she said she'd done it for some other reason. Not sure if that's true or not, but still.

"Anyway. That's where you first met me—keeping myself at the bottom of an ale keg, and the bottom of the rankings, while I was at it. It took time, but I think I've forgotten her. She's married now, with a kid, obviously."

"And you're sure the daughter's not yours?"

"She was born a year after we split. Not nine months, not ten, and not less." I shrugged.

Silence fell again, and Copper rumbled contentedly as Fieran ran his hand down her serpentine neck. He inhaled, and I looked at him, and it occurred to me that he looked hale and hearty, just tired.

The assassin had cured him, just as she'd promised. But had Fieran done the rest of what the assassin had asked? Or would the blood mage be coming for him again?

"So you know the whole thing," he said. "You know I'm the king's bastard."

"The assassin told me the night she injured you. Yes."

He scratched his smooth cheek. He knew what I wanted. *A secret for a secret. A friend to a friend.*

"You found out the rest... how? When I got hurt?"

"No. I just figured it out."

The nightweed root. The shaving cream. The prostitutes moaning against his door at all hours, when no one ever saw them go in.

Fieran looked at me, really looked at me. "It's my real name. Fieran. My mother raised me this way. She wanted...." He shook his head, a sneer flickering across his face.

"She raised me to pretend. She wanted a *prince*. She wanted me to take the throne, and she built a rebellion on that lie. There's a network of people out there who support me, without knowing the truth. The city general of Olinios, and its watch-master, are two of them.

"But gods, there are so many more. I don't even know about half of them. She built a little empire for me."

My stomach fluttered. Now *this*, I didn't know.

"The assassin went after all bastards," I said. "Do you think she knew about the network?"

He shook his head. "No. I think I was just another bastard to her, or else the King's Hand himself would be after me. She's just from the Blood Guild, if I had to guess. They're mercenaries, killers for hire.

"My mother warned me about them. She said that the king rewarded his inner circle for taking care of his *problems*... but that sort of thing is always hush-hush, never something to be publicized. And he had too many bastards to bother with it himself."

I whistled softly. "And your mother's still alive?"

"Yes, and she's still weaving her web for me. I want out, I do, I always have." He reached up, pulling his shirt aside to show his collarbone, where a white bite mark glistened pink in the light of new day.

"But she put a curse on me when I was a kid. A bite from her dragon. Because of it, I can't hide from her anywhere."

He dropped his shirt again. "So if I reveal myself, I die; if I do what she wants, I join a rebellion and *then* die. I played along, always training, losing myself in surviving. I know I was an asshole, but I hated the world. I think a part of me wanted someone to kill me, to end it... until the assassin.

"Then it felt real."

I slapped his knee with the back of my hand. "And now you want to live, do you?"

He looked at me again, his face hard with resolve. "Yes. I want to live."

"As a lost prince, though?" I said. "Or as a lost princess?"

Fieran closed his—*her* eyes, and laughed at me.

"How about you tell *me*, genius," she said. "Which one is gonna keep me alive?"

Chapter 76

Upkeep

I DIDN'T GIVE her an answer that morning, but we both left the rooftop feeling lighter than before. I did ask, though, if she was going to take the nightweed root. That would keep the assassin off her, at least.

"I want to. It shows in the blood," she told me. The assassin must have guessed Fieran's real gender while Fieran had gotten sick with the blood poison. Maybe Fieran had moaned in her sleep, or twisted the wrong way, or given too many clues to someone too smart—or maybe the assassin could tell when she used magic to filter Fieran's blood.

Either way, I didn't miss the fact that the assassin had offered her a way out. A bastard woman could inherit a throne, but only if she could bear children. A *barren* female bastard? That wasn't a threat.

The assassin had offered Fieran a way to keep her life, which meant there was good in the assassin herself.

Demons, I wish I knew her name.

"But... taking some root to make me barren leaves me with fewer options," Fieran concluded. "And my mother would kill me. *Literally,* she would destroy me, and find some other bastard kid to control.

"So I guess I'm between a dragon and a long drop right now." She paused. "What do you think?"

I smiled. "I still need a bodyguard." Copper growled. "Well, a page, anyway."

And so I had my friend back, the same as before. Things were different between us. We both knew it. But Fieran didn't have to pretend around someone for the first time in her life, and suddenly, she was less of an asshole. I couldn't say I minded the change.

She kept appearing in public as Fieran the guardsman, and a week passed from there with no appearance of the assassin. That was concerning, but several other decent changes occurred that improved my situation with the farm.

For one, I boarded up every window and entrance to the villa, much to Jolene's dismay. Renting in town would have been too expensive and just as dangerous as staying here, since we couldn't know which inn proprietors we could trust. Instead, I'd made the villa more secure.

The barn changed hands, and so did the few dragons within it. I had our new stable hands fill a guest bedroom with hay, and that was now serving as our nursery, but I didn't want to board the windows on the poor kiddos. Both eggs and hatchlings needed real light to thrive, so I let the nursery have one of only a few guarded windows—the guards being our other dragons, of course.

One of the stable hands changed the hot stones under our various eggs once every hour, and Dull, the little flame hatchling who'd taken a liking to me the first time I'd met Jolene, provided the heat with her fire breath.

We kept all of our new females, except for the pregnant horizon hybrid that Jo had been so excited about. Jolene proved herself rather good at selling dragons, provided Rachel accompanied her to help with the haggling.

The horizon female went for an exorbitant amount, *and* we would get the female back once her eggs were laid. The buyers assumed she'd be too wild to raise, and we didn't tell her she was as docile as a lamb around me.

All the males went for very high prices, as predicted, but we kept the clay Mount-class dragon we'd named Feldspar, and of course the little healing dragon, Tonic.

As a Combat-utility dragon, Feldspar should have been valuable, but Dasvilla didn't have a big market for that after all. So we'd kept him to help Copper with guard duty. We didn't dare to sell her.

Throughout the sales process, Jolene and Rachel were professional to each other, although Jolene was a bit cold due to the many inspections and tax threats she'd had to deal with in the past. Rachel pretended like that past had never existed, because to her, it had just been a job.

Regardless, she kept taking her "payments" in the form of bottled cloud breath, and I still wasn't sure what she was doing with the breath, or where the bottles were coming from. She'd agreed to rent a few bottles to Becki for a low cost, and she'd also given me a deferment on her 5% take on the rest of the business, until all its debts were paid off.

Aliese had taken to managing the villa like a dragon to a crag, and the place was cleaner than it had probably ever been. A chef materialized after the horizon dragon sold, and suddenly we were having three square meals a day, albeit cheap ones. Jolene handled the dragon side of things, while Aliese managed the villa and its human inhabitants.

Freed up from household duties thanks to Aliese, Becki had gone ahead and filled every spare room with rich people's stuff, and she was taking in a steady income that way. Her ale cart had been abandoned, but she'd pitched me an idea on how to use it again: Cage Tours.

It was a project we'd had in the works from the start, but now, we had time to make it happen. I now spent my mornings training our various dragons how to behave well around humans, and when Becki decided they weren't going to eat anyone, she would start giving tours of the property so that outsiders could see all of our dragons.

To pretty the place up for the future tours, Aliese and her brothers spent their spare work time dressing up the villa, at least on the outside. Becki had big dreams of turning it into a "Dragon Bed and Breakfast." I definitely had an entrepreneur on my hands.

For now, though, her storage business was bringing in consistent cash, which she funneled to me and Rachel. Rachel handled the books when she could get time away, from both her normal Keeper duties and from helping Jolene bargain with merchants.

I kept checking her books, and Jolene did too, but it all seemed above-board. Rachel was as straight-laced as they came, at least as far as I could tell. I had been too busy to get to know her much yet, but she was already keeping Pinnacle's secrets, so I'd long since decided to trust her.

She'd also told me some good news: that our debt-to-income ratio was slowly improving, especially with the sale of the fire-fruit. Apparently, we were bringing down the value of the fruit by increasing the supply in the marketplace, but the take was still substantial.

Orphans now milled in and out of the villa at all non-picking hours, conscripted into this task or that by Aliese, Rachel, the stable hands, and especially Becki. (I suspected she had a nice ale-delivery business running on the side, but I didn't ask.)

As for the orphanage itself, it had sent its thanks. I'd checked in with the headmistress once, to ensure the orphan Tiff was passing along the proper stipend. She was, but the headmistress hadn't said what the money would be used for. I found this suspicious, but it was far down my list of things to look into. I'd deal with it after this month.

Jolene also stayed busy outside of her sales duties. She handled all the feeding and grooming, coordinated the egg warming and monitoring, and designed each adult dragon's training schedule while giving them each a hatchling companion that could learn good manners from them.

I hadn't forgotten that the core of Pinnacle would always be its dragons, and that all these side businesses would one day be rendered moot. Because of that, I gave Jolene everything that she asked for. That included a chicken coop off the side corner of the house. (I was getting sick of hearing the roosters each morning, their crows leaching up through my floorboards.)

And my lenience with my pocketbook was already paying off. The dragons were apparently the fastest learners that Jolene had ever worked with.

Despite her wealth of knowledge and experience, however, the dragons did seem to listen better to me. I had them marching in lines, doing tricks, and learning basic verbal commands and associations, so that they could obey humans that *weren't* always me.

My success as a teacher was the reason Jolene had me train them in the morning: they listened to me, and the effects of my instruction lasted later into the day. I basically just went into their nests to lecture them, pet them, praise them, and get a better sense of each of their auras.

Communicating with them grew easier each time, and my senses grew stronger. It had been a nice week, all in all, with no setbacks. Pinnacle Dragons was rising out of its hole.

And that, unfortunately, had drawn notice. To most of the Parshil kingdom, a dragon farm was nothing but a breeding stable, where animals were trained to love the human masters who only *occasionally* let them wander free.

Pinnacle was not like that, and the population of Das had noticed. We had onlookers outside the gate every day (Becki gave them pamphlets about the upcoming Dragon Wagon tour, even though we had no wagon yet). The children *oohed* and *aahed,* but most of the adults paused only long enough to look worried before hurrying their children along again.

Like all the people in Parshil, the Dasvillian people feared the monsters of the jungles and wilds... but they also feared their own dragon pets. Seeing much larger, more free-roaming dragons like Ravager at the Cage made them nervous. In a lot of ways, I didn't blame them.

Jolene had also been skeptical about dropping the barn, but her prized dragons loved living under the sun, even if they were still technically inside a cage. Ravager, Copper, and Feldspar (the clay fighter male) now protected the old guard of dragons, falling into their own little patrol routes, depending on the time of day.

Every dragon that *could* serve a purpose at Pinnacle, did so. Almost all of them became workers or guardians, instead of lazy dragons in cages.

Even though the gate remained locked and the dragons at least *appeared* to be docile from the outside, I knew the city was getting complaints about our activity.

The guardsmen and the watchmaster were firmly on my side, though, thanks to a late-night round of drinks at one of the guardsmen's favored taverns and another late-night chat with the watchmaster.

For the first time in a decade of working in Dasvilla, the watch-master saw a way to actually *explore* the unconquered wilds that bordered Dasvilla. I lent them a dragon or two, to help clear more of the hotlands crags of their hidden minotaur and troll populations. No orcs or minotaurs attacked during that week, although we definitely attacked some of *them*. With every day that passed, more and more of the wilds were tamed.

I also treated the soldiers with respect, taking their names down for future paid work on their days off, so they could get ahead on their savings. Pinnacle would grow, and I'd need more hands eventually. I even paid a few men up front, provided they had the right knowledge to give me.

Meanwhile, Justicar Ormish hung in the shadows, lurking just out of sight. I was probably imagining that, but he did seem to hover about. Like the assassin, he was a bit of a mystery entity, but I had the strong sense that he wanted to strike. Why he wanted that, or who he really worked for, I wasn't sure... but trouble was brewing all around me, and I knew that—if I wasn't careful—it would boil over when I wasn't looking.

Chapter 77

Stolen Lands

DURING MY TIME on our farm, two caravans arrived safely from Ashkar, the walled city closest to Dasvilla. "Caravan" was a bad term, because they were really a mercenary unit with dragon lancers, crossbow troops, ballista turret mounts, and heavily armored shock troops.

They brought wagons laden with metal, their supplies far too heavy to carry via dragon. I myself felt safe on this edge of the wilds, although it helped that my swarm of dragons was not only loyal, but deadly.

And on the very rare hours where I had any time to myself, I started constructing a farmhouse on the wildlands that the Biscuits had granted us. Copper and the baby night dragon were my constant companions there.

While the baby dragon mostly stayed inside my shirt and grew, Copper proved to be both versatile and intelligent. She helped me dig through the rich soil and collect loose rocks, then level them into a basic foundation. Once I had a place out of the mud, I laid down boards and started raising the first barn.

It would be nothing more than three long walls and a slanted roof, and it wouldn't be massive, grand, or special, but it would fit dragons and the harvest, and it wouldn't leak. With the hot rains of summer sweeping down the mountains, building the back wall facing the Dasco volcano was my first priority.

On the last day of that week, I admit that I went feral, showering in the daily rain outside the farmhouse, eating delicious firefruit I'd picked myself (it was spicy and sweet, and I could see why lords liked it so much), and sending Copper out to hunt for her food.

One day, I'd fill this barn with farming utility dragons and start turning the soil over and making something of the place. The orphans had already started to call me the Wild Lord, and I didn't stop them.

All in all, the politics of the city vanished from my day-to-day life, and I found Jolene didn't miss it, either. Her personality had never been about luxury, riches, or status. Jolene was about the dragons, and while our early success was only slowly compounding, I had a feeling she was very happy with the direction Pinnacle Dragons was headed.

We sold fruit, cold ale, chicken eggs, storage, and the labors of our more renowned dragons (namely Tonic), and our little farm employed dozens every day.

Two more weeks, I told myself, watching the sunset from the unfinished farmhouse, a cold ale in one hand and Collette the half-ice dragon nuzzling the other. Becki lay beside me, wrapped up in the blanket she'd brought along for her so-called "naked picnic," her clothes scattered all around us. Her mere presence cooled me, due to whatever magical blood made her skin so cold, which was nice in these hotlands.

I let my gaze linger on her bare snow-white shoulder, smiling as I remembered those shoulders rocking in front of me while I took her from behind. While Aliese kept me well-attended at home, I liked the simplicity of Becki. When she wanted sex, she found me for it, no matter where I was or what I was doing. To her, it wasn't about pleasing me, it was about pleasing herself.

In that way, having two lovers had yet to cause me issues— except maybe with Jolene. Our stolen kiss had not yet repeated itself, but I wasn't pushing her for anything more.

When I had the time, I would court her the right way. Until then, I'd be living my life in whatever way I liked. After all, I might not stay a bachelor for much longer. I was having my fun while I still could.

I sighed, knocking back the rest of the ale, and rose to my feet. *Guess it's time to put clothes on,* I told myself. Today was the day we dealt with the balance sheet, and figured out whether or not there was any hope of paying all our debts and becoming profitable in only two more weeks' time.

"Copper, stay with Becki," I said. My old blue-haired friend was a night owl, so she had come to me in the early morning when I was just waking, but when she was just going to sleep.

"I'll walk back. Oh, don't growl at me like that. I'll take Collette with me. Okay?"

With Collette as my chaperone—Fieran left me alone when I worked on the farmhouse—I wandered back to the villa. In the den, I paused, startled. The young daughter of the Biscuits, Jasmine, sat poring over documents with Jolene at the cluttered foyer table we had moved to the den.

"Why, hello there, Viscountess Jasmine," I said, bowing slightly while she shot to her feet as if I'd just aimed a blade at her. "I apologize for my appearance. Had I known you'd be stopping by today, I would have been more prepared."

The rapidly paling young teenager stared at me, wide-eyed, and then flushed so badly that she appeared to be sunburned.

"Lord Orpheus-Minax!" she blurted. "I hadn't expected— Jolene said you were—"

"Occupied," Jolene said, straightening in her seat to look at me impassively. She probably knew Becki had come to me, since Becki's own room at the villa was empty and Aliese was probably moping this morning, since I hadn't given her the chance to give or receive any early morning pleasure.

"I *was* occupied," I said, "but today's Balance Day. I wouldn't miss it for the world."

Jolene's gaze slid past me. "And your shadow? The human one."

"Fieran hates numbers. And building farmhouses. And pretty much anything that doesn't involve wearing full armor and too many weapons," I said, and shrugged. "We need a day off from each other now and then, anyway. I didn't see Feldspar outside, so I'm guessing Fieran borrowed him for protection last night and had some fun in a tavern instead."

Jolene narrowed her eyes. Had she noticed how I studiously avoided all pronouns when I spoke to her about Fieran? I had promised not to lie to her, but it was Fieran's secret to keep.

"Anyway, enough about me! What is the lovely duke's daughter doing here?" I asked, shooting Jasmine my best winning smile.

The poor kid nearly fainted. "I... I was going... I...."

"She decided to volunteer her time to help teach me about complex business math," Jolene supplied, raising a warning eyebrow at me. I wasn't oblivious; Jasmine was smitten, but far too young for me. The Biscuits had probably encouraged her to come here, hoping she might distract me, but I wasn't that kind of man.

And they're shitty parents, I thought with a curl of my lip. *Seriously, how low can you go?*

The duchess especially should know by now that I never let people get close to me. I slept with a dragon every night to avoid entanglements of the heart.

Well, except for last night, with Becki. And that night in the wilds with Kenna. And having Aliese wake me up with love-making every day didn't count, and also that kiss with Jolene never consumed my thoughts and took me down a deep hole of what-ifs.

No sir, I was as heartless as they came.

"Well, it's very nice of Jasmine to share her knowledge with us," I said courteously. "I thought Rachel was running our numbers, though?"

"Not for the past few days. The Biscuits have all the Keepers busy with requisitions, permits, and fee waivers for their new barn. Which used to be *our* barn, if you'll recall."

I swallowed a groan. That was going to be a sore spot forever, even though I'd essentially traded that barn for Aliese's honor. You'd think Jolene would stop bringing it up.

To her credit, she did change the subject quickly. "You've come at a good time," she said, turning to the stricken Jasmine. "We were just tallying the last figures. Weren't we, Viscountess Jasmine?"

Jasmine jumped. "Yes! Yes, we were just doing that!"

While they went over the details a final time, I popped upstairs to check Fieran's room. Surprisingly, I found her up there, lying spread-eagled on her bed, fully clothed, an empty bottle on the floor beneath her hand.

Feldspar sat next to her, glaring with red-eyed boredom, loosing a grumpy sigh when he saw me. The warrior dragon wasn't friendly to anyone but Fieran and me, even though he seemed rather annoyed at having to sit around while she slept off her drink.

He wasn't hostile, but he did want himself and his charge to be left alone. His charge was usually Fieran, but every now and then I set him to watch one of our entry windows, and he protected it in much the same way.

I strode across the unfamiliar red rug—it hadn't been here yesterday, so Fieran might have won it in a card game—and loomed over the brownish-red dragon.

"You've grown, but not too much," I said. "Not like Copper or Star." Star was the name I'd given the baby night dragon, who was currently asleep in my shirt with only her black tail hanging out.

"You're still fast, though, so go grab me some breakfast." I nodded at the window. "Bring me back something that still breathes."

Feldspar perked up at the order, but Collette slunk up from behind me and started doing a happy dance, shuffling foot-to-foot, as if eager to win a prize. Feldspar shot her a distasteful look.

Marcus Sloss & Jace Cannon

"Sure, let's make it a competition," I said. "Not to eat, though. Show me your prowess instead. Get me something alive. First to bring a prize home gets a lamb."

"Wait, no! Lambs are expensive!" Jolene said from the hallway, but it was too late. The duo both took running starts toward the window—which was thankfully open, because otherwise I was dead sure they would have just plowed right through it—and together they launched off the sill, soaring up toward a couple of bent bars of the Cage that passerby couldn't see from the road.

They easily sidled through, especially the Shoulder-size Collette. Feldspar was a juvenile Mount, so he wouldn't be able to fit through that gap for long.

I turned to find Jolene in the doorway. "I'm guessing you and Jasmine are ready for me now?"

She still looked distressed about the lambs, and then her gaze slid to the knocked-out Fieran. She sighed.

"Some bodyguard he is," she said. "Yeah, we're ready."

"Cut him some slack. He's going through stuff," I replied, following her back down the stairs. "Besides, I gave him the night off so I could work on the farmhouse in peace."

"I'm still not sold on the farming idea, you know," Jolene commented. "The Biscuits gave you too big of a plot. It stretches too far into the wilds, and there's too much to cleanse of monsters."

"Isn't more land a good thing?"

"Not necessarily. Your progress is good, especially with the soldiers using our dragons to clear land, but it will take a year or more to clear the space Duke Biscuit gave you. He also has the right to take it back at any time and take credit for all your work. I've seen the paperwork, and it's only a land grant. I think that's what he's planning."

I didn't argue. She was right. The Biscuits weren't out to actually help me, but this land grant worked in their favor. I could clear the land, and they could legally take it back for a spurious reason, then claim *they* had cleared it. It would make them look good to the king.

It was a tale as old as Parshil. Land outside the walls was normally free to anyone that could hold it against monsters. But adventurers in the past had gone too far by angering hostile warlords. If the monster tribes amassed a war band, a large enough group of trolls could sack the city. Minotaurs or orcs could do extreme damage, too.

It had actually happened once, when I was a kid. A troll army, complete with ogre generals, had stormed the walls of Dasvilla only a few days after Mom's death. The city burned, part of the walls fell, and a few dozen people were whisked away while most hid in shelters or flew out of the city.

By the time all was said and done, scores of guardsmen lay dead amongst the invaders. The orphanage had only escaped damage because trolls preferred meatier targets.

Still, not even a month later, the wall of Dasvilla had been repaired, new recruits from other cities had arrived, and it was like the attack never happened.

In Parshil, attacks from the wilds were a fact of life, a thing to leave behind in the history books. Meanwhile, the land that belonged to those monsters practically glittered with potential. Every lord had their eyes on expanding, by whatever means necessary. The baron at Caliph was an extreme example, while Duke Biscuit was much lazier.

So yeah, he'd try to take my lands back eventually. I needed a plan to combat this by the time it happened—and already, I had an idea.

Chapter 78

Watch Out for Catastrophes

As I MULLED over my new plan, I wandered into the den, where Jasmine promptly interrupted my plotting.

"Okay, I think we've got it all straight now, Lord Warren," Jasmine said, wagging a stack of papers as I reentered the den. Several orphans now knelt on the floor next to her, sorting papers into different piles.

"You're paying them?" I asked her, eyebrow raised.

"Of course. Jolene told me that rule."

"Good."

Once we settled back at the table, Jasmine flicked through some of her own pages to find the one she wanted. "May I start with the summary?" she asked.

I dipped my head in agreement, having a good idea of how this would go.

"Expenses. Twenty-one gold."

Now, I'd never choked on air before, but I did at that number. I clutched my heart, feeling it pound against my chest in panic. Jasmine held up a finger.

"Income. Thirty gold." I glared at her with squinted eyes. I'd make sure the dastardly woman started with income next time.

"This includes your dues to the orphanage, and here is my summary. Your tireless work has already transformed the exterior lands of Dasvilla, but you're starting to drain the economy's ability to handle firefruit. I suggest we start charging the soldiers to rent our dragons, to mitigate this cost."

I scoffed. "Are you sure you're not related to Rachel?"

"No. I'm just good at everything," Jasmine said.

I started to laugh, but Jolene gave me a warning head-shake. "It's actually true," she said. "This kid's a genius. Her mother has her training with tutors all over Parshil, so she's almost never home—but she keeps graduating from their programs early and moving on to new tutors. Demons help us when she decides what subject is her favorite, because she'll be the best in the world at it in no time."

"Ah," I said, impressed but unsure what to say about it. Jasmine was already looking at me like she would hang off my next words. "Continue, then," I said.

Her face fell, and I did regret that, but she was sixteen.

"Okay, next topic. You've depleted your dragon reserves for a variety of uses and projects, but your farmland can't produce until you plant something, and you can't sell dragons that haven't been conceived yet.

"While it's not bad to focus on short-term gains through fire-fruit, dragon-hunting, storage sales, and reselling, at some point you need to turn a long-term profit. I suggest you turn these fertile fields into something. Anything.

"Even if you do, your ability to generate recurring revenue rests in having your dragons reproduce. If they aren't breeding, you aren't growing. Having them out tilling land or pulling rock shrubs is fine, but we want every female pregnant all the time."

I turned my attention to Jolene. "She's right. What's our status with that?"

Jolene hadn't sat at the table, but rather one of the empty cages the porters had dropped off a week ago.

"Not great," she replied, setting down a ledger she'd been poring through. "Like I said before, we need an alpha male in the Shoulder and Mount categories, otherwise our dragons will only mate with one or maybe two partners.

"Tonic and Feldspar are our new males, and Tonic and Collette seem likely to pair with each other after Collette lays her eggs. Becki already promised to give us the eggs in exchange for her free room and board.

"But Feldspar is too young to mate yet, and while Dune and Useless are bonded mates, Useless is past her prime for egg-laying. She is probably pregnant already, but she won't lay many, and they won't be as healthy as they could be. She is a case where renting her to the soldiers is more cost-effective than babying her to keep just a handful of eggs healthy."

"What about all the males we sold? Can we go around finding studs and renting them for a couple rolls in the hay?"

I had suggested harvesting sperm from our males before selling them, but Jolene said it was a dangerous, expensive procedure that also reduced their resale value.

Jolene scribbled a note on a pad of parchment bound in leather. "I'll figure out the most saleable pairings, and ask around," she said. "But it will be expensive. These first two weeks had a lot of set-up costs, thus the twenty-one gold in expenses, but if we keep doing expensive things like this, that number won't go down."

"Get an alpha male in the two smallest size classes. Got it," I said. Jolene didn't seem to hear me. She'd picked up a sheaf of papers and gotten very absorbed in it.

"You know, I've read about something that might help with that," Jasmine said. "Hmm. I'll look it up at the keep library and get back to you.

"For now, speaking of the higher expenses, you *do* pay more than anyone else, and you don't have to—"

I cut her off. "That's not negotiable. The orphanage gets what I say it gets."

"Fine," she said, rolling with my punches. "How about this, then. Now that you've set up the firefruit operation and given it a dragon's protection, we've noticed competition increasing as other parties innovate to pick fruit in greater numbers while your dragons are on the field.

"Everyone has figured out that the dragons will fly outside the orphans' designated picking zone if it means they get a snack for taking care of threats. You currently let others use this network of protection for free, but I think you could charge for it."

"Do it," I said. "But charge reasonably."

She scratched another note on her paper, and I realized I'd given her an order, despite the fact she didn't really work for me. Ten to one, she was a financial spy for her mother and father.

I opted to let the order stand, and see what happened. Rachel would step back into this position once she was done dealing with her current workload, and when she came back, she could go over Jasmine's work. That would tell me where her loyalties lay.

"That's it from me," Jasmine said, still writing. "And now I hand off the review to Jolene."

The dragon steward in question was still sitting on the open cage, swinging her legs in and out of its door, her attention consumed by a thickly bound leather book. Jasmine cleared her throat to get the woman's attention. Jolene startled.

"Uh, we need to go dragon shopping again to maintain our current cash flow, or we need to go hunting. Both work. Margins on firefruit were decent but have worsened, so we shouldn't expand on that side of the business. Our gold reserves will cover about a quarter of our debts, but our dragon numbers are lacking. I think it's time we did something different."

Only a quarter? Shit, I thought. We had only two weeks to make our gold reserves cover 100% of our debts, taxes, and fees —and *also* to prove Pinnacle was now profitable. To do that, we'd need to double our income, at least.

I sighed, shaking my head. "How big is our loss now that fire-fruit prices are so low?"

"A few silver a day. It'll add up," Jasmine said. "You need to focus on farming instead."

"A farm can't produce anything in only two weeks," I pointed out. "So, we charge for protection to cover the lost firefruit profits. Any other ideas?"

"Firefruit wine is in demand across the kingdom," Jasmine said. "Wine takes eight weeks minimum, though."

I tapped the table, thinking. "Beer can be forced out in two weeks," I said. "What about firefruit beer?"

She cocked her head. "Fruit beer? Hmm. That doesn't exist, as far as I know, but we can try it."

I slapped a palm to the tabletop. "Sounds like another job for Becki. She can spin anything to make it sound like a once-in-a-lifetime bargain. I'll have her split her focus: half our fruit now goes to fast-brew beer, and the other half to long-term wine."

"Knowing her, she'll sell the *future* wine," Jolene sniffed.

The idea made me grin, and I pointed at her. "Now *that* is a good idea."

"What about the orphans' take?" Jasmine asked. "We still need their labor."

"We can pay their silver still, for their labor, and make up a contract for the orphanage to get the same cut of the sales price later."

"The same amount? But firefruit prices are dropping. They shouldn't expect the same—"

"Yes, and we'll make *more* off beer and wine. It'll work out in our favor," I countered. If things weren't so tight, I'd still let the orphanage take half, but I'd defer for now. Besides, I wanted to know where the orphanage was spending its money before I got *too* generous.

"You have chronic Nice Guy Syndrome," Jasmine said, without disdain. "My mother wasn't kidding when she said you were strange. Anyway, that's all I've got for now."

I rubbed my hands together. "Great. It's all looking good, then?"

"It would seem so," Jolene said, "but it's a slippery slope. If even a small catastrophe happens, we could lose all our progress."

She wasn't wrong. "So we mitigate," I said. "Jasmine, you're the genius. Mitigate for me. I will pay you."

The kid bit her lip, her cheeks pinkening. "I can try. But I've got to go back to school in three weeks."

I thought about what Jolene had said about her. *She's a genius. Good at everything. But if she could just find her passion....*

"That's one more week than we need from you," I said. "Well, what are we waiting for? Let's hop to it!"

Chapter 79

A Whole Lot like Hell

JOLENE CHASED me out of the den, still holding her leather-bound book. I paused in the foyer, and she surprised me by tugging me into the shadows behind the wide stairs.

"There was one more thing I meant to tell you," she said, her voice low. She tapped the book against my chest. "This is an old storybook that my father used to read to me. I've been rereading it lately, you know, to cope. And I found something interesting."

I barely heard that last sentence. I laid my hand over hers, pressing both her hand and the book to my chest.

"I'm sorry, Jolene. I keep forgetting that you're still in mourning. How are you?"

Her mouth wafted open, then stayed there for a moment. She shook herself. "I'm fine. I'm honestly not thinking about it too much. There's a lot to keep me busy."

"Me, too. But you know that I'm here, right? If you need to talk?"

If I could be emotional support for Fieran, I could sure as hell do it for Jolene. Yet I hadn't been prioritizing that. I kicked myself for it now.

Jolene's jaw worked, and I realized she was angry before she even spoke.

"Stop it. Stop being so great all the time, when you're off... *with* other women. I can't deal with it."

Unhappy prickles ran up through my stomach. I let go of her hand and stepped back.

"I'm sorry," I said.

"No, you're not."

"I *am* sorry I'm hurting you," I said. "But you have to remember that we barely know each other. You're beautiful, Jolene, and we have a history, and I'm a lord now, and lords need noble-women for wives. Obviously I'd be a complete moron not to court you.

"*But*, we can be partners without being lovers, and you *know* that's what you need right now, right? Someone to save Pinnacle while also giving you something to do. Because what if I courted you, and it didn't work out? Could you take that heartbreak on top of losing your mother?

"Worse, how hard would it be to keep working together if we were former lovers who no longer got along?"

The words poured out of me the way similar diatribes usually tumbled out of Jolene. I actually made myself blink. I hadn't realized I'd been thinking all those things, and I laughed out loud.

"Damn. I've been building walls between us without realizing it, haven't I?" I said.

Jolene already had a knuckle to her eye. "Yeah. Me too."

I rubbed a tear from her eye. "It *is* best we just be friends. But neither of us wants that, do we?"

A long pause, and then she said, "No."

My heart thumped. *No.* She wanted me.

I ran my fingers along her jaw, tilted her chin up, and kissed her.

It was soft, her body pliant against mine, her breathless gasp like music in the shadows. Instead of pulling away, she wrapped her arms around me, the book bumping the back of my head.

I followed her lead, kissing harder, then parting her lips with my tongue. She swallowed another gasp as I guided her tongue into my mouth and pulled her hips against me with both hands.

I hardened. She felt it. She arched backward in my arms, and I took the invitation, kissing her as deep as my tongue and my hunger could go. She ground her body against my cock, moaning my name between kisses. I suddenly had her up against a wall.

That's what broke it, for me, the sudden stop and loud *thunk*. I drew back, and for a moment we just breathed hard, together.

"I want to be one of them," Jolene said. "One of your lovers. I hate that I want you bad enough to share you. I hate it so much. I keep trying to be angry at them, at you, but I can't."

The admission caught me off guard. "What? You mean you aren't angry?"

"No. But I should be."

I kissed her, just a weak brush of my lips against hers. Her chest rose sharply, pressed so tight against me. I imagined lifting her skirt and finding a path into her.

"Who says?" I replied, my voice rough.

"Everyone. Just look at Oscilla, always out of town, always bitchy. No one wants to be a man's second lover. Or fourth."

"Aliese and Becki and Kenna haven't minded."

"I know, and I'm so jealous I want to scream."

I ran a hand up her thigh. "I can make you scream."

"Warren...."

I stopped, but let my hand rest against the bare skin of her upper leg. Pressed close as I was, I could feel the heat of her, a distant call. I was absolute clay in her hands.

"We should wait," I rasped. "You're too vulnerable. I won't take advantage. I *can't*."

She nodded, swallowing loudly. It made me want to kiss her neck again, her tits, her nipples and then lower—

I had to force myself to shove away from her, but the tight band of passion between us didn't snap. It stayed there, tense and burning. I needed out of here before I ruined everything.

"You said you found something. In your book," I managed.

Jolene had her eyes closed, and she still pressed her back against the wall as if it were the only thing holding her up. The book inexplicably remained in her hand, and she held it to her chest, like it was armor against me.

"Yes. Yes, there was mention of a warrior in one particular legend. A hero of the ages, who had the power of a dragon. The book called him Dragon-Touched."

Dragon-Touched. "That sounds about right," I said. "The assassin said something similar."

"Yeah."

It was clear she had more to say. "Are there any more details? Anything we could learn from?" I asked.

She shook her head and finally opened her eyes, although she looked toward the front door instead of toward me.

"Not in that story. But I'll keep looking. It helps to have a name for it, anyway."

She lowered the book and exhaled, her breath shaky. "I just think we should tell the staff, that's all. They keep coming to me with concerns about how you... manage things. I keep telling them you are just a natural with dragons, but everyone is starting to suspect.

"It might be best if they know. They're more likely to have loose lips in a tavern if they don't realize they're sharing a secret."

That depends on what kind of person they are, I thought, but if the secret got out, there'd be uses for that, too. Better to have people telling truths than exaggerations.

"That's sound logic," I said. "How about this. I'll call a staff meeting, and I'll include the city watchmaster. Markam's plenty aware that my dragon connections aren't normal, and I trust him.

"Then we can tell everyone what's going on, maybe even get a few more hands on deck when it comes to understanding the things I can do."

She said nothing for a moment. "And what about us?" she whispered.

I couldn't bear to see her like this, torn between lust and good sense. I reached out and took her hand, pulling her into a chaste hug.

"I had always planned to court you later," I said. "But if you become sure of me before then, we can take things from there. But only if you're *sure.* I don't want you in my bed for anything but the *right* reasons.

"That means caring for me, not needing an escape or feeling weak or just wanting something physical. I will trust you to know when *and if* the time is right."

I kissed the top of her head. "How does that sound?"

"It sounds... acceptable," she murmured into my chest.

But I knew we were both thinking, *It sounds like waiting. And waiting sounds a whole lot like hell.*

Chapter 80

What Could Go Wrong?

JOLENE HELD UP A HAND, asking the collected staff to please give her a moment as she dug into a satchel at her side. She eventually fished out the book of hero tales, holding it high. I read the golden lettering: *A History of Dancing with Dragons*.

"Dragon-Touched," Jolene blurted. "I believe Warren is Dragon-Touched."

Her blue eyes drifted across the assembled workers, including Becki, Aliese, Aliese's two brothers Jayke and Jerem, Tiff the orphan, a very harried-looking Rachel, and the watchmaster, plus the watchmaster's right hand man, Narvi.

I hadn't invited Jasmine to this one, although she *had* come back from her parents' keep with some information I was about to make use of. Fieran was still down for the count, moaning and complaining in her bed. That was fine, since she already knew of my abilities, albeit not the official name for them.

Anyway, I'd had Aliese make sure Fieran was hydrated before closing the curtains and leaving her in peace.

As my staff and friends listened intently, Jolene went on to describe all that we knew about my abilities. She kept it simple, leaving a few things out, but the point soon got across.

"You are his biggest loyalists, so don't spread this information," she summarized. "Lord Warren's future is our future in many ways, and for now, this secret gives us all an advantage. An advantage that leads to more money, I might add, in case loyalty isn't a good enough reason."

The watchmaster, Markam, let out a bemused whistle. "And here I thought this was a discussion about wiping out a local troll nest."

"It is, in a way," I said. I'd fed him the nest idea to get him to meet me here, in the hatchling room of the villa, where the little babies rested or played on and around all our feet.

"Basically, I'm still going to ask for your help in clearing that nest," I said, "but I wanted you to know exactly what I brought to the table first. Trolls are no joke, and a crew of dragons like mine can't normally stop a war band of them. *My* dragons are more useful than that, though.

"However, I *will not* enter the wilds with your men unless we go in a group and treat the mission seriously. It's one thing for me to go solo, because I'm fast, trained in scouting, and able to handle myself in combat, but that's not everyone."

Markam stroked his salt-and-pepper beard, thinking. "We could start by scouting the nest in a large group, then attacking it. A sort of trial run. If it goes well, we proceed with smaller groups. With time, we might be able to start real incursions."

He harrumphed. "The Biscuits have never really tried to expand, but I'm sick and tired of sitting around."

Jolene sucked in a deep breath. She hadn't liked my troll nest idea, but my reasoning for it had been too logical to deny.

"I think that's a good idea, Markam," she said. "The Biscuits *have* been lax with their forces. We could develop both offense and defense, adding to attack prevention overall, and fostering goodwill with the community."

She turned to me. "Dragons generally avoid you in the wild, because you're Touched. I think they sense power in you, more than they feel they can beat. That said, every city has dragon attacks, and Dasvilla is no different. Have you witnessed many dragon attacks as a soldier or guardsman?"

I shrugged. "It's been a while, but that's why we have ballistae on the walls and towers. You don't really need me for defense."

"A talented dragon can still snatch people, smaller dragons, horses and more from streets with little warning," Rachel pointed out.

Jolene held up another parchment from her satchel. "I did some digging and made requests from the capital. You spent two years in Olinios, guarding the city. During that time, zero dragon attacks.

"Three years before that, in your station at the desert city of Grisol, zero attacks. Before that, you were in Komish, only one city away from the capital... during which time the capital got *forty-seven* dragon attacks, almost a thirty-percent increase.

"One can surmise that the dragons attacked the capital more often, because they didn't dare attack Komish, and flew right on past it."

My eyes widened as she spoke. I hadn't known that.

"Damn, did you fall in love with a mystical dragon woman or something?" Jerem, one of the twin stable hands, asked. "Because it seems like a spell got cast on you."

"Not that I know of." I cracked my neck. "Okay, I'm picking up the hay that you're laying down, Jo. We can work on defense as well as offense."

"I think you do it naturally," she said. "I'm more wondering about stretching the ability to work against trolls and ogres too." Those were the monsters we dealt with most in the hotlands.

"Fine," I said, "but I'm going to prioritize offense. Wiping out a nest is a pretty good deterrent."

Markam's right-hand man grunted at that. "Not many good lords willing to do more work than a common man," Narvi said. "Only been a month and a bit, but my men will be with you, m'lord. Provided the watchmaster is on board."

Markam nodded, crossing his arms. It was approval enough.

"Okay," I said, "then I'll get started. I'll begin by going scouting to the north. I need to get a feel for the hotlands before I head out there with a whole crew."

"You should take someone with you," Becki said.

"I will, but I've already got someone in mind."

"And while you're away, we shall till and plant the farm," Rachel said. "I have compiled a list of profitable plants. It will take a long time to grow them, but we must begin as soon as possible. I will of course lend you the seed money, pun intended."

I grinned. "Then let's get to work. I'll head out today; I'll just need to go into town for supplies."

"Remember to be careful of any Enforcers," Rachel said. "The guardsmen all adore you, but the Enforcers are following a different agenda."

I nodded. I knew she'd been looking into it, and Markam too, but Justicar Ormish and his goals remained a mystery.

"It's just one trip through town before I head into infested lands," I said. "Honestly. What could possibly go wrong?"

Chapter 81

This is Nothing

For once, nothing *did* go wrong. I was almost disappointed.

Feldspar and Collette hadn't returned from their hunt by the time I departed to pick up some basic supplies. I took a shield, a sword, my ever-present knives, a satchel full of clinking bottles, and no carriers or traps.

The idea was to fight or flee, not to hunt. The supplies in my bag were mostly camping gear and enough food to last a week in case something went wrong.

My farmland and the road to Ashkar, the nearest city, were on the south side of the city where human activity was normally the highest. That's the way any wagons or carts tended to go. No one went north unless they wanted to forage on foot in a single file line, all in the shadow of an active volcano. And that was why there was only a door in the wall to exit instead of a gate.

I'd expected to have Justicar Ormish take a swipe at me on my way out, or for Duchess Nola to intercept me before I could exit, but I was happy to have neither happen. Speed tended to come with advantages.

The guard who controlled the exit asked what my plan was, and I explained I planned to scout around and forage, which wasn't actually true. I didn't know yet which soldiers Markam and Narvi trusted to have along once I did find a troll nest, so I left out details. The guard had likely seen a lot of prospective foragers, because he wished me luck and sent me on my way.

I soon found myself two or three hours away from the city, walking a game trail that grew less and less used the farther I went. I'd stopped once to harvest some rare bluemelons, which grew low to the ground on a particular igneous shrub, but otherwise I kept my strides long while heading up the gradual incline toward the volcano.

Fires could be seen on this mountain on most nights, suggesting that trolls did indeed live here. A few dragoners had flown close enough to glimpse cave systems, so it's possible that *something* nested inside the volcano itself. Given trolls turned to stone during the day, it seemed a suitable enough place for them to live.

The gritty trail abruptly ended within an hour of climbing, not coming to a split or a fork or even a smaller path. Either I braved the unknown, or I turned around.

Marking the path with bluemelon juice—it would take weeks for even hot rains to wash off the blue substance—I continued on. Contrary to the logic of the northern cities, the forest thickened up the mountain instead of lessening.

The stonetrees grew denser, their black bark stretching fingers of carnelian stone in place of leaves. This strange red canopy allowed for beams of glassy daylight, but the black branches absorbed most of the sun. Today it was less muggy than normal, but still moist and humid.

The shrubbery thickened, the bark hardy and tough to cut through. The bushwhacking process was loud and grueling, so I watched for signs of magma truffles and dug up a few on the way, just to give myself the occasional break.

Eventually, I reached another trail that went uphill at an angle. I wasn't sure what I'd find or stumble upon, but the trail was wide enough to accommodate a troll, so I followed it, still marking my path the whole way.

I hadn't lied to the gate soldier, not really. I did indeed forage as I went along. After sticking around my farmland for a week, getting to move through the land was a breath of fresh air. Foraging was about exploring and getting to know an area, while making an extra few bucks on the side.

Sure, I could have hired a scout, but I'd never intended to go very far. And so I crept across the growing mountainside, exploring quietly, adding this and that to my bag and wondering how much it would all be worth.

As the sun began to descend, I located a scalecherry tree, stopping to pick the expensive fruit. The tree was rarer than firefruit, but easier to pick and much harder to cultivate. Because they were so prone to damage and had short harvest seasons, they could actually sell better than firefruit. I might have avoided leaving the city as a child, but growing up around Dasvilla had taught me a lot about fruit.

I was about halfway through filling up my bag when I heard rustling, low to the ground and coming closer. I kept picking, mostly because I could buy a yearling dragon with a scalecherry tree this bountiful. Every extra fruit mattered, and I wanted to get as many as I could before I fled or fought.

The sound neared, slow and steady, and I recognized it as slithering. I kept still so that the poisonous snake could wander past me, minding its own business. It wove along the rocky ground only a few paces from me. I watched it go before starting up my work again.

Once I finished, I turned around to find a pair of twin bronze orbs staring at me from only an arm's length away.

"Hey Copper," I said, waving at the dragon, who had successfully snuck up on me without my knowing. Her ability to move through the stonetrees without making a single sound was a testament to just how powerful and dangerous she was going to be.

"Did you find anything?" I asked her.

She glanced back towards Dasvilla. The dragon lowered herself, craning her neck around to stare at her back.

I patted her neck. "Sorry, girl. You're not big enough for me to ride you yet."

She chuffed at my face, but nothing came out of her mouth. She'd shown no sign of her breath ability yet.

"Don't worry. I can handle what's coming," I said. That worried look back toward Dasvilla had told me all I needed to know. Jolene and Becki had both insisted I not come out here alone, so I'd had Copper watching my back from the sky.

If she'd landed, that meant she'd seen something approaching, and I knew what it was—because there was a certain object missing from the front of my chest, and I was now a more desirable target.

If only Kenna had been here today, I thought, but the dragon captain only passed through Dasvilla on Sundays. She made for a great companion on hunts, and with how turned-on she got by watching monsters die, she was a battle reward just as much as a fighting partner.

Without her, though, I'd been left with an opportunity that I didn't want to waste.

"All right, Copper," I said. "How far back? In walking minutes."

She chittered about ten or fifteen times, too fast to count for sure, but I got the gist.

"Great. And where is the nearest concentrated troll scent coming from? Large enough to be a nest."

She leaned back and rose onto her hind feet, craning her neck skyward like a swan. Her head bobbed back and forth until she scented what I'd needed.

I'd told a white lie to the others about looking for a troll nest. With the help of my dragons, finding a troll nest was always going to be child's play. It had only been half the purpose of this trip.

Copper dropped onto all fours again and chuffed in a specific direction, chittering seven times. A seven-minute walk. That would work out just great.

I tossed her a piece of jerky, which she snapped out of the air. "You're one of a kind, Copper," I told her. "Now get back up there, and shoot me a screech when she's a few minutes from me, or if I'm about to come upon the troll nest. Wheel left for the first threat, wheel right for the second."

At first, the dragon seemed too busy with her jerky to respond to me, so I repeated the command until her eyes flashed with understanding. She took flight, and I headed in the direction she'd indicated.

Once she was out of sight, I pulled a clump of handkerchiefs from my chest pocket. It had been ages since I'd used that pocket for anything, since I usually had a certain something strapped across my chest.

Anyway, I needed to be quiet from now on, so I packed the handkerchiefs in between the bottles in my satchel.

When I was done, I set off, no longer clinking with each step. I grinned. My plan was coming together.

"Time to make another fortune, or die trying," I said—and a little voice inside my head argued back, *You've already died once. This is nothing.*

I cast off the thought, and headed into the forest.

Chapter 82

Recycling

Copper found the troll nest first, and I crouched low behind a boulder to give it a good look. Trolls turned to stone during the day, and the very boulder I was hiding behind might be a troll come nightfall, which was hours off yet. They transformed into plain rocks, not statues, so you could never tell a rock from a troll.

However, if trolls found shelter in caves like the one I was looking at, they could keep from transforming. Daylight merely had to touch them directly for them to change, but inside the safety of a cavern, they could go about their day.

I couldn't see very far into the cave, but I heard the grating rumbles of the troll language very clearly, and smoke streamed out of a hole in the rock that sloped above the yawning entrance. Copper landed quietly on top of the cave's entrance, out of sight of its occupants. Some gravel fell from her landing, and the voices within fell silent, but nothing else happened.

Since trolls couldn't be out in the sun, they couldn't really have guards, and they didn't have much to fear from anything dropping just a couple of pebbles.

Once I gave the signal that she was safe, Copper hunkered down to listen, too. She'd probably have better luck differentiating voices and counting the number of enemies. Her tail flicked after a time: one flick, two, three, all the way up to eight before stopping.

Eight trolls. Damn.

Like minotaurs, the creatures could stand eight feet tall, although not all of them did. They came in a variety of sizes and shapes, but their main claim to fame was how impenetrable they were.

Their skin remained stonelike even in daytime, so that both blunt and sharp instruments had little effect on them. Even their eyes were rock-hard. Only magic seemed to work.

So I had eight of these guys to kill, which would make me one hell of a pretty penny, if I could pull it off. At the same time, I also had something to rescue. I could feel the unmistakable aura of a dragon from the very back of the cavern. Its aura, like a fog I could sense only in my mind, was heavy and suppressed, likely from a long time of containment. The poor creature was being kept prisoner in this place.

Exactly as Jasmine had told me.

Suddenly Copper raised her head high, a signal that I was no longer alone. I turned and sat on the gravel under the stone tree nearest me, leaning back into the boulder and fishing in a pocket for a vial I'd brought with me. I held it out to the forest.

None too soon. The moment the vial appeared in my hand, a twig cracked.

"What?" I said. "Did I surprise you?"

Nothing moved among the trees, which were so sparse that nothing should have been able to sneak up on me. However, a person didn't train to become an assassin for nothing. I swung the blood around, wondering where the woman might appear from. I just had to make sure she saw it.

"A one-time-use invisibility spell?" I said. "Those are costly. Am I really worth so much?"

She appeared then, blinking into existence right next to me, a knife to my throat. My eyes went wide.

"Holy shit, you're good," I said. "You buy a silence spell, too?"

"You're still talking," the assassin growled. "If you're going to beg, do it now."

I moved my hand unthreateningly to one side, offering her the vial. "This is my blood. Take it. You can kill me with it anytime you like. All you have to do is hear me out."

She narrowed her eyes, then snatched the vial.

"You can take the knife away," I said.

"I'll take my chances, thanks," she replied, her voice low. Neither of us wanted to alert the trolls. "How did you know I was here?"

I nodded upward, rolling my eyes back toward Copper. "My dragon told me."

"Bullshit. That dragon's a hatchling. There's no way she's that well-trained yet."

"Well, my dragons act a little differently than most people's," I said. "You've probably heard the rumors. Anyway, I've had her watching for you since I left the city."

The knife tickled my neck, almost sensuous. "Oh, did you now?"

"Yes. I left your dragon's eggs behind. I didn't wear the bandolier. So I knew you'd be seizing your chance to kill me without harming them."

I could audibly hear her teeth grate. "You think you know me, do you?"

I finally dared to turn my head to look at her. That dark skin, those red eyes, and that sharp black tattoo of a knife down her face... where had she come from? How had she learned magic? Mages were rare, and for one to escape army conscription took real skill.

In fact, no one was even sure how a mage came to be, since their powers weren't hereditary, and few ever talked about their upbringing. Most seemed to be orphans, although I'd never heard of any of Dasvilla's orphans becoming mages. It only seemed to happen to *wealthy* orphans.

"I know you cared very much for your dragon, and for her eggs," I said. "I know that you have mercy in you. And I know you are curious about why someone has put a hit out on anyone with blood like mine."

Her lip curled. "Your point being?"

My gaze slid past her, and I blinked twice.

Copper huffed a breath against the back of the woman's hood.

The assassin's red eyes went wide, but true to her training, she went still.

"Unlike humans, dragons are perfectly capable of walking silently if they want to," I said evenly. *Especially dragons that can move through solid objects.*

"You brought another one," she said, her tone changing. She took the knife from my neck, very slowly, and held up both hands—although she didn't quite drop the knife.

I cricked my neck, then reached out and dropped the vial of my blood in her pocket. "Another dragon? No. It's the same one."

"But... but when did you signal her?"

Smart, that you were looking for signals, I thought. "I didn't signal her. We discussed it ahead of time."

"You can't discuss with *dragons,*" she replied.

I pulled a knife from my belt and handed it to her, pommel-first. "Look, Mrs. Knifey McBloodface or whatever your name is, I already said this: I'm not normal, and my dragons aren't normal. They understand me, they obey me, they communicate with me. I can pull off all kinds of stunts with them, and I've just invited you to have a front-row seat to the next one."

Her eyes darted to the knife I'd offered her. It was the one I'd stolen from her during her first attack on Fieran and I, way back in Olinios. The same one she'd used to cure the blood poison.

"Take it," I said. "Consider it an advance on your payment for a certain job I've got for you."

Her bloody eyes narrowed. "What job?"

I nodded to Copper, and the dragon walked backward, loudly this time, to let the assassin know she was backing off.

"First, my demonstration," I said. I tossed the knife at her feet, rising into a crouch to match hers. "You can kill me anytime you like, with that blood I gave you, so why not hear me out? Or should I say *watch* me out."

With that, I nodded Copper around the rock. I rose to my feet, well in sight of the trolls. Their voices stopped.

I laid my hand on Copper's flank, and allowed her aura to pool around mine.

It was as easy as mixing two clouds of mist together. All I had to do was sense Copper's aura—as golden as treasure, with copper and silver mixed in—and my own intense aura, a fierce orange. I pictured the color we would make when we mixed, and suddenly our aura bled into each other, creating a vivid yellow-orange.

But I let her color predominate, forming a shell around mine. When the change was complete, I opened my eyes to find Copper looked blurry, almost like a projection of an image of herself. She wasn't the only one that looked that way.

I'd become a shadow, too.

"Good girl," I said as the first roar of alarm went up within the cave. I tensed, and Copper tensed, and as one beast we lunged forward, racing into the cave.

We weren't invisible, just darker than normal, fallen shadows without any clear edges. Together we raced straight for the first troll—and through him. I felt the stone of him pass through my stomach and chest, and it instantly made me nauseous and my heart palpitate, but I kept my feet.

Another. Another. Another. We passed through each troll, and I marked their position and numbers as my eyes adjusted.

There were actually nine of them, not eight, but two were smaller, possibly children.

As we lurched deeper into the shadows of the cavern, passing through them became harder to bear. I would get dizzy any moment, maybe vomit. I felt like I might have a heart attack.

"Copper, stop here," I said, pulling up against a dark wall. The dragon whipped her tail through a few more trolls for good measure. They definitely felt the impact, and they staggered, but otherwise they seemed fine. The ones we'd already passed through were turning around.

Ever since Copper had saved our dragonflight by phasing into the flight dragon's eye, I'd been toying with her magic. She could slip through anything, but she couldn't reconstitute her body inside it safely unless it was weaker than herself.

This meant she could reappear in a feather or leaf or in a dragon's eye jelly, and be fine. She'd just destroy the material. But she couldn't manifest inside a troll; it would kill her. Stone was harder than flesh.

Which left us in the middle of nine trolls, all of them staring at us. In seconds, they would start attacking.

My blades were useless here, and my shield not much better.

So I pulled a bottle from my satchel, and threw.

Chapter 83

Who's the Alpha Now?

I THREW the first bottle at the head of the nearest troll, and it shattered. He shook his head, then started roaring, and then the roar died as his entire skull began melting.

That had been Shiny's contribution: Becki had collected just one bottle of her caustic breath, but it was enough to kill an adult troll.

Next, I threw a bottle of Collette's breath at another troll's legs, and the stone froze solid. For now, it would keep him from being a threat, but I threw a similar bottle at a third troll's head to see if the ice would be deadly.

It was.

The other trolls were scrambling forward now, raising their big clunky fists to hit us. They stomped right over the face-melted troll, and bowled over the frozen-leg troll so hard that his legs shattered from their weight. He screeched like an owl as he fell, his legs spurting black blood, thick as tar. He would bleed out.

Three down, six to go.

I shattered fire breath against one troll's chest, turning it red; the troll scratched at it, screaming. That had been a contribution of Dull, the flame dragon hatchling, but we'd only been able to get two bottles out of her.

I used the second one now, to intensify the heat, and the stone melted away as two more trolls reached us. They passed right through our shadow magic, striking the wall behind us. My stomach lurched, but I kept myself focused.

I threw a bottle of poison breath at my feet.

As shadows, the poison passed easily through us, but the two trolls that had attacked—and the two just behind them, that we'd stepped through to clear the spot—instantly breathed in the harsh fumes. They started coughing, a sound like mud bubbling.

"Solidify," I told Copper, and we came out of our shadow form. Copper chirped in pain. I'd drained a lot of magic from her, protecting us both from damage.

I pointed. "Knock that one into the indent there. Then sit on him and have a nice rest."

She rumbled, and her demeanor instantly changed from tired to excited as she launched herself at the smaller troll that had been smart enough to hang back.

Meanwhile, I threw a second and third poison bottle into the midst of the coughing trolls—courtesy of Ravager. Swamp dragons spat poison gas.

Like Tilly's cloud breath, this gas was useful in covering more area than a bottle of something more pinpointed, like flame, but it was far more dangerous to use. I'd tested the range to make sure we'd be safe doing this in a cave, but it could still spread, so I had to be careful.

The ground shook as Copper's prey landed. I turned and instructed her to flip the troll over, which she managed to do. This put his face into an indent in the stone floor.

I threw a bottle of water breath into the depression, courtesy of a spring dragon we'd been borrowing to stud, and water filled it up while Copper kept her weight on him.

At the same time, two of the poisoned trolls dropped, while two staggered toward me, their thick hands pressed protectively to their mouths. The final healthy troll had been asleep in the back, and it had just now gotten to its feet and was lumbering toward me.

I threw my last bottle of ice breath at his feet.

He hit hard and slid, crashing into the poisoned trolls, and they all went down in a thunderous heap. Finally, I used my last trick: a combination of breath from both Useless and Dune, the mated adults that had predated me at Pinnacle.

Dune, a blue beach dragon, could turn things to sand with his breath. I threw the first bottle onto the pile, and the healthy troll didn't even get a chance to roar as its torso collapsed into sand.

Useless, a gray-violet storm dragon, had the power of hurricane-force winds—so I threw her breath on the pile.

This was a mistake, as the explosive wind hurled me backward —but it also shoved one of the sick trolls against a wall, while the other shot back out of the cavern and into the light, where it instantly turned back to stone.

As for me, I came to a stop next to the very thing I'd come to retrieve: a dragon cage. It was as tall as I was, with a cowering Mount-class dragon inside, its mouth locked in a muzzle. With my body aching, stomach churning, and head spinning, I managed to fight to my feet, open the cage door, and reach for the dragon.

"Hey now, I got you," I said, tugging the muzzle off. I backed up, leaving the door open, as the dragon tilted its head back and bugled piteously. He was vivid orange and glowing, like fresh magma. Magma dragons were Hauler-class, so this had to be their smaller cousin, a lava dragon. He would be useful, once he'd rested up.

Suddenly, Copper chirped in warning. I turned in time to see the final, sickened troll diving toward me. It was too close, and I had no time to draw my shield to protect myself. All I could do was catch my breath and watch the stone come.

A blur of red, and in the next blink, there was a glaring hole in the center of the troll's head. Something red paused to hover in front of my face.

The troll dropped dead at my feet.

I blinked first at it, then at the hovering red thing.

My blood. That's my fucking blood!

A shadow moved closer, and the assassin materialized from the dark side walls of the cavern. As I stepped back from the ball of blood, she scooped it out of the air with an oilskin pouch.

"Got a little cocky, didn't you?" she said, tucking the pouch away in her cloak. I blinked at it.

"How did you—that *went through his head,*" I said. She must have sent my own blood flying toward me, as her blood magic worked that way, but since when could blood move through *stone?*

She tapped her own forehead with the blade of the strange knife I'd returned to her.

"Wyvern blade," she said. "The unique construction and components infuse any of *my* bloods with the blood of a wyvern. Wyvern fields cause magic negation, which allows any infused blood to bypass magic protections. Useful for an assassin."

I stared at the miraculous blade. "Or for killing magical monsters."

"Just so."

We held each other's gazes a moment longer, and then I let loose a shuddering breath and peered past her. Copper appeared to have gone to sleep on the small troll, which lay unmoving, successfully drowned.

Eight trolls. I'd just killed eight trolls, and incapacitated another. *Well, seven. The assassin killed one of them. I ought to thank her for that.*

"What's your name?" I said instead.

She curled only one side of her lips in a smile. "Why do you want to know?"

I held out a hand. "I want to know the names of people I hire."

She cocked her head, and I thought she might say something like *What makes you think I'll work for you?*

Instead, she shook my hand and said, "I'm Yavonne."

"Yavonne, then," I replied, feeling weirdly pleased. I nodded at the dead troll. "Well, Yavonne. What do you think?"

She looked back over the carnage. "I think you might be the craziest motherfucker alive."

"And...?"

"And maybe the strongest, too," she admitted, turning back. "That bottled magic... it all came from dragons?"

"Yep. *My* dragons."

"And you used your own dragon's magic?"

"Yeah. I still need practice with that, though. Anyway, as you can see, my abilities as a Dragon-Touched are something else. Can you imagine how many monsters people like me could clean up? How many people we could save and protect? How many dragons like Vital we could conscript to help us, without having to trap them and break their spirits and turn them into slaves?

"And here you are, trying to kill me for all this... after you killed other people with the same potential powers. Don't you think the kingdom is better off if we stay alive? If we *help*, instead of just die?"

Yavonne said nothing, watching me. Copper peeped behind her, a small noise of concern. Something was approaching. She peeped again.

I indicated the bodies. "If you can prise off the ears, these troll bounties are yours. It'll be a small fortune. In exchange, I would like you to do two things. One: leave Fieran alone for now, but keep other assassins off her.

"And two: find out who has a hit out on the Dragon-Touched."

She laughed. "That's a tall order."

"But a great payment."

She raised a finger. "Make it a *down* payment, and we have a deal. Half up front, and half after."

That made me chuckle, and I reached out to shake her hand again. "Fine, I'll make sure you get paid again on delivery of a name. Until then—"

Copper screeched, and I looked at her silhouette to see her back spikes all raised in alarm. At the front of the cavern, four shapes loomed, chirping. Yavonne spun.

"Wild dragons!" she said, drawing a knife in each hand. "Where did they come from? Shit!"

I grinned. "Don't worry. I got this." Turning around again, I coaxed the caged Mount out of his enclosure. "Come on, boy, chirp for me again, would you? Something nice and calming. No one will hurt you."

Instead of lowering his head to make a meek noise, the wild dragon raised his crown up high. Pride radiated off him as he rumbled. The Mount-class dragons at the entrance rumbled back.

I ran a hand down his rough flank. "Apparently, troll clans keep certain dragons as pets, because of their ability to call other dragons to their aid," I explained. "Trolls use this to scrounge up an army of guard dragons when they need one, for defense or for a specific attack. They let the trapped dragon cry out, then muzzle him again... it draws other dragons close, but keeps them from pinpointing the captured dragon's location.

"If the dragons are attacked while trying to find him, they will of course attack back. In this way, trolls can basically conjure very impressive guard dogs."

Yavonne's eyes shone in cold, calculating wonder. "I've never heard of that."

"Yes, well, it pays to have a genius with a crush on you," I said, mentally thanking Jasmine for the tip again. "Anyway, I've got to take this guy home with me. Are you all good to—"

"Wait. You said *certain dragons*. What dragon has the ability to call others to its aid? Aren't dragons normally solitary?"

I scratched the unmuzzled dragon's chin. He rumbled.

"You're right—they are. Unless they are alphas."

And I'd just captured my very first one.

i

Chapter 84

Something to Kill

"THIS IS SILLY," Becki said with a sigh. "I can never find alone time with you."

I chuckled, shaking my head. "Don't blame me. You're too popular. That's the reason this blew out of control."

She folded her arms, leaned against the wagon's seat, and grumbled, "Maybe."

"It was a good idea. No. A great one," I said with approval.

We sat in the middle of a fairly large caravan, surrounded by soldiers, residents, and seemingly everyone in Dasvilla that was eager to make a quick coin. But most of this big clump of slow-moving wagons *was* Becki's fault.

My little secret had "somehow" gotten out.

That might be because—after the capture of the first alpha—I'd found myself with a little more time to spare before anyone back home would be worried about me. With Copper's help, it hadn't been hard to locate three more troll nests—and with Copper's good eyes, we were able to peer into the dark caves and find out which nest had an alpha.

Only one of them had a dragon caged at the back, but luckily, the Shoulder-class beast had been poorly guarded. Although I'd been low on supplies, I'd had Yavonne to help me this time.

We'd made short work of the five trolls guarding the second alpha, and it was now eating a big fat dinner back at the Cage with a harem of females already clustered around it.

Anyway, no sooner had I returned from my *very* successful scouting mission, with not one but *two* alphas in tow, before a random stranger had run up to me and blurted, "Is it true you can ward off dragons?"

The proverbial hatchling was out of the bag, it seemed, and I figured out why as soon as I got home to find a line of merchants out the gate, ready to hire me. I bypassed them and entered my villa to find Fieran passed out on the couch in the den, with Becki moaning in a chair next to her. Jolene was feeding Becki a cup of tea.

I dropped my pack of truffles, bluemelon, and scalecherries to the ground by the door, cocked an eyebrow at Becki, and said, "Really?"

Becki's copper-gold eyes widened, and she tossed her head back and moaned, "Noooo. You weren't supposed to get back yet. I was going to do damage control!"

Jolene dropped the teacup on the low table beside the couch. "Sweetie, you and Fieran got into a drinking contest against Enforcers. Half the town was watching by the end. There is no 'doing damage control.'"

She cast me an exasperated look, and I only shrugged, not fighting the smile that tugged on the corner of my mouth. I could imagine Fieran waking up from her long, miserable stupor to find me long gone on my scouting trip. I'd intended to try to shock her into more responsible behavior, but I hadn't accounted for Becki and her insatiable need to make people feel better when they were down.

I was now imagining Fieran and Becki drinking their good sense away, well into the evening, with a crowd of commoners cheering them on. Fieran had done it to drown out (and apparently repeat) her embarrassment, but that reasoning had been balanced out by Becki, who had been there to have a good time and force Fieran into having one, too.

A part of me warmed at the idea of the two of them being friends. "Did you win the contest?" I asked.

"'Course we did," Fieran rasped from the couch. "Who do you think we are?"

"Idiots," Jolene huffed.

"Jo, it's fine. It was going to get out anyway," I said.

"But we *trusted them!* With a secret! And they let it slip within a single *day!*"

"Hey, now," Fieran groused. She hadn't moved from the couch, and faced away from me. "Those 'Forcers threw a demons-damned truthteller dragon in the pot. How was we to know that little bastard was gonna bite us?"

I let out a laugh. *Hungover Fieran forgets her grammar, I see.*

"So we won a truthteller dragon?" I asked. "What breed is that?"

"It's a quartz-desert hybrid. One in four chance of having that ability," Jolene said.

I nodded. "You really do know everything. But aren't those illegal for commoners to own?"

Jolene let out a whoosh of breath. "I *thought* they were, but Rachel says she checked the laws, and there's a nifty little loop-hole about dragons being given as 'prizes' not counting as a sale or gift. So buying, selling, or giving away the dragon is a no-no, but giving it as a prize is not."

"It's so easily-entertained rich bastards like the king can give away priceless dragons to people that win a fox hunt or juggle well or something," Fieran said.

"Huh. Well, it benefits us. Great," I said. "Honestly, a truthteller dragon is a pretty good trade for having my secret get out."

"You haven't heard the rest," Jolene said.

Turns out, the justicar had already sent Enforcers to reclaim the truthteller dragon, and now Rachel was locked in litigation with them while we hid the healthy little dragon away.

Meanwhile, the word "Dragon-Touched" had leached out into the town through the drinking game of the century, the word had stuck, and whispers had gotten out. Turns out, people really liked the idea of being safe from wild dragon attacks outside the city. So when Jolene sold all my foraged items the next morning, I'd joined her.

At the time, I had been either an unknown or a rumored entity to most of Dasvilla. When I wandered through the market that day with Jolene, though, I'd drawn a lot of attention. Word had spread about me mounting a campaign into the wilds while my powers reduced dragon attacks.

All I'd wanted was to purchase a quality aviary wagon. After I'd captured my new alphas, they had proved to be docile but moody beasts. Like every dragon I'd encountered so far, they listened to me, but they had their own unique personalities— and that included laziness and a tendency to mope instead of walk.

I would have given just about anything to be able to drag them home in a cart rather than coax them back at the end of a couple of leashes. If I was going to start actively hunting wild dragons like this—or even with traps—then I needed a way to get them home easily and quickly. Not to mention a nice wagon would mean an easier ride and a bit of safety whenever I had to sleep.

Anyway, that attempt to find a wagon had soon become an attempt to lead *twenty* wagons, all of whom paid Becki up-front for my protection. The principle was simple: a lot of humans grouped together were more capable of warding off threats. Sometimes they massed to destroy a growing orc or goblin nest that the military couldn't handle alone, but most of the time it was because something specific transpired, like a rare fish-spawning season, a valuable breed of dragons migrating, a bison stampede, and more.

In this case, the merchants all claimed to know of a wild scalecherry orchard in season on the west side of the volcano, which my own haul of the fruit had confirmed. The cherries would freeze well with the help of ice dragons, and frozen cherries shipped easily, meaning coins would flow from all nine dukedoms of Parshil to this one.

At the same time, the watchmaster and I could do our practice nest-scouting trip. It was a win-win for everyone.

Organizing the group was easy, even with only a day's notice. Dasvillians knew their fruit, and scalecherries could be picked by hand with no more than a ladder and a basket. You didn't need to endanger orphans or use iron files to harvest it, like you needed with firefruit. The trick was finding the stuff in season, and beating dragons to it.

It was also called scalecherry for a reason: anything with scales loved to snack on it. People believed the special oils in the scalecherry is what made dragons so shiny—and what made certain smaller reptiles so poisonous. I hadn't forgotten my little visit from the snake, so I made sure to bring an apothecary with us.

Anyway, Becki drove a hard bargain: people had to pay upfront, and they had to bring their own wagons and supplies, and the entry price was enough to clean out our debts if we had twenty wagons attending. Also, you had to come *the next day.* Either you joined the main party in the morning, or you had to catch up later, and no one wanted that.

I had to force Becki to stop at twenty wagons, because I wasn't confident in protecting more than that if my natural dragon-repellent ended up being coincidence.

And so the caravan came to be, with a mood that was jovial from the start, especially among my staff. Provided nothing went wrong, our debts were paid after this one week of travel, and we only had to prove profitability after that... although once we returned, we'd have only three days to prove that.

I'd left Rachel in charge with Jolene, Jerem, Jayke, and Aliese to assist, and my little-seen business partner was currently working the books to provide a solid argument for Pinnacle's viability.

As for the caravan, everything had gone smoothly so far. There was lots of laughter during the day, and someone played drums from a nearby wagon even when we were rolling. A bevy of my dragons surrounded the group, all of them calm and organized. I rode Ravager in a patrol around the caravan hourly, just to make sure the dragons weren't starting to go native.

Through all this, I learned more about the dragon maturity curve, simply by being in touch with individual dragons on a more personal level. I kept the hatchling night dragon in my shirt still, but now I had the supposed hatchling Copper, the juvenile Feldspar, two adult alphas, and all kinds of other adults, some of which were going into heat in the presence of the alphas.

With each day that passed, the younger dragons rapidly grew, while Feldspar more slowly matured toward his full size. I guessed the growth speed of the smaller allowed them to reach fighting age sooner, where they had enough claws, teeth, and bulk to protect them while they finished growing.

And nowhere was that more prevalent than with Copper. She almost doubled in size in just that week—and she was anxious for violence. That was a good thing, of course... or it could be.

We just needed to find something to kill.

Chapter 85

Loaded Question

COPPER RODE on the wagon's roof because I preferred her close to hand. The wagon itself was caged like a portable aviary, with a bunch of traps stacked high in half the space while the other half remained open for the orphans to alternate between walking and riding.

Becki glanced back at the kids from our seat on the front bench of the wagon. "I've never seen a wildlands caravan so damned *happy*. Four Demons, Markam even sent a company of troops to entertain the kids."

"Aye, he did, and they're singing one of my favorite marching songs," I said, leaning against the bench and watching the stonetree forest drift by as we rolled further away from the city. Two nice-looking horses pulled past us, having no issue with the light weight of their empty cart. "It's nice to listen to marching songs without actually having to march."

"I can't believe you used to do that without real protection," Becki mused, cuddling up next to me, her hand slinking onto my thigh. "You are *ever* so brave, Warren."

"Oh, stop giving him a big head," Kenna said from my other side. "Both literally and figuratively," she added, her voice low and in my ear now.

Suddenly I had a woman's hand on *both* my thighs. Pair that with the rumbling movement of the cart, and I might soon have to call for a break and pitch a quick tent.

"I'll give him whatever head I want," Becki replied, without venom. Honestly, it surprised me how flirtatious both my companions could be without pissing each other off. I had to guess that both women were used to fly-by-night relationships, but I didn't intend to be one—if I could help it.

Jolene did complicate my chances of taking on multiple partners, but the more time went on, the less I wanted Kenna, Becki, and Aliese to be temporary. I cared about them, and they deserved better than to be bed-warmers for my future noble wife.

"I'm just glad you were in town the day we left," I said, turning my head to kiss Kenna on the forehead. The muscular woman socked me in the arm afterward.

"Quit it with that tender shit," she said, grinning. "You'll ruin my reputation as a bad-ass bitch."

I snorted. "As soon as we pass back through and start clearing out those traps you set, any lost reputation will be gained back ten-fold."

Along the path to the wild orchard, I'd had Kenna use her dragon-hunting know-how to set traps near our path, in whatever places she thought most likely to catch either dragons or high-value bounty monsters. In exchange for this service, I was paying her in both orgasms and a week's worth of her guide salary.

"Jolene is going to freak out if you get a good haul," Becki commented. "Speaking of the lady of the villa, are you two...?"

I blew air out my lips, unsure the best way to answer. "No."

"But the attraction is there, right?" Kenna said.

I nodded. "Yeah, but we've been avoiding doing anything about it. Rushing into things seems more dangerous than doing them right, especially with her still being in mourning. I don't want to hurt her, and Pinnacle is our main goal right now anyway."

That wasn't to say there hadn't been a little bit more casual flirting, at least in the one day I'd been back.

"Yeah, but you're an eligible bachelor *and* a lord," Becki said. "If you don't take a noble wife soon, you'll get swarmed with suitors."

"What about a non-noble wife?" I asked.

She waved a hand. "No one would take her seriously, not as a first-wife. You need a noble first-wife. It's just how things are."

She said it so casually, as if she saw no world in which I might be interested in having *her* as my life-partner. Kenna acted much the same.

"What about having kids?" Kenna asked. "You need a legitimate wife to have heirs, but she needs to be noble if you want the kids to have ties to other lands and assets besides yours. Jolene's got a sister who married well, right? Your kids could join that merchant empire if you married her, even though she's got nothing herself."

I raised my arms up and laid them across both their shoulders, pulling them closer. "Yeah, I want kids, but I don't care about their bloodlines. I just want to be a father whose children know love."

"When you say stuff like that, it makes a woman's ovaries hurt," Becki said. "Speaking of which, you're doing more for Dasvilla than just helping the orphanage. Some of the kids who work for us have single mothers or poor parents."

"I... I know. I don't turn them away," I said with indifference. "They need to eat, everyone does, and everyone has a sad story and a special situation. Demons, a lot of those cursing parents I remember from our alley days. They had no options, and got pregnant young."

Becki crossed her legs, so she could anxiously bounce one. "We breed to survive, just like dragons."

"You remember when King Kurto put out a reward for birthing noble babies a few years back?" I asked. "I met a woman who thought it was the dumbest thing in the world. *It just encourages prostitutes to get pregnant,* she'd said.

"Then we got into bed, and suddenly she was begging me to give her a kid. *That bounty will pay for us to have a new life!* Yuck. No thank you on that one."

Becki gasped. *"No.* Did the princess say that?"

I stiffened, raising an eyebrow at Becki. How did she know about that?

"What's this about a princess?" Kenna said.

I didn't answer. "Becki," I warned, drawing the word out.

"Oh, fine!" she burst out. "I extorted the information from the duchess, okay? Don't worry, I haven't told Jolene, but you should."

Kenna cleared her throat. "I *said,* what's this about a princess?!"

Several minutes of both explanation and exclamation later, and I was a man suffering beneath a deluge of questions.

"But you could have been a prince!" Kenna said. "Why'd you leave?"

"Yeah. You could be next in line for the throne!" Becki added.

I shushed them both for the fifth time in so many minutes. "No," I said, the word hard as stone. "I'm no prince, I'm just Warren, the man on his farm with his dragons." I reached up to pet Copper on top of the wagon cage. She allowed it for a few seconds.

"Anyway, don't tell Jolene. She should hear it from me. I'll bring it up eventually."

"Oh Warren, you're such a big romantic oaf," Becki said, lying down across one end of the bench to put her head in my lap. Her eyes glittered red whenever there were breaks in the canopy of carnelian-tipped trees.

"You should tell her you're choosing her over a princess," she said. "Then she'll spread her legs for sure."

"I'm not interested in that," I said with a grunt, thumbing my mystery dragon's chin. "That's the sort of thing a guy like Garm would do. The sort of thing he *tried* to do with you."

Becki nodded, sitting there staring up for a good few minutes. "Garm stopped bugging me, did you know?" she said finally. "I ran into his wife the other day. Turns out, she wanted me around to take her kids off her hands once in a while.

"Shelly's her name, a sweet woman, used to be a baker. She hasn't gotten to bake in years because he keeps pumping her full of kids." She paused. "Apparently, you beat him up."

Kenna leaned away and slapped my chest. "You violent little devil! Now you're beating up *Enforcers* as well as orcs?"

I shrugged. "He was trying to force me to sell Star. But I've made nice with him. He was just following orders."

"Some orders," Kenna scoffed. "Oh, hold on, this is a good trap spot. I'll be back."

With that, she hopped off the bench and started instructing the orphans to pass her supplies from the back of the aviary cart. Becki giggled in my lap, batting her copper eyes at me, her smile coy.

"Now that she's gone... I do want to ask. I'm ready for kids, Warren. Will you be the father?"

Chapter 86

You Get a Conspiracy! And You Get a Conspiracy!

I STARED DOWN AT HER, speechless. My thoughts scattered and fled. Becki giggled, her head bobbing slightly against my cock, which was inexplicably starting to react to her.

"You're teasing me," I realized. "You're joking."

She shook her head. "I'm not."

I couldn't believe this. Kids? With *Becki?* Hell, kids with *anyone* was inconceivable to me... especially after Vanessa. When the princess had named her child like she did, just to spite me... it had left a sour taste in my mouth forever.

Then again, maybe it was time to change that. I was a noble now. I needed heirs.

"I know it must sound silly to you," Becki sighed, "but if I have a kid with you, it'll show I'm your mistress, and other guys like Garm will finally leave me alone. Besides, I can't think of anyone better."

"But you *just* said I ought to marry someone else!" I sputtered.

"So? Warren, every morning I'm with you, you ask how I slept. Every day I'm with you, you ask how I'm feeling, and I'm actually *listened to* when I respond. You have this way of brushing my hair out of my eyes or dusting me off, no matter how dirty the both of us are."

I went to open my mouth and she sat up and kissed me, because she wasn't finished.

"You check on me every chance you can. You ask what I need without ever putting yourself first. You shouldn't do that for a nobody like me, and you don't have to, but you do.

"And while Jolene may be oblivious, I know you check on us before you go to bed every night. If you can't, you have Copper do it and report back to you. It's the sweetest damn thing, because you aren't asked, told, or forced into it. I know that, with you, I'm loved."

She tweaked my nose, as if she were joking. But we both knew that kids were no joke.

"Becki," I said. "I... I don't know how to respond to that."

"Respond to what? There's no responding necessary. Brave Warren the street kid turned into a fine man, one I'd do anything for. I don't need to be a wife to love him. Too much responsibility and dinner parties and stuff anyway. It's better for us to work together than to tear each other apart fighting over the silverware, you know?

"Besides, it's very common around here to have a family unit— Shelly proves as much—so why not? I'll keep working on Jolene, and we can get her permission first, if you want."

"Yes. Of course I want that," I said quickly, without first processing everything else she'd said. Demons, was she really talking about *silverware?*

"But I just want you. Aliese feels the same, and Kenna doesn't seem to mind sharing, either," Becki said, leaning into me, her hand on my crotch as she added another long, tender kiss.

When our lips parted, I connected them again, just to let her know I cherished her. Our relationship was *never* going to be about dinner parties and silverware, but a mistress? She deserved a title, just like Jolene did.

All this, I tried to say with my mouth and my hands, because these were things I'd need to think about later. I couldn't propose marriage on a fucking wagon. I also couldn't do it with a woman I'd only just reconnected with, although damn, I wanted to.

Becki made me crazy with desire, but she also impressed me every day. Of everyone I knew here, she'd made me the most money. I owed her so much more than she knew.

After a bit of back-and-forth that started to get heated, Arkin, an older boy in the back of the wagon, cleared his throat.

I chuckled and broke our kiss, definitely guilty. "Sorry," I told the kid.

He grunted, and Becki giggled, deciding to snuggle into me again. I pulled her close, trying to ignore how hard I'd gotten. When I pitched my tent tonight, I was going to knock it down again fast, because I'd be mouth-fucking her against the main post until I had her screaming for more.

"Are you sure you want to tie yourself to Jolene for life?" I croaked, trying to dispel the image of her cold, magical sex against my lips. "You two are so different. She's so haphazard and emotional. You're protective and direct."

"The more different we are, the more rounded-out our little family will be." Becki kissed my cheek before seductively nibbling on my ear. "Okay, enough heavy stuff. I'm gonna dice with the kiddos. Just... thank you for coming home, Warren. Thank you for making all our lives better."

With that, she jumped off the driver's bench to head toward the back of the wagon. I watched her go, absently drumming my fingers on her empty spot—and a moment later, someone's random Shoulder-size dragon stole the space, landing on it with a flap and a chirp. The cerulean shoulder pet sat on her haunches and surveyed me with attentive blue eyes.

I patted the creature, wondering who'd lost their baby lake dragon. When a copper-skinned woman showed up ahead of me, wandering between wagons and glancing about, I hailed her with a wave and then pointed at my visitor. Her dragon scurried onto my shoulder as soon as the woman locked her violet eyes on it.

She raced over to us, her headscarf flapping, and her beaded skirts swishing and swaying. She must be dying in this heat, but she was clearly a noble of the foreign country of Kiloba, where nobles were always doing that. There was never any reason to leave your clothes of station behind, and their women dressed like they were attending a ball even while they were out hunting.

"Darty, what are you doing!" the woman cried, her voice thick with a musical accent. "Leave the handsome man alone!"

"It's quite all right," I said, grabbing her dragon by the scruff before setting it back down on the edge of the bench nearest her. She put a hand over her eyes and looked up at me, keeping pace with Useless, who was pulling our wagon.

"Oh, you're him. The Dragon-Touched," she said.

Becki shouted from the back. "That's Mistress Emiro of Kiloba. Single, almost twenty summers, rich as hell. Not sure what she's doing here, though."

"I'm completing my journeyman's application for the Kiloban ambassadorship," Emiro said in her lovely, lilted voice. "Come on, Darty, come back to Mother!"

"An ambassadorship?" I said. "What does that have to do with harvesting orchards?"

"Well, I have to prove I know Parshil well, if I'm going to secure the title of ambassador. This will look great on my application. It's so daring, you see... yes, yes, Darty, he's very pretty, can we go?"

Emiro gestured for the lake dragon to come, but Darty ignored her, cleaving to my leg.

"Go on, now," I said, nudging him. He instantly hopped off the bench to land on her shoulder. "Pleasure to meet you, future ambassador."

She guided the dragon across her shoulders, where it draped familiarly around her neck. She bowed her head at me. "The pleasure is all mine, Dragon-Touched," she said. "Thank you for this opportunity. I must go now, or my parents will worry."

I watched the woman go, her beads making noise the whole way. *The king needs a new ambassador to Kiloba?* I thought. *But what happened to the old one? He was young.*

I'd glimpsed the guy during my very short stay at the palace, after the princess and I had been forced to return. He couldn't have been thirty years old, yet he had retired? Or been killed? Why?

Shaking my head, I reminded myself that not everything had to be a conspiracy. I had enough mysteries to deal with as it was.

Chapter 87

Silver Lady

I STRETCHED awake after a solid nap, feeling refreshed even if my back hurt a bit. It took us two days to pinpoint and arrive at the orchard, with the dragons hunting to feed themselves as we went.

Baron Maki, whom Becki had conscripted as the caravan leader, asked all the trappers to leave before sunrise to set their traps around the orchard. This would further protect us from incursions by monsters on the ground, while supposedly, my presence was enough protection from air attack.

Once the defensive perimeter was set, the entire caravan would leave the wagons to help pick scalecherries. Under Maki, the process had some issues, but we managed. Soon we were all headed into the fruit trees, every wagon staking an equal claim by marking the same amount of trees with red paint.

The scalecherry trees rested on a slope, where a gap in the jungle transitioned into scrub. For the hundred-plus people, it was a fun, but exhausting event that transpired without issue.

Instead of gallivanting off into the jungle solo again, I worked tirelessly to collect cherries just like everyone else. After six or seven hours of picking, almost every wagon was laden with the fruit, including our own spare wagon which we'd dragged along behind the portable aviary.

After a long day of picking, we slept through the night with minimal revelry. Even with a woman to either side of me, I was asleep when my head hit the pillow.

Since I had traps to check, I rose early to make sure I was ready to leave in the afternoon, according to the caravan's rigid schedule. When I walked through the camp, I noticed quite a few people had found shade under some stone outcrops, where they were now getting a few hours of extra sleep. Most of the dragons had decided to group up on the ends of the road we'd formed in our passing, creating two barriers of protection.

I passed a guardsman who'd been keeping watch by constantly walking the camp, and I nodded to him with respect. A few sentry dragons perched near the perimeter, lounging quietly. They faced the jungle and paid attention, but seemed completely at ease.

At the far end of the orchard, I found a clump of guardsmen gathered by a group of lounging dragons that Maki had borrowed from the Biscuits in exchange for a cut of the profits. A few of the guardsmen held spears anxiously, and they talked in hushed whispers.

The officer in the group had a golden Mount dragon curled behind his feet. The pony-sized creature inspected me briefly, bowing its head in acknowledgment. I'd already seen that the dragon was great at hunting, but I doubted this officer used him very often for more than patrols.

Captain Narvi grunted, waving me over to his huddle when one of the guardsmen noticed me. They adjusted to let me in with grimaces and stern faces. Something was clearly bothering them.

"Morning. Why so glum?" I asked.

Narvi leveled a finger at an Airship-class dragon curled at one end of the dragon huddle, looming like a wall of gray flesh. It was one of the Biscuits' biggest, able to transport a dozen people, even though it wasn't yet fully grown. Apparently, Maki had charged for seats aboard the Airship in case an emergency exit from the caravan was needed.

"There's no doubt now," Narvi said. "The dragons are abnormally calm with you nearby. It's a blessing. Normally, we have to deal with nipping, busted leashes, an escapee or three, and fighting. But not everyone's happy about it."

The fourth-ranked guardsman next to him, an older man with a curled mustache, gripped his sword hilt tightly. "Son, while Captain Narvi is calm, I'm not. All of these dragons are raised from eggs, bonded or transfer-bonded."

He glared at the big gray Airship, whose head faced away, and growled, "But whose cursing dragon is *that?*"

"It's just the Airship that Maki's borrowing," I said, earning a few snickers that the veteran soldier didn't appreciate.

"No, actually, it's not," Narvi cut in. "That one's a female. She showed up last night."

I frowned. "Did more nobles come to join us?"

"Nope," he said, popping the *p*. He gave me a raised brow, rightly concluding I was at fault. "There's a wild dragon in our camp, Lord Warren."

I looked over the gray dragon again, but upon closer inspection, it was silver. The metallic scales were dull in the shade of the mountain where it rested.

"Hmm... I think I know who it is," I said after a moment. "Ready your weapons, and... well, look. I know you are all brave and hearty warriors, but you really ought to stand behind me."

More snickers quietly erupted from the soldiers, as if they didn't think I was serious. The veteran guardsman grunted, withdrew his sword and said, "Tease us all ya like. No one'll care if it's you being the bait."

Wouldn't be the first time, I thought, stepping into the flight of snoozing dragons and clapping my hands loudly. Dragons weren't heavy sleepers, so this caused just about every head to turn my way.

Feldspar and Copper appeared not a moment later, flanking my sides, landing with light thuds. They had probably been circling overhead, keeping eyes on me.

Most of the dragons here were Haulers, brought to pull wagons, although quite a few of them had limited fighting capabilities. I waved an arm, and the dragons made way for me as we headed toward the Airship. The three of us paused a dozen paces short of the creature. Unable to avoid me, she craned her head around to see my approach.

Sure enough, it was the big dragon I'd defeated in the arena, the same one who'd been sniffing around my traps in Caliph. She had taken a long journey to get here.

She didn't seem special or extraordinary; if anything, she seemed sad that I came with an aggressive dragon to each side of me, their hackles raised. The big Airship was being cordial and respectful despite this, just watching me calmly. At the same time, she was a very big dragon, more than capable of swallowing a man whole.

"Hello. I'm Warren." She snorted to let me know she already knew this. I placed a hand on Feldspar and Copper's heads; Copper's was now much higher off the ground than her nest-brother's. "We're going to check traps. Wanna come?"

Chapter 88

Bull People

THE AIRSHIP-CLASS DRAGON regarded me for a moment before lowering her head back down to rest. That was answer enough: she wasn't going to help me. But she wasn't going to bother me, either.

I frowned, turning around to walk back to the officers. None of the other dragons seemed upset by her presence. She wasn't doing much, which I figured was probably for the best.

"Hey, uh, I can't order you to put your weapons away, but she's calm. I don't think she's a danger to anyone," I said with a shrug.

"She needs a collar and something to chain her to," Narvi said, thumbing in a different direction. "Even Barton is normally chained."

I guessed the Biscuits' gray Airship male was resting off that way, although I couldn't see him in the trees.

"Let me talk to him," I said. "He's a male. Females typically defer to males in the wild, so long as no babies are involved."

With that, I followed Narvi's directions into the woods, and walked over and smacked Barton's spiky ass. The huge dragon grunted, flipping around to glare at me.

"If that silver Airship attacks, stop her," I said, pointing toward her. I was sure he was aware of her presence.

The Airship huffed with a quiet growl. I took it as agreement, and returned to the silver. Once again, she raised her head for me.

"You want a home?" I asked.

She mewed a yes, quiet, as if afraid to wake the camp.

"All right. If you behave, you'll be welcome in my nest," I said.

The dragon tilted her head curiously, her eyes gleaming with a sly happiness.

"I'm off to check traps," I told her. "If you need me, approach this red asshole, tell him you need Warren, and he'll fetch me." I patted Feldspar, and told him to stay with her. He didn't like it, but he obeyed.

"I... hmm," Narvi grumbled when I explained my precautions to him. "I'm not sure that'll make the men happy."

"I know, but I'm not going to fight her or run her off. She very well could end up saving us. It's not like we're going to go unnoticed by warlords," I said, not wanting to drag out the debate.

"But if she *is* being sincere, I just gained a hundred-gold dragon. If she's not, Feldspar will tell me. I'll stop her before she can eat anyone."

"Hey," the fourth-ranked guardsman grunted when I turned my back. "We respect ya. We do, but if ya start gettin' us killed...."

Even though he didn't finish his sentence, it was a sentiment I knew all too well. But Feldspar would watch the soldiers just as much as the Airship, so I wasn't worried about an attempt on her life.

Besides, with Copper at my side, I'd have a tool that could stop just about any conflict fast. All the other dragons seemed to obey Copper by default, and she could get them to attack and pester the Airship in no time, slowing her down until I had time to reach her and give one of my Dragon-Touched commands.

So I waved goodbye to the soldiers over my shoulder, choosing not to worry about them as I picked up a jog to head to my first trap. The stony vegetation welcomed me and Copper, but it was so thick it forced me to slow to a walk. I noticed an abnormal silence.

A flash of heat sent my arms tingling, and a light scent of unwashed flesh assaulted my nostrils to the point I felt like my senses were heightened.

"We're not alone," I whispered.

My sword scraped out of its sheath and I growled. Copper already seemed to be on edge, her large eyes darting about as she tried to find the threat. She scaled a tree no different than how a cat would, scurrying up until she could hop and glide between trunks, even though she was nearly as big as they were.

Not even thirty paces into the stonetrees, a minotaur burst out of an ambush point with a bellowing roar. The bull-headed, hairy humanoid stood twice my height, with bulging muscles from years of arduous training. Unlike a normal bovine, its large canines flared when its lips peeled back in a snarl.

Killing minotaurs was never easy, since they were larger and more intelligent than orcs. They almost always won versus humans in a fair fight. I'd faced one in the Dasvilla wilds only a few days after I started picking firefruit as a teenager, and I wasn't ashamed to admit that I ran for my life. Despite fleeing, I still managed to kill that one after a misplaced hoof caused him to stumble.

I'd killed plenty more since, but this brute was bigger than usual, with numerous scars from fighting. It appeared to be a male in its prime, with tree-thick biceps and a loincloth, but no breasts.

He carried a massive spear, capable of ripping a giant hole in anything it connected with. He wore no armor, but at his size, it probably would only hamper his speed. I knew his hide would be thick, not easily sliced like human skin.

The massive brute charged, knowing I didn't have to go far to reach allies. These bastards understood the value of the element of surprise.

Copper roared out a battle cry as the minotaur cocked his arm back and aimed at the dragon. I leapt to one side, getting behind the nearest tree. Not a half second later, the spear whizzed through the spot where I'd been, no more than a blur. It slammed into the jungle soil with a spray of dirt.

I'd correctly guessed that I was the target of a feint, but even if I hadn't been, Copper could have let the weapon phase through her.

I stayed firmly tucked behind the tree, wanting him to close the distance. The big brute had a big brain, though, and no hooves thundered closer. When I peered out, I glimpsed his backside crashing away through the forest.

I grunted at the wise move. He'd tried to get a strike on me, and then had turned to retreat to his allies. But Copper wasn't done with him, not when he had all that delicious, meaty flesh on his bones.

She dropped from her tree and lumbered after him, cracking branches and snapping shrubs. I brazenly followed her, instead of going back for more help; our noise would draw help soon, anyway.

When the vegetation got too thick, Copper once again sprung from tree to tree, vaulting forward until she soared like an arrow. I scaled a big rock just in time to see her smack into the minotaur's back. He snorted out a pained grunt, growling with raw hatred as she pinned him to the ground.

I leapt off the rock and widened my sprint, smacking through the hard quartz-bushes until I found Copper and the minotaur wrestling. I gave myself a running start off another rock, then leapt, bringing my sword down. The minotaur's large brown eyes caught my attack in time to yank Copper into the path of my blade.

Copper, now! I thought at her, a burst of instinct more than anything. She phased out, her outline fuzzing. I'd never know if she heard my mental cry, or if she was just that intelligent, but my strike passed through her. The blow unfortunately missed the minotaur, too, because he twisted just in time.

I landed on him and thrust myself off again, forced to leave my sword on the ground by his head. Once on solid earth again, I dug my heels into the tall grass behind the monster, trying to kill the momentum from my run.

By the time I regained my stance, the minotaur was trying to scramble away from Copper, deep gashes now running down his back. Blood oozed out, coating fronds and thorns all around him. Copper's jaw lashed out, and she snatched his ankle with all four of her feet anchored into the jungle floor. Without a single verbal command from me, she had successfully locked him in place.

But the minotaur wasn't done yet.

Chapter 89

Why Fight When You Can Stomp?

THE MINOTAUR ROARED in pain and yanked an axe off his belt, swiping aggressively at Copper's head. She reared back, avoiding the blow, and I crossed the distance, retrieving my sword and blocking his next attack with a loud *clang*.

Copper snapped her jaws above our tangled, straining weapons, and she closed her whole mouth on his head.

With a heaving twist of her body, the minotaur shot forward like a rag doll, smacking belly-first into a tree. His head was bloody, but remarkably intact. When he shook it to clear the stars from his vision, I drove a knife into his throat, loosing a bellow I didn't know I'd been building.

As soon as it pierced his jugular, I hopped back away. The blade exited with a wet *slurp*.

Copper retreated with me to sit on her haunches and watch. The minotaur rose to his feet, staggered toward us twice, then dropped to his knees. He lashed out indiscriminately as he tried to close the distance, sweeping his blade about. For a good minute he flailed, not willing to go quietly.

I glanced back toward camp, keeping one eye on the dying monster. The soldiers in the camp hadn't come streaming to help me, so they were likely rallying their defenses. However, Feldspar wasn't about to leave me alone here. He crashed through the canopy to land beside us, then picked his way forward, sniffing the corpse.

I was about to double-check that it was dead when a shadow fell across us. The big silver Airship dragon hovered overhead, wheeling in a tight circle, high above the canopy. When the minotaur stopped twitching, she broke a lush tree to land, dropped her head, and immediately stole the minotaur's body.

"Hey! I need that thing's ear, it's worth months of pay," I shouted at her, still thinking in soldier terms.

One second we watched him twitch, the next the silver was gone. She left behind a ruined tree and a pool of blood in the middle of the clearing we'd made. Copper roared after her, indignant. I flicked a hand at Copper.

"Go get that ear. I know you can do it, with your phasing," I said. "I'll get you another minotaur. After all, where there's one—"

Right on time, a different minotaur bellowed out a war cry from farther away. Copper launched into the air, and I hurled myself into the woods, crashing through the bushes with Feldspar following overhead.

The wilds were dangerous, and I knew that venturing into them came with risk, but I had the capability to kill these things single-handedly. While some would get past me, I'd thin the herd. The soldiers and caravan dragons could fight what was left.

Copper landed in front of me a minute later, immediately going still, hunching down. Just as she had when the assassin had come after me at the volcano, she wanted me to ride again— except now, a half-week later, she was already big enough to fit me.

"Fine, but we stay grounded. No flying!" I said, hopping on. I almost lost my seat as she immediately dashed forward, ripping through the sloped forest in huge bounds.

Then the trees cleared, and she jumped us right into the

middle of a half-dozen minotaurs. They stood in a circle, laying their spears on the ground in a star-shape.

It was a known pre-attack ritual. I gulped as we landed right in the middle of the circle, breaking several spears under Copper's weight.

They roared in surprise and toppled back as I brandished my sword. Up to this point, Copper had stayed silent, but at the sight of the overwhelming odds, she unleashed the deepest roar of any dragon I'd ever heard. It could probably have been heard back at Dasvilla. The rock beneath us actually *shook*.

My arm hairs rose, and the minotaurs braced as a unit, not charging for once.

Before any of us could react, Copper fled.

I held on for dear life as we smashed away, back into the stone forest.

"Where are we going!?" I shouted, bleeding from the hard-rock bushes and branches cutting me as she rushed past them.

Copper glanced back, but her eyes said one thing: *trust me.* Feldspar's shadow crossed my line of sight; he was still with us, also headed toward some distant spot deep in the woods.

No—he's leading us there.

Trees whizzed by with unrelenting speed that I knew had to come—at least in part—from Copper's magic. I hugged her neck while holding my sword flush to her flank, until we arrived in yet another clearing.

In the grassy field, Barton and the silver faced off against three minotaurs with swords and shields. The warrior-monsters lashed out, keeping both of the Airship dragons at bay, and it only took a second to see why they were worried. These three minotaurs were protecting a small herd of goats, all tied together with rope behind them. More minotaurs cowered among the goats, likely non-fighters.

The warrior minotaurs snarled, shouting at each other. The two dragons were already too much, but when we added a human and two fighting-type dragons, the odds turned against them even more. One of the minotaurs reached to his hip, grabbed a horn, and blew a long call. I knew exactly which group he was summoning: the ring of warriors we'd just left behind us.

Behind the three minotaurs, the females and children of the tribe peeked out from among the goats, afraid to see why the call had been given. When they saw that I'd joined the fray, they began a hasty retreat, leaving the goats behind.

In theory, it'd be a great win to take the goats as the defenders fled; judging by the flower garlands all over the goats, the minotaurs meant them as a sort of offering to someone or something. However, I wasn't in the kind of mood to settle on a few goats.

Humanity was at war with all minotaurs, and we weren't winning. We lived in cities that might as well be cages, plagued by attacks anytime we left the safety of our walls. These minotaurs would have no problem dining on the flesh of women and children themselves, so my ability to feel merciful didn't materialize.

I wasn't the only one who felt that way.

The instant the smaller minotaurs faded into the woods, the silver Airship struck. She lunged forward, snatched a goat, and dragged the whole string of goats into the air. The rest panicked and tried to run, but in a matter of seconds the silver yanked the entire herd out of the clearing.

With their departure, the three warrior-minotaurs' courage returned, and they stabbed their spears forward. The slightest of blurs caught my attention from the woods as a minotaur archer also took aim.

"Copper, down!" I cried, dropping clumsily off of her on one side as she lurched in the other direction. I landed hard, then twisted into a roll. An arrow *twanged* against the rock at my feet.

Meanwhile, Barton reared and launched, soaring over the warriors and diving into the woods where the youth and females had run. His tactic was simple: why fight when you could stomp?

Copper and Feldspar picked a minotaur each, and started striking and snapping. I struggled to catch up to them as terrified shrieks pierced the air.

The warrior directly in front of me bellowed out a challenge, his shield lowered. He crossed the clearing in a flash, striking me with a fancy sword that he must have gotten from a human. The weapon whipped across my shield with raw power and no finesse.

I grinned. *Time to do what I'm good at.*

That's when his first blow struck.

Chapter 90

Camping is Fun

THE MINOTAUR's hit sent me backward, my feet leaving trails of upended plants. I ducked beneath the next swing, only to see the warrior's knee race up to greet me.

The clever blow slammed against my shoulder, sending me flying back into a tangle of weeds and dirt. The strike ruined my grip, and my sword spun away into the tall grass, lost from my line of sight.

I was now at my enemy's mercy, but the minotaur's focus on me cost him dearly; as he was about to deliver the killing blow, the silver Airship pounced on his back.

The claws of just one of her feet raked his thick flesh, leaving gashes that put his bones on full display. He roared, unable to bear her weight. The crunch of his rib cage followed, and then stillness.

I scrambled to my feet and broke into a sprint to help my dragons with the other two fighters. Copper hopped off her injured minotaur and hissed at Feldspar's as the monster landed a hit on the clay dragon's tail, making Feldspar roar. But this left Copper open to attack, and I reached her in time to deflect a spear with my shield.

Shadows fell across us as Barton burst into flight from the forest, a massive female minotaur dangling from his teeth. He wheeled away, happy with his kill, and the silver dragon keened and chased after him.

Shit, I thought. Without the Airship dragons to help, we'd have trouble with these last two warriors—and the reinforcements would arrive any moment.

"Copper! Ears!" I called out as Feldspar landed next to me. He rocked on his feet, antsy, and I burst into a run. He followed.

Behind me, Copper shook the ground with another mind-blowing roar. I nearly lost my footing, and almost looked back from worry. While her phasing powers should help her collect ears from plenty of the minotaurs that Barton had stomped on, I hoped she didn't stay long.

Careful, Copper! More minotaurs incoming!

My heart beat hard against my chest until we tore out of the forest and onto the road. Its appearance startled me; I must have gotten turned around, because the caravan was far too close to our battle for comfort.

Soldiers surrounded the gathered wagons, blades brandished and shields out. Everyone appeared to be on edge, but they seemed surprised to see our arrival. Captain Narvi waved for us to hurry into defensive positions.

Feldspar didn't hesitate, running alongside me across the final distance until he slid to a stop inside the defensive line. I meant to join the soldiers, but Copper arrived as soon as we did, landing in front of me with an arrow in her back.

To reach her, I sidled past the soldiers and yanked the arrow out of my prized dragon. The tip ripped a copper-gold scale out of her flesh, and a decent amount of blood oozed out behind it.

"Copper, girl! Are you all—"

Before I could finish, Copper ducked her head forward and vomited out at least a dozen minotaur ears. She must have been keeping them in her throat pouch.

I stared in awe, but even after realizing some were left ears—the crown only accepted right ears—that still left at least eight, which was a small fortune all its own.

She cried out with a whine, and I shook myself. I stroked her neck. "You did good, Copper! You did great. Now let me find the apothecary for your wound—"

"Grillus, get the apothecary over here, now!" Narvi shouted behind me. He grabbed my shoulder to turn me. "You stay. Report."

I nodded and obliged. "Killed one close, then got beat back by their tribe in a clearing about five minutes away on foot, less if you fly. One healthy male and one wounded at the main tribe, six more were not far, but I think the horn sent them to protect their vulnerable members as they escape the area."

I rotated my sore shoulder while I spoke, and hissed at a sudden lance of pain. "Four Demons, that's gonna bruise."

"Your silver dragon dropped a body, then a string of mostly strangled goats," Narvi said, glancing back at the tree line. "She was super proud of herself," he added.

"They may come back," I said, scouring the stone forest for signs of movement. "Anyone missing?"

"Thankfully no, but I'm calling it. We're moving for home. This is a good haul anyway, and it's standard operating procedure to break for home after an ambush, attempted or otherwise. Besides, this was more or less scouting practice anyway."

He didn't wait for my agreement because he didn't need it, and he left me and started shouting commands. In the meantime, Becki and the apothecary had brought a bandage kit for Copper. The poor old apothecary, a frail man in his sunset years, trembled in front of Copper as he stammered directions to Becki.

As I watched, Becki stuffed a poultice into the arrow wound, making Copper keen and snap at her, although she didn't make tooth-fall. Copper knew that Becki was a friend.

"Come on, Copper, let's get you on a wagon," I said, waving her toward our aviary wagon, just visible at the back of the train of carts. She rumbled, ducking her head to follow me.

We met Baron Maki halfway as the man snaked between the wagons, trying to calm the worried commoners, most of whom crouched in terror among the barrels of fruit they'd just collected.

He shook his head when he saw me, and I knew an oncoming argument when I saw one. "Our traps are worth fighting for! Go tell the Captain to halt the retreat. We must reclaim our traps—"

A minotaur corpse cut him off by falling through the sparse canopy of the orchard and splattering on the road right next to him. The big silver landed beside the caravan, leaned over three whole carts, and started munching on the cadaver.

If I had to guess, she'd killed the one warrior minotaur that Feldspar and Copper had injured. She used a paw to push the head toward me, pausing her feast to look to me for approval.

I walked over to the corpse and removed what was left of its waistband and clothing. There was a satchel too, its strap torn but the rest of it miraculously intact.

Once I had the loot piled up, I chopped an ear off, laying it into a wet, bloody pocket with the rest of them. A dozen caravaners watched nervously as I walked up close to the wild dragon. When I held up a hand, the female's massive head dipped down for a scratch.

"Enjoy your meal," I said. "You earned it." To the humans, I waved an arm and shouted, "Go around her!"

By that point, Captain Narvi and Baron Maki were locked in a fierce debate about the traps. I jogged over to them, and for some odd reason, they looked at me as if I were some great decider.

Baron Maki cleared his throat and asked, "Well, Lord Orpheus-Minax... it seems you are now the proud owner of a wild Airship dragon. Congratulations."

This man was a lot less of a prick with a gigantic dragon feasting in front of him. I glanced back.

"Yeah, I probably need to name her. Quicksilver. Yeah, Quicksilver works."

As I spoke, the dragon bit down with enough pressure to snap the minotaur's spine with a reverberating crack. Once she separated the body in two parts, she tossed it into the air to gulp it down.

"Huh," I said. "Don't see that every day."

"We can't stay for the traps," Captain Narvi blurted. "It's not safe, milords."

I turned my attention back to him. "Let's retrieve the traps first," I said, more to test the waters than anything. Technically, Narvi didn't have to obey me any more than he had to obey Maki. He was an employee of the watchmaster, who was beholden only to the city general, the war generals, and the king himself.

Despite my lack of authority, I still wanted to see what would happen if I gave him an order.

"It's daytime," I explained, "so it won't take long to gather the traps. Also, I can almost guarantee the minotaurs don't want to fight our dragons any further."

I pointed to a caretaker a few wagons away, who was now inspecting Barton for damage. The big gray was covered in blood, but only some of it was his. "Assuming he agrees."

"The dragon? You can't be serious," Maki said.

"The *dragon* will walk us to our traps. I'll go too, and then we march out of here laden with cherries and hopefully a few extra dead monsters," I said, already slow-walking toward Barton.

"I don't like it," Captain Narvi grumbled, "but I trust you and your dragons. How can't I, after seeing that copper brat puke up all those ears?"

"I don't need your dragons," Maki snapped, turning to stalk toward his own private guards. He soon had them setting off into the woods, with their Mount-size clay dragons carving a path. Little did he know, I'd been having chats with them too. There was a reason they'd obeyed especially well on this trip.

I crooked a thumb at the forest behind me. "Come on, Feldspar," I said to the dragon at my side. "Let's see what we just caught."

Chapter 91

I Come Bearing Gifts

"Welcome home, milord," Jolene said with a bow.

She wore a lovely summer dress that hugged her curves. If I didn't know any better, I'd assume Jolene had a fancy meeting with Duchess Nola, but I was pretty certain she'd cleaned up for me.

The problem lay in the fact that I'd spent the last two hours unloading cherries, and I needed a bit of a break. I plopped onto the couch, noticing the distinct lack of dust clouds this time. Aliese was doing her job well. The den was spotless.

"I missed you," I admitted. "Quite a bit actually. How are you?"

"Well, I *was* nervous for your return, but it's not so bad now that I have you home," Jolene said.

I reached up toward her, and she held my hand with both of hers. "*Home is where the heart is*, or so Mom used to say," I told her. "Sorry, you look *so* lovely, and I really want to take you out somewhere. Just give me a few more minutes to rest."

She rubbed my hand, which I didn't realize was sore until that moment. "You can relax, Warren. But the entire town is abuzz about this Airship you befriended! Did you really have it fight minotaurs for you? Tell me all about her!"

"Her name's Quicksilver," I said, mentally girding myself for the retelling. "Yeah, she's a hero in her own right. She doesn't like to be petted, and she took one look at Dasvilla's Roost and made it very clear she won't be coming into the city, but she's nesting out on the farm. I tried to get on her back, but that's a no-no." I had the bruises to show for it. "She can help fight and do chores, though, so it could be worse."

"We won't be selling her then?" Jolene asked.

"I'd like to see you try," I said, kicking my boots off. "You get anywhere near that dragon with a collar, and she's liable to bite your head off. Anyway, Becki has even better news, but she wanted to deliver it herself."

I'd been watching Becki approach through the window as I spoke, and the main door squeaked open on cue. Becki entered with a dragon cage under each arm, both of them covered with blankets. She stopped when she saw us.

Her face lit up. "Heya, Jo! Lookie what we got."

Jolene ignored the cages to hug her friend. "Oh, Becki! It's good to have you back. I was so worried when I heard about the minotaurs."

I watched Becki stand there, cages still under her arms, as Jolene hugged her with genuine warmth. She seemed a little shocked by it. "You were worried about me?" she said.

Jo pulled back. "Of course I was! Becki, there were *minotaurs.*"

"We got paid for eight of them, by the way," I said. I didn't tell her that I got a warning telling me the king's accounts weren't limitless. My first instinct was to have a good laugh at that one, but it actually worried me. Why would the king stop paying bounties? Or was he targeting me, specifically?

"Two gold each, right?" Jolene asked, pulling out of the hug. I nodded. "Well, that *is* substantial. And how did other affairs go?"

Becki snickered. "You're nervous, Jo, but you look a sight."

"I don't know. I kinda miss the straw in her hair," I said, earning a blush. "Anyway, Becki, show Jo what you've got."

Becki finally set down the cages and flipped the blankets back. Jolene's hands flew to her mouth.

"A root dragon and spring dragon! Where did you find these?"

"By a hot spring between Dasvilla and the orchard," I replied. "You can thank Kenna for them later."

"By the Mountains, they're fat! And with eggs!" Jolene exclaimed. "Oh yes! Two more Shoulder breeders, already fertilized by a different male than our alpha!"

I knew that having a variety of pairings led to a variety of breeds and abilities, although these wild dragons had likely mated with a male of their same type.

"I'll probably fly to a new city soon to hunt for even more. Besides, every new dragon is one more to help with running and protecting the farm."

Jolene foolishly stuck her hands into both cages, got bitten, and jerked her hands out again. Her smile never even faltered. It was like a compulsion.

"Oh, this is such a treat, Warren. But enough about that, let me tell you what you missed!" she said, setting the covers back over the dragon cages.

"I'll go put them in the rookery," Becki said. The rookery was the top-floor room where we kept the pregnant dragons.

As she left, Jolene walked behind my couch and rolled right over the back of it. She ended up lying across the couch with her head in my lap.

She touched my cheek. "I missed you, Warren," she said. "A lot."

I didn't miss how intimate this position was. I had to focus on something else *right now,* or she'd know how crazy she was making me.

"I missed you too. Where are the kids?" I asked, glancing around. There was usually at least one orphan in here doing busywork for Jolene or Rachel.

"I sent them away for the day," Jolene said. "Anyway, now for *my* news. Have you ever met Caravan Master Urgo?"

"Can't say I have," I answered.

"Well, he wanted to load up on frozen scalecherries a few days ago. I told him we were about to have an influx, but we were low on fruit at the time. So you know what he asked about next? Stonetrees!"

I leaned to one side, reclining, pulling her with me until we lay side-by-side.

"Do go on," I told her.

Her face was close to mine now, and I could feel her words brushing my lips as she excitedly continued. "Well, apparently one of the scholars at the capital invented a new softening process, and now stonewood is actually viable in construction!

"Now Urgo wants a sample of every variety, so he can see which woods have the prettiest grains. He says if he can control the supply, he can turn the right wood into a luxury item."

I whistled. "What timing."

"I know, right! There are tons of stonetrees on your farm plot, and we have the right to sell them right away."

"There are even more in the hotlands," I said, curling an arm around her and spreading my palm against her back. "Duchess Nola will be on top of that, though. Knowing her, she's already instituted a local law saying foragers need lumber licenses."

Jolene deflated a little. "Yep. She was on that like scale on a hide. But it means Dasvilla can grow! Like *really* grow! With Caliph expanding like it is, it needs boards for fortifications, and we can provide them in spades—"

She stopped talking when my hand wandered southward, grabbed her butt, and squeezed it. I could swear that hand acted entirely on its own.

Her breath caught, making me instantly hard. "Warren...."

I brought my hand back up to her cheek. "I'm sorry. I just didn't realize how badly I missed you—all the *ways* I missed you—until I had you next to me."

Her blue eyes shimmered, so close to mine. I could feel every inch of her curves against me, but I wanted to feel it with no fabric between us.

That was up to her, though. She had to be ready—and *willing*. We could wait a year, and I could court her as my only wife... although the thought of giving up Becki now seemed absurd.

However, that problem would be solved if Jolene wanted my affections sooner than that. If so, she had to be *sure* that she was okay with Becki, Aliese, and Kenna. I hadn't talked much about Kenna, but I was pretty sure she knew we were sleeping together.

"I missed you too. In this way," she admitted. "But I'm not sure—"

I kissed her nose. "Then we won't do anything."

But she shook her head. "No. I want to do something. We've been managing this farm as a couple, Warren, and I—I want to keep building up to that," Jolene said. "I'm going to foolishly lay my heart on the table here, and just come out with it. I missed you so much it hurt, and I lay awake every night wishing you were next to me.

"So, I want you there. Next to me. I want to start sharing your bed. Not for... *that*. Just to see how I feel about it."

"Oh," I said, swallowing hard. Sleeping next to her without sex? That was going to be tough.

At the same time, it was a strange request, and I sensed it had something to do with her sharing me. She had to know I'd taken both Aliese and Becki in that bed. Sleeping there would remind her of that, and it might make her explode from jealousy—or it might make her warm to the idea of being one of several lovers.

"I'll give it my all," was what I finally said to her, because the idea of having Becki's fabled "happy family" was worth any discomfort. "But I might have to kick you out if I stop being able to trust myself," I added, meaning it. "I'm sure you can feel how hard this will be for me."

She went still, her eyes widening as she finally noticed my erection. Four Demons, sometimes she was so cute it hurt.

I kissed her on the mouth. "Don't worry. I'm a big boy. I can go without."

"Or you can go to Aliese," she said, her voice shrinking.

"No, Jo," I said, tightening my grip on her. "Never. I don't do that. When I want a woman, I want *that* woman. There is no replacement for you, in sex or in anything."

Her gaze fell into mine, and she smiled sweetly at me. "All right, Warren. I believe you."

Damn. I'd known that keeping off her was going to be hard, but it might be the hardest thing I'd ever do.

Chapter 92

The Master's Sword

I SURVEYED the two nests with a critical eye. They were ugly things, built from compacted bushes and thick clumps of mud. We'd let our two new pregnant dragons set up their nests in the back corner of the rookery, but they had probably damaged the flooring.

None of this was a permanent solution. In three more days, we had to prove Pinnacle was making a profit. Once we did, we could keep the business and grow it. Eventually, the dragons would get their barn back.

Fieran waited behind me, shifting her weight from foot to foot. "Yes?" I said, wiping bunny blood onto my dirty pants. The mothers had been letting me hand-feed them, even though they were still biting Jolene.

Fieran fidgeted and tried to bow. We'd decided to requisition her as my page, and the city general of Olinios had approved the request. Of course he had. He knew Fieran—and the rebellion she represented—would be safer with me.

"Duke Biscuit requests an audience, Lord Warren," she said, still using her raspy voice to hide her gender. "Duchess Nola is bringing an outfit for you first, though. Lady Jasmine said you weren't presentable this time of day." She smirked at me. "You know, since you're knee-deep in dragon shit."

Yeah. She wasn't the best page. Fieran was accustomed to being coddled, and to being the best in her rank. Deferring to anyone was not in her nature. She might just make a good princess one day, but I'd think about that potential rebellion later. I wasn't sure how I felt about it yet.

"I definitely smell like it," I said, sniffing my armpit and instantly regretting it. The duke had probably called on me knowing I'd be in a state. He wanted me off my game, but for some reason, Nola didn't. I was almost warming up to the woman.

Fieran wasn't sure what to do now that her message was delivered, so I nodded him back to the door. "Just hang out near entrances until I call on you."

"I'd rather guard the door."

"Yeah, and that's *really* what you're doing, but you need to look like a page doing it," I said. It wasn't normal for nobles to walk around with a single bodyguard, and I had enough rumors about me already.

After a quick dip in my cold shower, I headed down to the foyer in a robe and trousers. I found Becki waiting for me with neatly folded robes and a curious Jasmine hovering behind her. Once the teenager saw I wasn't wearing a shirt, she spun and retreated into the den, muttering something about checking Jo's numbers.

Becki leered at my shirtless chest. "You could stop a girl's heart with those muscles, Lord Warren."

"Well, it's a good thing I scared her off, then."

"I wasn't talking about Jasmine."

I grunted. "I'll stop your heart later." *Or at least make it stutter.* "Do you know why the Biscuits want me?" Becki was always tapped in to that sort of thing.

She handed the clothes over. "It's the stonewood thing, plus everything you've been up to. The kingdom is taking notice of the Dasco region, now more than ever. It's not *all* because of you, but a lot of it is. I think the Biscuits are trying to do damage control."

I snorted, accepting the robes. By *damage control,* she meant the Biscuits wanted to take credit for my work.

"It's Quicksilver that they ought to be treating with," I said, moving to a side room to dress. Some of our more trusted dragons—the ones we allowed to free-roam—had taken to sleeping near the Airship beast at the farmhouse. It was a sight to behold, and rumors had spread. "She cleaned up eight trolls last night alone. She's making the city ballistae look bad."

"Yes, but she's *your* dragon. And they haven't missed that you signed the entire orphanage into your banner. You've taken on vassals. One might call it overstepping, since you've barely been here a month."

I shrugged. As a lord, I could do a lot for those kids, but most of it was ceremonial. Still, those kids had a future now, and an income. Crime was going down in the city, and whenever a kid *did* get caught stealing something, I was now beholden to handle it myself. I could give them the grace that the Enforcers wouldn't.

Becki *tsk*ed, dragging a finger over the back of my robes. "I never did ask you about the scars you've got back here," she said, kissing my shoulder.

A chill went through me. I preferred not to think of the lash marks. "I'd rather not discuss it."

She took a step away. "Fair enough. Anyway, like I was saying, you're getting too famous. Quicksilver might be shaking down trees like they owe her money, but she is hardly the talk of the town. The whispers of a Dragon-Touched have taken over the court here, and now they've moved on to other cities."

Becki shifted to stand in front of me, fiddling with my robes until I looked proper.

"What do you think they'll want from me?" I asked.

"I think Duke Biscuit is a businessman at heart. You've proven you can do something special for this city. He'll probably want

617

to make some sort of deal." Becki rose on her tippy toes to kiss my cheek, then glanced over her shoulder at Fieran. "Get the Master's sword."

Fieran looked like she might tell Becki exactly where to shove the word "Master," but she bit her tongue. "Uh, which one?" she asked.

"The spear," I replied. "In the armory." I never used it, but it looked impressive.

He nodded and left to fetch the weapon. "Do we *need* to keep that guy?" Becki asked, once he was out of hearing range. "He's so uppity. You could train an orphan as a page, you know."

"I know, and I'll do that later. For now, I need Fieran around. Just trust me on it."

"Of course, Warren. I'd trust you with anything."

After I got my spear, I headed outside to find the Biscuits waiting to speak with me, surrounded on all sides by the duke's guard. These kinds of personal guardsmen were usually tournament winners, arena competitors, veterans with lots of experience, or lower officers waiting for promotions in the garrisons. Each of them would be talented and deadly.

Copper had already decided they were a threat. She'd jumped off the roof to face off with them, hissing low in her throat.

"The gardens are looking good, by the way," I said to Becki. She'd been cleaning them up in her off-time, and Jayke, Jerem, and Aliese had made a lot of progress while we were gone.

"Just you wait until my tours start," she said. "It's gonna be the best garden in the city. Now go on. You've got dukes to disarm."

Chapter 93

On One Condition

I PATTED Becki's hand and strolled toward the guards, handing my spear back to Fieran to carry, even though he had literally just handed it to me. Decorum was decorum, after all.

"Copper, back on the roof," I ordered.

She gave a sassy snort before launching into flight.

"She sure is something else," Duchess Nola commented from within the ring of armored men. "What breed is she?"

"No one seems to have any clue. Now, where are my manners? Welcome to Pinnacle Dragons. How may I help you, Your Graces?"

The duke stepped forward. "We have come to congratulate you on your increased reputation. Our dear Jasmine thinks quite highly of you—Four Demons, most folks do. Even some of your detractors have come around. Why, just this morning I heard Baron Maki telling the tale of your minotaur fight as if you were some sort of legend."

He unleashed a laugh at that, and I didn't miss that it came at my expense. *As if you could* possibly *be legendary;* that's what he meant.

"I'm just a humble lord, trying to do right by his estate," I said.

Biscuit's face fell into seriousness. "Yes, *doing right* seems to be a trait of yours. I've heard you took the entire orphanage as your vassals."

Before I could reply, Duchess Nola said, "Jasmine said you're teaching them trades?"

"Of course. All my staff have apprentices now, and several are assisting the lumber crews on my farm plot. Jasmine herself is doing some teaching as well, just general knowledge, but I don't think she realizes she's doing it."

The Biscuits exchanged glances at that, and it dawned on me that they might be here to ask what my intentions were with Jasmine. She had been over here quite often lately, but I assumed it was to spy for her parents.

But they didn't make any mention of marriage when they spoke next. "Well, that's all well and good, but Dasvilla is hardly the utopia you think it is," the duke said. "You are setting those kids up for a big disappointment, once you are forced to sell the farm to me. And that's in... hmmm... how many days was it, love?"

"Three," Duchess Nola supplied.

He chuckled. "Three! And here you've been, trying to 'clean up' the hotlands. Really, Lord Warren, people are going to forget how hard life is outside the walls if you keep—"

"Quicksilver brought me eight orcs just this morning," I said proudly. "I think she found a nest, and just dropped on it. The bodies are really quite flat."

Biscuit paled at that, but Nola was prepared for it.

"And if your dragons turn on us?" she asked. "Everyone knows they are wild. It is only because of some magic spell that they obey you, and if you don't know the source of it, how can you know how long it will last?"

I folded my arms. "You make a fair point, and we're working on learning more. We've also put precautions in place. If the dragons were to suddenly stop obeying me, they would still abide by their previous orders for some days. It's natural to them; commands remain embedded in their minds for over a week, with diminishing returns.

"That means we'd have a decent window of docility to shoo them out or evacuate the city, if they ever stopped listening to me. Jolene did a study on it while I was away."

Duke Biscuit opened his mouth, but I cut him off. "All that aside, dead orcs make people happy. *Most* people, anyway." I raised an eyebrow.

Biscuit's face reddened. His wife saw it too, and took over.

"Yes, we realize the value of a reduced monster population," she said quickly, "but King Kurto is concerned about the increased bounties coming out of our area. *We* know it's not fraud, but he doesn't."

Ah. So that's what this was about.

"You don't want me attracting the king's auditors out here," I surmised.

Nola's eyes darted to her guard. She probably didn't want them hearing that.

She held an arm out. "Walk with me?" she asked. "Please. Show me the changes you are making around here. I am always fascinated by a good renovation."

I knew a raft in a shipwreck when I saw one. I took the offered arm.

"I'll be right back, dearest," Nola said to her husband, but he was already turning around.

"See that you do," he said gruffly.

I led the duchess around the side of the house, where a herd of small chicks peeped within a wire-sided hutch, watched over by a couple of hens.

"You're raising your own feed now, I see," Nola commented.

"Yeah. Now I just need to figure out how to keep them alive. They're good at keeping the bugs down in this mess, but one dragon swoops down and *boom!* Feathers everywhere."

621

Duchess Nola said, "You need a carpenter, or ten."

I led her to the neat rows of old fruit trees along the back of the cage, where Jayke was busy constructing a gazebo.

"I've got one carpenter, but he'll do for now," I said, nodding to him. "Like I said, most of my staff are out assisting Quicksilver with the stonewood harvest."

Jolene and I had gone out this morning to see the progress. I'd practically leapt out of bed to do it, because waking up next to her had been a real test of will, and my first instinct was to flee to my farmhouse.

I'd been pleased with what I saw. A wide age range of workers had been stripping the uprooted trees, sawing off the roots, bundling sticks, and burning parts we couldn't use. At the time, four trees were being processed while a different team hooked the finished products up and dragged the trunks toward Urgo's warehouse.

It wasn't perfect, but it worked for now.

"Seems the farm is performing better than it was when you took it over," Nola said, pausing beside a dry fountain with blue tile along the bottom. The mosaic depicted the Four Demons, the famed Behemoth-size dragons that had supposedly founded Parshil by sharing their nests with humans, thus creating the first walled cities. Each one bit the tail of the next, forming a circle of dragonflesh in the basin.

I folded my arms. "What do you want, Nola?"

"Would you like more land?" she replied.

Without hesitation, I said, "Yes."

The Duchess watched Jayke work with interest. "We can double your plot. But only if you stop handing in bounties. And the farmland will remain yours even if you lose Pinnacle to us."

I didn't tell her that the farmland *was* Pinnacle—or, at least, it was the *future* of Pinnacle.

"That's a lot of money you're asking me to give up."

"And a lot of land you will get in return."

I folded my arms, tapping a finger as I considered her offer. "And your husband approves of this?"

"My husband will make the best choice for Dasvilla," she said, not answering the question. There was a reason she was here, and not him.

"Hmmm. The same way he chose a maid over his wife?"

Her gaze leapt to mine, bright with rage. I held my palms out. "Sorry, sorry. That was out of line."

"Yes, Lord Warren. It was. Now—do we have a deal, or don't we?"

I held my breath. What would Rachel say? Damn, I had no idea. I needed to spend more time with the woman. I'd only seen her once or twice since I'd made her a partner.

But that, too, was by design, wasn't it? She'd vanished because the Biscuits kept giving her work.

My eyes narrowed. "It's a deal, on one condition."

"And pray tell, what might that be?"

"The farmland stops being a land grant. It's mine. *Really* mine. I want to own it, and I don't want you to be able to snatch it away when it pleases you."

"You're mad," she snapped. "That's impossible."

I crossed my arms again, flexing my biceps and throwing my shoulders back. Standing like this, I could make most people feel small.

"If you want to keep the king's attention off Dasco, then you'll have to pay for it," I said. "Now, I don't know what the fuck you've got to hide, but I know it's got you worried. And in case you haven't forgotten, you squeezed me first. You can't complain that I'm squeezing you back."

The Duchess visibly seethed for a moment. It was as if a dark cloud had descended around her.

"Fine," she snarled. "Have it your way." She looked up, and I saw no trace of intimidation in her eyes. She poked me in my broad chest with one dainty finger. "But if you think *for one second* that I'd *ever* allow you to marry my daughter, you have got another think coming. As of now, she will no longer be coming over here, for any reason. I forbid it."

With that, she spun in her heels and stalked off toward the front of the house again. My eyebrows rose. So this *had* been about Jasmine, at least a little.

"Suits me," I said to no one. It saved me the trouble of letting Jasmine down easy.

I could only hope it wouldn't hurt her too much.

I shouldn't have worried about finding Rachel. Within an hour, Rachel found me.

She burst into my office, luckily when Aliese wasn't there. She rushed to my desk and slammed her palms down, leveling her gaze on me. Those hazel eyes were intense behind her glasses.

"Is this about the breath-collecting bottles I broke?" I asked. "Because I can pay you back later, I swear it."

"Forget the bottles," she said. "You *own* it. You *doubled* your land grant, and you *own it.*"

I grinned and brushed her nose with the end of my quill. "Correction: I own 95% of it. *You* own the other five."

She didn't seem to notice the quill at all. "How? *How?*"

Four Demons, she was intense. "I have my ways."

"Yes, fine, but how are you even going to *manage* that much land?"

"Easy," I said. "I'm going to build a wall around it."

The Keeper stared at me. That gaze was like getting sucked down a dragon gullet. I swallowed thickly, and opened my mouth—

"You're going to expand Dasvilla," she said. "You're going to wall off your property, and make it a part of the city. That much farmland will employ dozens of people, maybe hundreds. You'll own half of all the farmland in the region."

"Yes, and I'll own *all* of the *best* farmland in the region," I pointed out. "The soil outside the cities is rich from disuse—"

"You genius man. You genius, genius man."

She grabbed my collar, shoved closer, and kissed me.

Before I could do so much as kiss her back, she'd whipped back around and stormed from the room. Fieran, returning from an errand, had to jump out of her way.

"Whoa. What's gotten into the bookworm?" he asked.

I shook my head. "I've got no idea."

Chapter 94

Infestation

"Bloody Demons! It's infested," Jolene cursed, eyeing the scene below the walls of Ashkar, the city closest to Dasvilla.

A small siege blocked the road south of the city, although the blocking force wasn't exactly well-organized. It consisted mostly of goblins, led by orcs, all of whom were constantly shouting at each other. Right in the middle of their camp, they were building crude battering rams—pretty much just tree trunks with handles.

Their numbers had to be in the thousands, and they'd seemingly cropped up overnight, closing off the trade route from Ashkar to the inner kingdom. They thankfully hadn't blocked the north road leading to Dasvilla, but the sight of the enemy army was deeply troubling. This siege would soon have effects on Dasvilla's trade, if it wasn't stopped.

Ashkar was one of those rare cities built into a naturally protected valley, rather than a simple clearing. As such, they'd dared to expand outside their walls for generations. The landscape rolled with immature grains, and several quarries were built into the mountainous—but not volcanic—surroundings. All farming and mining had ceased, however, with the appearance of this army.

The city itself was fairly safe. It was made entirely of stone, thanks to the quarry. In the center, the keep rose higher than was typical, while most of the other interior structures stood multiple stories high. Kill zones were located outside each layered wall, and I could see how the layout was meant to buy defenders time if a wall was lost.

Since the city was near three rivers that fed an expansive lake, Ashkar attracted all sorts of wildlife. The stone and easy hunting made the area prime for settling. The city had fought the hordes hundreds of times over its storied history.

But even with strong walls that didn't burn, a determined enemy could scale or smash their way in, and many an orc or troll army had tried. More than a few times, the rulers had marshaled commoners to help reclaim the walls and return order. The people here were made of stern stuff.

However, the soldiers on the wall seemed almost bored. The siege had been ongoing for some time, yet reports of it had been vastly underplayed. Why wasn't this being dealt with? Half the city's trade had ground to a halt.

Copper watched inquisitively from the parapet at my side, studying the threats with her far-seeing eyes. Feldspar had stayed home to defend the farm, and I sorta regretted the decision. I wanted a dragon larger than Shoulder-size watching Jolene at all times, especially when things were looking suspicious, but the laws here hadn't allowed Ravager to leave the Roost after we'd landed. I had to pay a bribe just to have Copper with us.

As for Ravager, we'd flown here on the old green dragon, with Quicksilver tailing us. I'd guided Quicksilver to land in a field, one hill away from the sieging army. I could see her from here, a gray lump among bales of rolled hay. Although some goblin scouts had seen her, they hadn't made any moves. She could simply fly away if they tried to go after her, and she'd probably kill half of them first.

"Copper, take Jolene to the inner walls," I commanded. There were three sets of walls here, each one thinner than the last.

Jolene frowned. "What are you going to do?"

"I'm going to make you some shopping money. I don't think you have any idea just how expensive farming is," I teased. She rolled her eyes, and I kissed her forehead. "Please, I need you safe, and I promise not to leave the saddle."

"What saddle? You can't take Ravager, and Copper's still too small for flight riding."

I raised an eyebrow, flicking my eyes to our Airship female.

"What? You said she hates being ridden!"

"Then I'll have to make it worth her while," I said. The dragon *did* despise all forms of leather, but I could wrap some rope around her for stability. She was big enough to seat two dozen people, so staying on her back wouldn't be an issue—unless she tried to roll me off.

"Warren... do we really have time for this? We've got barely more than a day to get Pinnacle's affairs in order."

Now *that* made me smile: she wasn't worried about my safety. She was worried about my *time commitment*.

"My sweet maiden, please," I said, gesturing to the guide we'd hired upon landing. I'd flown us here to get *lunch,* for demonssakes, and this is what we'd found. My romantic getaway in the sweeping green hills had become a battle, and I wanted it over with, just as much as she did.

Jolene kissed my cheek and backed away. "I'll find you at the Roost when you're done."

With that, Copper pounced off the wall with a theatrical flare of her wings. The dragon wanted to kill, but I called after her, "To me, Copper! Don't go alone!"

She protested with a cry, but wheeled back to me. I raised up my arms, and her next cry was one of joy.

"Warren—Warren, what are you doing?" Jolene cried out, but she was too late. As Copper swooped low above me, I caught one of her front ankles in each hand. She tore me off the wall, her wings gusting.

She couldn't carry me, not yet-but she could glide just fine.

In the field near the army, my two dragons stared expectantly at me, a twinkle of violence in their metallic eyes.

"Snatch and drop," I ordered. "But take care not to hit any humans. Let's remind the good folks of Ashkar that these walls were built with blood."

I didn't need to say anything more before Copper was airborne, swirling high above me and Quicksilver. As I moved to climb the Airship's leg, Copper tucked her wings against her flanks, seemingly sucking speed from the air as she plummeted into a tight group of goblins.

Meanwhile, Quicksilver huffed, not keen on being ridden. As I settled in behind her head and tugged the ropes, I said, "This is only to keep me from falling, girl. I promise, no saddles in the future."

She rumbled in argument, and I said, "You really expect me to achieve anything out here alone? I'll be a sitting duck down here."

She puffed a blast of hot air out of her mouth, but apparently the discussion was over, because she spread her wings and leaned back to take flight.

Starting from the ground meant a slower rise into the air, and I was almost nauseous by the time she had us circling in place to gain altitude. I peered over Quicksilver's shoulder as we climbed, watching Copper dive near the battering rams. She ripped out of the crowd with a goblin, and the little greenskin shrieked as she carried him off toward the city. Once there, she dropped him, and the screaming stopped.

As she returned to the battlefield, she made a snap at a ballista meant for wild dragons, flying low and fast to the point the crew had to duck. She passed them harmlessly by, then rapidly reengaged the monster army. By now, the goblins had focused on her, hurling rocks, unleashing arrows, and trying to jump to catch her. She deftly avoided it all, stealing attention away from us.

Quicksilver tucked in her wings.

A squeak of joy escaped my lips before turning into a full-throated cry of excitement. Thankfully, I'd already wrapped the rope around my wrists numerous times, because now I was suddenly weightless, barely even touching the big dragon anymore.

I held on for dear life, savoring every second. Airship-class dragons could fight, but they were so valuable to the economy and structure of the kingdom, they were almost never used in battle.

Quicksilver wasn't some cage-fed princess, though. She was an intelligent killer. And while she might be small when compared to some larger Airship breeds, she positively *dwarfed* orcs and goblins.

Our free fall went mostly unnoticed, and for those who did see the looming doom coming toward them, well, they'd already used their weapons trying to knock down Copper. The big hatchling continued to taunt them as she scooped up another goblin.

The ground rushed up to meet us, and I expected Quicksilver to snatch an orc or two or to drop in their midst and wreak havoc.

Apparently, that wasn't her style.

She flared her wings, adjusted her heading for the road that the army was blocking. She somehow found a good angle, and then smacked into the stones, moving faster than a horse at full speed. Startled goblins splattered under her initial landing, but we were sliding now, bouncing violently, compressing dozens if not hundreds of foes as she caught them under her mass.

When her speed started to slow, she flapped hard. Right before she launched into the air, Quicksilver brought her front arms in tight to compression-hold another clump of orcs and goblins. As she took back to the sky, a few lucky ones dropped away. The rest fell to their deaths as we gained altitude, their shouts of panic fading beneath us.

I had the ropes in a death-grip as I shouted, "Damn, girl! That was something else!"

Quicksilver banked over the city, unleashing a mighty roar before she kicked a clinging foe off her back foot. From this angle, I couldn't see if it had been an orc or a goblin. They all sounded the same going down.

Heading back toward the army again, Quicksilver bugled out a different roar, unleashing it loud and long. Within seconds, a half-dozen wild dragons burst out of a nearby corn field. Quicksilver bugled again, and I guessed she was telling them about a free meal, because they cried out in delight and moved to copy Copper.

Soon, a rain of dragons were pestering the orcs and goblins, working in concerted effort. I'd never seen anything like it. This *never* happened with human-owned dragons, and wild dragons rarely attacked orcs or trolls while the monsters were wearing weapons.

Still, the dragons hadn't yet broken the orcs' will to fight. The monsters seemed to be regrouping, with goblins funneling weapons to their larger leaders.

"Looks like it's time for another run, eh girl?"

Quicksilver bobbed her head, and she dove.

Chapter 95

Fat Dragon, Happy Dragon

FIVE MINUTES after our second pass, the gates opened and guardsmen streamed out, riding Mount-class Combat dragons and horses, with more troops amassed on wagons. Whoever the watchmaster of Ashkar was, he'd prepared his troops for a quick repel, and he was capitalizing on the fact we'd just broken their formation.

What I want to know is why it took this long, I thought. I didn't suspect the watchmaster; he was beholden to the city general. However, because he was on the ground in a state of war, he had the right to act when certain opportunities presented themselves. I'd given him that opportunity, and he'd taken it— meaning the issue lay higher up the totem pole.

"All right, Quicksilver! You can drop me at the Roost now!" I shouted into the wind.

She keened in dismay, but obeyed, landing on the wide platform intended for dragons even bigger than she was. However, I could tell she wasn't finished. I slapped her leg with the back of my hand after dismounting.

"Go on," I told her. "Have fun."

She happily did so, taking flight again. I watched like a proud father as the big dragon soared higher and higher with each powerful flap of her silver wings. When the surging allied

633

troops crashed against the enemy's front lines, Quicksilver suddenly dove at a dizzying rate.

She whipped out her wings at the back of the soldiers' charge to glide over the allied forces by only a pace or two. A chieftain bellowed out to his orcs when he saw her coming.

A few of them managed to level spears at her, bracing for impact, but she flared her wings at the last second. Before I had a chance to be worried, she lifted out of spear range.

But with their eyes and weapons focused on her, the orcs had forgotten to prepare for the soldiers. The Ashkar troops smashed into them, a clean impact, shattering the rest of their resistance.

Quicksilver landed with a thud where the crowd was thinner, and she casually bit an orc in half, swallowing the upper torso while he still screamed. She tore into ranks from there, switching from flying to mauling, swiping with enough power to fling bodies off the road and into the corn field a quarter-mile away.

Over the next minute or two, she ate a dozen orcs, never sullying herself with the goblin flesh. The allied troops continued to expand the massacre; thanks to us, they had the upper hand for the entire engagement.

The fighting died down when the enemy retreated from the valley into the jungle, where chasing them made no sense. By that point, Jolene had returned to the Roost to find me.

"Um. Should we go to lunch now, then?" she asked.

I laughed. "I'd love to, believe me. But it's probably best we wait for someone to come ask us what happened. We don't want to look like we're trying to run off."

So we waited, and eventually an officer with a plume in his helm landed his Mount-class dragon on the Roost to meet us. By that point, Quicksilver had returned, so it was easy to tell where we were.

The man lifted his face visor, exposing a smile. His armor and mount were covered in blood, but he looked hearty as he spoke.

"I don't suppose you'd care to explain all that?" he asked.

I held out a hand. "I'm a guardsman, third-rank, should I wish to return to the defense of the realm. Most call me Lord Warren now."

"Once a guardsman, always a guardsman. Well met." He shook my hand. "Officer Fourth-Class Ernith. The watchmaster will want a word." He glanced over his shoulder, watching Copper drop a goblin over the city again. She kept flying into the valley and returning with the creatures. I think she enjoyed seeing people's reactions when a goblin splattered into the street just in front of them.

"Sorry about her. We think she's still a kid," I explained. "She likes to play."

"That's a messy way to play."

"Yeah, well, maybe the people need a reminder to actually deal with threats instead of ignoring them around here."

I expected his face to darken, but he laughed. "You've got that right. These cursing games they've got us playing, you wouldn't believe. You got anywhere to be? I can take you there, then to the watchmaster after. He'll be done doing cleanup by then."

I didn't envy the men who'd have to do that. Troops usually cleaned up monster battles by securing loot and tossing bodies into pyres. It was gruesome, smelly work.

"We meant to have a look at your market," I said.

Ernith nodded, dismissing his dragon and before leading us out of the Roost. As soon as we emerged at the bottom of the structure, a random Shoulder-size dragon landed on my shoulder. He had a lovely light blue coloration, so I let him claim me—no different than how a stray cat would.

"Is that a wild dragon?" Ernith asked, frowning.

I shook my head. "Nope, this is Alpine." The lie was light, and he had no way to prove it wasn't true. "How often are the roads blocked by monsters around here?"

Marcus Sloss & Jace Cannon

"To the south, weekly if not daily. They just show up, looking for a free meal, and too often our caravans feed them," Ernith said, turning down a wide road where several small crowds had gathered around two goblin bodies.

"They're just so numerous," he went on. "This group will be back in a few days, hopefully with fewer fighters. This *had* to put a dent in their numbers—but even if we whittle their forces down, a new camp will appear before long."

"And so your local dragons stay fat," I joked.

Like the good girl she was, Copper appeared to prove my point. She zipped by overhead, pained shrieks erupting from the young orc in her talons. A moment later, the monster plummeted earthward, and I whistled when it got skewered on a spire.

"Her aim is impressive," Jolene said. "Our ballistae operators could learn a thing or two."

A grin spread across my lips. For too long the enemy had felt overconfident against us. But now, with dragons able to understand humans and work together with us... anything was possible. We were changing the world, one battle at a time.

This is bigger than me, I realized. *Bigger than Pinnacle, bigger than all of us.*

But the Biscuits didn't want me to be big anymore, so I had to be careful. This game we were playing was a deadly one. I had survived before, with the princess, but I hadn't won. Maybe, this time would be different.

Or maybe, we'd all end up dead.

Chapter 96

Just One More

TURNS OUT, we blended into Ashkar just fine, looking like minor nobles with an officer friend wandering through the market after he got off a shift. Ashkar supported a much higher population than Dasvilla, with wider streets, nicer homes, and signs of progress everywhere I looked.

"It's nice here," I said, leaning close to Jolene. "You'd think they'd care more about protecting the place."

"It's their stone," she said sagely. "It's strong stuff, and plentiful."

In front of us, a woman suddenly ducked under a table displaying hairy fruits I didn't recognize. Every shadow that crossed the sky had the residents flinching, worried about falling goblins.

"The watchmaster is going to want to know who you are," Jolene warned me. "The Biscuits won't be pleased."

"I'll ask him to keep my identity secret," I said, knowing it was already hopeless. Running away would have only made the rumors worse, though. "What do we need at market? Nuts and bolts, hinges, nails, and bracing beams—"

"Forget the shopping!" she said, even as she paused at a saddle display, running a hand across the material. An older man rocked in a chair behind the display, watching us.

"We can't get complacent, Jolene. We need more dragons to prove our future viability. That's what Rachel said, anyway. She said paying debts and doing seasonal work isn't enough. The breeding part of the business needs to look reliable. We sold fresh eggs last week, but we need a consistent supply."

She ran a hand over the saddle, then turned away. "I know."

As soon as she faced the other direction, I leaned toward Ernith, who'd been giving us the space and quiet to talk. "Have that guy deliver this saddle to the Roost. I'll pay in full on delivery."

He nodded, a smile ghosting his lips, and hung back while I caught up to Jo.

"I am just worried about over-extending," she said. "Every dragon we own has an upkeep cost. We don't want to upset the balance."

"Leave the balance to Rachel. She can sell any unnecessary dragons tomorrow. Better to have too many, than not enough."

I didn't tell her my other reason for wanting more dragons: because this fight would come to us again, and when it did, I'd rather lead an army of dragons than wish I'd bought some instead of being cheap.

"Take me to another dealer you know. Let me guess, he'll be handsome and charismatic."

Jolene snickered. "As if the great Lord Warren—adventurer, womanizer, businessman, and war general of wild dragons—needs to worry about some merchant baron."

Maki hadn't felt like a threat to me, either, but I'd still wanted to stomp him flat for having courted Jolene.

I gestured across the wide market. "We'll see about that. But if he's *too* handsome, I might just sic a dragon on him. Be warned."

She giggled, grabbed my hand, and dragged me deeper into the market. She ignored any sellers trying to offload non-dragon wares, but I did pull her back when I saw some milk cows.

"What about a cow pasture? For their meat, and milk for the babies?"

She tapped her chin. "Milk isn't common in Dasvilla for a reason. The heat spoils it."

"Hmm... for fertilizer, then?"

She shook her head. "No, Dasco's soil is already rich. Especially on *your* land. Besides, you'd be inviting trouble. The real reason Duke Biscuit butchered our last herd was because minotaurs consider them sacred. We eat the cows, we piss off the minotaurs, and they turn back around and eat us. The fewer cows around, the less minotaurs come near the city."

That made sense. Minotaurs were fairly unique to the Dasco Region, preferring to stay close to the volcano rather than roam around like orcs and trolls. Still, I filed the information away for later. Bait could always be a useful tool.

"No cows, then? What about pigs?"

"Ogres love them. Like *really* love them, but pigs are escape artists. It's a real pain to keep them safe and enclosed. Sheep are better, but you'd need to get a big herd going. You'd have to build a barn just for them."

Damn, there was always more work to do. "How do the big farms handle feeding?"

Jolene dragged me over to a chicken farmer, where a bored teenage boy glanced up once, then ignored us. By this point, Ernith was shadowing us again. He gave me a casual all-good salute when I glanced his way.

Jolene said, "It's a cycle. A city's lord tends to control the surrounding land. Dragon farmers guarantee that the lord gets first rights to buy their leased land back from them, and they offer emergency defense of the realm, *and* they pay a high tax rate. In exchange, they get their pick of the land.

"To feed their dragons, though, they have to raise crops to feed livestock, so most dragon farmers are also regular farmers. As farmers, they are beholden to pay a tithe of their production to the city lord.

"The more dragons they have, the more they have to farm, the more land they need, and the more they have to share with their lord. It is actually more lucrative to the lord in some places than it is to the dragon breeders, even though they never actually pay for their land."

I grinned. I'd already solved this problem.

"Worse, lords have a lot of sway in deciding which dragons get bred, due to their first-rights agreements. If they want dragons with expensive upkeep, and they usually do, the breeder has to eat that cost.

"However, breeders do this for *money,* so they cut costs by paying really low wages, making commoners poorer with each passing year, often on dangerous lands and with dangerous work." She sighed. "It was a cycle my father had been trying to change. He never once tried to grow food, and yet he never struggled to feed his dragons when business was good. He bought all their feed locally, which enriched the town instead of enriching the Biscuits."

And maybe that's why he got killed, I thought.

"But of course, he made less money than most dragon breeders do," she admitted. "Most of them get into the work because they like money; he got into it because he liked dragons."

"Begging your pardon," Ernith said behind us, "but have you considered cats? They reproduce quick, and you can get them free anywhere." To make his point, he pointed at a stray that was currently sniffing at a cage of chicks.

"I'd rather raise *rats* than to feed cats to my dragons," I said coolly. "Come on, I see a blacksmith."

Over the next hour, we bought a crate of metal supplies, three dragons, six eggs, and lunch. I shook plenty of hands, paid in full every time, and made sure every vendor knew where they could send any dragons or eggs they weren't able to sell.

"If you've got a misbehaving dragon, I want it," I told them. "A clutch of dud eggs? I want that too."

It wasn't my city, nor was I the lord, but I wanted the word to spread that we were spending good money on so-called "bad product." That way, they'd start bringing dragons to me, instead of me having to go out and find them.

As Ernith showed us around the city, he also pointed out the fancy new scaffolding being used to create higher stone buildings. Some of our stonewood planks had already been shipped here for this purpose, so Urgo was definitely earning his commission. Jolene hung on my arm the whole way, until finally a messenger came for Ernith, to let us know the watchmaster wanted us.

"Just one more merchant, please," Jolene said, and Ernith nodded. She then pulled me out of the market toward a big warehouse building not too different from the barn where I first met Jolene. No sign hung over the door, and she rapped on it loudly. The door creaked open and Alpine shot in.

"Hey, no strays!" a wizened voice protested, and I pushed the door open to find an old man struggling with a pitchfork in the main aisle of the barn. He looked to be held together by horse glue and wrinkles, like a sack of human stuffed full of sawdust. One good gust of wind, and he'd probably fall over. He had no business handling a pitchfork.

Jolene spread her arms wide. "Garmond, you handsome devil!"

I'd never seen an old face light up so fast. The man threw his arms wide and cried, "Little Jo!"

Chapter 97

Alpine and Alabaster

I STOOD there awkwardly as the two old friends hugged. Ernith leaned close to say he'd wait outside.

"Watch that guy," Ernith warned. "He's crazy."

I shut the door behind him, just as Jo turned sideways to let me be seen.

"This is my mother's heir, Lord Warren," she explained to Garmond. "He's a former guardsman."

Before I could say anything, Alpine hissed from his perch on a ceiling beam.

"Oi! Whatcha doin' up there, beastie?" Garmond cried. "Stay away from the lady. Why's he hissing like he's feral?"

I closed the door and said, "Uh, because he is?"

"They let you buy a wild 'un and let it go 'round loose?" Garmond asked, squinting at Alpine with rheumy eyes. His face soured. "He's been roostin' in trees, look at him! Those scales are so—"

"Forget him, Garmond, he'll behave," Jolene said. "We're here to look at your babies!"

Garmond scoffed, waving us grumpily toward a line of pens where clans of tiny dragons chirped for food. I still hadn't even

643

spoken yet, and I thought it best to keep it that way. Garmond didn't seem the type to warm to strangers.

As we walked down the cages, I studied the animals as they studied me. An adult Shoulder dragon stood guard at a perch outside each door, and they all turned their heads so that one eye could track me.

Unlike Pinnacle Dragons' original barn, this entire building was packed with caged dragons. If I had to guess, it was the culmination of Garmond's life's work. My fingers rippled as I dragged them across the bars.

The old man pointed at Alpine without looking at me. "You say he's wild? Like flew-out-of-the-woods-this-morning, wild?"

I caught Jolene's eye, and she nodded at me. It was a look that said, *You can trust him.*

"Yep. Sometimes dragons just come to me." I patted my shoulder, and a baby dragon almost instantly escaped his pen to scurry towards my feet. "Not you, little one. You still need your mother."

The baby unleashed an adorable roar and begrudgingly returned to its pen.

"We think Warren is something called Dragon-Touched," Jolene said proudly, just as we passed a side exit. Scratching sounded at the door, making Garmond stop and grumble. He limped to the door, popped it open, and met Copper as she barged in sideways to get to me.

"Easy girl," I said. "Don't go bowling people over."

Garmond was fine, though—at least physically. His eyes had gone wide when he saw Copper, and he appeared to be trembling. Alpine suddenly left the rafters and landed on the old man's shoulder, but Garmond didn't even react.

It was probably the state Copper was in. I sat down on a bench, letting her stalk over like a panther and curl up at my feet. She was drenched in goblin blood and very tired, her swollen belly full of monster bits, if I had to guess.

"You... you're the mystery warrior who broke the siege," Garmond said. He limped over to sit beside me, completely fascinated by the big hatchling on his floor. "And you have a mine dragon? These are so rare that I've never even met one up close."

I glanced at Jolene. "A mine dragon?"

She spread her hands. She hadn't heard of them either.

"I've only seen one once, and it had to be put down because it was so violent," Garmond explained, his voice tinged with awe. "It had bonded to a human from birth, too. Taming one is like trying to tame a volcanic eruption. But Four Demons take me, she's a beauty...."

Copper squeaked out a long fart, not half so impressed with herself as Garmond was.

I chuckled. "I'm starting a farm outside the walls of Dasvilla, so I need dragons who can be violent. It's about time the wilds feared humans again."

"Well, with a dragon *that* size, you might just make it happen," Garmond mused.

I shared another look with Jolene. "She's an Airship-class, then?"

"As far as anyone knows. Mine dragons live underground. They're treasure hoarders. People rarely see them, and if they do, they don't live to tell about it."

I owned not one, but *two* Airship-class dragons? "Well, I'll be burned," I said.

"Anyway." Garmond still sounded breathless. "I'm far too old to get into some sort of crusade. Are you here to shop or not?"

Jolene brightened. "We were wondering if you had a dragon that can handle a fight, but also be happy outside without a chain."

"My girl, you just described all wild dragons," Garmond said. He sighed. "But I've got Alabaster. He's a dust dragon, slow and with limited stamina, and he's not very friendly either. I let him out at night with Branch and Rocky."

Garmond rose up off the bench, his knees popping in protest. He headed a few cages deeper into the rows and opened one up.

"Alabaster, meet Lord Warren."

I'd yet to hear what was actually *good* about this dragon, but when a pure white dragon with only one wing exited the cage, it was love at first sight. Copper opened a single eye, sized him up, then went back to her nap. The dragon stalked forward two steps, then just watched me.

"He's built like a damn wall," Garmond said. "Scales and spikes like diamonds, too. He attracts attention, but it's near impossible to damage him. Invulnerable to sharp impacts, heavy as all hell, and his breath ability is this weird sparkly dust. It can catch on the wind and draw monsters from miles away."

I strode up to the beast and touched his snout with a palm. He was taller than me, probably a big Mount-class. His eyes were a pale blue, almost white.

"And he likes to be outside?" I asked.

"Yep. I'd wager he'd pull trees down, since he's always digging. Not sure what he's after, but my back pasture's right torn."

Alabaster yawned without dislodging my hand. "He can't fly?"

"No dust dragon can fly," Jolene said. "Not after they're hatchlings. Their wings often get docked."

"Not on my dragons, they don't," Garmond snapped. "This guy lost his wing being an idiot. Tried to mate with a Behemoth, and failed."

That caught me by surprise. "I didn't know dragons mated outside their size classes."

"They don't," Garmond said. "He's a Behemoth, but he's a dwarf. Got a bad lot in life, but still cost me a fortune."

I lowered my hand. *He could be my first Behemoth! But to what purpose? Can he even mate?*

"How much?" I asked. "And how do I get him home if he can't fly?"

"I bought him for twelve gold. I've made that back twice selling his dust and lending him to masons to dig foundations."

Unlike regular dragon breath-which was mostly intangible—any breath ability that produced something physical, like dust, could easily be collected and sold.

I opened my purse, noting it only had nine gold in it. "I can offer nine gold, but only if he arrives to Dasvilla."

"He will."

"Nine gold? You're mad. Give me five," Garmond countered, earning a chuckle from us. "He's past his prime, and I think it's a good retirement for him. Also, this way, the taxes won't give me a heart attack."

I fished out the five gold, placing them in his palm. "I appreciate your time."

"How did you find her?" Garmond asked, stuffing his purse away. "The mine dragon."

"Near Caliph. She followed me back from a trapping trip."

"She *followed* you? You didn't catch her?"

I shrugged. "I think she had friends in the group of dragons I caught. She was watching over them."

Garmond rubbed his jaw. "Was she, now?"

I sensed he had more to say, but a knock sounded at the big door where we'd entered.

"I've gotta run," I said. "But they only need me. Jolene can stay here with you and the dragons for a bit, if you'd like."

Jolene grinned, and Garmond patted my shoulder. "Your girl and your dragons will stay cageless right here, son. As for the brass, good luck dealing with that lot." He grunted. "Trust me, you'll need it."

Chapter 98

Anything for Free Beer

A SERIES of guards escorted me toward the towering castle in the heart of the city. The grand stone structure, with its looming walls and rapidly increasing height, was the bastion of Ashkar.

If the enemy breached the city walls, which happened far too often, then the inner keep became a trap. The residents could enter a labyrinth below the city to wait for a counter attack, or they could climb the inside stairs of the walls and fly to safety.

Meanwhile, any invaders would be forced to bridge a moat, brute-force their way through numerous checkpoints, and try to scale smooth, impervious walls well beyond the height of a ladder.

The deeper they led me into the walls, the more guards I saw and checkpoints I passed. I wasn't a guardsman anymore, but I did still carry a sword and daggers, and at the last stop, I was forced to leave them behind with a guard.

A crier stood at the final checkpoint before our entry. I whispered my name, and he belted it out to the hundred-plus attendees who sat at long tables inside the main hall.

"Holy shit. A victory party already?" I asked, but the crier and guards did not answer.

649

Hmm. Maybe a pre-planned party, then? Did these people not even notice the battle?

I looked around to get my bearings, unsure what I was needed for. A heavy scent of glazed ham mingled with the smell of spilled ale, but despite this, the chatter was subdued.

The room was crowded with officers, nobles, and ladies in garb fit for comfort rather than grandeur. I nodded in approval, much preferring an atmosphere of camaraderie and laughter than the pretend posturing of the nobles I'd grown used to.

At the same time, no one danced, although a tiny dance floor had been built off to the side, with a raised platform for a bard in the corner. Attendants worked the tables, and guards stood at four entries where double doors swung constantly from the flow of workers.

A few of the guests turned at our arrival, but only one of them was moved by my name: one of the soldiers on duty spun his head to fixate on my face, and his jaw dropped when he recognized me.

"Taos!" I bellowed, striding toward him. The guards didn't stop me.

"Who's this?" a portly man with a messy brown beard demanded from the head table.

Officer Ernith raised his voice. "Lord Warren is our Dasvilla Champion. Without his dragons, we would have suffered the siege for much longer. Lord Warren is becoming known for such deeds. He also defeated a tribe of minotaurs just last week, and he's served a decade in the king's army."

"Seems you've still got a knack for killing," Taos said as I reached him. While the nobles started chattering at the tables, I shook his hand, then pulled him into a hug, smacking the back of his armor fondly. We pulled apart and smashed our foreheads with a solid *bang*.

Together, we'd cleared more than a few monster sieges so that caravans could reach safety, and while we weren't forever-friends, we were kindred spirits.

I turned to Ernith, who had followed me. Patting Taos on the shoulder, I said, "This one is too good to play guard at parties. He ought to be on a mission. I'm sure he's bored to death in here."

"Oi, now, don't ruin things for me," Taos said. "They give us free beer afterward."

I laughed, leaning against the wall to stand with my friend instead of sitting at the tables. To Ernith, I said, "Who am I supposed to be meeting? I thought we were headed to the watchmaster, but these guys are all nobles."

Before Ernith could answer, the noble with the tangled beard shouted, "Lord Warren, is it? Will you not sit?"

I faced him, guessing he must be the city's ruling count. "I appreciate the offer, but there was a battle barely an hour past. Men like Taos here bought that victory with their lives this day. I couldn't bear to sit and be merry, thinking of that. But!"

I caught the arm of a serving lad walking past me, grabbing two mugs of ale from his tray and raising them both. "I will happily give a toast! To the fallen!"

A beat passed, and then mugs rose in salute all across the room, and the throng of people echoed, "To the fallen!"

I drank my ale, and then drank the one I grabbed for Taos. "Sorry," I teased him. "You're on duty."

He chuckled. "And you're still a bastard."

The crier announced someone else, and people returned to talking amongst their table. The count had an open seat next to him, which I suspected was intended for me, but Ernith didn't push me to it. He looked uncomfortable, and I could swear I caught the foul stench of politics.

"How the Demons did you become a noble?" Taos asked. I snorted and turned back to him, telling the tale.

He winced at the end and whispered, "Do you think, you know, *she* set it up? I heard she's had troubles since your... falling-out."

My stomach soured. The *she* he referred to could be no one else. "I should never have told you about her," I groused, sipping more ale.

"Well, a man can't help what he says when he's right tossed," Taos replied. "Honestly, I'm surprised you didn't tell the whole world you fucked a princess. I would have bragged if it were me."

"Ugh," I replied, draining my third ale. "But no, I don't think it was Vanessa." Just saying her name made my stomach roil and my head feel fuzzy, and not just with drink.

"No, I think if it was anything *other* than luck, the King's Hand would have stopped it. I'm surprised he hasn't stopped it yet."

Taos leaned closer. "No matter what is at play, don't you find it odd you stumbled upon a night dragon? Those are for royalty. Even dud eggs shouldn't have gotten into a market."

I was impressed at Dasvilla's rumor-mongers. I barely ever took the baby night dragon out of the villa, yet people knew about her even here.

"Look, I'm just a man on a farm," I said. "Politics aren't my thing. If they were, I wouldn't be standing here, blowing off the count."

"Oh, he's got enough whores to do that for him," Taos joked, clapping a palm against my arm. "But I also heard you're building a farm outside the walls in Dasco. You're seriously doing that?"

I snorted, handing my empty mug away to a passing server. "If all these lords emptied their barns and roosts, they could have pushed back the hordes years ago. But we are all divided—soldiers, guardsmen, mages, Enforcers, dragons both public and private, guildsmen and merchants, nobles. I manage to join just *three* of those groups—dragons, guardsmen, and my little noble self—and I save a damned city while I'm going to lunch."

"You do realize you're making big people look bad?" Taos said with a heavy tone. "You can't defeat the hordes by yourself. Like actually *beat* them back permanently. You need support from *all* of those sources, and instead, you're pissing people off."

I crossed my arms. "Friend, I just want to be a farmer. It's everyone *else* making me something I'm not."

He had a point, though, so I made my goodbyes. We clasped forearms and I departed as a noble, finally wandering over to count. Within seconds of my sitting, I had a platter of pheasant and scalecherry in front of me, but I didn't much feel like eating.

Count Yeli leaned over. "The hero arrives!" he exclaimed, waving a fork at me. "I heard you commanded a wild Airship today. You *must* tell me how you achieved such a feat!"

I gave a polite answer, deferring, and over the next hour I repeated that same cycle over and over. Count Yeli would try to get me to boast or share secrets, and I'd downplay everything I'd done, and foist credit onto anyone else.

But no matter how much I waxed eloquent about the Biscuits or Ernith or the watchmaster I still hadn't met, the count wouldn't stop trying to make me the star of this ball. Apparently, it *had* been a pre-planned event to celebrate the wedding of his favorite cousin.

After three whole dessert courses had come and gone, and all the people closest to us had departed or taken bathroom breaks, I finally slammed a palm on the table.

"With all due respect, Count," I said, "could you *please* come out with what you really want to say?"

The big man crossed his arms and settled back in his plush chair, waving off another glass of wine with just his fingertips. This left us mercifully alone, with the party loud enough to cover most of our words.

"Parmisca remains lost to the kingdom," he said suddenly, referencing the walled city far to the west of us, which had been lost a year ago to a horde of trolls. "Now, you didn't hear this from me, but the losses we sustained were so great that King Kurto sees a need to double his troops. As such, he has been forced to draft soldiers into his service for the first time in over a decade."

I gritted my teeth. Another military draft? There had been one ten years ago. I'd been powerless to stop it.

This time, though, would things be different? Did I have the power to save all those lives?

Chapter 99

Not another Plot!

"A DRAFT? WHAT FOR?" I growled at the count. "The king didn't conscript enough people last time? Because if I remember right, *thousands* were killed."

Yeli shrugged. "Too much peace for too long has led to a soft kingdom. He is merely making us hard again."

I was too angry to make a comment about his phrasing, and that said a lot. Half the young men of Dasvilla were still serving the king against their will. He never let anyone go.

"I volunteered during the last draft, not that it goes on the paperwork," I said. "And I know one thing: a lot of good men died back then, but not fighting hordes. He had us on the roads all the time, protecting caravans, trying to establish routes and way stations. Barely half of it worked, but he's still dead-set on expanding in Caliph. I'm sure that's not the only place, either."

I nodded in the direction of the siege. "I'd even venture to guess that you're perfectly aware of this, and damned sick of it, too. You let that siege go on for too long. You want him to deal with the actual threat, not enrich himself with more expansion."

Yeli's face darkened. "That's a treasonous thing to say, boy."

"Pretend I never said it, then. But one thing I'm sure of: if the king is expanding his military, it's not to fight off the hordes. Parmisca was just an excuse."

655

The count took a sip of wine, ruminating. I could see no other reason for him to hold off on dealing with the siege, except to damage the king where it hurt most: in his pocketbook.

Of course, it had hurt Yeli's pocketbook too, but the draft had him scared. He needed the young men of his city to protect it, to help it thrive. Every duke and count had suffered ten years ago, when the draft drained half their best working population.

Also, he had two sons.

"It never ends," Yeli said.

"Nope. But you knew that already. And as much as I helped today, you could have done it without me. Your troops did admirably, and with minimal losses. I don't say that lightly. They're well-trained."

He nodded, then changed the subject. "Have you heard of the Kiloban Kingdom?"

I most certainly had. Kiloba was an island nation in the middle of the ocean, with no natural threats outside of water beasts who would attack ships. Unlike here, where hordes of enemies assailed our walls, Kilobans lived in relative peace from monsters. The place also happened to be a tropical paradise, a sort of fantasy location talked about amongst the troops.

But although the Kilobans lived in peace, their land was finite, their economy reliant on facilitating trade. Parshil didn't have a single port connecting us, and we never would unless the road from Caliph succeeded. It was a vacation destination reachable only by dragon.

"I've never been. The rumors say it's lovely," I said, curious about the question. Unable to help myself, I asked, "This has to do with Parmisca?"

"Yes and no.... How to best explain this? I like Duke Biscuit, but he doesn't meddle. He refuses to open a spy network, which makes him look harmless." Yeli shook his head. "I suppose that's the right strategy for a duke whose entire title rests on the fact his king has forgotten he exists. He wouldn't deny this, either, given the dice he has to play with. He's clearly spoken to you about not standing out."

"And what does that have to do with Kiloba?" I asked. I was getting tired of asking him to speak to me directly.

"Well, there's been an exodus of nobles from the outlying Parshil cities to the west. The ones bordering on Parmisca's lost lands. Many of the old families, the ones with vast sums of wealth, are selling their businesses and heading to Kiloba to retire.

"The truth is, today, we celebrate a victory the monsters never had a chance of winning. That rabble out there? It was just some small tribes coming together out of boredom. What happened in Parmisca was different, far different.

"The defenders were ambushed at night. The guardsmen failed to signal the alarm. The gate was opened before anyone knew anything. Worse, the ballistae were silenced before anyone even knew an attack was nigh.

"The enemy conquered the city cleanly, with strategy, economy, and ruthlessness. An elf called General Iskar was the leader of that force, and he still holds Parmisca, waiting for a counter offensive the king refuses to make. It's only a matter of time before Iskar presses close again. Scouts claim he's funneling hordes to the city, but it's hard to say, because Iskar dominates the air."

Yeli lowered his voice, raised his wine glass, and spoke into it. "It's rumored that, like you, this Iskar has bonded with dragons."

I swallowed. Now *that* was troubling.

It also explained why I was still alive.

"He'll need me. The king. He'll need me to fight this guy, this *Iskar*." Damn, it was a good thing Fieran and Becki had let that information slip, or else the Hand might have murdered me by now.

A cold stone dropped into my stomach. "Shit," I said. "The mass exodus of nobles...."

Yeli raised his glass in silent toast. "And that, young lord, is the great secret that's not a secret. We don't expect Parmisca to be recaptured, ever. The nobles of the nearby regions are fleeing. That happens just as you, a man despised by the king, suddenly appears as a Dragon-Touched."

I nodded. It all made sense.

"He'll send me there to die," I said. "Then he'll use my death as an excuse to let the other cities fall. I'd get the blame."

I thought of Caliph, and the other half of the story clicked. "Caliph is building roads to the east, to the coast, toward Kiloba and other foreign nations. When our Western cities fall, the king will have the spare population to start settling the East... to settle all those new outposts Caliph's count is building.

"Fuck! He's moving the whole kingdom east! He's abandoning the West and moving to the East, where it's more profitable. That's why Caliph is getting so much funding to build their road!"

Yeli pursed his lips and brooded, his eyes dark. He didn't counter a single thing I'd said.

I shook my head, astounded. And here I thought I'd be talking to Yeli about him being lazy with the hordes. Instead, I'd stumbled upon a conspiracy to abandon entire cities—a conspiracy hatched by the king himself.

Worse, I had a feeling I was about to be invited into a rebellion —and I wouldn't have a choice but to join. Either I helped hold those cities and all the innocents that dwelled in them, or—

"The fucking *draft*," I breathed.

"Cheers, kid. You're not stupid, at least," Yeli said.

The king was conscripting men. Fighting men. The most valuable population when it came to settling new areas. He was going to draft them out of the Western cities, and move them to the East, where they'd survive the slaughter of their families back home.

Because there *would* be slaughter. The king would send me in with all my dragons, all my glory, all my hype—and I'd fail, and the swarms would come for the barely-defended outer cities. I bet that, even now, the men stationed there were being replaced with older soldiers on the edge of retirement. Less-valuable assets for the king to lose.

Suddenly the count tensed, straightening, the contented wrinkles around his eyes vanishing as he saw something that had his complete attention. I turned to see it too, and my whole body went cold.

Lord Egrid, the Hand of the King himself, had just walked into the room.

Chapter 100

The Hand of the King

Lord Egrid gently set himself into the seat next to Count Yeli. He had not been invited.

"Lord Egrid! What a pleasant surprise," Yeli stammered. "Please, let me order you a drink—"

"No drinks, please, Count," the man said, his voice deep and throaty and as unsettling as always. "I've come because I have a message from the king." His silver gaze slid to me. "A message for you."

I swallowed all emotion, all the rage and hate and fear. This man had advocated heavily for my execution, and had only been satisfied when the king had given him leave to kill me if I ever tried to talk to Princess Vanessa again.

But I knew the guy would have taken that command loosely. By making myself slightly famous, that gave the Hand reason to say I was trying to gain rank so that I could speak to Vanessa. Luckily, I had other uses now, but he'd wanted me dead for years.

The Hand was a brooding man who almost never talked with people personally. One of his agents would slip you a scroll or whisper a warning, but the man himself was half-myth and half-ghost. I'd met him once and only once, fully expecting to never see him again—unless he was stabbing me in my sleep.

The count waved off an attendant who was trying to bring wine.

"We had a deal," Egrid said.

Yeli blinked, probably not in-the-know about my dalliance with Vanessa. "Yes, and I honored it," I said. "To the word, letter, and intent."

Egrid faced ahead again, so I could see a magically healed scar along his jaw. "I told him to kill you. You would one day realize what power you possessed, and you would surely use it against him.

"But no. He listened to his daughter plead for your worthless life. He believed her when she said you were harmless, as if you hadn't purposely wormed your way into her heart. But I know the truth. You were after the throne, and my king is a sentimental fool."

I barely heard anything beyond his second sentence: *You would one day realize what power you possessed.*

"What's this about the princess?" Yeli asked.

The Hand scoffed, and his pale hand reached into his robes, retrieving a scroll from under his sleeve. He handed it to me. I popped the seal and unrolled it.

I'll admit this: you've shown surprising tenacity, and I'm shocked you still live.
My Hand despises you, but you never gave him any excuse to end your life. He might think me weak, and I am sure he has said so as he was handing this very document to you—but the fact is, I wished you dead, too.
I saw his hate and fear as a tool that would end you just as surely as my own sword, but in letting him do the killing, I would preserve my only daughter's regard for me. So that is the route I took. This I admit freely.
That said, part of our agreement still stands. I won't be able to keep Essy from learning of you, but if you speak to her, touch her, even look at her, I will do everything in my power to make sure you die a very long and very painful death.

No dragons will be able to spare you that fate, no matter how much you enthrall them.

That line made me narrow my eyes. Did he have some counter against dragons that I didn't know of? Or was he just that confident in his own army of beasts?

That said, I am no warrior. I am a tactician. As such, I always use the tool best suited for any task. You have become that tool.
Parshil teeters on the edge of destruction. If our scouts and agents are truthful, war brews to the West. The army which took Parmisca is led by a Dragon-Touched enemy.
Imagine my surprise when I hear about a Dragon-Touched returned to his hometown of Dasvilla in glory.
Go to Parmisca. Rid the region of General Iskar, and I will make you the new duke of Dasvilla, one of only nine duchies in all of Parshil.
Fail in this at your peril, and the peril of those you care for. I have no issue killing you twice.
-His Majesty King Kurto, Second of His Name, Ruler of the Walled Cities of Parshil and Warden of All Lands Between

I folded the paper, but The Hand held out a palm. I gave it back to him. He wouldn't want me stowing it somewhere, to use as evidence later.

He asked, "And your answer?"

I sat still for a moment. *I have no issue killing you twice.*

So that really is how it happened, I thought.

I rose from my seat, stalked over to the nearest window, stuck my head out, and whistled.

"What are you doing?" the Hand asked sharply from behind, but I didn't have to wait long. Copper dove down in front of me, meaning she'd been perched on the roof this whole time. I could always trust her to be close by.

I looked both ways, found a balcony on the same floor, and pointed at it. "I'll meet you there!" I shouted, as Copper pulled up from her dive and laid eyes on me.

I withdrew to find the Hand behind me, with Yeli standing nervously beside him. I ignored them and moved toward the dance floor, where a pair of doors led to the balcony I'd just seen.

"Lord Warren? Where are you going?" Count Yeli asked, clearly concerned.

A laugh escaped my lips as I threw the doors open to find Copper already waiting. "Anywhere but here."

"And what is your answer?" the Hand countered.

I rounded on him, this pale ghost of a man. "How did you bring me back to life?"

The ghastly man curled his nose. "I have no idea what you mean."

"You know damn well the king whipped me for days without water or food. He covered me in scars, trying to find out who I was working for, what country had sent me to woo his precious daughter away from him.

"I never gave him anything, because there was nothing to give. I found her in the forest. I saved her life. We fell in love, and that was the story."

"Not many men talk to me in such a manner, and live," the Hand growled.

"And you deflect yet again," I said, pointing a single finger at his face. "I died in that place. I remember it. The dragon-tail whip cut into my neck, and I went beyond the point of no return.

"I've been telling myself for years that I imagined it, that I was just delirious, but it's true, isn't it? I died. But something brought me back.

"And that thing is what made me Dragon-Touched."

The Hand drew himself up. He was tall and thin, like a scarecrow dipped in tallow. "You are a madman. I should kill you for spreading such lies."

"Back to life?" Count Yeli blurted.

The Hand frowned, eyeing the man like he was a mouse sniffing at a trap. I faced the city, not afraid to turn my back with Copper present. The dragon had already stalked up beside me, watching the men with a bored stare.

"You would one day realize what power you possessed. You just said this," I said as Copper nuzzled my hand, no differently than a loving cat would. "You gave me that power. Or someone did. Someone who wanted me alive, who'd expend any magic to do it—"

I stopped speaking. There was only one person in all of this who had cared that much.

"Vanessa saved me." I turned. "How?"

The Hand scoffed. "I will not entertain the ramblings of a madman—"

"Oh yes you will," I said. "The kingdom is crumbling because the king is too weak. The people of Parshil need a hero, someone who will restore his image and defeat his enemies for him.

"I am the hope on the horizon, Lord Egrid, and the king will *entertain* my ramblings in exchange for that hope." *And for my sacrifice,* I added internally. I was the king's path to prosperity, to bringing all his plans to fruition.

"So how did Vanessa do it?" I demanded.

"I have had enough of this. Go, if you please, but remember well the king's warning. You have a task; perform it, or die."

With that, Lord Egrid pivoted mechanically in place and began to walk away, each stride precisely measured.

I turned to Count Yeli. "In exchange for my efforts, I want everyone to know I was detained and tortured for the crime of saving the princess from her own foolishness.

"I will tell the full story to you as I know it, and you will have your best rumor-mongers spread it. The king can deflect or decry it as a falsehood, but some will learn the truth, and that is enough for me."

Yeli had started to sweat. "You push him too far. He does need you for his plans, but publicly challenging him for breaking his honor—"

"Do it. I'll announce my campaign against Iskar as soon as I've secured my farm, and that will give him an end date for having to tolerate me. He will be able to keep from acting if he knows the day of my death." I paused, wondering just how much meat I was biting off here. "How long do you think I can get away with?"

Count Yeli considered this seriously, scratching at his beard. "Given the flight of the nobles and the state of the front... six months, at the most."

I patted Copper. "How about that, girl? Next spring?" She mewed. "Okay. We agree. I want the kingdom to know that the Dragon-Touched was betrayed once, and that I am not an agent of the king. However, I *will* fight to keep this kingdom safe."

"A fine story. The people will love you for it."

I nodded. Yeli understood.

"And how might I support you?" Count Yeli asked, his voice lower now.

I shot him a smile. "Easy. You tell me more about you, and others like you. Together, we will save the western cities.

"Together, we will bring down the king."

Chapter 101

We've Got Eggs!

Jolene departed Ashkar in absolute delight, because Count Yeli gifted her three adolescent dragons that his wife bought but didn't really need. They were Mount-class grazers, not too different from large oxen, just with more muscle, claws, and pitiful wings that barely lifted them off the ground.

I flew home with Quicksilver, because the time for proving Pinnacle's viability was so close, and I needed to be there. I instructed Copper to guard Jolene while she rode Alabaster and herded the three grazers back to Dasvilla over land. It would take her a full day to return, while a dragonflight was barely an hour.

Once Quicksilver and I arrived home, I dumped all our other purchases—mostly various metal and building implements— into the new barn outside the city. It would all go to good use, but I wouldn't be the one swinging the hammer or securing the bolts. With help from Becki, I'd hired a bunch of laborers who'd aged out of the orphanage to continue building the farmhouse so I could turn my mind to other prospects.

A lot of people needed me to create a better tomorrow, so the farmer in me had faded away once again, while the soldier in me surged back to the forefront.

When I arrived back to the Cage, my first stop was the rookery, where I retrieved my night dragon, Star. I kept hearing about the damned creature everywhere I went. People were either impressed that I owned her, or thought it was some sort of conspiracy.

Either way, the rumors helped me gain renown, so from now on, the baby was going to go everywhere with me. I stroked the deep purple webbing of her wings, and she curled around my neck and fell asleep, much like a cat curling into a ball before the hearth.

With that settled, the first person I visited was Duchess Nola, to tell her the sad truth. King Kurto was not supportive of Duke Biscuit's accomplishments, if he was eagerly willing to replace him with me.

She wisely called me silly, because in the game of politics, division was key. "He is only trying to pit us against one another. And we won't let that happen, will we?"

I bowed at the waist and assured her I would do no such thing, but I smiled at the ground while I did so. This information had been divisive, all right; it would divide the king and the duke. The fact that I told Nola immediately would make her think I wasn't after the duchy, and their anger and fear would go to the king instead.

At this point, I wanted the Biscuits as future allies, not enemies. Duchess Nola and her network of nobles and spies was something to contend with, and I'd rather be able to use it than have it used against me. And even if others thought that Duke Biscuit was a weak noble who wished to avoid the political arena, I knew his wife had other goals. While she worked to raise his power, I sought to secure it.

I didn't like the man himself, but Biscuit was greedy and *not* ambitious, a combination that would be easy for me to control over time. Offer him something he wanted and make it easy to get, and he would be clay in my hands.

While I was at the keep, I took the relatively small detour to the guard house and got a report from Captain Narvi. Apparently, his soldiers had carved up a small goblin camp just this morning, showing no mercy and pilfering as they went.

It was the first time they'd acted on their own in this way, and because they were renting Red for the purpose, they paid me a portion of the proceeds—including some of the bounties. Since I hadn't collected them directly, I saw no reason to say no.

However, the captain did have a job for me. "We've been setting troll traps along their known routes," he explained. "But recently we found one of these traps missing. It was a rope trap, the kind that's attached to trees. The ground was disturbed, with signs of a scuffle, and it wasn't hard to see which direction the thief went. We think he stole a trapped troll and ran away with it."

"Take me there," I said.

He nodded. "I'll have my best scout and my best ranger go with you. I can't do it myself, unfortunately."

I agreed, and we set off for the site. This wasn't what I should be doing with the rest of my evening, but at this point, there wasn't much I could do to improve Pinnacle's profitability overnight.

I was leaving the books with Rachel, who was pretending to be sick to avoid work while she tallied up all our numbers and planned income. After all, if Pinnacle failed, she would lose her 5%. It was down to the last talon now, but if anyone could make the ledgers ooze with profit, it was Rachel.

So I let the captain take me to the site of the stolen trap. After all, an enemy intelligent enough to disarm a trap was an enemy that we ought to be concerned about.

When I arrived, I bent down to look at the scrapes on the ground, trying to glean more information. "Hmm...."

Fieran whipped a bead of sweat from his forehead, crouching beside me. She hadn't come to Ashkar with Jo and I, since that was supposed to be just a lunch date, but now she was in "never let you out of my damn sight" mode once again.

While I crab-walked over the scene of the crime, she drank a long pull of water from a flask. At least, I hoped it was water.

Feldspar sniffed the air at her side, focusing on the direction the culprit had gone.

"I don't see any footprints," Fieran noted, tucking her water away.

Grayson, a First Rank Scout, checked the site alongside me. He swept the perimeter while another guy, Kreegor, watched our backs. He was a ranger, which meant he specialized in forest warfare.

I knew Grayson only in passing, but Kreegor was an older friend of mine. I'd filled his slot as protector of the alley kids when he'd departed to join the military at eighteen. He'd managed to make first rank, and was helping train up some of the locals in forest warfare as the watchmaster made more and more forays into the hotlands to clean out monsters.

Kreegor grunted, his stern face fixated on a patch of smoothed dirt. "Something's smoothed the tracks."

I rose to stand again. "It's not like it's hard to see where they went. They just hid their tracks to hide what they are." Trolls, minotaurs, and orcs weren't usually smart enough for that. "All right, lead the way, Feldspar."

We followed the trail of smashed bushes and fresh dirt for the next ten minutes at a steady pace. The drag marks transitioned into gritty rubble, heading up the mountainside. The bushes died down and the trees simply stopped at a lip.

The clearing was small, with a large pit slightly off-center. When I walked to the edge of the hole, a cavernous opening yawned at the bottom, big enough for a big Hauler to pass through. Quicksilver wouldn't fit, but all my other dragons would. Further up the mountain, most of this area sloped uphill, clashing with heavy stonewood forests.

I had no idea how this hole had been created, but it wasn't natural. Three rope ladders hung down into the hole, and I was about to climb down when I saw something move.

I cursed. "That's a *tail*."

The other soldiers leaned in, Fieran included. The tip of a dragon tail poked out of the cavern at the bottom, unmoving.

The ladders are for people, I thought. *But there's a dragon down there. Did it eat them, or are they keeping it here?*

Suspicious now, I rounded the hole to look at its interior wall from a better-lit angle. I pointed.

"There are other nests in the walls. Hard to see, because it's black on black."

Along the inner walls of the pit, dozens of shoulder-sized dragons rested in nests, hidden except for a couple of tail-tips sticking out. It made sense for them to use such a space as a hotel. The dragons were safe from Behemoths here; they could react quickly to hunters if the ladders started moving; and they had safety in numbers.

While my eyes scanned the nests, I noticed many of them revealed flickers of color.

A thrilled hiss escaped my lips, and I called out, "We've got eggs, boys, and lots of them!"

Chapter 102

Wonderful. Now Run!

"HOLY SHIT," Fieran whispered in awe. Every single nest in the pit showed a speckle of light, meaning some source of interior light was reflecting off dozens of the jewel-like dragon eggs.

I backed up, motioning for the rest of my team to pull back with me.

Once we were a good distance away, I brought them into a huddle. "Anyone got a piece of paper and pencil?"

"I do," Grayson said. Typical scout.

I took the page, scribbled a message to Becki on it, and sent Feldspar into the sky. "I'm sending for traps, reinforcements, Quicksilver, and Useless. There's either a big dragon down in that cave eating whatever your trap caught, or whatever we caught was strong and smart enough to dismantle the trap and drag it home. I would guess the former, though, since the drag marks go right up to the edge of the hole."

"You don't wanna just rush it?" Grayson said, earning a frown from the rest of us. "Not that I disagree, just curious. They definitely don't know we're here yet."

Pretty silly of these dragons not to have lookouts, I thought, remembering the guard dragons from the House of Cards nest. Maybe it was just nap time—or maybe they saw no purpose in being afraid, because their protection was just *that* good.

673

"They live in a pit. Quicksilver can block most of their exit with just her mass, so when she gets here, we can start," I explained. "We wait and do this right."

Over the next few minutes, the jungle settled back into an odd sort of harmony. The four of us hunkered down while waiting for Quicksilver, taking up defensive positions in the thick bushes surrounding the hole. Our line of sight into the pit was nonexistent, but we could see the edges. By air, it should only take about ten minutes for Feldspar to reach home, so I expected him and Quicksilver to return fairly quickly.

Whatever had dragged the captured prey into the pit, it had done so recently, so I had to hope they were still busy doing something with the body. We didn't talk or adjust for a good twenty minutes, sitting in silence. Just when I thought Quicksilver might arrive, one of the rope ladders creaked, grinding against the tree stump it had been hung from.

Kreegor smoothly shifted in place, nocking an arrow. I laid down, as did Grayson, while Fieran merely crouched, ready to draw her blade at a moment's need.

We waited in ambush, but with the sun descending on the far side of the clearing, I had a bad angle to see who rose out of the pit. I had to trust Kreegor to do the right thing; from his standing height, he should be able to see better.

My heart beat so loud it filled my ears with a constant thrum. The sound of someone walking across leaves moved away from us.

Kreegor gently tapped my boot with his. I rose to a crouch and he bent down.

He whispered, "Young green elf, male, carrying a bow. I could have taken the shot, but if I missed, he'd have us all dead in moments."

My brow drew low. An elf, in Dasvilla? That wasn't a good sign. Elves were one with the wildlands, and therefore savage at their core. I tended to think of them like the dire wolves of the ice territories. They were smart, opportunistic, and violent.

The big difference between wild wolves and green elves was that green elves could never be tamed into a hound. Even captured orc babies were more civil if raised in human society.

Factions of other elves lived in lavish cities in other corners of the world, but the green elves lived and died in raw nature. While they weren't common, they would attack humans to gain their supplies, and then feed the bodies to their dragons.

General Iskar, the supposed Dragon-Touched man who had taken Parmisca, was a green elf.

I didn't see the need to leave this threat in our midst, so when Feldspar landed quietly beside me a few minutes later, I instructed him to go after the elf.

"Kill. Bring me whatever he carries," I whispered, pointing in the direction the elf had gone. Feldspar should be able to pick up his scent from here.

The dragon stalked forward until he reached a point where the forest opened up a bit. Then the dragon burst into a galloping sprint, quickly vanishing from sight.

I returned to my hiding spot and waited.

"Kinda like cheating," Kreegor said with a snort. "Always wanted a dragon."

I dipped my head in agreement. "They have dragons too, so I expect this won't be one-sided."

"You think elves are keeping those dragons as farming animals and eating the eggs?" Kreegor asked. "I heard they eat dragon eggs like we eat chicken eggs."

I shook my head. "Those small dragons are their warning signal. Notice how none of them were distraught when the elf scaled the ladder. Not a single one made a peep. They live in harmony, and if we do anything more than peek over the edge, the nesting dragons will give warning to the cave residents."

"Residents? You think there are more of them?"

"One elf wouldn't have trained that many alarm dragons. He would have trained one."

675

"So we might have found a secret base.... What's the plan?" Grayson asked.

A high-pitched yell crashed through the forest before it abruptly stopped. We froze, hunkering back down.

That'll draw someone out, I thought.

Sure enough, a huge wyvern clambered out of the pit less than a minute later. Once the wings cleared the lip, the black, two-legged beast burst into a flight, heading directly toward the cry of the elf.

I sucked in a deep breath and growled in frustration. Wyverns were faster than dragons, with less weight and frame size, and they all had the same kind of magic: negation. They acted as equalizers in battle, preventing the use of magic, both natural and learned, whenever they loosed one of their thunderous cries. They mostly ate small dragons, like the shoulder-sized creatures in the pit, so it was odd to see one here.

As a juvenile, Feldspar was going to struggle against a wyvern of this size. Not only that, but he'd be slow to escape, unless he found a thicker part of the stone forest to hide in. I hoped he would have fled the scene already, but a few seconds later, Feldspar roared out a challenge, deciding to fight.

I groaned, sprinting from my hidden spot in the bushes to aid my ally. Where in the four hells was Quicksilver?

"What are you doing?" Grayson hissed, struggling to keep up. "We can't beat that wyvern! It's three times the size of the one dragon we've got!"

I ignored him, because he was right. I didn't exactly have a good plan. I also sensed I'd struggle to use my powers on the wyvern, because it was not a dragon at all.

The rock forest thinned the higher we went, the rubble taking over the landscape between thin trees and bushes. A blight must have passed through here decades ago, leaving dead trees that eventually wore away.

I sensed Feldspar's presence seconds before I burst onto the scene. In a ring of dead, craggy trees, I found the wyvern staring down at

Feldspar with teeth bared. The elf surprisingly still lived, but a random orc lay dead with an arrow in an eye further up the terrain.

Why Feldspar didn't flee was beyond me, because I knew he wasn't some die-hard who followed orders religiously. The dragon would undoubtedly disobey me if it suited him.

I skidded to stop next to Feldspar. The elven bow lay broken at his feet, and I finally pieced together what had happened. The orc had tried to ambush the elf and died. Feldspar stole the bow, but he'd spared the elf... why? To bait out the wyvern? Had he smelled the creature on the elf?

It was possible. I snapped at him, because he should have fled, but instead he postured aggressively and roared out another challenge, wanting a fight.

Wait... did I just snap *at him? What the hell?* I was starting to act like a damned dragon, but this wasn't the time to be worried about that.

With a puzzled tilt of his head, the wyvern chittered at me, much like a cat did to a mouse before it attacked. I gulped, raising my shield, wondering what the Demons Feldspar had been thinking, challenging something thrice his size.

The wyvern dropped down and lunged forward. I dove side-ways into a roll, feeling the air sway as teeth snapped closed only a finger's width away.

Feldspar pounced on the wyvern while it was distracted, using me as bait. The daft bastard clamped down on the wyvern's jugular with zero fear.

An arrow whizzed out of the trees behind me, passing an arm's length to my left. The projectile shot into the elf's chest, piercing his heart. The long-eared scout had been in shock up to this point.

As soon as the arrow pierced his flesh, he dropped to his knees while clutching the shaft. He started muttering, but I didn't hear what.

Two more dragons growled and snarled, back toward the pit. They weren't mine. The wyvern hadn't given a shout yet, so I could still sense their auras. They were enemies, yet Feldspar didn't release the wyvern to flee.

Instead of backing up, I charged the wyvern, bringing my sword in for a hefty swing. The wyvern flopped onto his side, thrashing, trying to escape Feldspar's clutches. Leveling my blade like a lance, I rammed the tip into the beast's chest. Metal cracked scales, and the blade sank deep with a *thud*.

Since the wyvern lacked front legs to swat at me, I managed to rake the blade up toward the head until I ran out of momentum. Blood surged right into my face, a fountain of black heat.

The wyvern panicked, one wing flexing as it lifted off the ground from its side. It gained a bit more height, but the weight of Feldspar and me proved too much.

A violent snap shattered the wing. To keep myself from being squished when it crashed down, I released the blade and leapt to hide behind the trunk of a nearby tree. The wyvern slammed to the stone rubble with its back legs flailing uselessly.

"Enough, Feldspar. Its allies come. We run," I ordered, using simple language the hyped-up dragon could understand.

"Arrggg!" came a shout behind me. When I glanced back, I found an arrow protruding from Grayson's shoulder armor. I dashed to get in front of him, raising my shield to stop the next arrow.

It came, ringing against the shield. It would have drilled him in the side of the head.

"I'm good. It didn't get through the chainmail," he grunted.

"Wonderful," I shouted. "Now run!"

Chapter 103

Forge the Sky!

KREEGOR FLUNG a dagger in the direction the arrow had come from, buying us a few seconds. We darted into the trees as Feldspar let the elves know he existed, bellowing out a triumphant roar.

The elves silenced his courage with a volley of arrows; I heard at least three twangs. He yipped in pain, followed by flapping. He had taken to the air to flee.

I grumbled angrily under my panting breaths, running up and away from the site rather than back toward the pit. I ditched my bag, as did the others, and we fled further up the slope, getting into more and more open territory. I wanted Quicksilver to see me when she arrived, but when would that be? She was already late.

Not even a few minutes into our mad dash, things got worse. We stumbled upon a makeshift orc camp that'd clearly been hastily assembled. No defenses had been erected, and none of the tents were suited to more than a quick sleep. Luckily, no orcs patrolled the site.

I ran right through the six tents where the orcs slept, not saying a word. Kreegor and Grayson followed me, slicing at anything that still moved under the collapsing tents. If I had to guess, that first elf scout had downed an orc day guard, and thanks to him, there was no one to alert the camp that we were coming.

On the other side of the orc camp, an orc exploded from between a pair of leaning boulders, roaring. His bellow became a gurgle when an arrow pierced his chest from behind.

"More elves!" I hissed, waving my companions into a stand of redpines, evergreen trees that glowed red with inner heat. Once we'd ducked behind them, I set my gaze on the choke point between the two boulders.

"Grayson, here," I commanded, stealing his sword when he turned to me. "I lost mine in the wyvern. How's the shoulder?"

"Sore. My aim'll be shit, but up close that won't matter."

I grunted in reply. "Kreegor and I will hold the choke, you and Fieran fire a round of arrows, then reposition... shit, where's Fieran?"

She wasn't with us. Grayson and Kreegor looked around.

"He was just here," Kreegor said. "I didn't see him go down."

I nodded. She might be trying to get another angle on the choke point.

The ground shook, trees cracking and crumbling behind us. I turned, flinging an arm up to shield myself from pebbles as Feldspar landed.

"Feldspar, clear our rear, then come back to help with the fight," I said.

As Feldspar bugled and took off once more, Kreegor and I raised our shields, bent our knees, and readied for whatever came next. A few cries of anguish erupted down the hill, but they didn't last long. Feldspar had finished the bowmen, but there were still two enemy dragons down there.

I tried to see through the choke point, foiled by the angle and the pine trees. A minute became five. *Quicksilver, damn it, where are—*

A mountainous, echoing screech ricocheted between the peaks far above us, and Quicksilver shot out above the rocks, finally revealing herself. She tore down the mountain toward the choke point with enough power to bend trees in her wake.

"Well, I'm glad she's on our side," Kreegor commented, as two elves darted through the choke point and tried to huddle behind the boulders for safety. My knives made short work of them, one in each neck, but more elves poured through just as Quicksilver reached us.

That's when, for the first time, she truly lived up to her name.

With a feral roar, she opened her jaws and spewed a beam of silver magic onto the elves. It wasn't flame, but instead a massive, instantaneous spell. Before the men could even blink, the fleeing elves turned to solid silver in front of us, clanking to the ground like upended statues.

Quicksilver landed in the open space beyond, although "landed" was a generous term. She seemed to collapse from the air, slumping to the earth, all the power gone out of her. For a moment, I was certain she'd been run through with a blade, but her aura remained bright. If she were in pain, it would tighten or shrink.

Her breath ability. It drained all her energy.

Of course it had. She'd made *silver*—or at least some sort of metal. Jolene would know what it was, and how it could and couldn't be used or sold.

Is that how dragonsteel is made?

A spear glanced off Quicksilver's head as I marveled, and an orc bulled through the gap between boulders. The dragon snapped at the orc, biting its arm and picking it up like a doll, before smashing it against a rock with a wet smack.

But more orcs were coming, and I was out of knives. I bolted for the boulders, but an orc had already come through with an axe, and Quicksilver was busy eating the first orc, trying to regain her strength. This left the side of her neck exposed.

"Quicksilver! *No—*"

Light flashed, and from between the two boulders, something spun and flipped—and landed square on the orc's back. It clanged off the beast, but not without leaving a bloody mark. The orc lost its footing and toppled forward before it could swing at Quicksilver. It bought me just enough time to cleave its head from its shoulders.

Sweating, I turned to see Fieran running up to retrieve her sword. "Sorry," she said. "I'm not good at throwing swords."

I clapped a hand on her shoulder. "Are you kidding? You hit him. That's what matters."

She smiled, gray eyes flickering, then nodded back at the boulders.

"Quick left a trail of dragonsteel corpses back there. When the elves went down, the orcs appeared. I think they were hiding the whole time."

"And you were waiting to catch the elves from behind when we attacked the choke point and distracted them," I guessed. She nodded. "Great thinking, Fier. You're not half-bad at this."

"I miss battle," she admitted. "A lot."

With a stone-splitting crash, Feldspar backed into the clearing, and we whirled around. An elf prodded at Feldspar with a spear, outmatched but defiant. The Mount-class dragon stayed out of the weapon's range, eager to win without taking damage.

Kreegor fired an arrow at the elf from the pines, unleashing it with the poise of a master archer.

The elf sidestepped the arrow as easily as water moves around a rock, stabbing again at Feldspar, as if a nearby archer didn't concern him.

"That was my last one!" Kreegor shouted, but I was already running.

"Quicksilver, back leg down, now!"

The enormous dragon splayed out her back leg, and I raced up her ankle to her knee to her monstrous thigh, dashed between her back-spikes, and leapt.

Whatever magic protected the elf from projectiles alerted him again, and he sidestepped, but it wasn't enough to escape the complete arc of Grayson's sword in my hands. It was no expert move, just a wild swipe to take up as much space as possible, but I slashed the elf across his lower back.

He cried out, dropping his spear as I landed. I kept spinning the blade, losing my footing and falling even as I brought the sword through the backs of his knees.

I crashed, losing my grip, but an unearthly *crunch* cut off the elf's next scream. By the time I scrambled back to my feet, Feldspar had bitten deep into the elf's neck.

The dragon spat out the elf, then lunged into the forest, knocking over another, larger clay dragon as it began to emerge. The two red beasts tussled, and then Feldspar raised a paw and cratered the other dragon's throat. I blinked, astounded at the sheer power of the strike. The other dragon loosed a sad bugle, and fell.

I ran up to Feldspar, keeping an eye to the woods—but I heard shouts now, human ones, in my own language. Reinforcements had arrived.

"Four Demons, boy," I said. "How'd you know to hit him there?"

He rumbled at me, pressing at my cheek. For the first time in an hour, I remembered Star was still curled around my neck. Fesldspar was nuzzling *her*, not me.

I patted her. "Good girl. You kept your cool, didn't you?"

"Clay dragons," Fieran said, running up next to me. "They're weak at the throat. They normally keep their heads down, since their entire bodies are impervious to metal or stone weapons, so they're usually used at the front of any attacking party. Their breath ability also enhances their smell and taste, so they sometimes have their heads down, tracking enemies."

I raised an eyebrow. "Since when are you the dragon expert?"

"Every Vanguard learns about clays. We fight with them on the front lines all the time." Fieran threw a thumb at Quicksilver. "And I recognize that one, too. You've got yourself a forge dragon. They're rare as hell, and the state heavily guards them, so I wouldn't advertise that you've got one. Prince Zelkar's got a male, and it's common knowledge he's been looking for a female to mate it with."

A forge dragon, eh? I thought. That would be valuable indeed.

"Noted," I said, turning to face the noise of crashing feet in the forest. Becki appeared, riding Tilly, with Collette flapping along beside her.

"Thank the Demons," Becki said. "I'm sorry, we got your message but it took ages to rally the troops without Jolene. They won't take us seriously without a noble around, but I finally got to Captain Narvi when Quicksilver made a fuss. I think Feldspar told Quick what was happening."

Quicksilver looked up with blood dripping down her mouth. Feldspar hopped onto the dead elf proudly, chirping a string of dragon words.

"Should we harvest the ears on everything?" Grayson asked.

I surveyed the fallen. So many. It would be worth a small fortune—which I no longer had access to.

"Yeah, the bounties are all yours," I said. "But first, let's check the pit."

Chapter 104

An Official Tally

By the time we arrived to the pit, about a dozen soldiers were standing at my back.

"Narvi!" I called out, waving to him. "I've got a proposal for you!"

He jogged out of the regiment, his face flushed from battle. Apparently, a half-dozen elves and one dragon had emerged from the hole, and they'd been waylaid taking them down. My dragon, Dune, had helped. The blue Mount dragon was nearly full-red with blood.

"Yeah?" Narvi asked.

"You and your men take the bounties. I take any spoils from this pit."

He grinned. "You sure about that? The bounties on green elves are astronomical right now."

Narvi wasn't aware yet that I'd sworn off taking bounties. I pointed into the hole. "There might be eggs down there, or dragons, or nothing. It could mean a fortune too."

The captain looked to Kreegor and Grayson, who nodded. "None of us went in," Kreegor said. "So we don't know what's down there. Could be a total wash, or a trove."

As Narvi nodded, Kreegor winked at me. He knew I'd seen eggs, and lots of them, but he had my back. Once an alley orphan, always an alley orphan.

"Fine. This was mostly your fight anyway," Narvi said. "Let's have a look."

I took the lead, edging up to the lip of the hole, keeping my shield up. When I peered down into the dark, the rope ladders were gone, and the Shoulder dragons had all abandoned their nests. I reached a hand up to Quicksilver, and she let me dangle off her chin spikes as she lowered me down into the hole.

The eggs in the nests all remained, abandoned. It was a beautiful hoard, showcasing more varieties than I knew what to do with, with eggs of every color and size. Some of the Shoulder-size dragons might have been nursery dragons, tasked with watching the eggs of other breeds, like the ones I'd seen at the House of Cards formation.

Either way, Pinnacle Dragons had officially become profitable, the Biscuits be damned.

I landed at the bottom, still marveling, as Feldspar climbed down to join me. He landed with a thud and stormed into the massive cavern opening where we'd seen a big dragon's tail.

No sound emerged from the darkness, and a minute or so later, Feldspar returned with a bored grumble. He launched himself back up the inner walls of the pit, climbing up while avoiding the nests.

"All clear," I shouted. "And Becki?"

"Yes?"

"You'd better go back home and get some crates full of hay." I looked around at all the holes, each one glittering with color. "Lots and lots of crates."

When I climbed back out of the hole, I handed Grayson back

his sword with the handle extended. "Nice work, First-Rank Scout Grayson."

The man smiled, his brown eyes crinkling. "Many thanks, Lord Warren."

"What's in there?" Narvi asked, nodding at the cavern below. He absently extended a hand, holding the bag I'd dropped in my run through the stonewood. I took it.

"Dozens of eggs. But in the extended cavern?" I shrugged. "Who knows. I'm not going in there with no light."

"But it's empty? Of enemies?"

"That's what Feldspar seems to think."

He nodded, and set to forming an expeditionary team.

"That's going to be one helluva score," Kreegor said with a grunt. "But green elves, in our lands? That's new."

I was about to say that this worried me, too, when a distant roar raced over the jungle. When Feldspar heard it, he roared back. I squinted against the sunset to see another flight of dragons approaching from the west, with Duke Biscuit's gray Airship-class, Barton, in the middle.

While they approached, I borrowed a torch and went on ahead of the expeditionary party, determined to see the spoils before Biscuit's agents could claim them all. I tied a rappelling harness around my waist, then secured the rope to a tree before I descended. As I slowly dropped down, a baby dragon left its nest and landed on my head, grabbing my hair to curl up in a ball.

I reached the bottom, shimmied out of the harness, and stuffed the baby into the main pouch of my bag. The little yellow dragon went in without a complaint, and when I heard it eating my jerky, I couldn't help but sigh.

Inside the cavern I saw the signs of a recent kill.

A full-grown Mount dragon lay in the first chamber with its throat slit. The elves or the wyvern must have dragged it from the trap. Its legs had been bound, and they'd collected its blood in buckets next to the neck. Its flanks had been halfway butchered by the time we arrived and interrupted the process.

The wyvern appeared to have eaten all the best organs, too. It had stopped at the stomach parts, barely picking them over.

But the most important discovery was impossible to miss, waiting for me at the very front of the cavern: a nest with four wyvern eggs. I knew they were wyvern because they looked similar to dragon eggs, but had no auras.

The wyvern we killed had been a male, meaning the mother had to be out there somewhere. Behind the egg, I found shelves, beds, end tables, a dining area, and a fire pit. Green elves were civilized, to a point.

Feldspar landed behind me with no stealth. Four arrows stuck out of his red-brown scales, with a line of missing scales behind his head from a bite. As usual, the arrows had stuck in his skin the way they might stick into clay, doing no damage and drawing no blood. I could easily pull them out, so I did.

"Does the mother wyvern live?" I asked.

He sourly huffed, chittering a string of profanities. At least that was how I interpreted his attempt to talk. In the end, I assumed that he'd chased some elves, but lost them due to wyvern magic. A wyvern could dispel magic in a certain range, negating Feldspar's smell-enhancing breath ability, making it much harder for him to track them. I doubted they would launch a counter attack, given how badly we'd routed them.

I waved Feldspar over to lie down in the nest.

He eyed the eggs, huffed in annoyance, then lay down to keep them warm. I doubted I'd have the same control over the hatch-lings that I had over dragons, but I could still hatch and bond them like the elves had.

Unfortunately, wyverns were worthless in Parshil, because the king outlawed their use except in the case of special permits. He didn't want them interfering with Parshil's day-to-day life, which often relied on dragon labor and magic.

Once Feldspar had settled, I walked back to the bottom of the pit, finding Duke Biscuit already standing far above me.

"Oi, is the young lord Warren? What's down there, boy?" he asked.

I gritted my teeth. He still insisted on calling me *boy,* did he? *Just wait until you find out what fortune your men promised me —because they know bloody well I deserve it, and you don't.*

"Four wyvern eggs," I said, "and an elf camp. They appeared to be entrenched here, but they've now fled. If I had to guess, orcs had recently discovered them in the area, and were amassing for a conflict. We got in the middle of it."

"There must be a hundred Shoulder-class eggs here. Very nice find," Duke Biscuit said.

"Um, sir," Narvi cut in. "About that...."

I grinned, then turned away, walking around the nest to do a more thorough inspection. I found eight bows, at least a hundred fine arrows, a decent sword, and then a chest full of silver coins, more unique weapons, and jewelry that had definitely belonged to human nobles, given its craftsmanship. I even saw a piece from the artisan Jolene had liked, the woman called Gem whose works were all marked with a tiny diamond, and I pocketed it.

So it seemed the elves were civilized, but they had the stolen goods of dead humans. When I inspected a coin, I found it was the real deal, just with a king on the stamp I didn't recognize.

I headed out, having seen enough. "You want an official tally of my treasure?" I asked a red-faced Biscuit. "Or is this going to be another legal battle?"

Duke Biscuit scoffed. "The word of a captain is hardly binding."

"Oh? Would you rather I hand in all the elf ears myself, then, since either me or my dragons killed most of them?"

Duke Biscuit looked like he might spontaneously combust.

"Look, boy. How about this. You apparently have a war to win with some foreign Dragon Lord, so you can have the eggs. In six months they'll be an army, half-grown at least. Or you can sell them in exchange for adult fighters, I don't care. But we split the other loot."

I smiled. "Soldier's Code, Section Eight, Addendum Two," I recited. *"In the case of a combined combat effort with another non-soldier party of allies, the highest-ranked officer on site has the right to dispense the spoils of war as he sees fit.* Unfortunately, Your Grace, everything in this cave belongs to me. Captain Narvi promised it to me, and all of his men were witness."

After Rachel had defeated her boss, Illowyn, by so beautifully inventing a law on the spot, I'd gone ahead and looked up a few relevant laws myself. Given I'd already started doing combination kill-and-loots with the watchmaster's soldiers, it was only good sense that I'd memorized this one.

Even though I could barely see his face, I could tell that Duke Biscuit seethed.

I raised a finger. "Counterpoint," I said. "I could forfeit my entire find to you, in exchange for Pinnacle Dragons being recognized as a viable, profitable company, thus leading to a nullification of my ownership contract with you." I waved a hand at the walls of eggs. "In addition, I could promise to purchase all of these eggs back from you at full market rate, bulk sum."

The duke fell to stammering. "Why you... you...."

"This is worth quite a bit more than my current estate value," I said. "And as such, it is quite fair."

After all, even though the eggs were worth a great deal of money to Pinnacle, they didn't prove *viability*. They were a random find from a random event, not a result of any service of breeding provided by Pinnacle Farms.

In this way, I could prove viability without having to hope Rachel had made the numbers look good enough. There was always the chance she would fail.

The duke kicked the edge of the hole, scattering dirt on me. I closed my eyes and let the clods hit and fall off again. Really, it was nothing to me.

"Your business is worth twice the loot in this cave, and you know it!" the duke raged.

I opened my eyes again. "So you admit, before all these men, that Pinnacle Dragons is a valuable-and therefore profitable—company? I retract my offer, then. All this loot is now mine."

There was a pause, heavy with the scent of a storm. Feldspar gloated behind me with a soft, earthy chirrup.

"I'll get you for this," Duke Biscuit said lowly.

I smiled. "Whatever you say."

Chapter 105

Titles Galore

LAST YEAR, an elf had smashed a human city to pieces using dragons.

This year, I had defeated an encampment of elves—also with dragons.

It didn't balance the score, not even close. But it was a start, and I let that thought carry me—and all of my loot—right back to Duchess Nola. I thought it prudent to warn her that her husband had effectively given up his hold not only on Pinnacle Dragons, but on a dragon's weight in loot value.

Also, it was *her* that I didn't want to have as an enemy. Duke Biscuit was a cowardly, lecherous, opportunistic man. His wife was none of those things—except perhaps opportunistic.

"Glad you could join us," Duchess Nola said.

I stretched across her sitting-room couch, somewhat drowsy from my evening battle. "My pleasure," I said.

Duchess Nola sat on her own lavish couch, sunken into the seat, while a motherly figure sat primly beside her. Jasmine sat at the desk in the corner of what seemed to be a study, attending to paperwork. I caught her glancing at me more than once.

Nola said nothing more while a series of servants set down fresh tea and then retreated again.

The duchess used an underhand gesture to signal the couch beside her. "This is Second Matron Helin. Helin, this is Warren. I remove titles for a reason."

"And that reason?" Becki asked astutely. I'd asked her to come, in place of Jolene.

"Changes are coming to both Dasvilla, and to your position in it. Let me start with this," Duchess Nola said.

She had obviously coached Jasmine about this meeting, because the sixteen-year-old immediately started to read out loud,

By order of King Kurto and the Parshil Kingdom, all men of birth, noble or not, between the ages of fifteen and thirty summers, are hereby ordered to submit their name for a formal war draft.
Those selected will be commanded to sharpen their blades, tighten their bows, and ready their spears. If any such man is without a weapon, he must see his lord to gain one. Anyone seen to flee this draft will be put to death.
If you find yourself concerned by this decree, have courage. While the threats outside the walls of Parshil are substantial, our great people are up to the task.
As your king, I humbly ask for you to prepare, to understand, and to answer the call to save those you cherish, when that call comes.
In this, and in all things, your king thanks you.
Your humble servant,
King Kurto.

I let out a long and low whistle. "That was fast," I said. I'd had advance notice of the draft only this afternoon, but apparently it hadn't been *that* advanced.

"He released this after his Hand returned home from a disastrous meeting with *you*," Nola said. "Sent to all city leaders instantly via mushroom dragon."

"Can't say I'm shocked," I replied. "Smart of him to not mention me yet, either. That way, things can get dark before he offers me up as a golden scapegoat for my inevitable failure to kill an entrenched Dragon-Touched with twice the army and dragons that I have."

Nola eyed me, clearly not believing all these thoughts were my own. I didn't blame her. I could play the dumb brute with the best of them.

I turned my head. "Back to our guest, though. Nice to meet you, Helin. I assume you're here for a reason?"

"Indeed," the elderly woman said, nodding her head to Jasmine.

Duchess Nola flashed a warm smile. "My husband does not know it yet, but he will be taking his second-wife to her home to be with her family during these trying times, leaving me in charge of the estate." Her middle-aged face tightened at the mention of the Lady Oscilla. "Before he leaves, however, he will approve some changes I requested."

The duke's daughter procured a piece of parchment with a flourish, and began reading: "'I, Duke Biscuit, hereby certify that Lord Warren is promoted to Viscount Warren of Dasvilla. With his change in title, he is hereby granted one villa at Seventh Street, address Fourteenth. With his change in title, he is hereby granted one barn on Lilo Street, address Eleventh. His taxes are hereby altered, his responsibilities adjusted to suit his title, and his purpose correctly aligned to match his stature in the Parshil Kingdom."

Becki's eyes shot wide, and her fingernails dug into my shoulder from shock. I gently removed her hand before I stood and walked over to the desk, my hand extended.

Jasmine handed me the parchment and then an inked quill a second later. I signed the paperwork before returning to my seat. I stared at Duchess Nola for a good minute without saying a word.

"My husband has been embarrassed thoroughly," she finally said, "and with this new influx of elf ears, no matter who hands them in, he will gain attention that he does not want. We must therefore shift blame. *You* will take that blame, in exchange for this title. *My husband was away. You were left in charge. Elves encroached on our land during your tenure here.* Is that understood?" she said.

"Sure thing," I replied, because this wouldn't damage me at all. The king already wanted me dead. What else could this do? Make him want me *double*-dead?

"It was my idea, actually," Jasmine said with a cocky grin. "Now, I'll be able to work for you. It wasn't fitting for a duke's daughter to be serving under a lowly lord, and I didn't want to be in Caliph, where I already had a man try to force me into his home without a chaperone present. Within my first week!"

I turned to her, concerned, and replied, "Your virtue shall be protected with me." I eyed her mother and emphasized, *"Completely."*

Duchess Nola breathed out, tension visibly going out of her shoulders. I had the feeling that her wily daughter had her worried. Jasmine didn't seem like she'd be easily controlled, but if she fell for every handsome lord she looked at, she was a disaster waiting to happen.

"As a viscount, you will have your own militia," Jasmine piped up. "This gives you leeway to assign these new draft conscripts to local positions and training. Those conscripts will have no loyalty to the king or duke that has drafted them. They will be angry.

"However, you are beloved here in Dasvilla, and they will follow you better than they would follow my husband. This is how you solidify the southlands. This is how you protect our people."

"I'm part of your transition," Helin said, straightening her back. "I've served the Lord and Lady of Dasvilla as their head steward for many years, and now Duchess Nola will pass me on to you. I will lead your household servants, who—"

"Sorry Helin, but I have a head maid already."

I could almost see the woman's hackles rising. "It is required of a lord to have an experienced head steward," she declared. Apparently, Helin had zero issue giving me moxie.

"You. Are. The. Dragon-Touched," she enunciated. "You can't deny it. Your estate must be ready to entertain dignitaries, you must have a guard, you must process taxes. You will stay alive by having a series of servants who are assassins. When you are on the front lines, your loved ones will need to be kept safe in your absence. Your current head maid, Aliese, is not qualified to manage such things."

I found myself nodding slowly. "You do make good points. But I thought Lady Etonia used to be the Biscuit's steward? Are you new?"

"I worked in tandem with Etonia, as her superior," the woman said smoothly. "As for Aliese, she may still manage your home. In fact, I will train her in my craft. I don't have many years left, and it is time I took on an apprentice," Helin conceded.

"Fine. I'm honored. But is all of this strictly necessary? "

"Yes, Warren, it is," Jasmine said. "You need a proper framework in place to run this city, if you want to fly off to war without leaving your loved ones vulnerable to attack while you're away."

Becki cleared her throat and looked at me. "You're going to go away?"

I hadn't had a chance to tell anyone but Jolene about the king's likely call for me to fight General Iskar.

"Okay, so I'm a viscount," I said, deflecting. "What house am I supposed to move into, then? I don't want to be far from the Cage."

"I am preparing it," Helin said. "It'll be fit for a king shortly."

I stood. "And Pinnacle?"

Jasmine practically leapt from her seat, as if she'd been waiting for this exact question. She practically threw herself at me in an attempt to hand me a sheaf of papers—the Pinnacle contract I'd made with the Biscuits, marked *null and void,* with Duchess Nola's signature.

"Father will sign when he's back," Jasmine said, hopping from foot-to-foot like a dog who'd seen a treat. "If he doesn't, Mother says you can sue and win."

I frowned and looked at Nola. "How can you be so sure?"

She smiled. "Because we got Rachel's paperwork just today, and it's airtight. You didn't need my fool husband to declare your business viable, Lord Warren. Not when you have a sea-dragon like Keeper Rachel on your side."

Chapter 106

Break Out the Bubbly!

ON MY WAY out of the keep, I stopped through one of the Biscuit's kitchens, swiped two bottles of bubble-wine off a shelf, shot the cook a wink, and stepped out again. If the cook wanted to tell on me, let her.

We made it. Pinnacle is viable!

I had a skip in my step all the way out the door, where Fieran met me, since they hadn't allowed her to come in. She dropped a cigar and rubbed it into the dirt with a foot, saluting the page on staff. I expected the stuffy young noble to scowl at her, but he just laughed and saluted back.

"Making friends, I see?" I asked her.

"You can bond with anyone over a good smoke and some boredom," she replied, raising an eyebrow at my bottles. "Good news?"

I grinned. "Pinnacle is viable. One month in, and the business has proven itself."

She huffed. "Give me one of them bottles."

I passed it over, and she surprised me by untying the wire net and popping the cork within five seconds. She didn't even break her stride.

"What?" she said, taking a swig. "You think I was *sober* all those nights I spent faking orgasms against my own bedroom door?"

"Ha! I ever tell you how convincing you were?"

She grinned. "Wouldn't you like to know."

"Maybe," I said, shrugging. "I do wonder what you'd look like actually dressed as a woman."

"Meaning, would I be fuckable?" she replied. "Because at the rate you're going, you'd just about fuck anything that moves."

I belted out a laugh and shoved her in the arm, and she shoved me back. We strode the rest of the way into town, swapping swigs of the wine. I was feeling pretty good by the time the Cage came into view, a cubic shape of black outlines against the evening twilight.

"Oh, shit. We got a pack of dogs coming."

The last leg of the journey was about to take us past two Enforcers walking toward the keep. We fell quiet and let them by without comment. They didn't seem to notice us, buried in their own conversation.

"Something tells me they're up to something," Fieran said.

I nodded. "Yeah. But they've kept under the horizon for a while now. I think the justicar's got plans, but he's been keeping out of things since he tried to have Garm shake me down for my night dragon."

Her gaze followed the Enforcers' backs. They continued heading for the keep. "Maybe he's waiting to see who'll come out on top in Dasvilla?" she suggested. "So he can know who to target with his scheming."

"Maybe. Now if we only knew what that scheme was."

"You think he might be working for the king, with his expansion plan?"

"Probably, but thankfully that has become a six-month plan, so we don't have to deal with it now. I'll put eyes on it soon, now that Pinnacle is settled. What about you, though? Where are you gonna be in six months?"

"You mean if the assassin doesn't kill me for not taking the nightweed root?"

"You won't need to worry about that," I said.

Fieran raised an eyebrow.

"Trust me," I added.

She nodded slowly, falling silent for a few more strides, until we reached the gate of the Cage.

She stopped. "You want to know if I'll help with the rebellion out of Ashkar."

I stopped with her, setting down our now-empty bottle. I dropped a hand on her shoulder.

"Look," I said. "I'm not trying to pressure you. But if you took your allies—the rebellion cult your mother built—and turned them to your side, *as yourself,* then you could support Vanessa when the time comes. She and I are no longer a thing, but I know her. She's a good woman. She won't like what her father is doing.

"With your support as her long-lost sister, you could support her claim to the throne without earning yourself the bastard treatment." By that, I meant assassination, and she knew it. "You wouldn't be king or queen or whatever, but you'd be able to live your life, and you'd probably be someone important."

She sighed, and before she could speak, I patted her shoulder. "Just something to think about. This stuff is far off."

"Yeah. Far off," she agreed. "I'll consider it. Now go on inside and celebrate with your ladies. I'll stand guard until Copper and Jolene get back, and I'll make sure to get the new dragons settled at the farmhouse."

"Thanks, Fier. You're the best page a guy could ask for."

She outright punched me in the arm. "Oh, shut up."

I chuckled and left her there, trudging across the newly groomed front courtyard, up the steps, and into the foyer. Jolene wouldn't arrive for some time yet, but Becki and Aliese should be home, and I still had one bottle of wine.

"Oh *laaaadddiiiies,*" I called out.

"In here!" Becki called from the den, while Aliese giggled. I followed the light and sound of a crackling fire into what had effectively become Jolene's office, although all the papers had been shoved aside to make room on the table for a game of Dragoness. Aliese and Becki sat on opposite sides, and while Aliese rose to hurry over to me, I saw Becki surreptitiously switch two pieces around.

"Hi Warren! Where's Fieran? Oooh, is that wine?"

"Is there a special occasion?" Becki said. "Oh, and Aliese—*checkmate.*" She stabbed the dragoness piece down, knocking over Aliese's dragon with aplomb.

Aliese gasped in theatrical rage. "Oh, Becki. How could you?"

"By cheating," I said, untwisting the wire net on the second bottle. "That's how."

Becki shot to her feet. "Warren! You dare make such accusations?"

I popped the cork loudly and tossed it at her. "Forget the game. Guess what dragon breeding company just proved itself today?"

Aliese's eyes went wide, and Becki grinned. Then, as if they had rehearsed it, both women threw themselves at me, hugging me so hard that I staggered back and fell on the couch. They followed, toppling onto me, giggling. I barely managed to keep the wine upright.

"Girls, girls, girls! Save the drunken theatrics for *after* the wine!"

"But, oh Warren, that's great news!" Aliese said, dropping a knee between my thighs and leaning into my face to kiss me. I blinked as she put tongue into it, tilting her head to taste the wine on my breath.

"Mmm, you got started without us," she purred, one of her hands sinking into my thigh. "But you chose a good vintage."

I glanced at Becki, but she had crawled right up next to me. She curved a hand under my chin, then around my jaw, pulling my face towards her.

"Now you have to choose something else," she said, flicking her cold tongue into my ear. "Let's celebrate properly. One of us gets the wine, and the other gets you."

With that, she slid her tongue into my mouth, so hard and breathless that I had no defense. While Aliese's hand fumbled for my belt buckle, Becki pressed up tight against me, her tongue exploring spaces around my tongue that I hadn't known existed until now.

She broke away, reaching for my thigh. I looked down in time to see Aliese retrieve my cock from my underclothes, and start stroking it.

"Well, aren't you both forward tonight," I said, as stunned as I was horny.

Becki's hand slithered into my clothes, where she squeezed my balls lightly while Aliese kept working. Neither one seemed to care that the other was there. It was all smiles, all flushed cheeks and short breaths.

"Come on," Aliese said, leaning close to speak into my ear while she gripped me. "Let me take care of Master tonight. You can bend me over this couch and celebrate inside me."

I laughed, but Becki kissed the sound away, then whispered against my lips, "Or you could let me chill your cock in this hot, hot room. Maybe I'll make you explode, just like that glass candlestick did."

Something inside me shuddered, and my balls shuddered right along with it. "You want me to choose between you? I'm not doing that."

"Oh, no. Not between us," Aliese said.

Becki reached for the bottle and took a swig. She breathed out in harsh satisfaction and said, "Just choose which of us will go first."

Chapter 107

Well that was Unexpected

I LOOKED from one woman to the other, Aliese keeping her hand hard on the top half of my shaft, going fast, and Becki with her lips glistening from the wine.

"Becki, hand her the wine and get down on your knees," I said thickly. "Aliese, take off your dress, and then drink."

As they both smiled, stepping off the couch to comply, I hurried to thrust off my shirt. How much time before Jolene got home?

Why am I counting? I told her no lies. There's no sense in hiding anything from her.

Aliese set down the bottle, then deftly wiggled her big tits out of her tight maid's uniform, leaving her in a simple corset and panties. Meanwhile, Becki tugged my pants down over my hips. I took my shirt off, enough to feel the warmth of the fire on every inch of me.

I scooted forward on the couch, until my balls hung slightly over the edge. Becki took my cock in her hand.

"Drink," I said. "Both of you."

Aliese smiled softly and reached for the bottle again, while Becki took my cock in her eerie, cold mouth.

I moaned from the feel of it, my body hot from desire while her mouth was so chill. There was nothing unpleasant about it—the sensation sent me over the moon, leaving me half-mindless. Becki took me to the back of her throat, hacked loudly, then did it again.

Meanwhile, Aliese took a second swig, licking first the mouth of the bottle, then her lips. I tugged her closer by the panties, then slipped my fingers into them. I parted the lips of her sex with my knuckles, making her sigh.

I closed my eyes, allowing both women to sway against me for a few more strokes of both cock and pussy. My hand came to rest on Becki's head, and the next time she deep-throated me, I pulled her off.

"Pants off and drink," I said. "Shimmer, Master's cock is dirty again. Make sure you clean it up good."

The women switched off, Becki taking the bottle and Aliese kneeling in place. While Aliese's hot mouth met my cold, stiff dick, Becki took a swig and undid her trousers at the same time.

I reached into them, and flicked two fingers into her pussy. She rocked against me, swallowing more wine, while Aliese practically *sipped* at my cock, gently playing with the tip, kissing and sucking, licking off beads of seed with her tongue.

I kept my eyes open this time, watching the way Becki sagged against me, forgetting the wine, letting it fall to the side of her thigh. She let her head roll back, mouth open, breaths heavy as I pleasured her with my hand. Aliese took swigs of me, her cheeks puffing, tongue circling. She traced a circle around the ridges of my head.

"Aliese. Your corset. Becki. Down."

They switched again, and this time Aliese started working off her corset one ribbon-loop at a time, while Becki moaned her mouth onto my cock. Her throat rumbled around my shaft.

Aliese wrangled out of her corset, throwing it down and exposing that gorgeous dragon tattoo to the front of my face. I felt it again—that strange sense of memory—when I saw it. *Scales under my hand as I felt her power. Human skin against my snout as I felt his.*

"Oh, Master. That feels good," Aliese said, dropping forward, one hand on the couch back as my fingers played inside her. The closeness of her big tits shot me back out of the memory, and the moisture of her sex made me ache.

"I'm going to make you come," I whispered against her neck. She quivered against me, then pressed the wine to my mouth and tipped the bottle back. I drank.

Becki popped off my cock, then stroked it, hard and fast. "You're too big for just me, Warren. My throat's getting sore."

"Let me help her," Aliese whispered. "Please...."

I moved faster inside her, my thumb catching her nubbin. "Come, then. As fast as you can."

She nodded, set the bottle aside, and then climbed right up onto the couch and planted a foot on the couch back behind my head. Catching her drift, I pulled out of her and slid my hand around her thigh, ducking closer. I clamped my mouth onto her clit and flicked my tongue down her folds.

"Oh, *Tallan*," she gasped, using her old nickname for me.

"Shimmer," I said against her clit, and then I started spelling the alphabet onto it with my tongue.

"Oh, my girl's stepping her game up, huh?" Becki said. "Well, two can play at that game."

With that, she sank her mouth to my base, getting me slick so her stroking could go smoother. Then she combined the two actions, sucking and stroking, keeping me wet and hard.

I held like that for a good minute, until I felt my high starting to build. Aliese was dripping wet now, and I was just about to tell her *fuck your orgasm, I want you first,* when we all froze in place.

The front door had opened.

My eyes went wide, and Aliese stumbled back from me while Becki shot to her feet. We all spun toward the door, but I knew exactly who had arrived. I could feel Copper on the front lawn, yawning from her long ride, and Alabaster being led out through the gate.

"Jolene," I said, stunned. She stood just inside the foyer, staring through the opened glass doors to the den.

Where she saw Aliese in her panties, a pants-less Becki, and my cock pointed straight up in the air.

"Shit," I said, scrambling to get up. *This was a bad idea, bad idea—*

Jolene held up a hand in front of her, a commanding gesture, which seemed so odd on her. Her face showed nothing. It was dangerously blank.

"Jo, I'm sorry—"

"Don't be," she said. "This is who you are, Warren." Her eyes darted to Becki, then Aliese, and she swallowed loud enough for me to hear from a room away. Her hand fell, but I made no move toward her. *Message received: stay the fuck away.*

I had no idea what to say, but she beat me to it, setting down the satchel she'd carried all the way back from Ashkar. She looked at it carefully the whole time, as if it were of extreme interest to her. All three of us didn't so much as twitch.

"You've all been busy while I'm gone," she said flatly. "Doing everything without me. Well, I'll show you."

She straightened and looked us over, one by one.

"Jo," I croaked, unsure how to feel. Did I feel bad that it turned out like this? Or awful, because there was no other way it could have happened?

She's right. This is just who I am.

"I'm tired of pretending," Jolene said, closing her eyes. "I'm so fucking tired of pretending this isn't hot to me. It's so hot. I feel like I'm burning."

Time stilled. I could have sworn it was magic.

Did she just say this was hot?

I thought back to her jealousy, to her stolen kiss, to the want she expressed behind the front stairs. It dawned on me then: if she was the type of woman who couldn't share, she would have given up on me weeks ago.

Instead, she'd held on. She'd built up to *this*.

"Would you... care to join us?" I asked.

Chapter 108

I Did Warn You that Nobles were Crazy

HER EYES OPENED, as blue as the sky.

"I thought you'd never ask."

Then Jolene left, up the stairs, with all of us standing there, in different states of naked and aroused. We looked at each other, unsure, only to hear her run back down again. She turned the corner, holding a basin of water.

"It's been a long trip," she told me. "I'll wash up while I watch. When you've made them both happy, I'm next."

With that, she dropped the bowl next to an armchair—and started untying the bow at the lower back of her dress. That ribbon would lead to the corset back, to a slow unlacing, to a fall of fabric to the floor... and to a very naked Jolene.

"Go on, Aliese, preserve my modesty," Jolene said. "Cover his eyes. You know with what."

Aliese jumped, making her tits hop; then she eyed me. I sat down, held out a hand, and nodded her forward. Whatever magic this was, I didn't want to spoil it. I'd do what Jolene asked, and just see what happened next.

As Aliese pulled her sex back against my mouth, Becki also knelt to lick my shaft with her cold tongue. The heat of Aliese against my lips and the cold on my cock was an erotic combination, but I was so much more distracted by the idea of what I was missing by not being able to see Jolene.

This can't be real, I thought. I'd planned to court her originally, to go through the chaste and noble process, and to set aside all other women for her. Since then, I'd fallen in love with Becki and Aliese both. I knew I couldn't leave them, and I wouldn't give up Kenna either. I wanted to get to know them all better.

In a way, I'd sworn off Jolene as a possibility. But why? She'd been sleeping in my bed every night lately, even though she knew my intentions with other women. I'd thought she was trying to love me despite my flaws—but was she just discovering she loved me *because* of them?

Did she find all this as erotic as I did? As *all of us* did?

Had I really lucked out onto the best situation any man alive could ever hope for?

Well, far be it from me to fuck it up, I told myself, gripping one cheek of Aliese's butt and putting more effort into my tongue work. If Jolene wanted a show, I'd give it to her... and if *I* wanted a show, I had to make Aliese come, so that she could fall back and expose Jolene.

So I put in my best, albeit somewhat drunken, effort. I wrote *poetry* on that poor maid's clit. I had her moaning my name, had every thought out of her head in mere moments. She'd forgotten Jolene could see her, she'd forgotten Pinnacle was solvent, she'd forgotten everything but my tongue on her sex and her own need to keep upright.

The curtain rod groaned as she seized a curtain, using it to hold herself up as she thrust against me, mad with building pressure. With the curtain moved, I wondered if we could be seen from outside, but at the same time, I didn't care.

As Becki kept her own ministrations slow and steady, her fingers pulsating rhythmically against my balls and her mouth dipping over my head, I went wild on my beloved Shimmer.

"Tallan... *Tallan,*" she moaned, more breathless each minute. "You're gonna make me... you're...."

"*Shimmer,*" I breathed against her, before starting again, but it was already too late. That one word, that one change of pace made her thigh clamp against one side of my head.

She cried out, first loud and then louder. I reached inside her with two fingers to feel the tension of her coming, while Becki moved faster, trying to get me there, too.

As Aliese went limp, I helped her down to the couch, where she fell back with a gasp. Her panties remained on, but they were soaked through. Her tits rolled as she breathed heavy breaths, and I had to appreciate her beauty in that moment. At any other time, I would have told Becki to stop and had my way with Aliese, to completion.

But my attention was drawn back to the armchair, and to Jolene, curled up inside it.

She was naked, but not to me. She'd undressed, and her bare shoulder and collarbone glistened with bathwater, but she'd found the time to curl up in the fine wool blanket that she liked to use when she worked late. All the best parts of her were covered, with only her head, neck, shoulder, and feet showing. She'd pulled herself into a ball on the chair, her eyes hooded as she watched Becki work.

And falling between the breasts I couldn't see was a single gold chain. My gaze alighted on it.

I'd seen it before. Did she always wear the same chain?

Her eyelashes fluttered, drawing my attention, and her blue eyes met mine, as vast as the sea. She pulled the blanket aside to reveal one perfect breast, exactly the size of a hefty handful, with a rigid pink nipple—and my mother's turquoise pendant curled beside it, at the end of the long golden chain.

I stiffened. *She still has that? Impossible. She kept it all these years?*

I had barely remembered the memory myself. I'd been so

young. Yet Jolene wore the heirloom now, tonight, in this place where I wouldn't be denied.

Is that why she said she couldn't wear that necklace in Caliph? Because she was already wearing one that she couldn't take off?

My heart swelled. With that semi-precious gemstone, she was saying all she needed to say: *I have always loved you.*

Jolene smiled, and in a rough voice, she said, "One woman down. Another to go." She nodded at Becki, who'd never once slowed her work. In fact, she'd brought me all the way to my crest, and if I gave her so much as three more sucks, I'd be done for. Seeing Jolene's bare breast was making muscles tense in my cock.

I suddenly felt like I was noticing every twitch of my own skin, and if Jolene threw off that blanket right in this moment, I'd be making a fat mess inside Becki's mouth.

"Becki, up. Your turn," I rasped, gripping her shoulder.

She popped off and looked up at me with those surreal copper eyes. Her dark blue hair hung furiously about her face, and she looked like a wild creature with those slightly blue, puffed lips.

"Where do you—" she started to say, but I scooched back on the couch and tugged her with me. She crawled into my lap and tried again. "What can I—"

I pushed her panties aside, found her hole, and thrust my hips up to get into her. She gave a short, rapturous scream, then sank onto me, gripping the back of the couch with her hands.

"Lord Warren," she breathed. "I always forget how deep you—"

"Fuck me," I said, gripping her fine ass with one hand and thumbing her nub with the other. The bead was already slightly engorged with pleasure. "Let's see who can come first."

She nodded and rose up, her thighs tensing on either side of mine as she lifted her own weight and sank down again. I kept up a steady flick on the bead of her sex, exactly how I knew she liked it, but I was close. Especially when I could see Jo over

Becki's shoulder, her hand working between the shapes of her legs under the blanket. Her blue eyes had gone hazy again.

Becki looked over her shoulder. "Fuck, that's hot," she breathed. "It's hot to be watched." She faced me. "I want to make you come, Warren... so let's come together, for Jo."

Chapter 109

You Liked That, Did You?

I NODDED, wordless, and kept fingering her, trying to focus beyond the cold hard pleasure of her inner walls riding me. It took longer with Becki because of the magical coldness, but that also made it better—it just lasted and lasted and lasted, feeling so different the whole time.

She missed a beat in her rocking. "Oh, Warren... *there....*"

The strangled word was direction enough. I held to the current motion of my finger to her clit, and she breathed in sharply, then again, then again even louder, fucking me each time, until she let out all the pleasure in a long and tumultuous cry.

I pushed her off me, but it was too late. I groaned between my teeth as I came right against her outer lips, and when she put her weight down on my cock, I slid back into her and finished there. Jolene hissed from her chair, her hand working more frantically than ever, but my gaze was drawn to Becki.

"Mmmm," she moaned, rolling her head back and exposing her throat to me. "That feels good."

I spurted again, and she twitched as she felt it. I felt like my chest was melting into my stomach.

"I was already coming outside of you," I whispered. "You didn't need to do that."

She finished unbuttoning her shirt and pressed her sweet tits to my face. "But I wanted to. I'm sorry." She laughed. "You said before that you trusted me because I *didn't* try to have your baby. So I guess you won't trust me anymore."

I sighed, turning my head to tuck a nipple between my teeth and suck it. She shuddered.

I might have just fathered my first child, I thought. But as a noble, I'd need an heir—especially as a noble that everyone else wanted dead. Might as well start making babies now, especially when Becki had already agreed to be my second wife.

As for my first wife... she had no complaints.

Becki caught my eyes wandering and ducked down to kiss my forehead. "Go to her," she whispered. "I'll take Aliese out. This night should belong to you both."

I nodded, and Becki rose off my cock, stepped away, and gathered up a still-insensate Aliese. The two staggered out of the den, closing the glass doors behind them.

I rose from the couch, my cock slackening. If only Becki hadn't been so good at what she did—then I could take Jolene right this moment.

"You liked that, did you?" I asked, crossing the small rug to drop a hand on the arm of her chair. I leaned over her, and she tilted her head back so our mouths were close. She nodded at me, her hand still working beneath the blanket.

"Yes, milord. I'm so wet over it. I get wet every time I hear them moan."

I reached for my cock, held it carefully, and started doing my best to get it working again. Her gaze flicked to my head, popping up inside my fist.

"Show me how beautiful you are. And make yourself come for me," I said. "And I'll fuck you the way I know you've been dreaming of."

She nodded, and she curled the delicate fingers of her free hand around the edges of the blanket and began to lower it to one side. Both her gorgeous tits were there for the grabbing now, and then her flat stomach with the gentle indent of her navel, then the triangle of shaved hair....

Shaved? I raised my eyebrows. "When did you find time to do that?"

Her lips had parted, her eyes watching my face as I looked over every exposed part of her with rabid hunger.

"Ever since we started sleeping in the same bed, I've kept it up... I just never had the courage... I wasn't sure...."

When she couldn't seem to finish the sentence, I asked, "And you're sure now?"

She parted the blanket over her pink sex, over her pale thighs spread slightly in the chair. Her other hand worked between them, several fingers deep inside her while the heel of her palm worked her bead. My cock twitched, getting there.

"Yes," she breathed.

I dropped my weight onto my elbow, drawing closer to her, and freeing my hand up to touch the turquoise pendant.

"You've loved me all this time?" I asked.

She didn't hesitate. "Yes."

"Get up, Jo. Right now."

Hastily she took her fingers out of herself, and no sooner had she gained her feet than I gripped the outsides of her shoulders and pushed her roughly across the room to the nearest expanse of undecorated wall. She went willingly, and as soon as I shoved her against the paneling, I dropped to my knees.

She came about one minute later.

"Warren!" she screamed. "Yes, Warren!"

I'm sure it was all in my head, but she tasted like sugar. It was hard to draw away from her, but my cock was ready again. I don't know what madness had possessed me to be ready so quickly. Maybe I'd been getting too much practice.

"Do you want me, Jolene?" I whispered into her ear.

She seemed to be crying as she looped her arms around my neck. "Yes."

I lifted first one of her legs, then the other, heaving her back against the wall. "Tell me how you want me."

"Inside," she said. "Inside all the way. And finish there. Please. Make me your wife. Give me everything you've got left."

"You like that, do you? You like my leftovers?"

"Yes. Please Warren, I'm so hot. I need you."

I positioned my hips, found her entrance, and swung into her.

I'd intended to keep it slow, to make her mad with the meandering pace of it, but as soon as I felt the tender flinch of her lost maidenhood, I had to thrust again, and again, and *again*.

She never so much as grunted in pain, just that one faint hiss and then a wild moan on every single captured breath as I fucked her with all my might against that wall. Her thighs taut to my hips, her hole slick and tight, the way she tensed and loosened and scrabbled to keep hold of me, the prodding of her nipples against my chest—

I went until my legs shook, giving it to her the way I'd nearly done on accident on the dragonflight. She never stopped moaning. The sounds she was making made my mind spin out of control, a barrel roll in my head.

I started sweating and grunting, my expression forceful as I focused on holding her up, on filling her, on sinking to my base, on merging my hot core with hers....

"Jo," I exhaled.

"Warren, I love you."

I lost control then, and I came.

In that moment, I felt my future pour into her—my children, my household, my new noble line. The house of Orpheus-Minax, of Warren the Dragon-Touched. Would my children be Dragon-Touched, too?

"I love you too, Jolene," I breathed. "I love all of you, with all of me."

"I know," she replied. "I know, Warren."

I had to ask now, while my legs were still working. "Will you marry me, Jo? Will you be my first wife?"

She tightened her grip, clinging tight. We didn't want this to end.

"Oh, Warren. You know that I will."

———

I woke the next morning with Jolene stretching in the bed beside me. It was like all our recent mornings had been, only better. So much better.

She rolled to face me, nuzzling her nose against mine. "I'll never get used to this," she said.

I pulled her close. "I refuse to. I want every time to feel like our first."

With that promise made, I kissed her deeply, and just as I tensed to roll on top of her, she gasped.

"Oh, Warren, I forgot!"

I gave her a few inches of space, although it was hard for me. "Forgot what?"

"While I was coming back to Dasvilla! I finally had time for some reading, and I read a story in a children's book I found in my old bedroom. I learned something new about the Dragon-Touched!"

My lust suddenly flared and died, as if it had been lit aflame and then doused. All my attention was on her next words.

"Jo, tell me."

She seemed to deflate a little. "Well, it's not much," she said. "But apparently, creating a Dragon-Touched requires the sacrifice of a Behemoth dragon. It's not hereditary."

I frowned. "A sacrifice—?"

"Wait! Before you let that upset you," Jolene blurted, "you should know that it was worded oddly. According to the story, a powerful dragon had to 'pour out its heart and sacrifice its own memory' to create a Dragon-Touched."

Pour its heart out. Sacrifice memory.... I let the words wander through my head, but they made no sense.

"I've never even met a Behemoth dragon, except for Alabaster," I said. "How could one have sacrificed for me?"

She snuggled against me again. "I'm sorry, Warren. I don't know. It might have just been flowery language."

Maybe. Or maybe not.

"Either way, we can think about it later," I said. "For now, I want to make this beautiful morning last. Tell me... have you got any ideas?"

Chapter 110

Dragon versus Dragon

COPPER SNARLED AHEAD OF ME, snapping at any person dumb enough to get in range of her. I sighed. Old man Garmond in Ashkar had been right—these so-called mine dragons were violent. If she was like this with a Dragon-Touched keeping her in line, I can't imagine what she'd be like in the wild.

Still, it made her useful, and it made me stand out in Dasvilla's thriving market, as did the royal night dragon on my shoulder. The more I stood out, the better. As we walked, whispers trailed me.

"Who is that? Everyone's whispering."

"He's Lord Warren Orpheus-Minax, you dunce. The Dragon-Touched who's gonna kill the other Dragon-Touched."

"Is that a night dragon around his neck? I didn't believe those rumors."

"Well, the copper dragon's real. What is that breed, anyway?"

"Do you think he can win in six months?"

I needed to make friends everywhere that I went over the next half-year, so that if the enemy Dragon-Touched did happen to kill me, at least a few people would question the story they were told about it. And if I succeeded and went on to expose the king's treachery, I could use all the support I could get.

"Be nice, Copper," I said after she nearly took a kid's ear off when he got too close to me. Luckily, the kid thought it was hilarious. He ran into an alley to meet his friends, laughing and pointing back at Copper, as if she'd somehow blessed him with a love-nip or something.

Nobles took the treatment worse, occasionally following us and spouting off obscenities. I ignored them, because I cared more about the approval of commoners than useless nobles, some of whom were already complicit in the king's plot to sacrifice his western cities.

"Aren't you itchy in that shit?" Fieran asked, at my right side and one step back, still playing page.

For once, I'd entered a market wearing fine robes fit for a king, and it felt ridiculous. I felt like a walking coat rack, with two shirts and two coats, each one buttoned up in different places. My belt was barely able to carry a sword; it was more decorative than anything.

"Not itchy. Hot," I admitted.

Copper liked the clothes well enough, though, since my viscount colors were purple and black with a copper-colored dragon emblem over the heart. I'd wanted to honor both my royal night dragon and Copper, who went with me nearly everywhere now.

"You'll have to get used to that," Jolene said, hanging on my left arm, wearing a dress that matched my obscenely voluminous clothing—though for some reason, she had less material on than I did. *Because I'm not Viscountess yet,* she'd explained. *When I take that title, trust me, they'll make me into a tent.*

And you'll get dragon droppings all over it, I'd replied. *And probably hay up the sleeves.*

Behind me, one of my guards gave a shout. A full six men now protected me from all sides but the front, since Copper refused to share that duty.

As we progressed through the various sections of the market, our party garnered a lot of attention. Most of the people in the lower dragon market weren't noble, and yet Star, my night dragon, was clearly visible on my shoulder.

We also dragged a massive wagon loaded with eggs between my guards. Alabaster, the white dwarf Behemoth from Ashkar, had insisted on being the pack horse for this trip, even though it wasn't a task he'd ever taken up before I'd bought him. And by *insisted*, I meant he'd stuck his head through the harness and growled threateningly at anyone who made moves to take it off again.

I had to give him credit, though: he had the low and terrifying growl of a Behemoth, if not the size of one. I'd thought it best to let him have his way.

When we arrived at the vacant lot where we'd made our appointment, I spread my arms wide at the old lady standing there with her arms folded.

"Missa!" I boomed. "So good to see you."

She grunted, unimpressed. We walked across one empty market lot to reach a sales wagon the next plot over. Missa stopped next to the window on the wagon, which she could use to sell her wares on the road.

"Don't roar niceties at me," the merchant said sourly. "The Dragon-Touched title has gone to your head. You're just here 'cuz I hired you to be here. A hired man, that's all you are."

With that, she pushed open the side panel of the wagon, exposing six long lines of eggs. These were rejects, which she'd purchased as part of our agreement for today. After my promotion and the celebration that followed it, it was now time to start forming my dragon army. I had to decide which dragons to keep, which to sell, and which to breed.

Jasmine had taken up the mantle of this particular task, comparing breeds, composing graphs and charts and columns, and creating a theoretical, rounded-out army of dragons with a variety of useful abilities. I was here to collect the remaining dragons on her list.

As for the money-making side of the business, that would continue in the original barn, which I had purchased back from Duke Biscuit at the promised double rate. In there, our alphas and a couple of select bonded mates would be hard at work producing best-selling hybrids to generate income for the rest of our work.

Feldspar was now one such bonded male. He'd fallen in love with one of the females that Count Yeli had gifted to Jolene, and he hadn't been good for much else since then. Apparently he was old enough to breed, even though he wasn't full-size yet.

I could hardly blame him. My partners had been keeping me busy nearly every night since that first time with Jolene. I was starting to worry that my legs and arms would give out, and I wasn't even married yet.

"So?" Missa asked. "Which ones is good?"

"Can I go in the back?" I replied. "It's easier if I'm close."

The old woman obliged, entering the attached tent—which was stuffed with crates, so I had no clue where the woman slept— and opening the back door of the traveling wagon. I stepped up into the tight space, ducking.

"Don't bump anything," Missa called after me. "You break it, you buy it."

I grunted in reply and moved gingerly among her collection of supposedly dead eggs. I passed five different eggs to her after finding their auras alive and well.

"There's others that are decent, but may not make it," I said, pointing them out. She picked them up and stowed them in a crate separate from the first five.

"And their varieties?" she asked.

I looked through them, and she marked three eggs with chalk as I identified them. "I'm not familiar with the rest yet," I said, "but ask me again in a year."

"In a year, you'll be dead," she replied. It should have darkened my mood, but it just made me laugh. Trust Missa to never be happy.

When I stepped out of the wagon, Jolene said, "That went well. Inspecting eggs for a fee—who would have thought of it?"

"Who else but Becki?" I said.

She giggled. "You're right. She's quite the entrepreneur. Selling *future* rides on Star... I still can't believe she got away with that. And now she's opening her dragon tour business in less than a week. It'll probably make a fortune, knowing her."

"Yep. Rachel says I need to give Becki a five-percent cut, too, instead of free rent. *'Becki might work hard for good cock and a room, but she'll work even harder for good cock and a fortune.'*"

Jolene hid a snort behind her hand. "Oh, that accountant really is something else. But it sounds like a good idea to me."

I nodded. *A ring, a wife title, and 5% of the profits.* I hadn't told Jolene yet, but that was my plan for Becki and Aliese both. And Kenna, too, but she'd be harder to convince. She didn't like to be tied down.

Either way, I'd have to tell Jolene eventually—and there was no telling how she might respond.

"Well, if that's all the service yer givin' me, m'lord, here's your fee," Missa said, handing a pouch of coins to Fieran, now that I was too noble to dirty my hands with it.

I shook thoughts of Jolene as a spurned lover from my head. After last night, we were a family, and this was a family business. Nothing would break us. I would make sure of it.

Things could only get better from here.

Chapter 111

A Golden Aura

"THANK YOU," I said to Missa, my heart warmer now. I waved a hand at my own wagon. "Now if you'd like to have a look at my wares, perhaps we can—"

Before I could get the words out, something tugged hard at my mind. It had to be a dragon, deeper in the market. The yellow aura was different from anything else I'd ever experienced, and incredibly powerful.

My chest tightened with a strange pain, like a sadness so deep it burned a hole through my sternum. My knees caved, and I gripped the wagon to stay upright.

"Oi! Jo, yer man's swooning," Missa said with a snap of her fingers.

Jolene had been looking over the eggs I'd identified, but now she rushed over. Fieran beat her to me, of course, sliding under my arm to support me. I stabilized quickly and looked up, only to give a start. Copper's face was inches from mine, and she looked unaccountably sad.

She blinked twice, accepted a pet from my free hand, then lay down in front of me and chuffed.

"You good?" Fieran asked, her voice low and more feminine than usual.

I let her lift me up, with Jolene taking my other arm. "Yeah, I think so." Whatever that aura-blast had been, it remained in the area, but it had stopped hurting once I turned toward it.

I knew I shouldn't go gallivanting off into the market to chase down the yellow aura, but I couldn't risk it getting away.

"Jo, I need you to stay here and get us established," I said. "The market plot is paid for and you've got all the permits, so you don't need me. Missa might have advice, if you need it. Pay her whatever she asks for as a consultant's fee."

Her face fell. "But I thought you were going to help?"

"I'll be back," I assured her. "I just have to check something real quick. Setting up a stall is too important to neglect, though. The war isn't going to fund itself. Come on, Fieran, you're with me."

The plan was to sell at a discount with a sign that said no reasonable offer would be refused, and it just so happened to be on a day Kenna had offered a free flight to the Dasvilla market for all dragon merchants in Caliph. Because of that bright idea, I didn't expect Jolene to be here for too long.

Once we had a nice reserve of profits, I planned to spend them in Ashkar, where we'd buy armor and gear for my new command of soldiers, and hire a baker, farmer, another carpenter, and a dragonsteel smith. After all, the war effort against the Dragon-Touched wouldn't *just* require dragons.

One of my guards was already setting up behind Jolene. I recognized him as Andon, Becki's brother. I hadn't had a chance to speak to him yet, but I'd asked for him when Narvi had put together my guard. *He can buy from a drunk and sell to a merchant, and still make money,* Becki had assured me.

The man was proving this now. As he set up the tables, he started shouting, "Come get yer egg inspections by the renowned Dragon-Touched! First two are free. Ride the legendary Copper, slayer of a hundred fiends! Buy eggs confiscated from an elf farm, recently raided and demolished! One rare wyvern egg for sale!"

Already people had stopped to watch. I turned to go—only to stop dead.

That aura, the presence... it's gone.

My shoulders slumped. I'd already wasted too much time.

"Never mind," I told Jolene. "It's too late anyway. All right, what's left to do?"

By the third time Andon shouted about me being Dragon-Touched, a crowd had gathered, the tables were ready, and Baron Maki had arrived, parting the crowd with a warm smile that I didn't trust for a minute.

A beautiful woman in her early twenties carried a large black-scaled egg behind him, cradling it on a tasseled pillow. Like a professional, Maki raised his hands to get attention.

"This is Jorgia, my competitor, who thought the stories of Lord Warren were fabricated. I have not touched this egg, and we all know how serious she takes her business. All right, Dragon-Touched, what's in the egg?"

I scattered hay to make a trail to get to Copper's saddle, stealing a glance at the egg.

"No legs yet, so don't crack it. Two rich green Mount-class dragons, twins; that's why the egg seems abnormally large. Next!"

A different man arrived with a white Behemoth egg he could barely carry. I glanced up and said, "Nothing lives in that one. Just empty space. You've been cheated, sir. Next!"

"But there is movement in the light," he protested.

I shrugged. "I call it as I see it. I have no idea why it moves, but it's not alive."

He grumbled, then dropped the egg.

I blinked. *Holy hells, he really believed me, just like that?* I'd expected him to keep the egg until it started rotting, just to prove me wrong.

But I wasn't wrong. Sure enough, a long dead dragon spilled out of the cracked white egg, bringing a rancid smell with it. People murmured in astonishment.

He was right. He was right!

Holding his nose, the man grabbed the dead beast by the tail to drag it out of the area. I scoffed at his behavior. The poor dragon deserved better—

My heart fluttered again, and I looked up.

The aura. It's back. Coming closer....

Before I could act, Quicksilver surprised everyone by diving into our market plot, flaring her wings at the last second before she landed. She craned her head back and unleashed a light burst of her dragonsteel beam, the first she'd ever done in public. One very unlucky bird dropped from the air with a clank.

She kept her wings flared, because if she didn't, she'd probably flatten a house. Thank goodness we'd rented a double plot.

Feldspar arrived not long after, followed by Alpine, Collette, and Alabaster, who had to walk in with Jerem accompanying him. There was no room for the one-winged dragon, so Jerem led him to a nearby roof to stand watch. I'd told him to pay the inhabitants if we ever needed to do that, and thanks to Quicksilver, we were very tight on space.

The crowd *oohed* and *aahed,* rather than growing nervous. As each dragon arrived, a new round of cheers went up. These people knew they were witnessing wild dragons who answered to the Dragon-Touched.

Their awe baffled me, while it seemed to make Maki gloat. The baron hadn't left yet, because my wares were too good of a value for him to ignore.

"What are you grinning at?" I asked him.

He tucked his hands into his opposite sleeves. "Oh, nothing. It's just that I'm a little worried for you, milord. The Royal Guard won't like this show of force."

"Oh, yeah? If the king or his guard aren't here, who's going to tell him? You?"

"Who says they're not here?" Maki replied.

Before I could answer, the man turned away.

Chapter 112

Fear the Reaper!

I GRITTED MY TEETH. *The Royal Guard, in Dasvilla? Impossible.* Why would they come all the way out here? To see *me,* the person they either hated or spurned? I highly doubted that this was the case.

Damn these counts and barons and dukes, I thought bitterly. I was tired of the politics that were now permanent in my life. Jolene slung an arm around my waist in support, watching Maki scurry away.

"I can't believe I ever considered marrying that toad," she said. "Anyway, Warren, what happened back there? Why did you fall? Why did you want to leave?"

I looked over her shoulder to see a hooded figure arriving. I could tell it was Becki by the way she moved, although she dressed as a common worker with her hood drawn tight.

I pretended she was inconsequential and told Jolene, "We will find out soon enough." I raised my voice. "Does anyone have an egg that's ready to hatch?"

A young boy of eight or so raised an egg the size of his head. "This one, milord. My Momma said it's dead since it never naturally hatched."

I roared out a laugh, waving him forward. "Nope. But he can't get out. He's dark red and healthy, but his shell is too tough."

"What species?" a random woman shouted.

I shrugged. "I'm still learning how to discern that. I'm Dragon-Touched, not an expert." I threw a thumb at Jolene. "That's her."

Jolene curtsied and listed off a few dragon types known to be dark red. When she finished, I told the boy, "All right, my friend. Drop it. I'll pay his full value if he dies."

The kid's eyes went wide. "Like... *drop it,* drop it?"

A chant echoed across the crowd. *"Drop it! Drop it!"*

While somewhat morbid, he found strength in their words. The casing was solid, too solid, and he'd never help that dragon out without intense force. After the chant reached a fever pitch, his arms spread wide and the egg plummeted.

It shattered with a dramatic crash. A second later, a baby red dragon struggled to fly toward me. It ran right by me and curled up near Copper, squawking at her.

To my disgust, she vomited out a nice little meal for him: a partly digested arm from something she'd eaten on her morning hunt.

The boy shouted, "Awesome! It's a red boy!"

"Could be luck," another man said, offering two eggs, both ready to hatch.

"Light purple, Mount class, something that likes killing. Don't drop it, bring it here and set it there. I'll buy her," I said with a grunt.

"She's five gold," the man said, frowning.

"Demons to that. Not paying that much, not when I get them for free," I said with a grunt, pointing at the other egg, which was enormous. "A wind dragon, Hauler class, but it's weak. Despite that, she's ready to come out. You can drop her."

The man dropped the second egg. The casing shattered, and the little gray girl slithered forward with a stunted wing. She'd never fly, and the look of disgust on her owner's face was evident. The wind dragon saw the regurgitated arm and started slapping her way toward it, perfectly happy to eat beside the red baby.

"Want it?" the man asked me.

"Most certainly," I said. To Andor, I said, "Give him the spiel and the prices."

I rubbed my chest, once again having to turn toward the nearing yellow aura. It was starting to zigzag through the city, but always drawing closer. A series of dragons flew underneath Quicksilver's raised wing, carrying the litter of some sort of dignitary between them. I let them join the back of the line.

As I inspected an egg for a young woman, the yellow aura deviated from its winding path, heading directly toward me. I handed the woman the egg, giving her my report. She opened the egg in excitement, setting her dragon down to eat with mine. Copper didn't care. She, too, was focused on the massive golden aura.

When it arrived, I figured it'd be a dragon of some legendary quality. Instead, a young girl in a yellow dress appeared, a pink bow poised on top of her rich red hair. Dark freckles dotted her pale face, contrasting with her appearance in a way I knew all too well.

I sighed, noting she carried a tiny golden egg. Was it the egg with that aura, or the girl? I waved her forward, and she grinned in that way only innocent kids can.

Jolene glanced around with a deep frown. "Where's your momma?"

The little girl shrugged.

Jolene looked the kid up and down. "You look familiar... what's your name, sweetie?"

The anxiety in my chest spiked, and I crouched down in front of the girl before she could reply.

"It's best if you stay in one spot so your handlers can find you," I said. "I need a helper though. Can you be that helper?"

737

"Handlers?" Jolene asked, while the girl eagerly nodded.

"Will you hatch my dragon?" the girl asked, offering me her egg.

I smiled weakly, lowering myself to my knees. I placed the egg in front of her and held my palms above the casing.

The aura was coming from here.

This egg is so small, but the aura... it's as big as Copper's aura, maybe bigger.

The baby was also eager to be free, and when I called to it, the little yellow dragon burst from the egg with an adorable little screech, much to everyone's delight.

What are you, little one? I thought. The dragon peeped at me.

"Name her Camilla," I said softly. "That was my mother's name."

"What!? That's my name, too!" the little girl squealed, bouncing on her heels in excitement.

I sighed, looking away. Of course I'd known the kid's name—everyone in Parshil knew about the precious little Princess Camilla. Vanessa had named her after my mother, but I never understood why. She'd been born a full year after Vanessa and I had parted, so she couldn't be mine.

But seeing her now, fawning over her dragon... I had to wonder if that timeline had been faked. Maybe the name *Camilla* hadn't been a subtle way for Vanessa to tell me she would always remember our love. Maybe the name was a clue as to this girl's real parentage.

She could have been born nine months later, and then hidden from the world. Why had that never occurred to me?

As these thoughts burned through my head, Camilla scooped up the dragon, fast but gentle. "She's just so perfect! Thank you! But I shall call her Chunks. No, wait, she doesn't like that.... She has to be Gary... Gray... something. So I'll call her Graychunks then! And Chunks for short!"

Did she just say the dragon vetoed its own name? I laughed as she giggled, but that was new. *Can the two communicate somehow?*

I was about to press gingerly for more information when I heard the sound of armor, clanking fast as it raced in this direction.

So Maki wasn't just blowing smoke, I thought, sighing. *The Royal Guard really are here today.*

"I... I must say, young lady, you've got quite the dragon there," I told her, and she seemed to fully agree, because her entire focus was caught in the dragon's yellow gaze. The two stared at each other, bonding fast and tight. The golden aura only grew larger.

Becki appeared out of the crowd, darted forward, and grabbed my arm. "It's time to go," she hissed.

I withdrew while Jolene was distracted. Meanwhile, Copper popped her neck, then launched into the air as the Royal Guard drew close. Camilla flinched, but quickly returned to snuggling on her baby dragon. Armored men poured into the market plot from a side street, but by then I had slowly retreated behind our sales wagon.

Jolene and Becki stayed near the little girl as the Royal Guard arrived with a very anxious mother in tow.

Oh shit. If the king finds out I've seen her....

But the thought vanished as Vanessa arrived.

She looked exactly as she had the day I'd left her. Dark red hair in a tight braid against her back, emerald eyes shining above a scatter of freckles, and a light tan adorning her skin.... Her father hated that tan, because it made her look foreign, but no one could ever keep Vanessa indoors.

They hadn't kept her leashed today, either. She was here to see me.

I steeled myself. *This is going to hurt.*

Chapter 113

Reunion

JOLENE WAVED, hailing the princess, definitely not making the connection that Becki had.

"Your Highness! What a wonderful surprise!" Jolene gasped, whipping around and frowning when she didn't see me with her. "Your daughter wanted to hatch her dragon," she said uncertainly, before turning her full attention back to Vanessa. "We kept her—"

A gruff officer with a flowing cape growled at Jo. "There is a copper-colored dragon irritating our protection wing," he snapped. "Is it yours?"

"Oh, that would be Copper..." Jolene said, trailing off. She clued in on the little girl again. Her eyes went from Vanessa to the daughter, then back to Vanessa. "Shut the Demon's door. She looks like—"

In the sky, Copper nipped at the night dragon whose only intention was to keep the princess and her daughter safe. My metallic dragon was infuriating the massive violet-black dragon, so big it could double as a storm cloud.

I didn't dare shout. *Copper, stop! What are you doing? Those dragons aren't enemies!*

Princess Vanessa drew herself up. "Control your beast. Rakor will eat her if she doesn't cease."

741

Looks like Copper can't read my mind after all, I thought.

"Copper, enough!" I bellowed, loud and clear.

The Royal Guard drew weapons at my command, bending their knees, pulling shields up around the princess. In response, my six guardsmen immediately formed into a makeshift formation behind me.

To Vanessa's men, I said, "Please stand down. We are not your enemy."

"I'll do no such—" Vanessa's lead officer started to say, but Princess Vanessa touched his forearm, an immediate and egregious breach of protocol. "Princess?" he said softly, concerned.

Vanessa abruptly fell to her knees, and the man struggled to catch her. She stared up at me in muted shock. Copper landed directly beside Quicksilver, watching with feigned boredom now that she couldn't pester the other dragons.

"These are wild dragons," Maki warned from behind the guards. "They cannot be trusted around Her Highness."

"For he is the prince of the wilds, a man who only needs a sword and his heart to conquer any challenge," Vanessa said, her words washing over the crowd. "You died. You're dead." She finally seemed to notice Jolene. "Wait! Who is she?"

I removed my belt, tossing it away. My sword clattered to the ground along with it. "You named her Camilla," I said.

"Where the… where have you been?" Vanessa demanded, her voice still ghostly. "If you didn't die… then where have you been?"

I narrowed my eyes. *Did Kurto tell her I was dead?*

Of course he had. *Of course.*

Had she really not forgotten me after all?

That's when I saw something far more disturbing. "Turn your head to the side," I commanded.

She shook her head, instantly doing what I wanted by refusing.

There was a bruise under her eye, faint and covered by makeup, but I could see it as she moved.

Vanessa touched it, paling. "An old bruise," she said.

"Please rise, Princess," the gruff guard said. "It will not do for you to kneel like this."

"Can someone tell me what's happening? Because I'm lost as hell," Andor whisper-hissed behind me.

I half-turned toward him, but my words were for everyone. "Over five years ago, Princess Vanessa ran away from home."

I instantly had the crowd's full attention.

"She ran into an arachne nest on her fourth day," I went on. "A brave scout came across her while on his mission, and he saved her, thinking she was nothing more than a common woman in distress. For weeks, she forced him deeper into the wilds, but he willingly protected her, giving her his heart over his duty.

"The weeks turned into months and we... *they* journeyed across the realm, until someone finally recognized her.

"I was that guardsman," I declared.

"Oh shit," Vanessa's head guard whispered.

My chest tightened. *Couldn't have said it better myself.*

I threw back my shoulders. "I'm Viscount Warren, and I am no longer a mere scout. The princess is marked with a bruise. *Who struck her?*"

As I made this demand, every single one of my dozen dragons roared out in primal fury. For the first time, the Royal Guard seemed to notice Quicksilver looming over them. She'd been so still, that they must have taken her to be a great silver statue.

The head guard raised his sword again, but Vanessa stood up, grabbing her daughter and pulling her against her skirts. She strode to my side in a very surprising move, towing the child along with her. Both Becki and Jolene backed out of her way.

I wasn't sure if she'd hit me or hug me.

743

"What happened?" Vanessa said, her voice low and shaky. She stopped within arm's reach of me. "Father said you died trying to get vengeance on the arachne to prove your worth."

Camilla poked at her mother's skirts. "Mama? What's going on? Did you see I got a new dragon?"

"Yes darling, I see. She's your favorite color, too! Let's hear my friend's story, okay?" Vanessa said, sounding strained.

The little girl put down her dragon, which wandered away toward the orc arm. A random cat had joined the dragons to pick at the remains, providing a new shiny for Camilla to give attention to. She wandered off, and two guards automatically peeled away to go with her.

I cleared my throat, taking an extra step back from Vanessa. My mind raced. This was all happening too fast. It wasn't going to plan at all. It was too soon. It would anger the king.

But I would never get this opportunity again, so I raised my hands and unbuttoned my coat.

"What are you doing?" Vanessa said.

I flipped my coat open, dropping it, and reached for my under-coat. "Showing you the truth," I replied.

The guards tried to move in again, but Vanessa stayed them with a gesture. I threw open my second coat, then pulled off both my shirts. Once my chest was bare, I turned to let my full audience take a long look.

"King Kurto pulled me into his dungeon after I returned with the princess," I said. "He ordered me to tell his daughter that I was using her for position and power.

"I refused.

"He told me to lie. I refused. He told me I never loved her. He was wrong, and I refused. Each time I refused, I felt the lash. Not once did I waiver, not once did I lose faith.

"I loved that stubborn redhead, and no father in the world could change my conviction. I never faltered, never failed her. Over and over I suffered. I never gave up on Vanessa—

not until the final lash took my life after a week of brutal torture."

I turned back to her. She was crying.

"And then I awoke. I felt different, whole, as if I had been healed by some great force. I still do not know what it was.

"The Hand advocated for my death, but the king hadn't intended to kill me to begin with. Now, here was an opportunity to spare his daughter pain. He let me go free, on the condition that I would never contact her again, nor ever become noticeable in the public eye.

"He told me that he allowed you to watch me leave the castle alive, but I... I could never verify that.

"Five years passed. I hoped for a letter, for a word, for anything. Now I know why: the king lied to you. He convinced you I was dead in some other way, not by his hand.

"And you believed him. You *believed*."

The bitterness surged up in my heart. This revelation should have brought me joy, but after everything we had been through, Vanessa had given up on me at the first opportunity. Worse, she'd married immediately and borne a daughter. There was no doubt about whose daughter it was, or about why she had married so quickly.

"I believed? I *believed*? Of course I believed!" the princess cried, her surprise and tears turning to rage. "They brought your sword and the head of the arachne. A month later, I knew I carried your child. What choice did I have?"

"Your Highness!" a woman shrieked, from somewhere behind the guards. The princess was giving all her secrets away.

But she never stopped her tirade. "Could I leave the palace and chase after you, after evidence of your death had been given to me?" Her face twisted into a sneer. "You, of all people, should know how *worthless* I am, alone out in the woods. And without Iggs? Do you think me mad?"

I frowned. Who was Iggs? Some other paramour?

"No," I replied softly. "I don't think you mad. I think you *economical*."

Her hands gripped her skirts so hard the threads were separating. "I married Prince Zelkar to protect our daughter. Surely you can see that this was the wisest choice?"

"Your Highness!" the woman shouted again.

"Four Demons," Fieran breathed, sidling up next to me. Once again, she'd stepped away without my noticing. I glanced at her, worried about what she'd been doing. After all, she was Vanessa's blood sister.

Thankfully, the two looked nothing alike, but Fieran knew the leaders of a sect of rebels, and I still didn't know where she stood on that front. There hadn't been time to discuss it.

Meanwhile, the crowd gaped in stunned silence.

I couldn't blame them. They had just heard of the king's betrayal and Vanessa's shame very publicly.

My eyes narrowed. *Her shame....* I looked over at the child. *She married the prince to protect Camilla, then just threw her under the wagon in front of all these people? How does that make any sense?*

I had come here to expose the king's treatment of me, but I had never intended to expose my damn kid. I'd known about her, of course. Her name was *Camilla,* after all, precious daughter of Prince Zelkar.

However, her birth had been announced over a year after we'd parted. I'd thought that Vanessa meant to honor me with the name, but I'd never had any clue that Camilla was mine.

Even now, there was no way to tell for sure. Yes, we looked alike, but coincidences happened. She looked more like Vanessa than anyone.

"And who are *they* to you?" Vanessa asked softly, nodding to Becki and Jolene.

"They're my future wives," I replied. "And they aren't a part of this conversation. Tell me, why would you tolerate a man who hits you?"

Vanessa's face darkened, and as beautiful as she was, the expression changed her. This was not the woman out of my memory.

She really *had* given up on me—and it would be best if I didn't forget that, before I fell for her all over again.

Chapter 114

I Don't Like This

CAMILLA TUGGED on her mom's leg, and her expression smoothed out. Smiling at her daughter, Vanessa said, "What is it, darling?"

"Momma, you're scaring me," Camilla said in a small voice.

"Camilla, this is Viscount Warren of Dasvilla. Say thank you to the nice man."

Tears were glittering in the child's gray eyes, but she turned to me and bowed. "Thank you, Sir Viscount, for helping me with Chunks." She winced. "Graychunks, I mean."

Above us, Copper suddenly gave a pained cry as the night dragon bit into her wing, tearing the membrane. I straightened and reacted on instinct.

"You there! Night dragon!" I roared, racking my brain. Rakor... *Rakor* was his name, the personal night dragon of the princess. She hadn't owned him when we were together, but night dragons were public members of the royal families they belonged to, so I'd heard his name around.

"Rakor!" I shouted. "Leave the mine dragon alone at once. Land at the Roost, that way." I pointed.

The big violet dragon didn't hesitate, dipping low with an ear-ringing roar so intense the hairs on my arm rose. He flared his wings, then flapped them, rising into the air and heading to the Roost. He reached it in moments, landing so aggressively that he ripped a wall off and one of the captured wild dragons broke free and fled.

"Mama, where's Rakie going?"

Vanessa rolled her eyes, her knuckles still white as she fisted her skirts. "Wherever he damn well pleases, Cammy."

Camilla looked like she might cry again, so I pulled an egg off my cart and tossed it into the air. My orange-hued aura burst outward in demand, and the egg shattered in the middle of its arc. A lovely golden dragon glided out, landing on my shoulder.

"Oh, it looks like Chunky! Again!" Camilla shouted with glee.

I watched closely as Vanessa glanced between me and her daughter, and I noted every shift of her expression as it suddenly warmed. Her cheeks flushed, and her hand spread across her stomach. She looked back at me.

"Warren... I've been cruel. I am sorry."

I took a deep breath to level my emotions, picking up another egg for Camilla. I hatched it for her in a smooth, practiced motion, and she clapped as the brown dragon slid into her arms and started earnestly chewing her hair.

"Maybe one day, I will come to understand how I could so freely sacrifice so much for us, while you could not," I said. "Until then, I will accept your apology."

Vanessa reached for my hand. "Please, Warren—"

I withdrew my hand from her reach.

Her eyes welled again, and now she spoke low, in a voice meant only for me. "I loved you. *Love* you. This is just... it's so much. Please, I beg of you. Visit me tonight...."

She trailed off, and it was impossible to tell what was going on behind those eyes. She turned her gaze to the people gathered here, to Quicksilver, to her daughter.

"No," she said slowly. "Do not visit me tonight. Instead, I shall visit you."

She raised a hand and snapped her fingers. "Izmon, come here," she commanded. Instantly, a man broke from the Guard, and three more guards joined him.

Vanessa held up a stopping hand. "No, just Izmon. The rest of you may leave. You will no longer be allowed to protect me or my daughter."

I gave Izmon a once-over. His most obvious feature was the Shoulder-class dragon on his shoulders, sand-colored. I racked my memory for what it was.

A desert dragon. Their breath can make illusions.

"Wait, what?" an oblivious guard said to Vanessa. "You're not coming with us, after you just pulled all this drama?"

I blinked away from Izmon. This random guard dared to speak to royalty in that way? Just what the hells was going on here?

Vanessa pointed a finger at the man. "I shall do as I please. I am Princess of Parshil, First of my Name, Heiress of Demons and Matron of the Realm. You shall not speak to me in that way. Begone. Go back to my worthless husband, and crawl back up his ass where you belong."

The guard scoffed, tossing his hands in the air. To the head officer, he said, "It'll be just like when she escaped the first time. You can't let this happen."

The head officer looked impassive. He watched Vanessa raptly, as if daring her to give the order a second time.

Vanessa rolled her eyes and strode up to him. "Fine. Take this letter to my husband, then."

I saw paper flash as she tapped a scroll against the officer's chest. He took it. Something about the moment snatched my interest, but the guard stuffed the scroll away without further argument.

He sniffed and said, "Fine. Let the bitch go." He turned in

place, and his men all turned with him. They began marching away.

"Vanessa," I said lowly. "You cannot burden me with this."

The infernal woman smiled, and my heart melted to see it. She reached out again, and this time I didn't pull away as she ran her palms up my arms.

"I burden you with nothing. I am my own woman, and I have my own will." She paused, then turned her head to Jolene and Becki, who both looked stricken. Becki had come here to play my surreptitious onlooker, hoping to get a feel of the loyalties of all the merchants and nobles attending my sales event. Instead, she'd been met with royalty, and she remained so stunned that she'd forgotten to keep up her disguise.

"My dearest lord, I require you to introduce me to your loyal ladies," Vanessa said. "I must thank them for caring for you so."

"Vanessa," I said, trying to add weight to my words, "the kingdom is already on the edge of rebellion. This will not improve things."

"Nonsense," she replied, facing me. "In fact, my favor will protect you. My father would never dare to harm me."

Somehow I doubted that. The king had too much profit to lose, and he'd had two new sons since I'd left the palace. Surely his beloved daughter had fallen out of his favor.

"You're not exactly rich without your father," I said. "I won't be able to provide for you. I need to raise funds to buy armor, weapons, and so forth."

"Very well, Viscount Warren, street-boy-turned-hero. I shall be destitute in your care, and I will be happy all the same. So, tell me: what is next?"

I glanced around and sighed. The Royal Guard was gone, and some of the tension had faded from the market. Copper, however, was growling directly at the man who had stayed, Izmon.

I couldn't blame her. If he had a desert dragon with him, and if I was remembering correctly what they could do, then he might well be in disguise, casting an illusion of some other person he was pretending to be.

"I see you still doubt my devotion," Vanessa said. With a flourish that drew gasps and whispers from the gathered commoners, she removed her marriage band from her wrist, kissed my cheek, then turned to bow to a very flustered Jolene and a worried Becki. Fieran dropped a hand on my shoulder and leaned close while Vanessa made formal introductions.

"I don't like this," Fieran whispered.

"I know," I said, "but she's royal. I can't exactly tell her what to do." I turned my head and raised an eyebrow at my page. "Where were you?"

"Just alerting some friends," she replied. "They wouldn't want to be anywhere near the Royal Guard."

"Now!" Vanessa said, clapping her hands. "I'm told we are here to sell eggs. And thus, we must sell them!"

I eyed Jolene, then Becki, and fought against looking at Fieran. After a moment, I swallowed. "Well, all right then."

The first few customers were hesitant, but they paid, marveling at Vanessa before they moved on with their day. As I went through the eggs offered to me for inspection, Camilla began guessing them too. She got each one wrong, and she said nothing suspicious about auras or colors, so I didn't think she was Dragon-Touched like me. Yet it seemed her golden dragon had communicated with her, or something? I didn't like how strange this all felt.

At the same time, it warmed me to my core to have Camilla at my side, loving every egg, every dragon that passed before her. Over the next hour, we sold eggs, identified breeds, clasped forearms, and annoyed Copper to no end. She still played the grumpy warrior as she growled at Izmon and his Shoulder dragon.

Overall, my party made the most of the situation, and by the end of the sales day, I had enough gold to depart for Ashkar with two new tag-alongs.

By that point, one suspicion had grown in me. As I took my last coin in payment, and the purchaser walked away, I said to Vanessa: "Duchess Nola put you up to this."

She smiled, but said nothing, which only confirmed my suspicions. This was why Duchess Nola had prepped Helin as my head steward, and why she'd given me a new estate.

It had all been for Princess Vanessa. Nola had known all along that my lost love wouldn't let me out of her grasp again. I should be angry at Nola. I felt manipulated somehow.

My heart ached, and I wasn't sure why.

Chapter 115

Behind Closed Doors

"I FEEL RIDICULOUS," Jolene said, walking with stiff limbs because the armor definitely felt foreign to her. "Like, how am I supposed to do anything?"

"You're supposed to stay on the dragon's back, shouting out any danger from above, behind, or to the sides," I replied, flicking her shoulder armor and listening to the *tink* sound it made.

"Ha! That didn't hurt, but I guess that's the point. I just feel so... goofy," Jolene grumbled. "The helmet is cute though."

"Never change," Becki teased with a grin. "Never cursing change."

We stood in a private changing room back at the villa, where Becki and Jolene could get into battle armor. I'd commissioned the armor only yesterday, but a local smith had coopted existing pieces to procure the sets for me overnight.

This wasn't something we needed to do with Vanessa standing by, hovering like some sort of observing goddess. However, I didn't mind the distraction. It felt strange to have this woman here, so close to me, after so many years.

"Izmon retrieved my gear-set and no one stopped him, so..." Vanessa spread her armored arms with a shrug. "How do I look?"

She'd sent her single bodyguard out of the room as soon as he'd handed her the armor. I was personally glad to have the guy gone, because he'd kept his eyes on me like I was a hungry, muzzled dragon about to snap Vanessa up at any moment.

"It looks like it fits," Becki said. "Even the tits look good."

Vanessa pursed her lips at the shameless comment, then nodded. "It's quite expensive, and I used to hate it, but it fits again after Camilla."

She sighed and looked around. "I hope she's sleeping well. Thank you for providing the guest room. She's had a very long day."

"No problem. And I'd love to take her to the farm tomorrow, if that's all right. She doesn't look like she sees the sun much," I said, trying not to sound accusatory.

"Yes, and we can change that, but it won't be easy. If I had to guess, Duchess Nola won't let her run rampant outside of her estate," Vanessa said with a scoff. "And thank you for the compliment," she added, speaking to Becki. "I am devilishly proud of these tits."

All of us laughed, but my laugh felt weakest. I rubbed the back of my neck. "I apologize. I should have been the first to compliment you. I've always thought you were beautiful, Nessa. I'm not keen to admit it, but dammit, I feel out of place."

"Oh, I do imagine so," she replied tritely. "After all, I just divorced my husband and entrusted our daughter to you. This will surely be considered a rebellion, but Duke Biscuit shall take the blame."

My gut churned. *Was that Nola's game?*

"Oh, don't look so worried!" she said, wrapping me in a luscious hug. I sank into it, fool that I was. "Nola and I understand the politics, so that you won't have to."

I swallowed. "I've done pretty well so far."

Vanessa opened her mouth, but Jolene spoke first. "Yes. He has," she said.

That same darkness cracked across Vanessa's face again, but she brightened a moment later. "How about you sit down then, milord? I will happily show you how silver my tongue is. And perhaps your ladies might help me?"

My heart beat faster, but a deeper, cooler part of my mind ran slow. I showed nothing on my face, but a beast reared its head in the back of my mind.

I turned to my other lovers. Aliese was away on some errand for Helin, so it would just be Becki and Jo. Jo's defensiveness had already vanished from her face, leaving behind a flushed excitement. Becki, however, met my eyes. A knowing look passed between us.

We were both thinking the same thing: *This makes no sense. Why would she suddenly be okay with you having multiple wives? Why would she go home with you, starting a war just like that? And try for sex the first chance she got?*

All of it seemed to lead to this, to sex, and I couldn't help but think one horrible, dark thought: *Is being Dragon-Touched hereditary? Is Vanessa only here to try again, because Camilla doesn't have my powers?*

I had to try to figure it out, so I sat in the room's only armchair. Becki followed, hovering behind me. At the same time, Vanessa knelt in between my knees. She couldn't have been any more obvious.

"I missed you more than you'll ever know, Warren," Vanessa whispered, her breasts heaving against my crotch as she leaned forward. "As long as I'm alive, I'm your wife, and will never leave your side again."

My heart yearned to believe her—but I couldn't. *You're not my wife. You gave up on me. You got pregnant, then you threw me away.*

I reached up to take Becki's hand off my shoulder, but although I made the touch look gentle, I squeezed the webbing between her thumb and forefinger. It was an old alley-kid's trick. It was supposed to look like *get your hands off,* but it really meant, *go get me a distraction.*

Becki rose and excused herself, smiling. "I'll just leave you two to get reacquainted, then. Jo? Don't hover over her the first time she's here. Come on."

My voyeur's eyes widened as if she were emerging out of a haze. "What? Oh, yes, of course... of course...."

Becki hurried her future sister-wife out of the room, through the back door leading to the servant's quarters.

Vanessa smiled, reaching for my belt. "Now, where were we—"

Someone knocked on the door.

I suppressed the urge to breathe out in relief. Becki must have raced from the servants' hall to the front foyer in record time—

"Milord!" Fieran called. "Milord, you are needed!"

My stomach dropped. That wasn't Becki.

I rose and cinched my belt. "Give me a moment!"

Vanessa opened her mouth, likely to express disappointment, but Fieran burst into the room before I could give her leave.

"Fieran!" I said. "How many times have I told you, you can't just—"

"Dragons," she cried, her voice shrill and feminine. "Warren, there are dragons attacking Dasvilla! We have to go! We have to go *now!*"

Chapter 116

Behind Very Closed Doors

WHAT? Dragons? How?

I shoved past Fieran and raced across the foyer to the villa's front door. I reached for the handle—

A hand grabbed my shoulder, spinning me. "Warren, wait! Where are you—"

It was Vanessa, behind me. I opened my mouth.

At that exact moment, the whole world went gray.

I looked up, around, and my brain struggled to process what I was seeing. Everything—*everything*—was suddenly gray. The walls, the floor, the door, even the windows had a sheen of it that made the glass more opaque. I spun back around on the door and grabbed the handle, but it didn't open. I twisted the handle, but it didn't move.

"What the—" I said, backing away. My own hand, all our bodies still had color. "What is this?"

I might have stayed in that haze another full minute, if not for the sudden thunderous shake of the ground. The entire room, silver though it was, rumbled as a small quake ran through it. Behind me, Vanessa screamed so loud that it made my head throb, and I covered my ears as I fought to keep my footing.

It ended just as quickly as it had begun.

"Warren, look!" Fieran said, standing at the window. She pointed and I dashed to her side. I sensed Jolene and Becki behind me again, too, as well as Aliese and one of her brothers —all of the people currently in the house, except for Camilla. The poor kid was probably waking up, terrified—

The thought died. Right there on my front lawn, visible through the now-hazy window, was Quicksilver. My big, beautiful forge dragon.

Dead.

I could tell immediately. No aura, no nothing. She lay there, still and lifeless.

I suddenly understood what all the grayness was.

"She turned the villa into dragonsteel!" I said, recoiling from the window. "Quicksilver used her breath on the house, and it was too much power...."

It must have drained the poor dragon, and she'd collapsed. The weight of her huge mass had caused the ground to shake when her body dropped out of the sky.

No, not Quicksilver, no....

Jolene threw herself at the window, palms slapping against the grayed glass. "What? No!"

I drew my sword, gripping the blade carefully, and told Jolene to move. She did, barely noticing as I slammed the sword's pommel against the window. The resonant *thunk* made all of us flinch, but the glass didn't crack. The dragon breath must have reinforced it.

"We can't get out," I said. "She's trapped us here."

Another scream rent the air beyond the door.

Fieran spread a heavy hand on the window. "Or maybe she was saving us from—"

"No." Jolene straightened, her stricken face suddenly calm. "No, that's not Quicksilver. It's a male."

I looked out the window again, but I couldn't tell for sure if she was right. "Are you certain?"

"Yes," she said. "That's not Quick." She bent her knees and peered up, then said, "And it rent a hole in the top of the Cage to get in. Quick would have known to just push on the gate. We don't lock it."

I bent down to confirm. "Fuck. We have an enemy dragon here, then?"

"Zelkar," Vanessa whispered.

I whipped around. "You think this is your husband's doing? How did he get your letter so fast?"

She looked flushed, intense, nothing like the extremely pale face of Becki beside her. It was that rage building again. I could see it.

"He has his ways," she said lowly. "And he's got a male forge dragon."

"Warren, those are highly regulated," Jo said, grabbing my sleeve. "There aren't very many in the realm."

I nodded. So this was Zelkar.

Vanessa suddenly gasped and tore for the stairs. "Camilla!"

"Shit." I threw an arm at the stairs. "Fier, go with her. Protect them."

Fieran said nothing, just raced after my former lover and child.

"Aliese," I said, turning, "get everyone else into the cellar. *Everyone.* This whole thing screams 'trap.'"

If Zelkar had literally sacrificed an entire Airship dragon just to enclose me here, then something big was about to go down. In fact, it already was—the screams outside were increasing in both number and volume, spreading across the city. Buildings flickered with flame, blurry through the reinforced window. Beams of lightning struck out of the sky, evidence of a royal night dragon at play.

My own dragons are already out there, I realized. *They're fighting. I have to get to them.*

"But what about you?" Jolene said, still hanging off my sleeve. "You can't go out there alone!"

"I have to get out there to begin with," I said. "I'm going to find a way to break the dragonsteel. Somehow. I'll come for you when I do."

With that, I followed Fieran and Vanessa up the stairs, but broke in another direction on the mezzanine. After another flight of stairs, I approached the rookery.

In my head, I flipped through the pages upon pages of information I'd been trying to memorize about dragons, going over every breed I had in the rookery, every ability they all had. What ability could break through dragonsteel, without killing the dragon that used it?

Melting anything is transformative, but dragonsteel? I'd need too much power. I'd kill a small dragon instantly, and probably not even make a small hole. Damn, there's gotta be something else—

I gripped the door handle of the rookery and thrust it open, arriving to chaos. The eggs remained still on their heating stones, although some had been upturned—and one unlucky one smashed—as all the nursery and hatchling dragons freaked out.

They whizzed about the room, bugling incoherently. They knew a dragon war raged close by. I could feel it too, the sense of huge clouds of auras clashing with others. A storm of souls had taken over Dasvilla, and I had to get outside to end it.

My eyes darted, identifying each dragon as it flew past me. Only two seemed remotely calm—Collette and Dull, the flame hatchling, although she'd grown bigger over this past month since I'd met her. The two of them rushed over to me and curled protectively about my legs, looking up, as if for reassurance.

Seeing them—*fire, ice*—and seeing the shattered egg... these three things together made me remember that moment of passion with Becki. The shattered glass candlestick... it gave me an idea.

Damn, it just might work! I thought, pointing the two dragons at the window. I should go downstairs and try on a ground-floor window, but that would only waste time if this failed.

"Collette, Dull, I need you to use your breath on the glass, right here." I pointed. "Collette, you first, five seconds. Then Dull, you go next, five seconds. Repeat."

The alternating heat and cold should shatter the window, even if it was reinforced. The glass had not turned fully gray, meaning it was likely weaker than the walls of the house, and still had some of the weaknesses of real glass.

The dragons chirped, and Collette stood up with her paws on the window sill. She opened her mouth, and her head jerked forward.

Nothing happened. She did it again. No magic breath came out of her mouth.

Chittering fearfully, she turned back to look at me, her pink eyes wide. It wasn't working? How?

"Dull, you try," I commanded, and she did. The same thing happened. Her flame didn't work.

But how? That wasn't possible, unless—

"Wyverns," I said aloud.

I shook my head, leaning into the window to check the sky. Shapes passed before the stars, moon, and clouds, but I couldn't tell if any had only two legs.

They had to. There was no other way this could happen. A wyvern had cast a negation spell over the villa.

We were trapped, and we couldn't use magic.

There was no other way out.

٢

Chapter 117

Never the King

I LEANED my forehead against the window, trying to think of any other solution. But there was nothing, nothing at—

Thunk.

I opened my eyes and jerked back from the window. Something small had just struck it.

Squinting, I saw a hooded figure in the courtyard. It pulled an arm back, and threw. Another pebble struck the glass.

Who is that? It's so dark. Darker than usual, like my eyes have gotten worse—

But as soon as the person knew they had my attention, they threw their hood back. My eyes went wide. It was Yavonne, the assassin.

My pulse thudded to a stop, and then seemed to start running in reverse as hope burgeoned again in my chest. I didn't question this gift. I didn't ask why she was here right now, of all times. I just gestured for her to meet me at the front door.

Yavonne nodded, then darted out of sight beneath the window. I spun around and practically crashed down the stairs, arriving to the front door in record time. I saw no one, not Fieran, not Vanessa or Camilla. It worried me, but I shoved the worry back.

Get out of here first. Worry later.

"Warren! Your house—"

"I know," I replied, startled that I could hear Yavonne's voice. I pressed close to the crack between the door and its frame. It had kept its shape, not melting together, so I could still hear her through the tiny gap. Yet the handle didn't move.

Someone must have melted the lock first, after Fieran got here, but before the building was transformed, I thought. *Otherwise, it should still be functional, just made of steel.*

Dragonsteel didn't melt stuff, it just converted it into a whole new material. None of the shape or details were lost. I knew that well enough after having to cart out all the perfectly-preserved dead elves from the stonewood forest a day ago.

"Warren, the princess, is she—" Yavonne started to say.

"Here, she's here. Yavonne, I need your help."

"Is she in the room with you?"

"No. She's safe. There's no time." I told her what to do, and she nodded and backed away. I did too, only a few steps. I had to stay in position.

But the moment I moved, another ear-shattering scream ripped out of the upper floors of the house. I twisted, but didn't move my feet, as red light flared on the door. It took all my will to hold back from running until Yavonne's blood magic had seared through the bolt.

Almost any other magic wouldn't have worked, but with Yavonne's special knife, she could infuse human blood with wyvern blood, which did two things.

One, it made the blood maneuverable even within a wyvern's negation field.

Two, it could burn through existing magic, because the wyvern blood itself could function in that way.

Which meant that my own wyvern-infused blood, when shot toward me through the door, could melt through a dragonsteel deadbolt. After all, dragonsteel was magical.

The moment the door swung inwards—a mere inch as Yavonne started to heave against its weight—I said, "I have to go! I'll be in the rookery!"

"Warren, wait! The prin—"

I missed the rest of what she said as another scream sounded. I was halfway up the stairs now, and I recognized the sound as coming from a storage pantry for the second-floor kitchen. Fieran must have gotten hold of Vanessa and Camilla, but they had all holed up inside the pantry instead of going all the way down to the cellar.

If Fieran had done that, it meant something had been attacking them from the outside. There were no windows in the pantry.

Yet, as I surged toward it, I felt a draft breezing past me. The pantry door hung open, and I heard words in the screaming now, and two distinct voices.

"Oh shit... *aaaaghgh!*" Fieran's cry shot up in volume, and I recognized the sound of pain. "Help... me. Princess, help...."

"*Cammy!*" Vanessa wailed. "*Cammy!*"

Then, a roar.

That roar was a strained, mindless screech which could only belong to one beast. I nearly slid past the door in my rush to get into the room, banging my shoulder so hard against the frame that I dislocated it with a pop I couldn't hear.

Well, breaking the walls down was no longer an issue. By use of its own negation magic, a wyvern had scraped a hole out of the wall of the pantry, negating the dragonsteel and melting it away. The beast had its two back paws clutched to the shorn opening, and in its jaws—

It held Fieran's arm.

I lunged for her, seeing no one else, but as soon as the wyvern saw me, it beat its wings and shot backwards. Fieran met my eyes, her gray gaze tear-stricken with pain and exhaustion, and my fingers brushed hers before she was gone.

"No!" I shouted, reaching after her, but even my best leap would only get me killed. Fieran swung and screamed, held in the wyvern's jaws by a single arm. She had no weapon in her other hand, and the wyvern itself was armored. I glanced back into the room and found Fieran's sword and shield on the other side. She must have tried to fight it off, but she'd been outmatched.

Gritting my teeth, I shot one last look at Fieran's fading form, expecting to see her fall. But she didn't.

It could drop her so easily, but it's taking her hostage. It's being controlled by someone else.

Kicking stone away from the ledge, I rounded on Vanessa, who knelt in the corner with Camilla in her arms. "Why didn't you help—" I started to say, storming up to her.

Then I stopped.

No... no!

The little girl in Vanessa's arms was limp, too still. The gash of a wyvern claw glistened with arterial blood in a thick line from her ear, across her neck, to her left collarbone. Her freshly-hatched golden dragon quivered against her, its head resting on her unmoving chest.

"No," I heard myself say, dropping to my knees. I fumbled for my breast pocket. "No."

"Why weren't you here?" Vanessa screamed at me, not inches from my face. She shoved Camilla's limp body at me. "She's your daughter! How could you let her die?"

When Camilla's body came against me, I stopped digging into my coat. I knew death when I felt it.

This child—my only daughter—was gone.

I held her to me, shaking. The little hatchling keened. Vanessa shot to her feet and screamed at me again. I don't know what she said. She stalked away. I closed my eyes. The tears built behind them.

Then a hand landed on my shoulder. Someone leaned close. I turned to look back at Vanessa—

Only to see her jerk sideways, crashing to the floor, her weight coming off my shoulder again.

She slid toward the opening in the wall as I lurched to my feet, my child still in my arms. My eyes darted to Yavonne, who stomped a foot down as my gaze landed on her.

She kicked Vanessa. She just kicked Vanessa.

I tensed, but Yavonne met my eyes. "I was trying to tell you, Warren. I found the person who's been calling for Dragon-Touched to be killed." She pointed her wyvern knife at the princess.

"It was never the king or his Hand. Warren, it was *her*. She's been trying to kill you all along."

Chapter 118

The Dragon's Sacrifice

MY THOUGHTS SPUN, a vortex, and trying to catch one thought was like trying to capture a leaf on a breeze.

Vanessa had been leaning on my shoulder. After screaming at me, after running. Had she come back to comfort me?

No.

With my eyes on Vanessa, I lowered Camilla to the ground. The elder princess was rising, and in her hand—a knife.

"It took some doing, but I found her," Yavonne said, backing slightly away from me, her knife ready for defense if I didn't believe her. "She's had a hit out on Dragon-Touched since a little after she met you. Four people have been killed, Warren. Four people that *weren't you.*"

"Don't believe her! *She's a liar!*" Vanessa shrieked.

No. I can't believe this. She gave up on me, sure... but wanting to kill me? After her father spared me for her sake? This can't be right.

"But Prince Zelkar is attacking the cit—" I started to say, then stopped. Zelkar *did* own a forge dragon, but it wasn't the only male forge dragon in existence. There was no reason Vanessa couldn't have one, too, and no reason she couldn't use her husband's dragon if she wanted.

And I had seen a night dragon, in the sky, shooting lightning. How could one of Zelkar's dragons have gotten here so quickly?

It was Vanessa's dragon, Rakor. The one I sent to the Roost.

And where was her guard, the disguised man? Izmon? She'd sent him out of the room when she'd tried to seduce me, but I hadn't seen him since.

Someone melted the lock from the other side....

"It's her, Warren," Yavonne pleaded. "She was trying to slit your throat just a minute ago. You have to believe me."

"Liar! Warren, please—I don't even know this woman—"

"Shut up!" I drew both my knives and stared her down. To Yavonne, I said, "I believe you. This hasn't been right from the start."

As Vanessa bit back her next words—as her face softened into the beautiful, sweet young woman I'd fallen for—I knew right then who the real liar was. The evidence had been there from the beginning.

But she was the first woman I'd ever loved. I wanted it all to be real.

Her anger when she first saw me... it wasn't anger at me. She was angry because I had escaped her assassins, even though I was standing there in front of her in broad daylight.

Damn. I had been such a fool.

Her sudden switch in temperament, too... acting all loving.... She had wanted to get me alone.

The proof came fast, now that I was looking for it. *This is why she aired all our dirty laundry. Because she planned to burn Dasvilla to the ground anyway. She never expected word to get out.*

And the scroll she gave to her royal guardsman, for Zelkar... it had already been written.

There was also no seal. The guardsmen would be allowed to read it. That's why he'd walked away, because it was a message, a code only the two of them knew.

She hadn't sent her men away. She'd sent her men to do *this*. To attack Dasvilla, call the wyverns, lock me here, and—

"Warren," Vanessa said, her voice soft and serious. "You *know* me. That woman is tricking you. Surely you must see—"

She cut herself off this time, looking toward Camilla's body. Golden light flared behind me, and I didn't miss the flash of hunger in Vanessa's eyes. I'd seen that same craven hunger between the sheets, in the grass beneath the sky, up against trees or with her mouth on my cock.

Now I saw it for what it was: avarice, pure and simple. It had never, not ever, been love.

I glanced back, not daring to take my eyes off Vanessa. The golden glow seared my eyes, but faded just as fast. Camilla remained still and cold, but not her dragon—her poor dragon—

It lay across her stomach, its colors dulled. It was dead.

"Fucking *finally*," Vanessa said.

I spun, throwing a knife out, but Vanessa was nearly as fast. The moment my blade struck her shoulder, she released her own knife.

I taught her that, I thought. *On her adventures, I taught her.*

But she'd never been a very good student.

In that split second of time, I knew Vanessa would miss me. The blade cut low, where it was going to strike the floor, or even—

A blur jumped out in front of my knees, low to the ground. Yavonne took the knife so that it wouldn't strike my dead daughter's corpse. She screamed.

I threw my second knife.

This one, too, hit Vanessa in a shoulder. I'd taught her to throw, but also how to avoid. She'd known to twist and dart, to mess with her enemy's aim. And she was darting now, for the hole in the wall.

She staggered forward, reeling from the impact, one knife sticking out of each shoulder, each one protruding from a different direction. She crashed against the edge of the hole in the steel, and flipped to face me.

No. Not me. Yavonne.

"Demons damn it," she said, when she saw where the knife had gone—into the assassin, not the child. She raised her perfect, naive, endless gray eyes to mine.

"You ruin everything, don't you?" Vanessa said.

I didn't understand. But I still drew my sword.

Behind me, somebody coughed.

I knew that sound. A small sound. A sound heard a thousand times in the streets, whenever my friends got sick. And before so very many of them died.

It was a child's cough. Not Yavonne's. *No. It can't be.*

I turned, and Camilla's eyes were wide open.

In that second, I took it all in.

The gash in her neck had healed over, replaced by a bright mark of gold flesh. She was struggling to sit up, her face stricken with terror.

"Lady, are you... Chunks? Chunky, *no!*"

A swish of fabric was my only warning, and I swung my sword around before me—but Vanessa hadn't been leaping for my throat. Instead, she'd flung herself backwards, out of the hole—

And she'd landed squarely on the back of a wyvern.

The beast was there one moment, gone the next, a mere flicker of time. It was moving even as Vanessa landed on it. She grasped its reins with one bloodied arm.

The whole thing had the look of a practiced maneuver—because that's exactly what it was.

She and that wyvern are bonded... the way that me and Copper are bonded. They're bound together by magic too extreme to be normal. There's no other way that could happen.

My mind reeled from the implications. Vanessa must have targeted Fieran, to get rid of her. She'd instructed her wyverns to put a hole through this wall.

And when she'd screamed earlier, the way it made my head hurt... that hadn't been a normal scream.

She screamed like a wyvern. A negation call. That's why Collette and Dull couldn't do magic.

The instant the truth dawned on me, I leapt for the opening, but once again, my mark was long gone. The wyvern soared away into the night, a rapidly shrinking shape. I shouted for a dragon, *any* dragon of mine, then turned back to the scene in the corner.

Camilla sat hunched over her poor dragon's body. Yavonne lay utterly still.

That's when I finally saw where the blade had struck her—the lower back.

A fatal blow.

"Shit," I said, dropping to my knees. I hovered my hands over the blood mage for a moment, afraid to touch anything. She rasped, and my heart soared for a moment. *She's still alive....*

But not for long.

I fumbled for my pocket as she fought to look at me. Her dark skin looked washed out, all the blood drained from her face.

"The kid... glowing. She was hunting—"

"Vanessa was hunting Dragon-Touched, I know. Now be still."

She shook her head feebly. "No. It's over for me, Warren. Take the kid and—"

"Who the fuck's gonna raise Vital's babies with you gone?" I snapped. "Now sit. Fucking. Still."

She laughed. "Where else am I gonna go? You big weird softie. Just let me die in—"

Her eyes went wide as I pulled out the knife.

As a scream built behind her mouth, I popped the cork in my hand, and shoved the entire bottle of healing breath right into the wound.

I would never forget that scream, not as long as I lived. It broke the night, a death knell, a choked sob, and then life.

I pulled out the bottle as the wound closed, and rolled the bloody thing in front of Yavonne's face. "Bottled breath, from that dragon, the one that healed Fieran," I explained. "I had Becki bottle it for me the morning after you fixed Fieran's blood."

Her whole body spasmed, and she started to get up. "It's not... it can't be—"

"You're healed, Yavonne. You're going to be fine."

I patted her shoulder as wing beats sounded outside the room. One of my dragons was about to land for me—Copper. I'd know that enormous aura anywhere.

I turned to my daughter. "Are you all right, Camilla?"

The little girl had stopped weeping. Instead, she stared at the dead dragon, still held in both her small hands.

"I don't... where'd he come from?" Camilla said. She looked up at me. Her eyes were hazy, edged in fading gold magic.

"Where'd who come from?" I asked, confused.

She held the dragon out. "Him. Why am I holding him? Why is he dead?"

My brow dropped low. Hadn't the dragon been female? Why was she calling it male?

I leaned close and gripped her arm gently. "Camilla. This is Graychunks. Chunky for short. You just named her today. Remember?"

She shook her head, her tears dried, a bizarre look on her face. "I don't know—"

"Who are you?" I asked her. "Who am I?"

She startled as Copper landed in the room and bugled, but I moved in front of her and repeated the question.

"I'm... I'm Camilla. Princess Camilla," she said. "And you're Viscount Warren, and that's Copper, and...."

Her face scrunched up. It was too much. She was about to start crying.

But this didn't make sense. How could she remember me, and Copper, and her own name, and not remember the dragon whose name she'd screamed only moment ago? How could that be—

My chest felt as if it sudden turned to vapor.

How could she forget?

How can this be?

I recoiled, my eyes burning. "Iggs. Ignace. *Iggs!*"

To create a Dragon-Touched, Jolene had told me, *a powerful dragon has to sacrifice its own memory....*

I ran both hands back through my hair. *How can this be?* I shook my head. *How could I forget?*

Suddenly the memories were right there, right in front of my eyes, as real as the aura flaring around me. The memories rolled through my body, feminine, a voice real and yet not.

What are we doing out here, in another infernal field?

The arachne will attack any moment.

When this is over, her father will berate me.

So will Pantalain.

Fuck Pantalain.

My magic flared in a halo, flame-orange and gargantuan. The molten power roared inside me, and I heard it, the roar of the creature that had died to save me in that prison, when my heart had finally given out.

Ugh, this princess... I so tire of these antics.

If she wants to leave the palace, she can fly anywhere on my back.

So why does she prefer to bait monsters, and watch as I kill them?

There's something seriously wrong with this woman....

It hadn't been the king, or the Hand, or Vanessa who had saved me. It had been Vanessa's dragon, a beast I'd forgotten—because she had died to merge her life force with mine, wiping all memories of herself from my head.

"Ignace," I said. "You were Ignace. The Behemoth. The *Demon.*"

No, not I. We were Ignace.

This time, the voice was no memory. It rose in my thoughts, finally able to speak. All I had to do was remember it.

I'd say it was nice to see you again, Warren, Ignace said, *but you took fucking forever, and I'm bored as shit.*

So pretty please, can we go murder something?

A scream sounded in the night. Dasvilla still burned.

I grinned. "I've got just the thing."

<<< END >>>

Check This Out!

Follow Marcus Sloss on Amazon here and Jace Cannon here

More from Marcus Sloss:
Check out Dinosaur Warlord and Minotaur's Maze of Monster
Girls.

For more Harem Lit Adventures:

Check This Out!

Made in United States
Troutdale, OR
12/29/2024

27367132R30435